Para Junot, mi lobo...este libro no existiría sin ti.
~ Marjorie

For everyone who has their own journey.
~ Sana

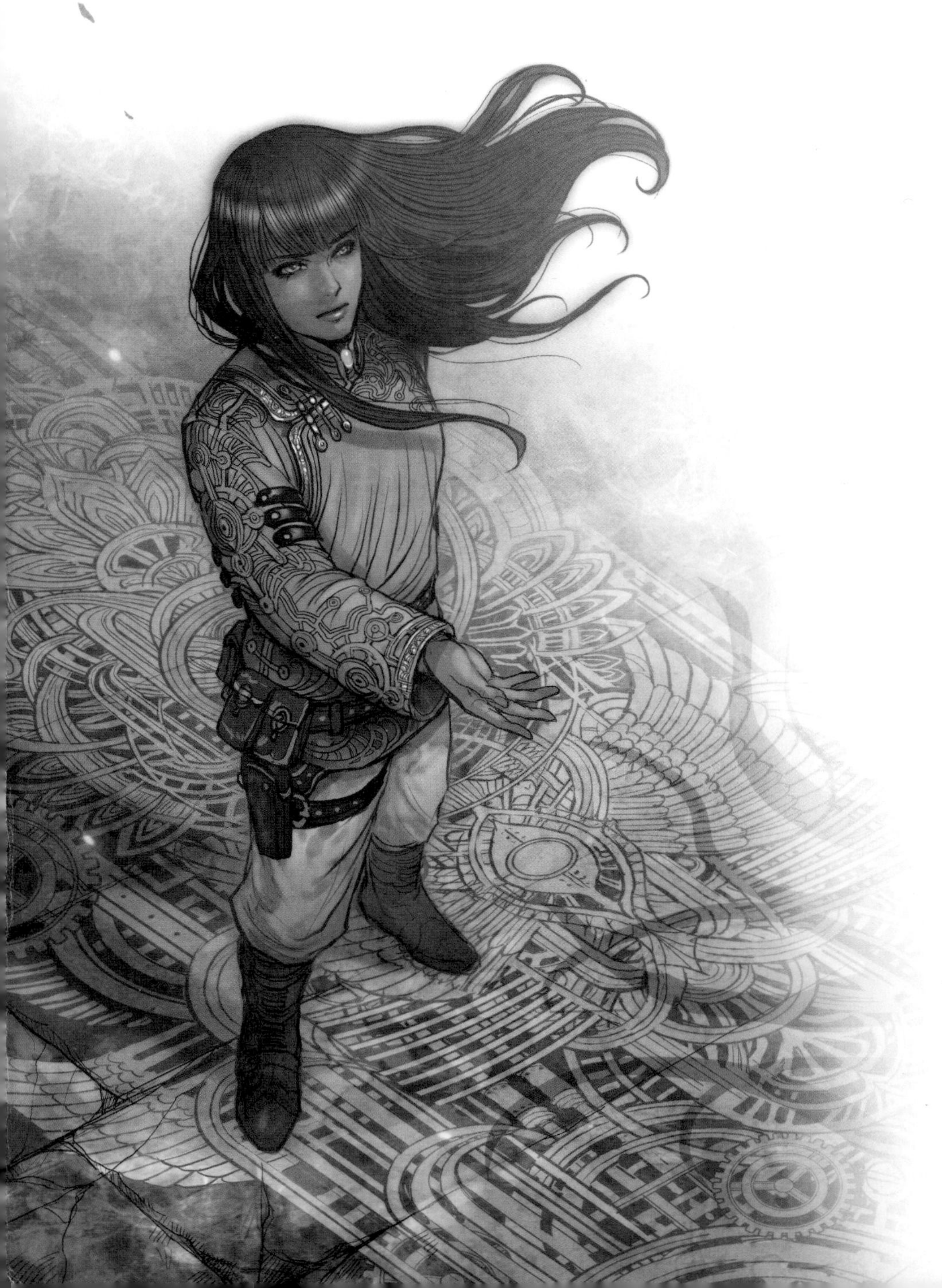

MONSTRESS

VOLUME ONE
AWAKENING

Collecting
MONSTRESS
Issues 1 - 6

MARJORIE LIU
WRITER

SANA TAKEDA
ARTIST

RUS WOOTON
LETTERING & DESIGN

JENNIFER M. SMITH
EDITOR

CERI RILEY
EDITORIAL ASSISTANT

MONSTRESS
created by
MARJORIE LIU &
SANA TAKEDA

CHAPTER ONE

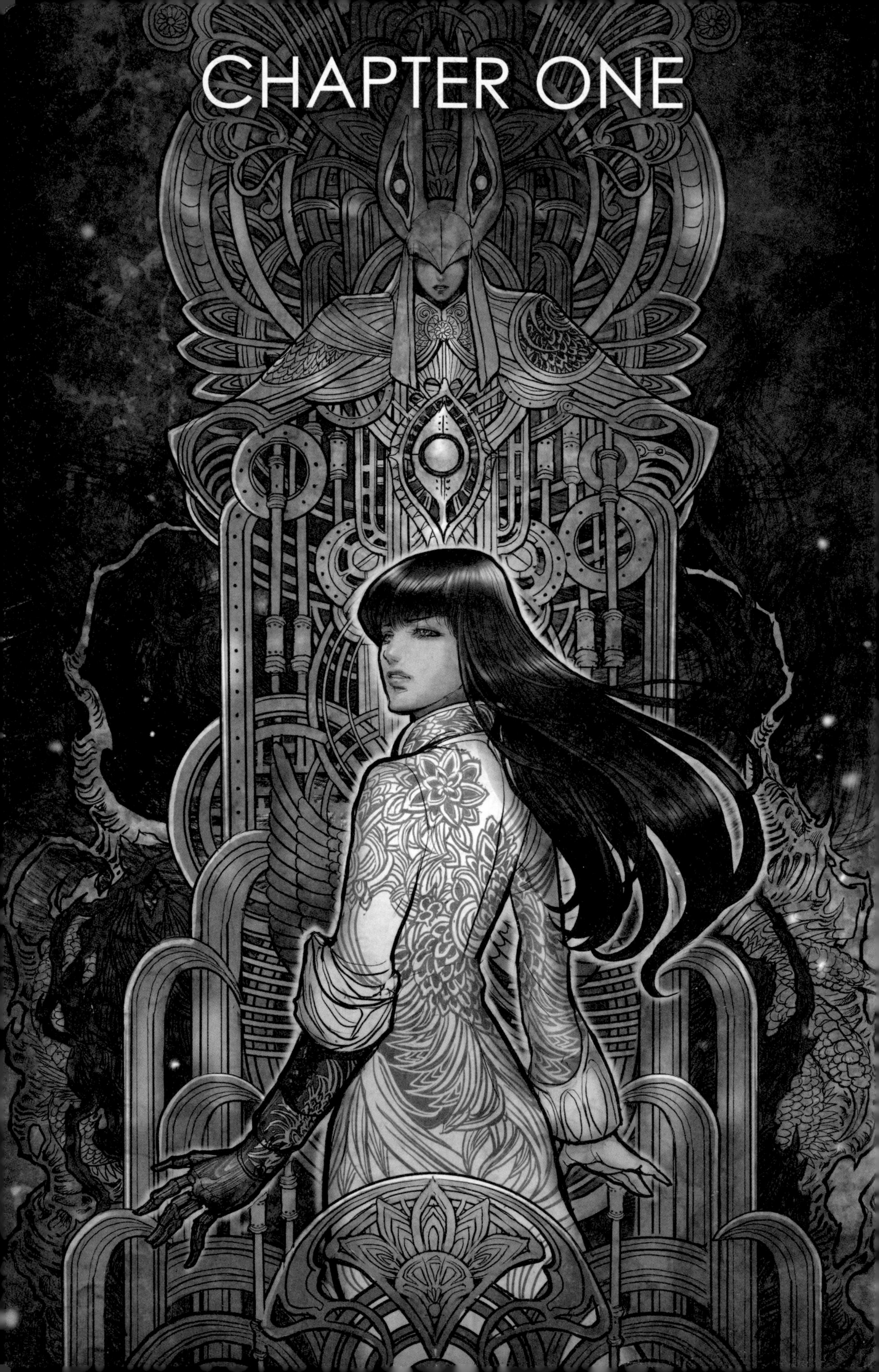

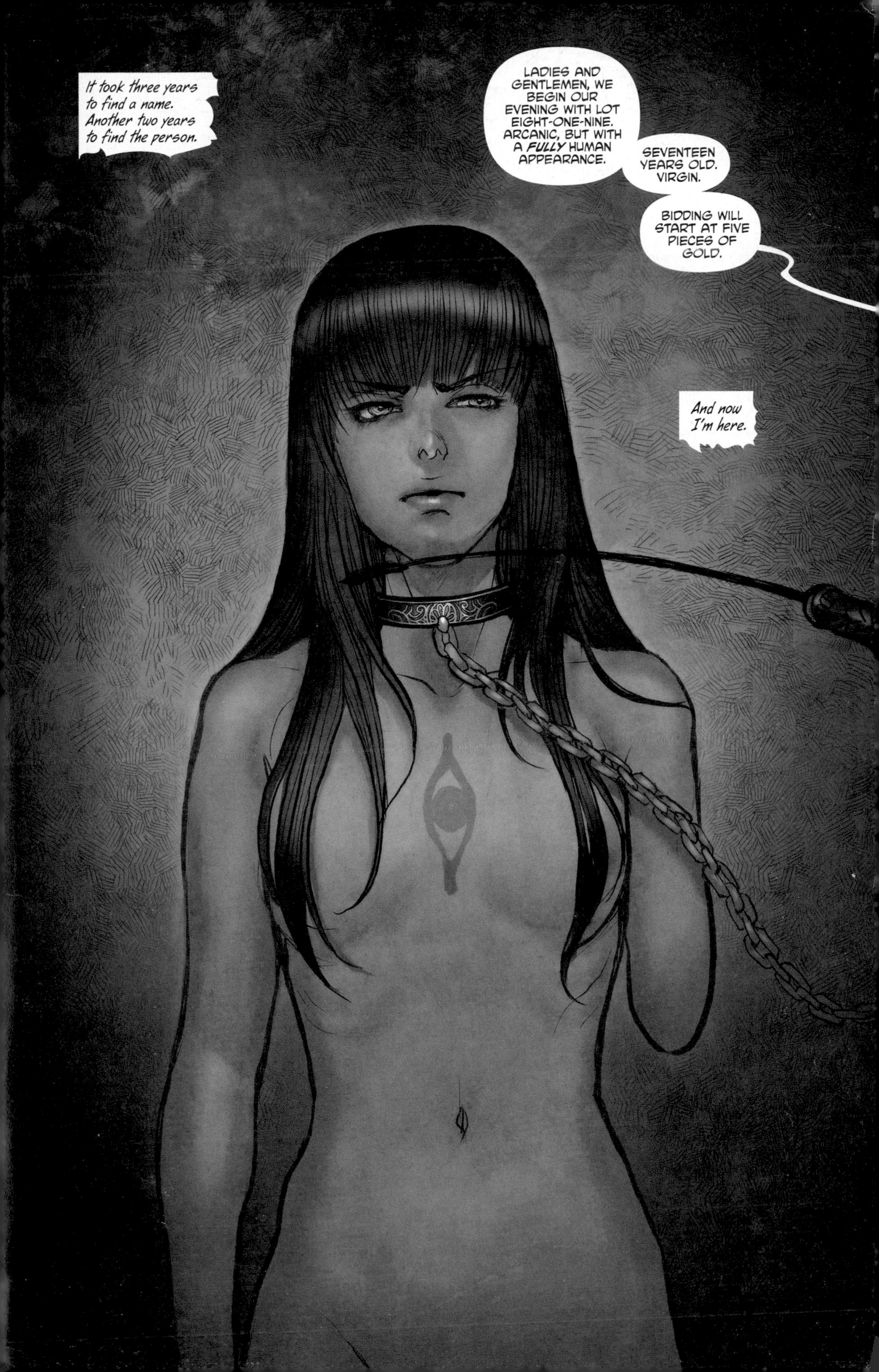
It took three years to find a name. Another two years to find the person.
LADIES AND GENTLEMEN, WE BEGIN OUR EVENING WITH LOT EIGHT-ONE-NINE. ARCANIC, BUT WITH A *FULLY* HUMAN APPEARANCE.
SEVENTEEN YEARS OLD. VIRGIN.
BIDDING WILL START AT FIVE PIECES OF GOLD.
And now I'm here.

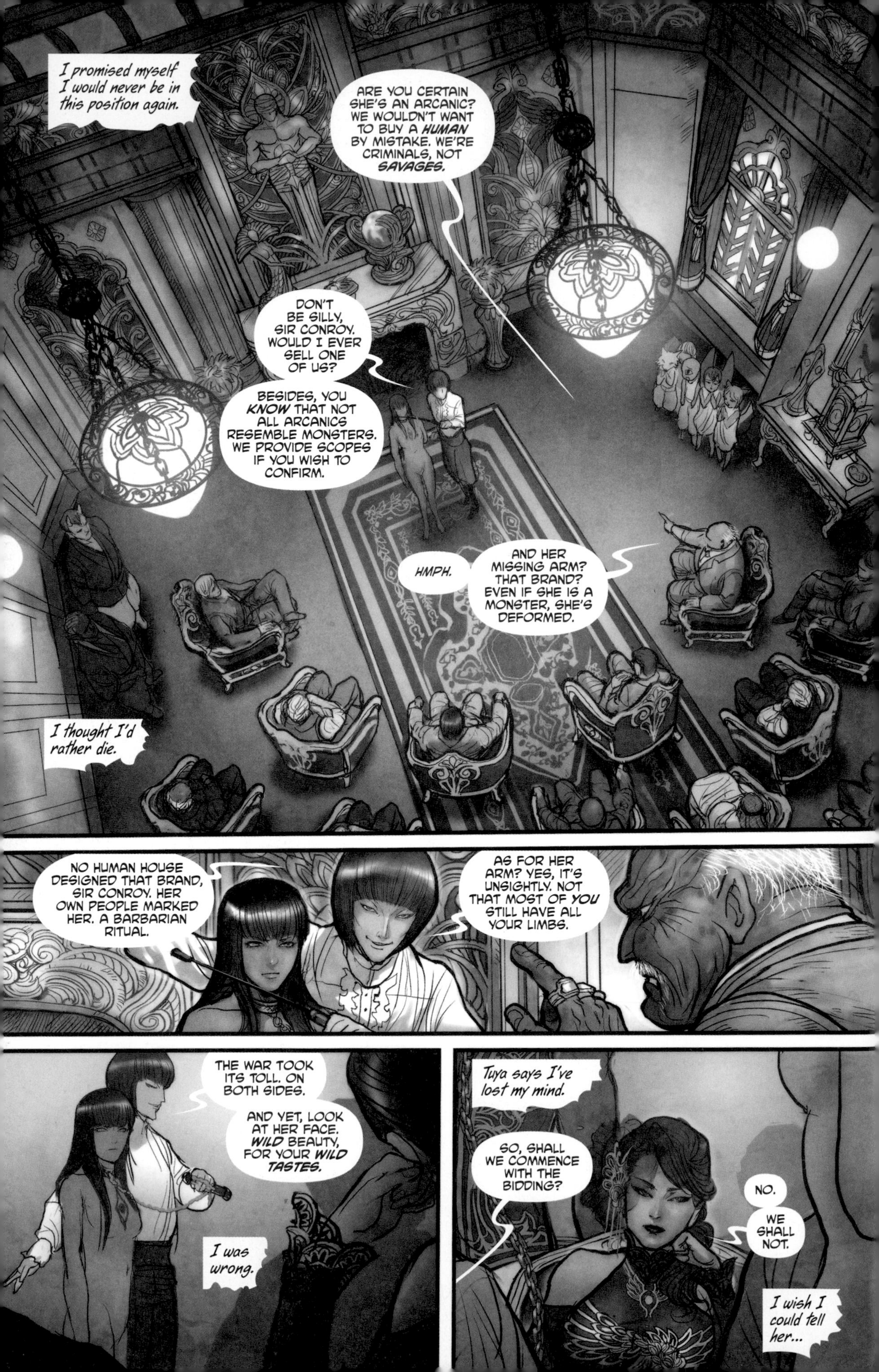
I promised myself I would never be in this position again.
ARE YOU CERTAIN SHE'S AN ARCANIC? WE WOULDN'T WANT TO BUY A HUMAN BY MISTAKE. WE'RE CRIMINALS, NOT SAVAGES.
DON'T BE SILLY, SIR CONROY. WOULD I EVER SELL ONE OF US?
BESIDES, YOU KNOW THAT NOT ALL ARCANICS RESEMBLE MONSTERS. WE PROVIDE SCOPES IF YOU WISH TO CONFIRM.
HMPH.
AND HER MISSING ARM? THAT BRAND? EVEN IF SHE IS A MONSTER, SHE'S DEFORMED.
I thought I'd rather die.
NO HUMAN HOUSE DESIGNED THAT BRAND, SIR CONROY. HER OWN PEOPLE MARKED HER. A BARBARIAN RITUAL.
AS FOR HER ARM? YES, IT'S UNSIGHTLY. NOT THAT MOST OF YOU STILL HAVE ALL YOUR LIMBS.
THE WAR TOOK ITS TOLL. ON BOTH SIDES.
AND YET, LOOK AT HER FACE. WILD BEAUTY, FOR YOUR WILD TASTES.
I was wrong.
Tuya says I've lost my mind.
SO, SHALL WE COMMENCE WITH THE BIDDING?
NO.
WE SHALL NOT.
I wish I could tell her...

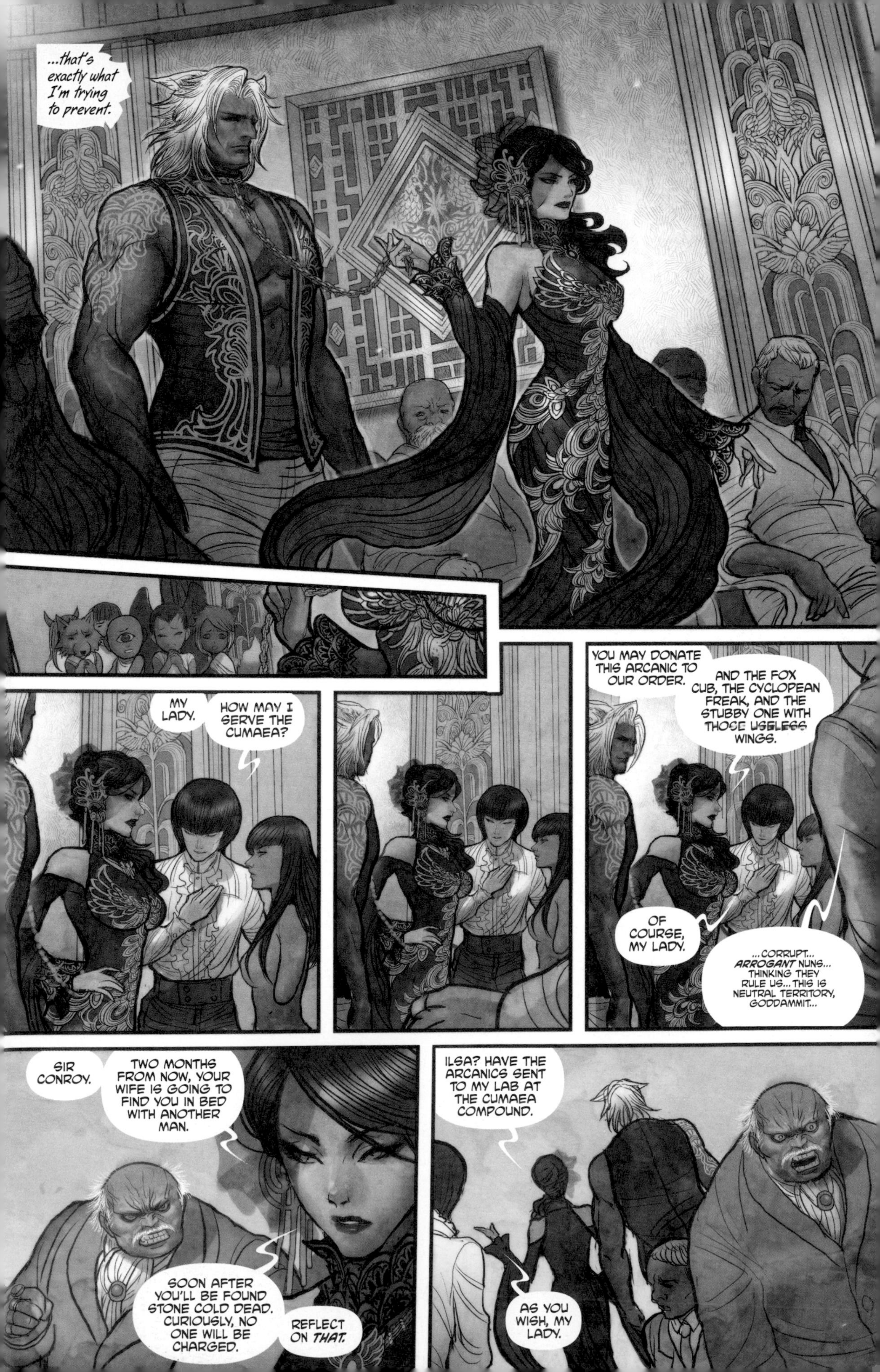
...that's exactly what I'm trying to prevent.
MY LADY.
HOW MAY I SERVE THE CUMAEA?
YOU MAY DONATE THIS ARCANIC TO OUR ORDER.
AND THE FOX CUB, THE CYCLOPEAN FREAK, AND THE STUBBY ONE WITH THOSE USELESS WINGS.
OF COURSE, MY LADY.
...CORRUPT... ARROGANT NUNS... THINKING THEY RULE US... THIS IS NEUTRAL TERRITORY, GODDAMMIT...
SIR CONROY.
TWO MONTHS FROM NOW, YOUR WIFE IS GOING TO FIND YOU IN BED WITH ANOTHER MAN.
SOON AFTER YOU'LL BE FOUND STONE COLD DEAD. CURIOUSLY, NO ONE WILL BE CHARGED.
REFLECT ON THAT.
ILSA? HAVE THE ARCANICS SENT TO MY LAB AT THE CUMAEA COMPOUND.
AS YOU WISH, MY LADY.

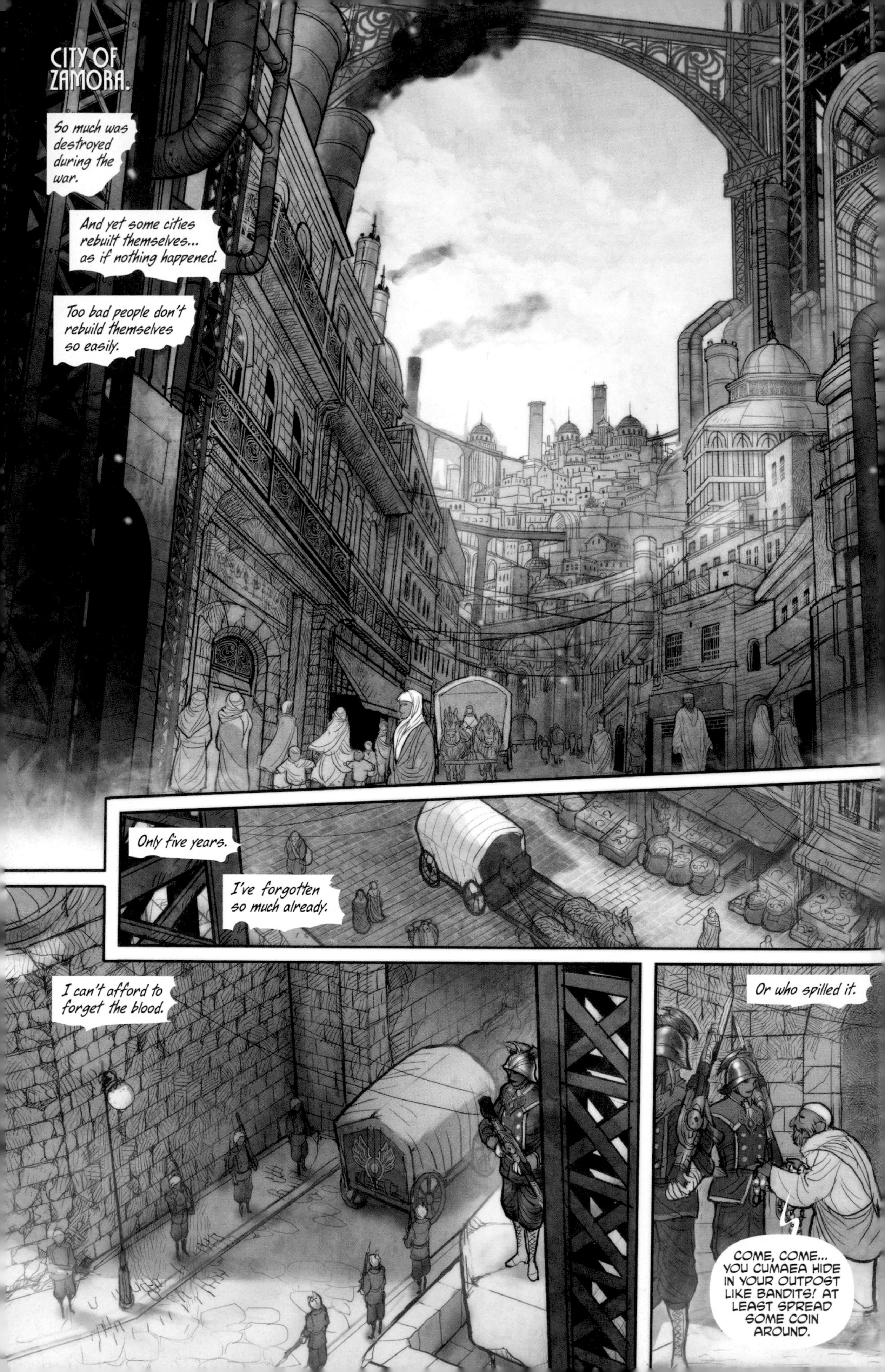
CITY OF ZAMORA.
So much was destroyed during the war.
And yet some cities rebuilt themselves... as if nothing happened.
Too bad people don't rebuild themselves so easily.
Only five years.
I've forgotten so much already.
I can't afford to forget the blood.
Or who spilled it.
COME, COME... YOU CUMAEA HIDE IN YOUR OUTPOST LIKE BANDITS! AT LEAST SPREAD SOME COIN AROUND.

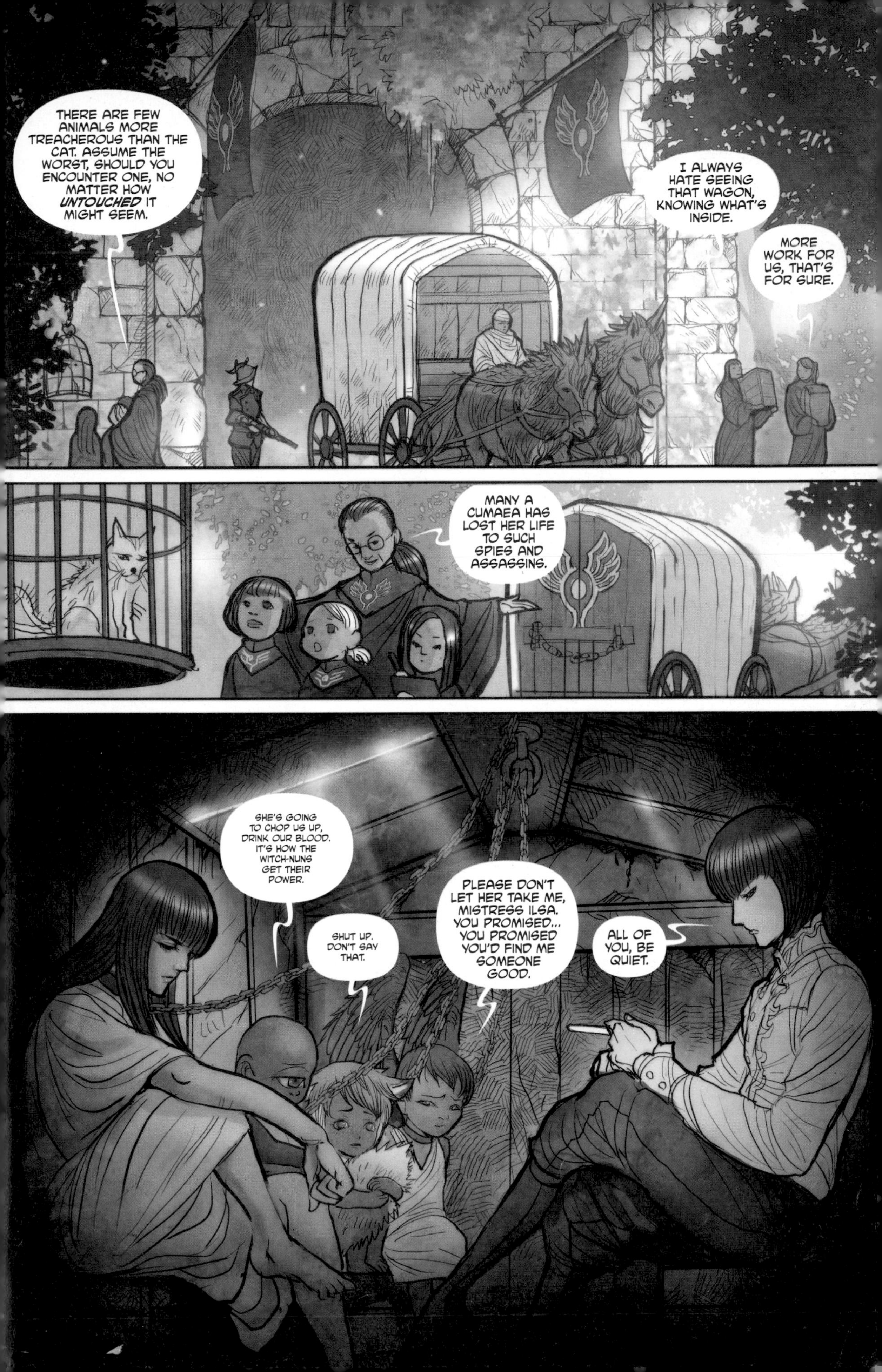
THERE ARE FEW ANIMALS MORE TREACHEROUS THAN THE CAT. ASSUME THE WORST, SHOULD YOU ENCOUNTER ONE, NO MATTER HOW UNTOUCHED IT MIGHT SEEM.
I ALWAYS HATE SEEING THAT WAGON, KNOWING WHAT'S INSIDE.
MORE WORK FOR US, THAT'S FOR SURE.
MANY A CUMAEA HAS LOST HER LIFE TO SUCH SPIES AND ASSASSINS.
SHE'S GOING TO CHOP US UP, DRINK OUR BLOOD. IT'S HOW THE WITCH-NUNS GET THEIR POWER.
SHUT UP. DON'T SAY THAT.
PLEASE DON'T LET HER TAKE ME, MISTRESS ILSA. YOU PROMISED... YOU PROMISED YOU'D FIND ME SOMEONE GOOD.
ALL OF YOU, BE QUIET.

WHAT, NO CRYING?

GOOD. SHE LIKES THEM BRAVE.

IS THAT WHY YOU ONLY DEAL IN CHILDREN?

WATCH YOUR FUCKING MOUTH. YOU'RE A SLAVE. AN ANIMAL PIECE OF SHIT ON THE WRONG SIDE OF THE WALL. IF THERE WEREN'T A STALEMATE IN THE WAR, THERE WOULDN'T EVEN BE A WALL AND ALL YOU INHUMAN FREAKS WOULD BE IN CHAINS.

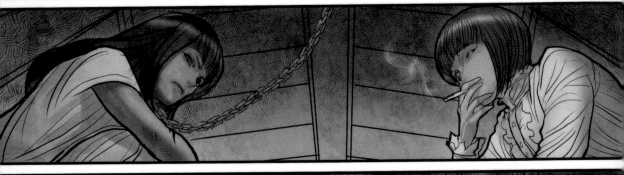

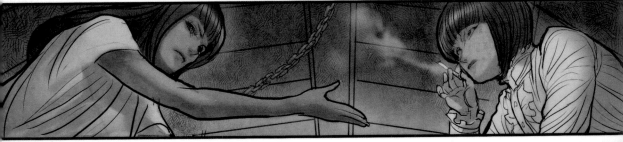

SHE'S GOING TO KILL YOU. EVEN AMONG THE CUMAEA, SOPHIA FEKETE IS KNOWN FOR HER KNIVES.

YES.

I NEVER WANT TO SEE THOSE KNIVES.

THAT'S YOUR CHOICE, ILSA.

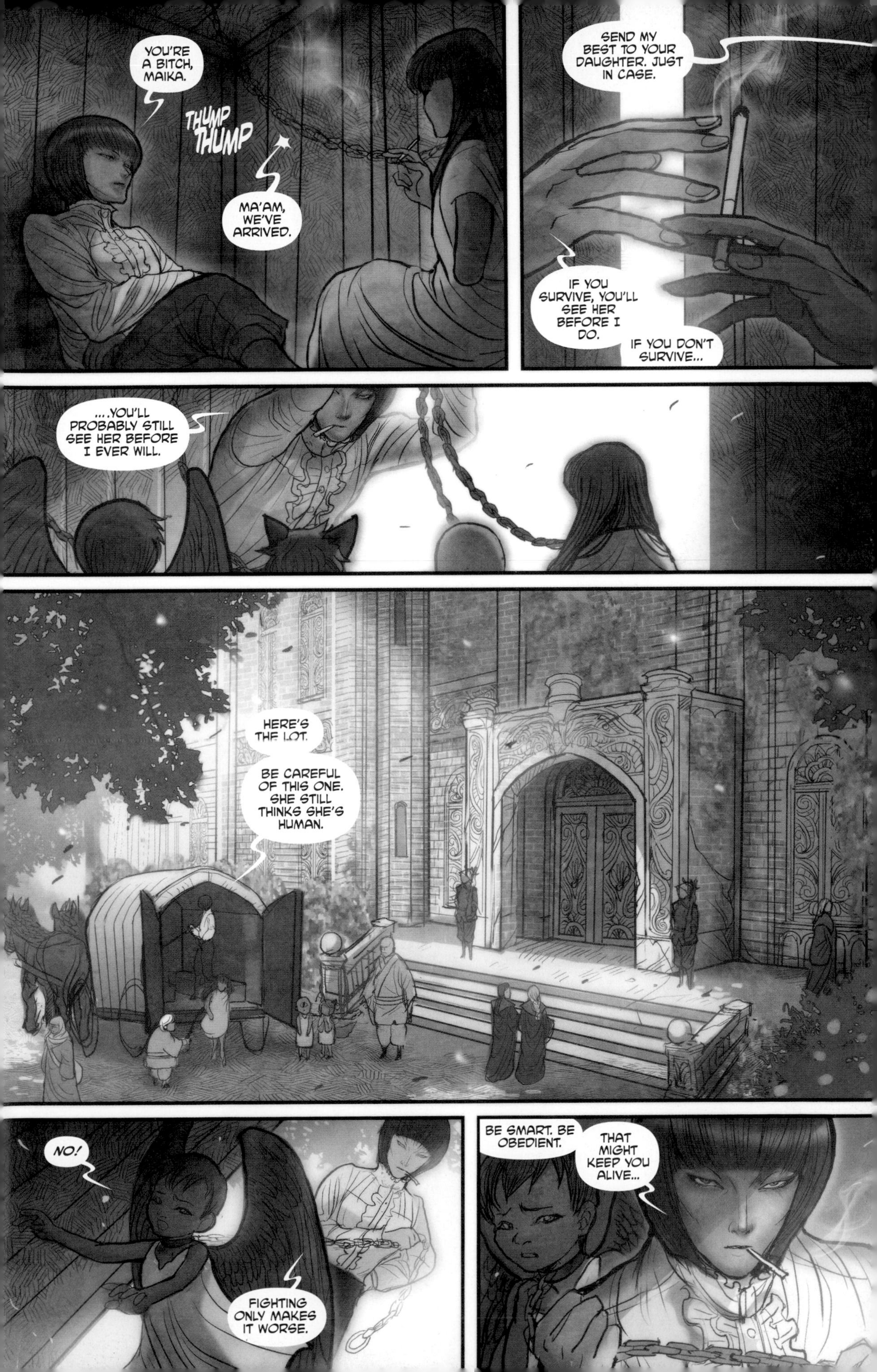
YOU'RE A BITCH, MAIKA.
THUMP THUMP
MA'AM, WE'VE ARRIVED.
SEND MY BEST TO YOUR DAUGHTER. JUST IN CASE.
IF YOU SURVIVE, YOU'LL SEE HER BEFORE I DO.
IF YOU DON'T SURVIVE...
....YOU'LL PROBABLY STILL SEE HER BEFORE I EVER WILL.
HERE'S THE LOT.
BE CAREFUL OF THIS ONE. SHE STILL THINKS SHE'S HUMAN.
NO!
FIGHTING ONLY MAKES IT WORSE.
BE SMART. BE OBEDIENT.
THAT MIGHT KEEP YOU ALIVE...

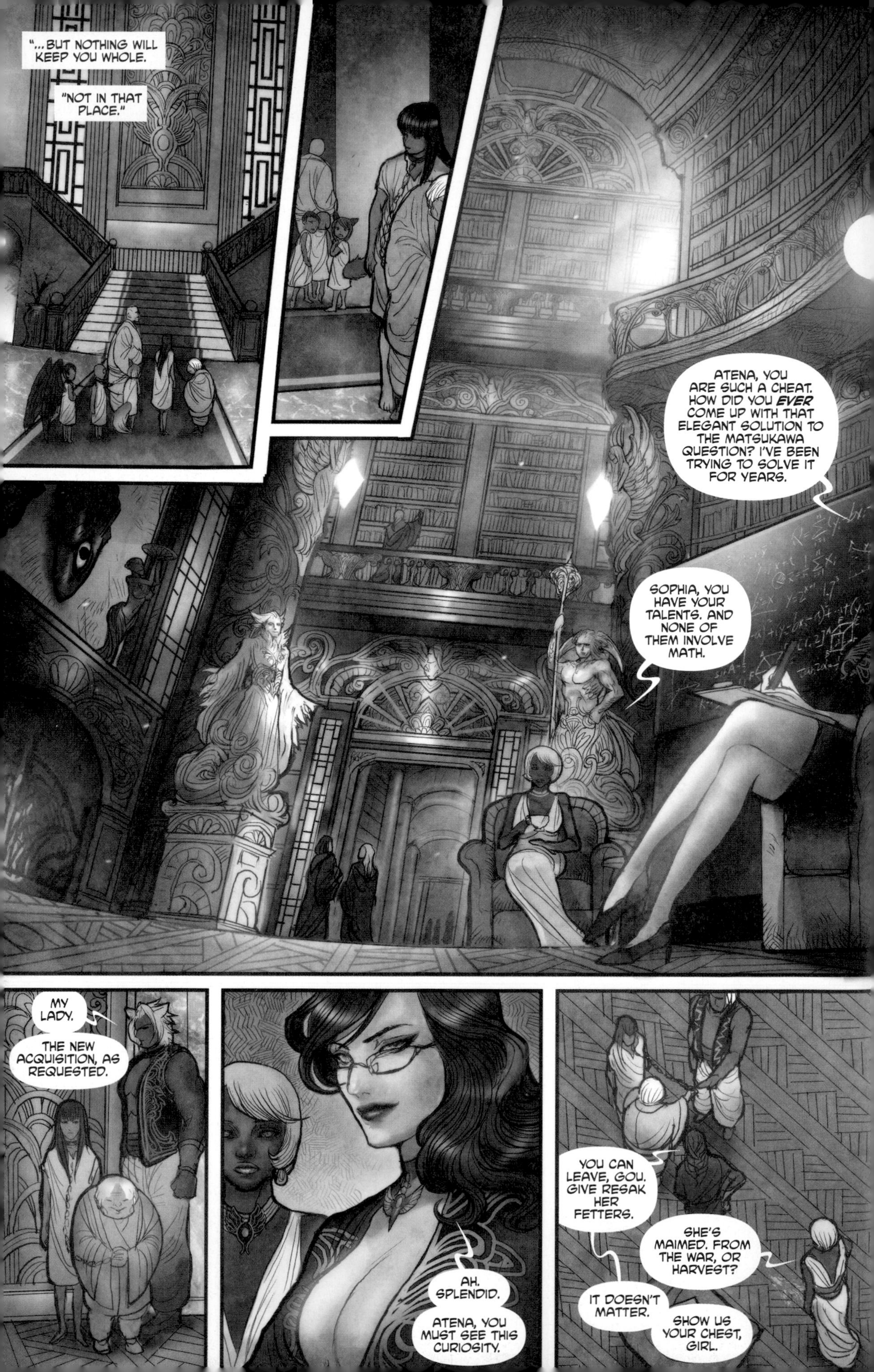

"...BUT NOTHING WILL KEEP YOU WHOLE.
"NOT IN THAT PLACE."
ATENA, YOU ARE SUCH A CHEAT. HOW DID YOU EVER COME UP WITH THAT ELEGANT SOLUTION TO THE MATSUKAWA QUESTION? I'VE BEEN TRYING TO SOLVE IT FOR YEARS.
SOPHIA, YOU HAVE YOUR TALENTS. AND NONE OF THEM INVOLVE MATH.
MY LADY.
THE NEW ACQUISITION, AS REQUESTED.
AH. SPLENDID.
ATENA, YOU MUST SEE THIS CURIOSITY.
YOU CAN LEAVE, GOU. GIVE RESAK HER FETTERS.
SHE'S MAIMED. FROM THE WAR, OR HARVEST?
IT DOESN'T MATTER.
SHOW US YOUR CHEST, GIRL.

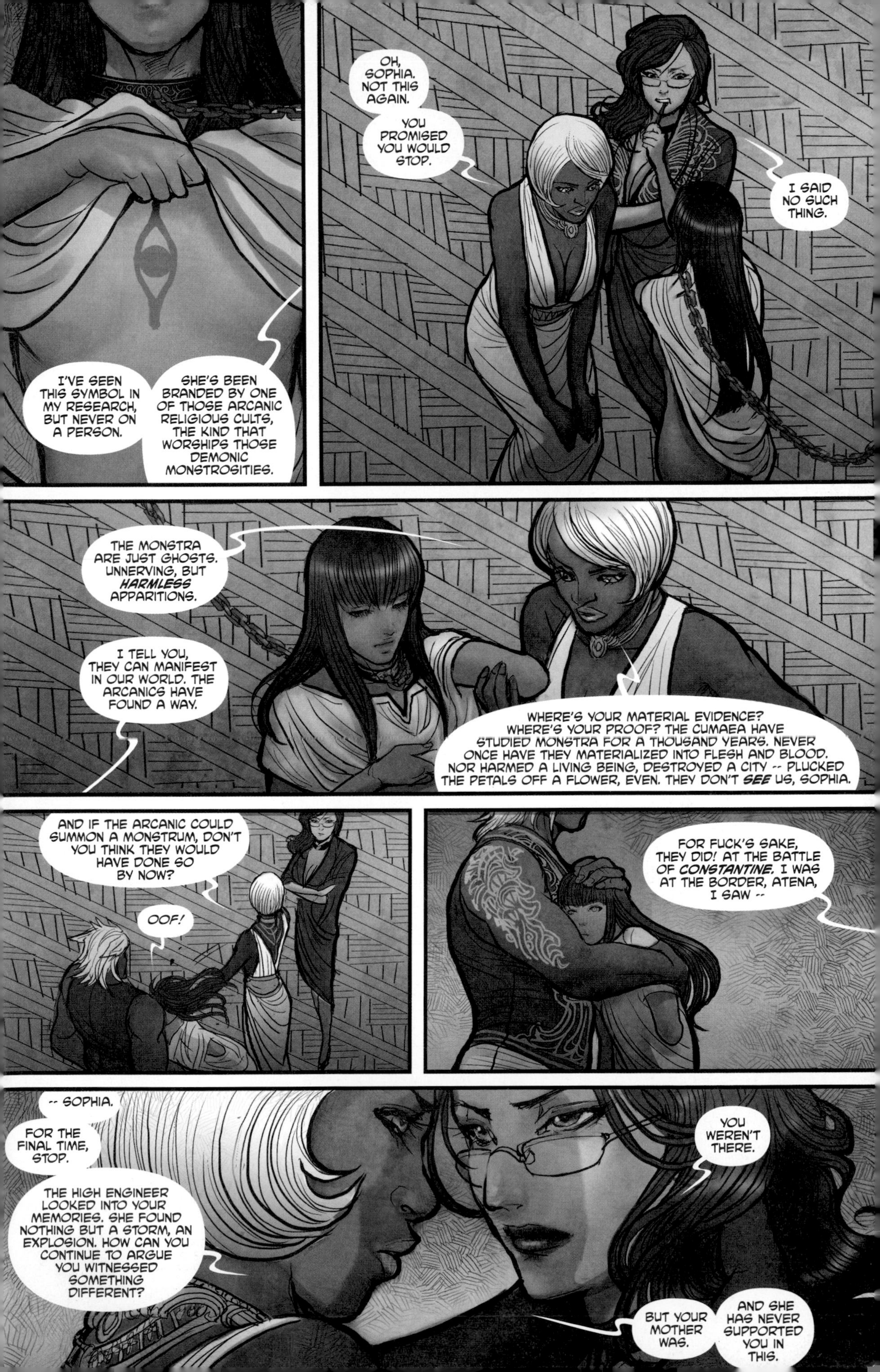
I'VE SEEN THIS SYMBOL IN MY RESEARCH, BUT NEVER ON A PERSON.
SHE'S BEEN BRANDED BY ONE OF THOSE ARCANIC RELIGIOUS CULTS, THE KIND THAT WORSHIPS THOSE DEMONIC MONSTROSITIES.
OH, SOPHIA. NOT THIS AGAIN.
YOU PROMISED YOU WOULD STOP.
I SAID NO SUCH THING.
THE MONSTRA ARE JUST GHOSTS. UNNERVING, BUT *HARMLESS* APPARITIONS.
I TELL YOU, THEY CAN MANIFEST IN OUR WORLD. THE ARCANICS HAVE FOUND A WAY.
WHERE'S YOUR MATERIAL EVIDENCE? WHERE'S YOUR PROOF? THE CUMAEA HAVE STUDIED MONSTRA FOR A THOUSAND YEARS. NEVER ONCE HAVE THEY MATERIALIZED INTO FLESH AND BLOOD. NOR HARMED A LIVING BEING, DESTROYED A CITY -- PLUCKED THE PETALS OFF A FLOWER, EVEN. THEY DON'T *SEE* US, SOPHIA.
AND IF THE ARCANIC COULD SUMMON A MONSTRUM, DON'T YOU THINK THEY WOULD HAVE DONE SO BY NOW?
OOF!
FOR FUCK'S SAKE, THEY DID! AT THE BATTLE OF *CONSTANTINE.* I WAS AT THE BORDER, ATENA, I SAW --
-- SOPHIA.
FOR THE FINAL TIME, STOP.
THE HIGH ENGINEER LOOKED INTO YOUR MEMORIES. SHE FOUND NOTHING BUT A STORM, AN EXPLOSION. HOW CAN YOU CONTINUE TO ARGUE YOU WITNESSED SOMETHING DIFFERENT?
YOU WEREN'T THERE.
BUT YOUR MOTHER WAS.
AND SHE HAS NEVER SUPPORTED YOU IN THIS.

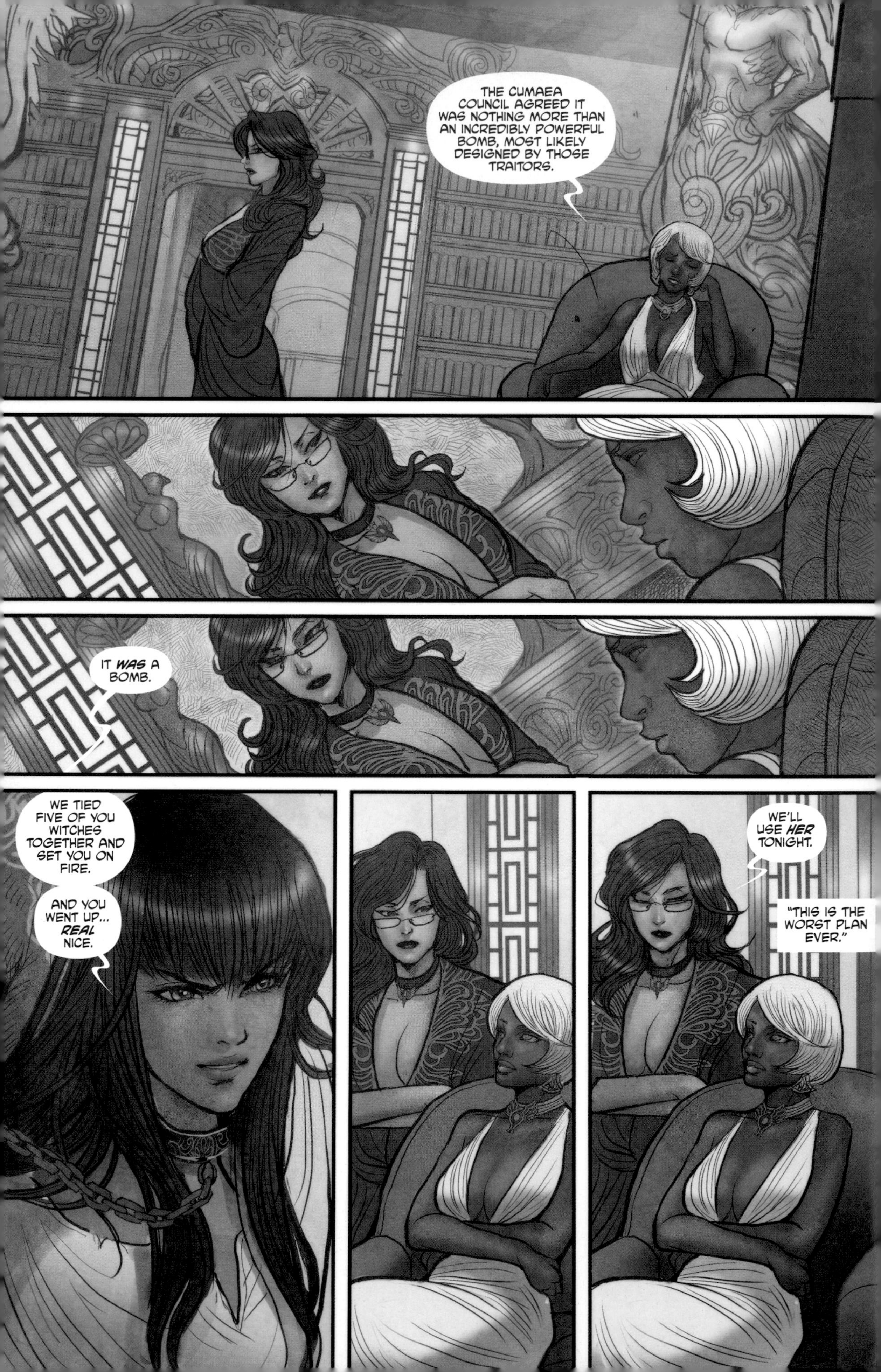
THE CUMAEA COUNCIL AGREED IT WAS NOTHING MORE THAN AN INCREDIBLY POWERFUL BOMB, MOST LIKELY DESIGNED BY THOSE TRAITORS.
IT *WAS* A BOMB.
WE TIED FIVE OF YOU WITCHES TOGETHER AND SET YOU ON FIRE.
AND YOU WENT UP... *REAL* NICE.
WE'LL USE *HER* TONIGHT.
"THIS IS THE WORST PLAN EVER."

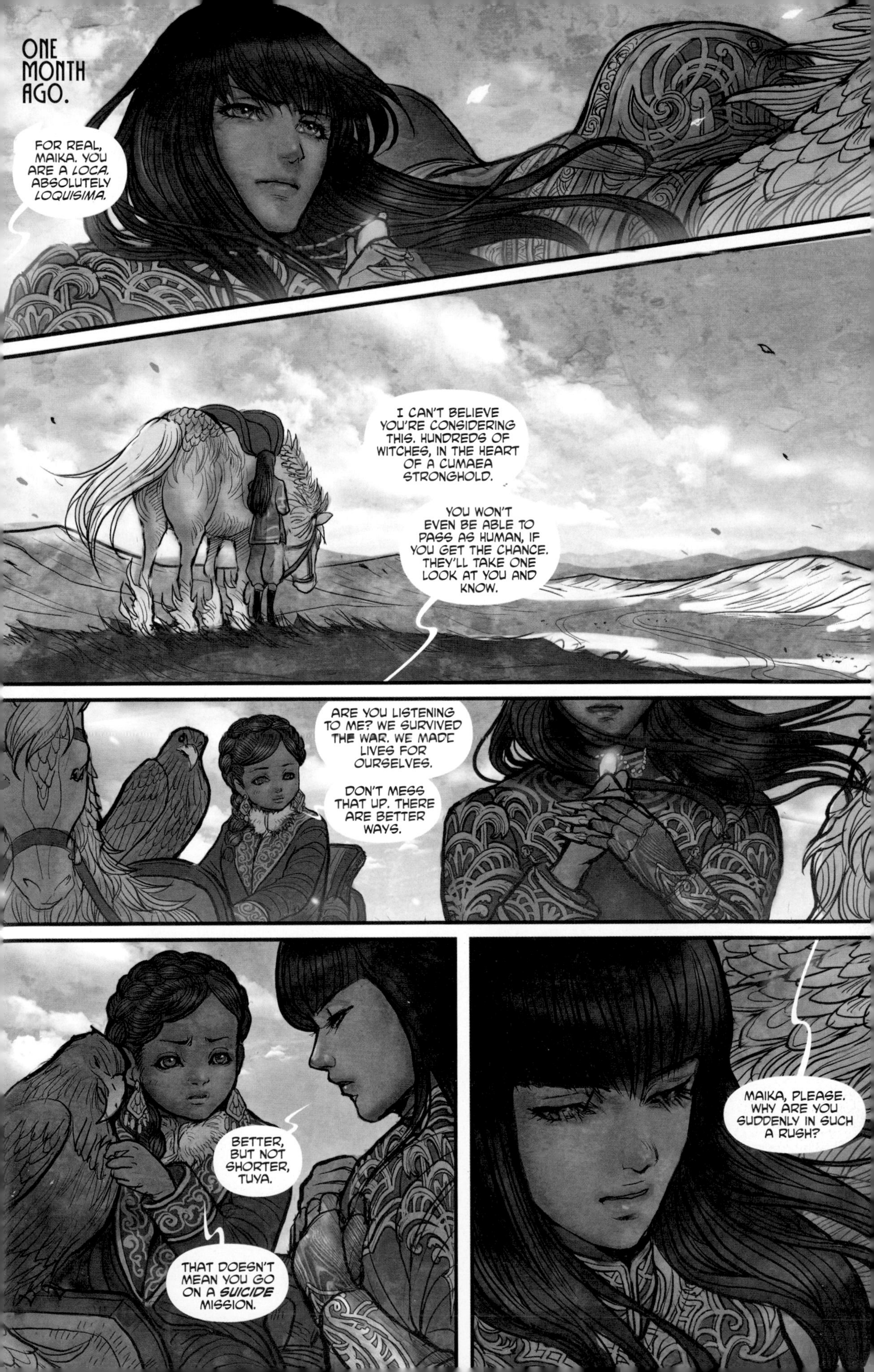
ONE MONTH AGO.
FOR REAL, MAIKA. YOU ARE A *LOCA.* ABSOLUTELY *LOQUISIMA.*
I CAN'T BELIEVE YOU'RE CONSIDERING THIS. HUNDREDS OF WITCHES, IN THE HEART OF A CUMAEA STRONGHOLD.
YOU WON'T EVEN BE ABLE TO PASS AS HUMAN, IF YOU GET THE CHANCE. THEY'LL TAKE ONE LOOK AT YOU AND KNOW.
ARE YOU LISTENING TO ME? WE SURVIVED THE WAR. WE MADE LIVES FOR OURSELVES.
DON'T MESS THAT UP. THERE ARE BETTER WAYS.
BETTER, BUT NOT SHORTER, TUYA.
THAT DOESN'T MEAN YOU GO ON A ***SUICIDE*** MISSION.
MAIKA, PLEASE. WHY ARE YOU SUDDENLY IN SUCH A RUSH?

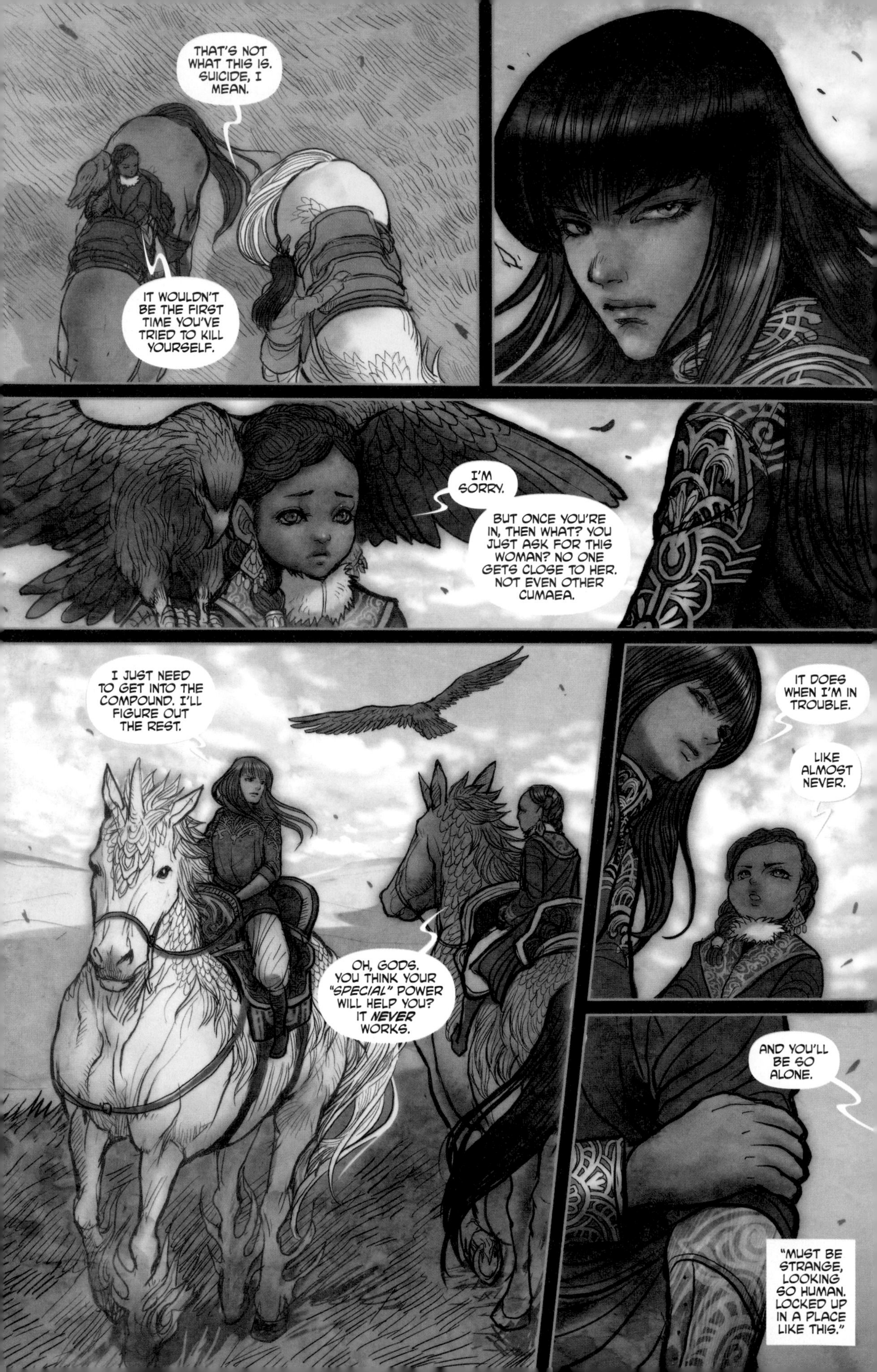
THAT'S NOT WHAT THIS IS. SUICIDE, I MEAN.
IT WOULDN'T BE THE FIRST TIME YOU'VE TRIED TO KILL YOURSELF.
I'M SORRY.
BUT ONCE YOU'RE IN, THEN WHAT? YOU JUST ASK FOR THIS WOMAN? NO ONE GETS CLOSE TO HER. NOT EVEN OTHER CUMAEA.
I JUST NEED TO GET INTO THE COMPOUND. I'LL FIGURE OUT THE REST.
OH, GODS. YOU THINK YOUR "SPECIAL" POWER WILL HELP YOU? IT NEVER WORKS.
IT DOES WHEN I'M IN TROUBLE.
LIKE ALMOST NEVER.
AND YOU'LL BE SO ALONE.
"MUST BE STRANGE, LOOKING SO HUMAN. LOCKED UP IN A PLACE LIKE THIS."

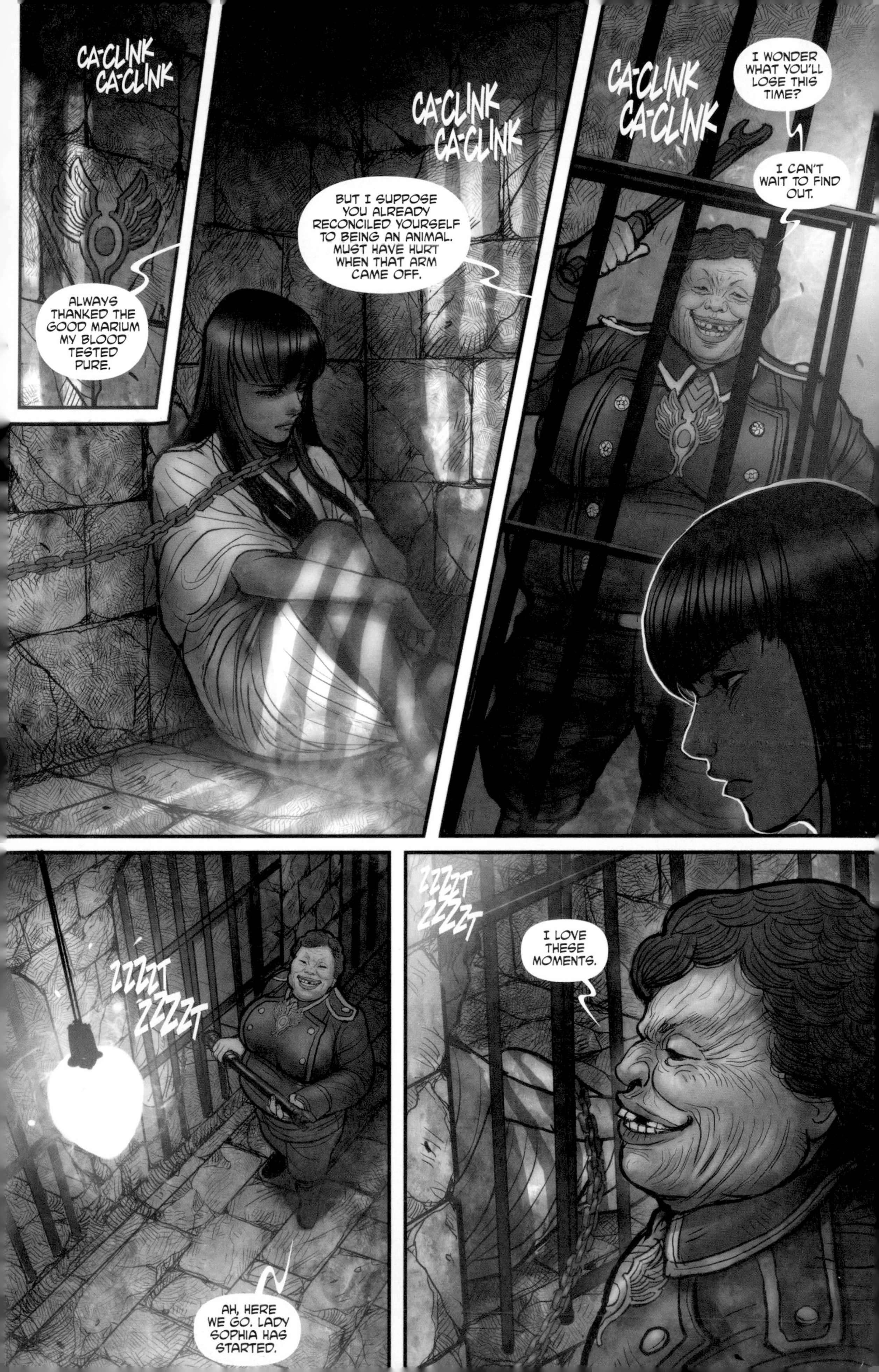
CA-CLINK CA-CLINK
ALWAYS THANKED THE GOOD MARIUM MY BLOOD TESTED PURE.
CA-CLINK CA-CLINK
BUT I SUPPOSE YOU ALREADY RECONCILED YOURSELF TO BEING AN ANIMAL. MUST HAVE HURT WHEN THAT ARM CAME OFF.
CA-CLINK CA-CLINK
I WONDER WHAT YOU'LL LOSE THIS TIME?
I CAN'T WAIT TO FIND OUT.
ZZZZT ZZZZT
AH, HERE WE GO. LADY SOPHIA HAS STARTED.
ZZZZT ZZZZT
I LOVE THESE MOMENTS.

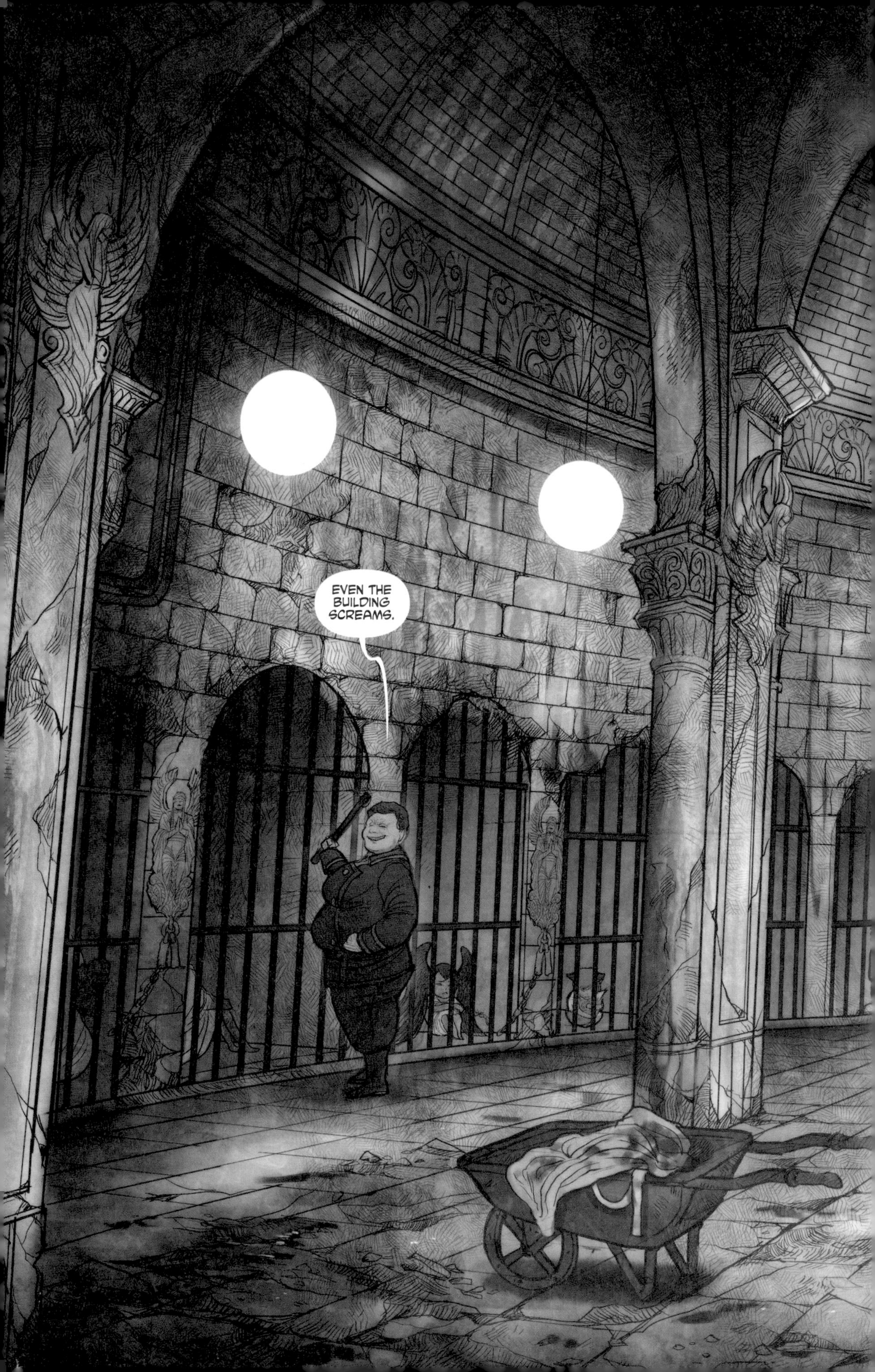
EVEN THE BUILDING SCREAMS.

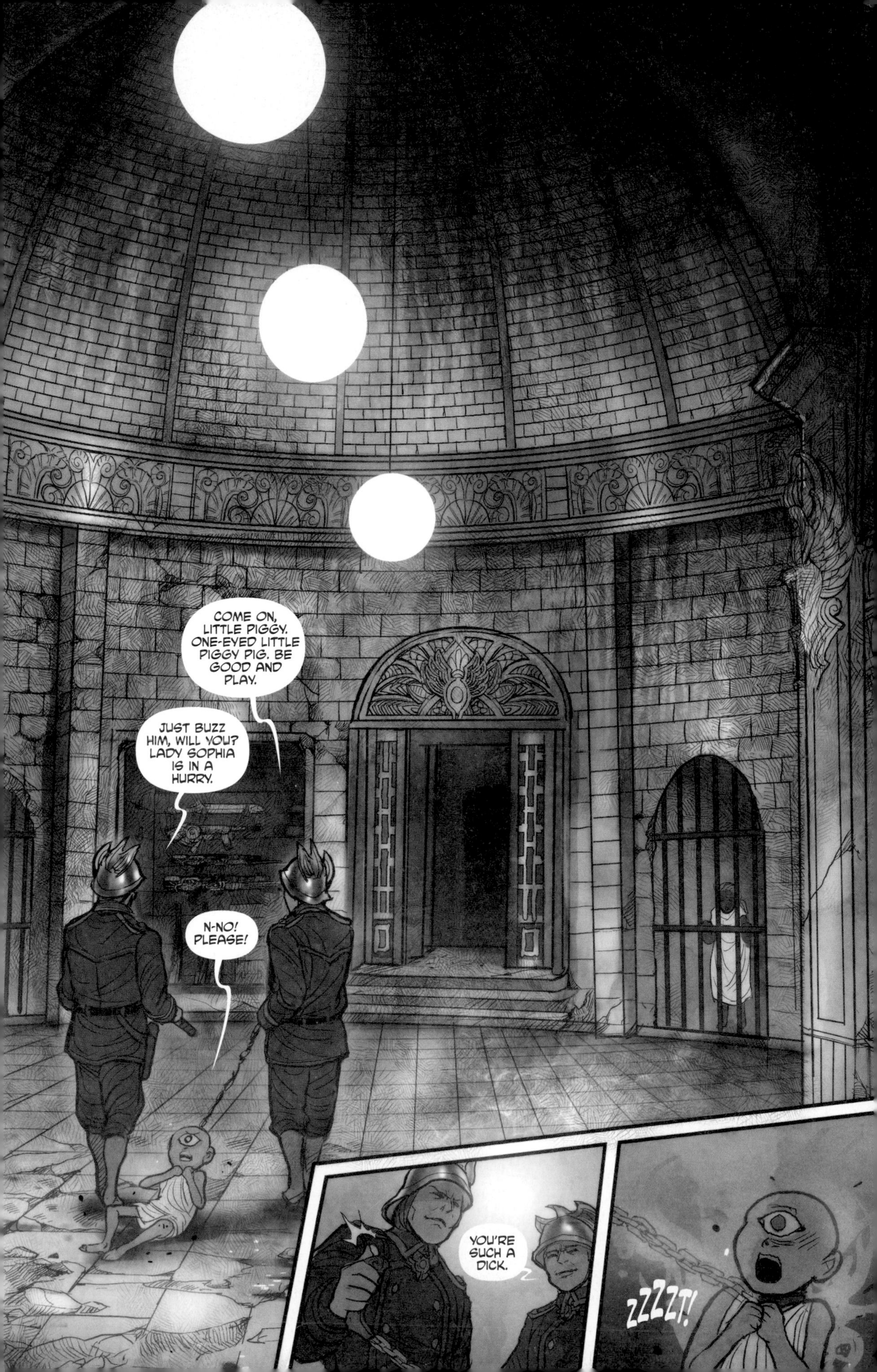
COME ON, LITTLE PIGGY. ONE-EYED LITTLE PIGGY PIG. BE GOOD AND PLAY.
JUST BUZZ HIM, WILL YOU? LADY SOPHIA IS IN A HURRY.
N-NO! PLEASE!
YOU'RE SUCH A DICK.
ZZZZT!

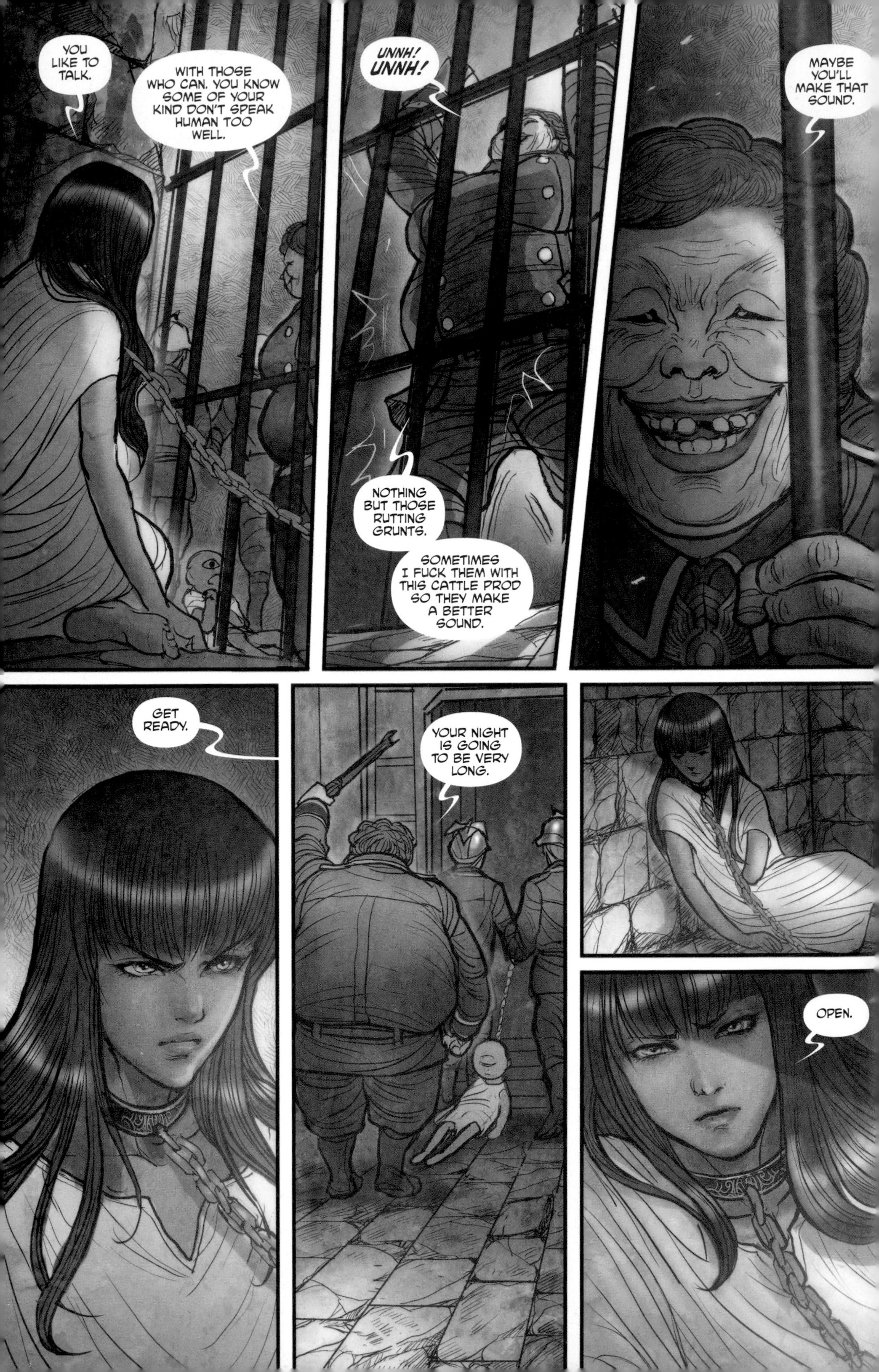
YOU LIKE TO TALK.
WITH THOSE WHO CAN. YOU KNOW SOME OF YOUR KIND DON'T SPEAK HUMAN TOO WELL.
UNNH! UNNH!
NOTHING BUT THOSE RUTTING GRUNTS.
SOMETIMES I FUCK THEM WITH THIS CATTLE PROD SO THEY MAKE A BETTER SOUND.
MAYBE YOU'LL MAKE THAT SOUND.
GET READY.
YOUR NIGHT IS GOING TO BE VERY LONG.
OPEN.

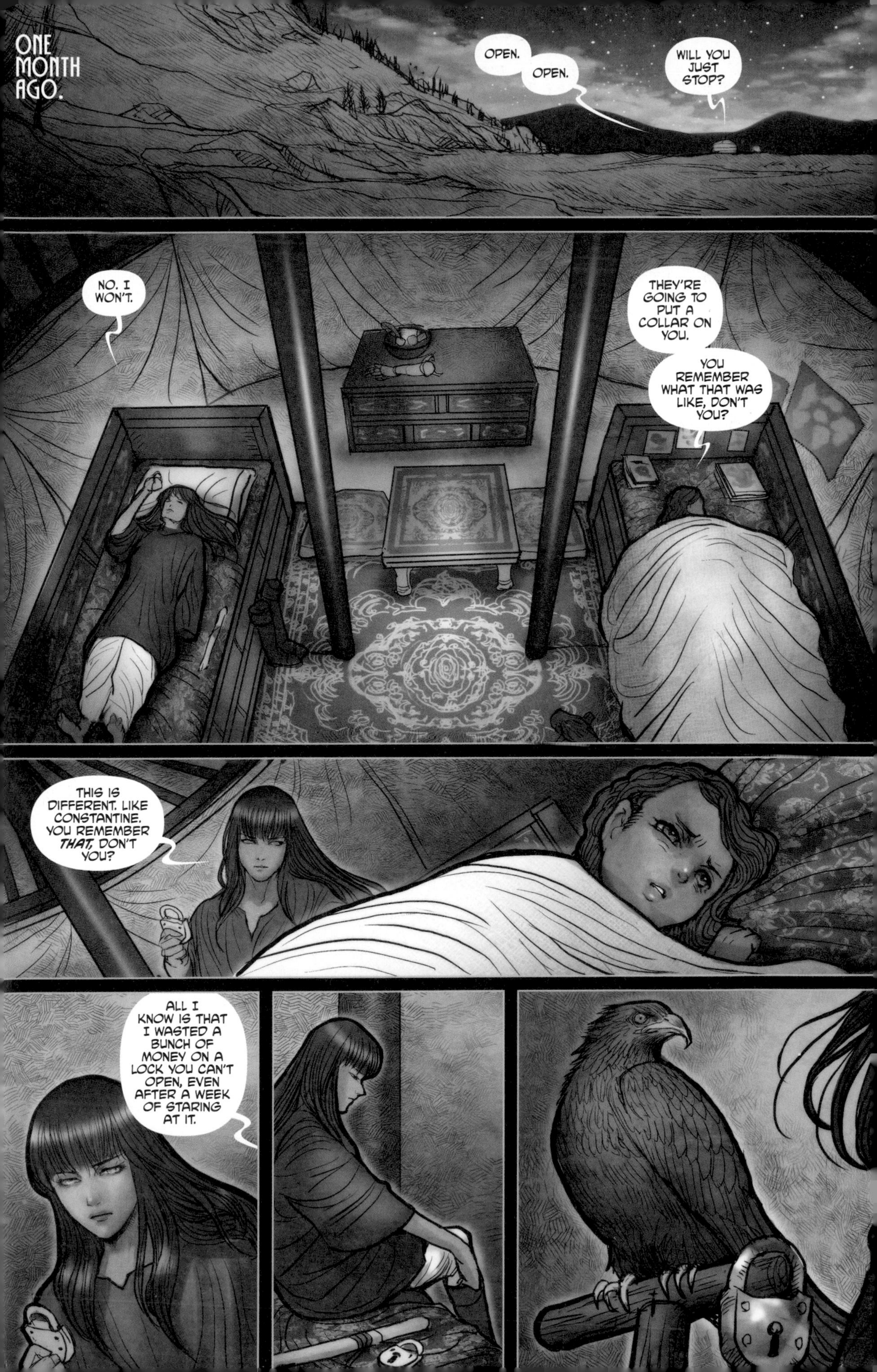

ONE MONTH AGO.
OPEN.
OPEN.
WILL YOU JUST STOP?
NO. I WON'T.
THEY'RE GOING TO PUT A COLLAR ON YOU.
YOU REMEMBER WHAT THAT WAS LIKE, DON'T YOU?
THIS IS DIFFERENT. LIKE CONSTANTINE. YOU REMEMBER *THAT,* DON'T YOU?
ALL I KNOW IS THAT I WASTED A BUNCH OF MONEY ON A LOCK YOU CAN'T OPEN, EVEN AFTER A WEEK OF STARING AT IT.

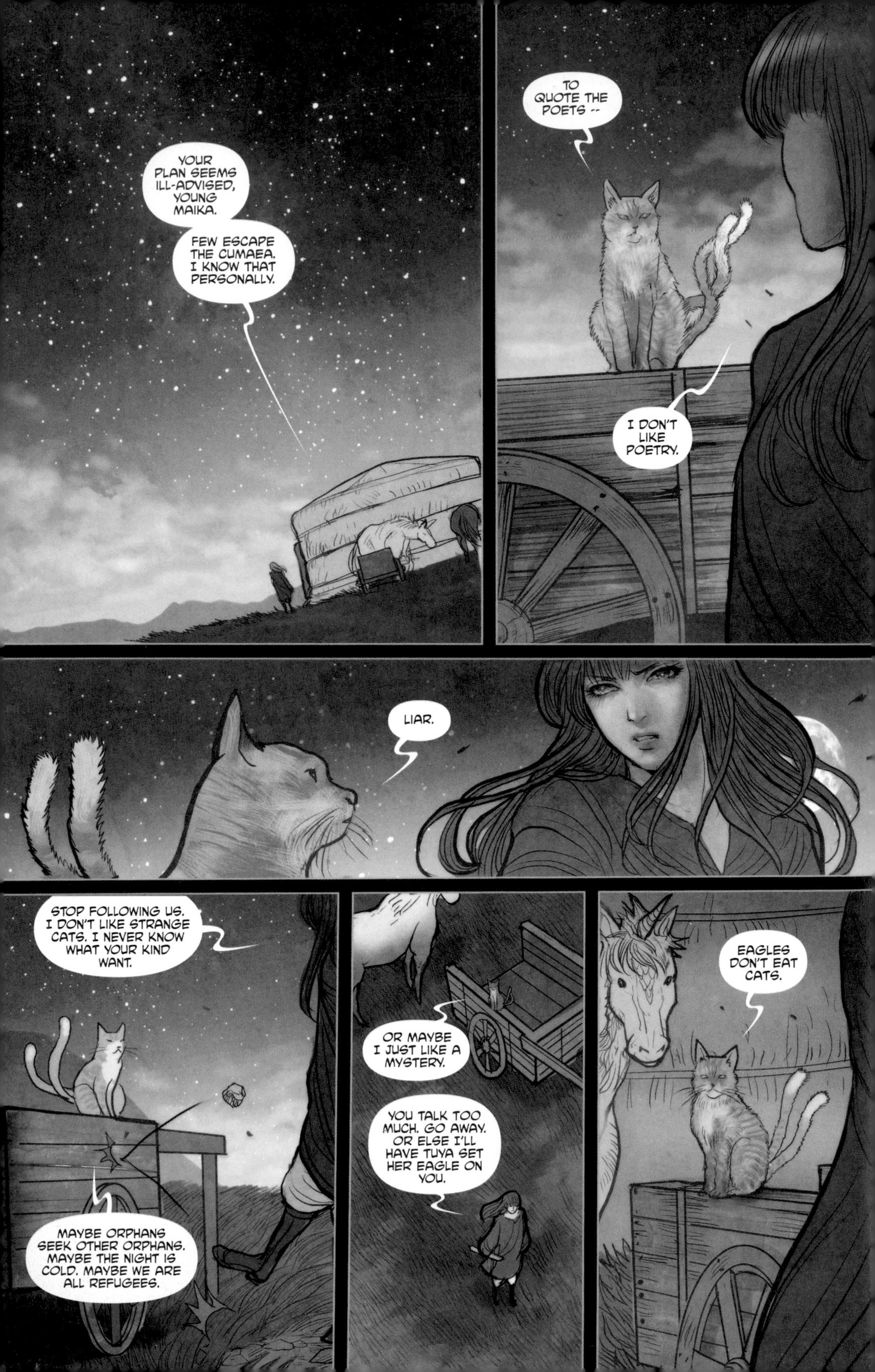
YOUR PLAN SEEMS ILL-ADVISED, YOUNG MAIKA.
FEW ESCAPE THE CUMAEA. I KNOW THAT PERSONALLY.
TO QUOTE THE POETS --
I DON'T LIKE POETRY.
LIAR.
STOP FOLLOWING US. I DON'T LIKE STRANGE CATS. I NEVER KNOW WHAT YOUR KIND WANT.
MAYBE ORPHANS SEEK OTHER ORPHANS. MAYBE THE NIGHT IS COLD. MAYBE WE ARE ALL REFUGEES.
OR MAYBE I JUST LIKE A MYSTERY.
YOU TALK TOO MUCH. GO AWAY. OR ELSE I'LL HAVE TUYA SET HER EAGLE ON YOU.
EAGLES DON'T EAT CATS.

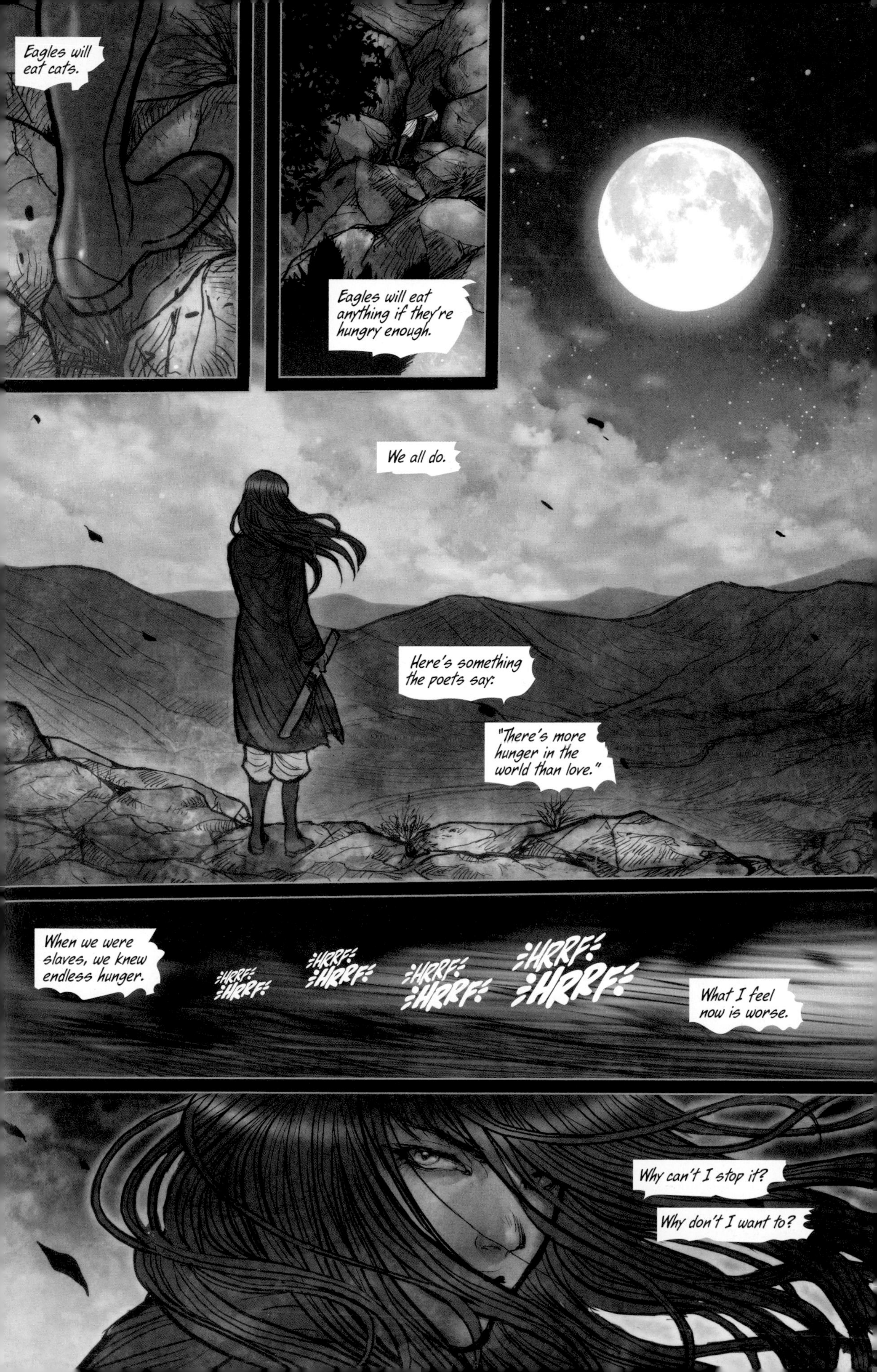
Eagles will eat cats.
Eagles will eat anything if they're hungry enough.
We all do.
Here's something the poets say:
"There's more hunger in the world than love."
When we were slaves, we knew endless hunger.
HRRF HRRF
HRRF HRRF
HRRF HRRF
HRRF HRRF
What I feel now is worse.
Why can't I stop it?
Why don't I want to?

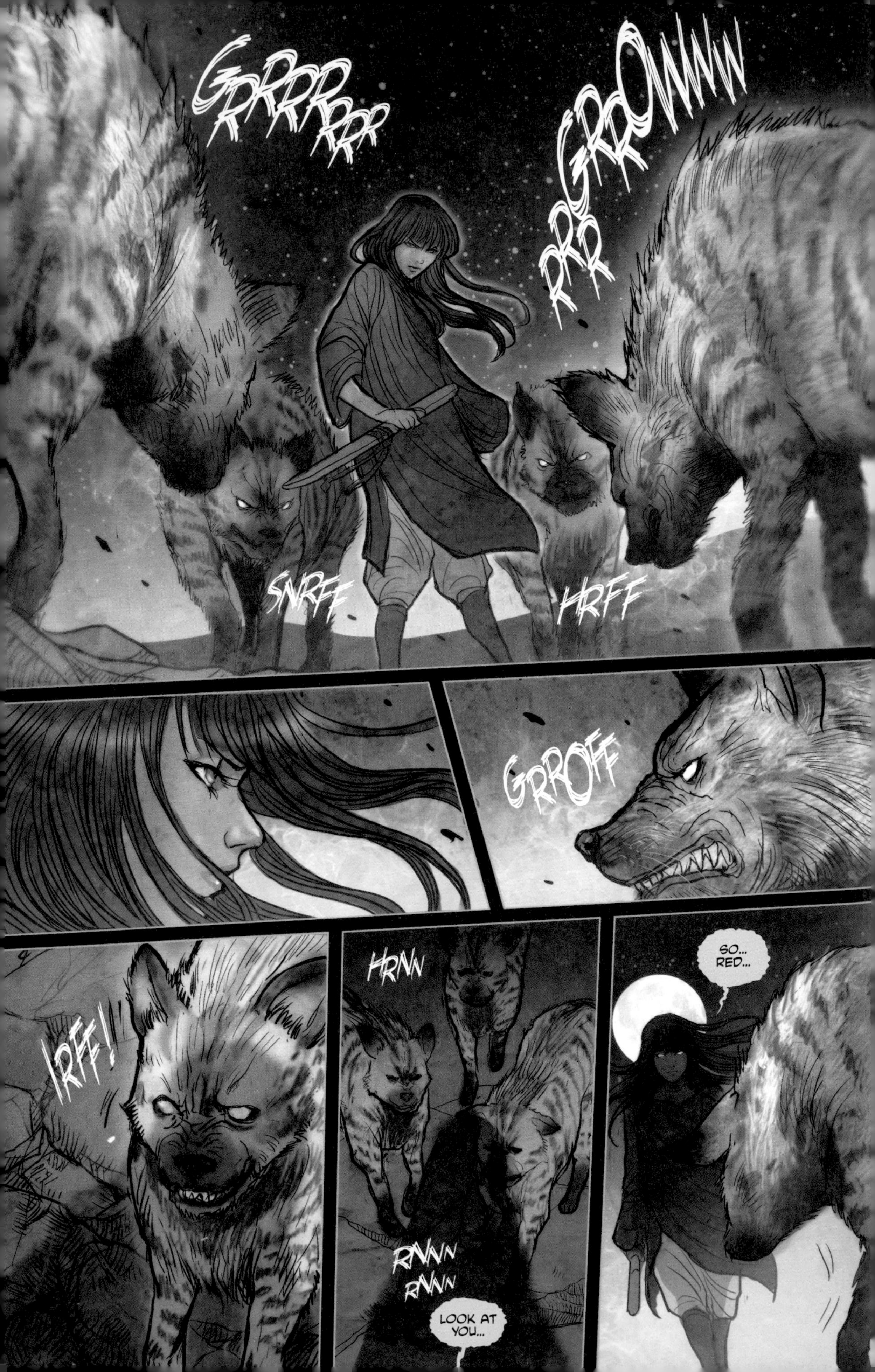
GRRRRRRRR
RRRGRROWWW
SNRFF
HRFF
GRROFF
IRFF!
HRNN
SO... RED...
RNNN RNNN
LOOK AT YOU...

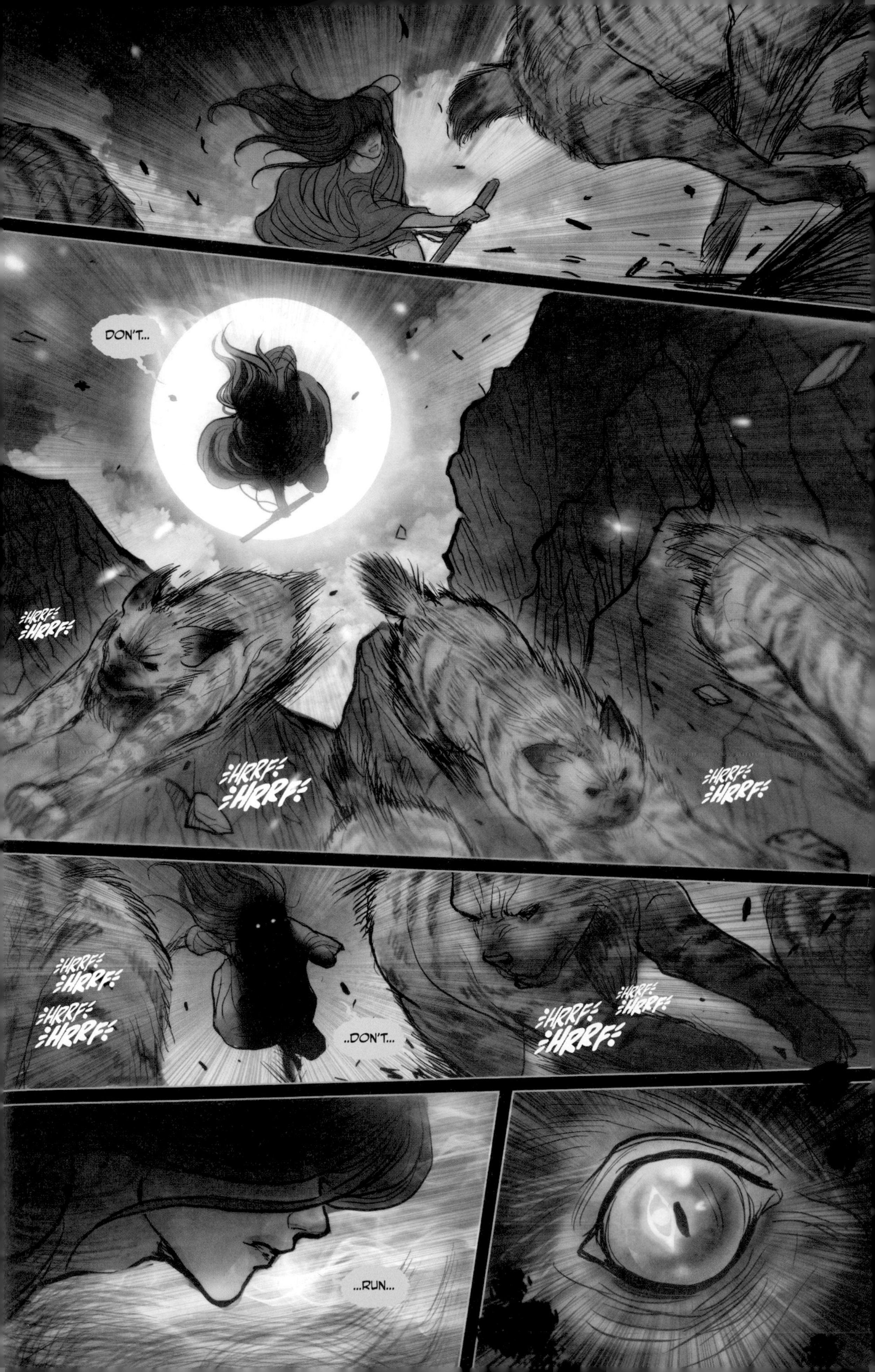
DON'T...
HRRF HRRF
HRRF HRRF
HRRF HRRF
HRRF HRRF
HRRF HRRF
..DON'T...
HRRF HRRF
HRRF HRRF
...RUN...

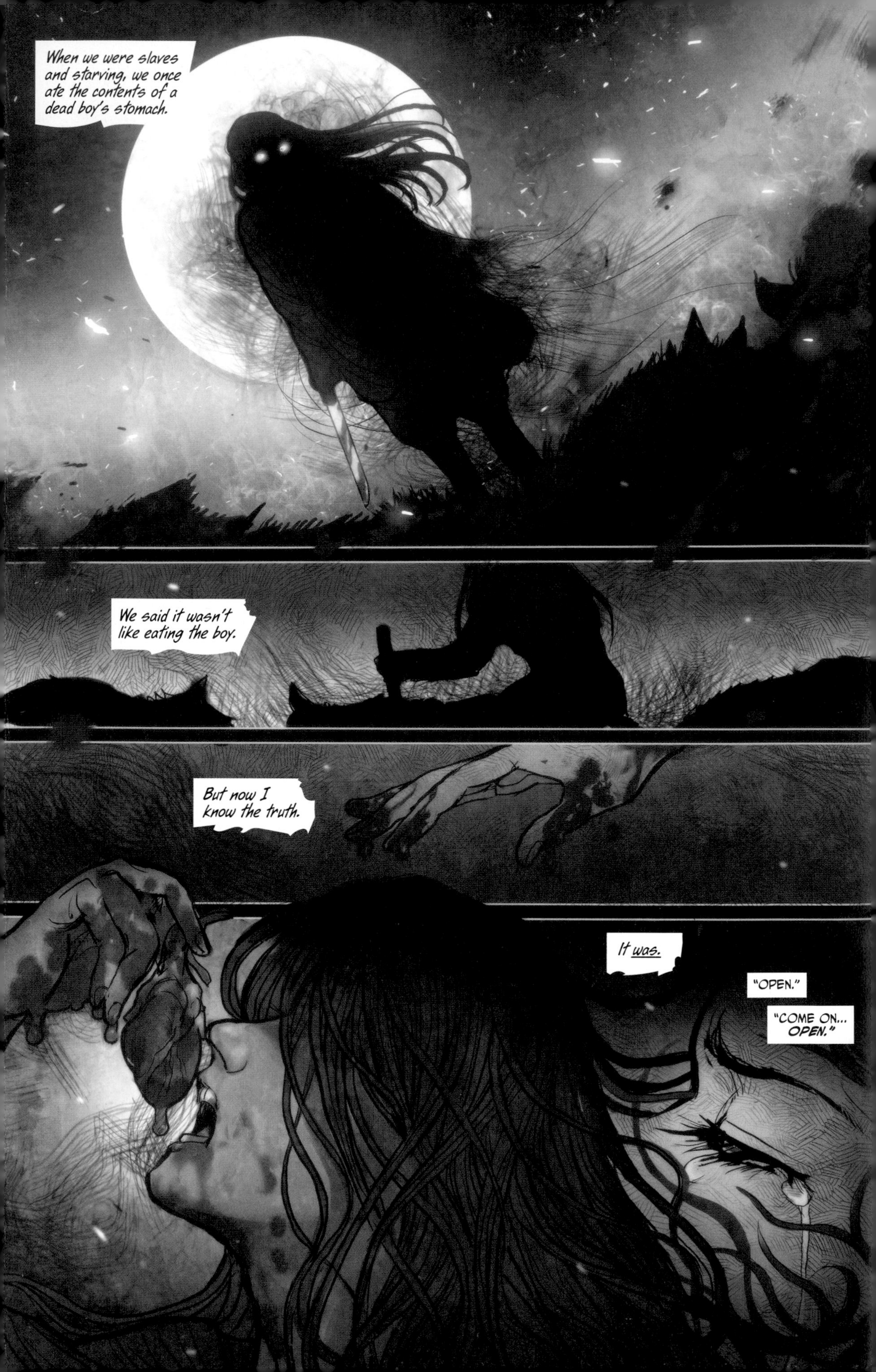
When we were slaves and starving, we once ate the contents of a dead boy's stomach.
We said it wasn't like eating the boy.
But now I know the truth.
It was.
"OPEN."
"COME ON... OPEN."

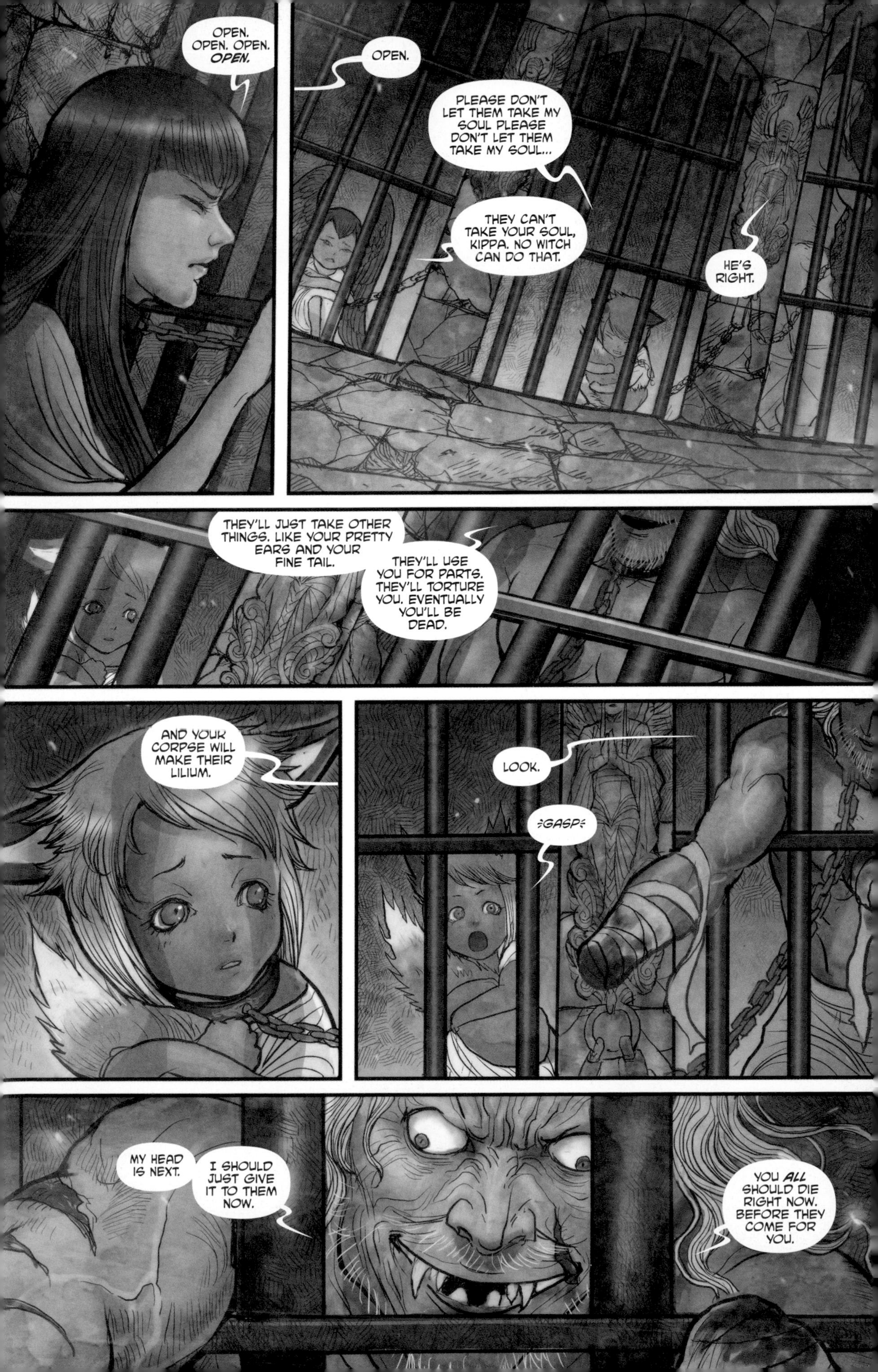

OPEN. OPEN. OPEN. *OPEN.*
OPEN.
PLEASE DON'T LET THEM TAKE MY SOUL PLEASE DON'T LET THEM TAKE MY SOUL...
THEY CAN'T TAKE YOUR SOUL, KIPPA. NO WITCH CAN DO THAT.
HE'S RIGHT.
THEY'LL JUST TAKE OTHER THINGS. LIKE YOUR PRETTY EARS AND YOUR FINE TAIL.
THEY'LL USE YOU FOR PARTS. THEY'LL TORTURE YOU. EVENTUALLY YOU'LL BE DEAD.
AND YOUR CORPSE WILL MAKE THEIR LILIUM.
LOOK.
GASP
MY HEAD IS NEXT.
I SHOULD JUST GIVE IT TO THEM NOW.
YOU *ALL* SHOULD DIE RIGHT NOW. BEFORE THEY COME FOR YOU.

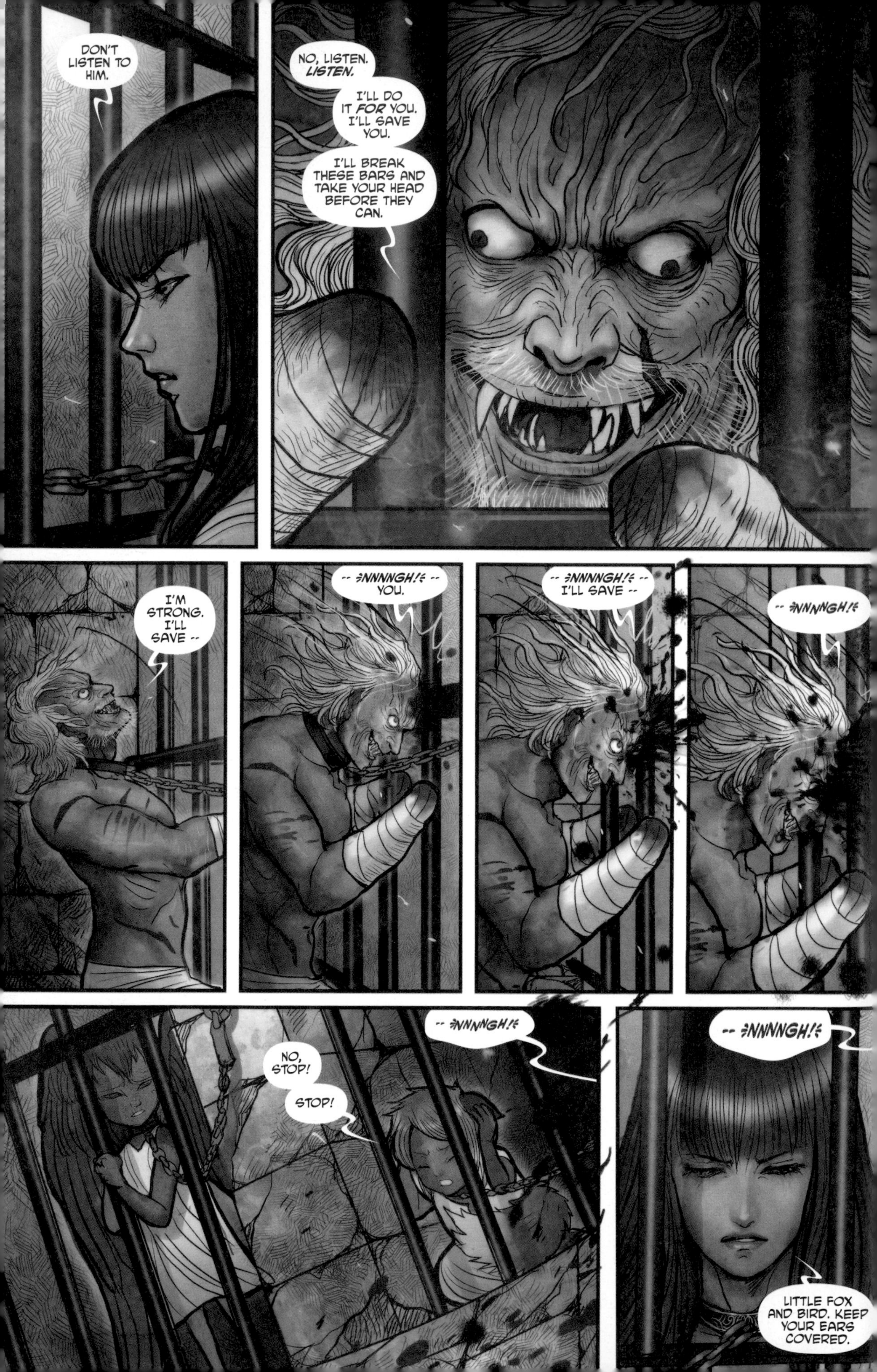
DON'T LISTEN TO HIM.
NO, LISTEN. LISTEN.
I'LL DO IT FOR YOU. I'LL SAVE YOU.
I'LL BREAK THESE BARS AND TAKE YOUR HEAD BEFORE THEY CAN.
I'M STRONG. I'LL SAVE --
-- NNNNGH! -- YOU.
-- NNNNGH! -- I'LL SAVE --
-- NNNNGH!
NO, STOP!
STOP!
-- NNNNGH!
-- NNNNGH!
LITTLE FOX AND BIRD. KEEP YOUR EARS COVERED.

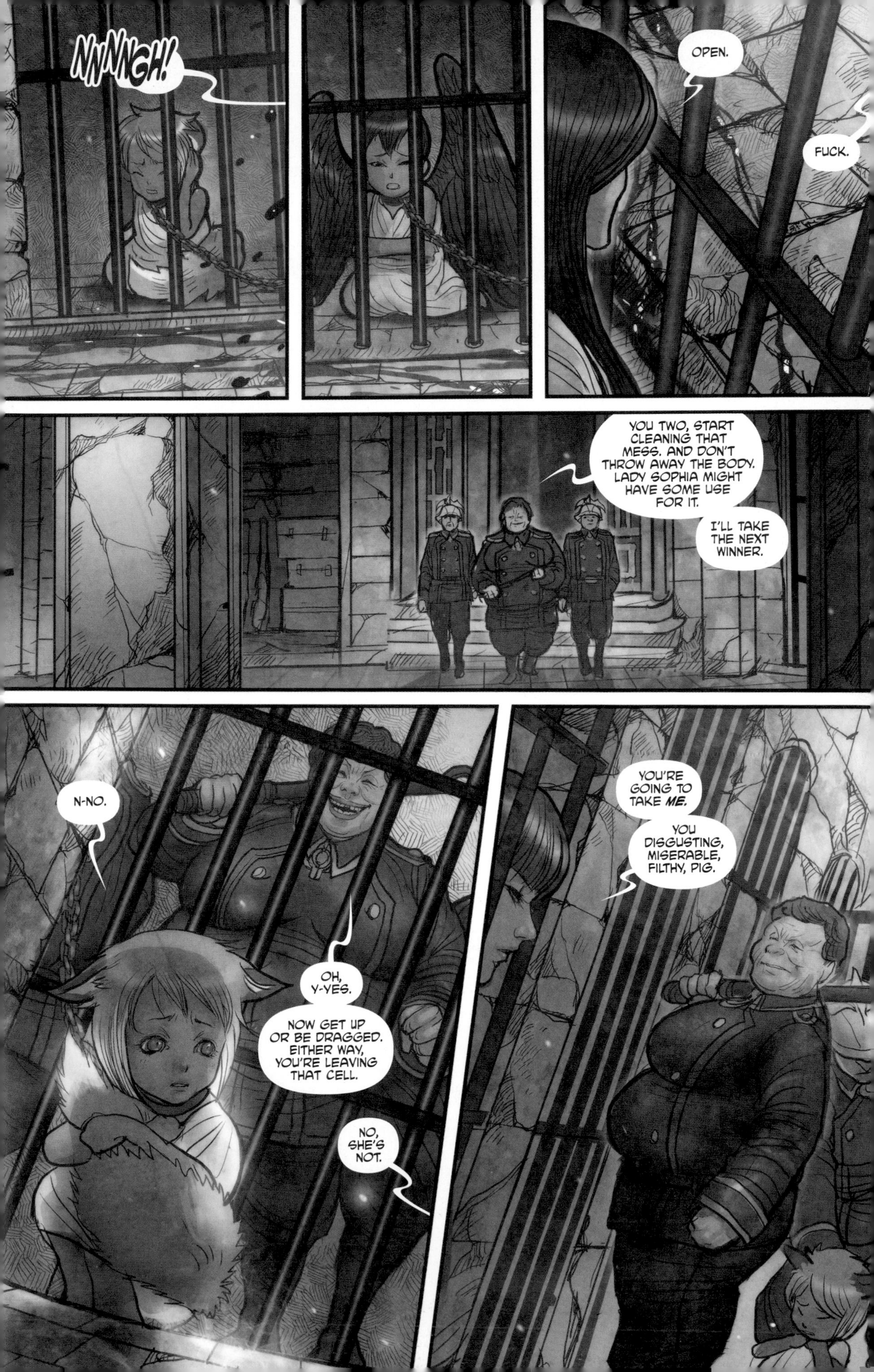
NNNNGH!
OPEN.
FUCK.
YOU TWO, START CLEANING THAT MESS. AND DON'T THROW AWAY THE BODY. LADY SOPHIA MIGHT HAVE SOME USE FOR IT.
I'LL TAKE THE NEXT WINNER.
N-NO.
OH, Y-YES.
NOW GET UP OR BE DRAGGED. EITHER WAY, YOU'RE LEAVING THAT CELL.
NO, SHE'S NOT.
YOU'RE GOING TO TAKE *ME*.
YOU DISGUSTING, MISERABLE, FILTHY, PIG.

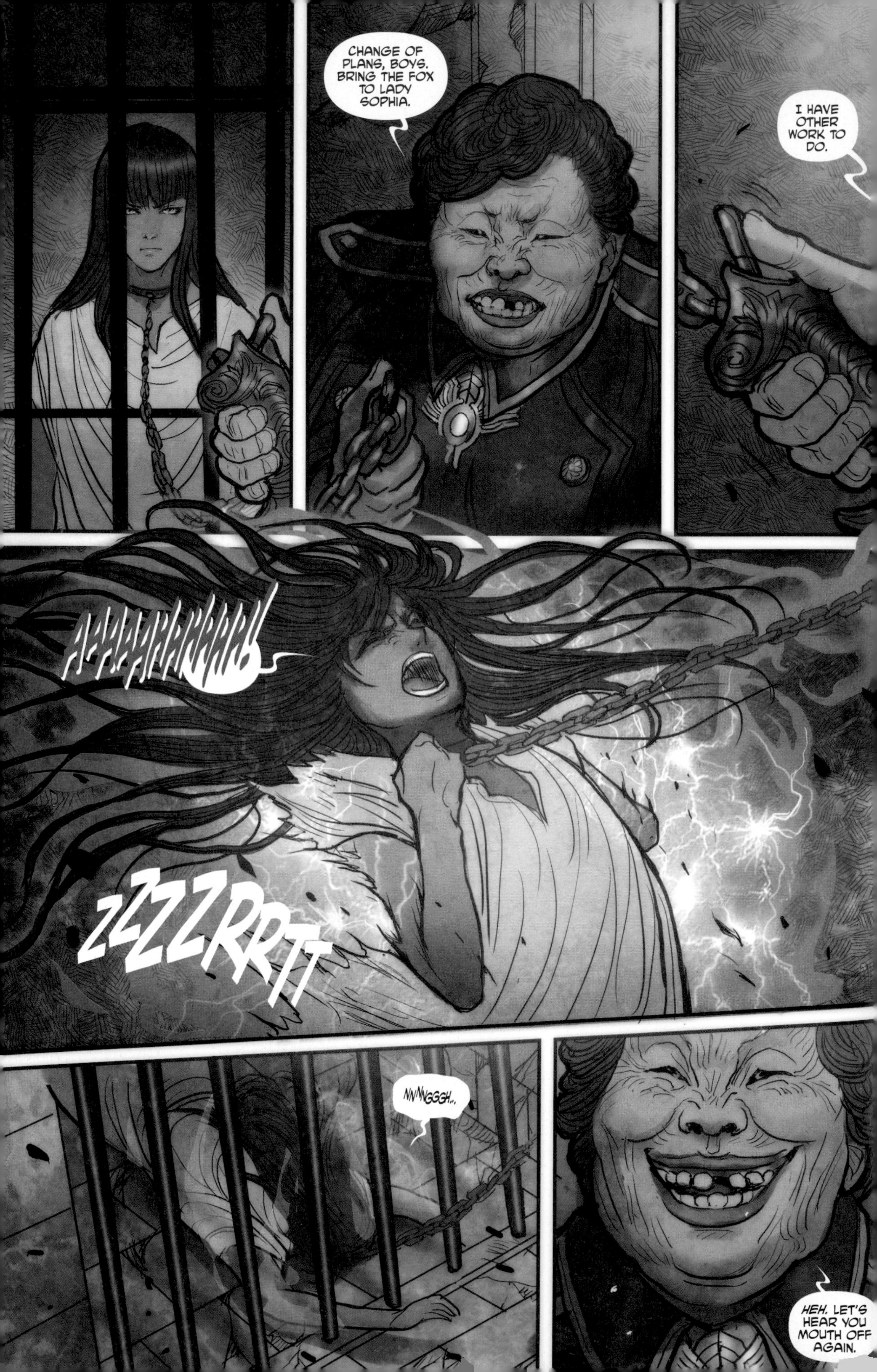

CHANGE OF PLANS, BOYS. BRING THE FOX TO LADY SOPHIA.
I HAVE OTHER WORK TO DO.
AAAAAHHHHHHH!
zZZZRRTT
NNNNGGGH..
HEH. LET'S HEAR YOU MOUTH OFF AGAIN.

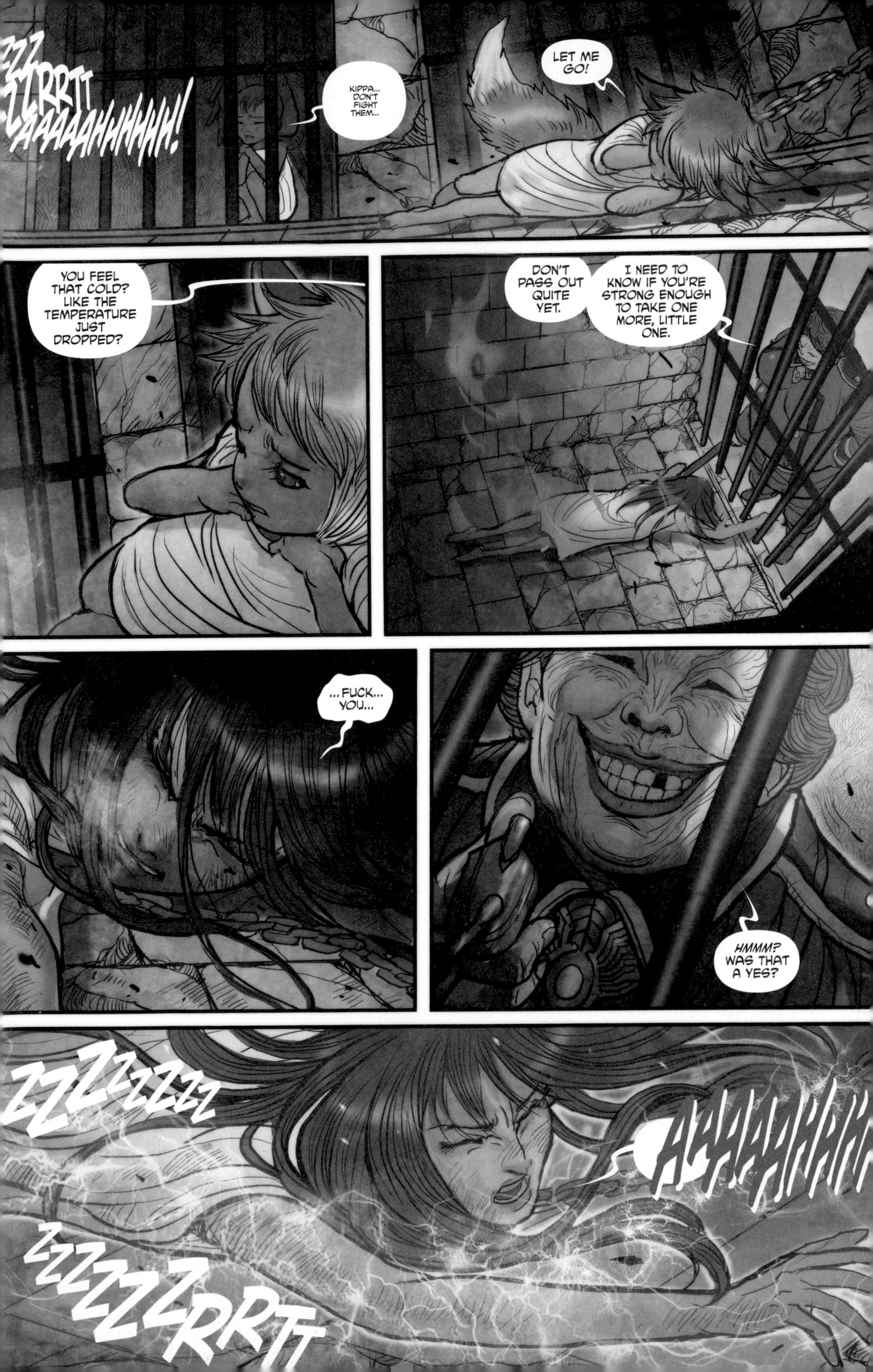
ZZZ ZZRRTT
AAAAAHHHHH!
KIPPA... DON'T FIGHT THEM...
LET ME GO!
YOU FEEL THAT COLD? LIKE THE TEMPERATURE JUST DROPPED?
DON'T PASS OUT QUITE YET.
I NEED TO KNOW IF YOU'RE STRONG ENOUGH TO TAKE ONE MORE, LITTLE ONE.
...FUCK... YOU...
HMMM? WAS THAT A YES?
ZZZZZZZZZZ
AAAAAHHHH
ZZZZZZZRRTT

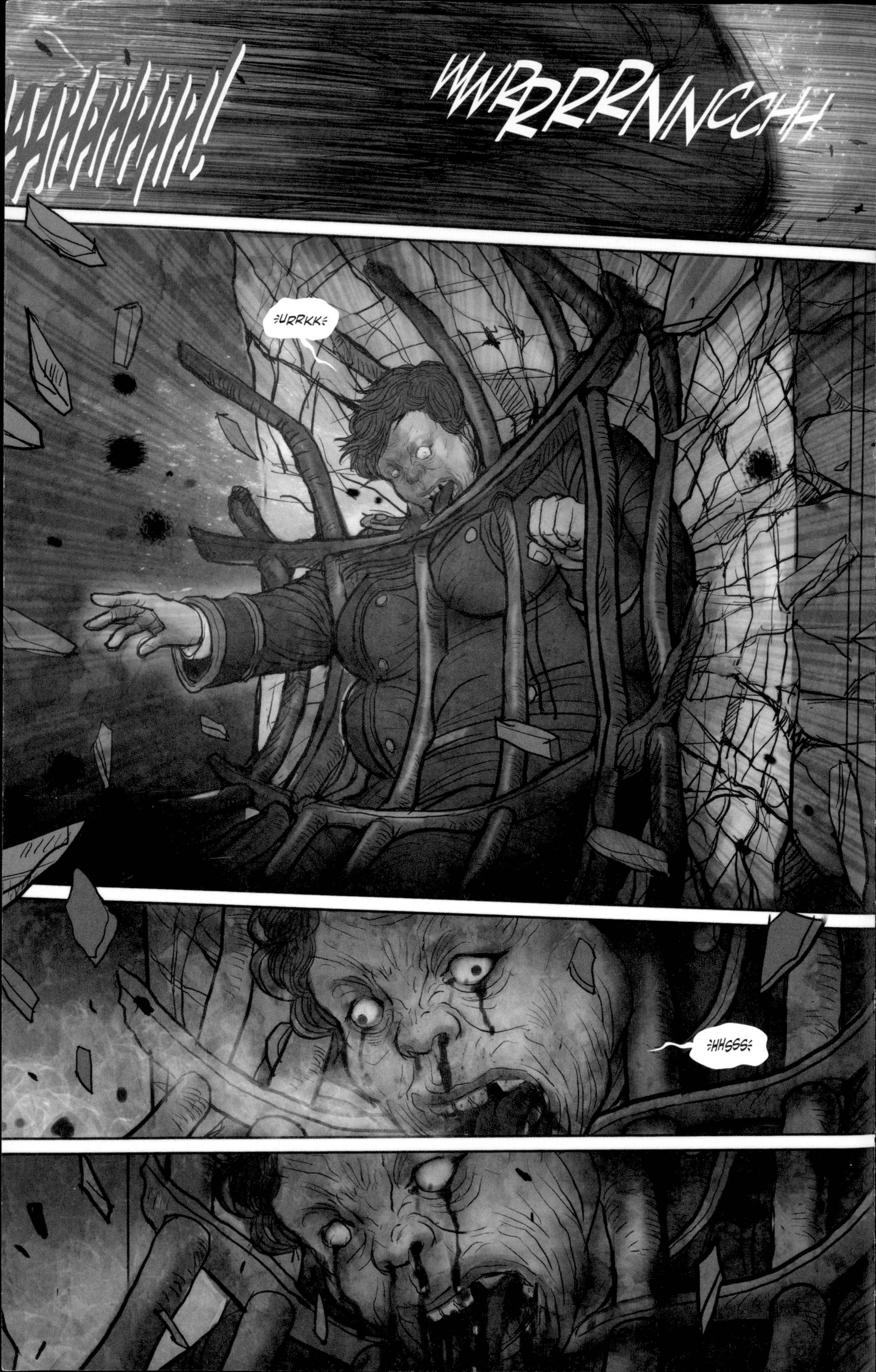
AAAHHHHHH!
WWRRRRRNNCCHH
URRKK
HHSSS

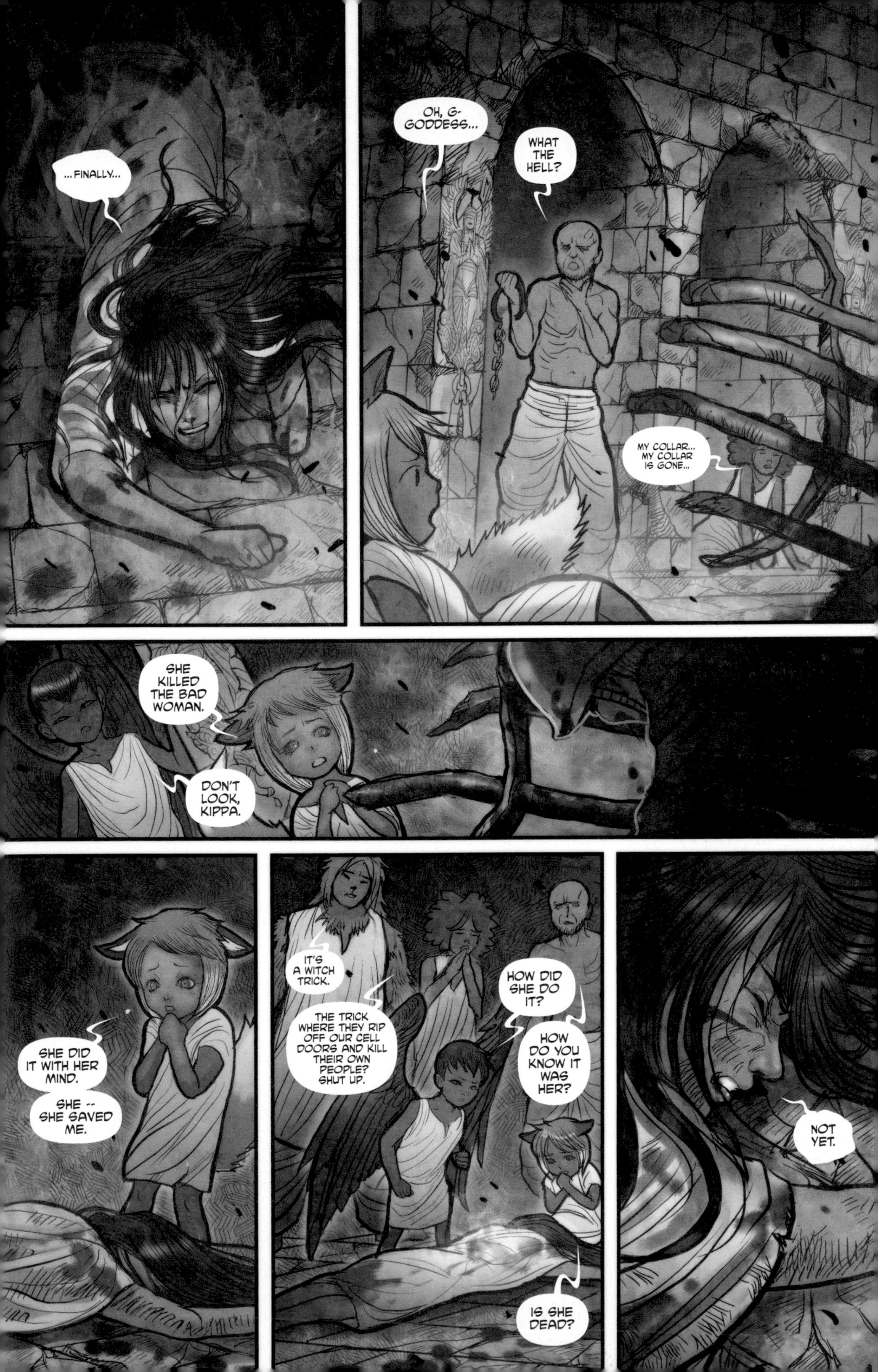
...FINALLY...
OH, G-GODDESS...
WHAT THE HELL?
MY COLLAR... MY COLLAR IS GONE...
SHE KILLED THE BAD WOMAN.
DON'T LOOK, KIPPA.
SHE DID IT WITH HER MIND.
SHE -- SHE SAVED ME.
IT'S A WITCH TRICK.
THE TRICK WHERE THEY RIP OFF OUR CELL DOORS AND KILL THEIR OWN PEOPLE? SHUT UP.
HOW DID SHE DO IT?
HOW DO YOU KNOW IT WAS HER?
IS SHE DEAD?
NOT YET.

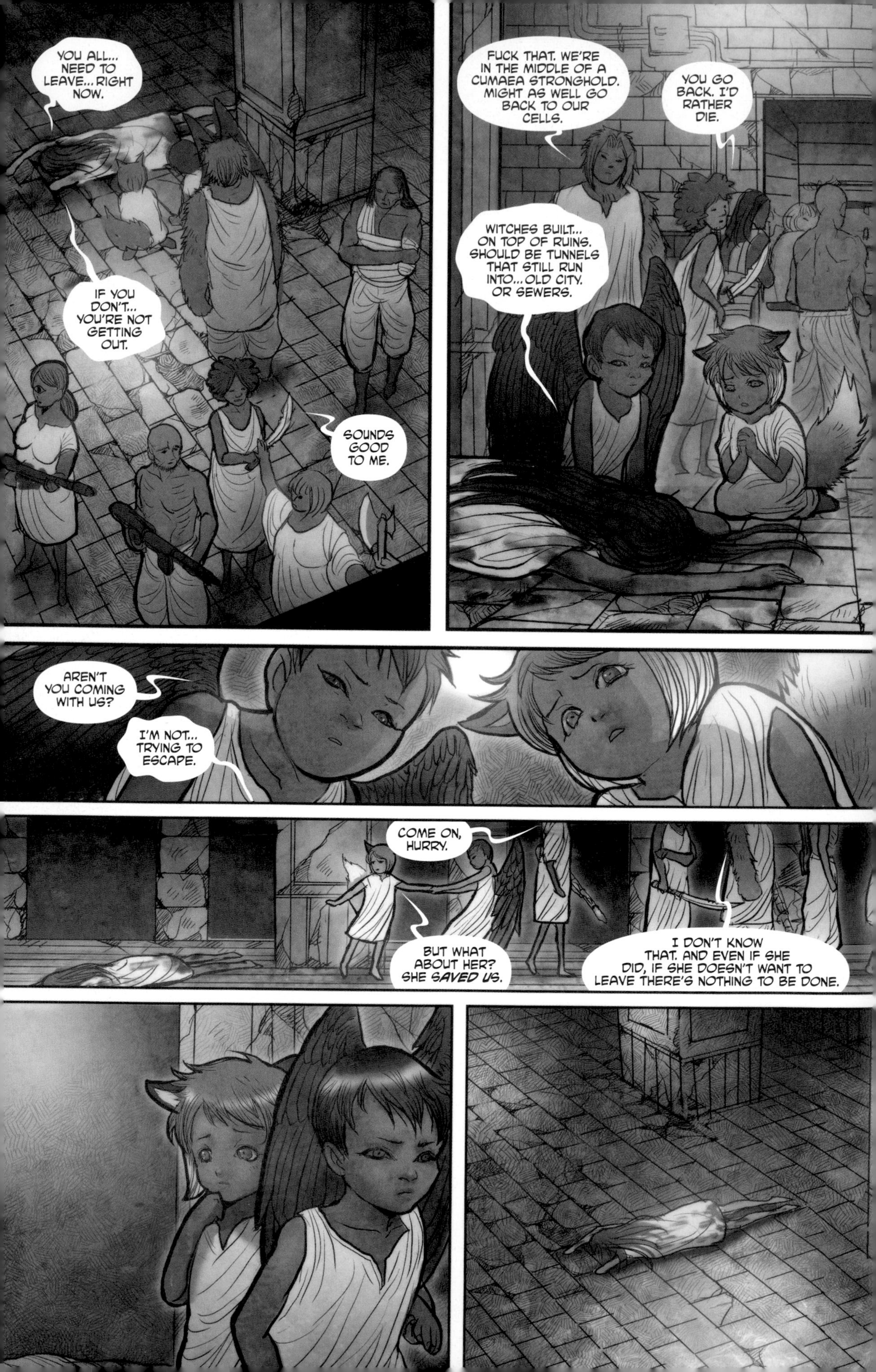
YOU ALL... NEED TO LEAVE... RIGHT NOW.
IF YOU DON'T... YOU'RE NOT GETTING OUT.
SOUNDS GOOD TO ME.
FUCK THAT. WE'RE IN THE MIDDLE OF A CUMAEA STRONGHOLD. MIGHT AS WELL GO BACK TO OUR CELLS.
YOU GO BACK. I'D RATHER DIE.
WITCHES BUILT... ON TOP OF RUINS. SHOULD BE TUNNELS THAT STILL RUN INTO... OLD CITY. OR SEWERS.
AREN'T YOU COMING WITH US?
I'M NOT... TRYING TO ESCAPE.
COME ON, HURRY.
BUT WHAT ABOUT HER? SHE SAVED US.
I DON'T KNOW THAT. AND EVEN IF SHE DID, IF SHE DOESN'T WANT TO LEAVE THERE'S NOTHING TO BE DONE.

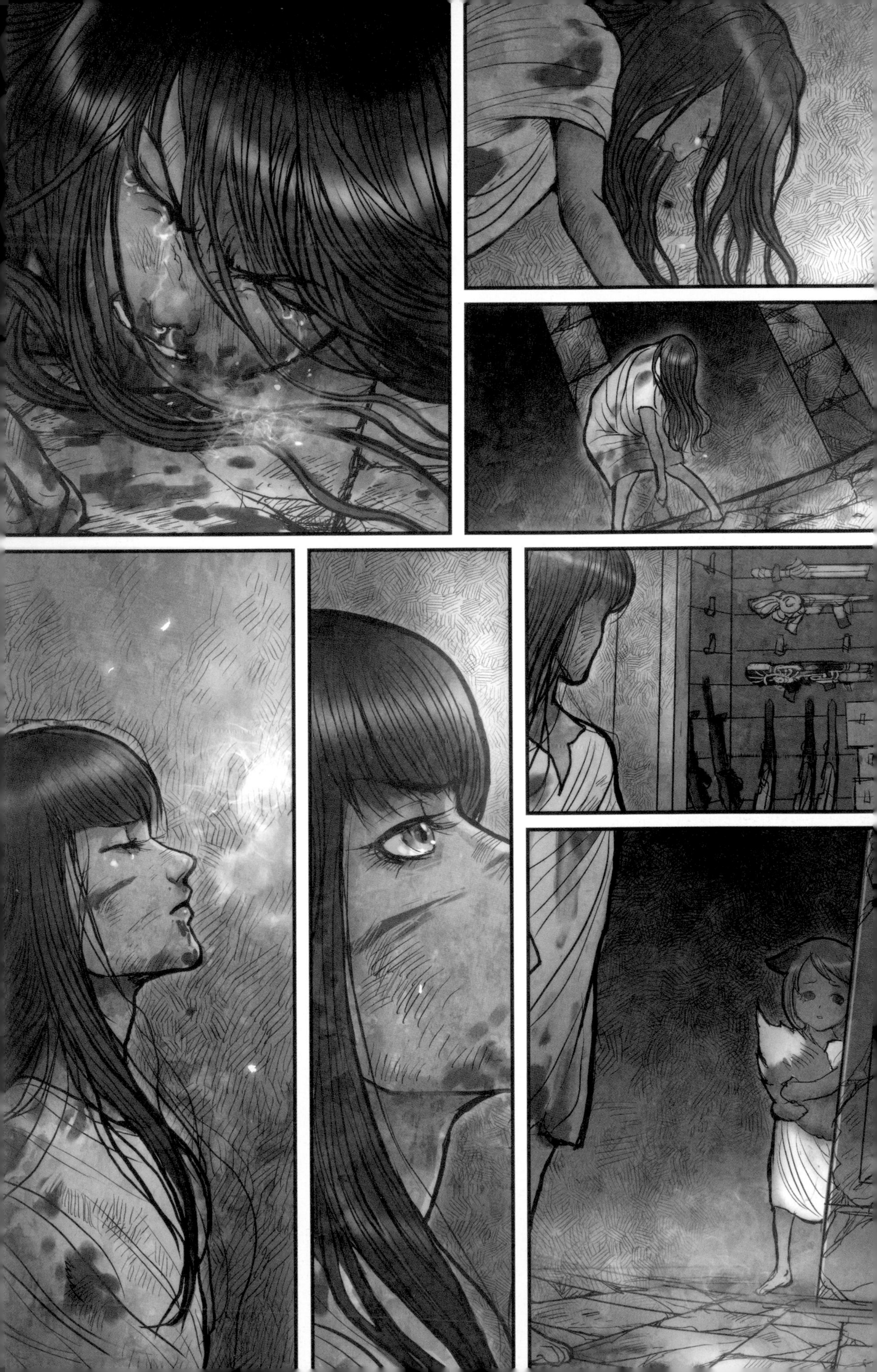

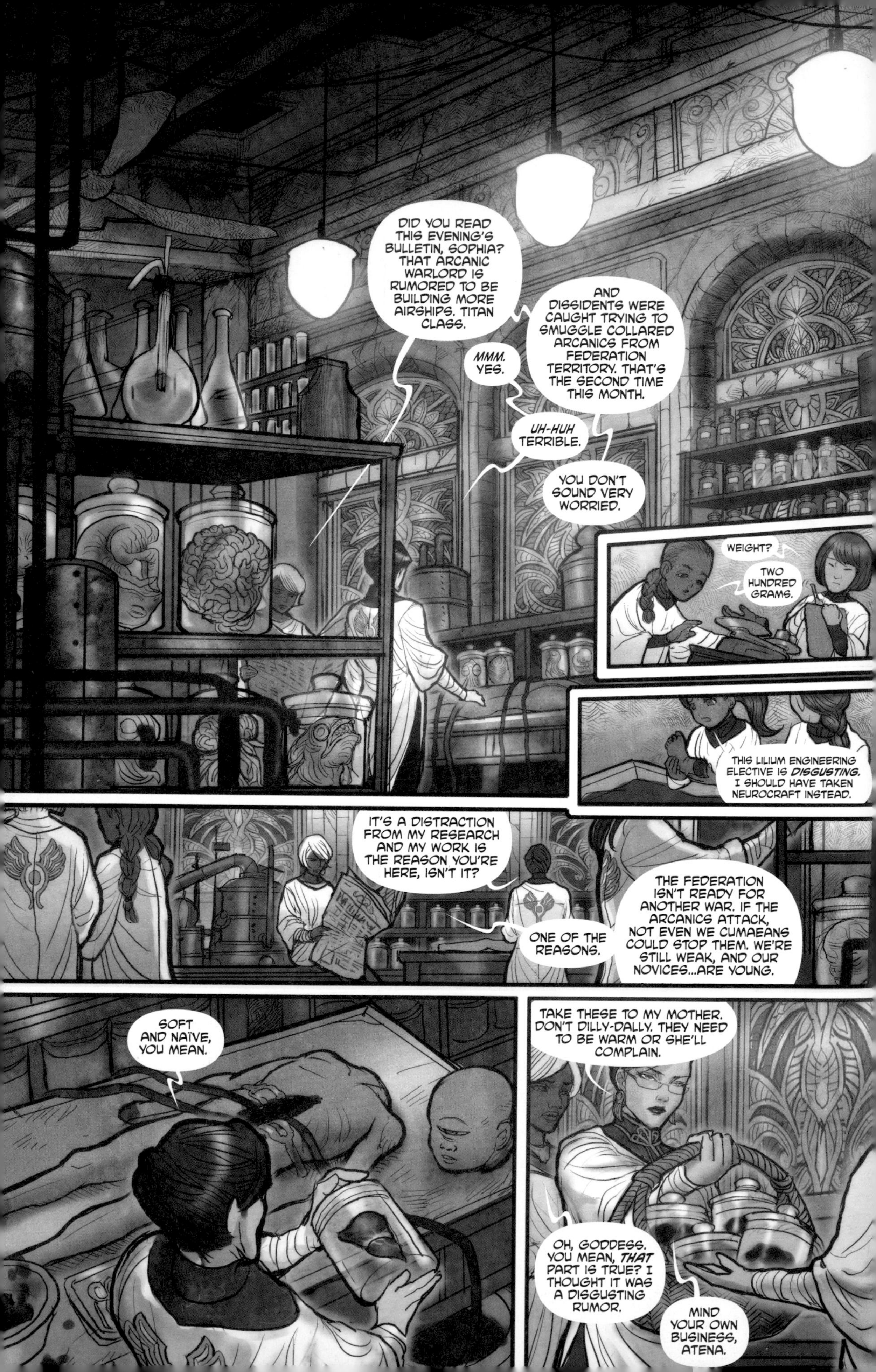
DID YOU READ THIS EVENING'S BULLETIN, SOPHIA? THAT ARCANIC WARLORD IS RUMORED TO BE BUILDING MORE AIRSHIPS. TITAN CLASS.
MMM. YES.
AND DISSIDENTS WERE CAUGHT TRYING TO SMUGGLE COLLARED ARCANICS FROM FEDERATION TERRITORY. THAT'S THE SECOND TIME THIS MONTH.
UH-HUH TERRIBLE.
YOU DON'T SOUND VERY WORRIED.
WEIGHT?
TWO HUNDRED GRAMS.
THIS LILIUM ENGINEERING ELECTIVE IS DISGUSTING. I SHOULD HAVE TAKEN NEUROCRAFT INSTEAD.
IT'S A DISTRACTION FROM MY RESEARCH AND MY WORK IS THE REASON YOU'RE HERE, ISN'T IT?
ONE OF THE REASONS.
THE FEDERATION ISN'T READY FOR ANOTHER WAR. IF THE ARCANICS ATTACK, NOT EVEN WE CUMAEANS COULD STOP THEM. WE'RE STILL WEAK, AND OUR NOVICES...ARE YOUNG.
SOFT AND NAÏVE, YOU MEAN.
TAKE THESE TO MY MOTHER. DON'T DILLY-DALLY. THEY NEED TO BE WARM OR SHE'LL COMPLAIN.
OH, GODDESS. YOU MEAN, THAT PART IS TRUE? I THOUGHT IT WAS A DISGUSTING RUMOR.
MIND YOUR OWN BUSINESS, ATENA.

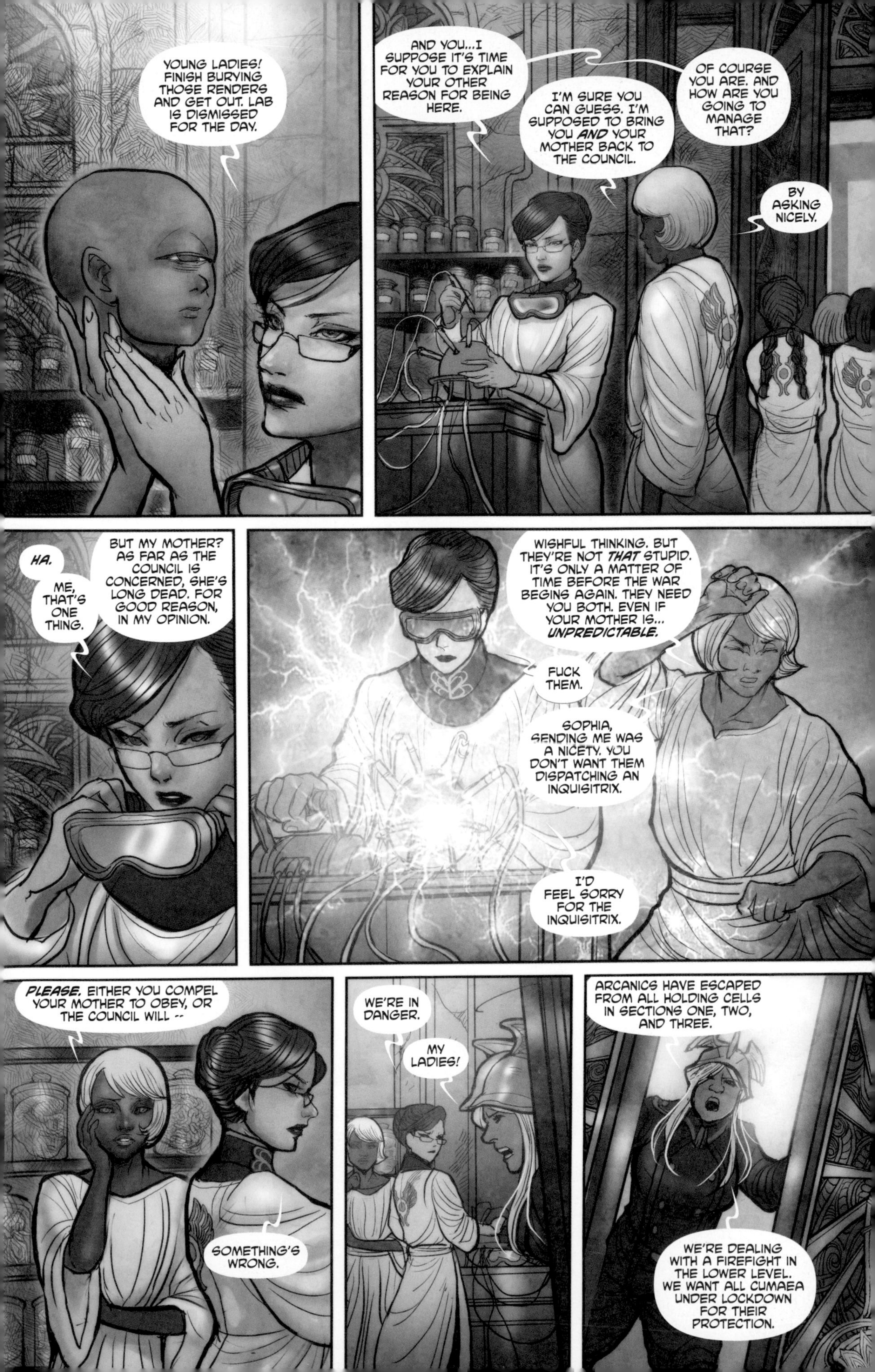
YOUNG LADIES! FINISH BURYING THOSE RENDERS AND GET OUT. LAB IS DISMISSED FOR THE DAY.
AND YOU...I SUPPOSE IT'S TIME FOR YOU TO EXPLAIN YOUR OTHER REASON FOR BEING HERE.
I'M SURE YOU CAN GUESS. I'M SUPPOSED TO BRING YOU AND YOUR MOTHER BACK TO THE COUNCIL.
OF COURSE YOU ARE. AND HOW ARE YOU GOING TO MANAGE THAT?
BY ASKING NICELY.
HA.
ME, THAT'S ONE THING.
BUT MY MOTHER? AS FAR AS THE COUNCIL IS CONCERNED, SHE'S LONG DEAD. FOR GOOD REASON, IN MY OPINION.
WISHFUL THINKING. BUT THEY'RE NOT THAT STUPID. IT'S ONLY A MATTER OF TIME BEFORE THE WAR BEGINS AGAIN. THEY NEED YOU BOTH. EVEN IF YOUR MOTHER IS... UNPREDICTABLE.
FUCK THEM.
SOPHIA, SENDING ME WAS A NICETY. YOU DON'T WANT THEM DISPATCHING AN INQUISITRIX.
I'D FEEL SORRY FOR THE INQUISITRIX.
PLEASE. EITHER YOU COMPEL YOUR MOTHER TO OBEY, OR THE COUNCIL WILL --
SOMETHING'S WRONG.
WE'RE IN DANGER.
MY LADIES!
ARCANICS HAVE ESCAPED FROM ALL HOLDING CELLS IN SECTIONS ONE, TWO, AND THREE.
WE'RE DEALING WITH A FIREFIGHT IN THE LOWER LEVEL. WE WANT ALL CUMAEA UNDER LOCKDOWN FOR THEIR PROTECTION.

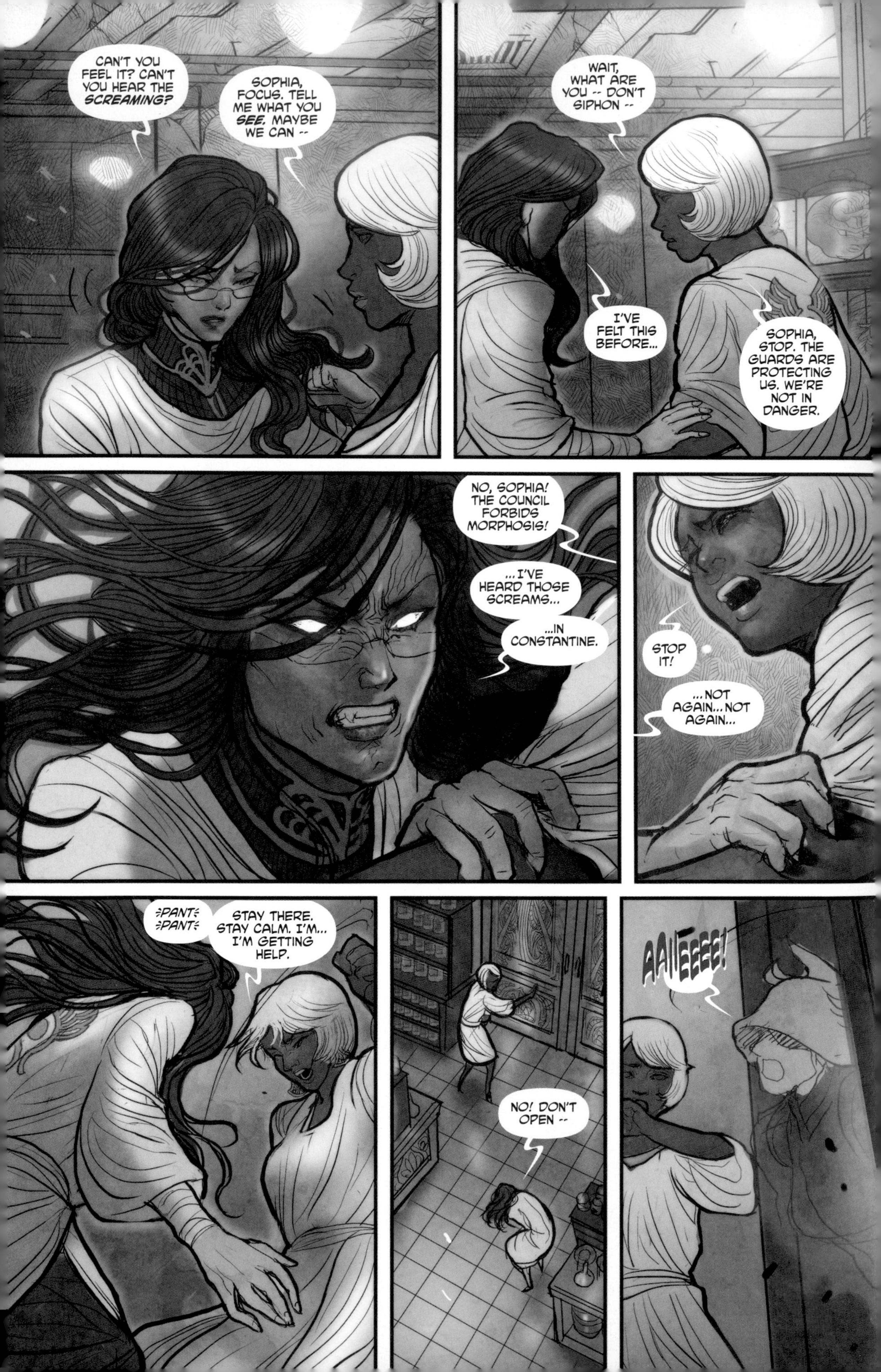
CAN'T YOU FEEL IT? CAN'T YOU HEAR THE *SCREAMING?*
SOPHIA, FOCUS. TELL ME WHAT YOU *SEE.* MAYBE WE CAN --
WAIT, WHAT ARE YOU -- DON'T SIPHON --
I'VE FELT THIS BEFORE...
SOPHIA, STOP. THE GUARDS ARE PROTECTING US. WE'RE NOT IN DANGER.
NO, SOPHIA! THE COUNCIL FORBIDS MORPHOSIS!
... I'VE HEARD THOSE SCREAMS...
...IN CONSTANTINE.
STOP IT!
... NOT AGAIN... NOT AGAIN...
PANT PANT
STAY THERE. STAY CALM. I'M... I'M GETTING HELP.
NO! DON'T OPEN --
AAIIEEEEE!

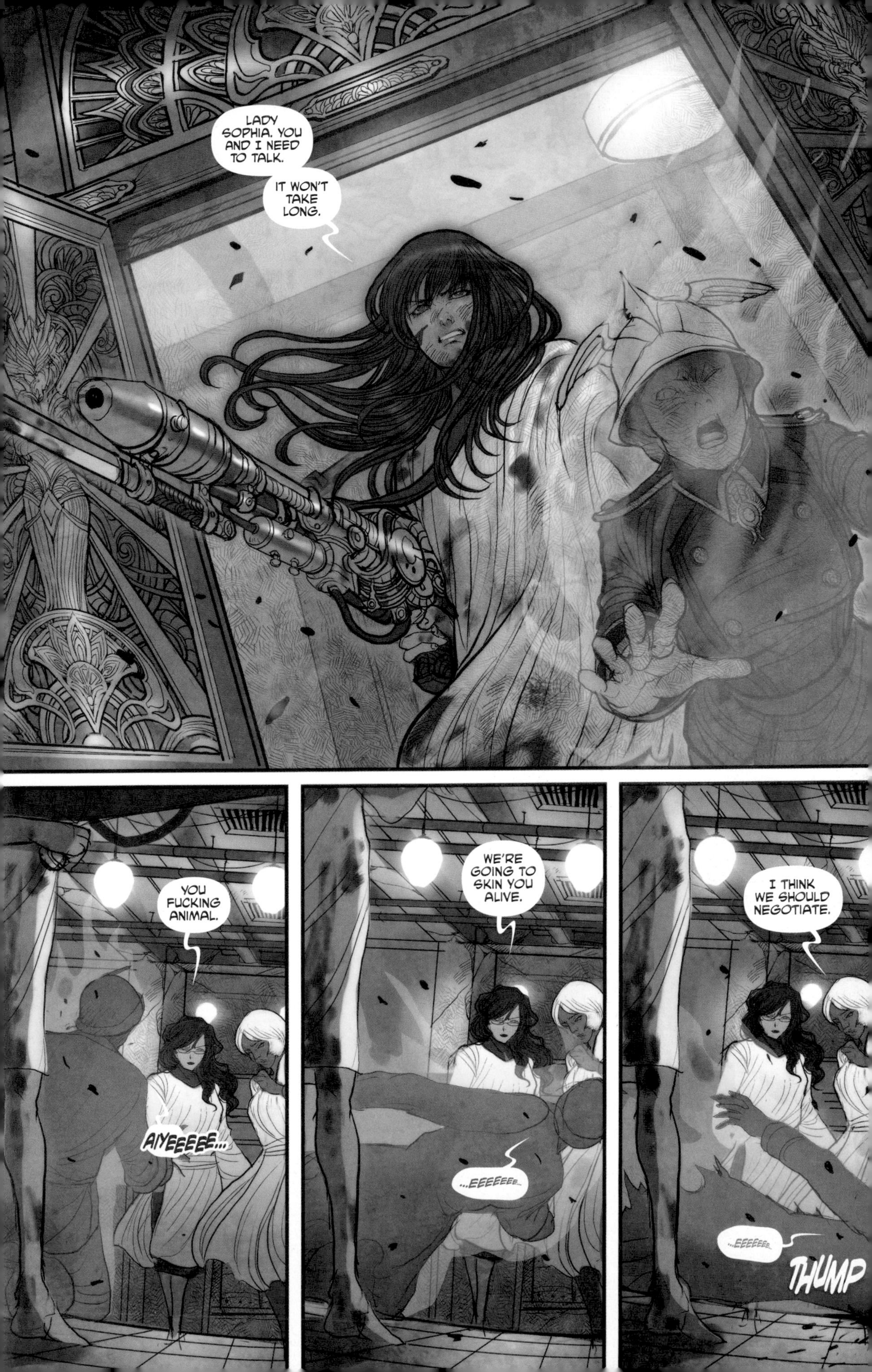
LADY SOPHIA. YOU AND I NEED TO TALK.
IT WON'T TAKE LONG.
YOU FUCKING ANIMAL.
AIYEEEEE...
WE'RE GOING TO SKIN YOU ALIVE.
...EEEEEEE...
I THINK WE SHOULD NEGOTIATE.
...EEEEEEE...
THUMP

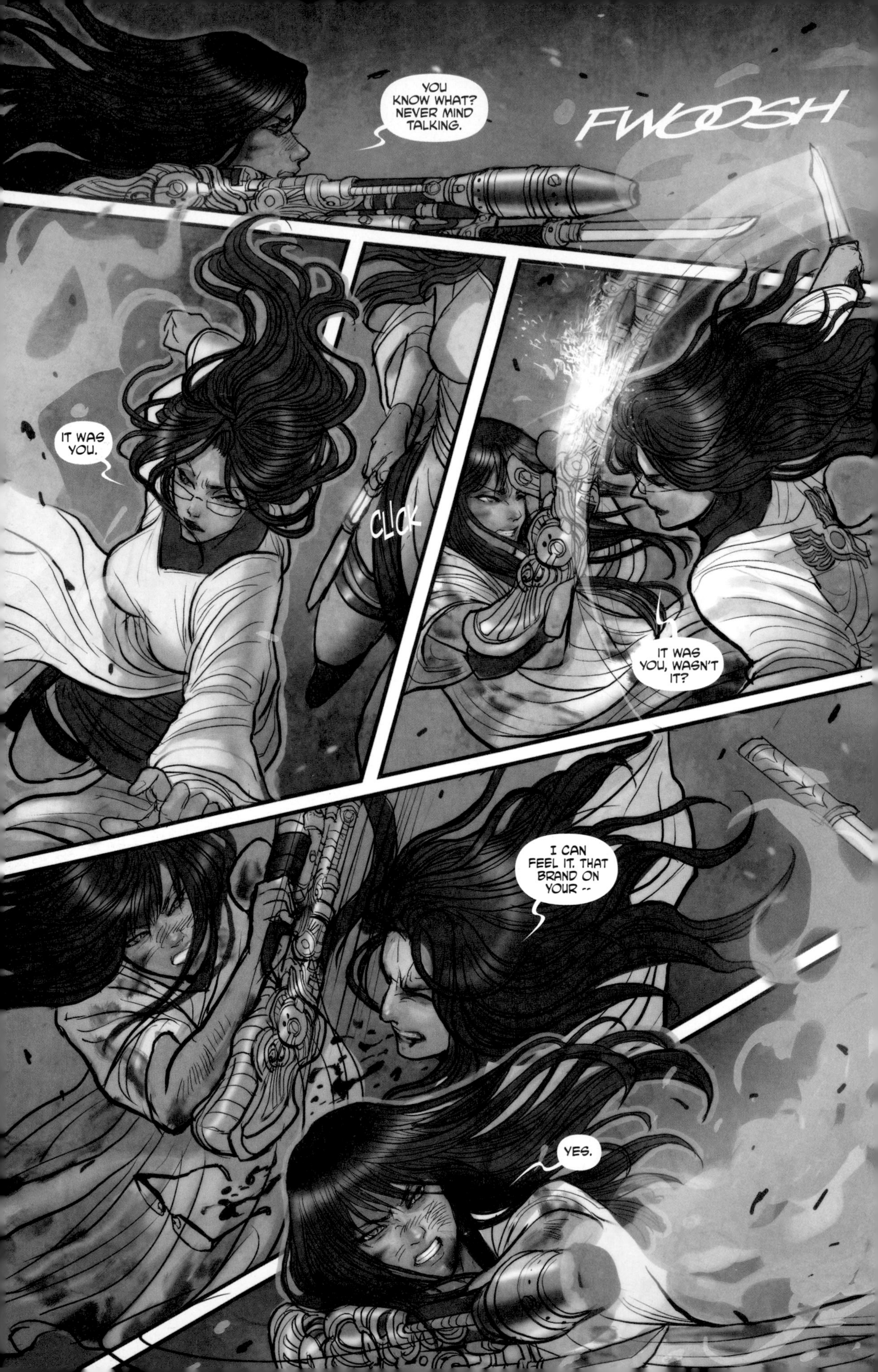
YOU KNOW WHAT? NEVER MIND TALKING.
FWOOSH
IT WAS YOU.
CLICK
IT WAS YOU, WASN'T IT?
I CAN FEEL IT. THAT BRAND ON YOUR --
YES.

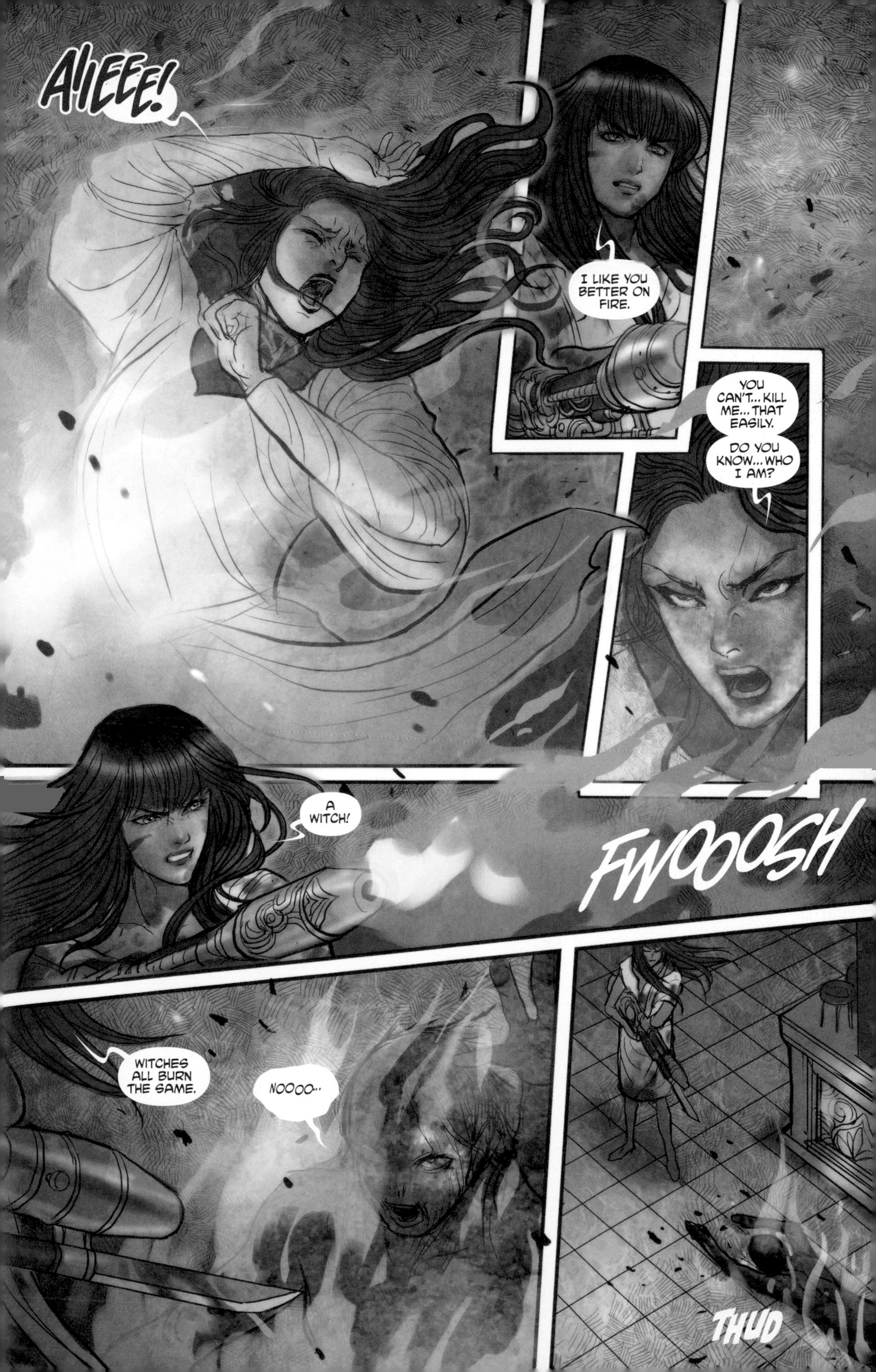
AIIEEE!
I LIKE YOU BETTER ON FIRE.
YOU CAN'T... KILL ME... THAT EASILY.
DO YOU KNOW... WHO I AM?
A WITCH!
FWOOOSH
WITCHES ALL BURN THE SAME.
NOOOO...
THUD

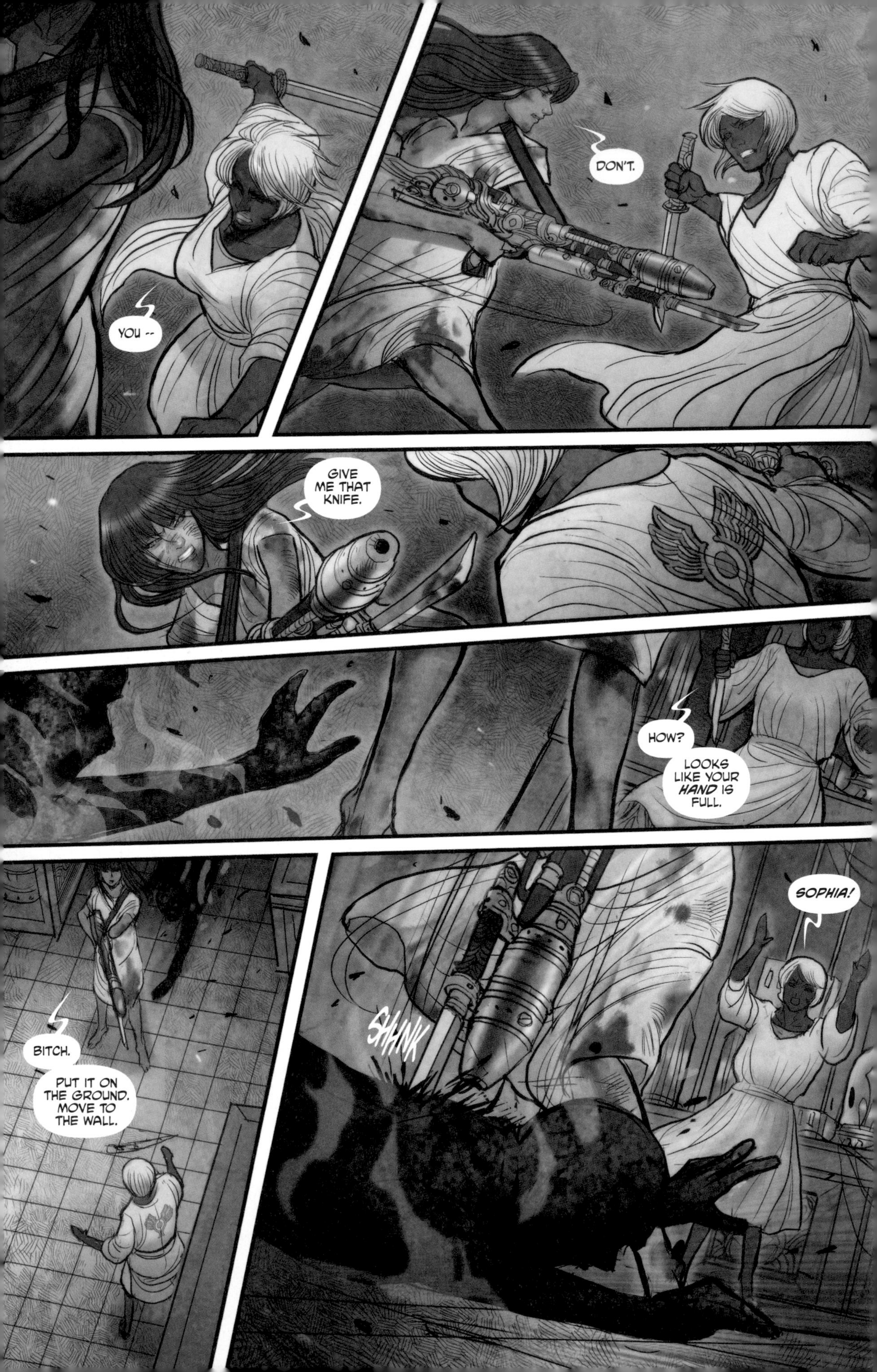
YOU --
DON'T.
GIVE ME THAT KNIFE.
HOW?
LOOKS LIKE YOUR HAND IS FULL.
BITCH.
PUT IT ON THE GROUND. MOVE TO THE WALL.
SHHNK
SOPHIA!

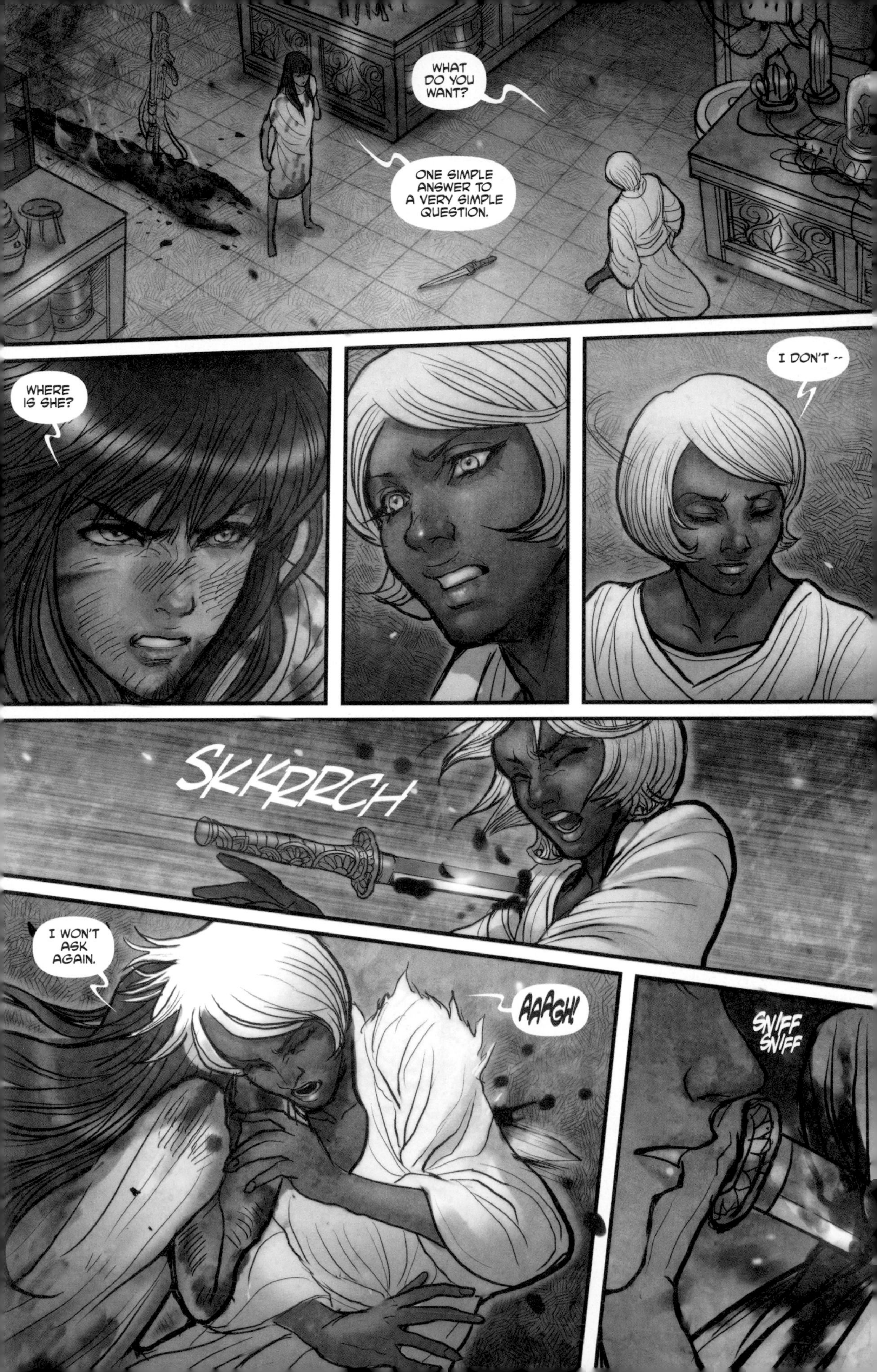
WHAT DO YOU WANT?
ONE SIMPLE ANSWER TO A VERY SIMPLE QUESTION.
WHERE IS SHE?
I DON'T --
SKKRRCH
I WON'T ASK AGAIN.
AAAGH!
SNIFF SNIFF

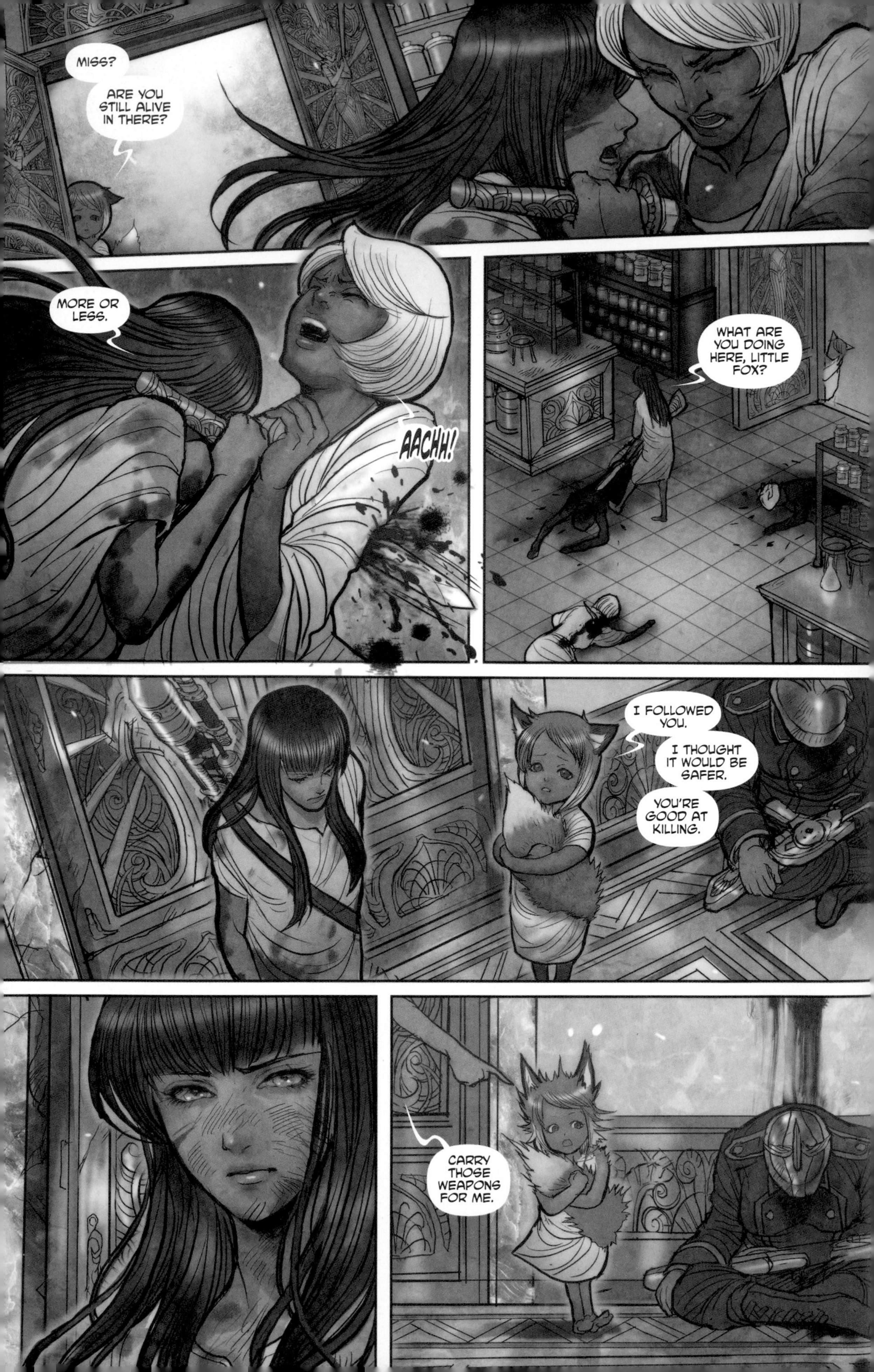
MISS?
ARE YOU STILL ALIVE IN THERE?
MORE OR LESS.
AACHH!
WHAT ARE YOU DOING HERE, LITTLE FOX?
I FOLLOWED YOU.
I THOUGHT IT WOULD BE SAFER.
YOU'RE GOOD AT KILLING.
CARRY THOSE WEAPONS FOR ME.

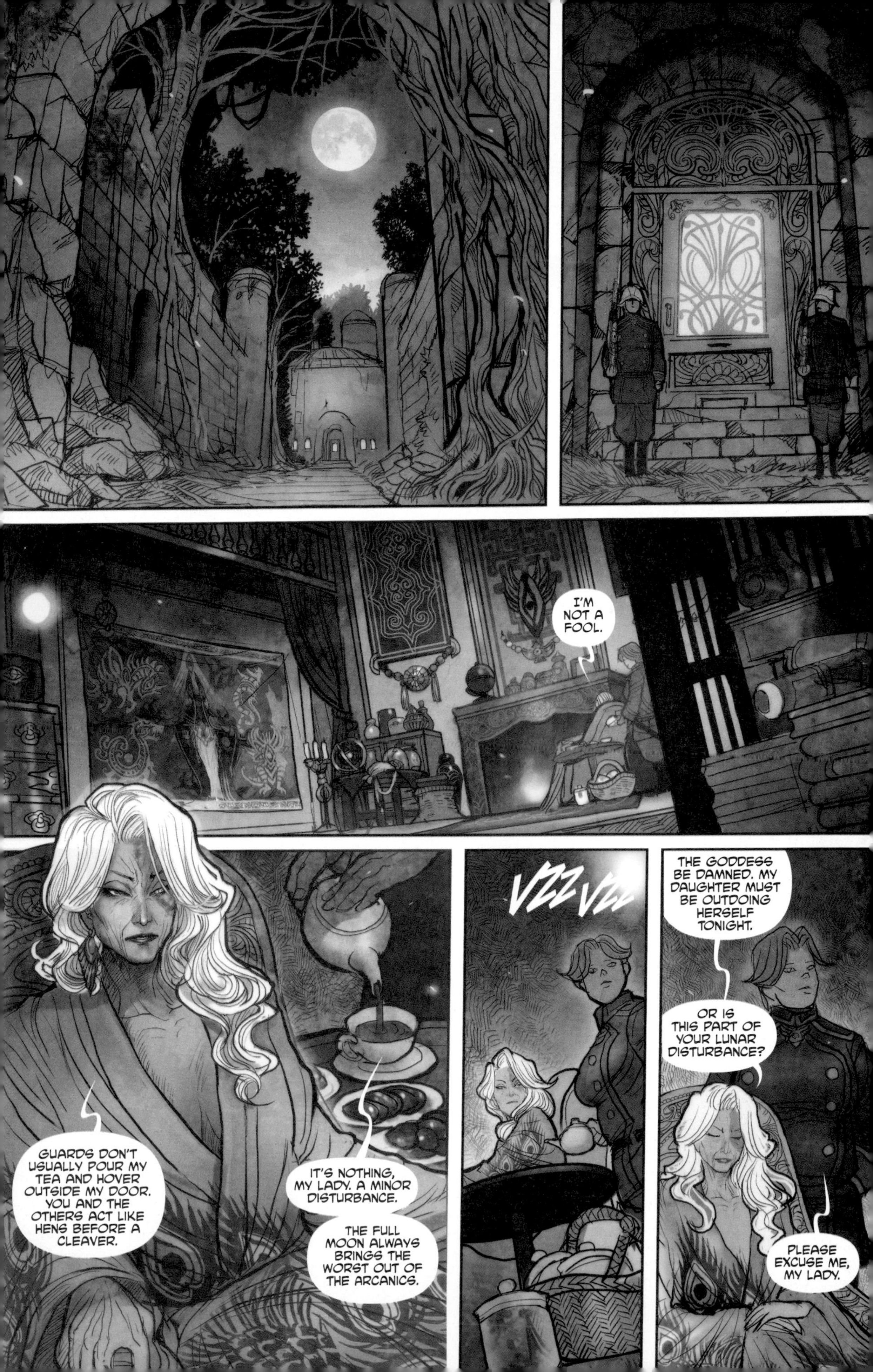
I'M NOT A FOOL.
GUARDS DON'T USUALLY POUR MY TEA AND HOVER OUTSIDE MY DOOR. YOU AND THE OTHERS ACT LIKE HENS BEFORE A CLEAVER.
IT'S NOTHING, MY LADY. A MINOR DISTURBANCE.
THE FULL MOON ALWAYS BRINGS THE WORST OUT OF THE ARCANICS.
VZZ VZZ
THE GODDESS BE DAMNED. MY DAUGHTER MUST BE OUTDOING HERSELF TONIGHT.
OR IS THIS PART OF YOUR LUNAR DISTURBANCE?
PLEASE EXCUSE ME, MY LADY.

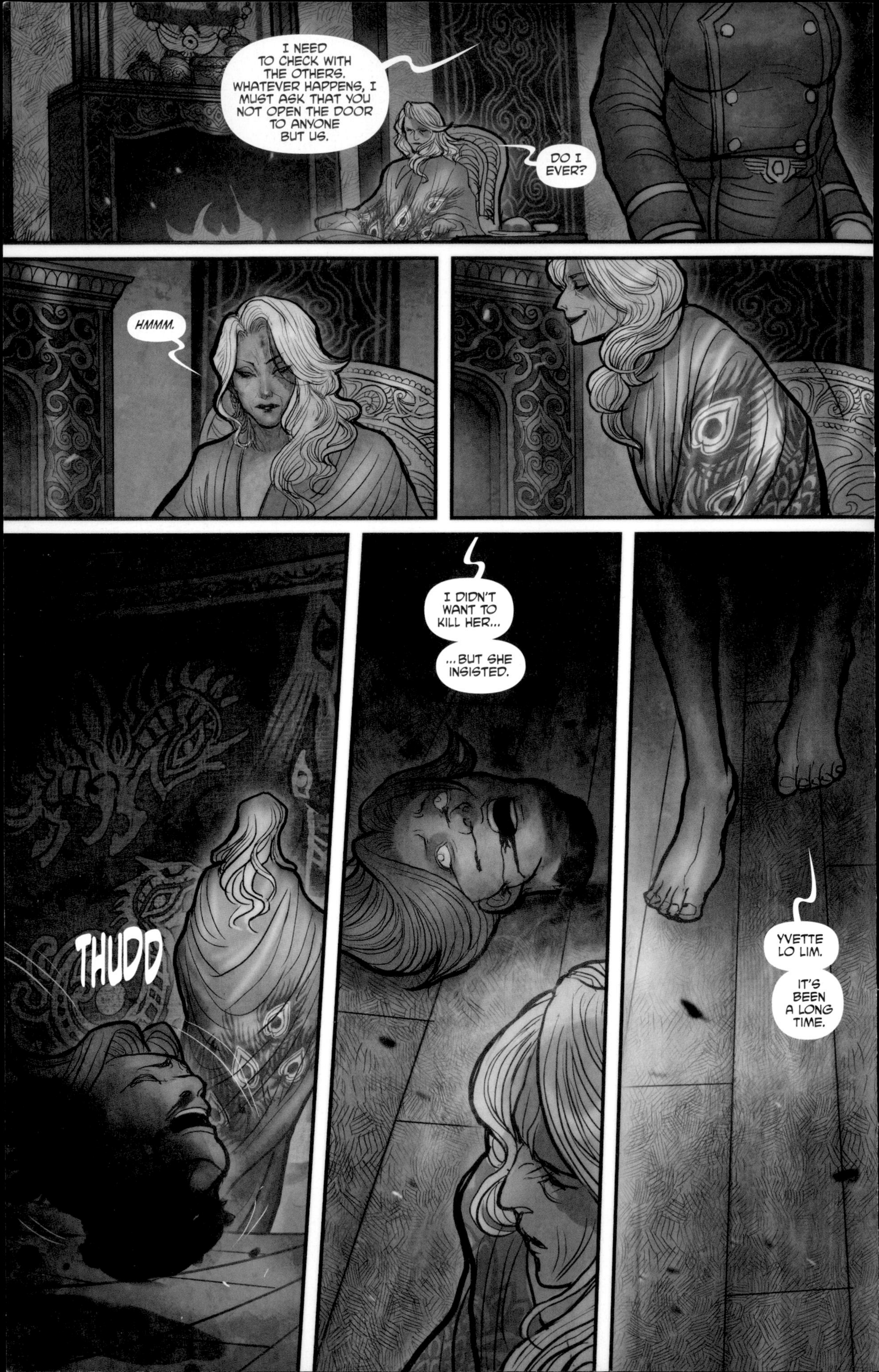

I NEED TO CHECK WITH THE OTHERS. WHATEVER HAPPENS, I MUST ASK THAT YOU NOT OPEN THE DOOR TO ANYONE BUT US.
DO I EVER?
HMMM.
THUDD
I DIDN'T WANT TO KILL HER...
...BUT SHE INSISTED.
YVETTE LO LIM.
IT'S BEEN A LONG TIME.

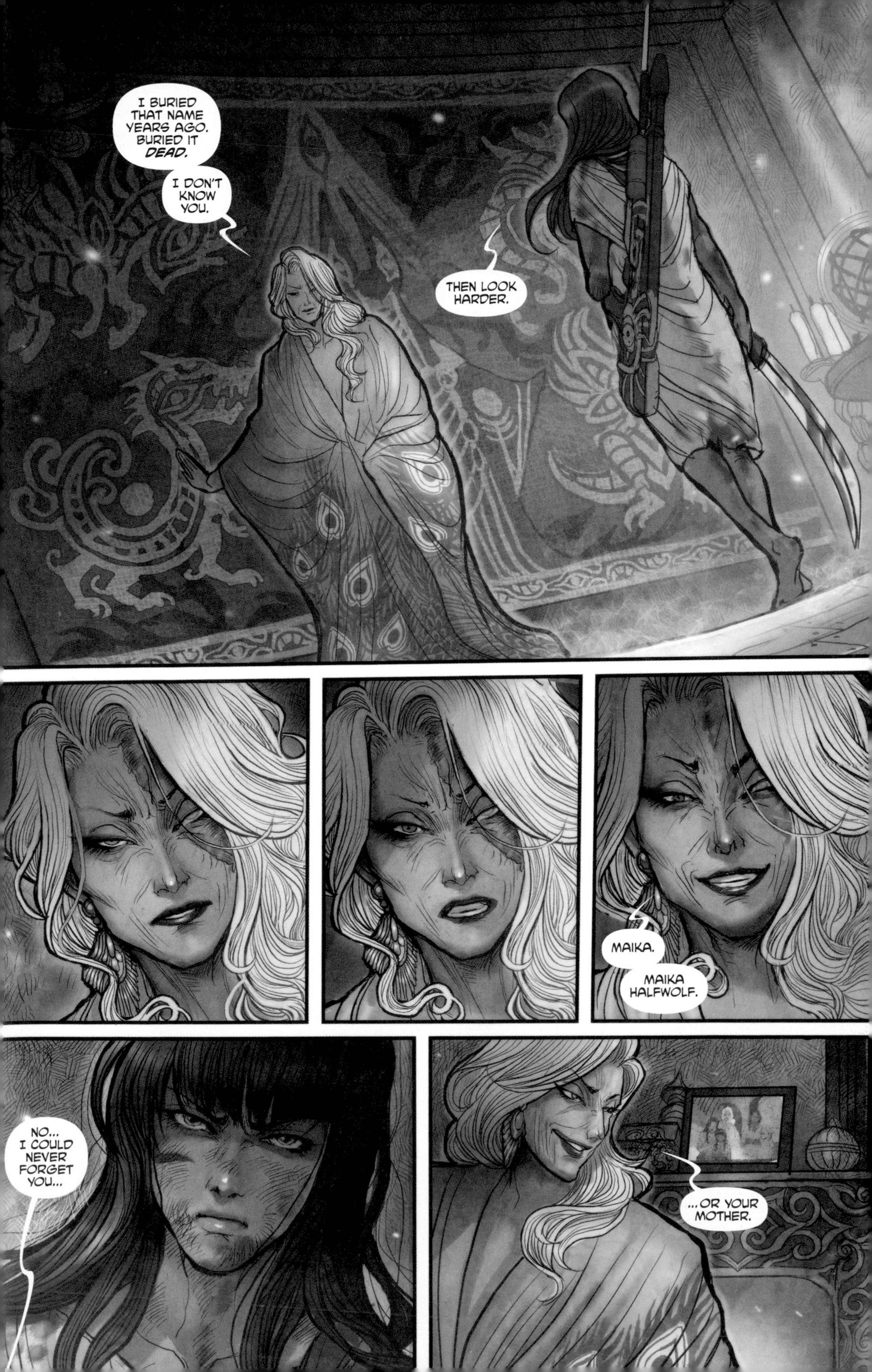
I BURIED THAT NAME YEARS AGO. BURIED IT DEAD.
I DON'T KNOW YOU.
THEN LOOK HARDER.
MAIKA.
MAIKA HALFWOLF.
NO... I COULD NEVER FORGET YOU...
...OR YOUR MOTHER.

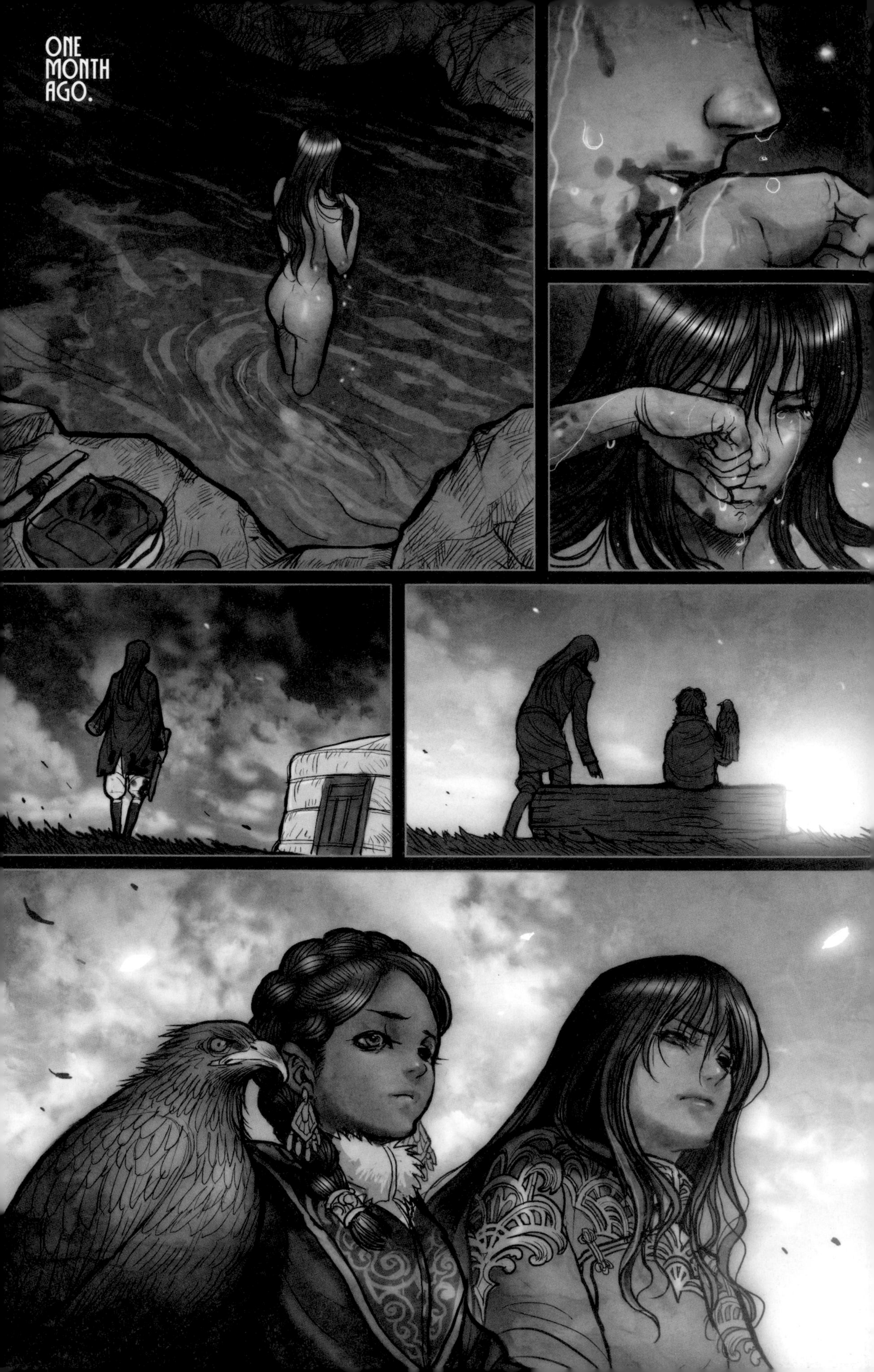
ONE MONTH AGO.

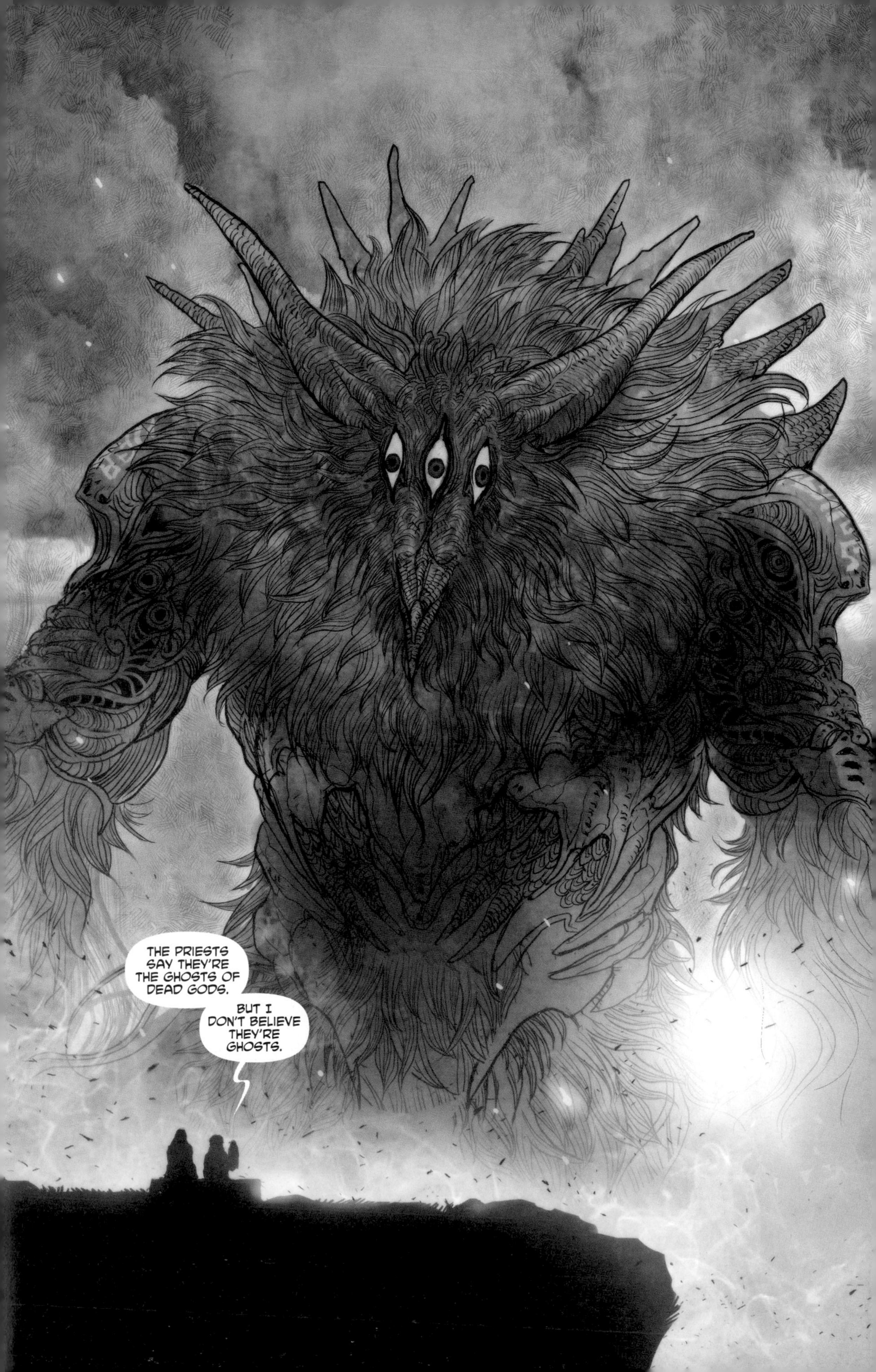
THE PRIESTS SAY THEY'RE THE GHOSTS OF DEAD GODS.
BUT I DON'T BELIEVE THEY'RE GHOSTS.

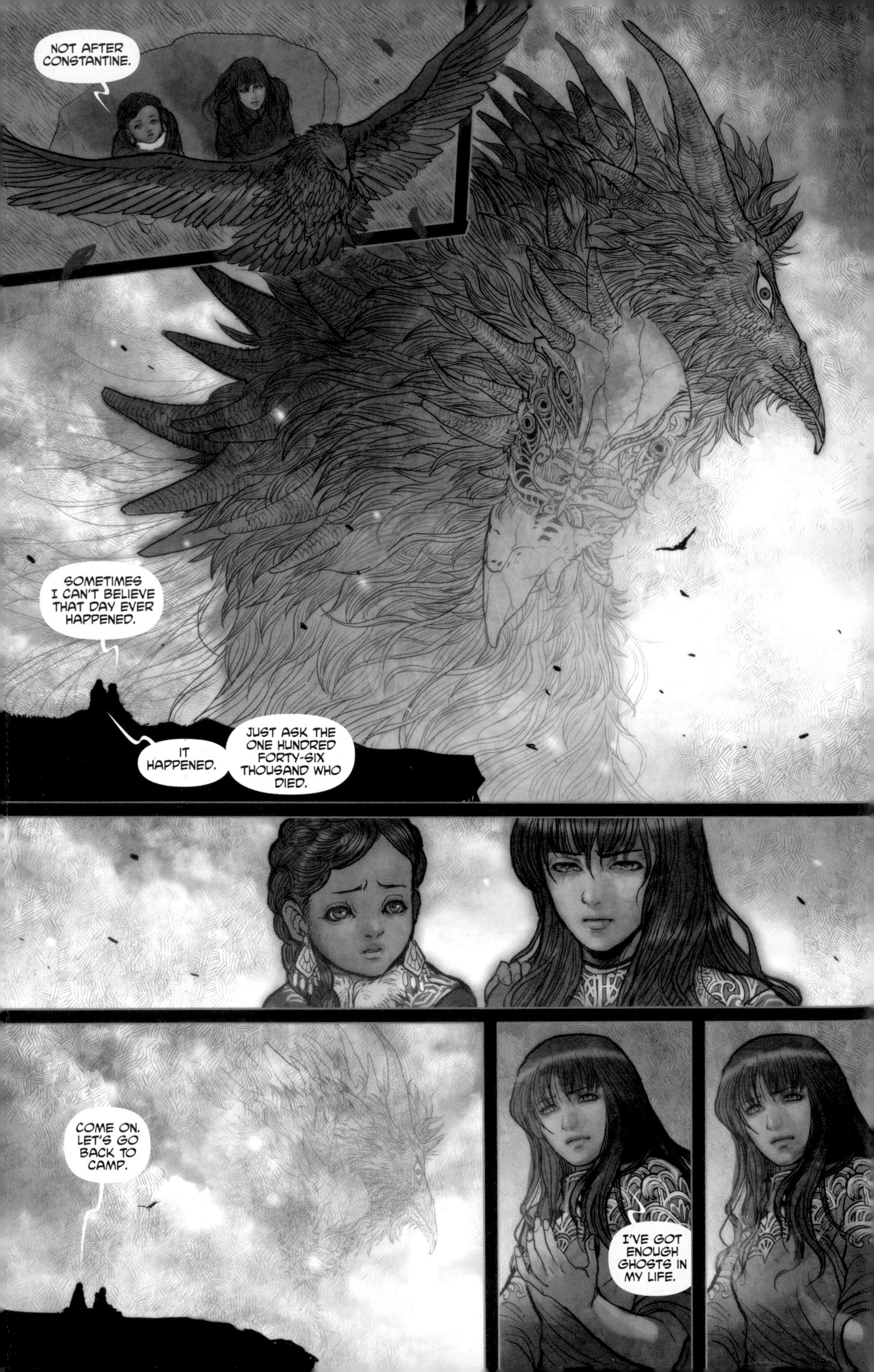
NOT AFTER CONSTANTINE.
SOMETIMES I CAN'T BELIEVE THAT DAY EVER HAPPENED.
IT HAPPENED.
JUST ASK THE ONE HUNDRED FORTY-SIX THOUSAND WHO DIED.
COME ON. LET'S GO BACK TO CAMP.
I'VE GOT ENOUGH GHOSTS IN MY LIFE.

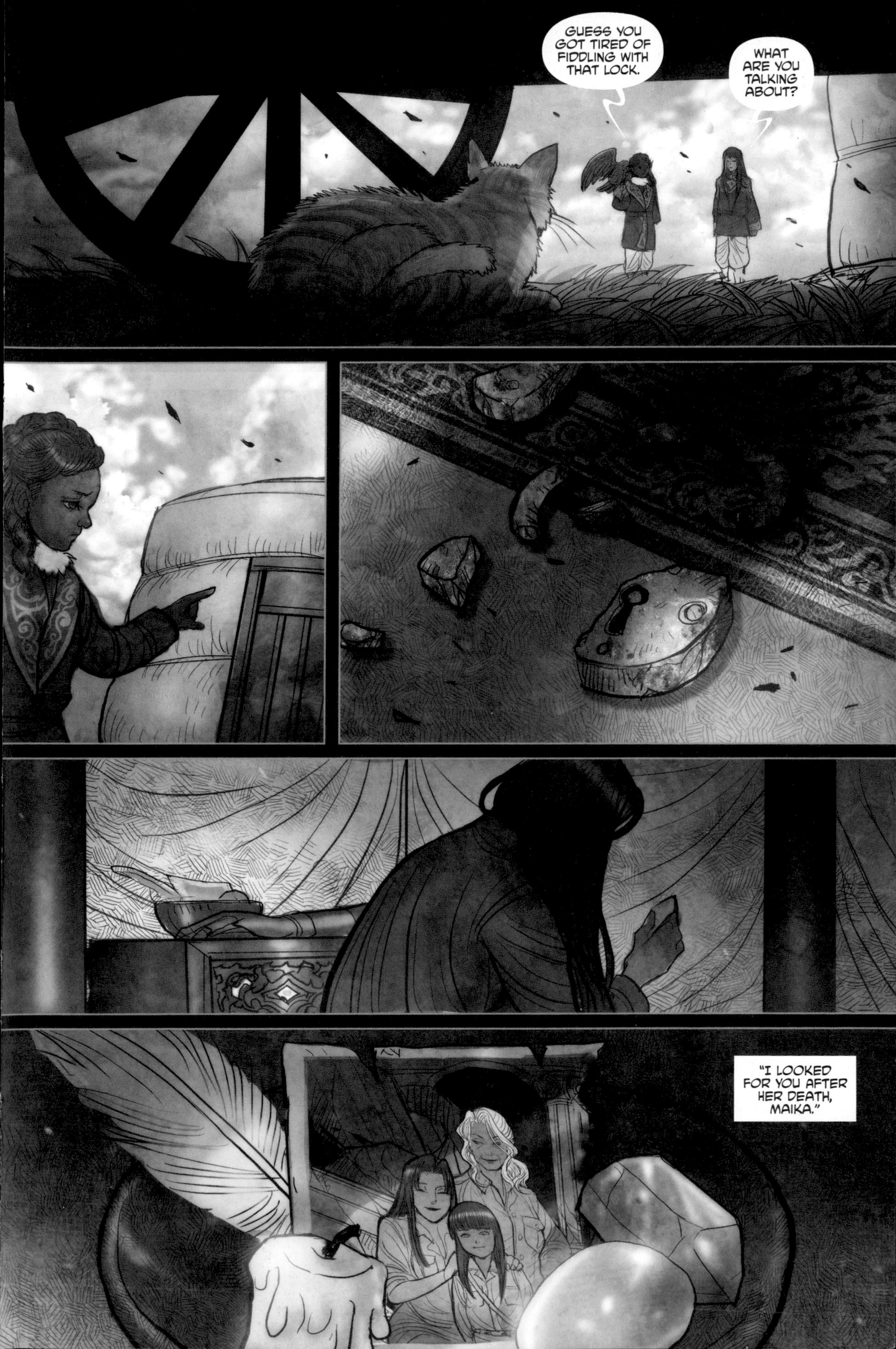
GUESS YOU GOT TIRED OF FIDDLING WITH THAT LOCK.
WHAT ARE YOU TALKING ABOUT?
"I LOOKED FOR YOU AFTER HER DEATH, MAIKA."

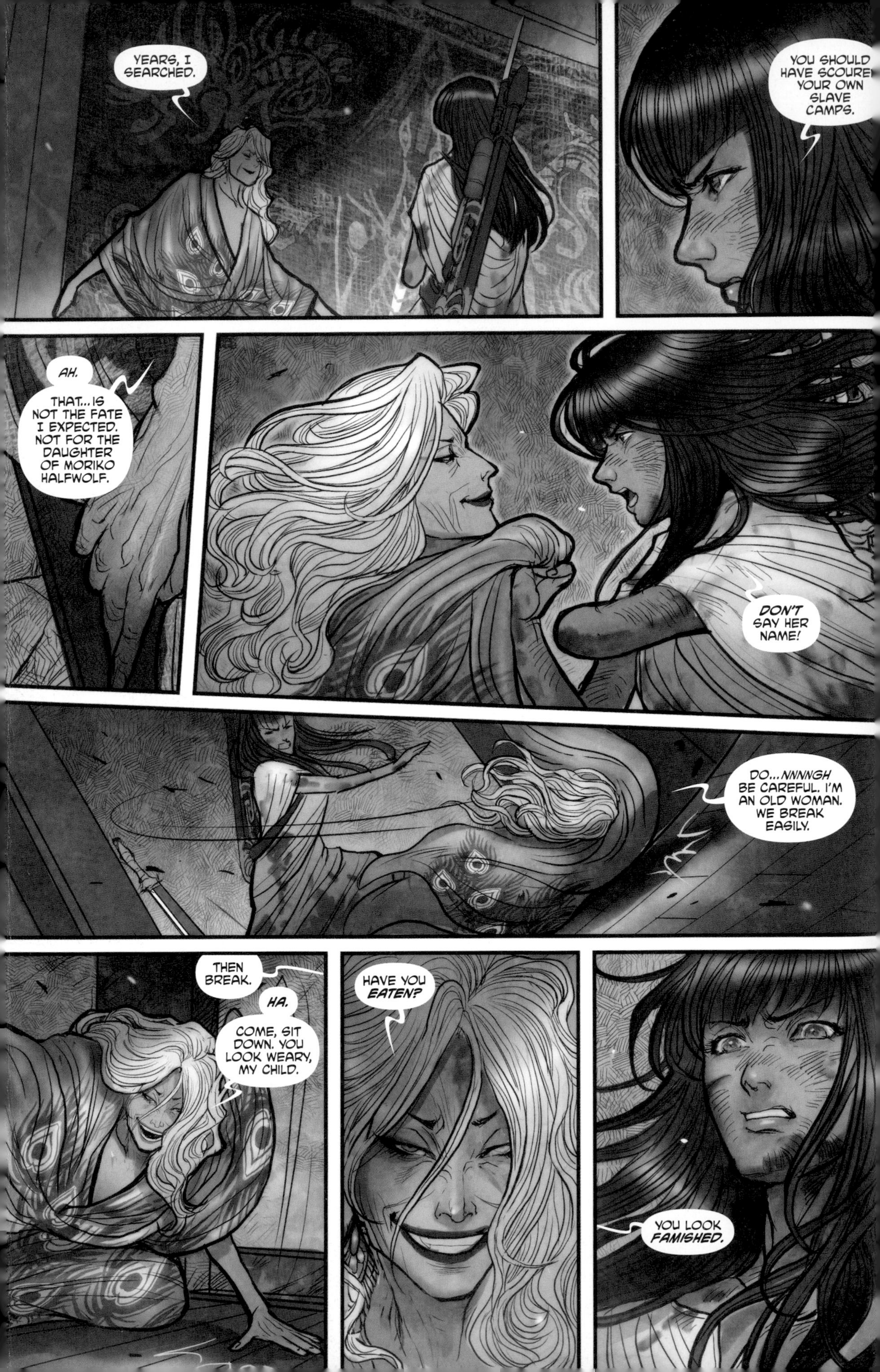
YEARS, I SEARCHED.
YOU SHOULD HAVE SCOURED YOUR OWN SLAVE CAMPS.
AH.
THAT... IS NOT THE FATE I EXPECTED. NOT FOR THE DAUGHTER OF MORIKO HALFWOLF.
DON'T SAY HER NAME!
DO... NNNNGH BE CAREFUL. I'M AN OLD WOMAN. WE BREAK EASILY.
THEN BREAK.
HA.
COME, SIT DOWN. YOU LOOK WEARY, MY CHILD.
HAVE YOU EATEN?
YOU LOOK FAMISHED.

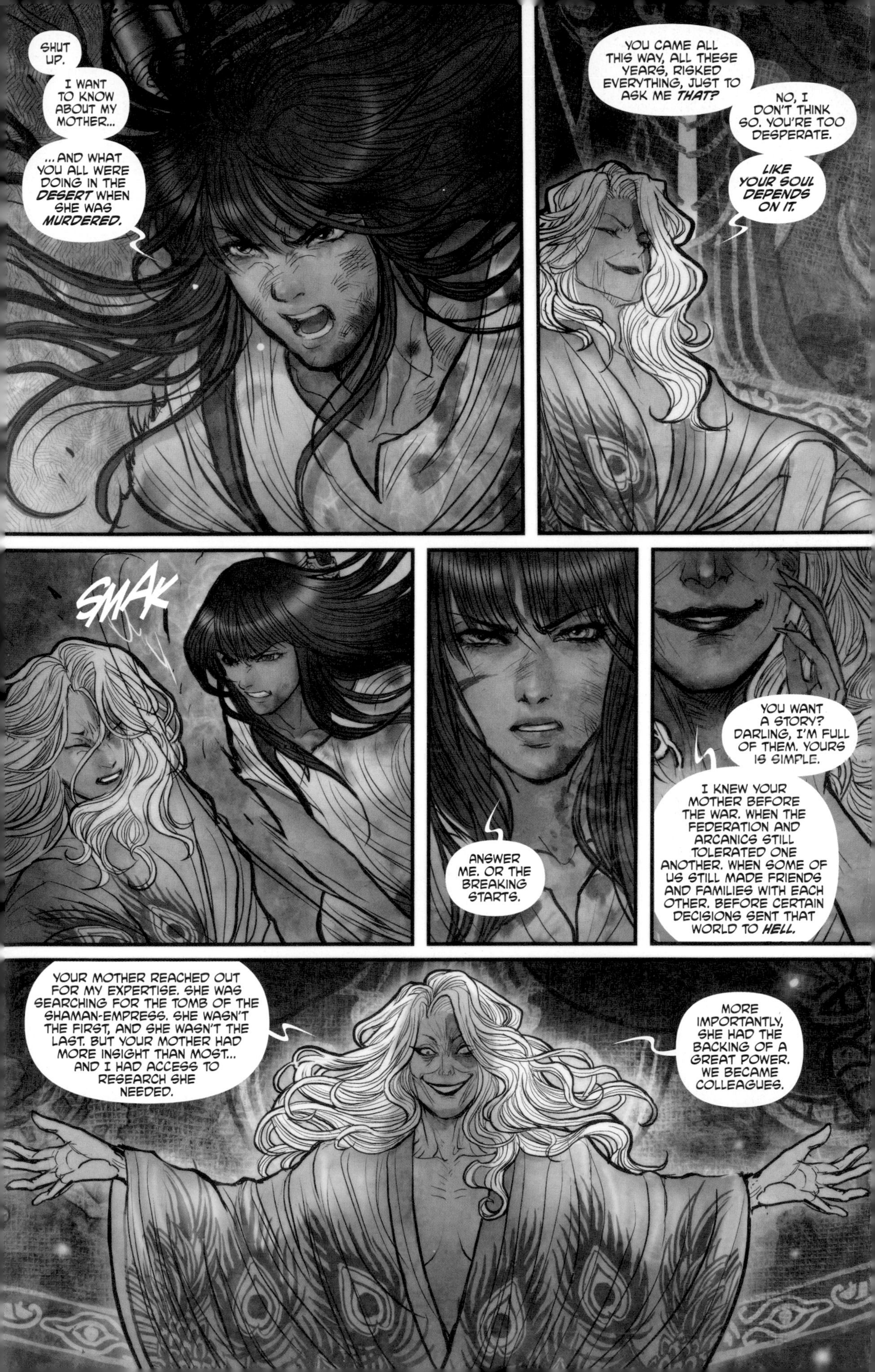
SHUT UP.
I WANT TO KNOW ABOUT MY MOTHER...
...AND WHAT YOU ALL WERE DOING IN THE DESERT WHEN SHE WAS MURDERED.
YOU CAME ALL THIS WAY, ALL THESE YEARS, RISKED EVERYTHING, JUST TO ASK ME THAT?
NO, I DON'T THINK SO. YOU'RE TOO DESPERATE.
LIKE YOUR SOUL DEPENDS ON IT.
SMAK
ANSWER ME. OR THE BREAKING STARTS.
YOU WANT A STORY? DARLING, I'M FULL OF THEM. YOURS IS SIMPLE.
I KNEW YOUR MOTHER BEFORE THE WAR. WHEN THE FEDERATION AND ARCANICS STILL TOLERATED ONE ANOTHER. WHEN SOME OF US STILL MADE FRIENDS AND FAMILIES WITH EACH OTHER. BEFORE CERTAIN DECISIONS SENT THAT WORLD TO HELL.
YOUR MOTHER REACHED OUT FOR MY EXPERTISE. SHE WAS SEARCHING FOR THE TOMB OF THE SHAMAN-EMPRESS. SHE WASN'T THE FIRST, AND SHE WASN'T THE LAST. BUT YOUR MOTHER HAD MORE INSIGHT THAN MOST... AND I HAD ACCESS TO RESEARCH SHE NEEDED.
MORE IMPORTANTLY, SHE HAD THE BACKING OF A GREAT POWER. WE BECAME COLLEAGUES.

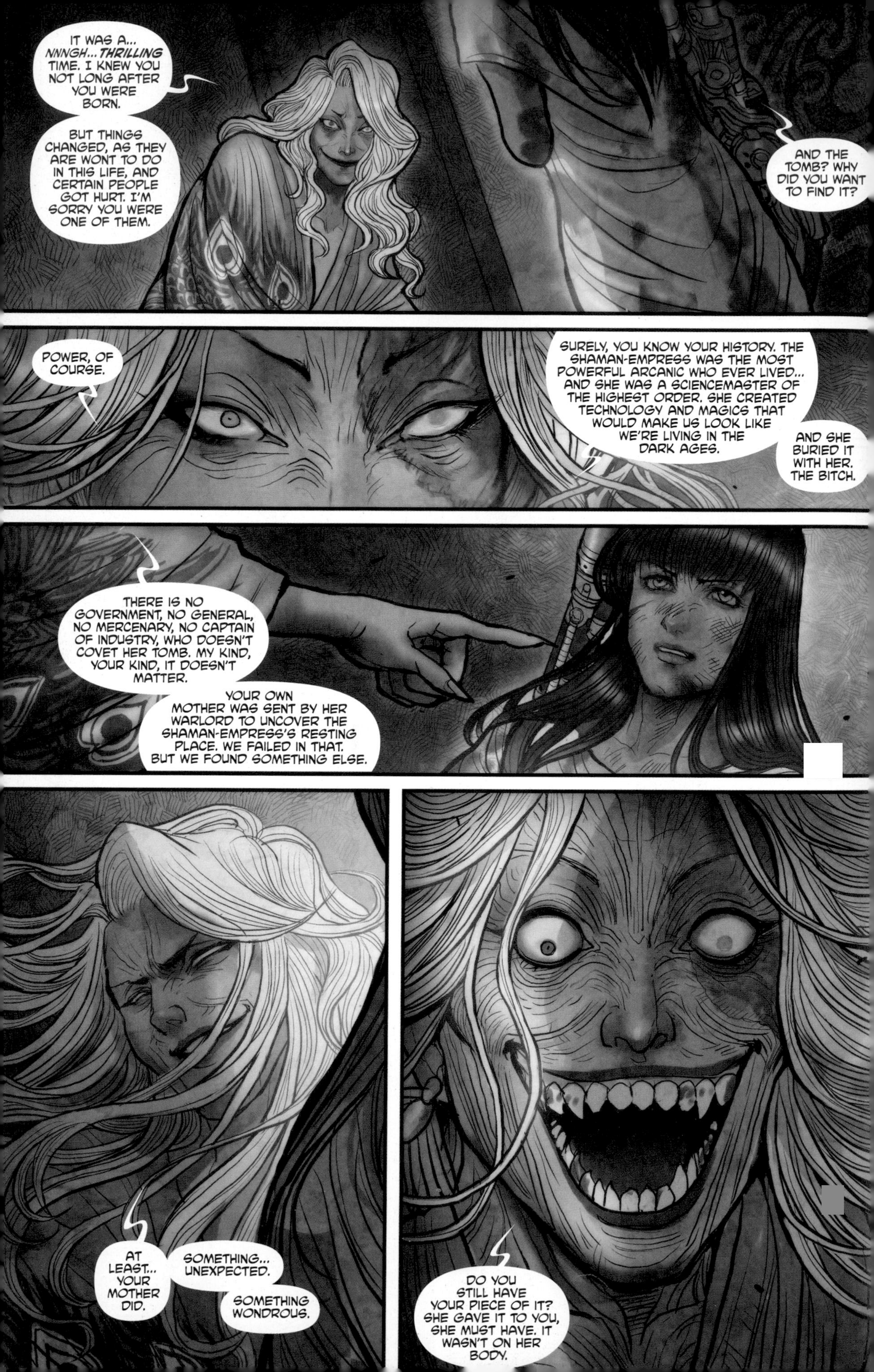
IT WAS A... NNNGH... THRILLING TIME. I KNEW YOU NOT LONG AFTER YOU WERE BORN.
BUT THINGS CHANGED, AS THEY ARE WONT TO DO IN THIS LIFE, AND CERTAIN PEOPLE GOT HURT. I'M SORRY YOU WERE ONE OF THEM.
AND THE TOMB? WHY DID YOU WANT TO FIND IT?
POWER, OF COURSE.
SURELY, YOU KNOW YOUR HISTORY. THE SHAMAN-EMPRESS WAS THE MOST POWERFUL ARCANIC WHO EVER LIVED... AND SHE WAS A SCIENCEMASTER OF THE HIGHEST ORDER. SHE CREATED TECHNOLOGY AND MAGICS THAT WOULD MAKE US LOOK LIKE WE'RE LIVING IN THE DARK AGES.
AND SHE BURIED IT WITH HER. THE BITCH.
THERE IS NO GOVERNMENT, NO GENERAL, NO MERCENARY, NO CAPTAIN OF INDUSTRY, WHO DOESN'T COVET HER TOMB. MY KIND, YOUR KIND, IT DOESN'T MATTER.
YOUR OWN MOTHER WAS SENT BY HER WARLORD TO UNCOVER THE SHAMAN-EMPRESS'S RESTING PLACE. WE FAILED IN THAT. BUT WE FOUND SOMETHING ELSE.
AT LEAST... YOUR MOTHER DID.
SOMETHING... UNEXPECTED.
SOMETHING WONDROUS.
DO YOU STILL HAVE YOUR PIECE OF IT? SHE GAVE IT TO YOU, SHE MUST HAVE. IT WASN'T ON HER BODY.

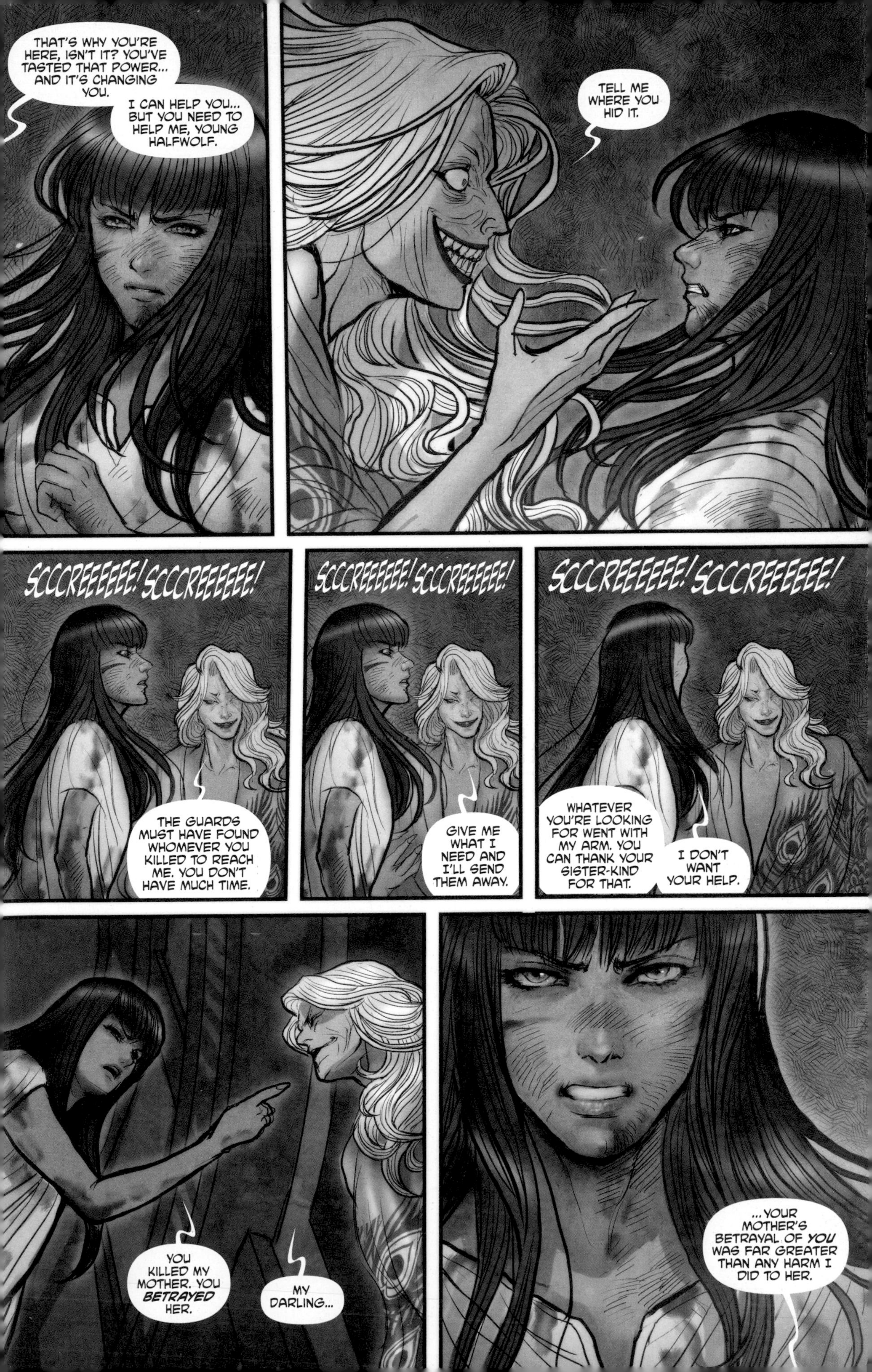
THAT'S WHY YOU'RE HERE, ISN'T IT? YOU'VE TASTED THAT POWER... AND IT'S CHANGING YOU.
I CAN HELP YOU... BUT YOU NEED TO HELP ME, YOUNG HALFWOLF.
TELL ME WHERE YOU HID IT.
SCCCREEEEEEE! SCCCREEEEEEE!
THE GUARDS MUST HAVE FOUND WHOMEVER YOU KILLED TO REACH ME. YOU DON'T HAVE MUCH TIME.
SCCCREEEEEEE! SCCCREEEEEEE!
GIVE ME WHAT I NEED AND I'LL SEND THEM AWAY.
SCCCREEEEEEE! SCCCREEEEEEE!
WHATEVER YOU'RE LOOKING FOR WENT WITH MY ARM. YOU CAN THANK YOUR SISTER-KIND FOR THAT.
I DON'T WANT YOUR HELP.
YOU KILLED MY MOTHER. YOU ***BETRAYED*** HER.
MY DARLING...
...YOUR MOTHER'S BETRAYAL OF *YOU* WAS FAR GREATER THAN ANY HARM I DID TO HER.

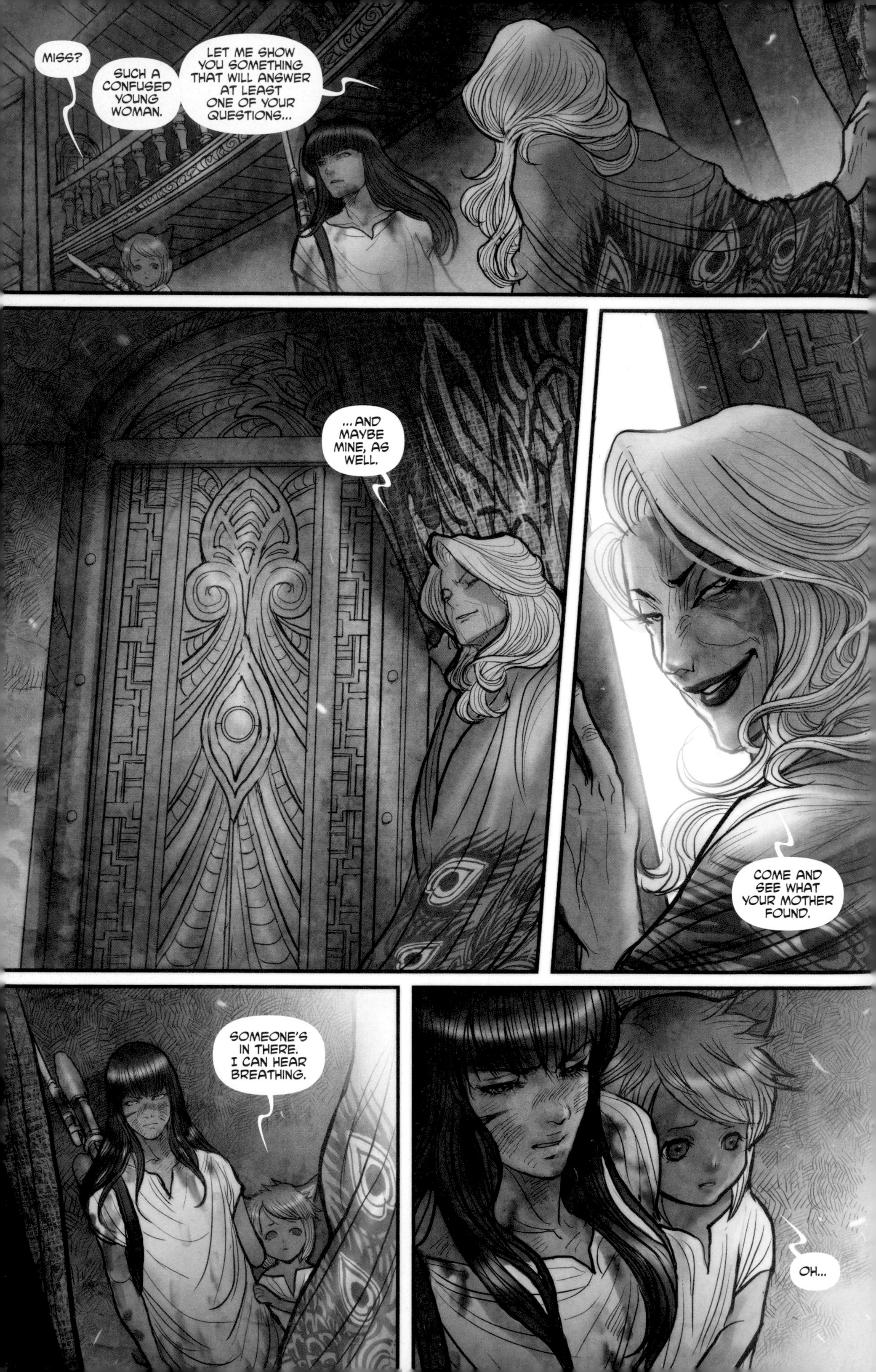
MISS?
SUCH A CONFUSED YOUNG WOMAN.
LET ME SHOW YOU SOMETHING THAT WILL ANSWER AT LEAST ONE OF YOUR QUESTIONS...
...AND MAYBE MINE, AS WELL.
COME AND SEE WHAT YOUR MOTHER FOUND.
SOMEONE'S IN THERE. I CAN HEAR BREATHING.
OH...

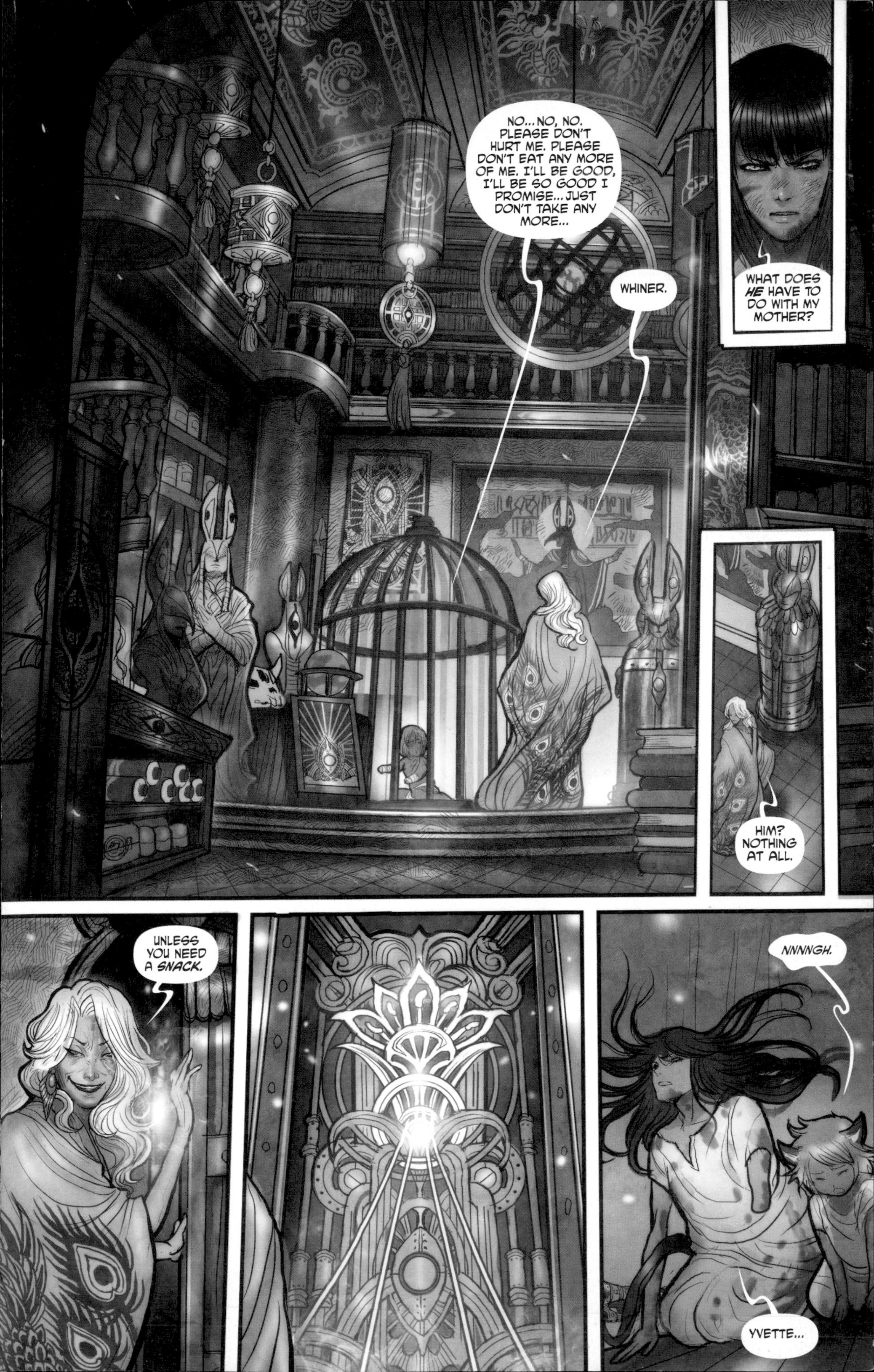
NO... NO, NO. PLEASE DON'T HURT ME. PLEASE DON'T EAT ANY MORE OF ME. I'LL BE GOOD, I'LL BE SO GOOD I PROMISE... JUST DON'T TAKE ANY MORE...
WHINER.
WHAT DOES *HE* HAVE TO DO WITH MY MOTHER?
HIM? NOTHING AT ALL.
UNLESS YOU NEED A *SNACK*.
NNNNGH.
YVETTE...

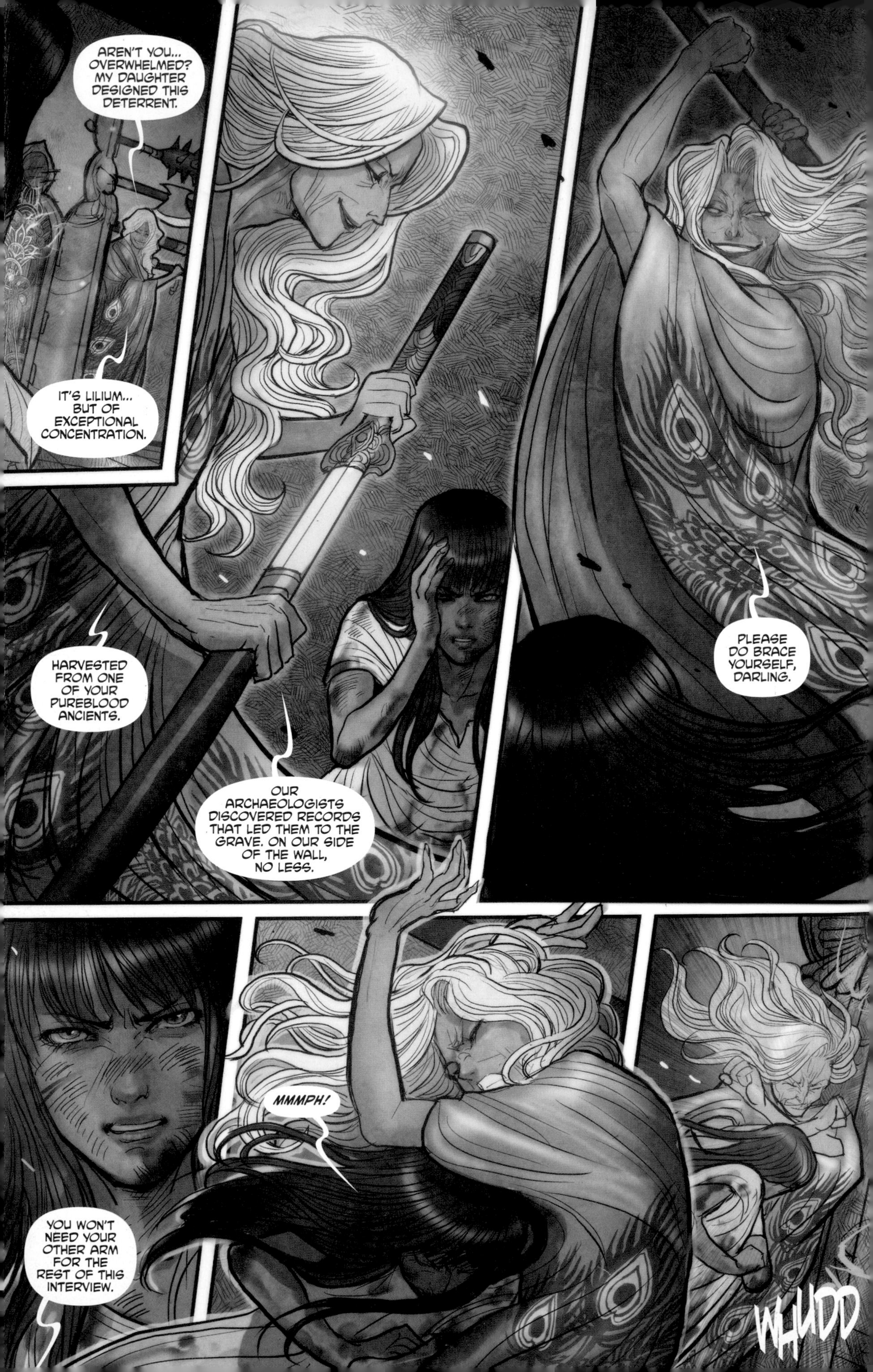

AREN'T YOU... OVERWHELMED? MY DAUGHTER DESIGNED THIS DETERRENT.
IT'S LILIUM... BUT OF EXCEPTIONAL CONCENTRATION.
HARVESTED FROM ONE OF YOUR PUREBLOOD ANCIENTS.
OUR ARCHAEOLOGISTS DISCOVERED RECORDS THAT LED THEM TO THE GRAVE. ON OUR SIDE OF THE WALL, NO LESS.
PLEASE DO BRACE YOURSELF, DARLING.
YOU WON'T NEED YOUR OTHER ARM FOR THE REST OF THIS INTERVIEW.
MMMPH!
WHUDD

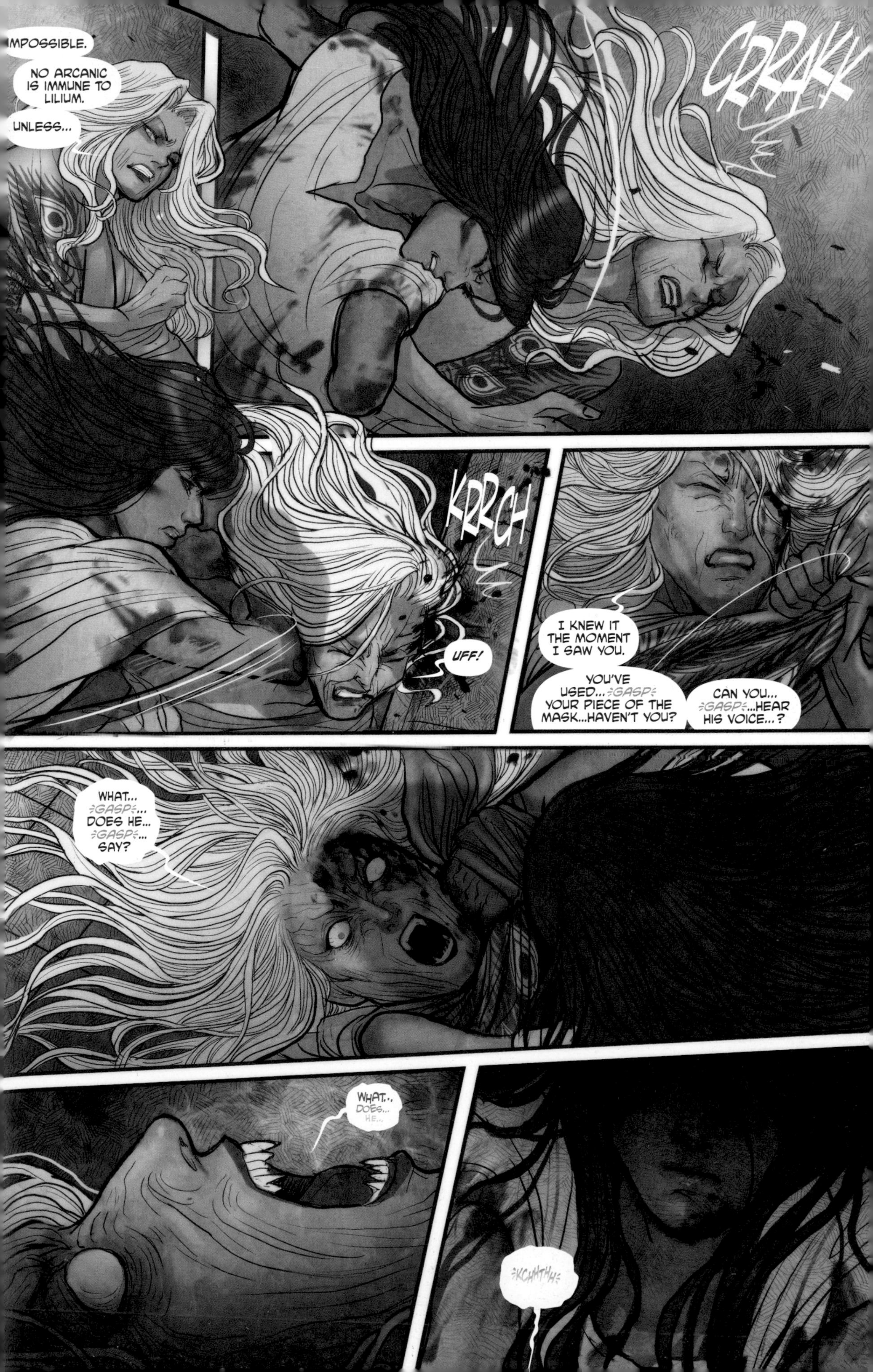
IMPOSSIBLE.
NO ARCANIC IS IMMUNE TO LILIUM.
UNLESS...
CRRAKK
KRRCH
UFF!
I KNEW IT THE MOMENT I SAW YOU.
YOU'VE USED... GASP YOUR PIECE OF THE MASK...HAVEN'T YOU?
CAN YOU... GASP ...HEAR HIS VOICE...?
WHAT... GASP... DOES HE... GASP... SAY?
WHAT... DOES... HE...
KCHHTHH

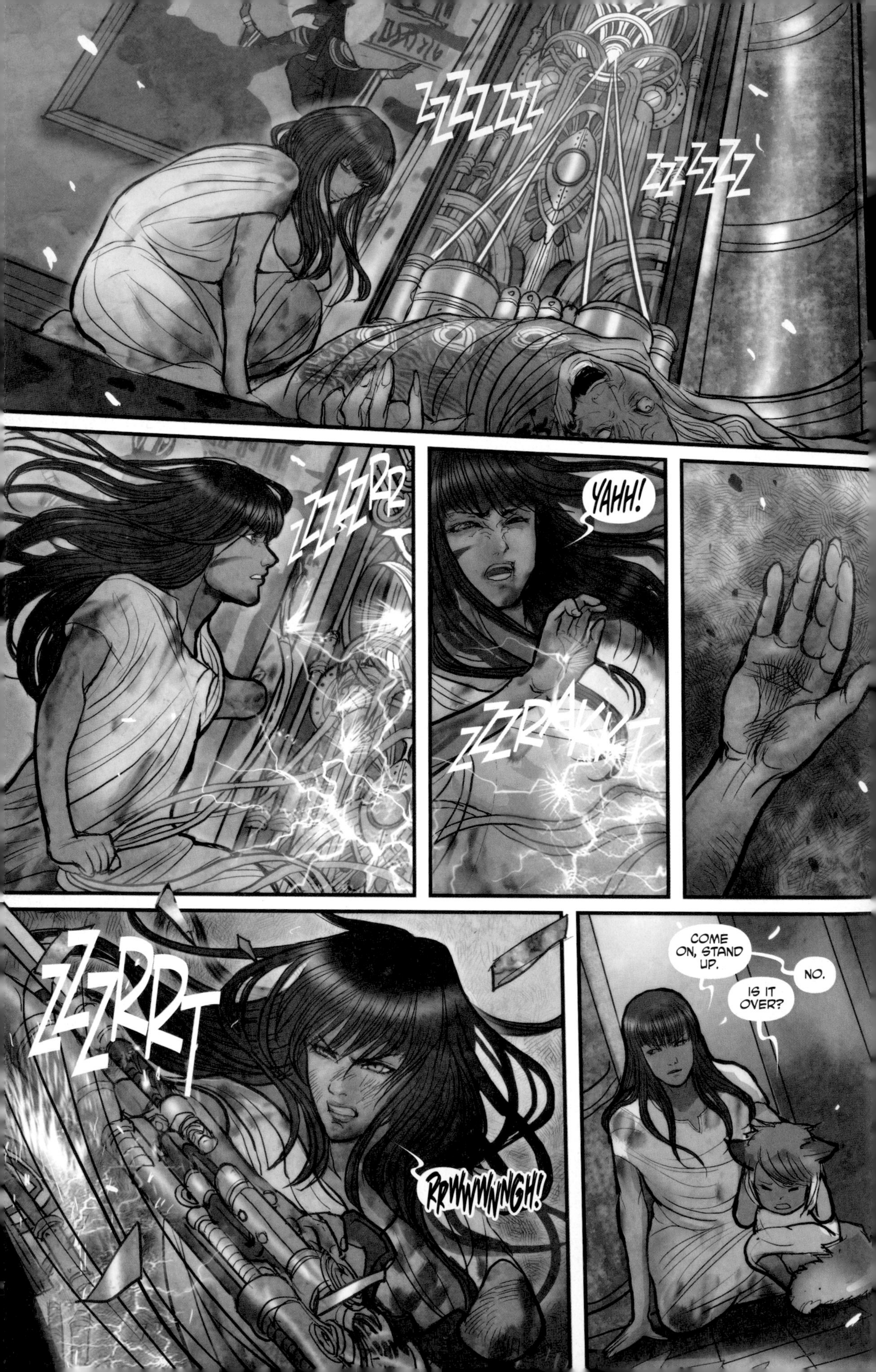
ZZZZZZZZ
ZZZZZZZ
ZZZZZZRRR
YAHH!
ZZZRAKKT
ZZZRRRT
RRWWWNNGH!
COME ON, STAND UP.
NO.
IS IT OVER?

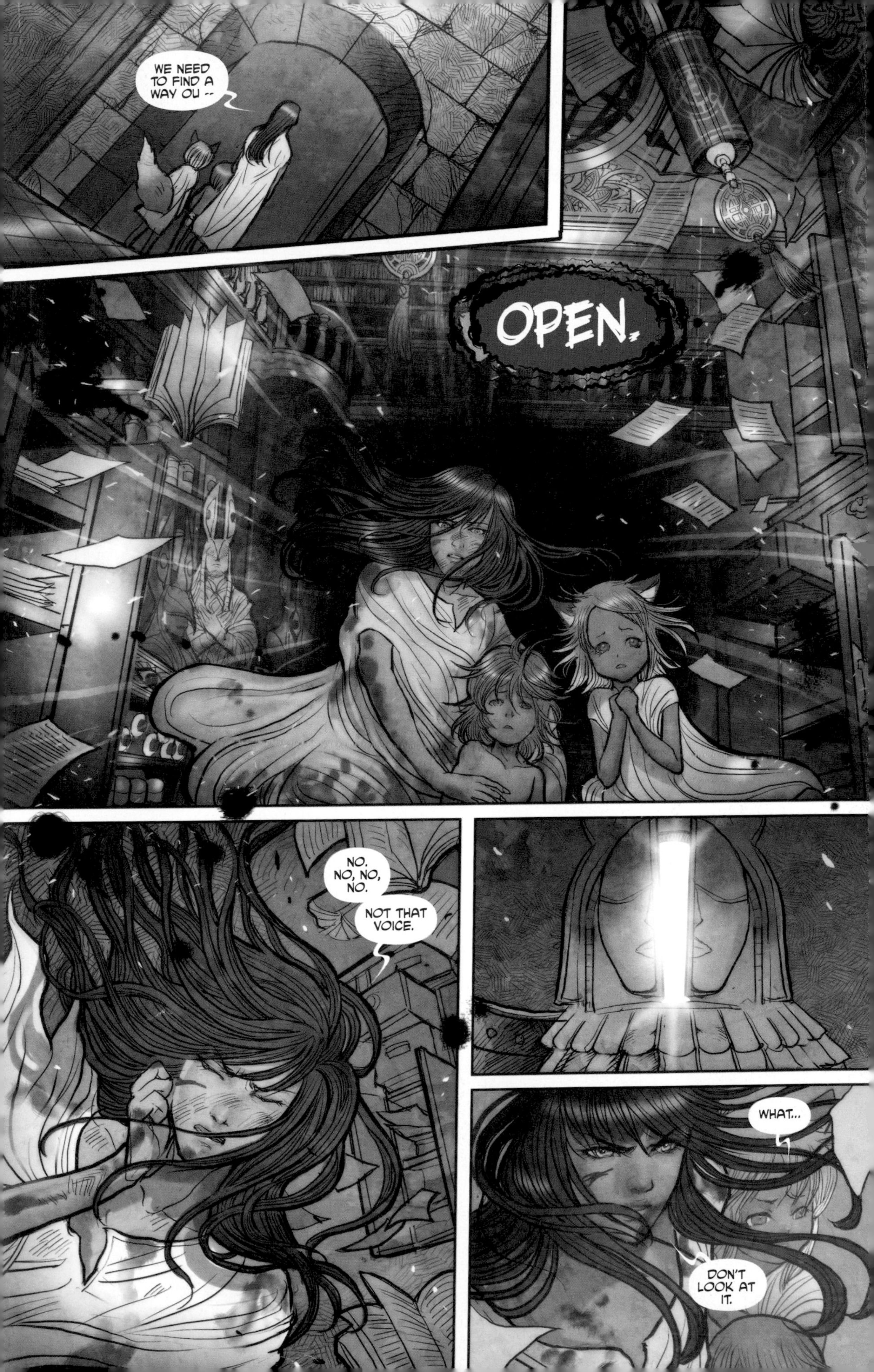
WE NEED TO FIND A WAY OU --
OPEN.
NO. NO, NO, NO.
NOT THAT VOICE.
WHAT...
DON'T LOOK AT IT.

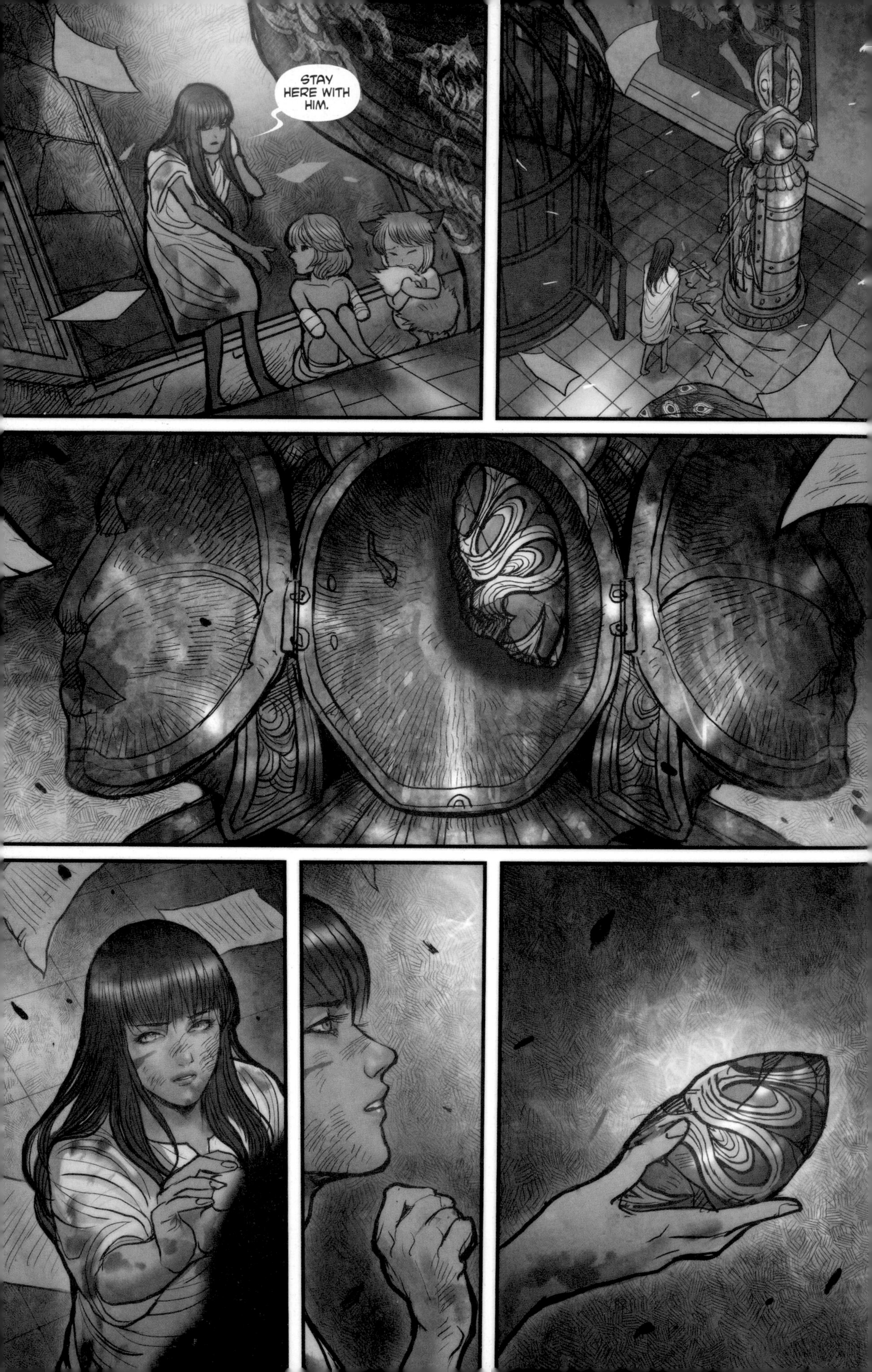
STAY HERE WITH HIM.

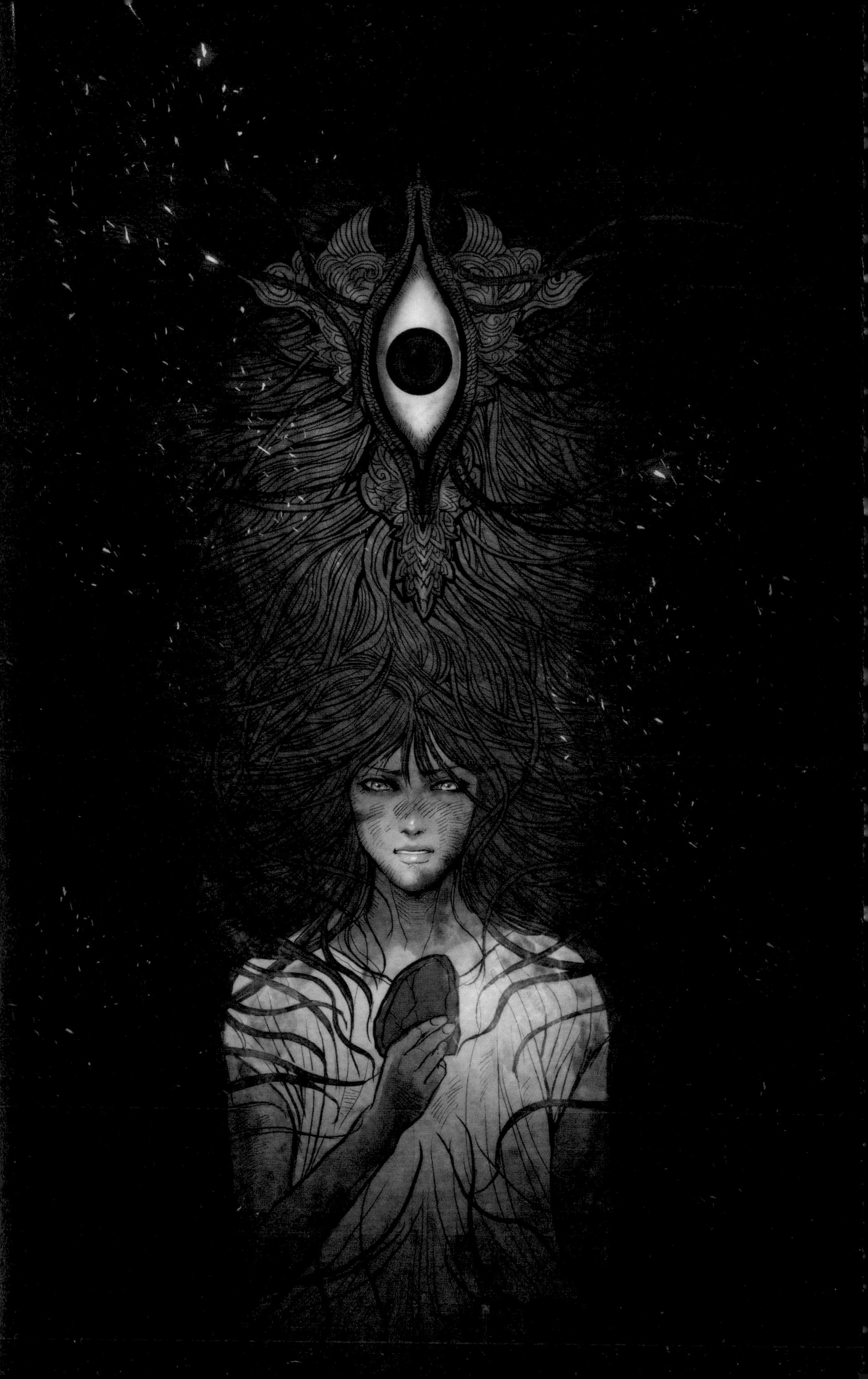

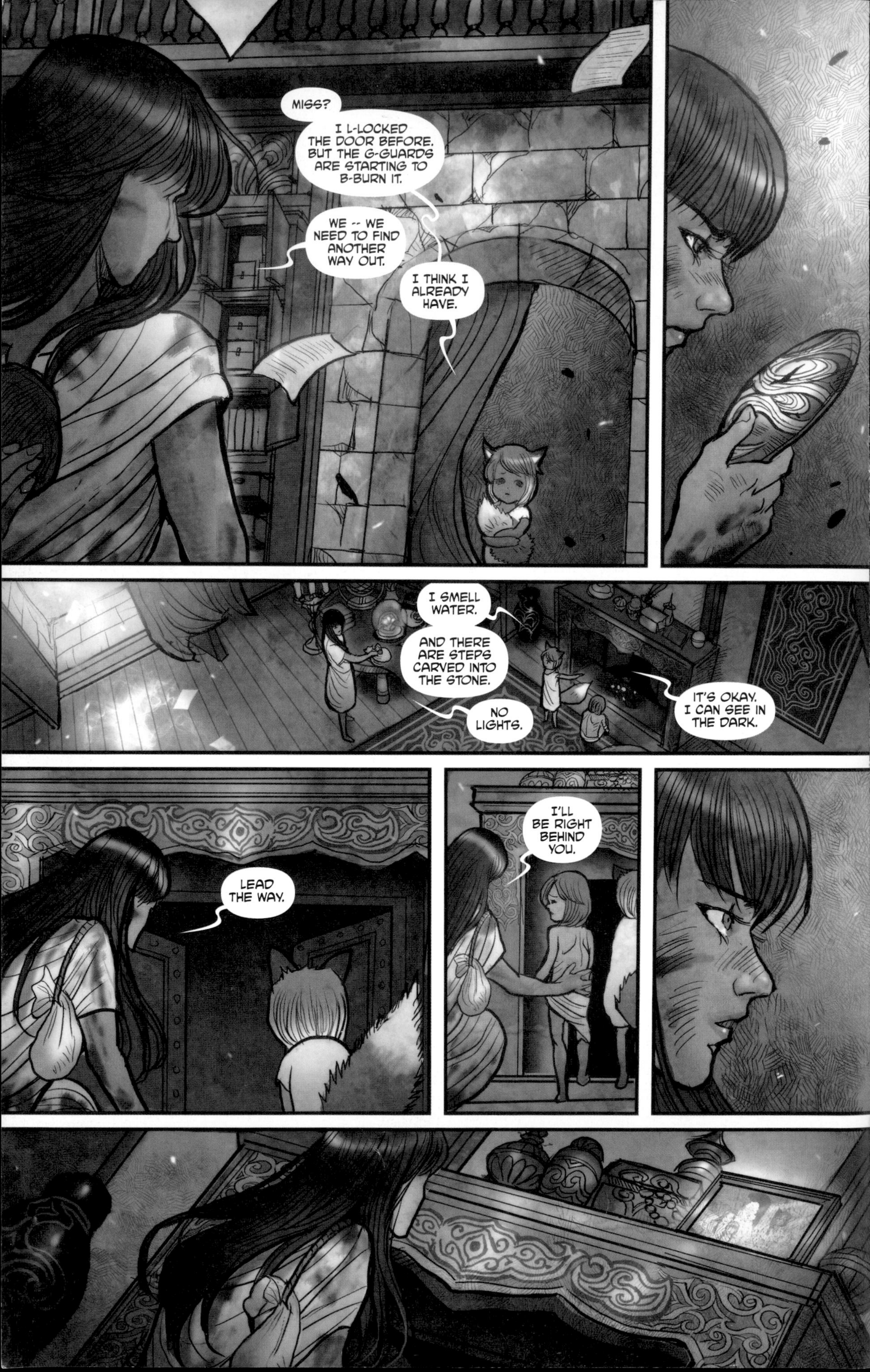
MISS?
I L-LOCKED THE DOOR BEFORE. BUT THE G-GUARDS ARE STARTING TO B-BURN IT.
WE -- WE NEED TO FIND ANOTHER WAY OUT.
I THINK I ALREADY HAVE.
I SMELL WATER.
AND THERE ARE STEPS CARVED INTO THE STONE.
NO LIGHTS.
IT'S OKAY. I CAN SEE IN THE DARK.
LEAD THE WAY.
I'LL BE RIGHT BEHIND YOU.

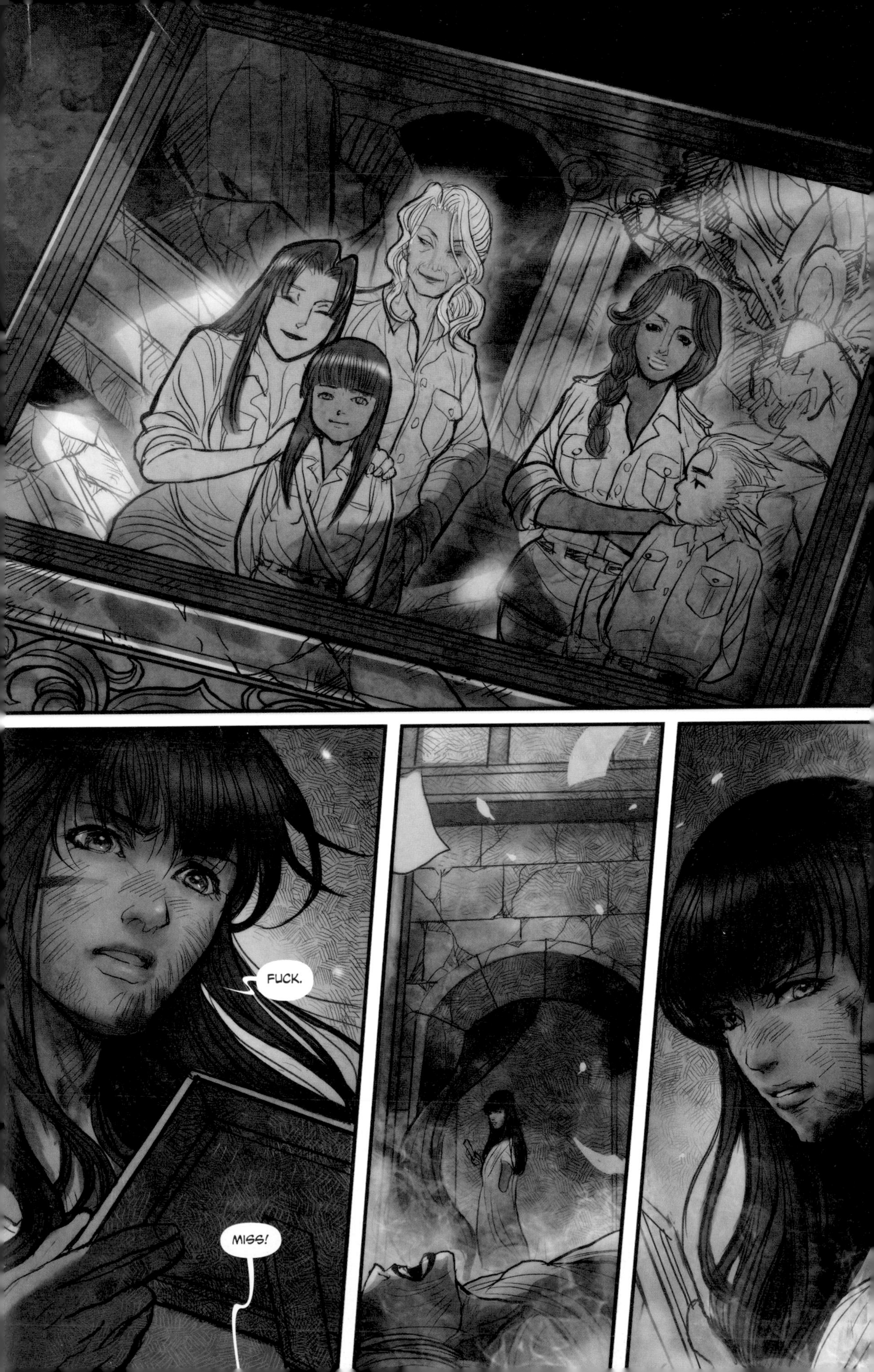
FUCK.
MISS!

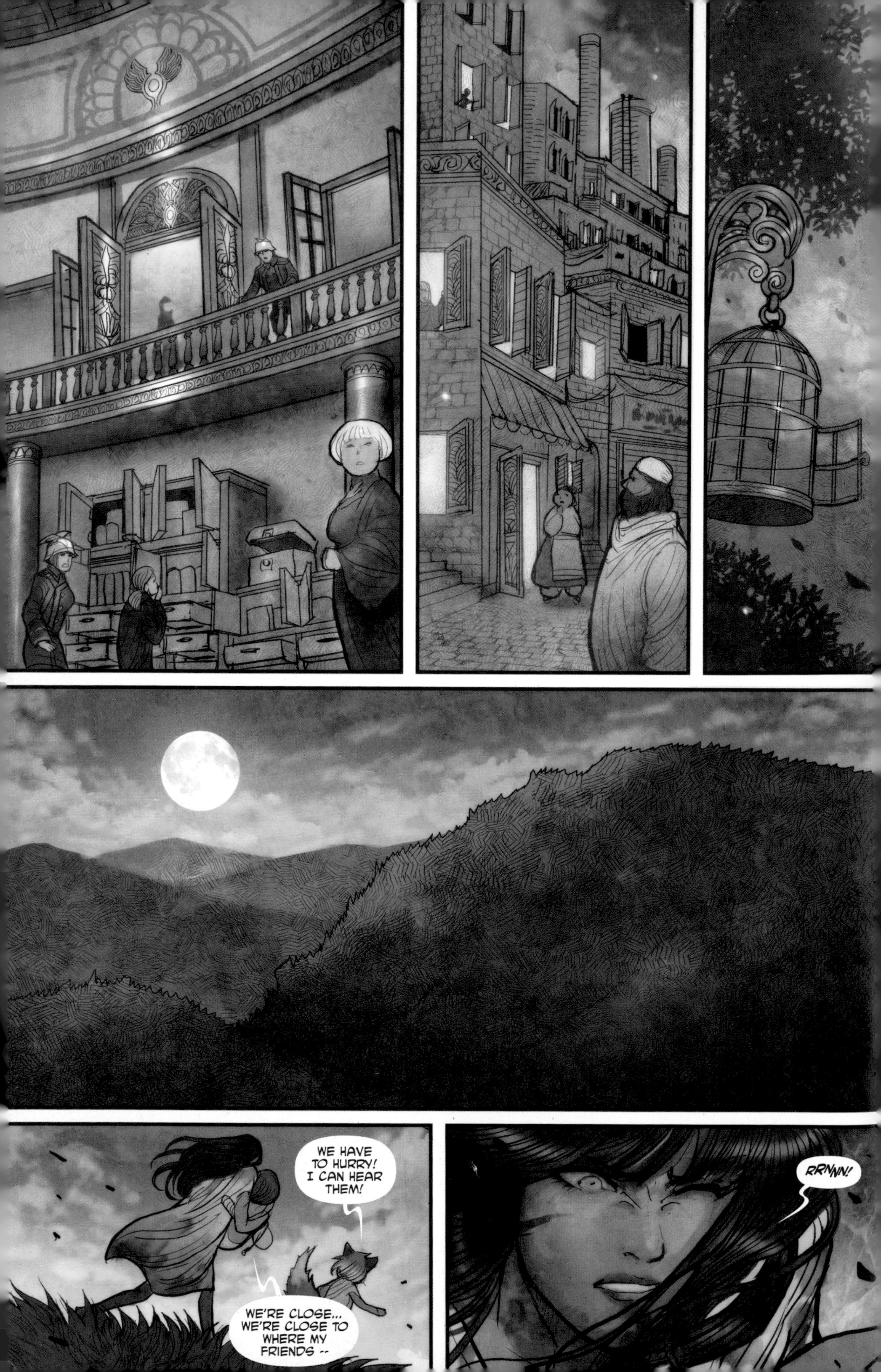
WE HAVE TO HURRY! I CAN HEAR THEM!
WE'RE CLOSE... WE'RE CLOSE TO WHERE MY FRIENDS --
RRNNN!

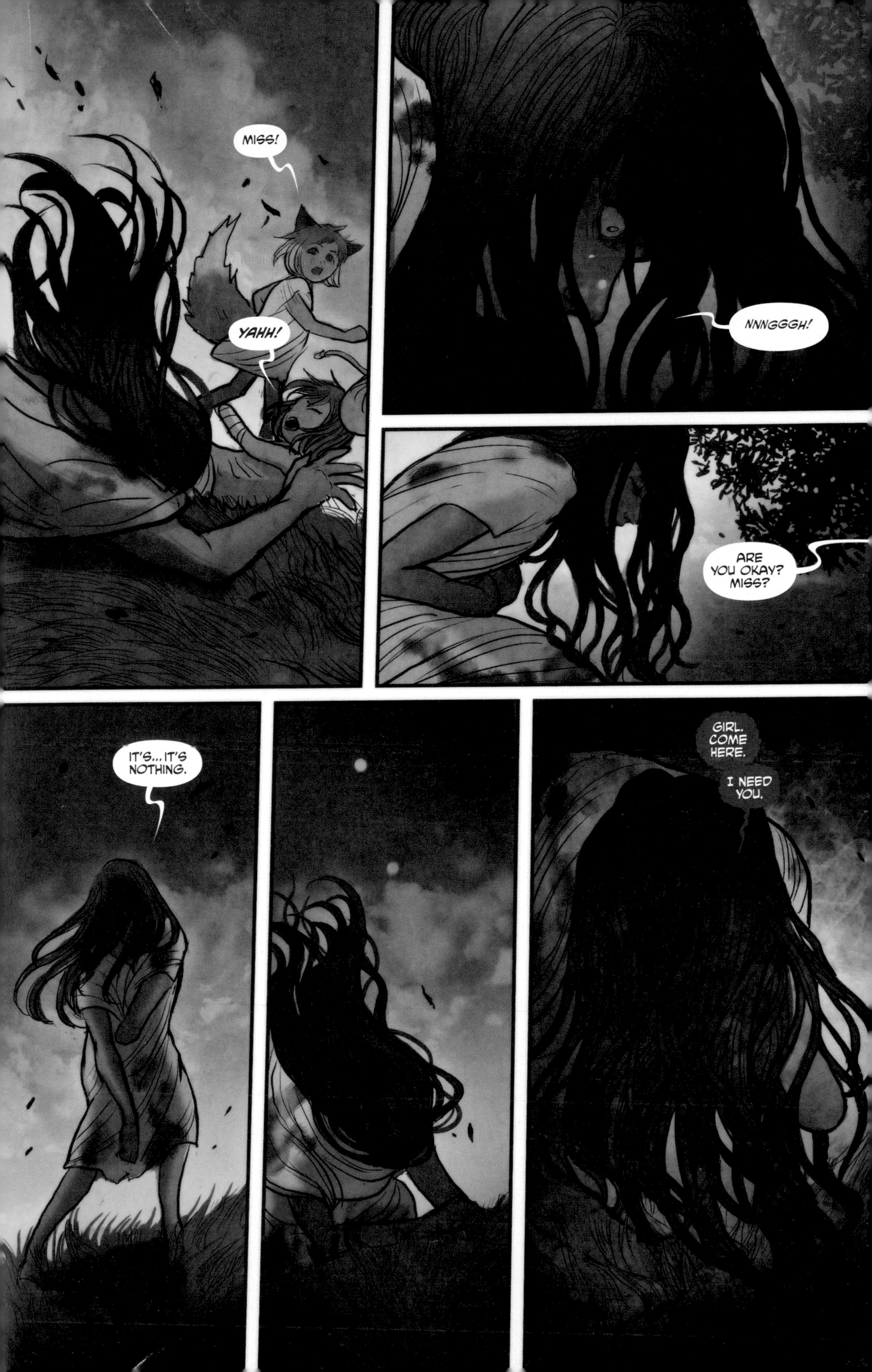
MISS!
YAHH!
NNNGGGH!
ARE YOU OKAY? MISS?
IT'S... IT'S NOTHING.
GIRL. COME HERE.
I NEED YOU.

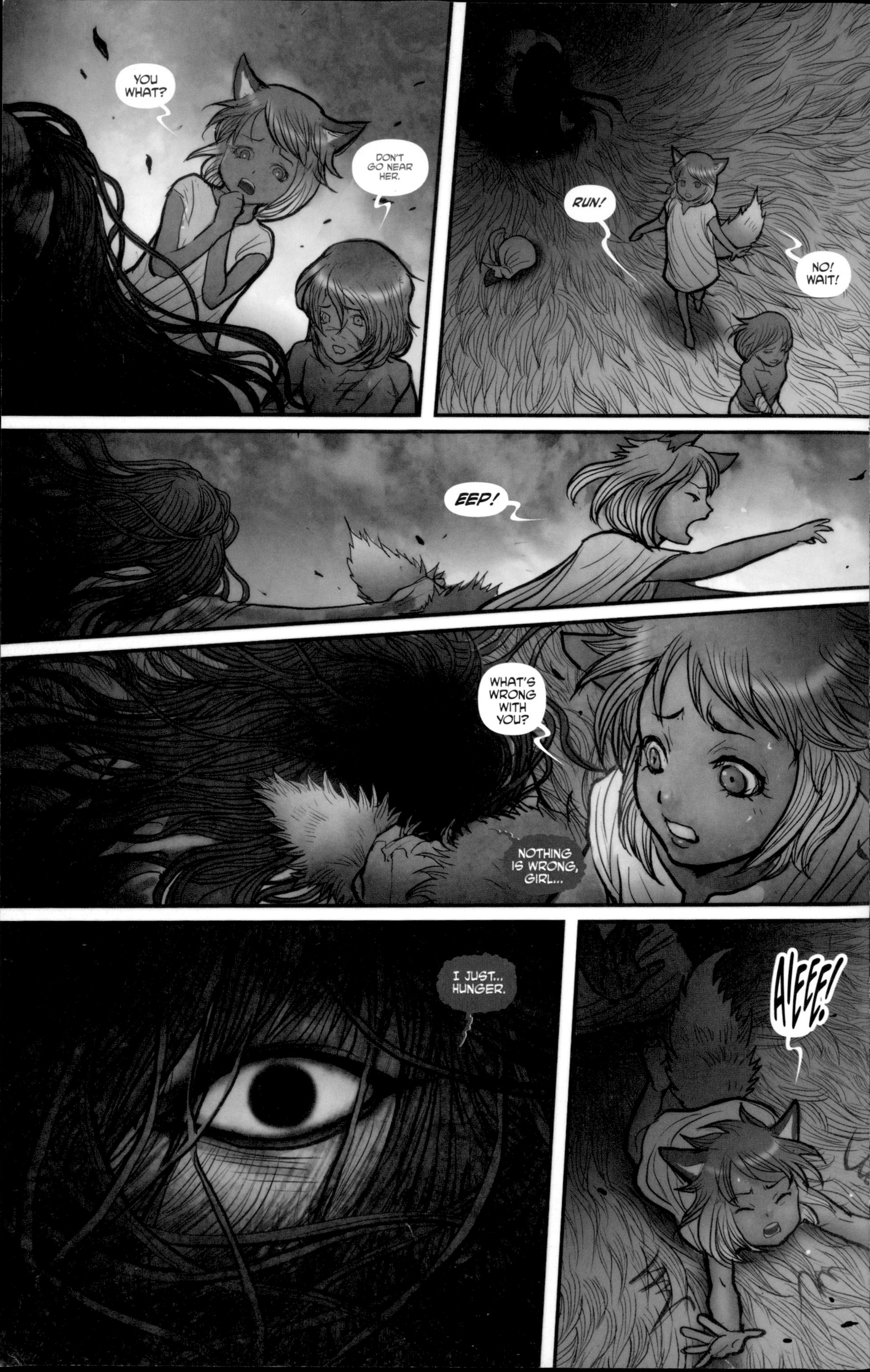
YOU WHAT?
DON'T GO NEAR HER.
RUN!
NO! WAIT!
EEP!
WHAT'S WRONG WITH YOU?
NOTHING IS WRONG, GIRL...
I JUST... HUNGER.
AIEEE!

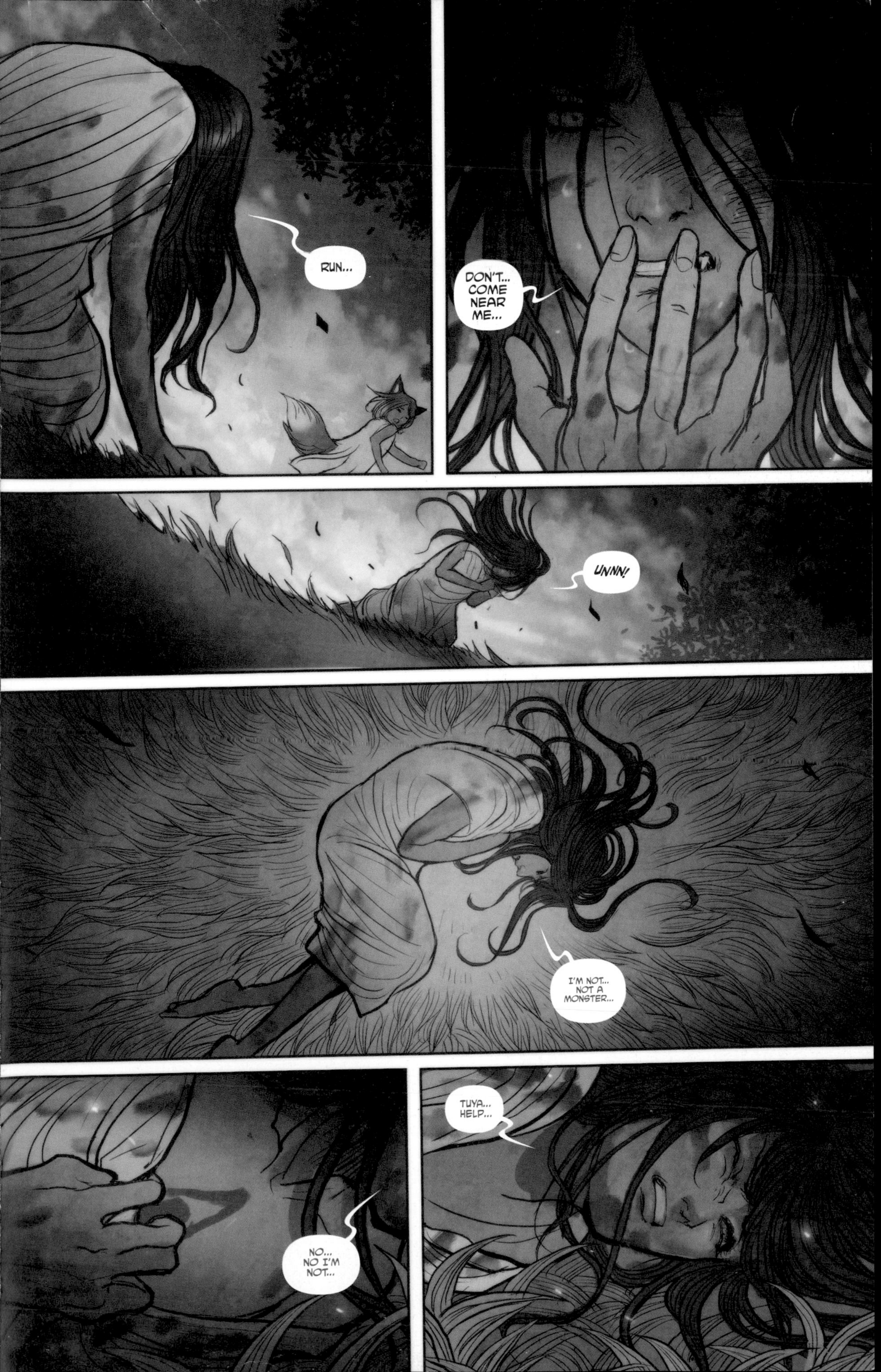
RUN...
DON'T... COME NEAR ME...
UNNN!
I'M NOT... NOT A MONSTER...
NO... NO I'M NOT...
TUYA... HELP...

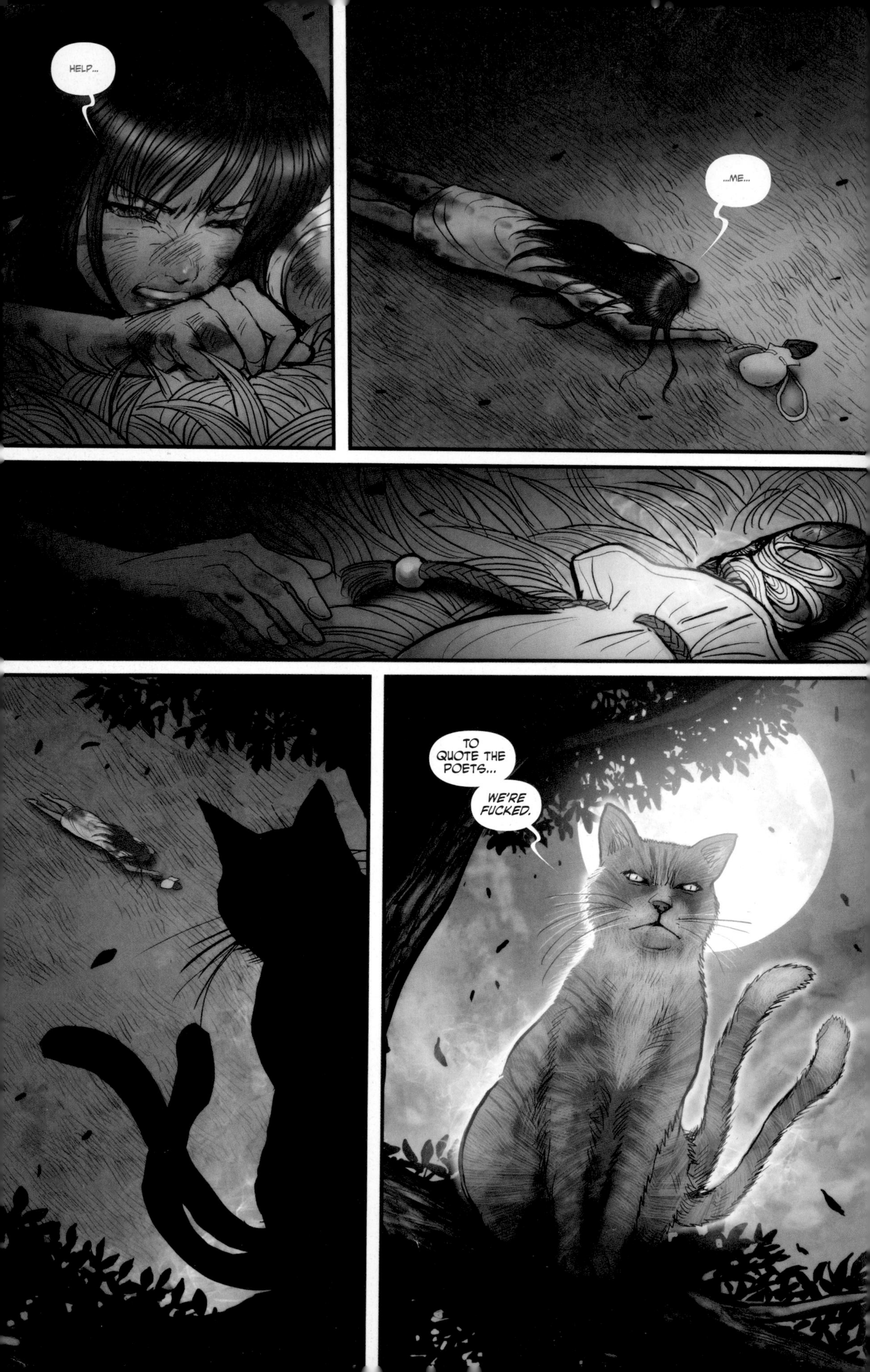
HELP...
...ME...
TO QUOTE THE POETS...
WE'RE FUCKED.

CHAPTER TWO

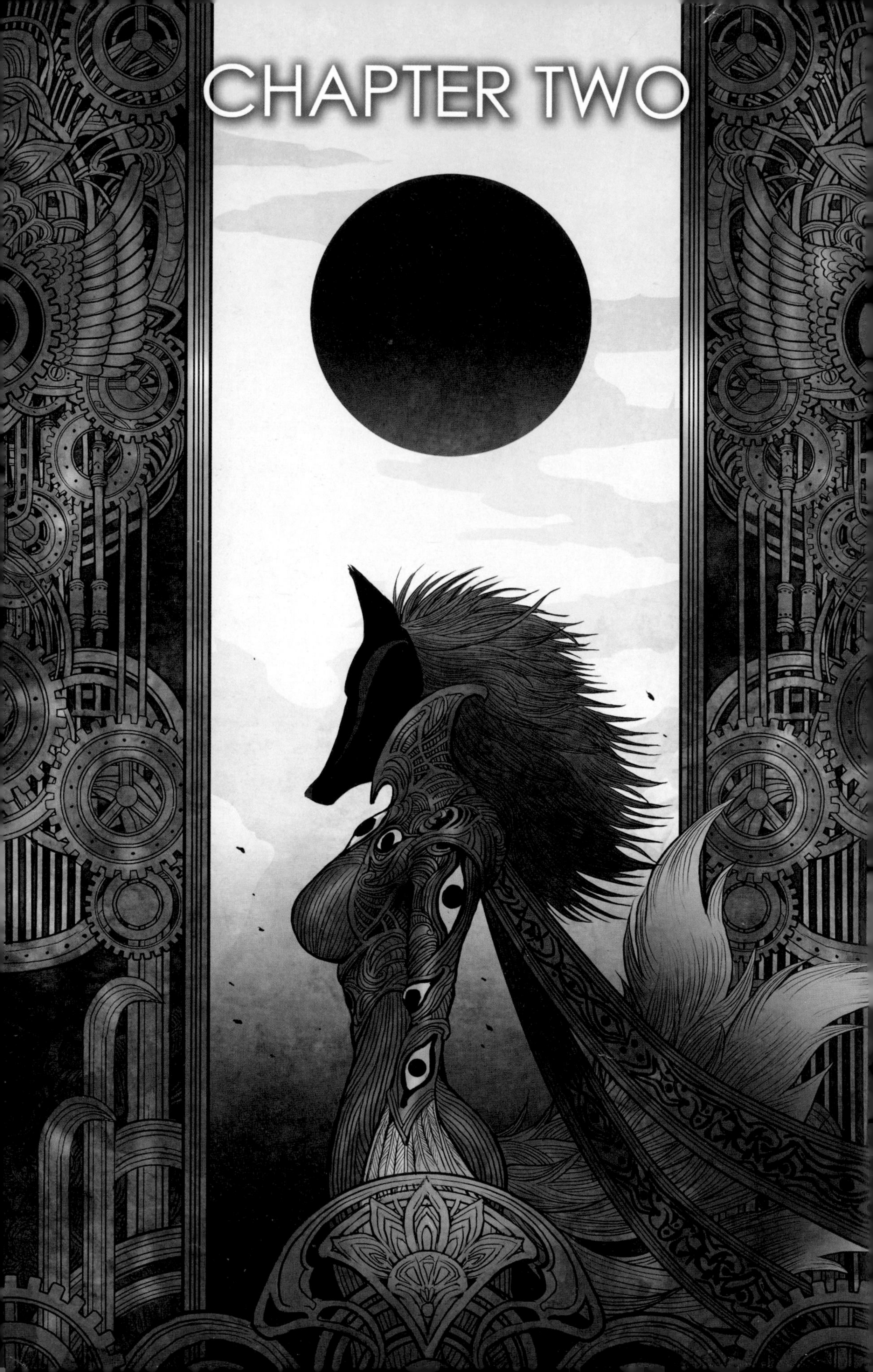

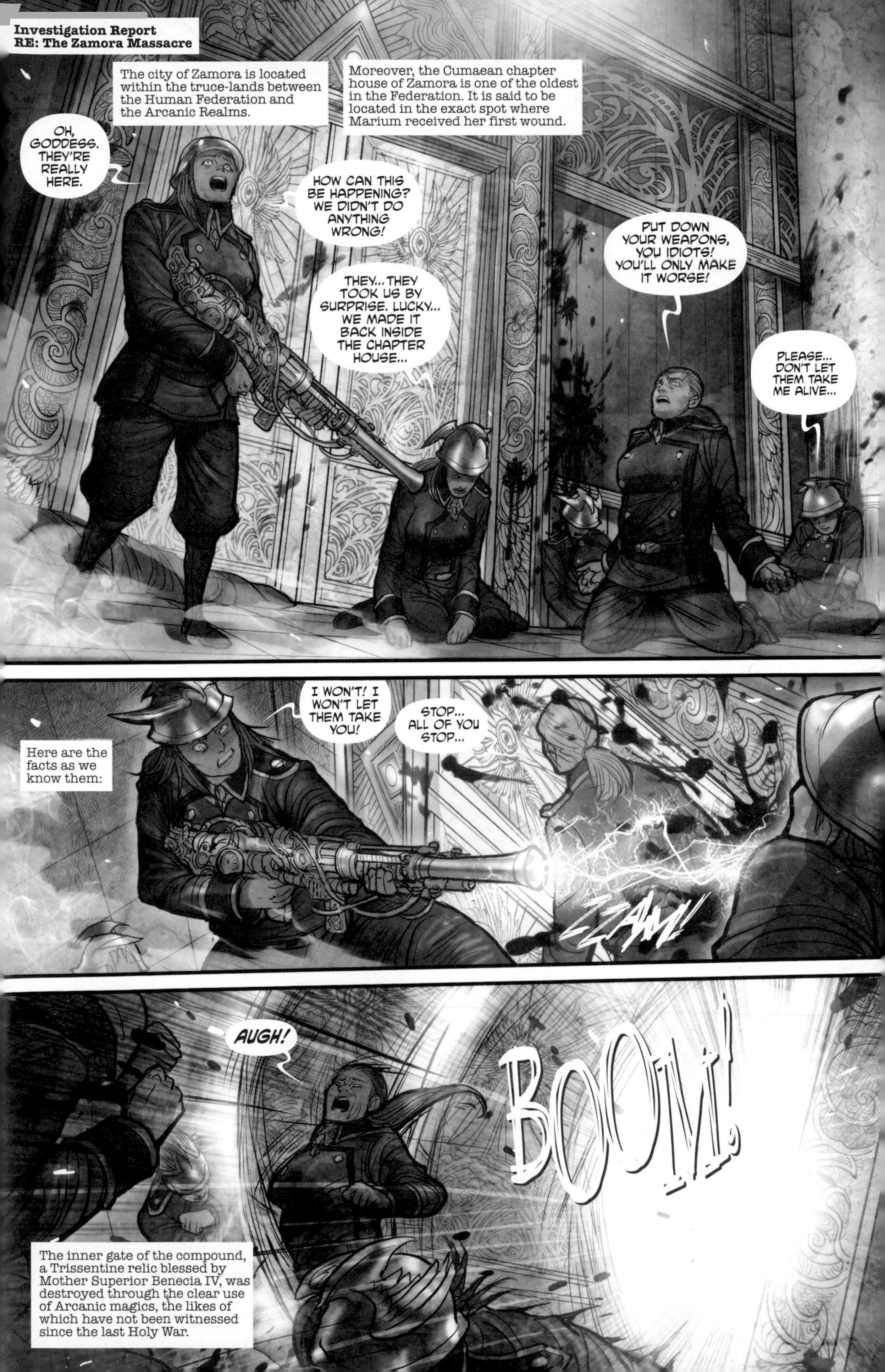
Investigation Report
RE: The Zamora Massacre
The city of Zamora is located within the truce-lands between the Human Federation and the Arcanic Realms.
Moreover, the Cumaean chapter house of Zamora is one of the oldest in the Federation. It is said to be located in the exact spot where Marium received her first wound.
OH, GODDESS. THEY'RE REALLY HERE.
HOW CAN THIS BE HAPPENING? WE DIDN'T DO ANYTHING WRONG!
THEY... THEY TOOK US BY SURPRISE. LUCKY... WE MADE IT BACK INSIDE THE CHAPTER HOUSE...
PUT DOWN YOUR WEAPONS, YOU IDIOTS! YOU'LL ONLY MAKE IT WORSE!
PLEASE... DON'T LET THEM TAKE ME ALIVE...
Here are the facts as we know them:
I WON'T! I WON'T LET THEM TAKE YOU!
STOP... ALL OF YOU STOP...
ZZAM!
AUGH!
BOOM!
The inner gate of the compound, a Trissentine relic blessed by Mother Superior Benecia IV, was destroyed through the clear use of Arcanic magics, the likes of which have not been witnessed since the last Holy War.

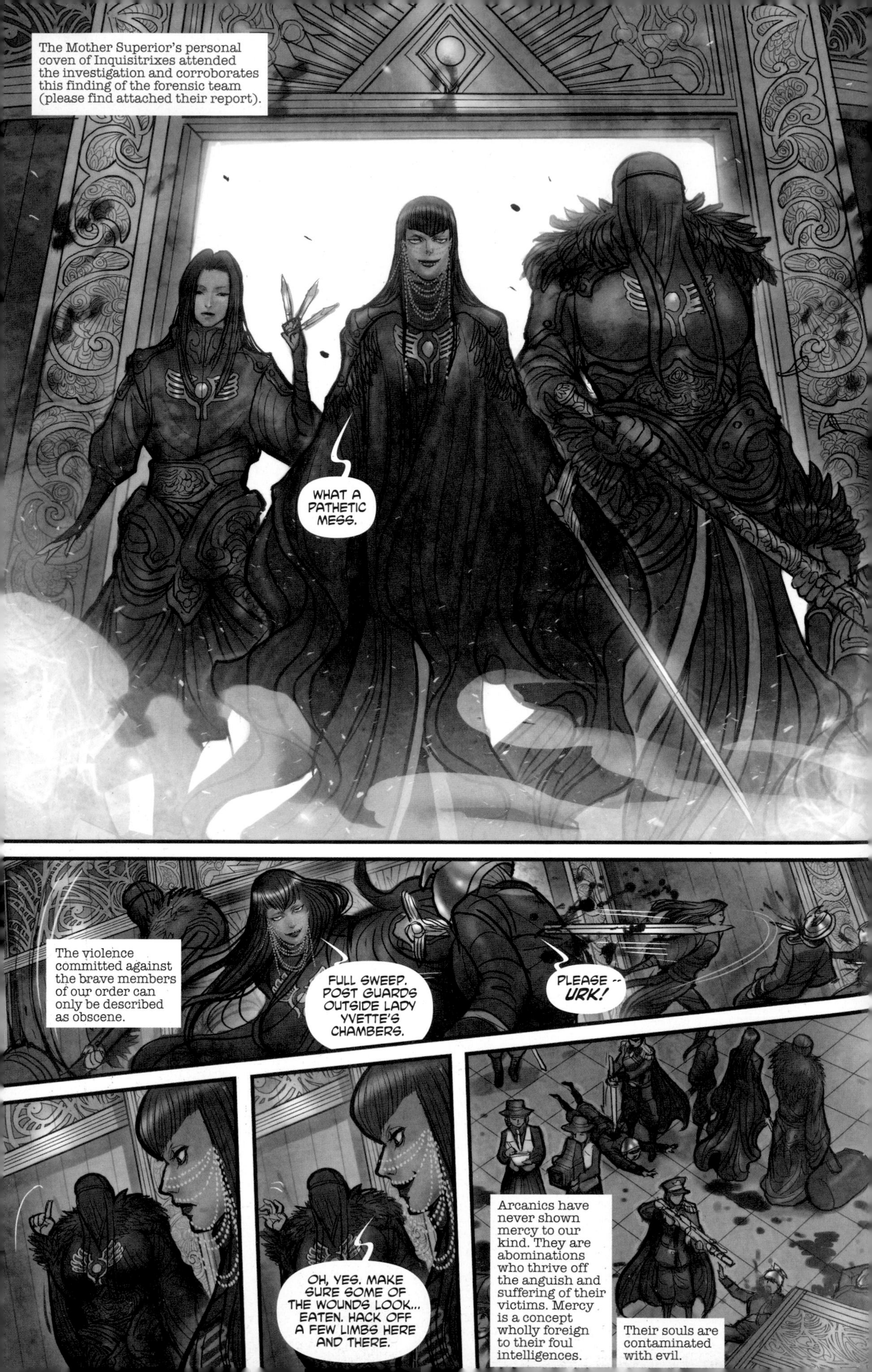
The Mother Superior's personal coven of Inquisitrixes attended the investigation and corroborates this finding of the forensic team (please find attached their report).
WHAT A PATHETIC MESS.
The violence committed against the brave members of our order can only be described as obscene.
FULL SWEEP. POST GUARDS OUTSIDE LADY YVETTE'S CHAMBERS.
PLEASE -- URK!
OH, YES. MAKE SURE SOME OF THE WOUNDS LOOK... EATEN. HACK OFF A FEW LIMBS HERE AND THERE.
Arcanics have never shown mercy to our kind. They are abominations who thrive off the anguish and suffering of their victims. Mercy is a concept wholly foreign to their foul intelligences.
Their souls are contaminated with evil.

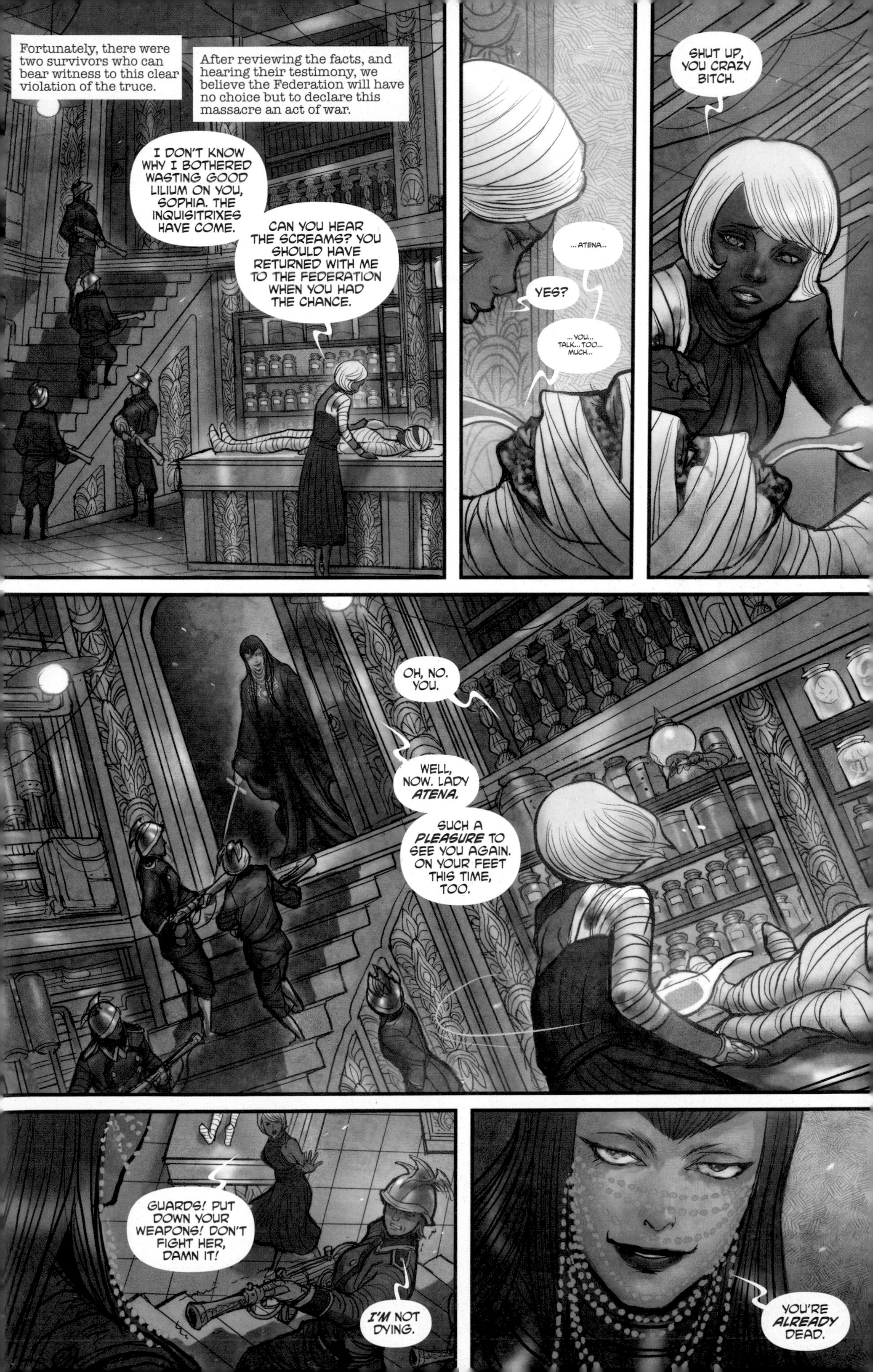

Fortunately, there were two survivors who can bear witness to this clear violation of the truce.
After reviewing the facts, and hearing their testimony, we believe the Federation will have no choice but to declare this massacre an act of war.
I DON'T KNOW WHY I BOTHERED WASTING GOOD LILIUM ON YOU, SOPHIA. THE INQUISITRIXES HAVE COME.
CAN YOU HEAR THE SCREAMS? YOU SHOULD HAVE RETURNED WITH ME TO THE FEDERATION WHEN YOU HAD THE CHANCE.
...ATENA...
YES?
...YOU... TALK...TOO... MUCH...
SHUT UP, YOU CRAZY BITCH.
OH, NO. YOU.
WELL, NOW. LADY *ATENA.*
SUCH A *PLEASURE* TO SEE YOU AGAIN. ON YOUR FEET THIS TIME, TOO.
GUARDS! PUT DOWN YOUR WEAPONS! DON'T FIGHT HER, DAMN IT!
I'M NOT DYING.
YOU'RE *ALREADY* DEAD.

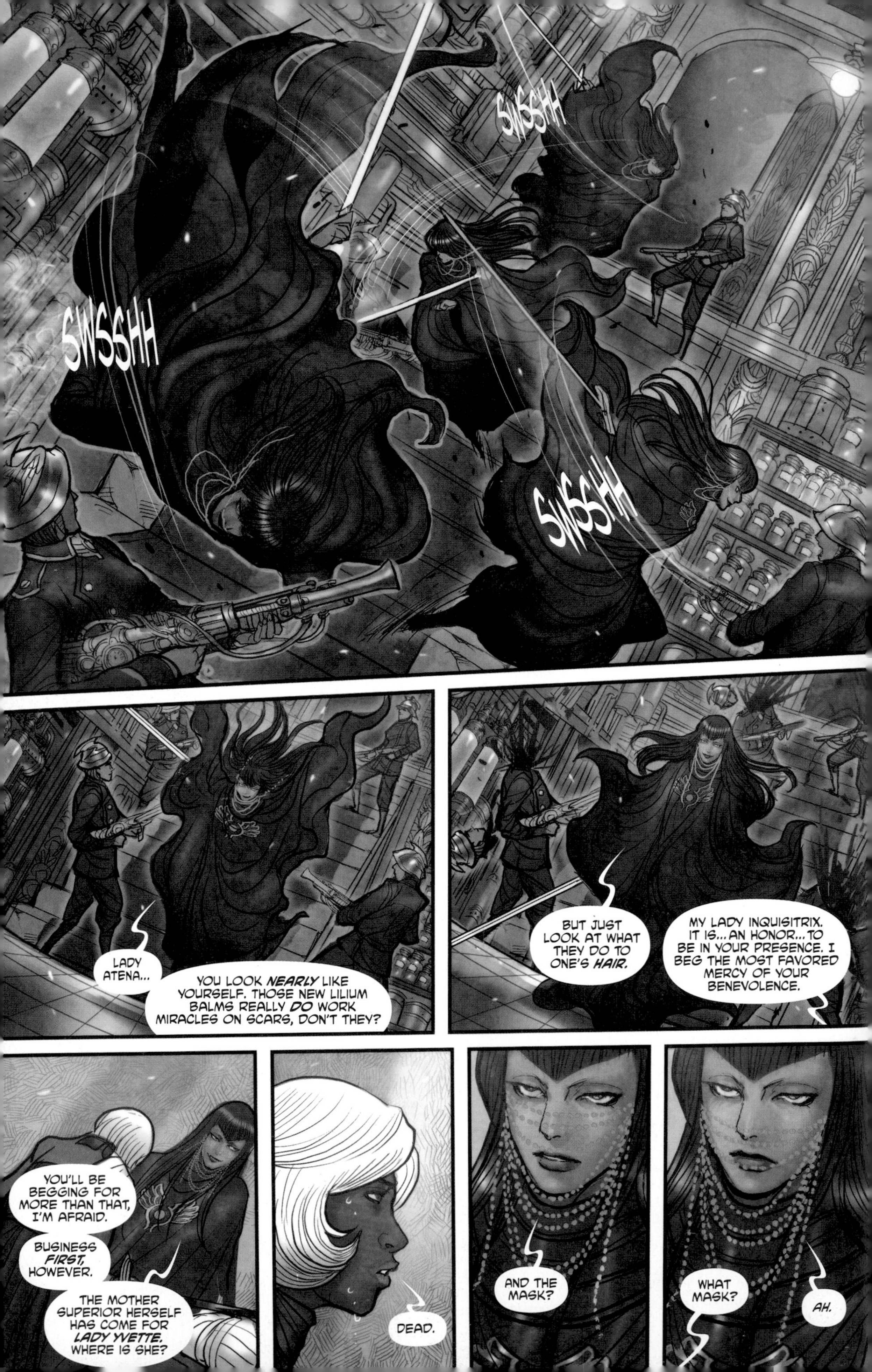
SWSSHH
SWSSHH
SWSSHH
LADY ATENA...
YOU LOOK NEARLY LIKE YOURSELF. THOSE NEW LILIUM BALMS REALLY DO WORK MIRACLES ON SCARS, DON'T THEY?
BUT JUST LOOK AT WHAT THEY DO TO ONE'S HAIR.
MY LADY INQUISITRIX. IT IS... AN HONOR... TO BE IN YOUR PRESENCE. I BEG THE MOST FAVORED MERCY OF YOUR BENEVOLENCE.
YOU'LL BE BEGGING FOR MORE THAN THAT, I'M AFRAID.
BUSINESS FIRST, HOWEVER.
THE MOTHER SUPERIOR HERSELF HAS COME FOR LADY YVETTE. WHERE IS SHE?
DEAD.
AND THE MASK?
WHAT MASK?
AH.

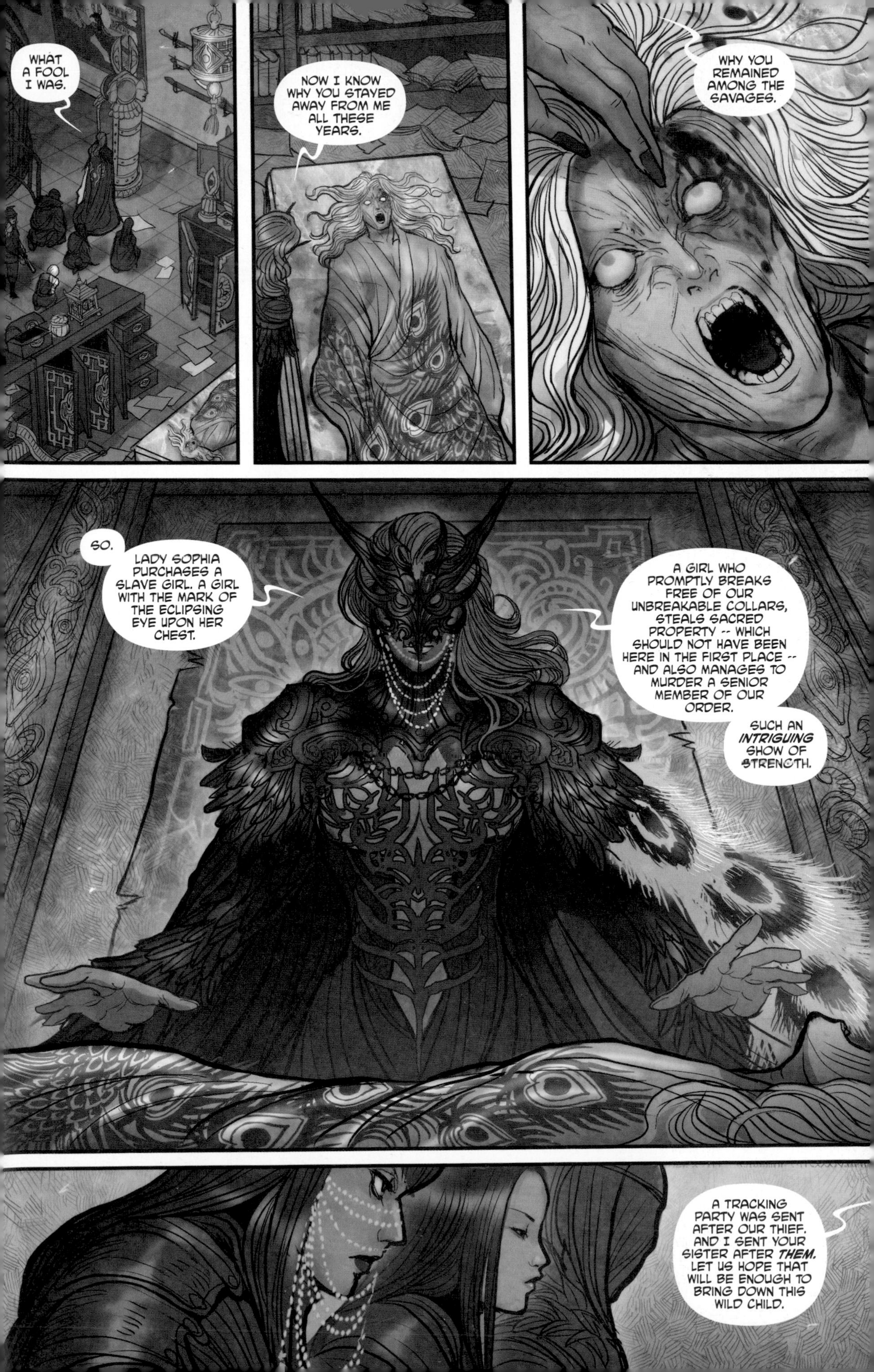
WHAT A FOOL I WAS.
NOW I KNOW WHY YOU STAYED AWAY FROM ME ALL THESE YEARS.
WHY YOU REMAINED AMONG THE SAVAGES.
SO.
LADY SOPHIA PURCHASES A SLAVE GIRL. A GIRL WITH THE MARK OF THE ECLIPSING EYE UPON HER CHEST.
A GIRL WHO PROMPTLY BREAKS FREE OF OUR UNBREAKABLE COLLARS, STEALS SACRED PROPERTY -- WHICH SHOULD NOT HAVE BEEN HERE IN THE FIRST PLACE -- AND ALSO MANAGES TO MURDER A SENIOR MEMBER OF OUR ORDER.
SUCH AN *INTRIGUING* SHOW OF STRENGTH.
A TRACKING PARTY WAS SENT AFTER OUR THIEF. AND I SENT YOUR SISTER AFTER *THEM.* LET US HOPE THAT WILL BE ENOUGH TO BRING DOWN THIS WILD CHILD.

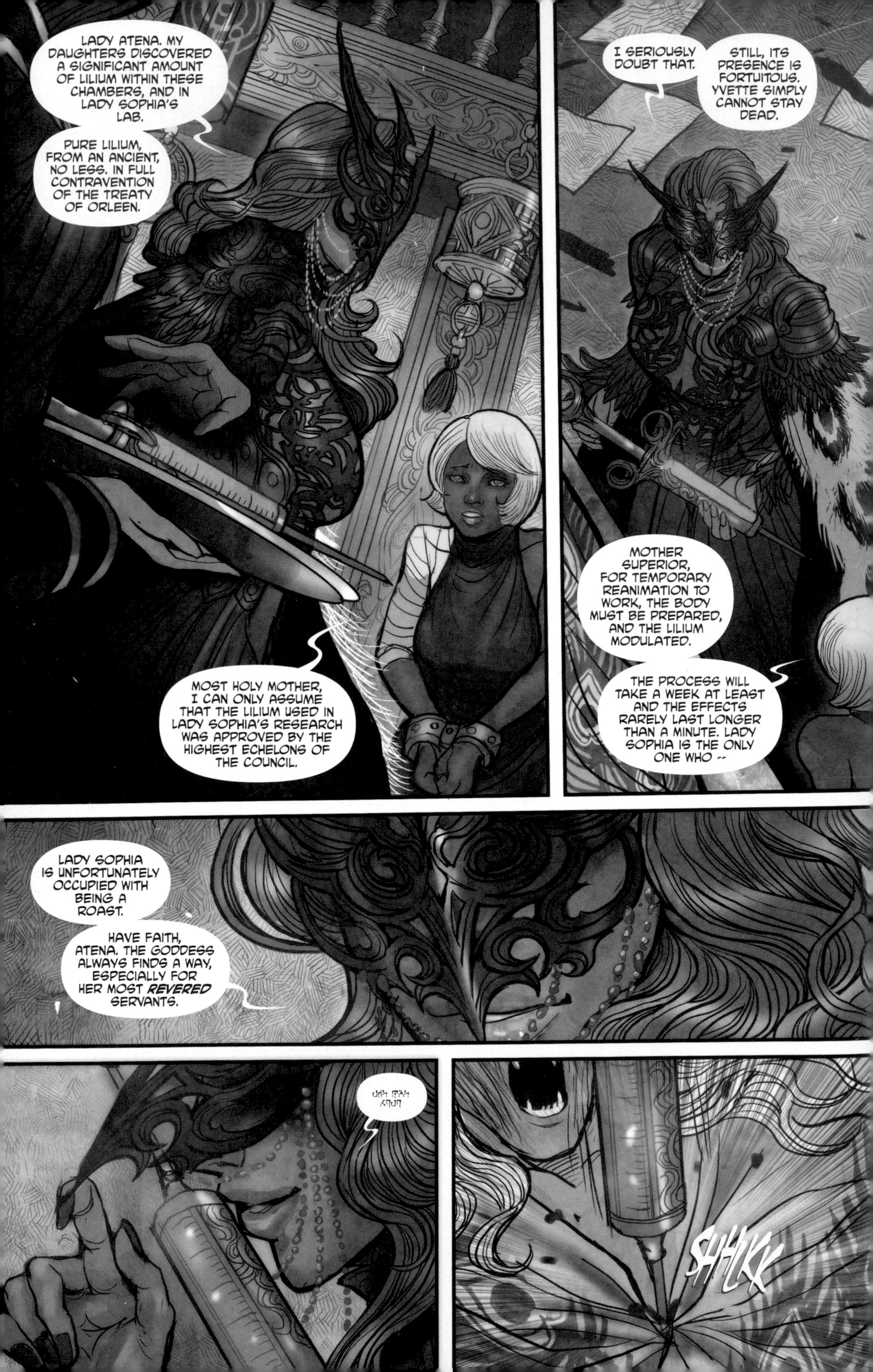
LADY ATENA. MY DAUGHTERS DISCOVERED A SIGNIFICANT AMOUNT OF LILIUM WITHIN THESE CHAMBERS, AND IN LADY SOPHIA'S LAB.
PURE LILIUM, FROM AN ANCIENT, NO LESS. IN FULL CONTRAVENTION OF THE TREATY OF ORLEEN.
MOST HOLY MOTHER, I CAN ONLY ASSUME THAT THE LILIUM USED IN LADY SOPHIA'S RESEARCH WAS APPROVED BY THE HIGHEST ECHELONS OF THE COUNCIL.
I SERIOUSLY DOUBT THAT.
STILL, ITS PRESENCE IS FORTUITOUS. YVETTE SIMPLY CANNOT STAY DEAD.
MOTHER SUPERIOR, FOR TEMPORARY REANIMATION TO WORK, THE BODY MUST BE PREPARED, AND THE LILIUM MODULATED.
THE PROCESS WILL TAKE A WEEK AT LEAST AND THE EFFECTS RARELY LAST LONGER THAN A MINUTE. LADY SOPHIA IS THE ONLY ONE WHO --
LADY SOPHIA IS UNFORTUNATELY OCCUPIED WITH BEING A ROAST.
HAVE FAITH, ATENA. THE GODDESS ALWAYS FINDS A WAY, ESPECIALLY FOR HER MOST ***REVERED*** SERVANTS.
SHHLKK

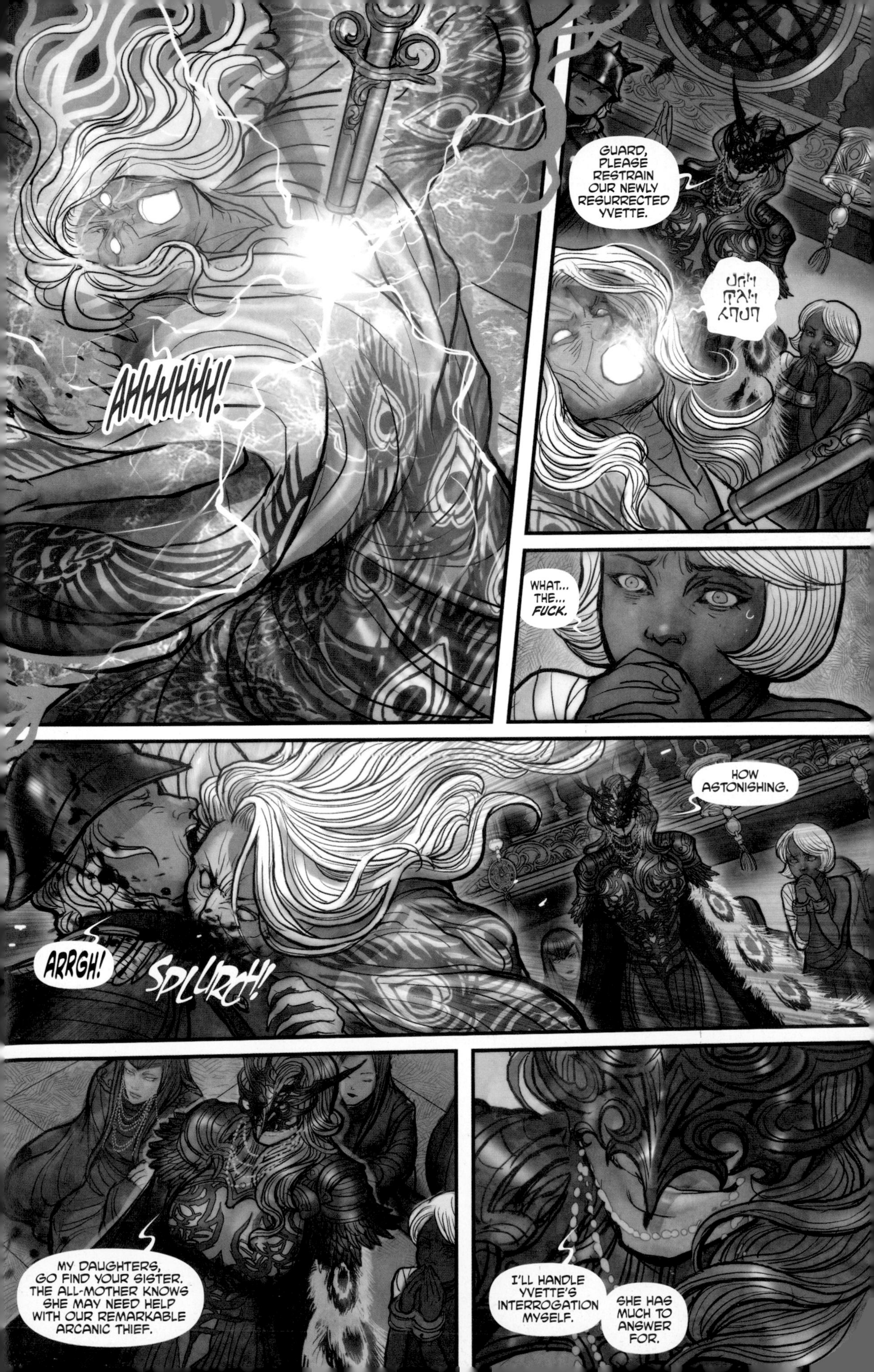
AHHHHHH!
GUARD, PLEASE RESTRAIN OUR NEWLY RESURRECTED YVETTE.
WHAT... THE... FUCK.
ARRGH!
SPLURCH!
HOW ASTONISHING.
MY DAUGHTERS, GO FIND YOUR SISTER. THE ALL-MOTHER KNOWS SHE MAY NEED HELP WITH OUR REMARKABLE ARCANIC THIEF.
I'LL HANDLE YVETTE'S INTERROGATION MYSELF.
SHE HAS MUCH TO ANSWER FOR.

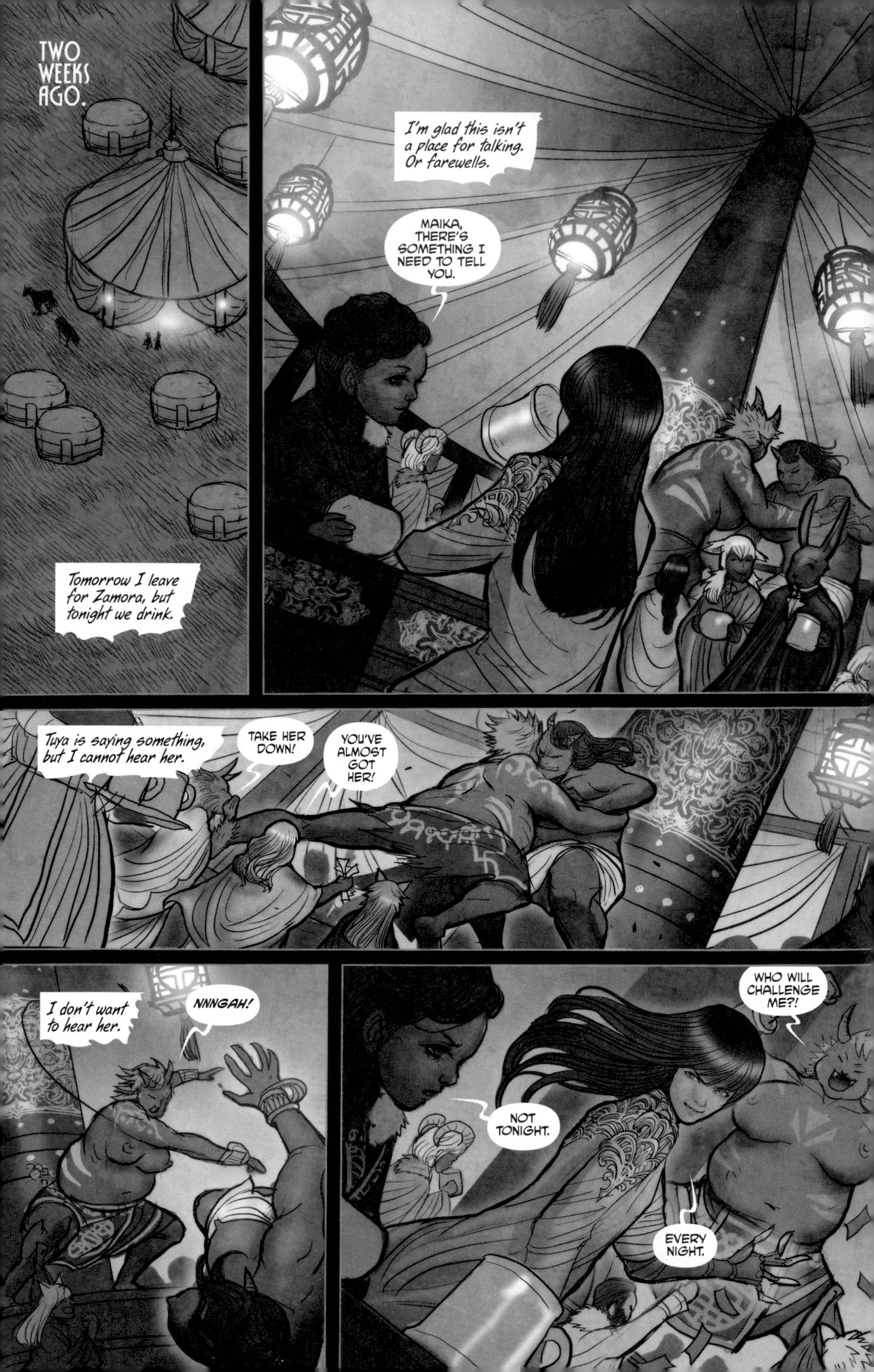
TWO WEEKS AGO.
Tomorrow I leave for Zamora, but tonight we drink.
I'm glad this isn't a place for talking. Or farewells.
MAIKA, THERE'S SOMETHING I NEED TO TELL YOU.
Tuya is saying something, but I cannot hear her.
TAKE HER DOWN!
YOU'VE ALMOST GOT HER!
I don't want to hear her.
NNNGAH!
WHO WILL CHALLENGE ME?!
NOT TONIGHT.
EVERY NIGHT.

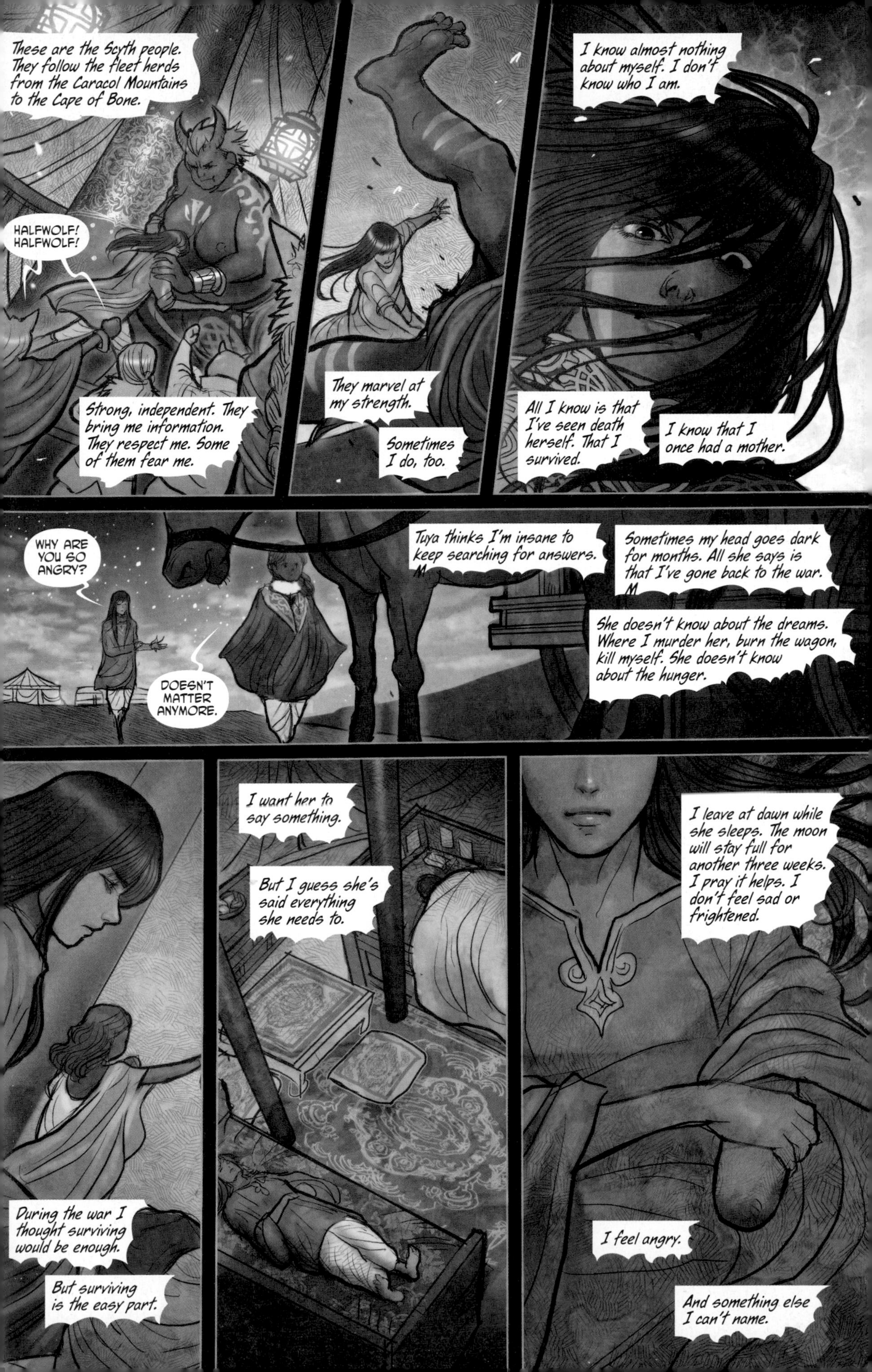
These are the Scyth people. They follow the fleet herds from the Caracol Mountains to the Cape of Bone.
HALFWOLF! HALFWOLF!
Strong, independent. They bring me information. They respect me. Some of them fear me.
They marvel at my strength.
Sometimes I do, too.
I know almost nothing about myself. I don't know who I am.
All I know is that I've seen death herself. That I survived.
I know that I once had a mother.
WHY ARE YOU SO ANGRY?
DOESN'T MATTER ANYMORE.
Tuya thinks I'm insane to keep searching for answers.
Sometimes my head goes dark for months. All she says is that I've gone back to the war.
She doesn't know about the dreams. Where I murder her, burn the wagon, kill myself. She doesn't know about the hunger.
During the war I thought surviving would be enough.
But surviving is the easy part.
I want her to say something.
But I guess she's said everything she needs to.
I leave at dawn while she sleeps. The moon will stay full for another three weeks. I pray it helps. I don't feel sad or frightened.
I feel angry.
And something else I can't name.

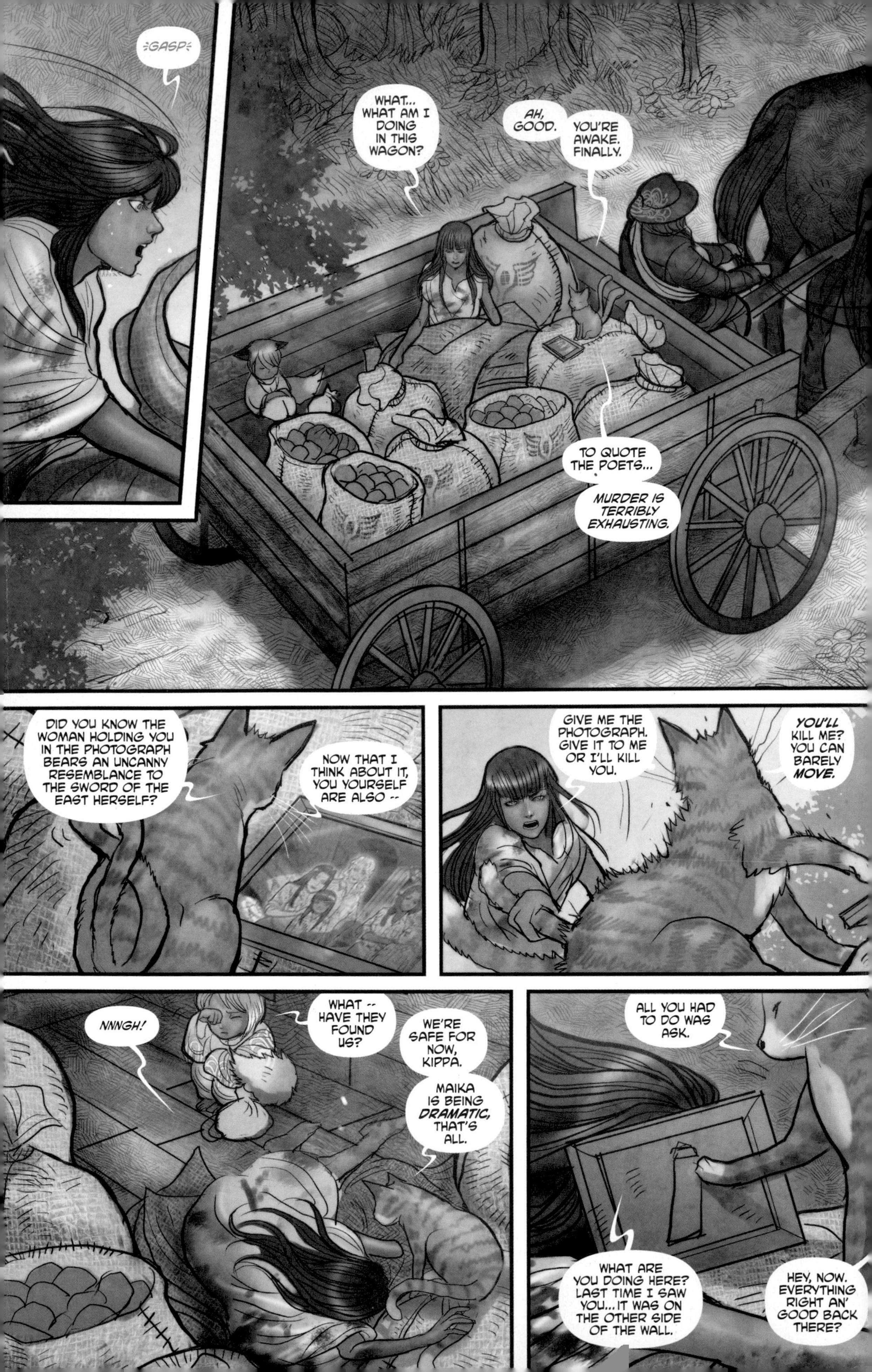
GASP
WHAT... WHAT AM I DOING IN THIS WAGON?
AH, GOOD.
YOU'RE AWAKE. FINALLY.
TO QUOTE THE POETS...
MURDER IS TERRIBLY EXHAUSTING.
DID YOU KNOW THE WOMAN HOLDING YOU IN THE PHOTOGRAPH BEARS AN UNCANNY RESEMBLANCE TO THE SWORD OF THE EAST HERSELF?
NOW THAT I THINK ABOUT IT, YOU YOURSELF ARE ALSO --
GIVE ME THE PHOTOGRAPH. GIVE IT TO ME OR I'LL KILL YOU.
YOU'LL KILL ME? YOU CAN BARELY MOVE.
NNNGH!
WHAT -- HAVE THEY FOUND US?
WE'RE SAFE FOR NOW, KIPPA.
MAIKA IS BEING DRAMATIC, THAT'S ALL.
ALL YOU HAD TO DO WAS ASK.
WHAT ARE YOU DOING HERE? LAST TIME I SAW YOU... IT WAS ON THE OTHER SIDE OF THE WALL.
HEY, NOW. EVERYTHING RIGHT AN' GOOD BACK THERE?

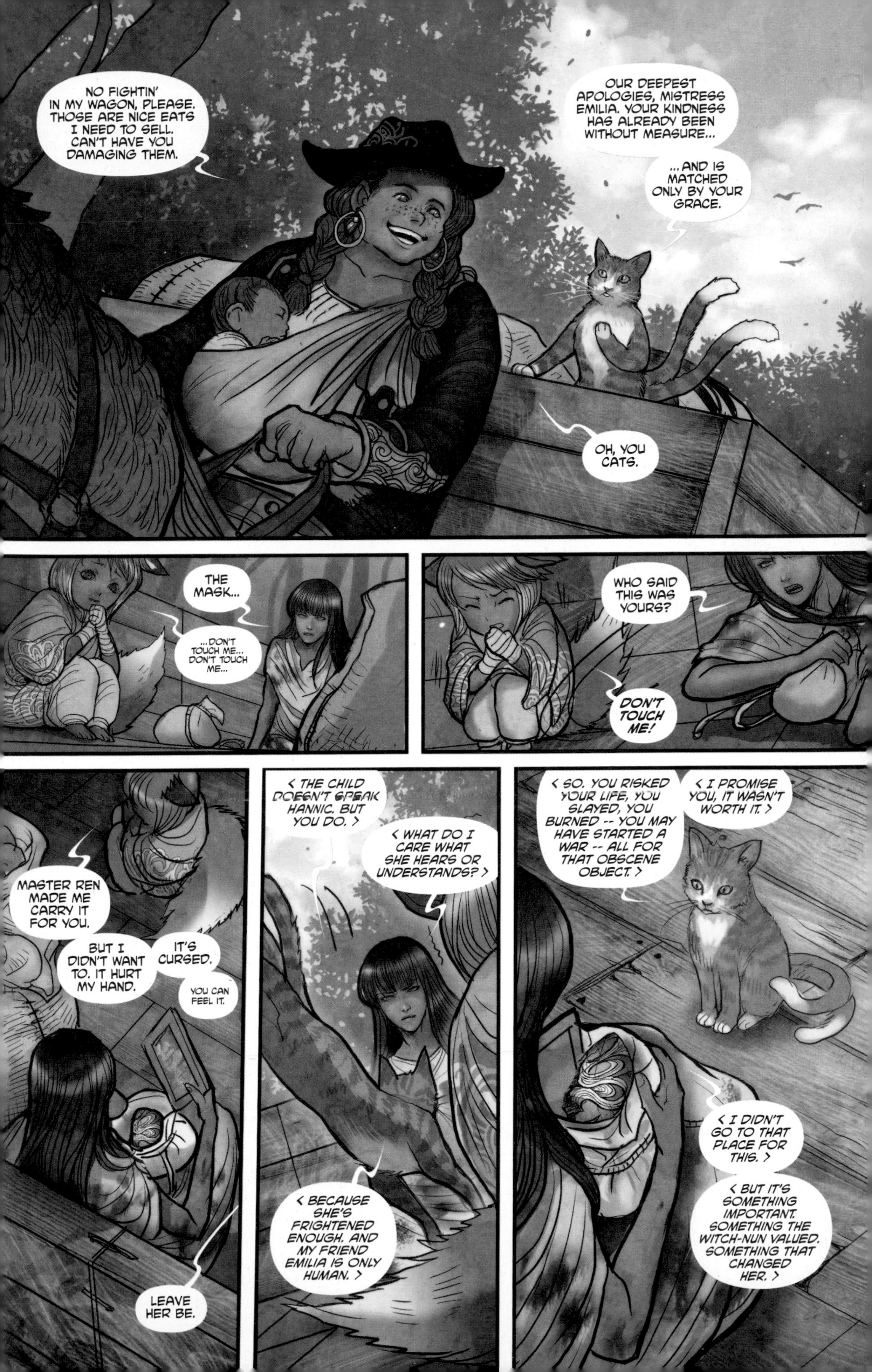
NO FIGHTIN' IN MY WAGON, PLEASE. THOSE ARE NICE EATS I NEED TO SELL. CAN'T HAVE YOU DAMAGING THEM.
OUR DEEPEST APOLOGIES, MISTRESS EMILIA. YOUR KINDNESS HAS ALREADY BEEN WITHOUT MEASURE...
...AND IS MATCHED ONLY BY YOUR GRACE.
OH, YOU CATS.
THE MASK...
...DON'T TOUCH ME... DON'T TOUCH ME...
WHO SAID THIS WAS YOURS?
DON'T TOUCH ME!
MASTER REN MADE ME CARRY IT FOR YOU.
BUT I DIDN'T WANT TO. IT HURT MY HAND.
IT'S CURSED.
YOU CAN FEEL IT.
LEAVE HER BE.
< THE CHILD DOESN'T SPEAK HANNIC. BUT YOU DO. >
< WHAT DO I CARE WHAT SHE HEARS OR UNDERSTANDS? >
< BECAUSE SHE'S FRIGHTENED ENOUGH. AND MY FRIEND EMILIA IS ONLY HUMAN. >
< SO. YOU RISKED YOUR LIFE, YOU SLAYED, YOU BURNED -- YOU MAY HAVE STARTED A WAR -- ALL FOR THAT OBSCENE OBJECT. >
< I PROMISE YOU, IT WASN'T WORTH IT. >
< I DIDN'T GO TO THAT PLACE FOR THIS. >
< BUT IT'S SOMETHING IMPORTANT. SOMETHING THE WITCH-NUN VALUED. SOMETHING THAT CHANGED HER. >

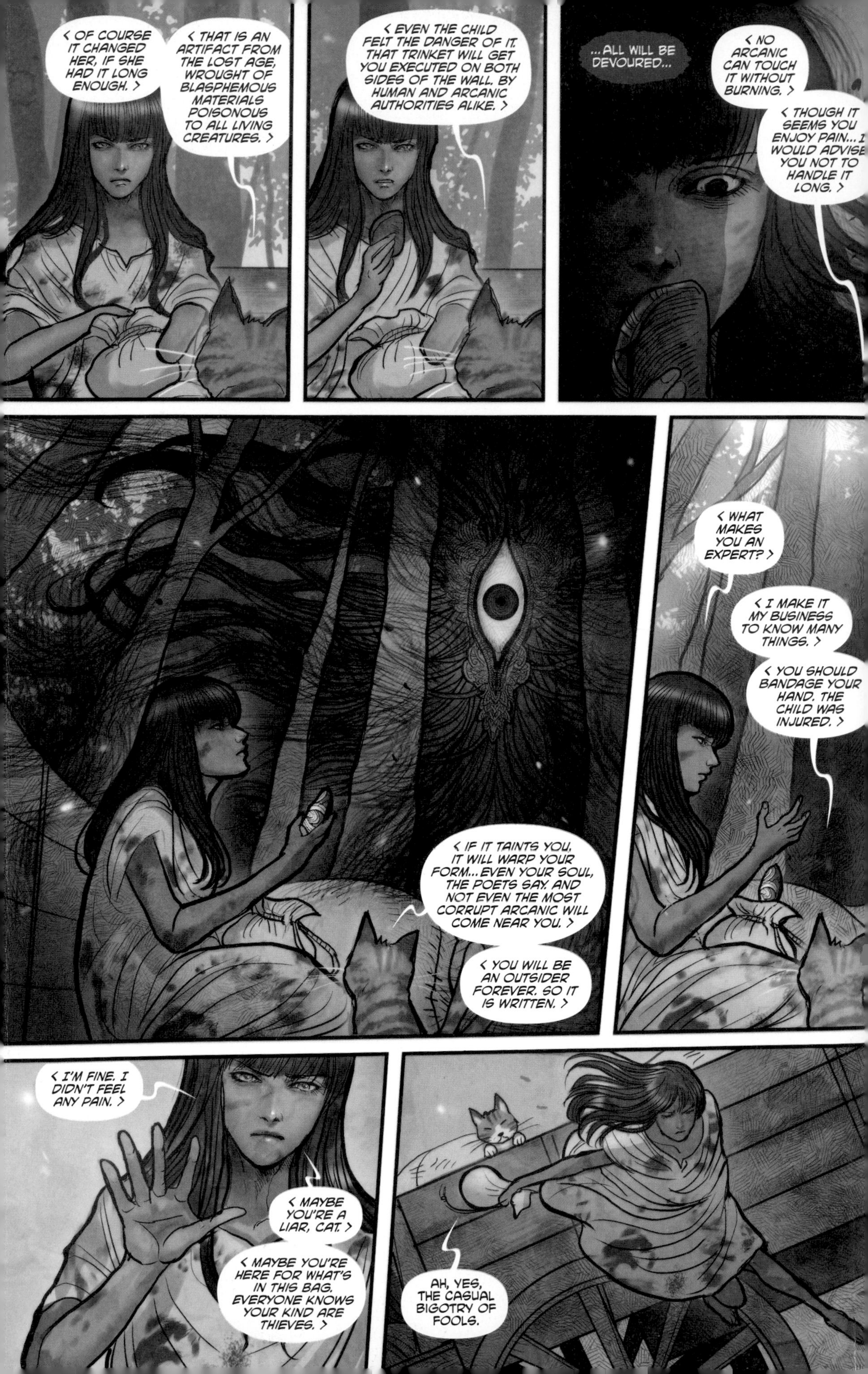
< OF COURSE IT CHANGED HER, IF SHE HAD IT LONG ENOUGH. >
< THAT IS AN ARTIFACT FROM THE LOST AGE, WROUGHT OF BLASPHEMOUS MATERIALS POISONOUS TO ALL LIVING CREATURES. >
< EVEN THE CHILD FELT THE DANGER OF IT. THAT TRINKET WILL GET YOU EXECUTED ON BOTH SIDES OF THE WALL. BY HUMAN AND ARCANIC AUTHORITIES ALIKE. >
...ALL WILL BE DEVOURED...
< NO ARCANIC CAN TOUCH IT WITHOUT BURNING. >
< THOUGH IT SEEMS YOU ENJOY PAIN... I WOULD ADVISE YOU NOT TO HANDLE IT LONG. >
< IF IT TAINTS YOU, IT WILL WARP YOUR FORM... EVEN YOUR SOUL, THE POETS SAY. AND NOT EVEN THE MOST CORRUPT ARCANIC WILL COME NEAR YOU. >
< YOU WILL BE AN OUTSIDER FOREVER. SO IT IS WRITTEN. >
< WHAT MAKES YOU AN EXPERT? >
< I MAKE IT MY BUSINESS TO KNOW MANY THINGS. >
< YOU SHOULD BANDAGE YOUR HAND. THE CHILD WAS INJURED. >
< I'M FINE. I DIDN'T FEEL ANY PAIN. >
< MAYBE YOU'RE A LIAR, CAT. >
< MAYBE YOU'RE HERE FOR WHAT'S IN THIS BAG. EVERYONE KNOWS YOUR KIND ARE THIEVES. >
AH, YES, THE CASUAL BIGOTRY OF FOOLS.

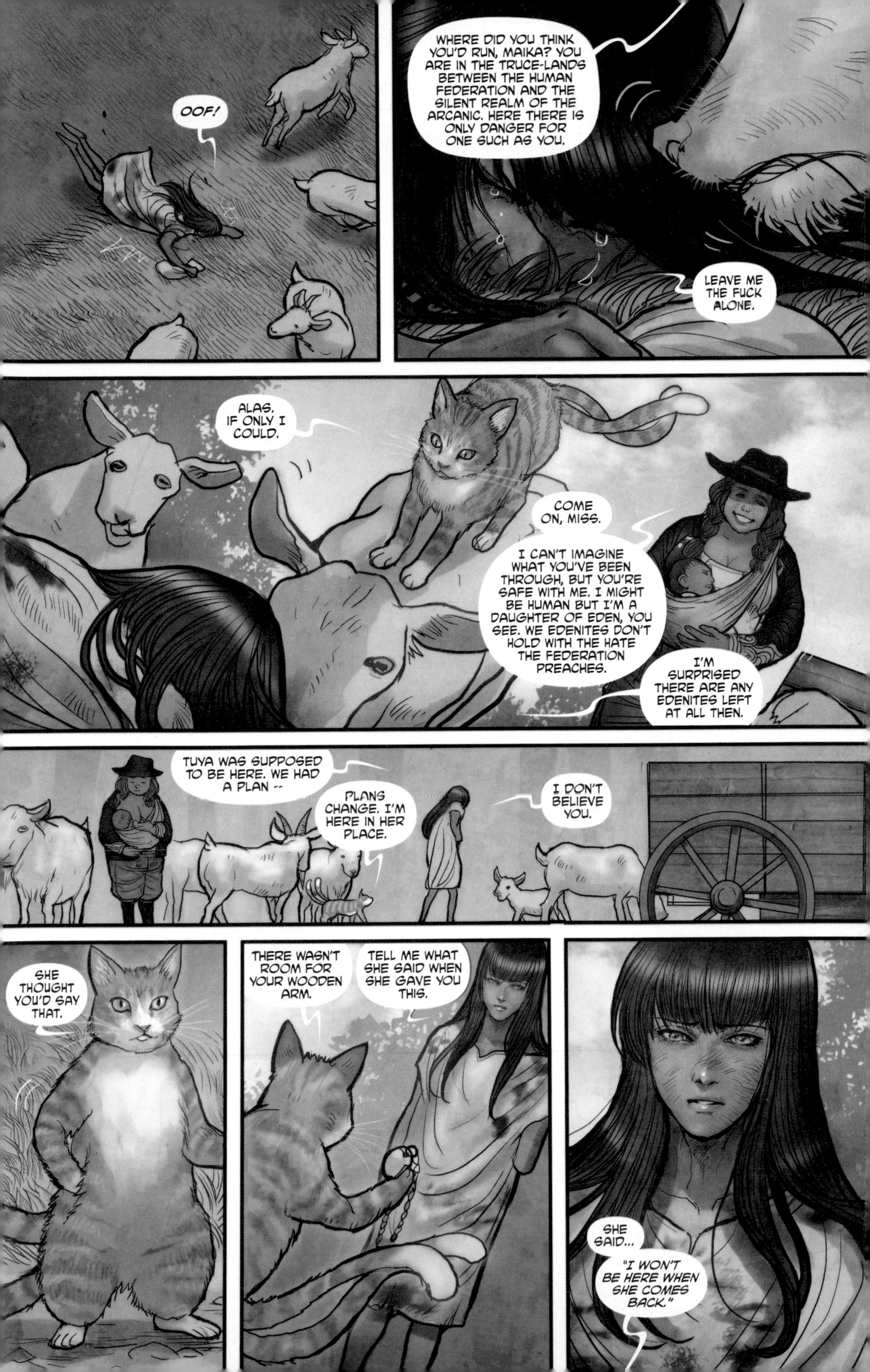

OOF!
WHERE DID YOU THINK YOU'D RUN, MAIKA? YOU ARE IN THE TRUCE-LANDS BETWEEN THE HUMAN FEDERATION AND THE SILENT REALM OF THE ARCANIC. HERE THERE IS ONLY DANGER FOR ONE SUCH AS YOU.
LEAVE ME THE FUCK ALONE.
ALAS. IF ONLY I COULD.
COME ON, MISS.
I CAN'T IMAGINE WHAT YOU'VE BEEN THROUGH, BUT YOU'RE SAFE WITH ME. I MIGHT BE HUMAN BUT I'M A DAUGHTER OF EDEN, YOU SEE. WE EDENITES DON'T HOLD WITH THE HATE THE FEDERATION PREACHES.
I'M SURPRISED THERE ARE ANY EDENITES LEFT AT ALL THEN.
TUYA WAS SUPPOSED TO BE HERE. WE HAD A PLAN --
PLANS CHANGE. I'M HERE IN HER PLACE.
I DON'T BELIEVE YOU.
SHE THOUGHT YOU'D SAY THAT.
THERE WASN'T ROOM FOR YOUR WOODEN ARM.
TELL ME WHAT SHE SAID WHEN SHE GAVE YOU THIS.
SHE SAID...
"I WON'T BE HERE WHEN SHE COMES BACK."

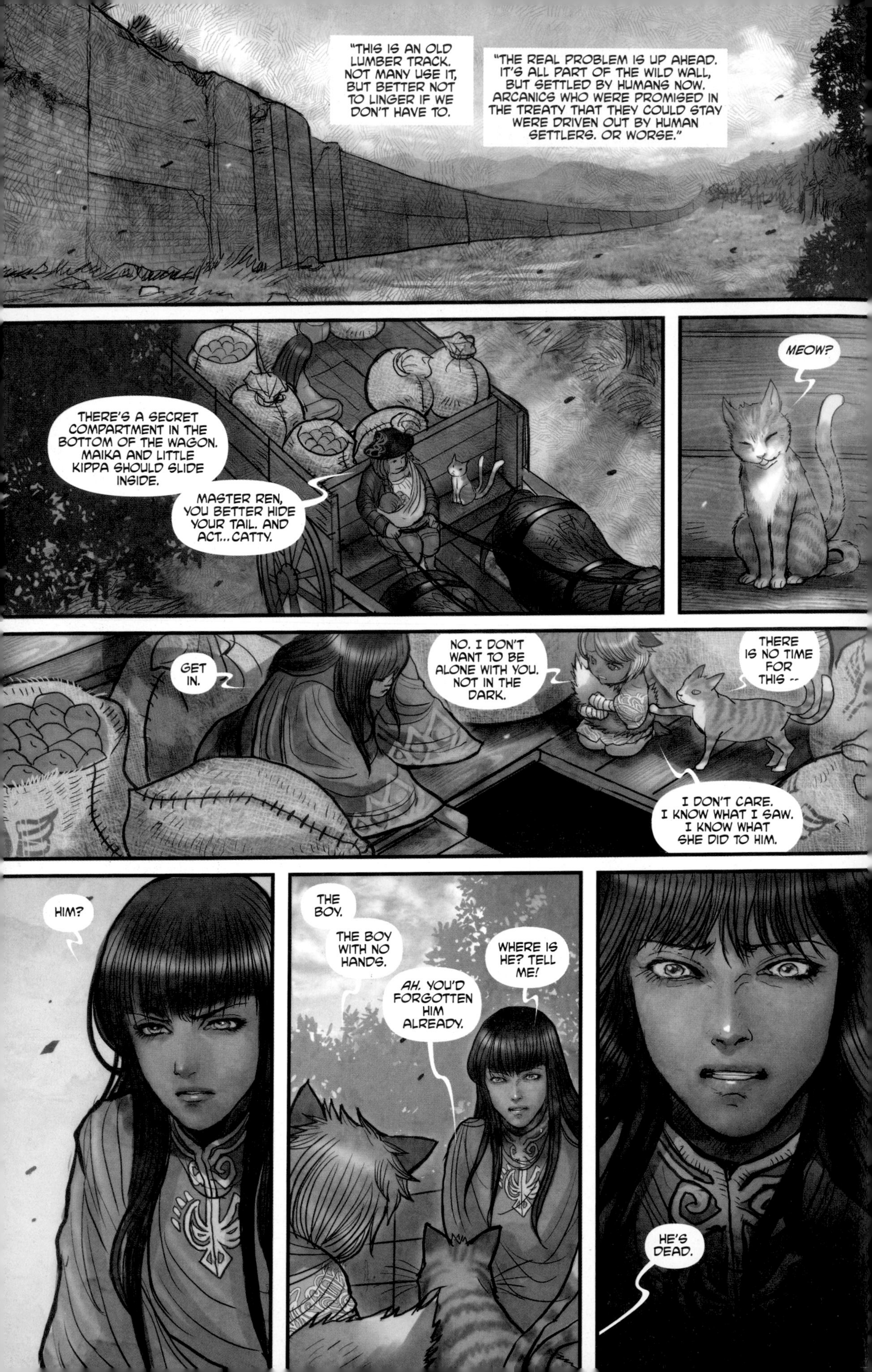
"THIS IS AN OLD LUMBER TRACK. NOT MANY USE IT, BUT BETTER NOT TO LINGER IF WE DON'T HAVE TO.
"THE REAL PROBLEM IS UP AHEAD. IT'S ALL PART OF THE WILD WALL, BUT SETTLED BY HUMANS NOW. ARCANICS WHO WERE PROMISED IN THE TREATY THAT THEY COULD STAY WERE DRIVEN OUT BY HUMAN SETTLERS. OR WORSE."
THERE'S A SECRET COMPARTMENT IN THE BOTTOM OF THE WAGON. MAIKA AND LITTLE KIPPA SHOULD SLIDE INSIDE.
MASTER REN, YOU BETTER HIDE YOUR TAIL. AND ACT... CATTY.
MEOW?
GET IN.
NO. I DON'T WANT TO BE ALONE WITH YOU. NOT IN THE DARK.
THERE IS NO TIME FOR THIS --
I DON'T CARE. I KNOW WHAT I SAW. I KNOW WHAT SHE DID TO HIM.
HIM?
THE BOY.
THE BOY WITH NO HANDS.
AH. YOU'D FORGOTTEN HIM ALREADY.
WHERE IS HE? TELL ME!
HE'S DEAD.

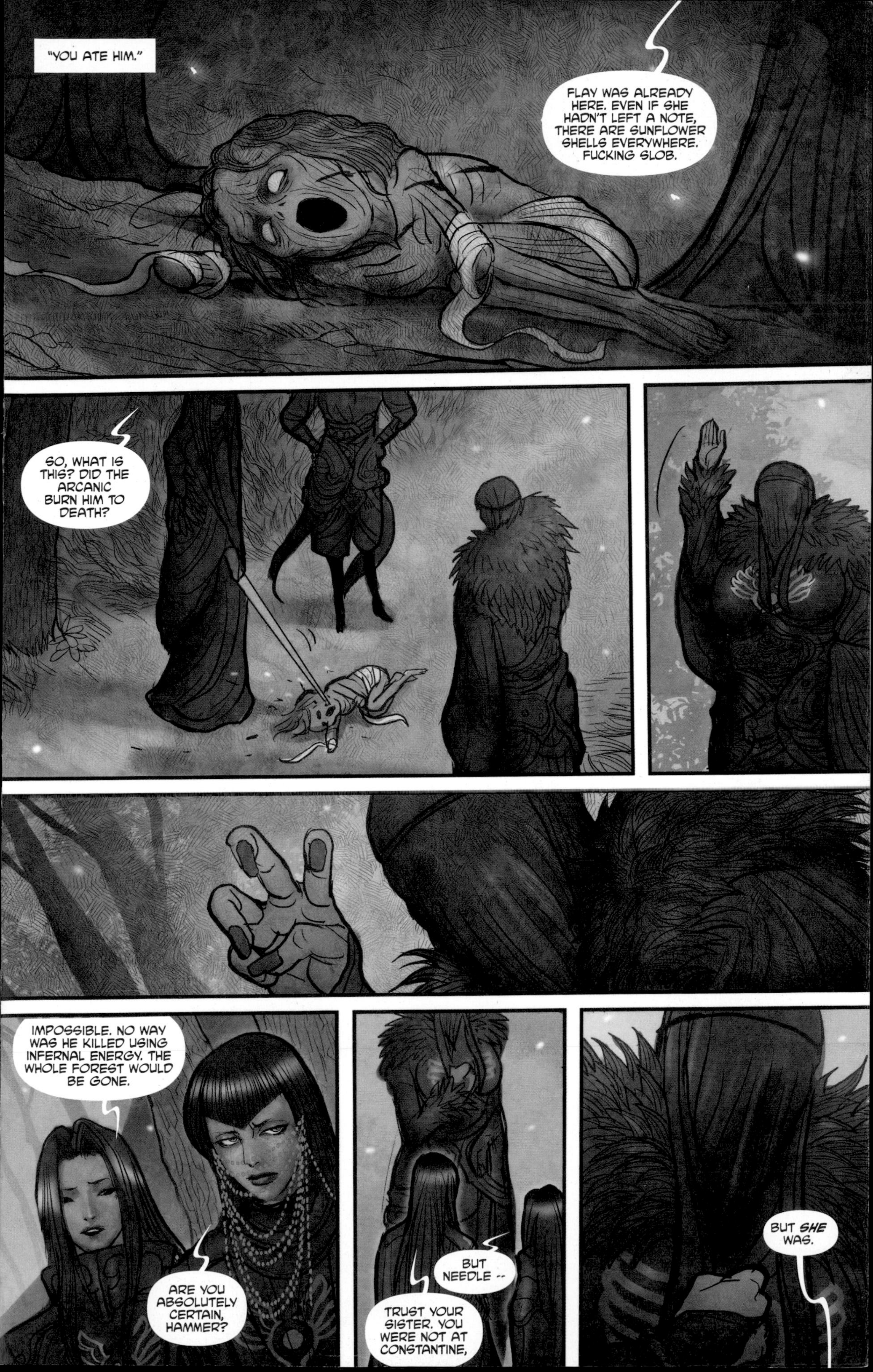
"YOU ATE HIM."
FLAY WAS ALREADY HERE. EVEN IF SHE HADN'T LEFT A NOTE, THERE ARE SUNFLOWER SHELLS EVERYWHERE. FUCKING SLOB.
SO, WHAT IS THIS? DID THE ARCANIC BURN HIM TO DEATH?
IMPOSSIBLE. NO WAY WAS HE KILLED USING INFERNAL ENERGY. THE WHOLE FOREST WOULD BE GONE.
ARE YOU ABSOLUTELY CERTAIN, HAMMER?
BUT NEEDLE --
TRUST YOUR SISTER. YOU WERE NOT AT CONSTANTINE,
BUT SHE WAS.

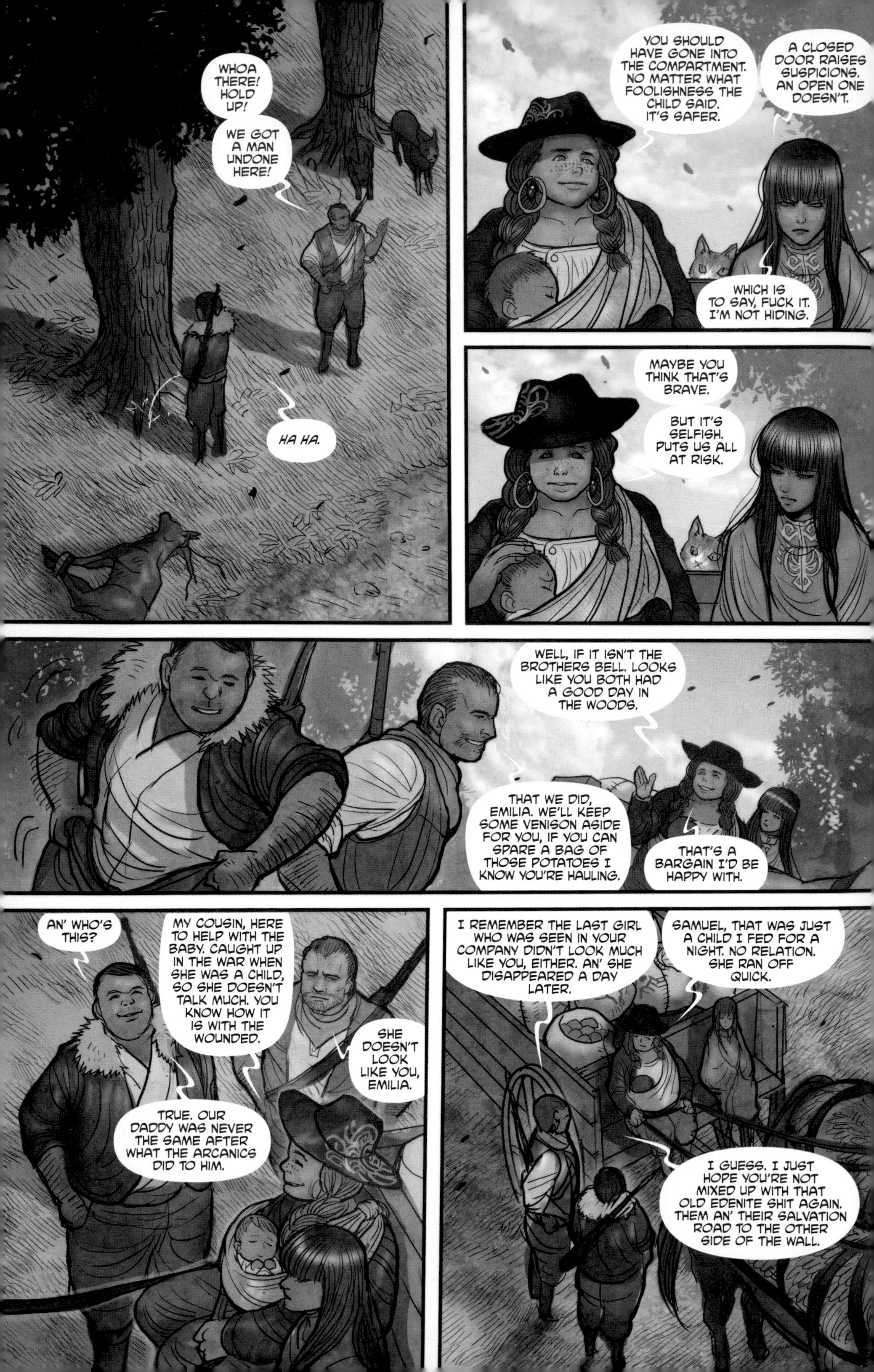
WHOA THERE! HOLD UP!
WE GOT A MAN UNDONE HERE!
HA HA.
YOU SHOULD HAVE GONE INTO THE COMPARTMENT. NO MATTER WHAT FOOLISHNESS THE CHILD SAID. IT'S SAFER.
A CLOSED DOOR RAISES SUSPICIONS. AN OPEN ONE DOESN'T.
WHICH IS TO SAY, FUCK IT. I'M NOT HIDING.
MAYBE YOU THINK THAT'S BRAVE.
BUT IT'S SELFISH. PUTS US ALL AT RISK.
WELL, IF IT ISN'T THE BROTHERS BELL. LOOKS LIKE YOU BOTH HAD A GOOD DAY IN THE WOODS.
THAT WE DID, EMILIA. WE'LL KEEP SOME VENISON ASIDE FOR YOU, IF YOU CAN SPARE A BAG OF THOSE POTATOES I KNOW YOU'RE HAULING.
THAT'S A BARGAIN I'D BE HAPPY WITH.
AN' WHO'S THIS?
MY COUSIN, HERE TO HELP WITH THE BABY. CAUGHT UP IN THE WAR WHEN SHE WAS A CHILD, SO SHE DOESN'T TALK MUCH. YOU KNOW HOW IT IS WITH THE WOUNDED.
SHE DOESN'T LOOK LIKE YOU, EMILIA.
TRUE. OUR DADDY WAS NEVER THE SAME AFTER WHAT THE ARCANICS DID TO HIM.
I REMEMBER THE LAST GIRL WHO WAS SEEN IN YOUR COMPANY DIDN'T LOOK MUCH LIKE YOU, EITHER. AN' SHE DISAPPEARED A DAY LATER.
SAMUEL, THAT WAS JUST A CHILD I FED FOR A NIGHT. NO RELATION. SHE RAN OFF QUICK.
I GUESS. I JUST HOPE YOU'RE NOT MIXED UP WITH THAT OLD EDENITE SHIT AGAIN. THEM AN' THEIR SALVATION ROAD TO THE OTHER SIDE OF THE WALL.

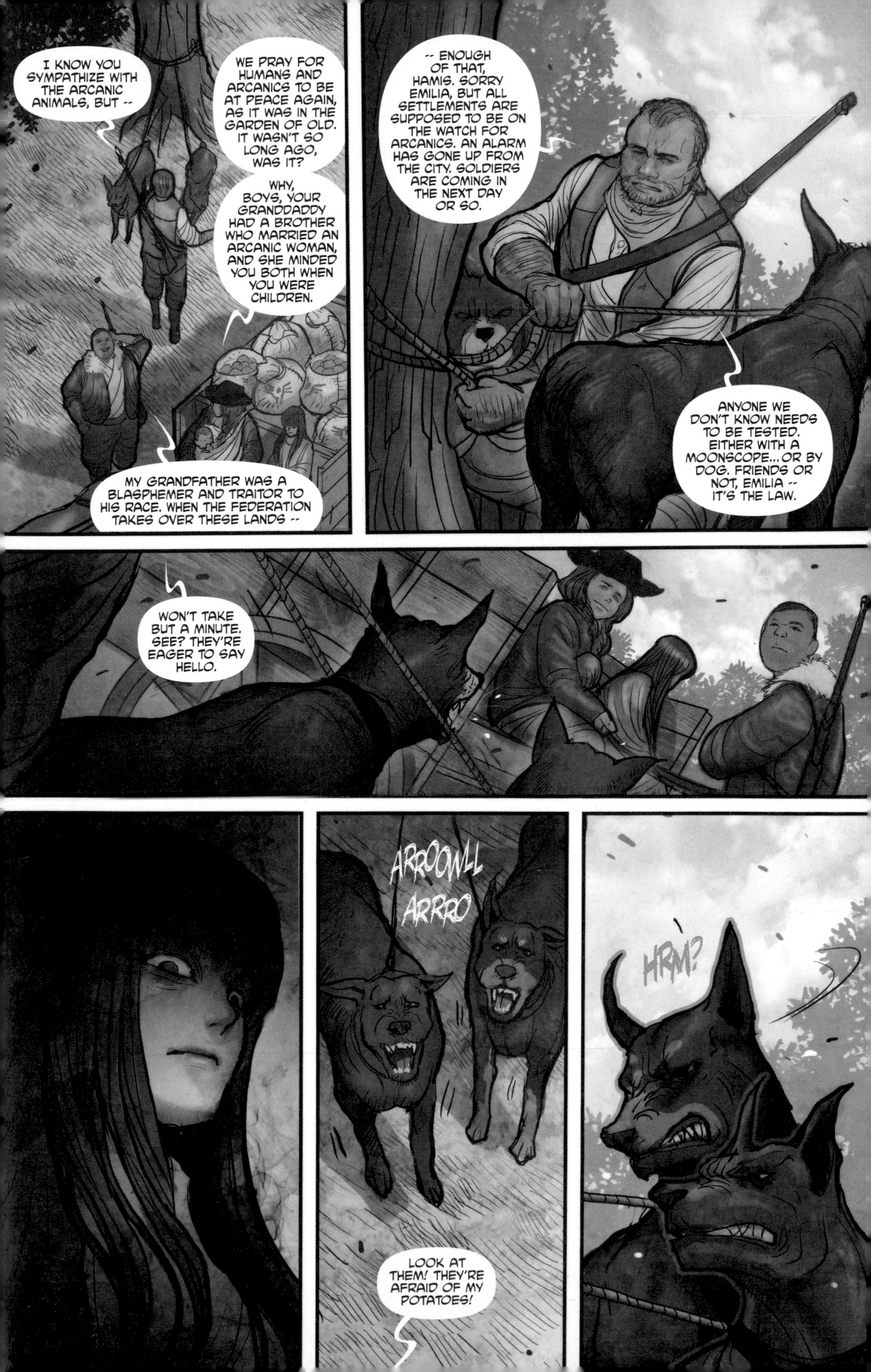
I KNOW YOU SYMPATHIZE WITH THE ARCANIC ANIMALS, BUT --
WE PRAY FOR HUMANS AND ARCANICS TO BE AT PEACE AGAIN, AS IT WAS IN THE GARDEN OF OLD. IT WASN'T SO LONG AGO, WAS IT?
WHY, BOYS, YOUR GRANDDADDY HAD A BROTHER WHO MARRIED AN ARCANIC WOMAN, AND SHE MINDED YOU BOTH WHEN YOU WERE CHILDREN.
MY GRANDFATHER WAS A BLASPHEMER AND TRAITOR TO HIS RACE. WHEN THE FEDERATION TAKES OVER THESE LANDS --
-- ENOUGH OF THAT, HAMIS. SORRY EMILIA, BUT ALL SETTLEMENTS ARE SUPPOSED TO BE ON THE WATCH FOR ARCANICS. AN ALARM HAS GONE UP FROM THE CITY. SOLDIERS ARE COMING IN THE NEXT DAY OR SO.
ANYONE WE DON'T KNOW NEEDS TO BE TESTED. EITHER WITH A MOONSCOPE...OR BY DOG. FRIENDS OR NOT, EMILIA -- IT'S THE LAW.
WON'T TAKE BUT A MINUTE. SEE? THEY'RE EAGER TO SAY HELLO.
ARROOWLL
ARRRO
LOOK AT THEM! THEY'RE AFRAID OF MY POTATOES!
HRM?

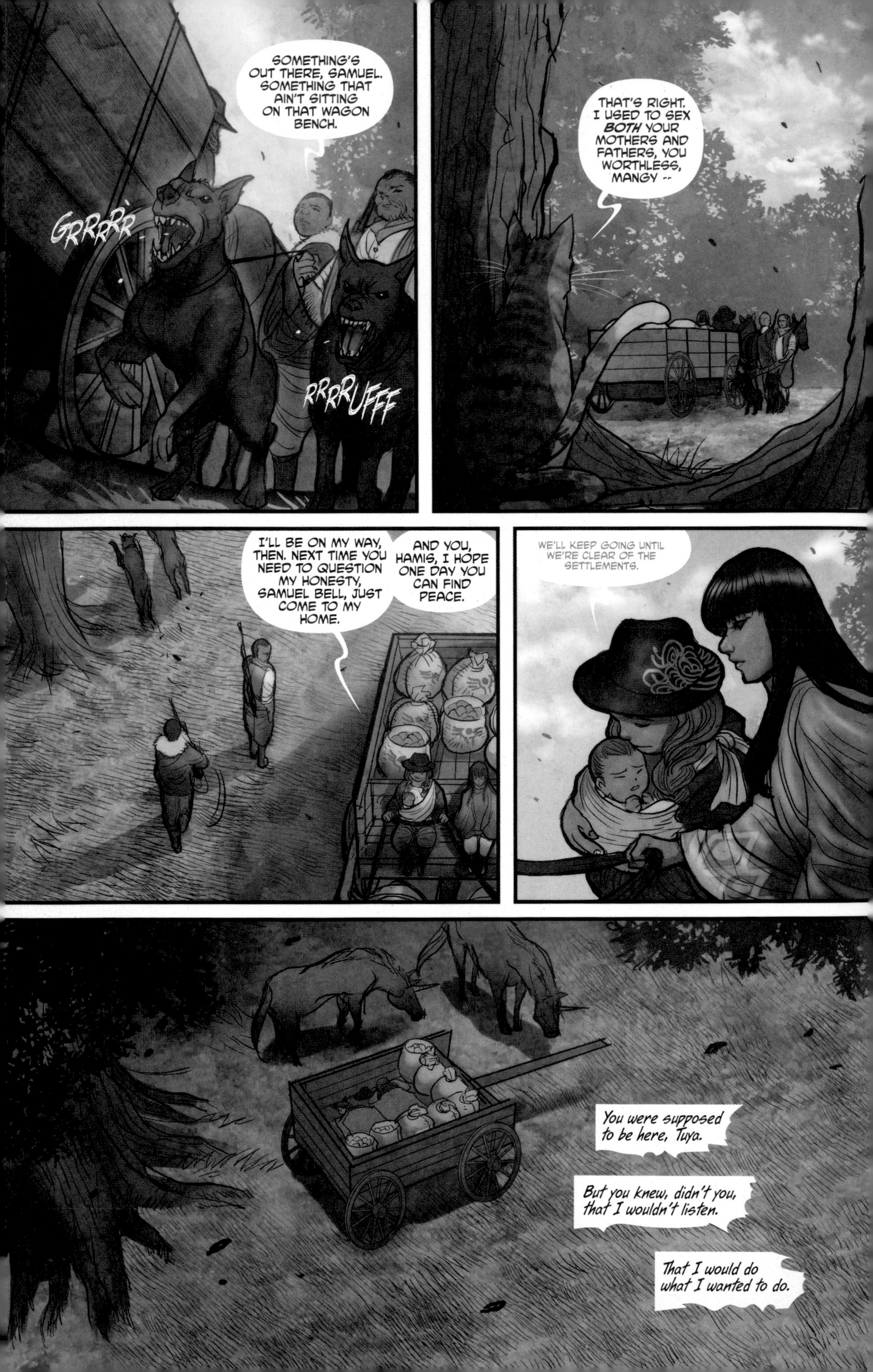
SOMETHING'S OUT THERE, SAMUEL. SOMETHING THAT AIN'T SITTING ON THAT WAGON BENCH.
GRRRRR
RRRRUFFF
THAT'S RIGHT. I USED TO SEX BOTH YOUR MOTHERS AND FATHERS, YOU WORTHLESS, MANGY --
I'LL BE ON MY WAY, THEN. NEXT TIME YOU NEED TO QUESTION MY HONESTY, SAMUEL BELL, JUST COME TO MY HOME.
AND YOU, HAMIS, I HOPE ONE DAY YOU CAN FIND PEACE.
WE'LL KEEP GOING UNTIL WE'RE CLEAR OF THE SETTLEMENTS.
You were supposed to be here, Tuya.
But you knew, didn't you, that I wouldn't listen.
That I would do what I wanted to do.

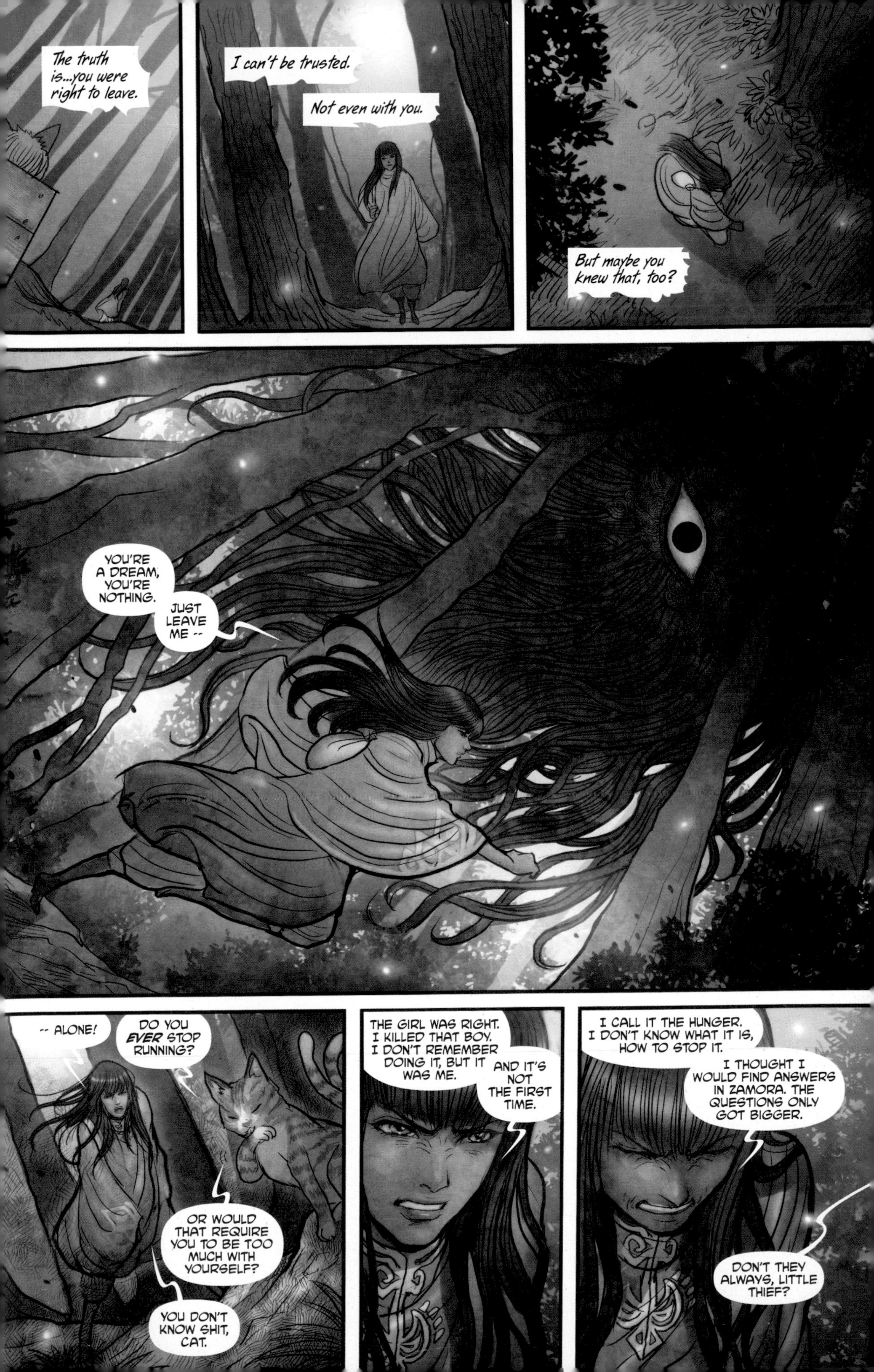
The truth is...you were right to leave.
I can't be trusted.
Not even with you.
But maybe you knew that, too?
YOU'RE A DREAM, YOU'RE NOTHING.
JUST LEAVE ME --
-- ALONE!
DO YOU EVER STOP RUNNING?
OR WOULD THAT REQUIRE YOU TO BE TOO MUCH WITH YOURSELF?
YOU DON'T KNOW SHIT, CAT.
THE GIRL WAS RIGHT. I KILLED THAT BOY. I DON'T REMEMBER DOING IT, BUT IT WAS ME.
AND IT'S NOT THE FIRST TIME.
I CALL IT THE HUNGER. I DON'T KNOW WHAT IT IS, HOW TO STOP IT.
I THOUGHT I WOULD FIND ANSWERS IN ZAMORA. THE QUESTIONS ONLY GOT BIGGER.
DON'T THEY ALWAYS, LITTLE THIEF?

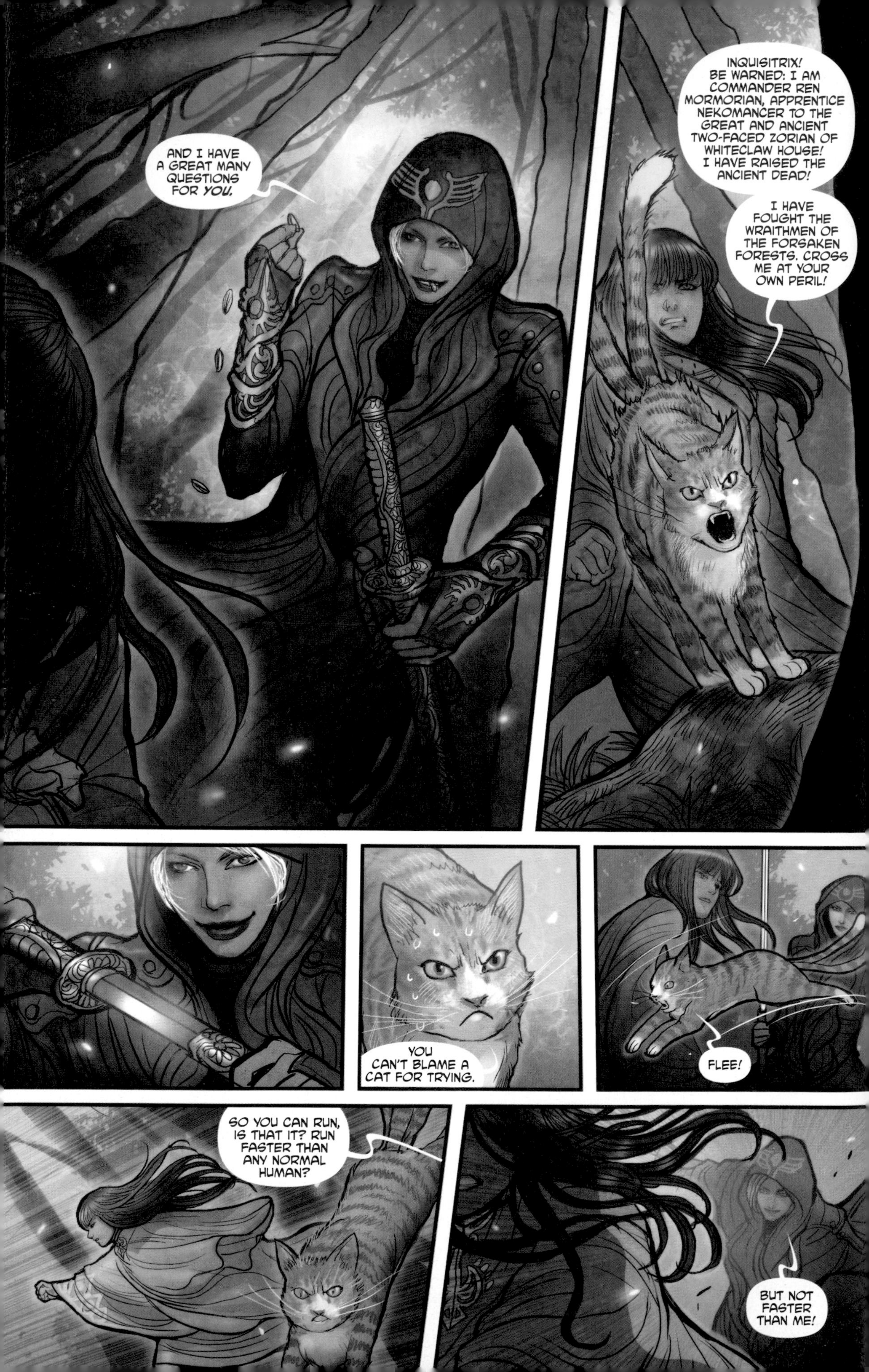
AND I HAVE A GREAT MANY QUESTIONS FOR YOU.
INQUISITRIX! BE WARNED: I AM COMMANDER REN MORMORIAN, APPRENTICE NEKOMANCER TO THE GREAT AND ANCIENT TWO-FACED ZORIAN OF WHITECLAW HOUSE! I HAVE RAISED THE ANCIENT DEAD!
I HAVE FOUGHT THE WRAITHMEN OF THE FORSAKEN FORESTS. CROSS ME AT YOUR OWN PERIL!
YOU CAN'T BLAME A CAT FOR TRYING.
FLEE!
SO YOU CAN RUN, IS THAT IT? RUN FASTER THAN ANY NORMAL HUMAN?
BUT NOT FASTER THAN ME!

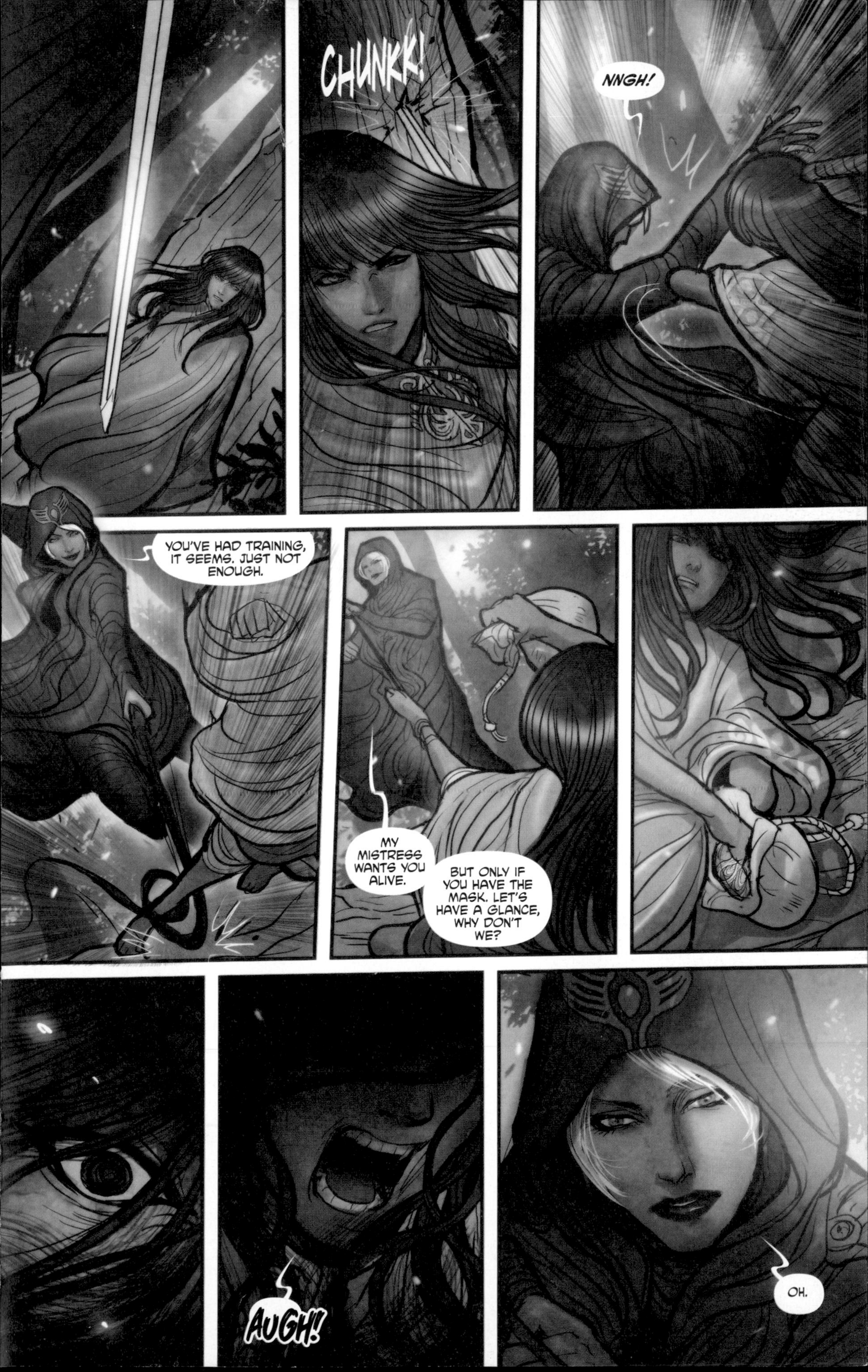
CHUNKK!
NNGH!
YOU'VE HAD TRAINING, IT SEEMS. JUST NOT ENOUGH.
MY MISTRESS WANTS YOU ALIVE.
BUT ONLY IF YOU HAVE THE MASK. LET'S HAVE A GLANCE, WHY DON'T WE?
AUGH!
OH.

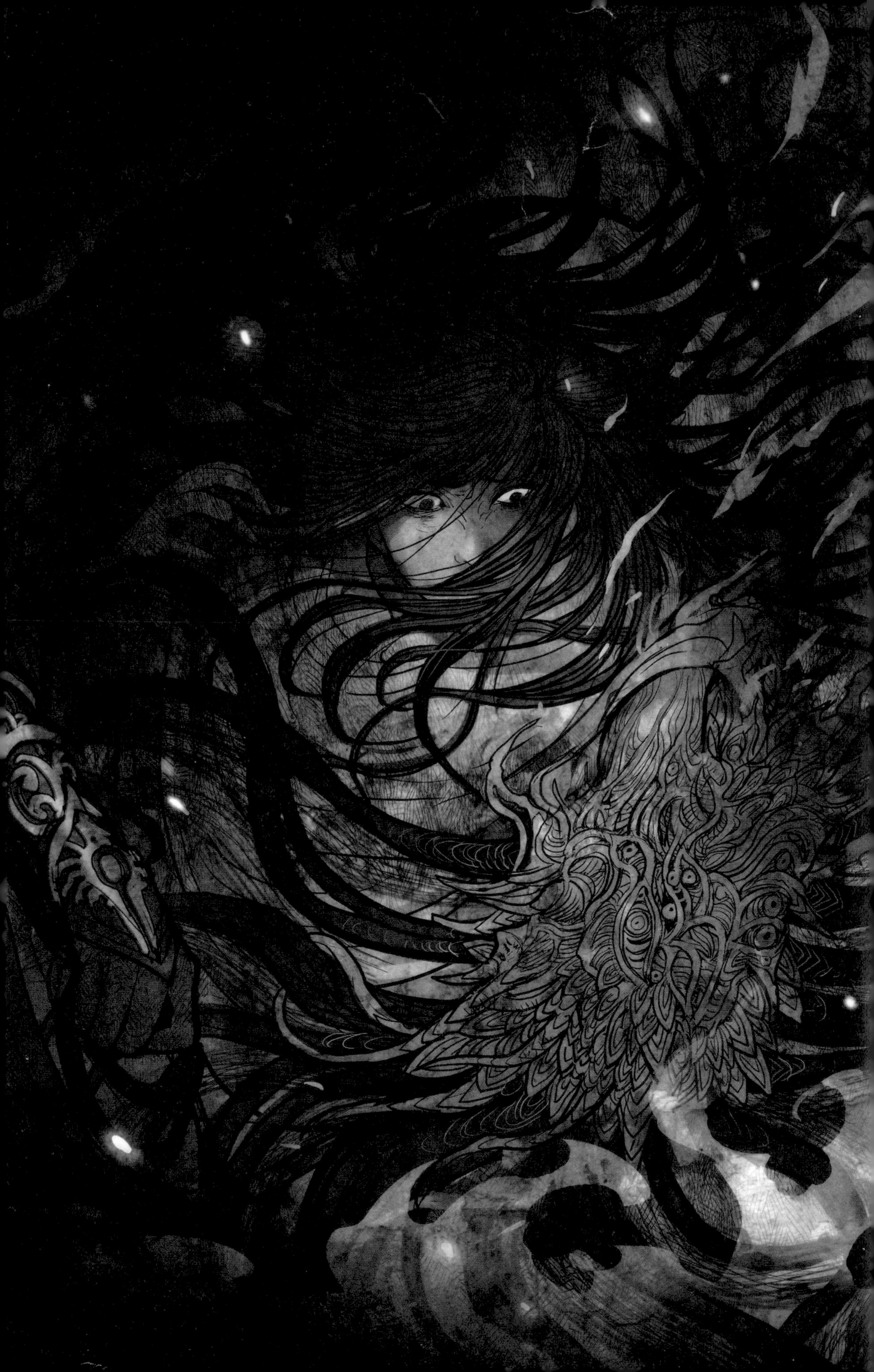

AN EXCERPT OF A LECTURE FROM THE ESTEEMED **PROFESSOR TAM TAM**, FORMER FIRST RECORD-KEEPER OF THE IS'HAMI TEMPLE, AND LEARNED CONTEMPORARY OF NAMRON BLACK CLAW...

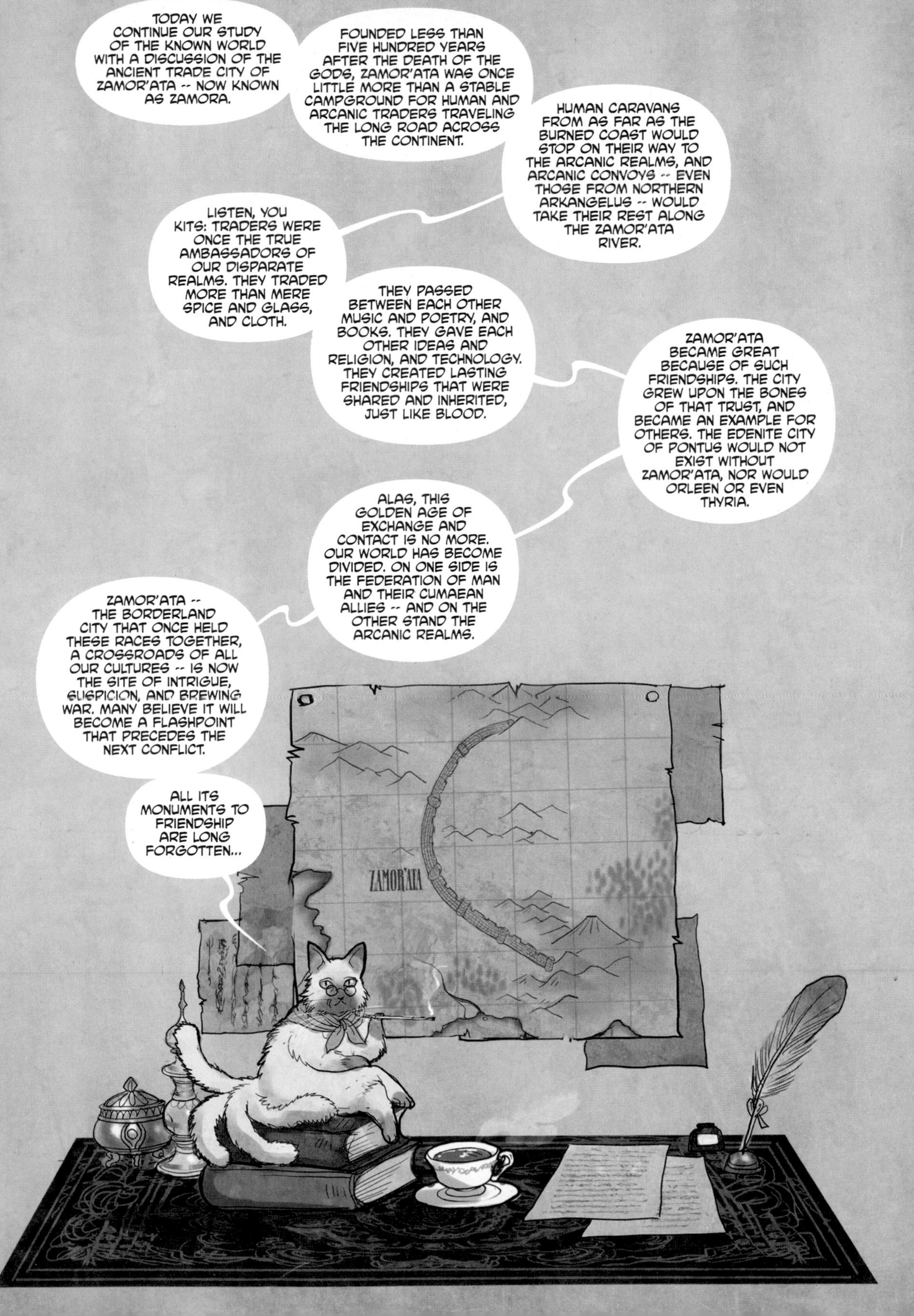

TODAY WE CONTINUE OUR STUDY OF THE KNOWN WORLD WITH A DISCUSSION OF THE ANCIENT TRADE CITY OF ZAMOR'ATA -- NOW KNOWN AS ZAMORA.
FOUNDED LESS THAN FIVE HUNDRED YEARS AFTER THE DEATH OF THE GODS, ZAMOR'ATA WAS ONCE LITTLE MORE THAN A STABLE CAMPGROUND FOR HUMAN AND ARCANIC TRADERS TRAVELING THE LONG ROAD ACROSS THE CONTINENT.
HUMAN CARAVANS FROM AS FAR AS THE BURNED COAST WOULD STOP ON THEIR WAY TO THE ARCANIC REALMS, AND ARCANIC CONVOYS -- EVEN THOSE FROM NORTHERN ARKANGELUS -- WOULD TAKE THEIR REST ALONG THE ZAMOR'ATA RIVER.
LISTEN, YOU KITS: TRADERS WERE ONCE THE TRUE AMBASSADORS OF OUR DISPARATE REALMS. THEY TRADED MORE THAN MERE SPICE AND GLASS, AND CLOTH.
THEY PASSED BETWEEN EACH OTHER MUSIC AND POETRY, AND BOOKS. THEY GAVE EACH OTHER IDEAS AND RELIGION, AND TECHNOLOGY. THEY CREATED LASTING FRIENDSHIPS THAT WERE SHARED AND INHERITED, JUST LIKE BLOOD.
ZAMOR'ATA BECAME GREAT BECAUSE OF SUCH FRIENDSHIPS. THE CITY GREW UPON THE BONES OF THAT TRUST, AND BECAME AN EXAMPLE FOR OTHERS. THE EDENITE CITY OF PONTUS WOULD NOT EXIST WITHOUT ZAMOR'ATA, NOR WOULD ORLEEN OR EVEN THYRIA.
ALAS, THIS GOLDEN AGE OF EXCHANGE AND CONTACT IS NO MORE. OUR WORLD HAS BECOME DIVIDED. ON ONE SIDE IS THE FEDERATION OF MAN AND THEIR CUMAEAN ALLIES -- AND ON THE OTHER STAND THE ARCANIC REALMS.
ZAMOR'ATA -- THE BORDERLAND CITY THAT ONCE HELD THESE RACES TOGETHER, A CROSSROADS OF ALL OUR CULTURES -- IS NOW THE SITE OF INTRIGUE, SUSPICION, AND BREWING WAR. MANY BELIEVE IT WILL BECOME A FLASHPOINT THAT PRECEDES THE NEXT CONFLICT.
ALL ITS MONUMENTS TO FRIENDSHIP ARE LONG FORGOTTEN...
ZAMOR'ATA

CHAPTER THREE

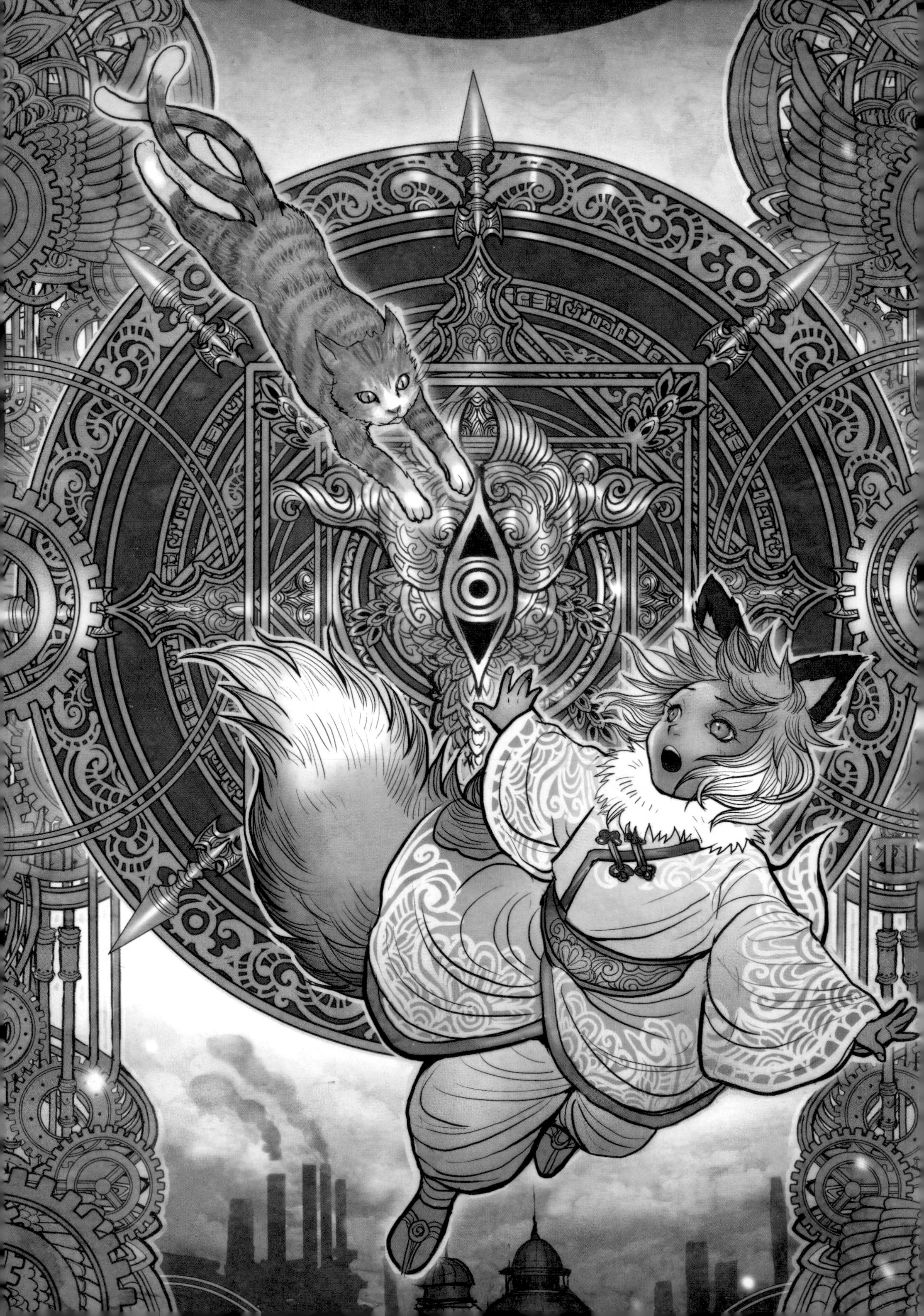

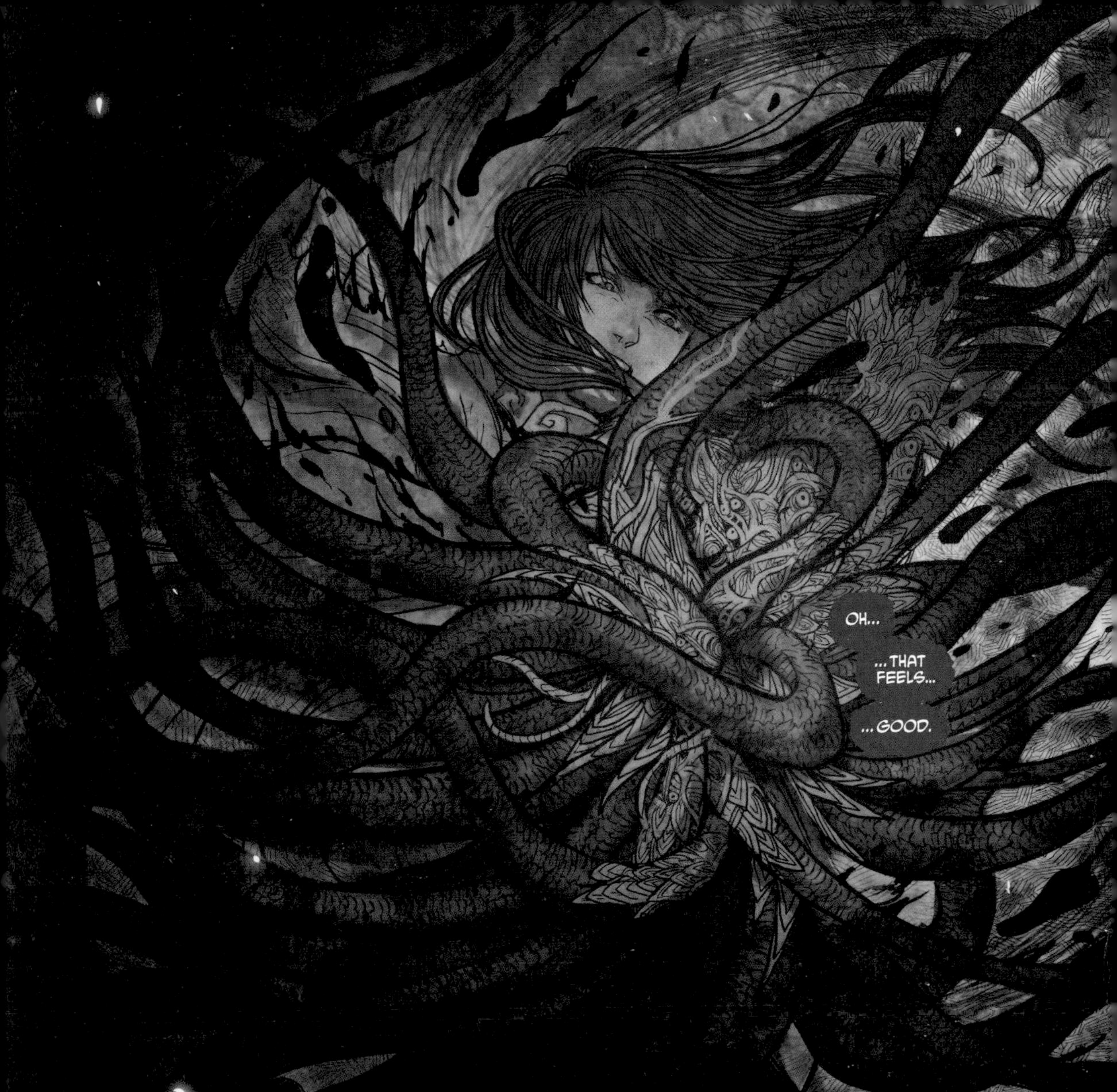
OH...
...THAT FEELS...
...GOOD.
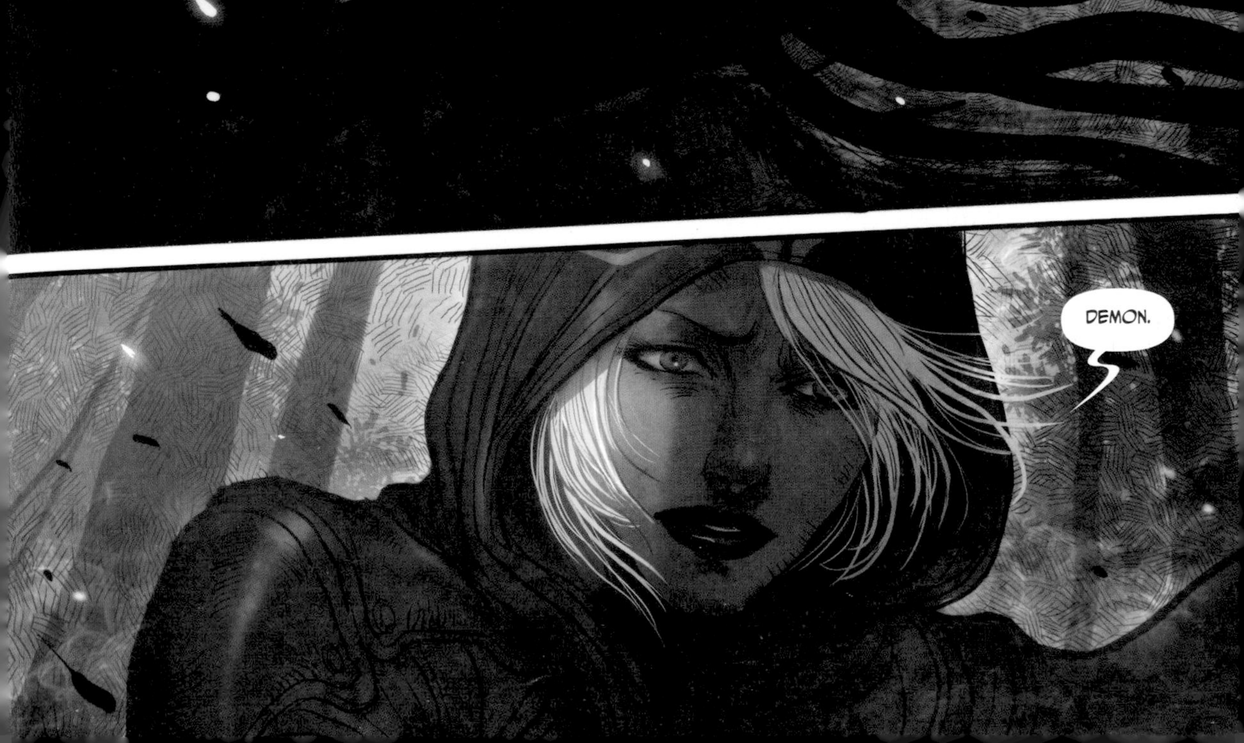
DEMON.

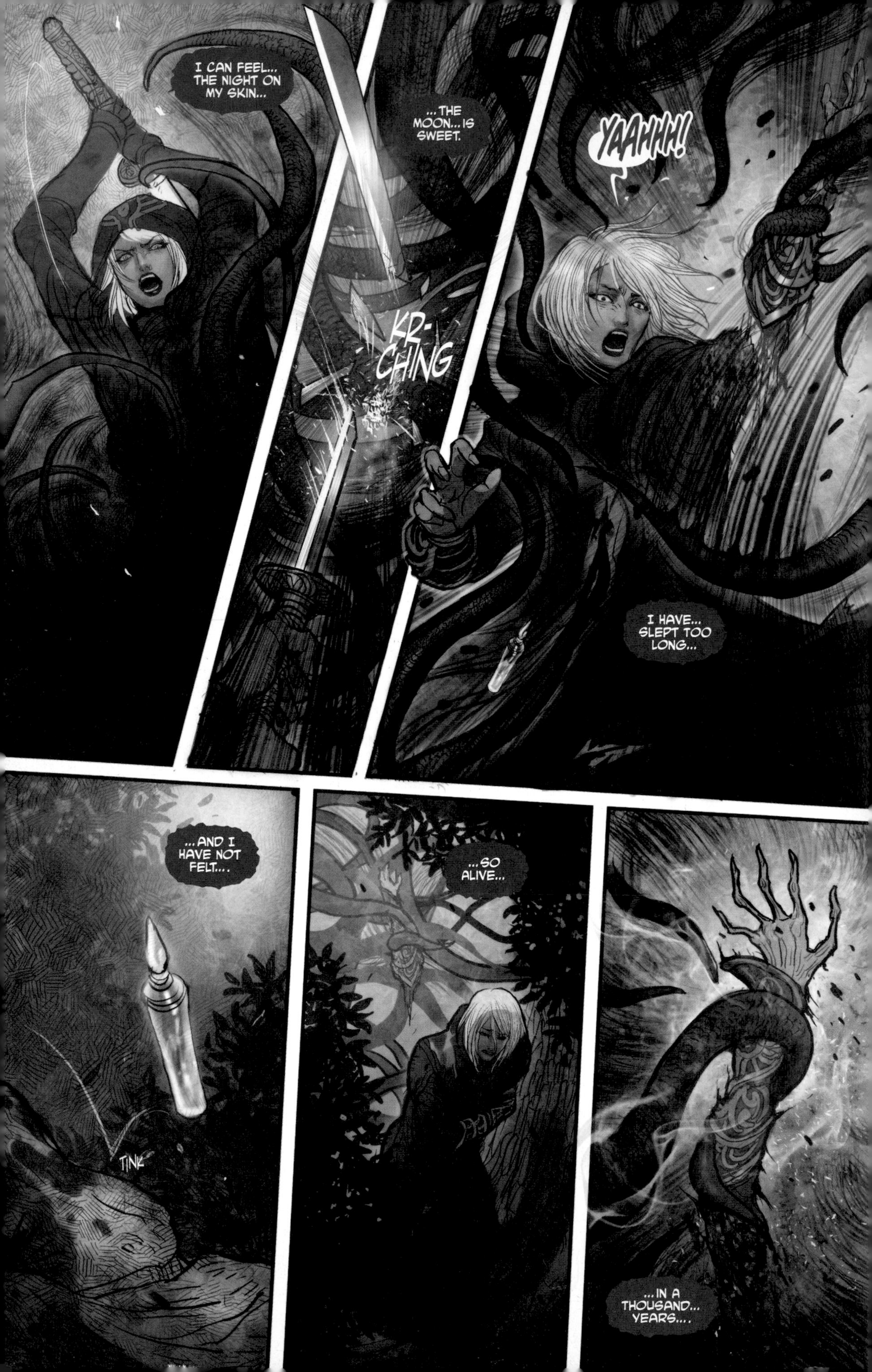
I CAN FEEL... THE NIGHT ON MY SKIN...
...THE MOON... IS SWEET.
KR-CHING
YAAHHH!
I HAVE... SLEPT TOO LONG...
...AND I HAVE NOT FELT....
TINK
...SO ALIVE...
...IN A THOUSAND... YEARS....

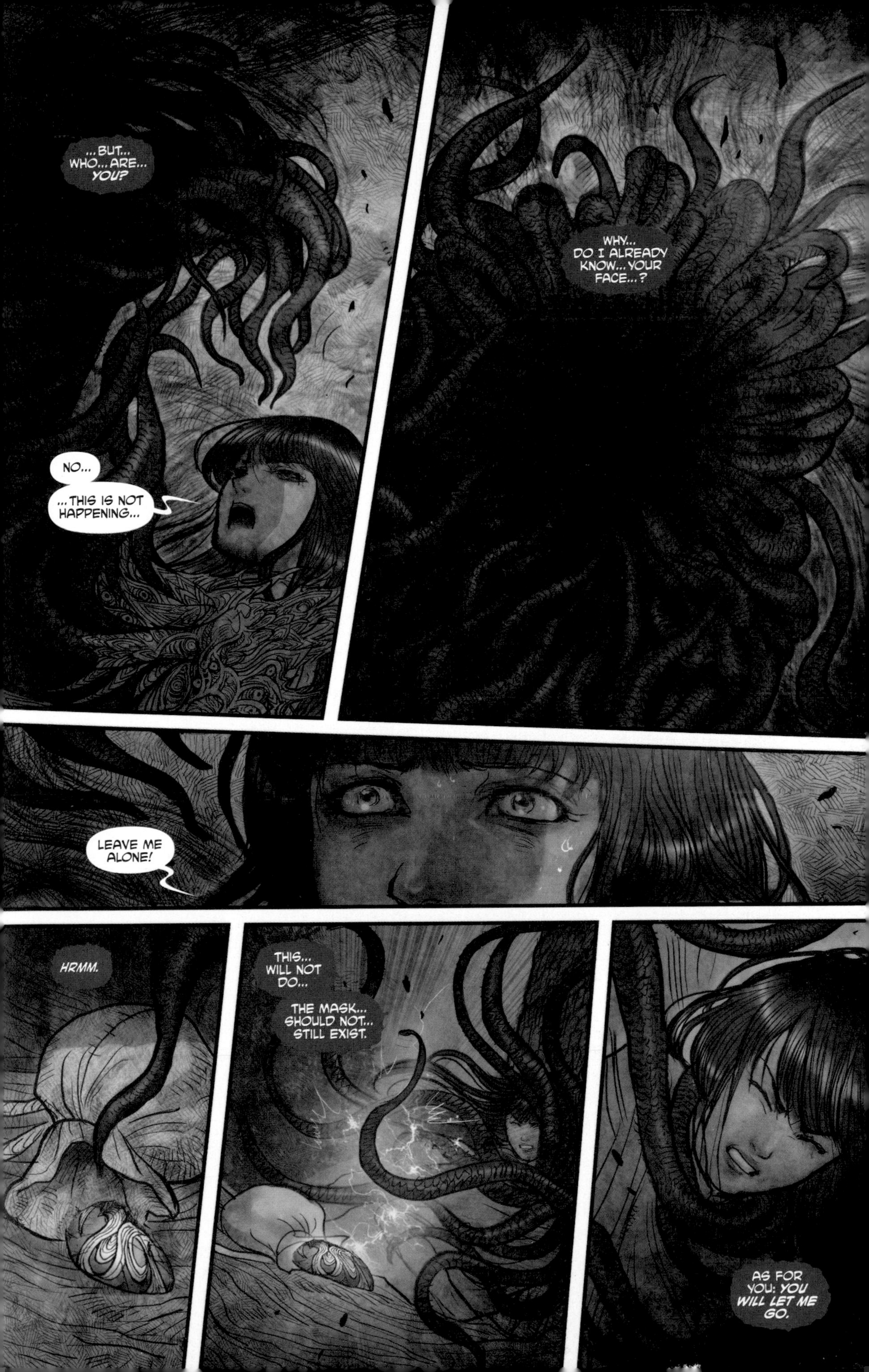
...BUT... WHO... ARE... YOU?
NO...
...THIS IS NOT HAPPENING...
WHY... DO I ALREADY KNOW... YOUR FACE...?
LEAVE ME ALONE!
HRMM.
THIS... WILL NOT DO...
THE MASK... SHOULD NOT... STILL EXIST.
AS FOR YOU: YOU WILL LET ME GO.

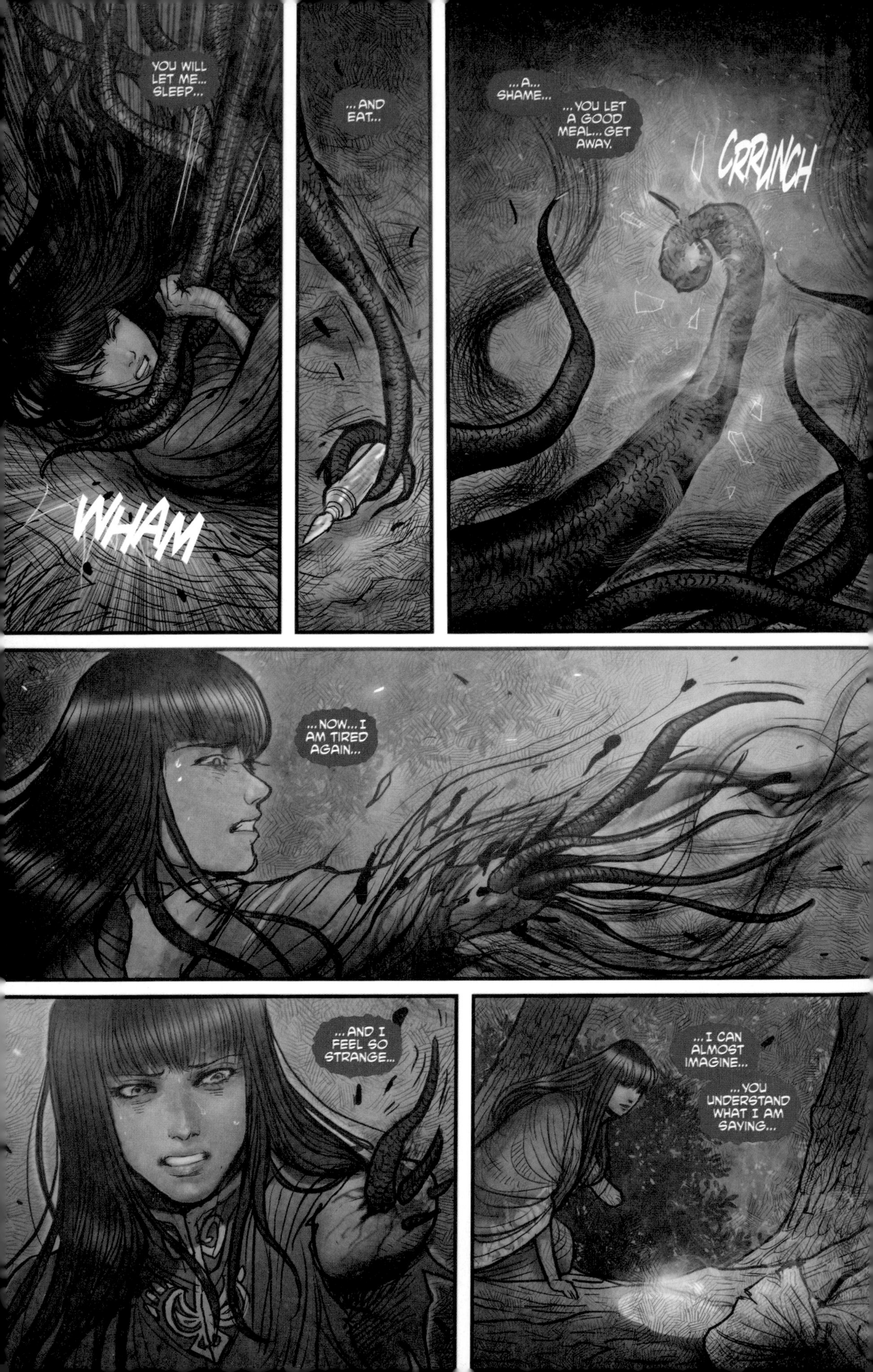
YOU WILL LET ME... SLEEP...
WHAM
...AND EAT...
...A... SHAME...
...YOU LET A GOOD MEAL... GET AWAY.
CRRUNCH
...NOW... I AM TIRED AGAIN...
...AND I FEEL SO STRANGE...
...I CAN ALMOST IMAGINE...
...YOU UNDERSTAND WHAT I AM SAYING...

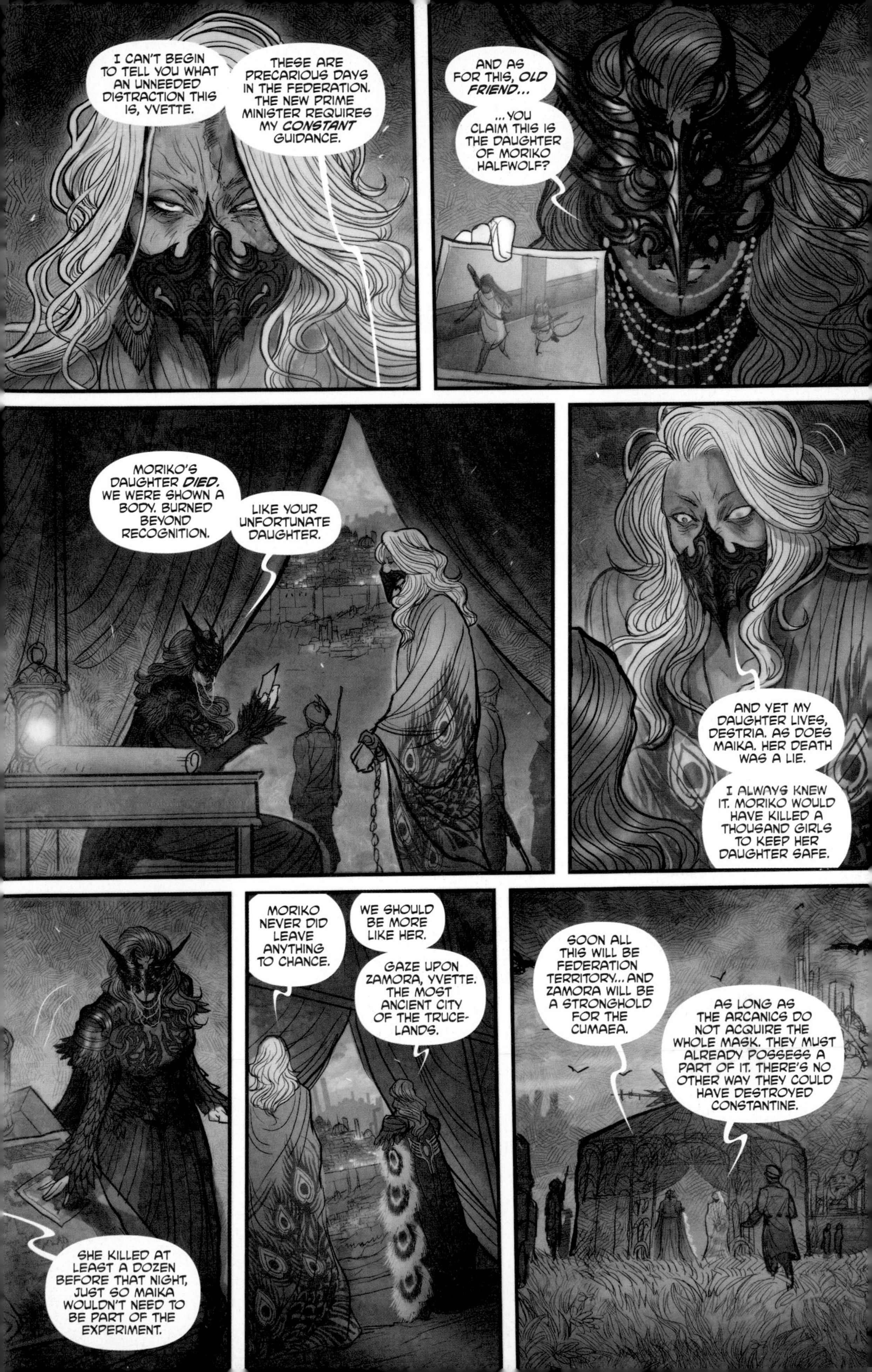
I CAN'T BEGIN TO TELL YOU WHAT AN UNNEEDED DISTRACTION THIS IS, YVETTE.
THESE ARE PRECARIOUS DAYS IN THE FEDERATION. THE NEW PRIME MINISTER REQUIRES MY CONSTANT GUIDANCE.
AND AS FOR THIS, OLD FRIEND...
...YOU CLAIM THIS IS THE DAUGHTER OF MORIKO HALFWOLF?
MORIKO'S DAUGHTER DIED. WE WERE SHOWN A BODY. BURNED BEYOND RECOGNITION.
LIKE YOUR UNFORTUNATE DAUGHTER.
AND YET MY DAUGHTER LIVES, DESTRIA. AS DOES MAIKA. HER DEATH WAS A LIE.
I ALWAYS KNEW IT. MORIKO WOULD HAVE KILLED A THOUSAND GIRLS TO KEEP HER DAUGHTER SAFE.
SHE KILLED AT LEAST A DOZEN BEFORE THAT NIGHT, JUST SO MAIKA WOULDN'T NEED TO BE PART OF THE EXPERIMENT.
MORIKO NEVER DID LEAVE ANYTHING TO CHANCE.
WE SHOULD BE MORE LIKE HER.
GAZE UPON ZAMORA, YVETTE. THE MOST ANCIENT CITY OF THE TRUCE-LANDS.
SOON ALL THIS WILL BE FEDERATION TERRITORY... AND ZAMORA WILL BE A STRONGHOLD FOR THE CUMAEA.
AS LONG AS THE ARCANICS DO NOT ACQUIRE THE WHOLE MASK. THEY MUST ALREADY POSSESS A PART OF IT. THERE'S NO OTHER WAY THEY COULD HAVE DESTROYED CONSTANTINE.

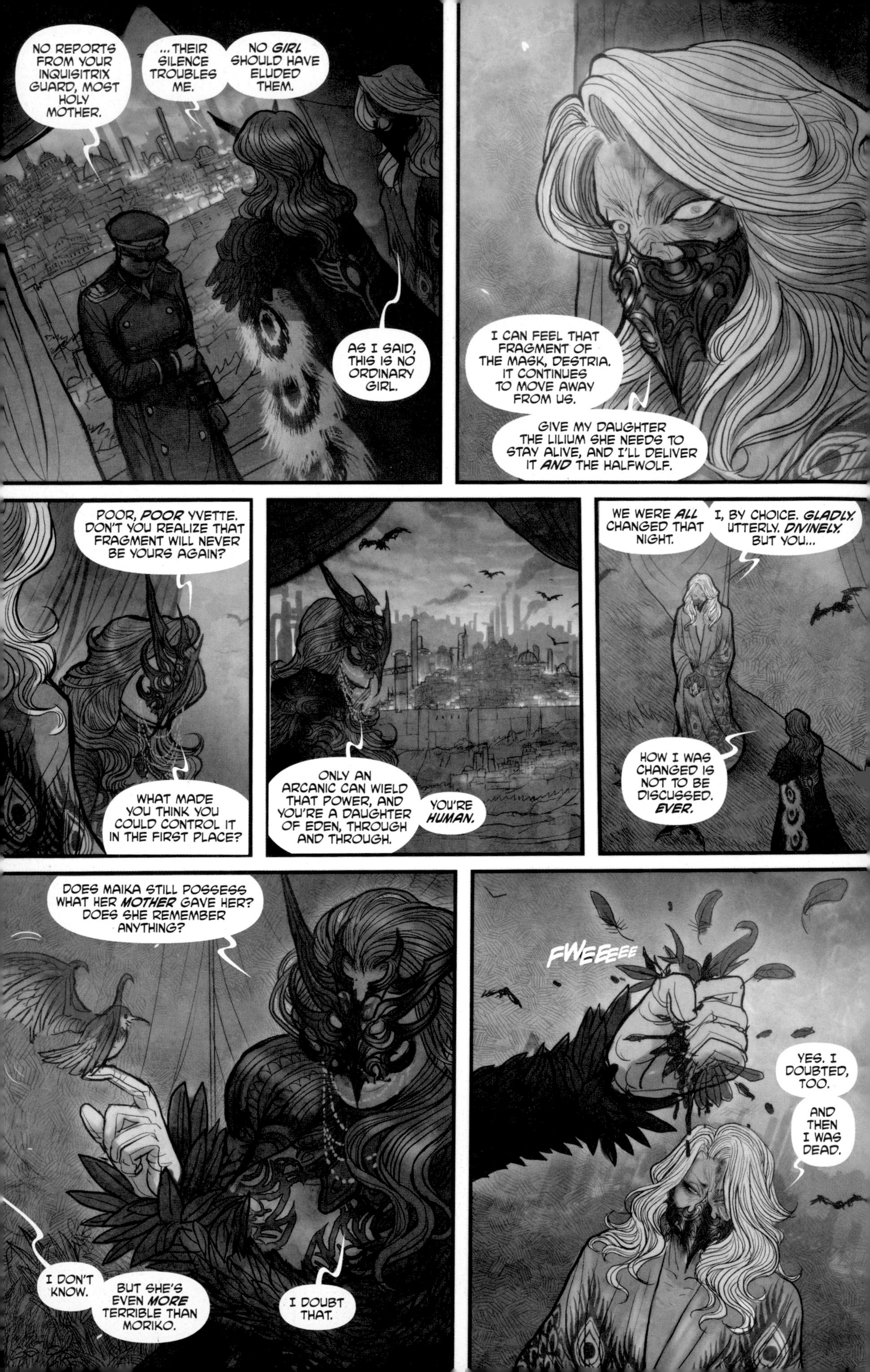
NO REPORTS FROM YOUR INQUISITRIX GUARD, MOST HOLY MOTHER.
...THEIR SILENCE TROUBLES ME.
NO *GIRL* SHOULD HAVE ELUDED THEM.
AS I SAID, THIS IS NO ORDINARY GIRL.
I CAN FEEL THAT FRAGMENT OF THE MASK, DESTRIA. IT CONTINUES TO MOVE AWAY FROM US.
GIVE MY DAUGHTER THE LILIUM SHE NEEDS TO STAY ALIVE, AND I'LL DELIVER IT *AND* THE HALFWOLF.
POOR, *POOR* YVETTE. DON'T YOU REALIZE THAT FRAGMENT WILL NEVER BE YOURS AGAIN?
WHAT MADE YOU THINK YOU COULD CONTROL IT IN THE FIRST PLACE?
ONLY AN ARCANIC CAN WIELD THAT POWER, AND YOU'RE A DAUGHTER OF EDEN, THROUGH AND THROUGH.
YOU'RE *HUMAN.*
WE WERE *ALL* CHANGED THAT NIGHT.
I, BY CHOICE. *GLADLY.* UTTERLY. *DIVINELY.* BUT YOU...
HOW I WAS CHANGED IS NOT TO BE DISCUSSED. *EVER.*
DOES MAIKA STILL POSSESS WHAT HER *MOTHER* GAVE HER? DOES SHE REMEMBER ANYTHING?
I DON'T KNOW.
BUT SHE'S EVEN *MORE* TERRIBLE THAN MORIKO.
I DOUBT THAT.
FWEEEEEE
YES. I DOUBTED, TOO.
AND THEN I WAS DEAD.

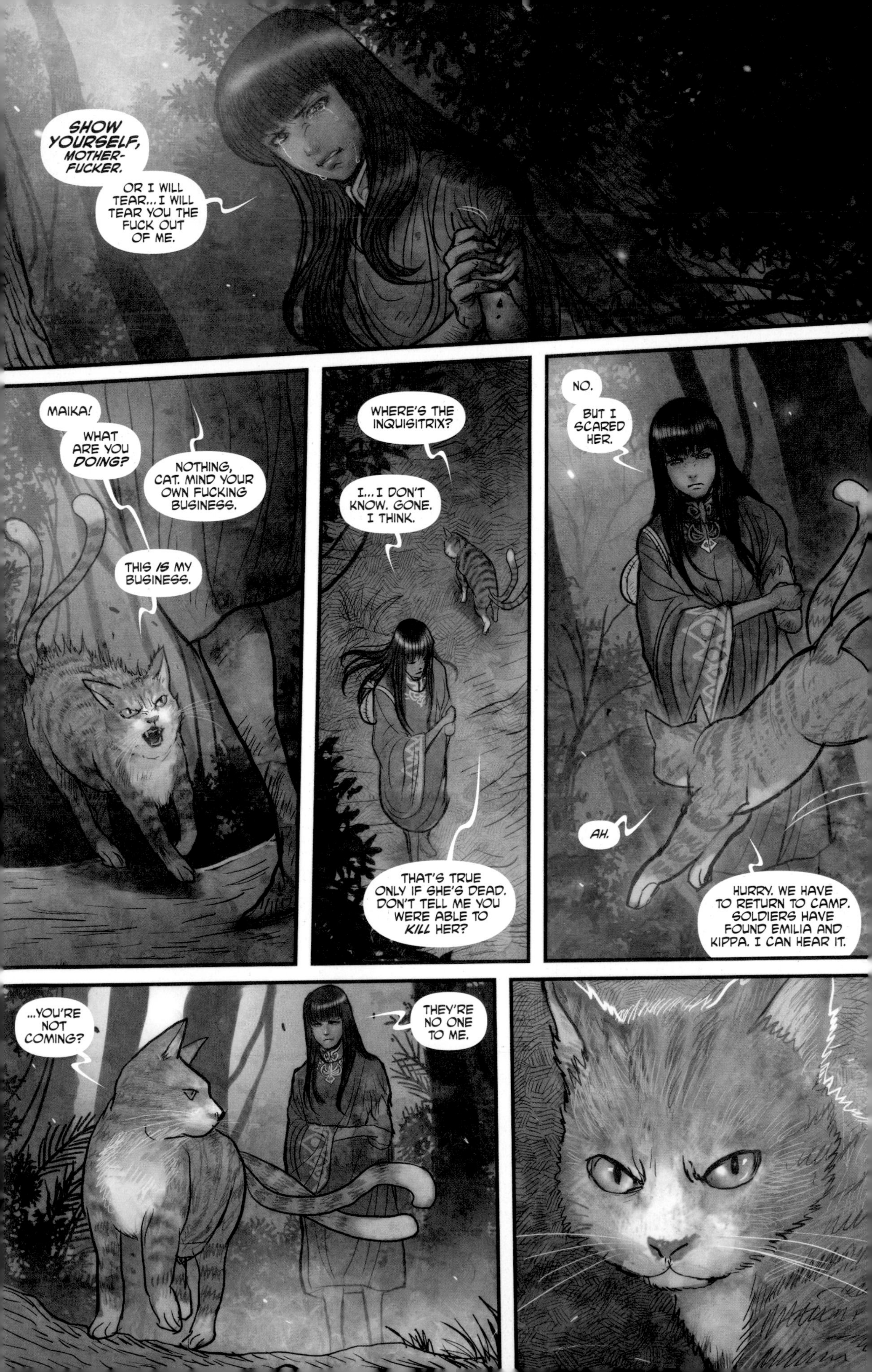
SHOW YOURSELF, MOTHER-FUCKER.
OR I WILL TEAR... I WILL TEAR YOU THE FUCK OUT OF ME.
MAIKA!
WHAT ARE YOU DOING?
NOTHING, CAT. MIND YOUR OWN FUCKING BUSINESS.
THIS IS MY BUSINESS.
WHERE'S THE INQUISITRIX?
I... I DON'T KNOW. GONE. I THINK.
THAT'S TRUE ONLY IF SHE'S DEAD. DON'T TELL ME YOU WERE ABLE TO KILL HER?
NO.
BUT I SCARED HER.
AH.
HURRY. WE HAVE TO RETURN TO CAMP. SOLDIERS HAVE FOUND EMILIA AND KIPPA. I CAN HEAR IT.
...YOU'RE NOT COMING?
THEY'RE NO ONE TO ME.

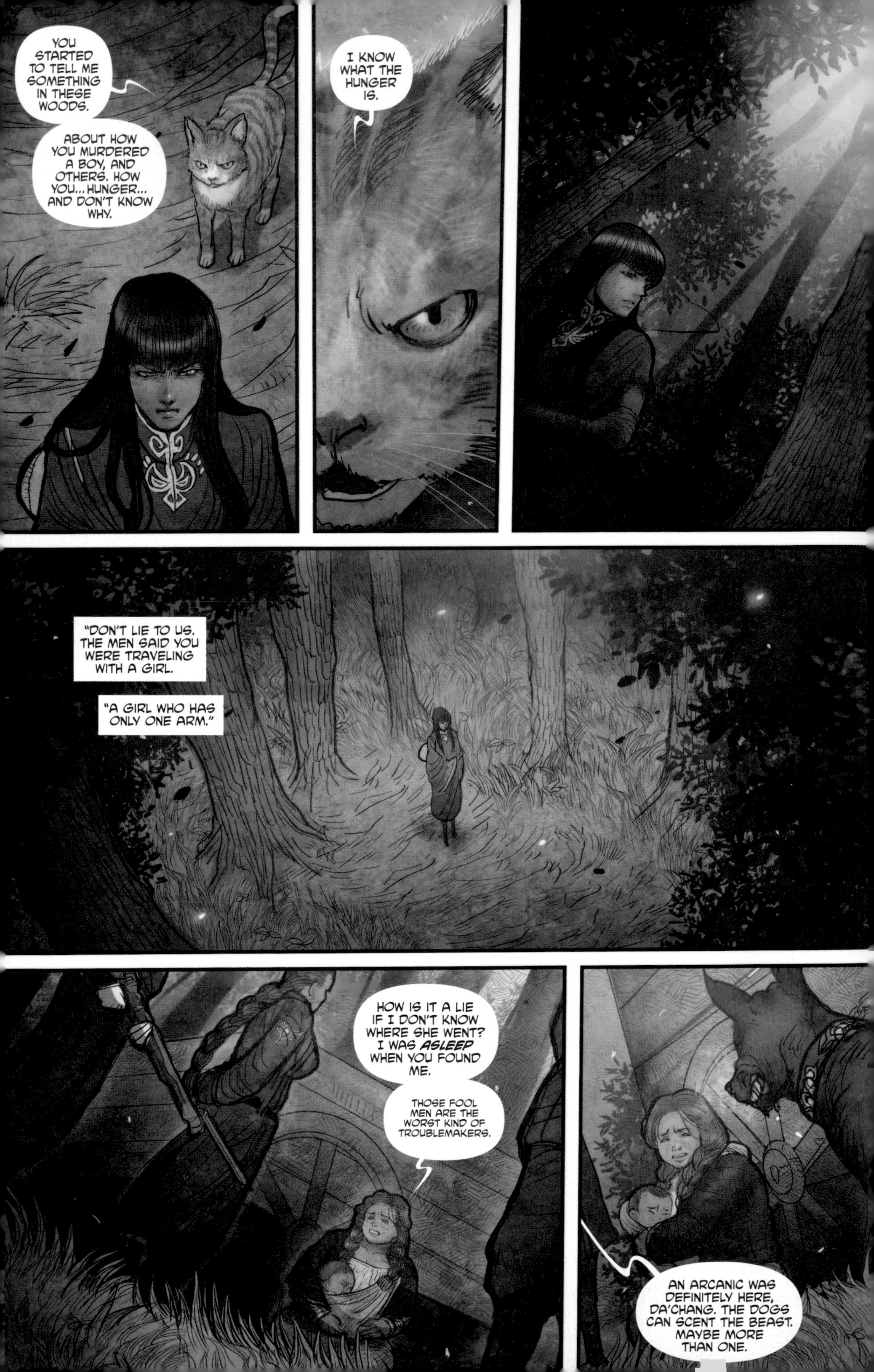
YOU STARTED TO TELL ME SOMETHING IN THESE WOODS.
ABOUT HOW YOU MURDERED A BOY, AND OTHERS. HOW YOU... HUNGER... AND DON'T KNOW WHY.
I KNOW WHAT THE HUNGER IS.
"DON'T LIE TO US. THE MEN SAID YOU WERE TRAVELING WITH A GIRL.
"A GIRL WHO HAS ONLY ONE ARM."
HOW IS IT A LIE IF I DON'T KNOW WHERE SHE WENT? I WAS *ASLEEP* WHEN YOU FOUND ME.
THOSE FOOL MEN ARE THE WORST KIND OF TROUBLEMAKERS.
AN ARCANIC WAS DEFINITELY HERE, DA'CHANG. THE DOGS CAN SCENT THE BEAST. MAYBE MORE THAN ONE.

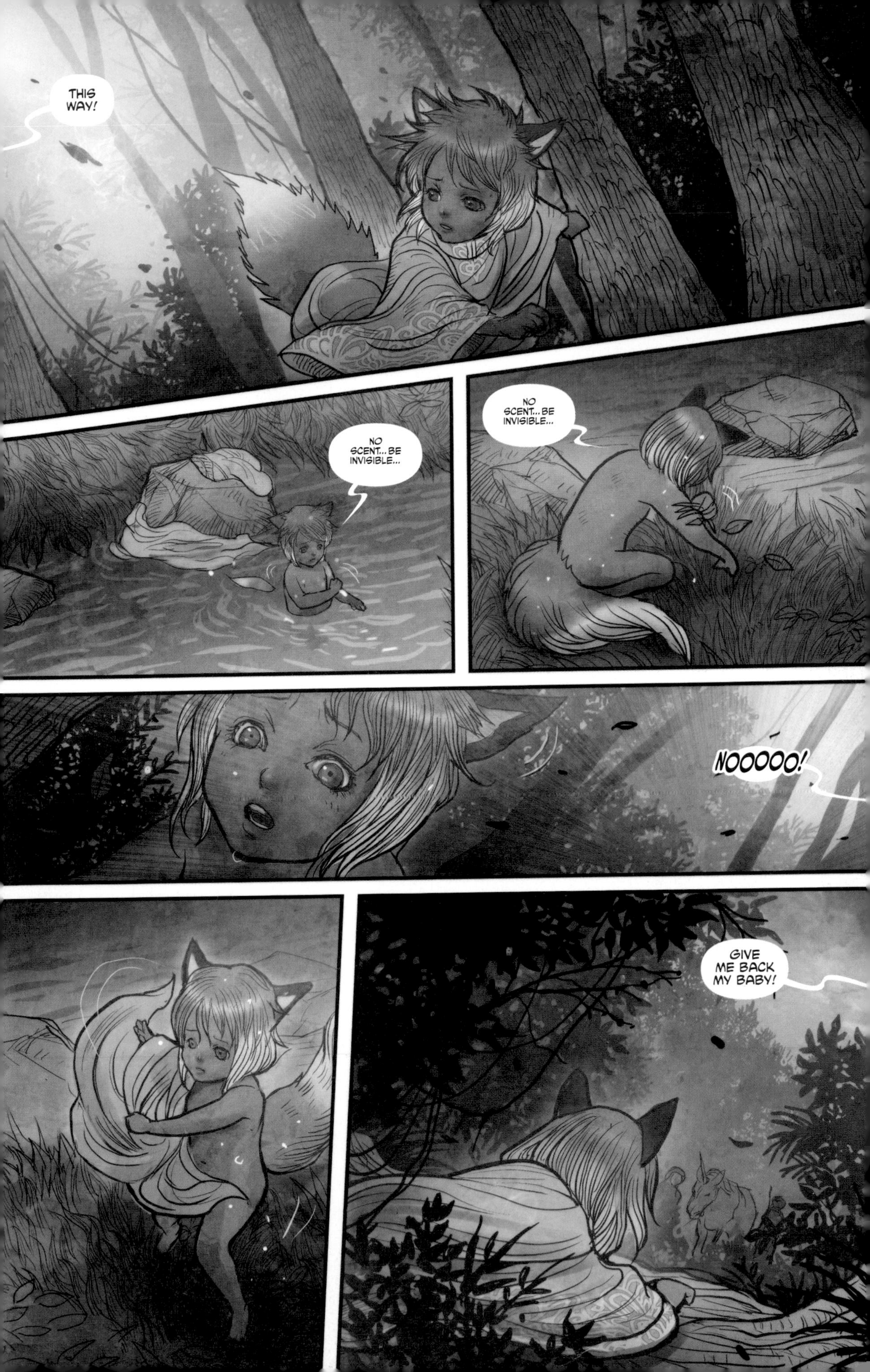
THIS WAY!
NO SCENT... BE INVISIBLE...
NO SCENT... BE INVISIBLE...
NOOOOO!
GIVE ME BACK MY BABY!

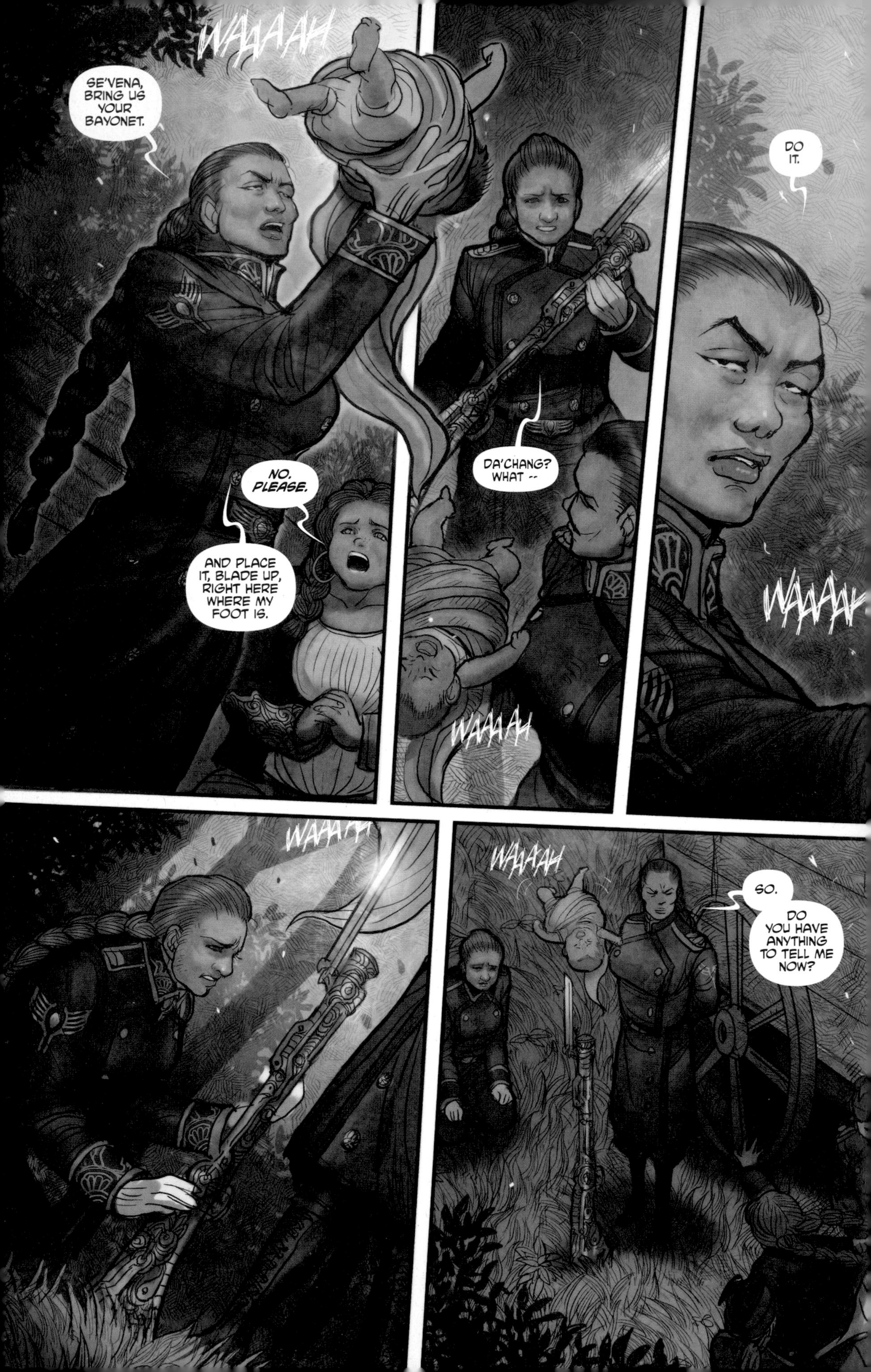
WAAAAH
SE'VENA, BRING US YOUR BAYONET.
AND PLACE IT, BLADE UP, RIGHT HERE WHERE MY FOOT IS.
NO. PLEASE.
DA'CHANG? WHAT --
WAAAAH
DO IT.
WAAAAH
WAAAAH
WAAAAH
SO.
DO YOU HAVE ANYTHING TO TELL ME NOW?

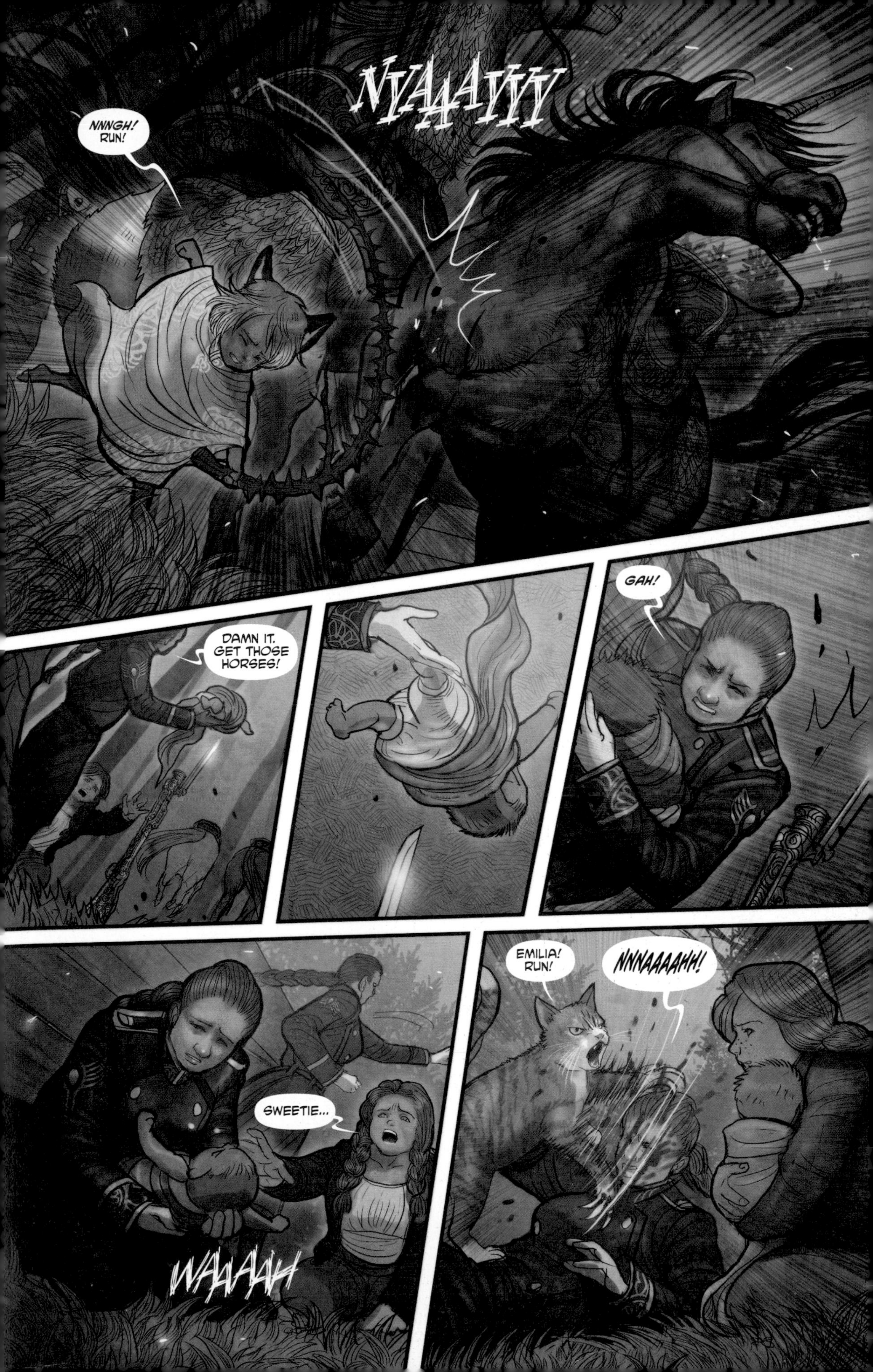
NNNGH! RUN!
NYAAAYYY
DAMN IT. GET THOSE HORSES!
GAH!
SWEETIE...
WAAAAH
EMILIA! RUN!
NNNAAAAHH!

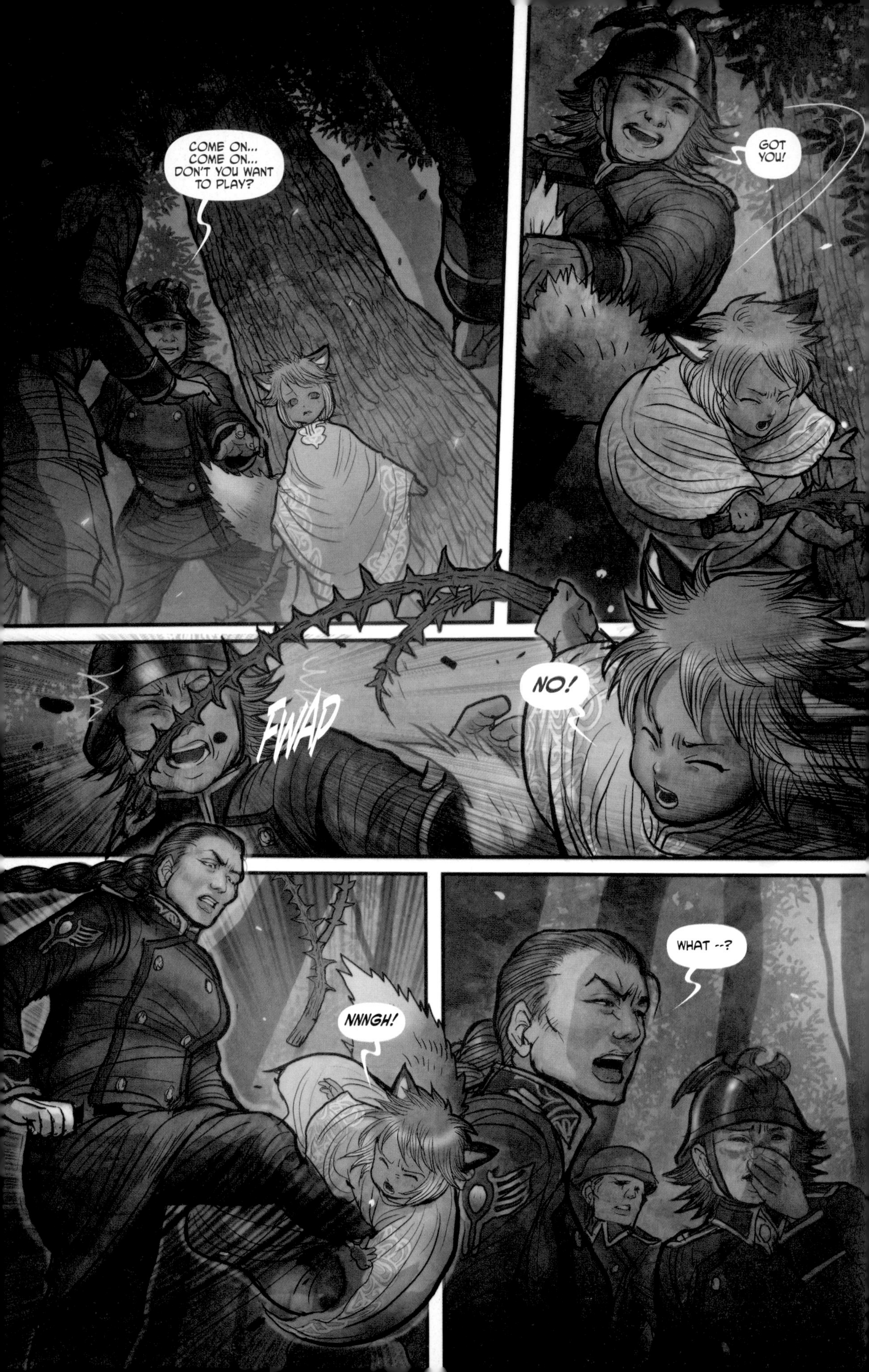
COME ON... COME ON... DON'T YOU WANT TO PLAY?
GOT YOU!
FWAP
NO!
NNNGH!
WHAT --?

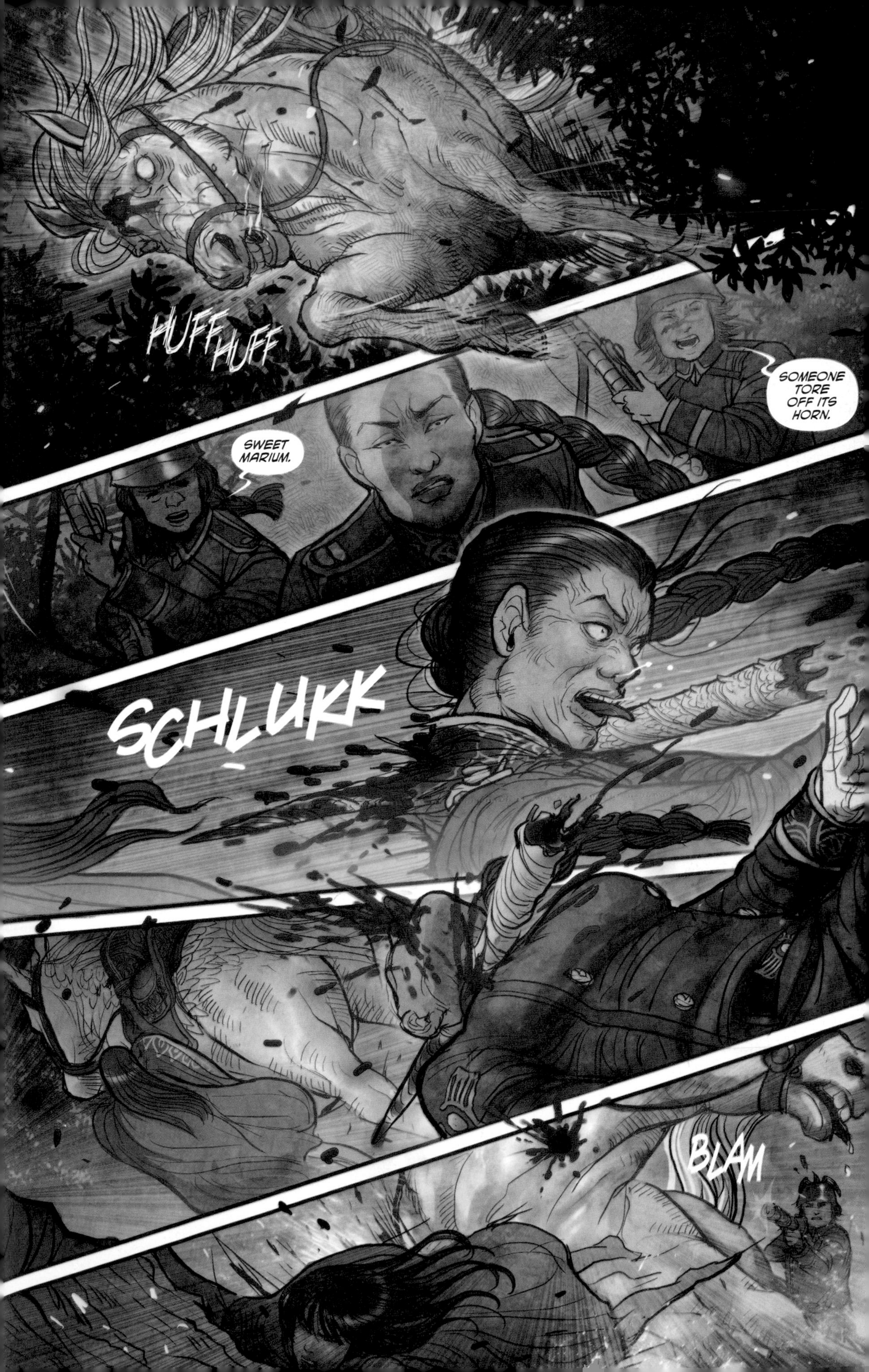
HUFF HUFF
SOMEONE TORE OFF ITS HORN.
SWEET MARIUM.
SCHLUKK
BLAM

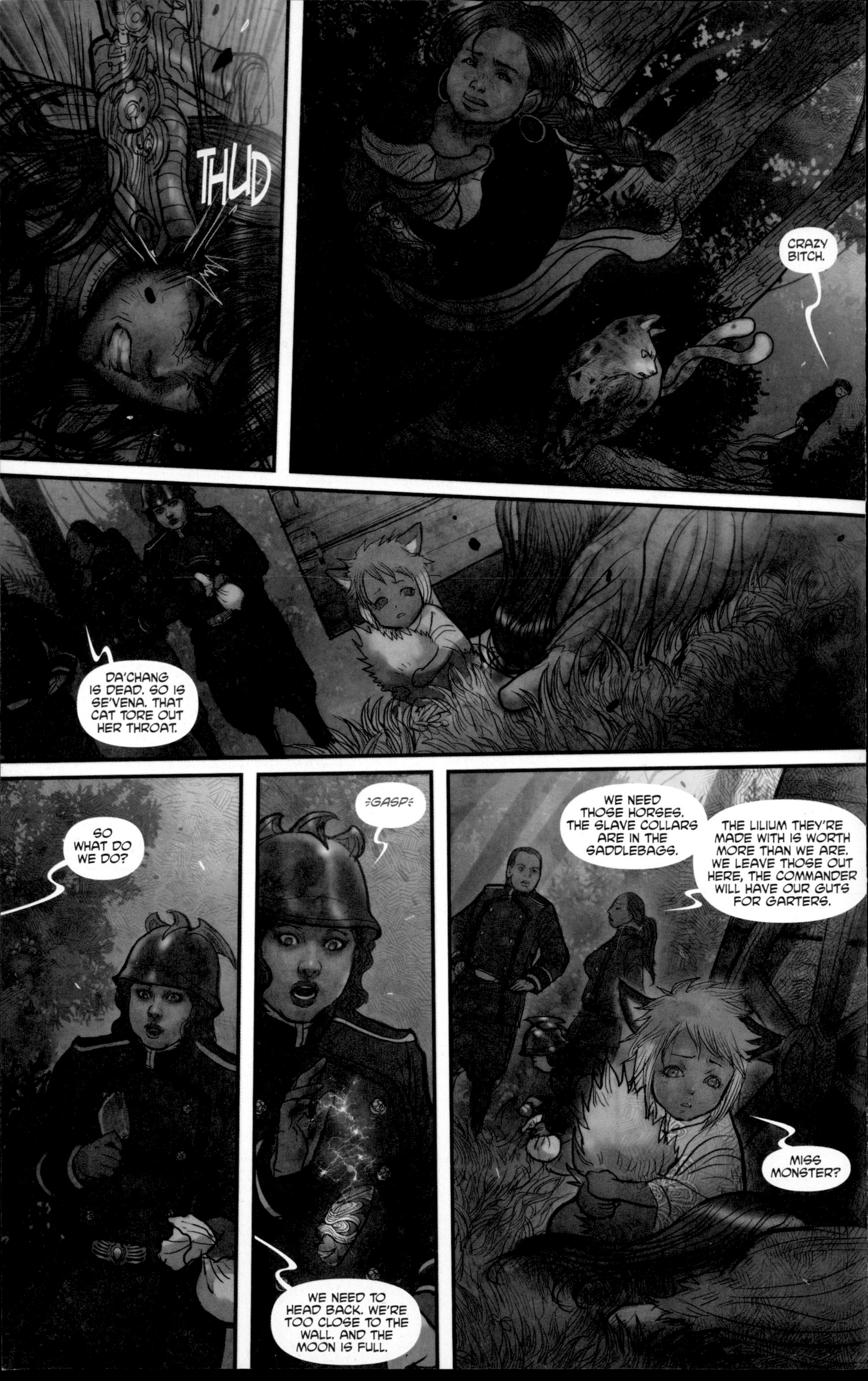
THUD
CRAZY BITCH.
DA'CHANG IS DEAD. SO IS SE'VENA. THAT CAT TORE OUT HER THROAT.
SO WHAT DO WE DO?
GASP
WE NEED TO HEAD BACK. WE'RE TOO CLOSE TO THE WALL. AND THE MOON IS FULL.
WE NEED THOSE HORSES. THE SLAVE COLLARS ARE IN THE SADDLEBAGS.
THE LILIUM THEY'RE MADE WITH IS WORTH MORE THAN WE ARE. WE LEAVE THOSE OUT HERE, THE COMMANDER WILL HAVE OUR GUTS FOR GARTERS.
MISS MONSTER?

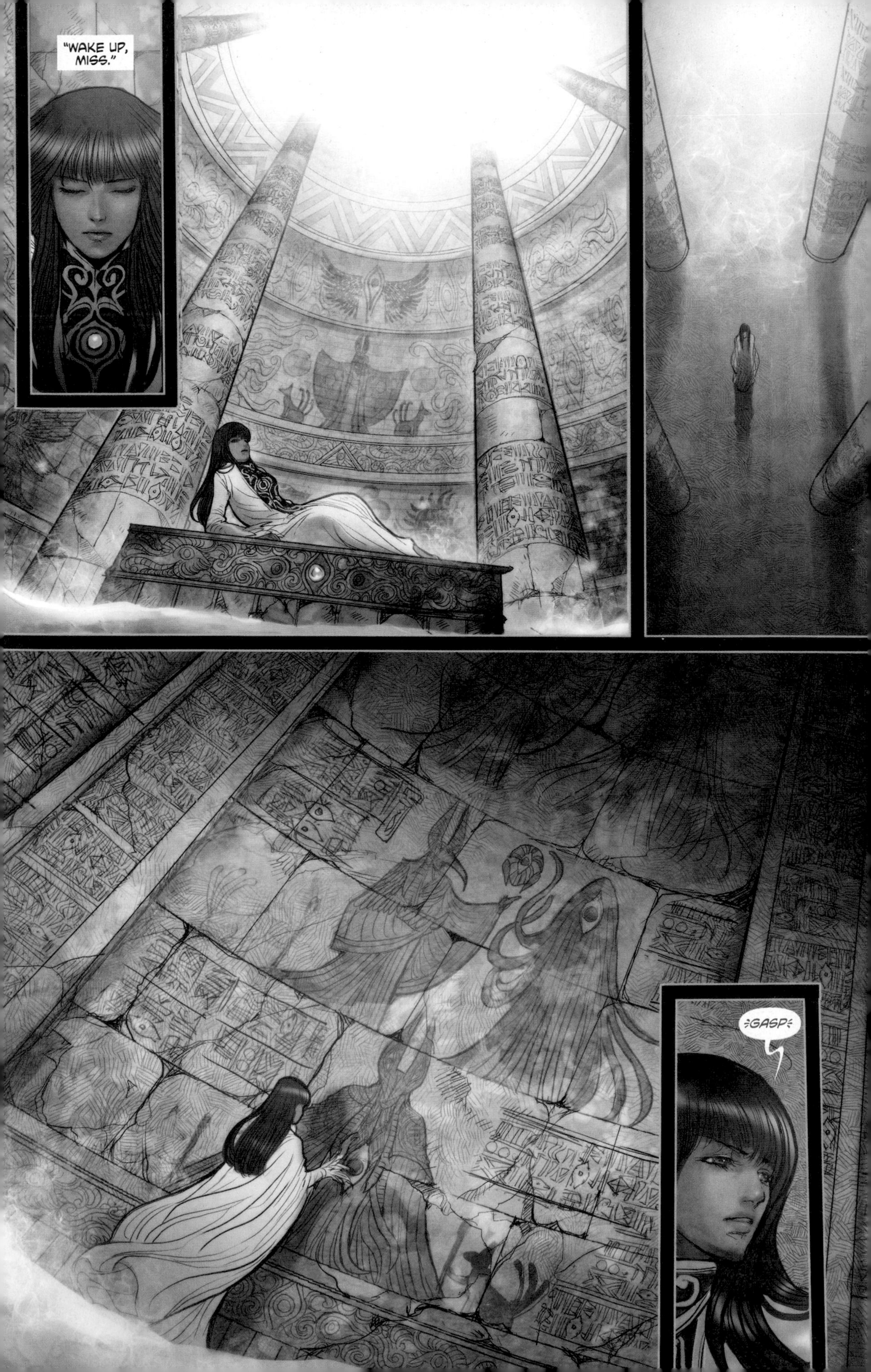
"WAKE UP, MISS."
GASP

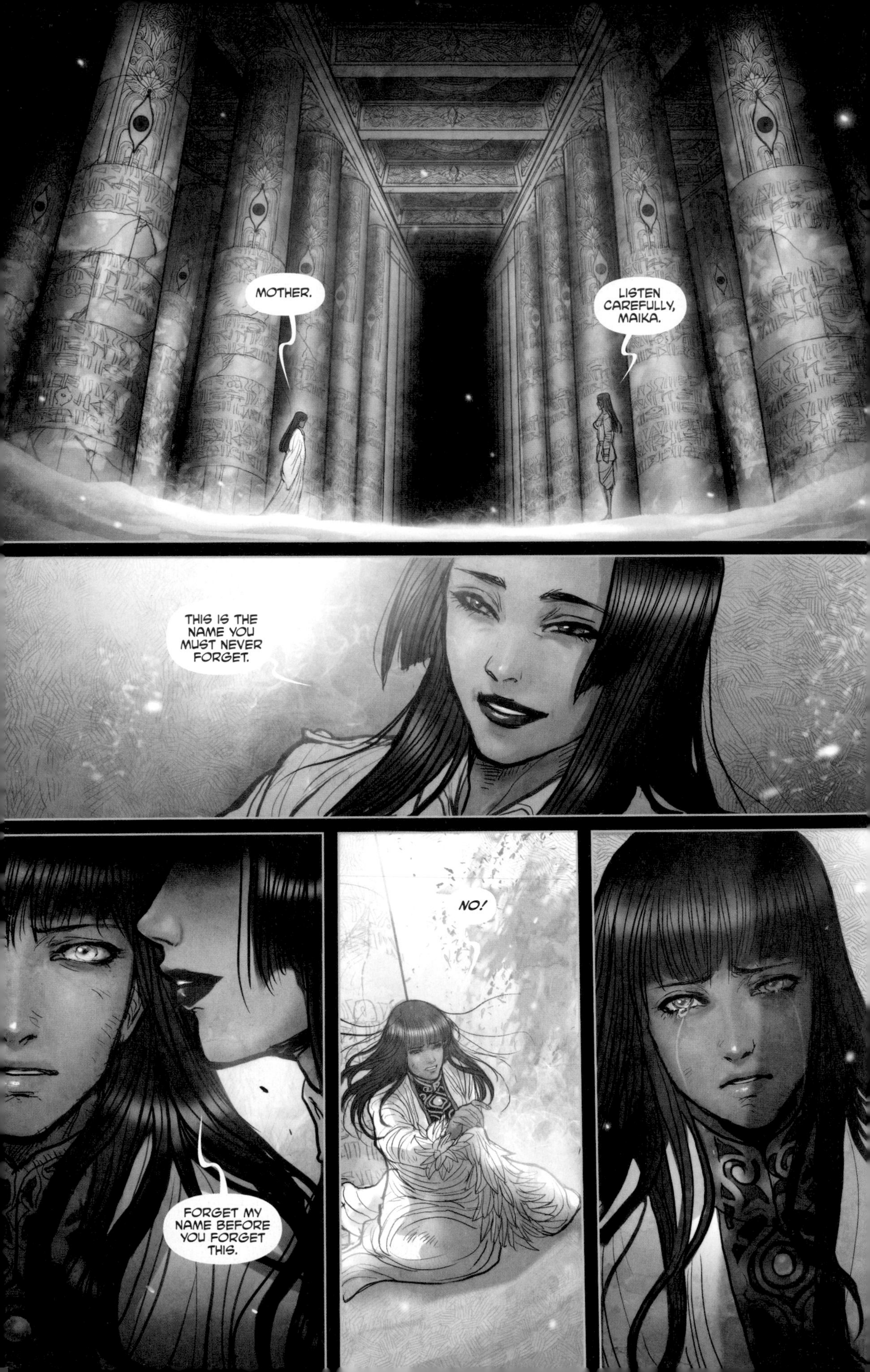
MOTHER.
LISTEN CAREFULLY, MAIKA.
THIS IS THE NAME YOU MUST NEVER FORGET.
FORGET MY NAME BEFORE YOU FORGET THIS.
NO!

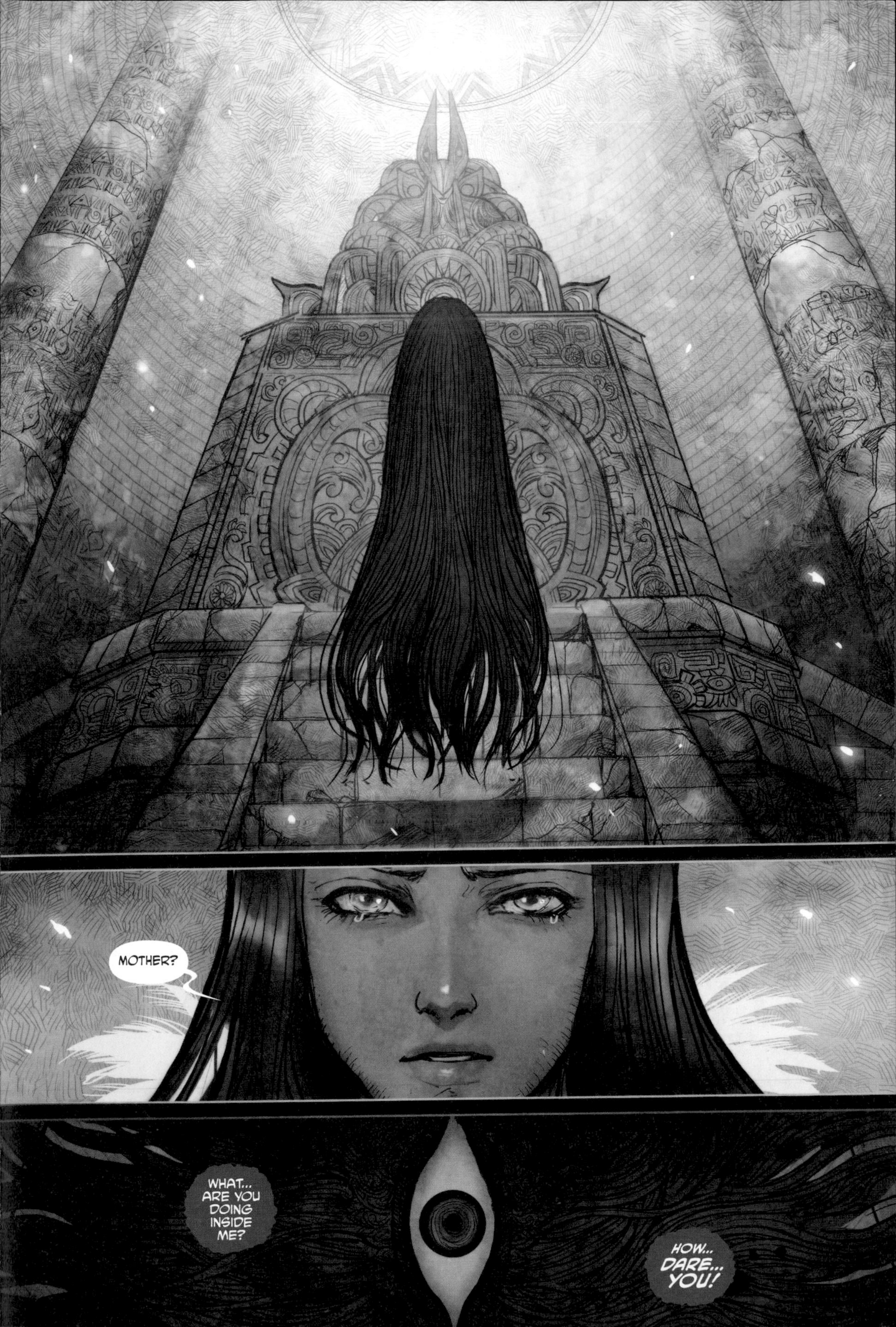

MOTHER?
WHAT... ARE YOU DOING INSIDE ME?
HOW... DARE... YOU!

≠UNH≠

WHERE ARE WE? WHERE ARE ALL THE SOLDIERS?

WE'RE ≠SNIFF≠ NEXT TO THE WALL, MISS.

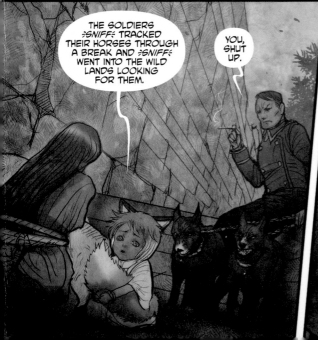

THE SOLDIERS ≠SNIFF≠ TRACKED THEIR HORSES THROUGH A BREAK AND ≠SNIFF≠ WENT INTO THE WILD LANDS LOOKING FOR THEM.

YOU, SHUT UP.

WHERE ARE MY THINGS?

HEY! DOWN ON YOUR KNEES!

I ASKED YOU A QUESTION.

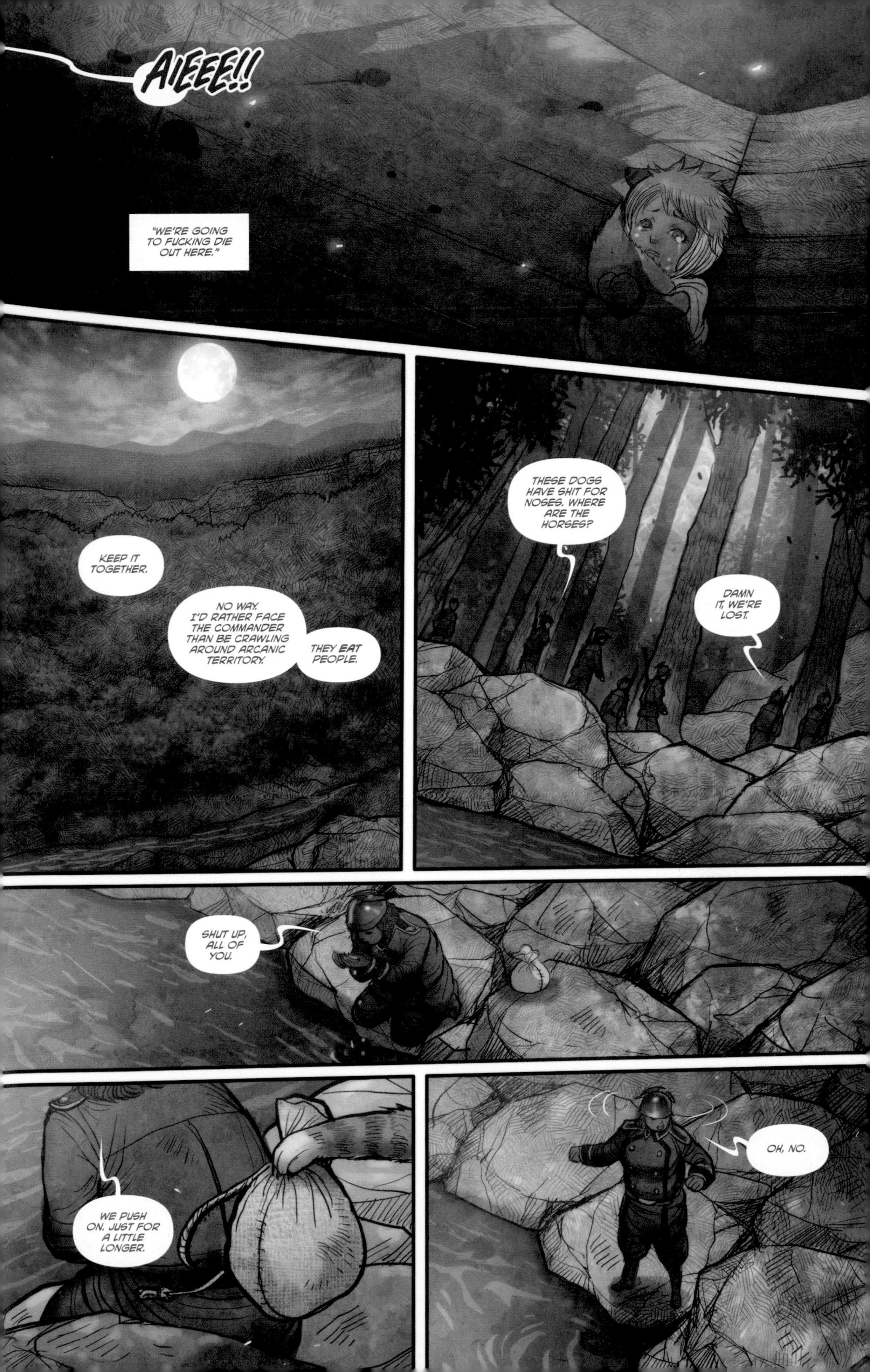
AIEEE!!
"WE'RE GOING TO FUCKING DIE OUT HERE."
KEEP IT TOGETHER.
NO WAY. I'D RATHER FACE THE COMMANDER THAN BE CRAWLING AROUND ARCANIC TERRITORY.
THEY EAT PEOPLE.
THESE DOGS HAVE SHIT FOR NOSES. WHERE ARE THE HORSES?
DAMN IT, WE'RE LOST.
SHUT UP, ALL OF YOU.
WE PUSH ON. JUST FOR A LITTLE LONGER.
OH, NO.

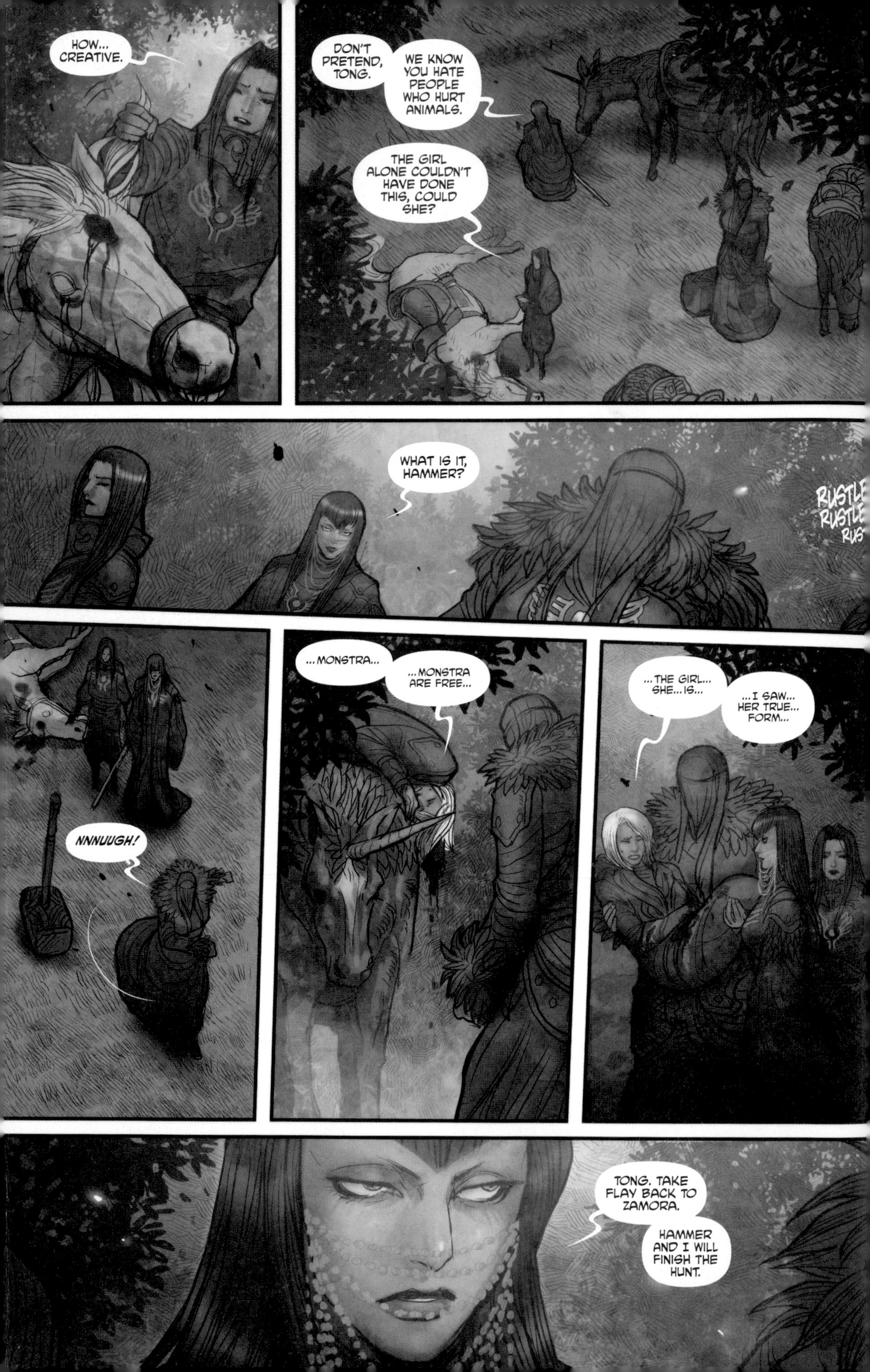

HOW... CREATIVE.
DON'T PRETEND, TONG.
WE KNOW YOU HATE PEOPLE WHO HURT ANIMALS.
THE GIRL ALONE COULDN'T HAVE DONE THIS, COULD SHE?
WHAT IS IT, HAMMER?
RUSTLE
RUSTLE
RUS
NNNUUGH!
...MONSTRA...
...MONSTRA ARE FREE...
...THE GIRL... SHE... IS...
...I SAW... HER TRUE... FORM...
TONG. TAKE FLAY BACK TO ZAMORA.
HAMMER AND I WILL FINISH THE HUNT.

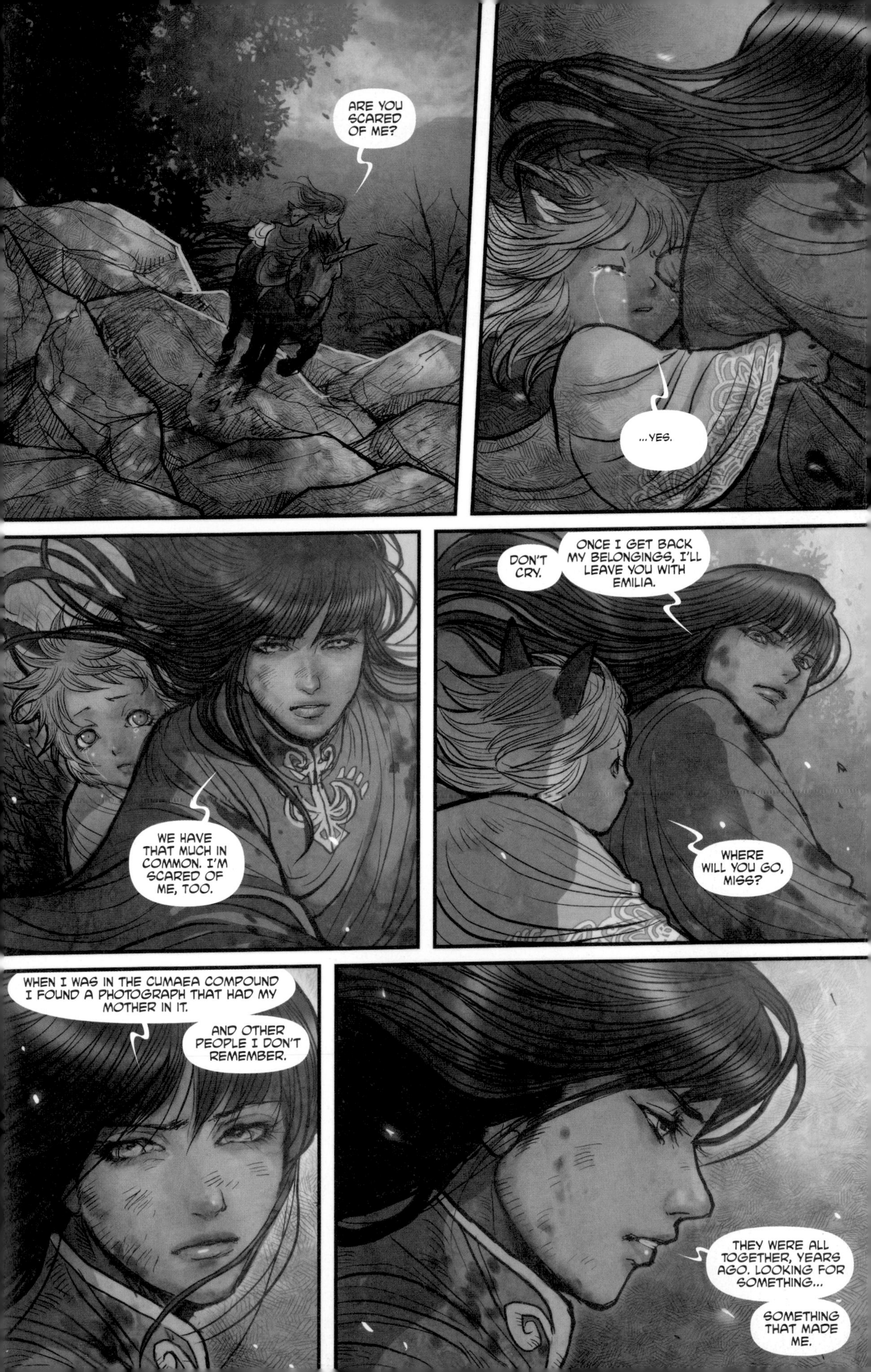
ARE YOU SCARED OF ME?
...YES.
WE HAVE THAT MUCH IN COMMON. I'M SCARED OF ME, TOO.
DON'T CRY.
ONCE I GET BACK MY BELONGINGS, I'LL LEAVE YOU WITH EMILIA.
WHERE WILL YOU GO, MISS?
WHEN I WAS IN THE CUMAEA COMPOUND I FOUND A PHOTOGRAPH THAT HAD MY MOTHER IN IT.
AND OTHER PEOPLE I DON'T REMEMBER.
THEY WERE ALL TOGETHER, YEARS AGO. LOOKING FOR SOMETHING...
SOMETHING THAT MADE ME.

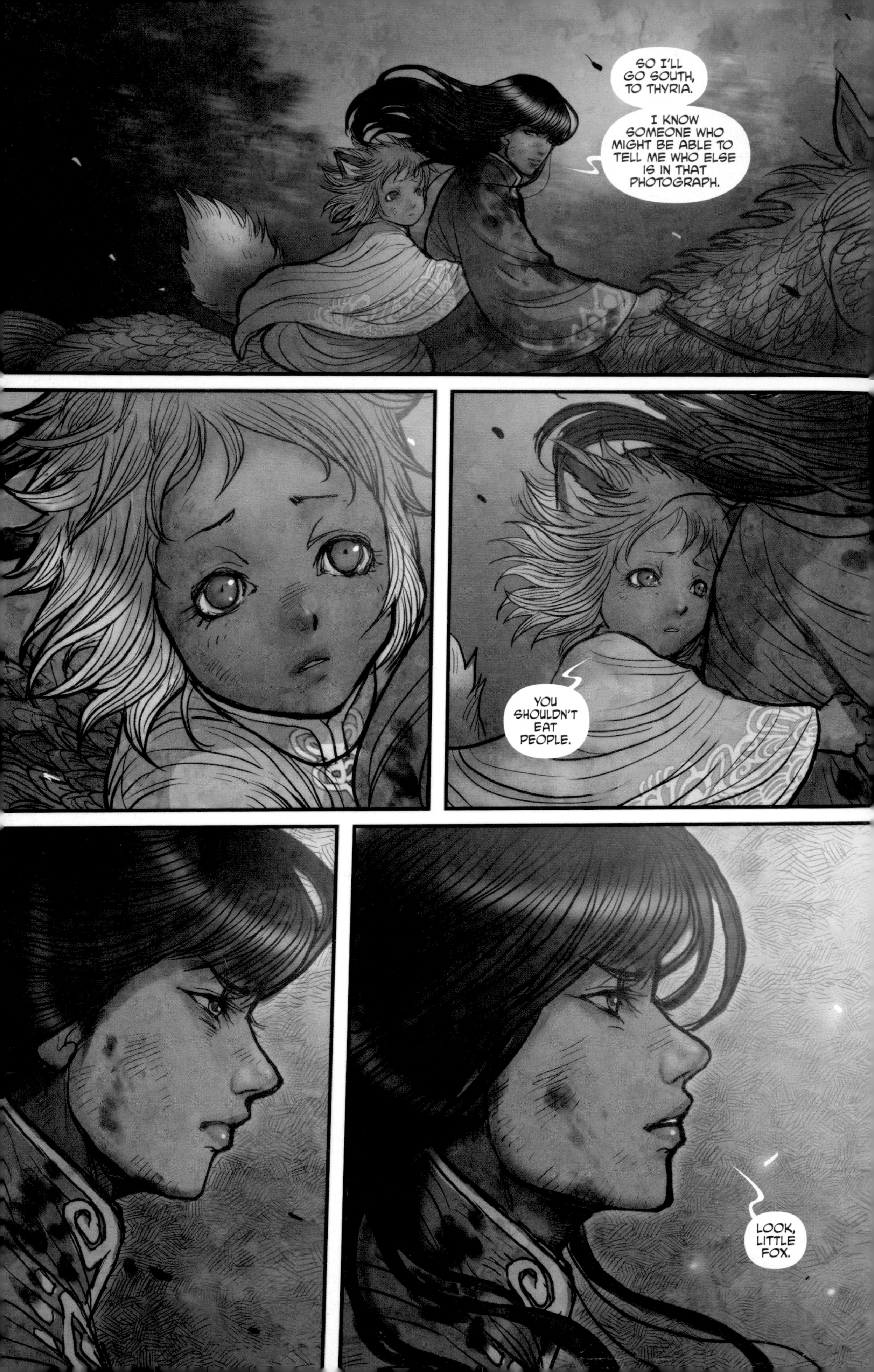
SO I'LL GO SOUTH, TO THYRIA.
I KNOW SOMEONE WHO MIGHT BE ABLE TO TELL ME WHO ELSE IS IN THAT PHOTOGRAPH.
YOU SHOULDN'T EAT PEOPLE.
LOOK, LITTLE FOX.

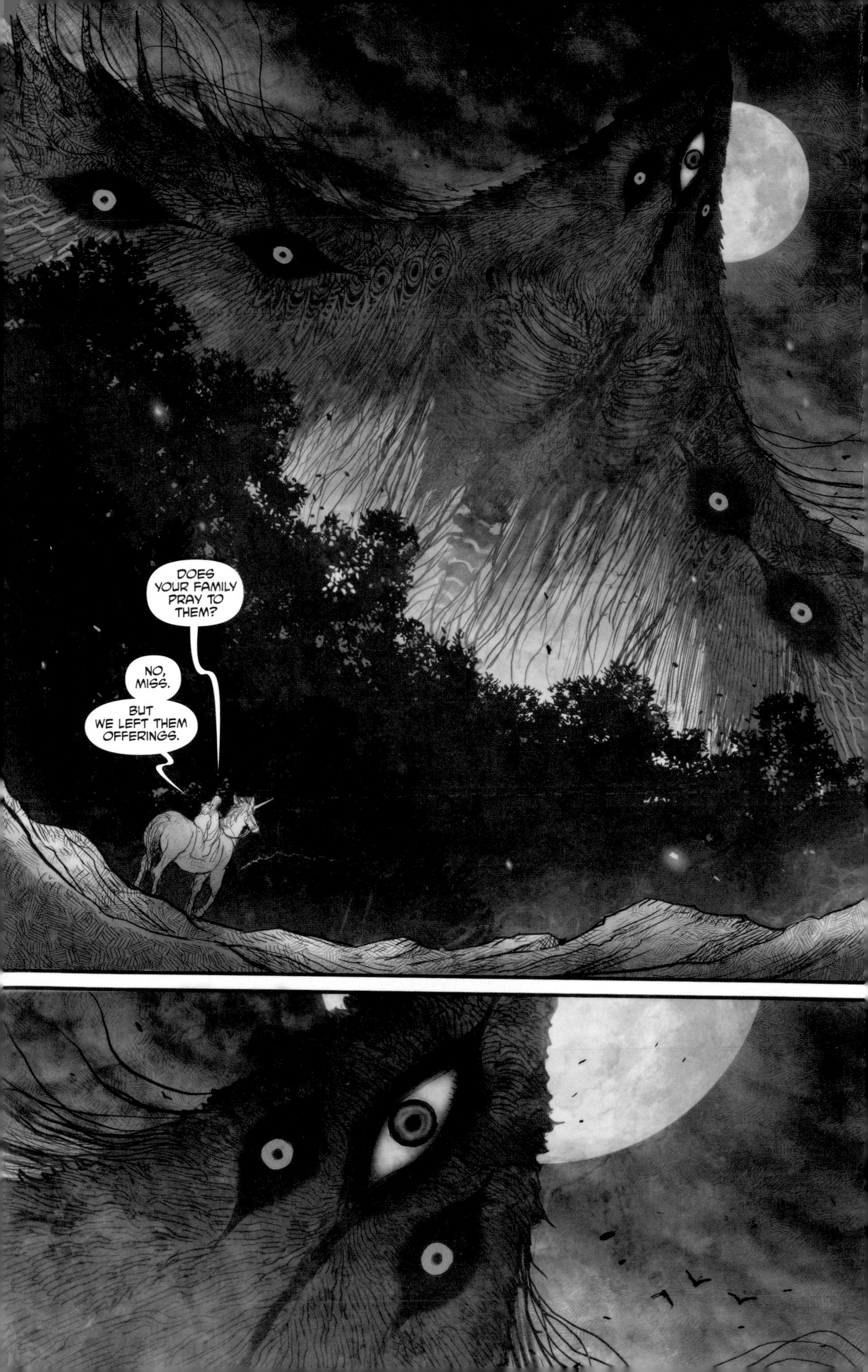
DOES YOUR FAMILY PRAY TO THEM?
NO, MISS.
BUT WE LEFT THEM OFFERINGS.

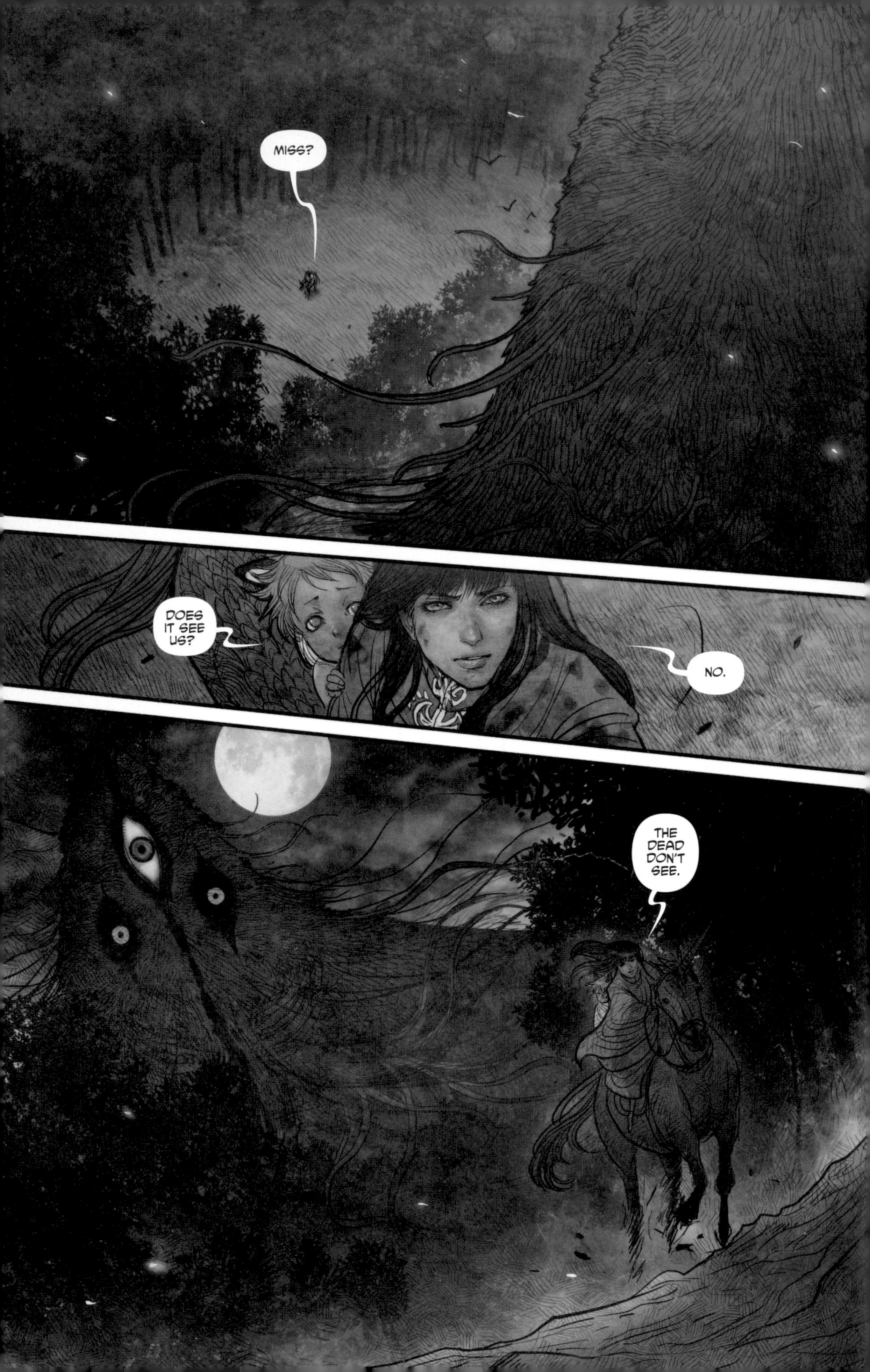
MISS?
DOES IT SEE US?
NO.
THE DEAD DON'T SEE.

An excerpt of a lecture from the esteemed **Professor Tam Tam**, former first record-keeper of the Is'hami Temple, and learned contemporary of Namron Black Claw...

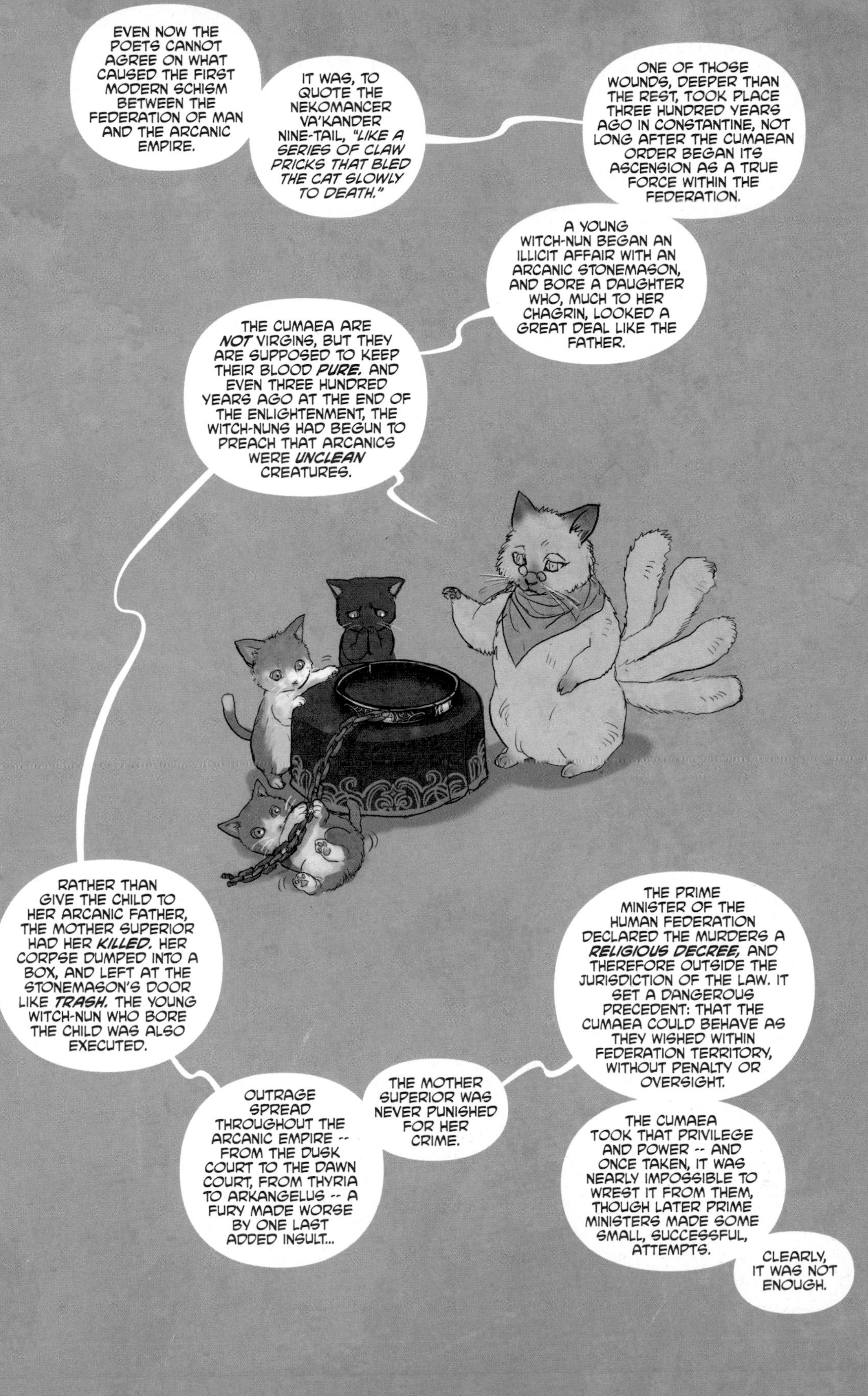
EVEN NOW THE POETS CANNOT AGREE ON WHAT CAUSED THE FIRST MODERN SCHISM BETWEEN THE FEDERATION OF MAN AND THE ARCANIC EMPIRE.
IT WAS, TO QUOTE THE NEKOMANCER VA'KANDER NINE-TAIL, *"LIKE A SERIES OF CLAW PRICKS THAT BLED THE CAT SLOWLY TO DEATH."*
ONE OF THOSE WOUNDS, DEEPER THAN THE REST, TOOK PLACE THREE HUNDRED YEARS AGO IN CONSTANTINE, NOT LONG AFTER THE CUMAEAN ORDER BEGAN ITS ASCENSION AS A TRUE FORCE WITHIN THE FEDERATION.
A YOUNG WITCH-NUN BEGAN AN ILLICIT AFFAIR WITH AN ARCANIC STONEMASON, AND BORE A DAUGHTER WHO, MUCH TO HER CHAGRIN, LOOKED A GREAT DEAL LIKE THE FATHER.
THE CUMAEA ARE ***NOT*** VIRGINS, BUT THEY ARE SUPPOSED TO KEEP THEIR BLOOD ***PURE.*** AND EVEN THREE HUNDRED YEARS AGO AT THE END OF THE ENLIGHTENMENT, THE WITCH-NUNS HAD BEGUN TO PREACH THAT ARCANICS WERE ***UNCLEAN*** CREATURES.
RATHER THAN GIVE THE CHILD TO HER ARCANIC FATHER, THE MOTHER SUPERIOR HAD HER ***KILLED.*** HER CORPSE DUMPED INTO A BOX, AND LEFT AT THE STONEMASON'S DOOR LIKE ***TRASH.*** THE YOUNG WITCH-NUN WHO BORE THE CHILD WAS ALSO EXECUTED.
OUTRAGE SPREAD THROUGHOUT THE ARCANIC EMPIRE -- FROM THE DUSK COURT TO THE DAWN COURT, FROM THYRIA TO ARKANGELUS -- A FURY MADE WORSE BY ONE LAST ADDED INSULT...
THE MOTHER SUPERIOR WAS NEVER PUNISHED FOR HER CRIME.
THE PRIME MINISTER OF THE HUMAN FEDERATION DECLARED THE MURDERS A ***RELIGIOUS DECREE,*** AND THEREFORE OUTSIDE THE JURISDICTION OF THE LAW. IT SET A DANGEROUS PRECEDENT: THAT THE CUMAEA COULD BEHAVE AS THEY WISHED WITHIN FEDERATION TERRITORY, WITHOUT PENALTY OR OVERSIGHT.
THE CUMAEA TOOK THAT PRIVILEGE AND POWER -- AND ONCE TAKEN, IT WAS NEARLY IMPOSSIBLE TO WREST IT FROM THEM, THOUGH LATER PRIME MINISTERS MADE SOME SMALL, SUCCESSFUL, ATTEMPTS.
CLEARLY, IT WAS NOT ENOUGH.

CHAPTER FOUR

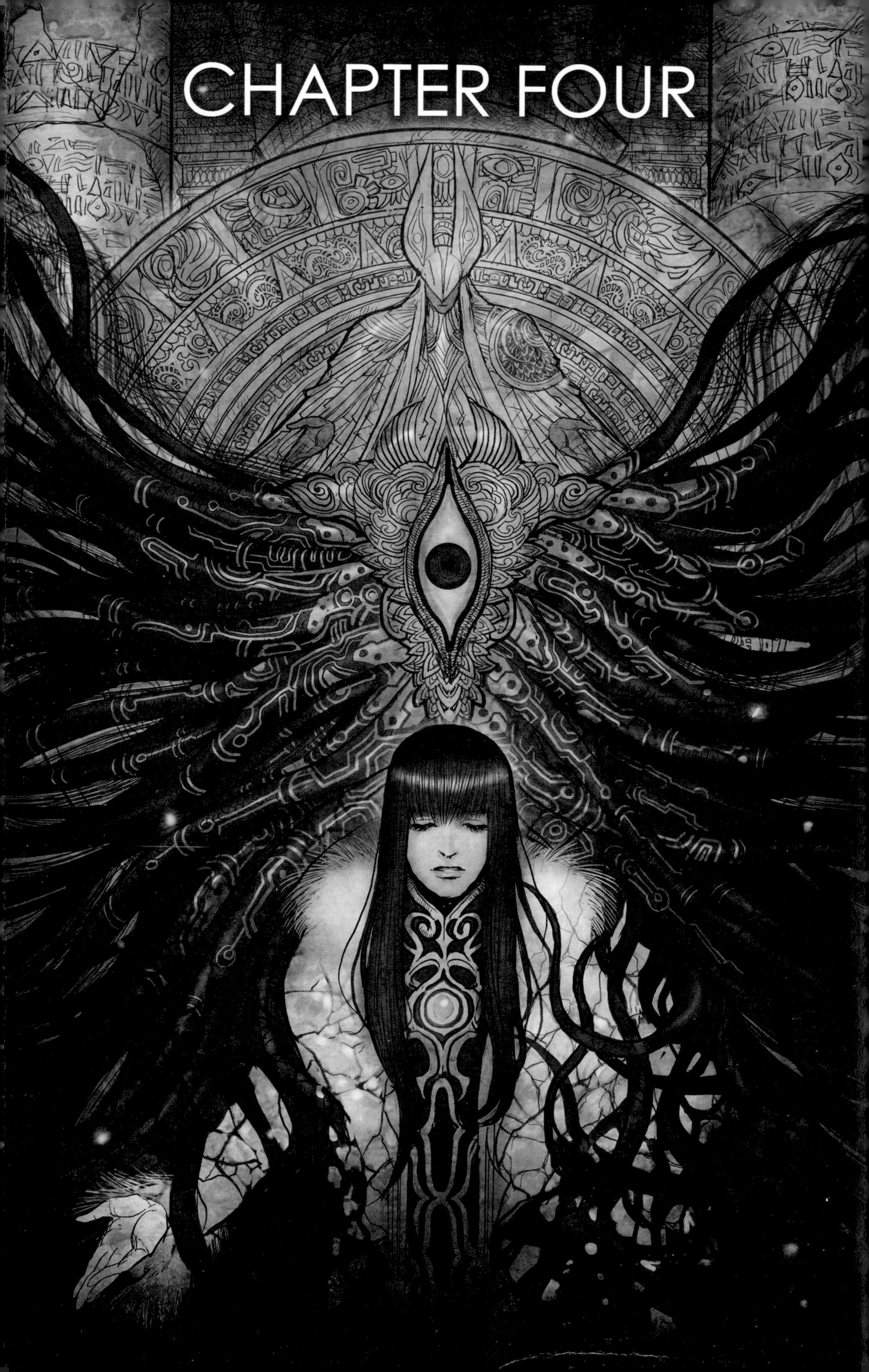

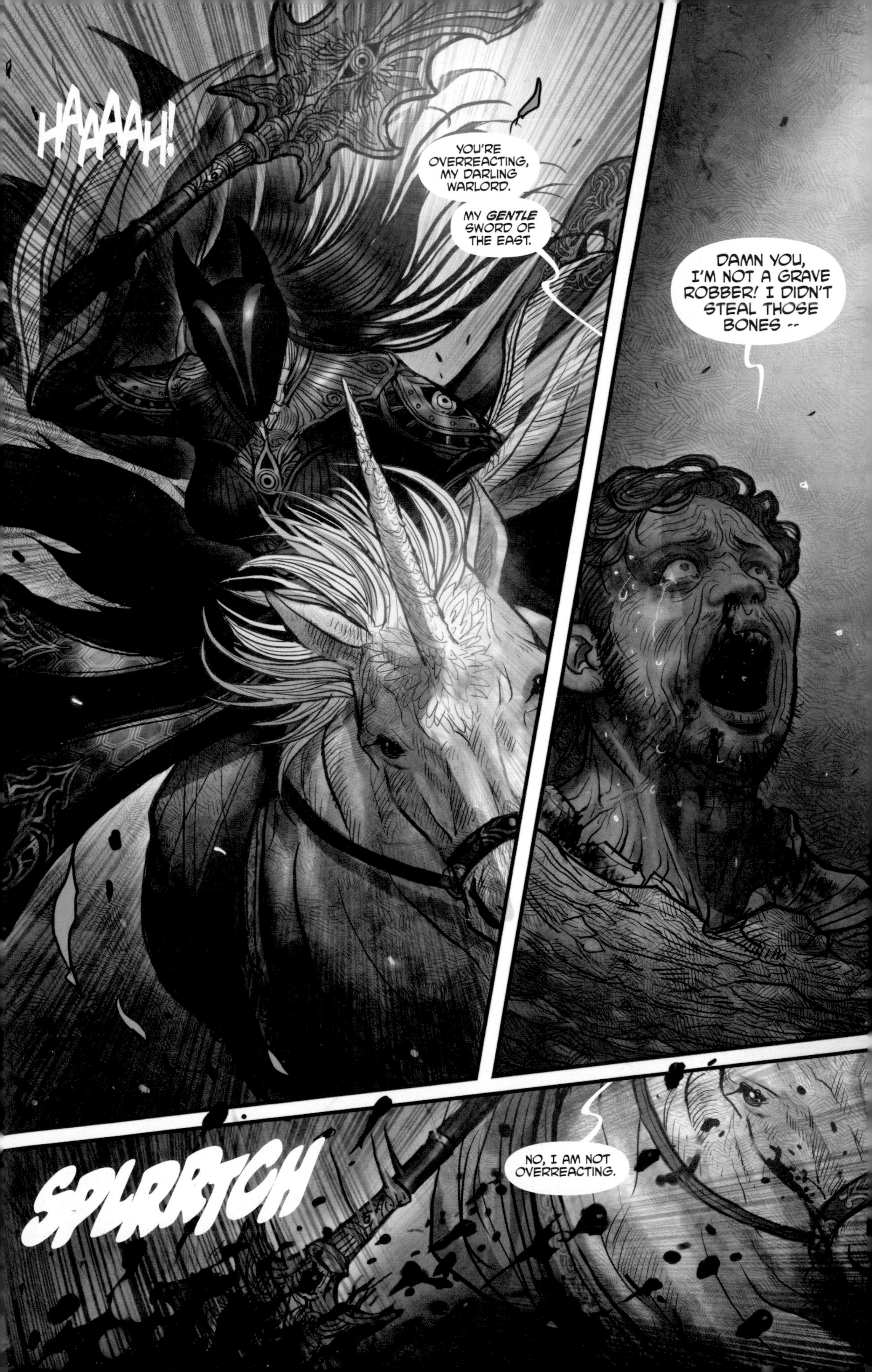
HAAAAH!
YOU'RE OVERREACTING, MY DARLING WARLORD.
MY GENTLE SWORD OF THE EAST.
DAMN YOU, I'M NOT A GRAVE ROBBER! I DIDN'T STEAL THOSE BONES --
SPLRRTCH
NO, I AM NOT OVERREACTING.

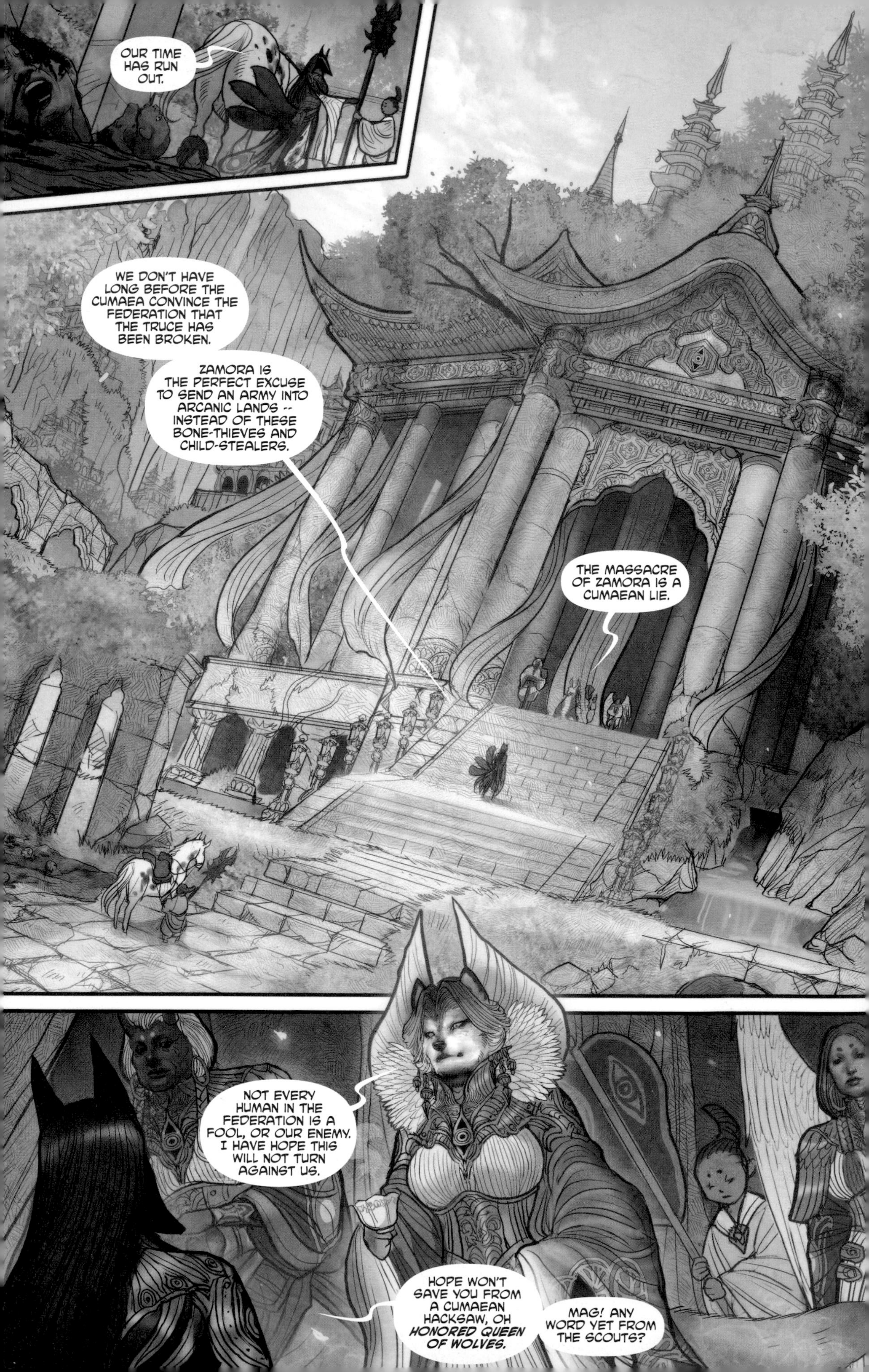
OUR TIME HAS RUN OUT.
WE DON'T HAVE LONG BEFORE THE CUMAEA CONVINCE THE FEDERATION THAT THE TRUCE HAS BEEN BROKEN.
ZAMORA IS THE PERFECT EXCUSE TO SEND AN ARMY INTO ARCANIC LANDS -- INSTEAD OF THESE BONE-THIEVES AND CHILD-STEALERS.
THE MASSACRE OF ZAMORA IS A CUMAEAN LIE.
NOT EVERY HUMAN IN THE FEDERATION IS A FOOL, OR OUR ENEMY. I HAVE HOPE THIS WILL NOT TURN AGAINST US.
HOPE WON'T SAVE YOU FROM A CUMAEAN HACKSAW, OH ***HONORED QUEEN OF WOLVES.***
MAG! ANY WORD YET FROM THE SCOUTS?

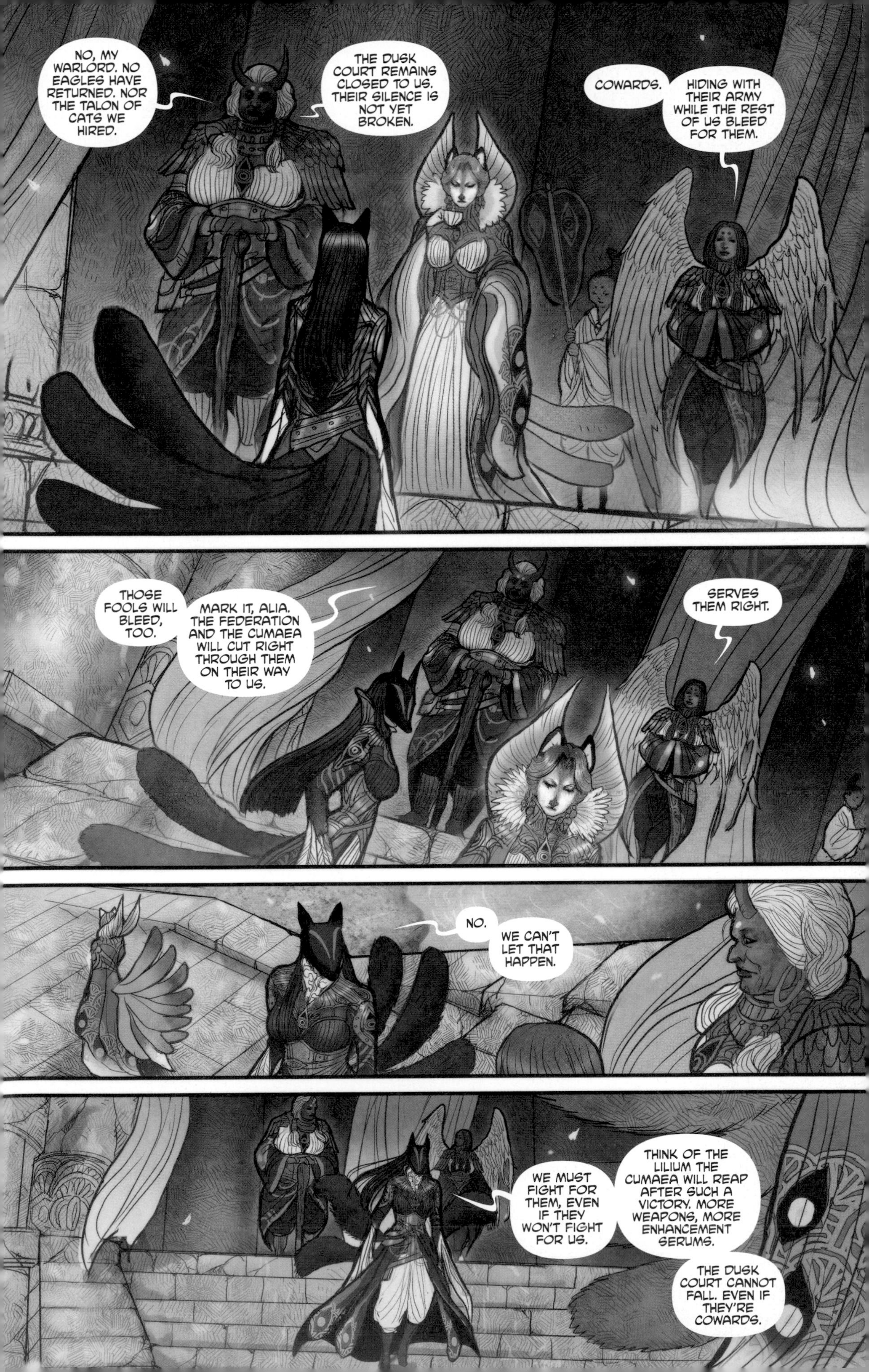
NO, MY WARLORD. NO EAGLES HAVE RETURNED. NOR THE TALON OF CATS WE HIRED.
THE DUSK COURT REMAINS CLOSED TO US. THEIR SILENCE IS NOT YET BROKEN.
COWARDS.
HIDING WITH THEIR ARMY WHILE THE REST OF US BLEED FOR THEM.
THOSE FOOLS WILL BLEED, TOO.
MARK IT, ALIA. THE FEDERATION AND THE CUMAEA WILL CUT RIGHT THROUGH THEM ON THEIR WAY TO US.
SERVES THEM RIGHT.
NO.
WE CAN'T LET THAT HAPPEN.
WE MUST FIGHT FOR THEM, EVEN IF THEY WON'T FIGHT FOR US.
THINK OF THE LILIUM THE CUMAEA WILL REAP AFTER SUCH A VICTORY. MORE WEAPONS, MORE ENHANCEMENT SERUMS.
THE DUSK COURT CANNOT FALL. EVEN IF THEY'RE COWARDS.

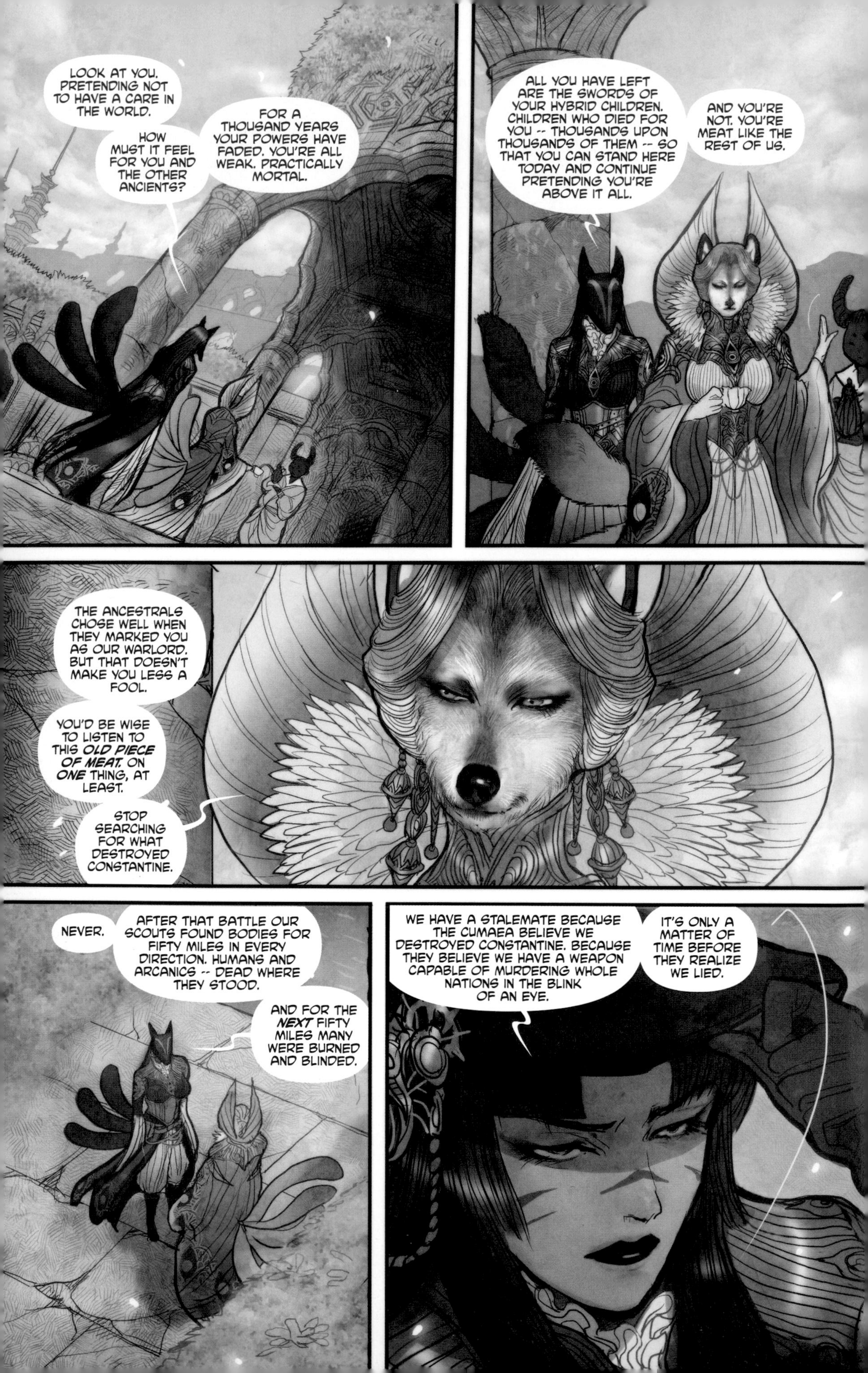
LOOK AT YOU. PRETENDING NOT TO HAVE A CARE IN THE WORLD.
HOW MUST IT FEEL FOR YOU AND THE OTHER ANCIENTS?
FOR A THOUSAND YEARS YOUR POWERS HAVE FADED. YOU'RE ALL WEAK. PRACTICALLY MORTAL.
ALL YOU HAVE LEFT ARE THE SWORDS OF YOUR HYBRID CHILDREN. CHILDREN WHO DIED FOR YOU -- THOUSANDS UPON THOUSANDS OF THEM -- SO THAT YOU CAN STAND HERE TODAY AND CONTINUE PRETENDING YOU'RE ABOVE IT ALL.
AND YOU'RE NOT. YOU'RE MEAT LIKE THE REST OF US.
THE ANCESTRALS CHOSE WELL WHEN THEY MARKED YOU AS OUR WARLORD. BUT THAT DOESN'T MAKE YOU LESS A FOOL.
YOU'D BE WISE TO LISTEN TO THIS OLD PIECE OF MEAT. ON ONE THING, AT LEAST.
STOP SEARCHING FOR WHAT DESTROYED CONSTANTINE.
NEVER.
AFTER THAT BATTLE OUR SCOUTS FOUND BODIES FOR FIFTY MILES IN EVERY DIRECTION. HUMANS AND ARCANICS -- DEAD WHERE THEY STOOD.
AND FOR THE NEXT FIFTY MILES MANY WERE BURNED AND BLINDED.
WE HAVE A STALEMATE BECAUSE THE CUMAEA BELIEVE WE DESTROYED CONSTANTINE. BECAUSE THEY BELIEVE WE HAVE A WEAPON CAPABLE OF MURDERING WHOLE NATIONS IN THE BLINK OF AN EYE.
IT'S ONLY A MATTER OF TIME BEFORE THEY REALIZE WE LIED.

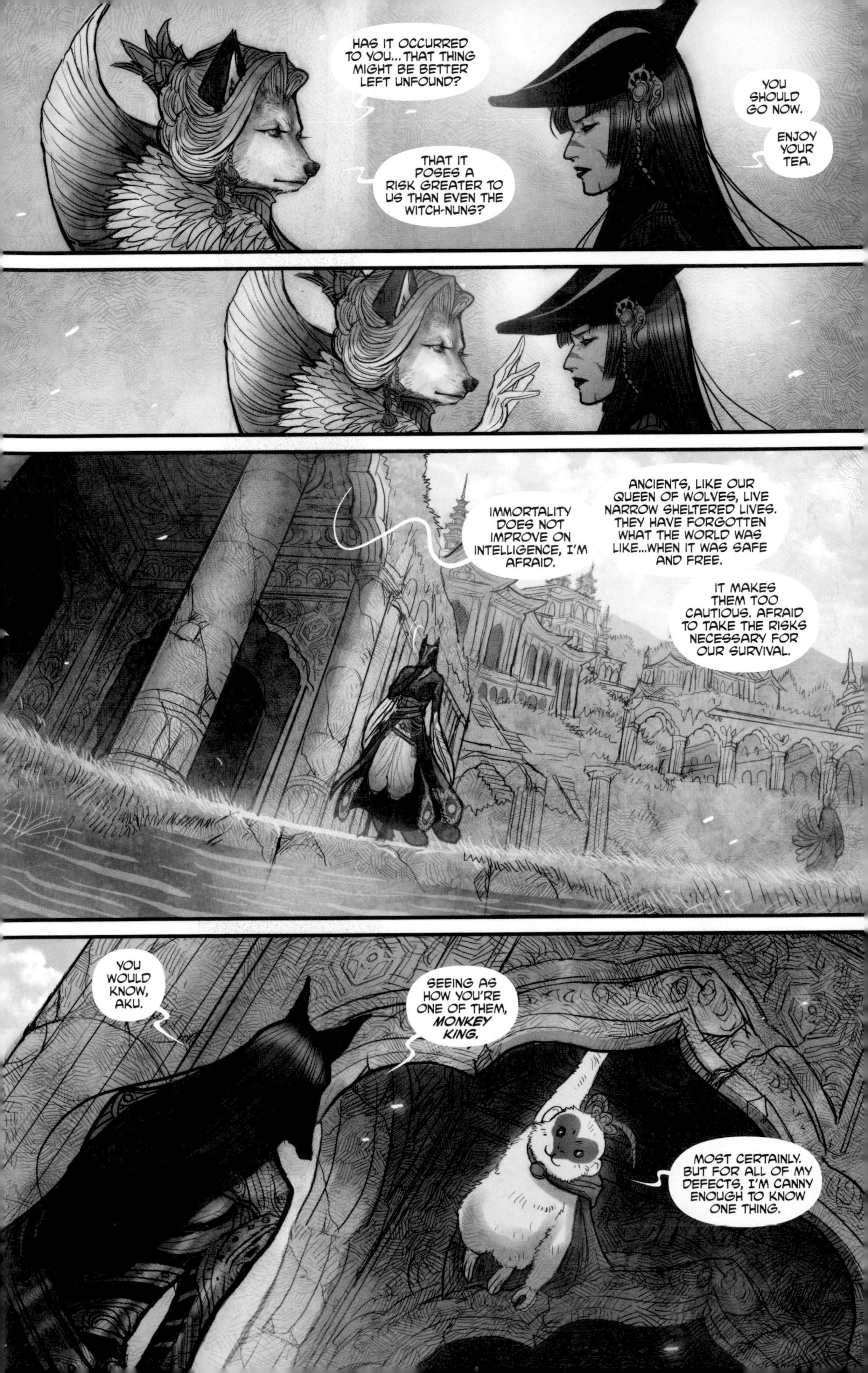
HAS IT OCCURRED TO YOU... THAT THING MIGHT BE BETTER LEFT UNFOUND?
THAT IT POSES A RISK GREATER TO US THAN EVEN THE WITCH-NUNS?
YOU SHOULD GO NOW.
ENJOY YOUR TEA.
IMMORTALITY DOES NOT IMPROVE ON INTELLIGENCE, I'M AFRAID.
ANCIENTS, LIKE OUR QUEEN OF WOLVES, LIVE NARROW SHELTERED LIVES. THEY HAVE FORGOTTEN WHAT THE WORLD WAS LIKE...WHEN IT WAS SAFE AND FREE.
IT MAKES THEM TOO CAUTIOUS. AFRAID TO TAKE THE RISKS NECESSARY FOR OUR SURVIVAL.
YOU WOULD KNOW, AKU.
SEEING AS HOW YOU'RE ONE OF THEM, *MONKEY KING.*
MOST CERTAINLY. BUT FOR ALL OF MY DEFECTS, I'M CANNY ENOUGH TO KNOW ONE THING.

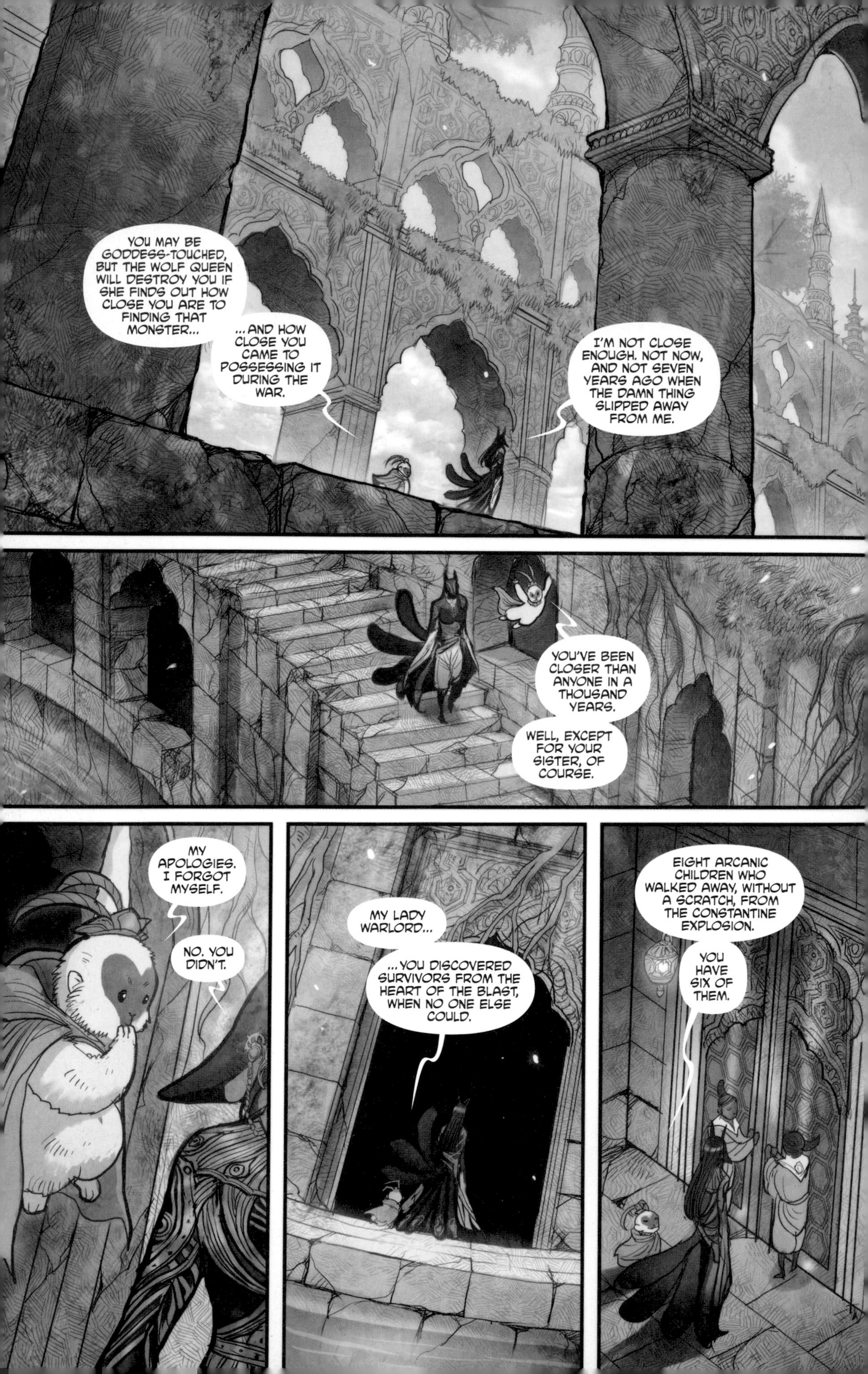
YOU MAY BE GODDESS-TOUCHED, BUT THE WOLF QUEEN WILL DESTROY YOU IF SHE FINDS OUT HOW CLOSE YOU ARE TO FINDING THAT MONSTER...
...AND HOW CLOSE YOU CAME TO POSSESSING IT DURING THE WAR.
I'M NOT CLOSE ENOUGH. NOT NOW, AND NOT SEVEN YEARS AGO WHEN THE DAMN THING SLIPPED AWAY FROM ME.
YOU'VE BEEN CLOSER THAN ANYONE IN A THOUSAND YEARS.
WELL, EXCEPT FOR YOUR SISTER, OF COURSE.
MY APOLOGIES. I FORGOT MYSELF.
NO. YOU DIDN'T.
MY LADY WARLORD...
...YOU DISCOVERED SURVIVORS FROM THE HEART OF THE BLAST, WHEN NO ONE ELSE COULD.
EIGHT ARCANIC CHILDREN WHO WALKED AWAY, WITHOUT A SCRATCH, FROM THE CONSTANTINE EXPLOSION.
YOU HAVE SIX OF THEM.

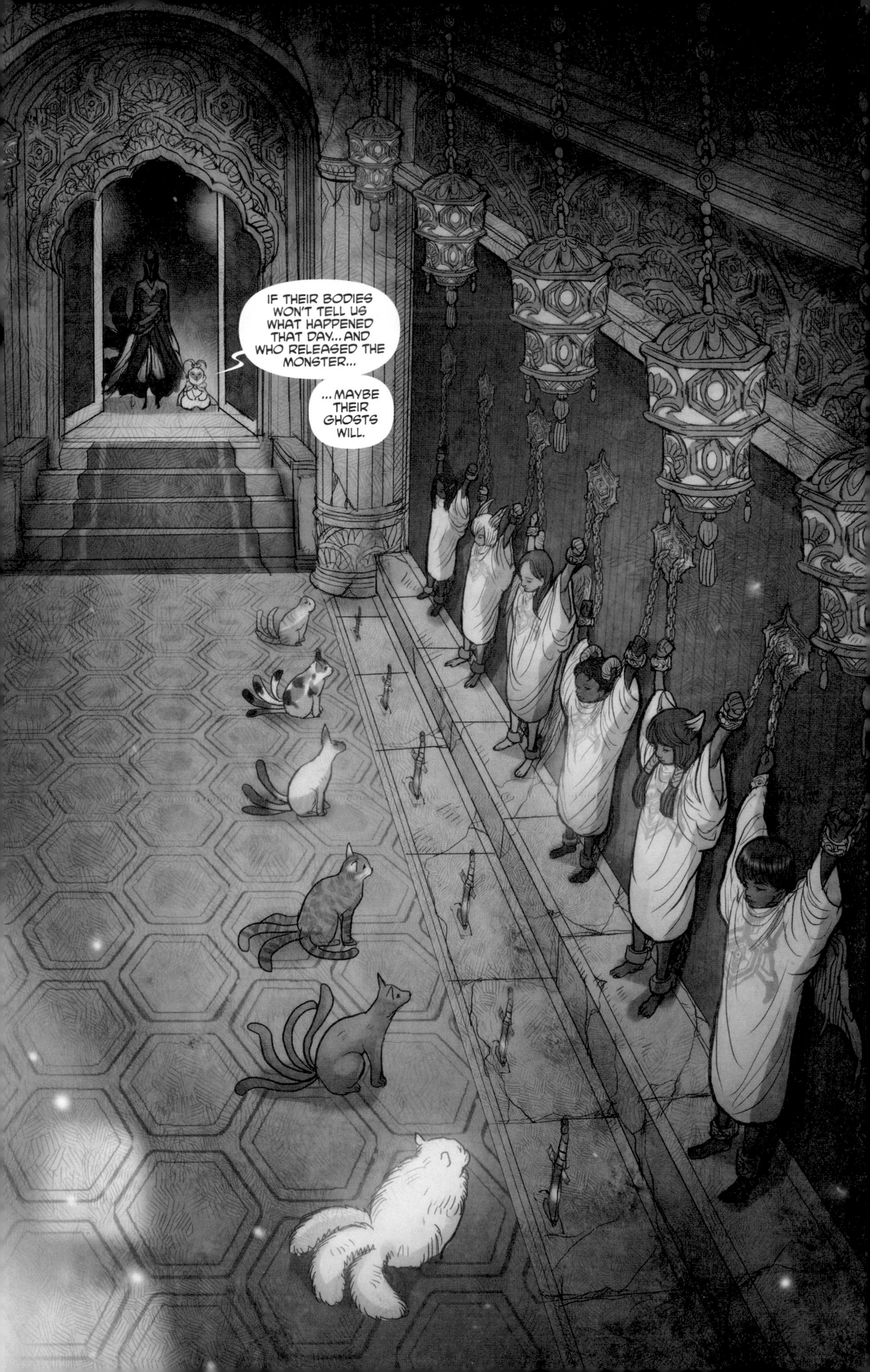
IF THEIR BODIES WON'T TELL US WHAT HAPPENED THAT DAY...AND WHO RELEASED THE MONSTER...
...MAYBE THEIR GHOSTS WILL.

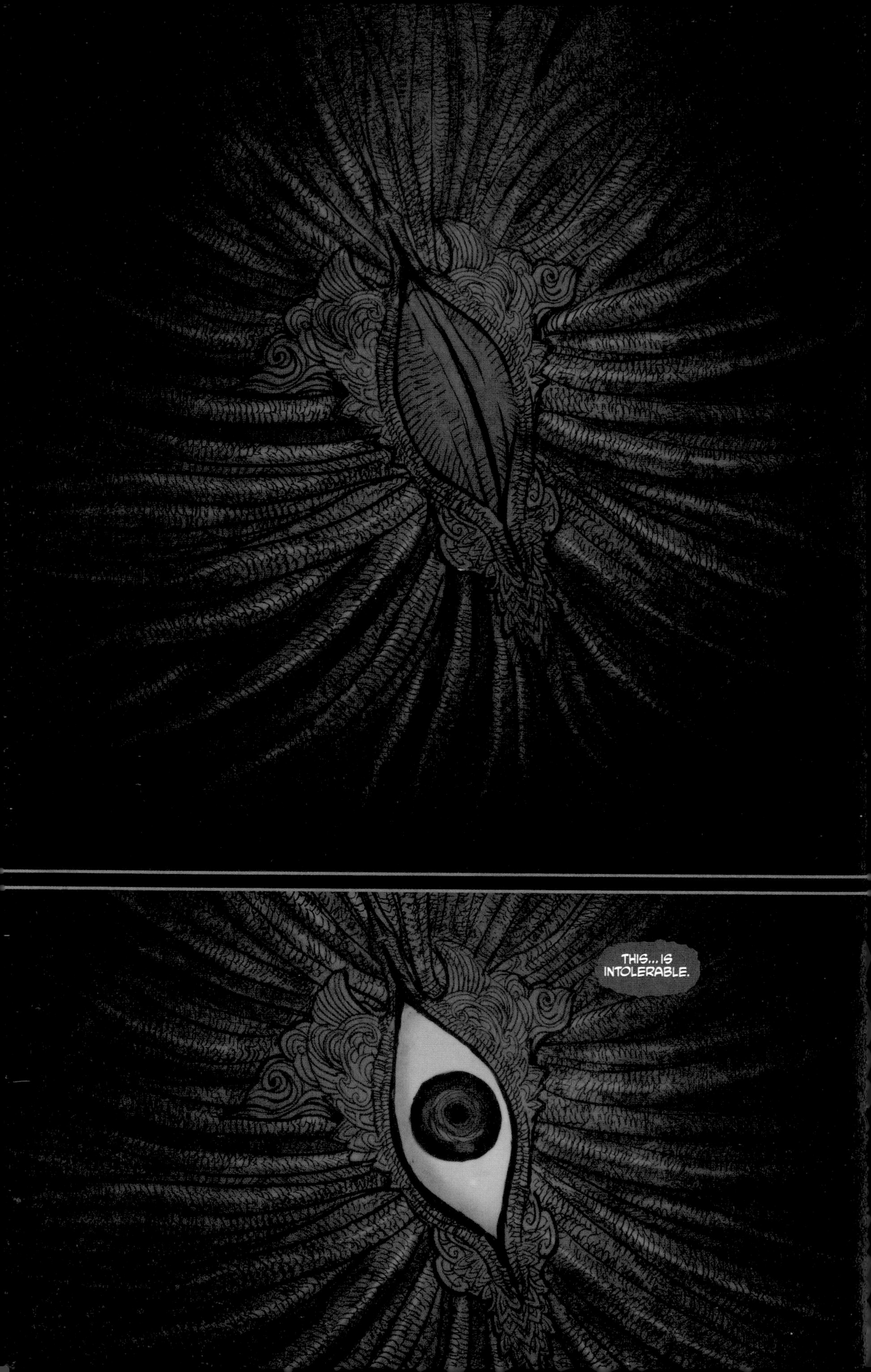
THIS... IS INTOLERABLE.

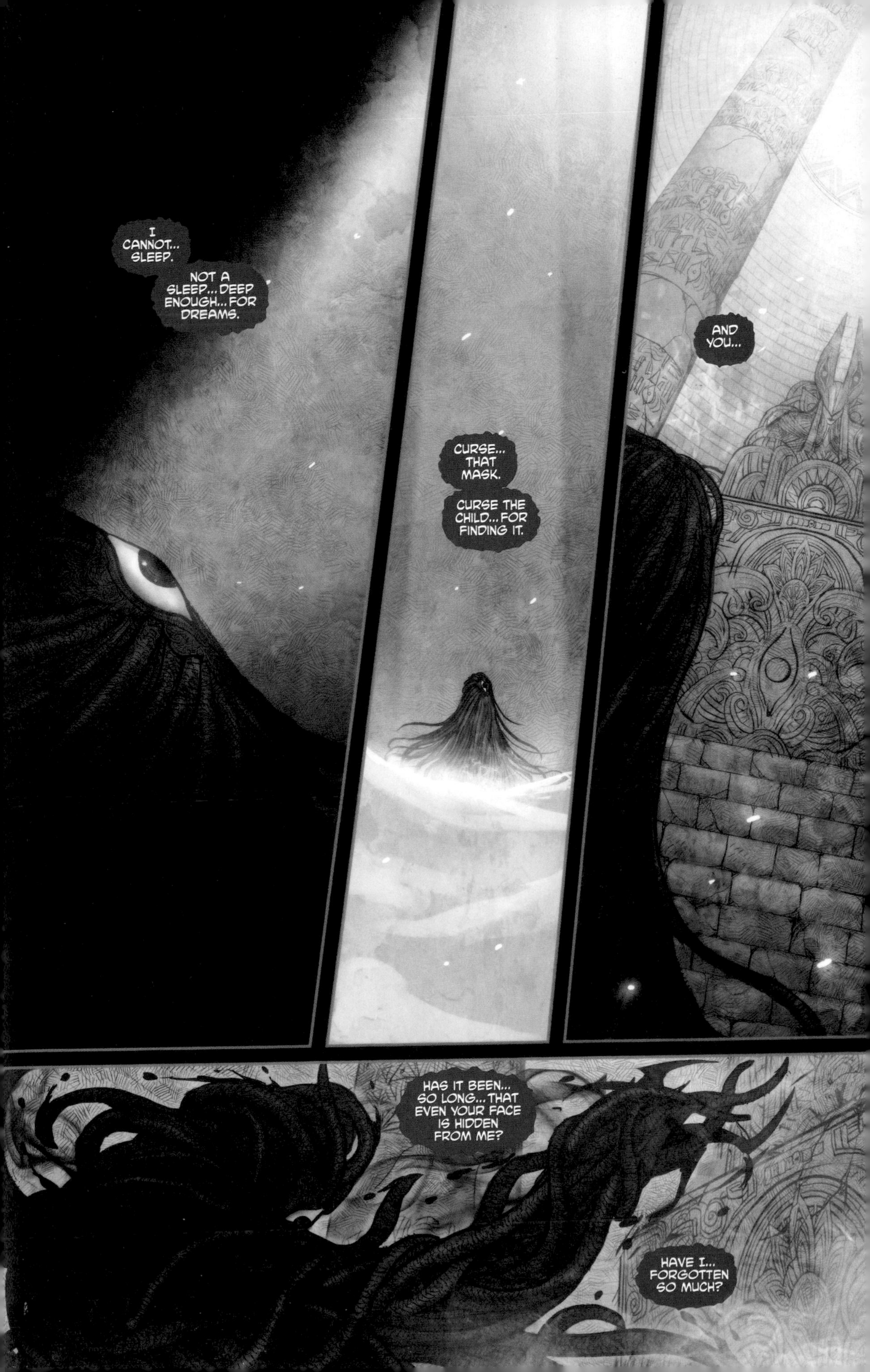
I CANNOT... SLEEP.
NOT A SLEEP... DEEP ENOUGH... FOR DREAMS.
CURSE... THAT MASK.
CURSE THE CHILD... FOR FINDING IT.
AND YOU...
HAS IT BEEN... SO LONG... THAT EVEN YOUR FACE IS HIDDEN FROM ME?
HAVE I... FORGOTTEN SO MUCH?

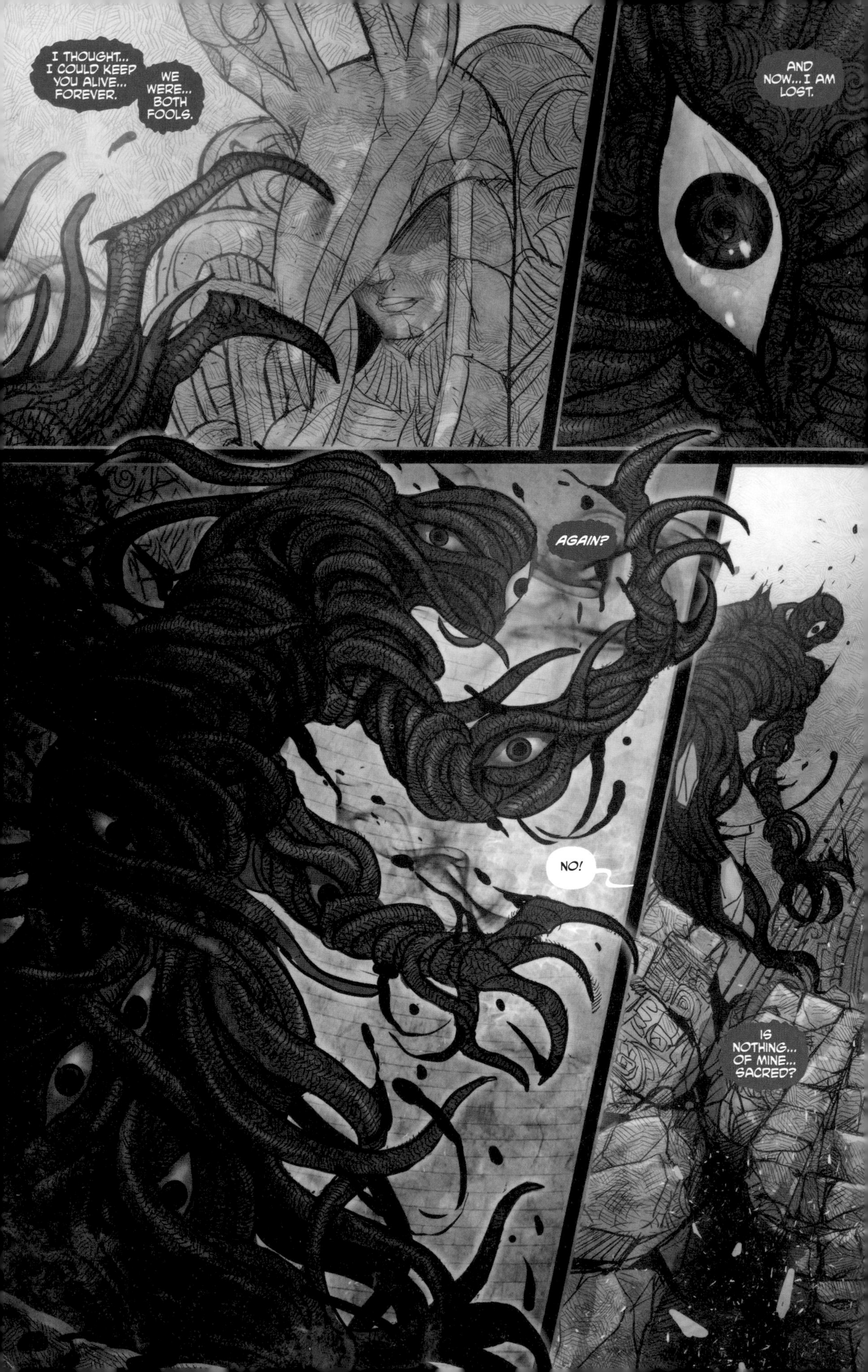
I THOUGHT... I COULD KEEP YOU ALIVE... FOREVER.
WE WERE... BOTH FOOLS.
AND NOW... I AM LOST.
AGAIN?
NO!
IS NOTHING... OF MINE... SACRED?

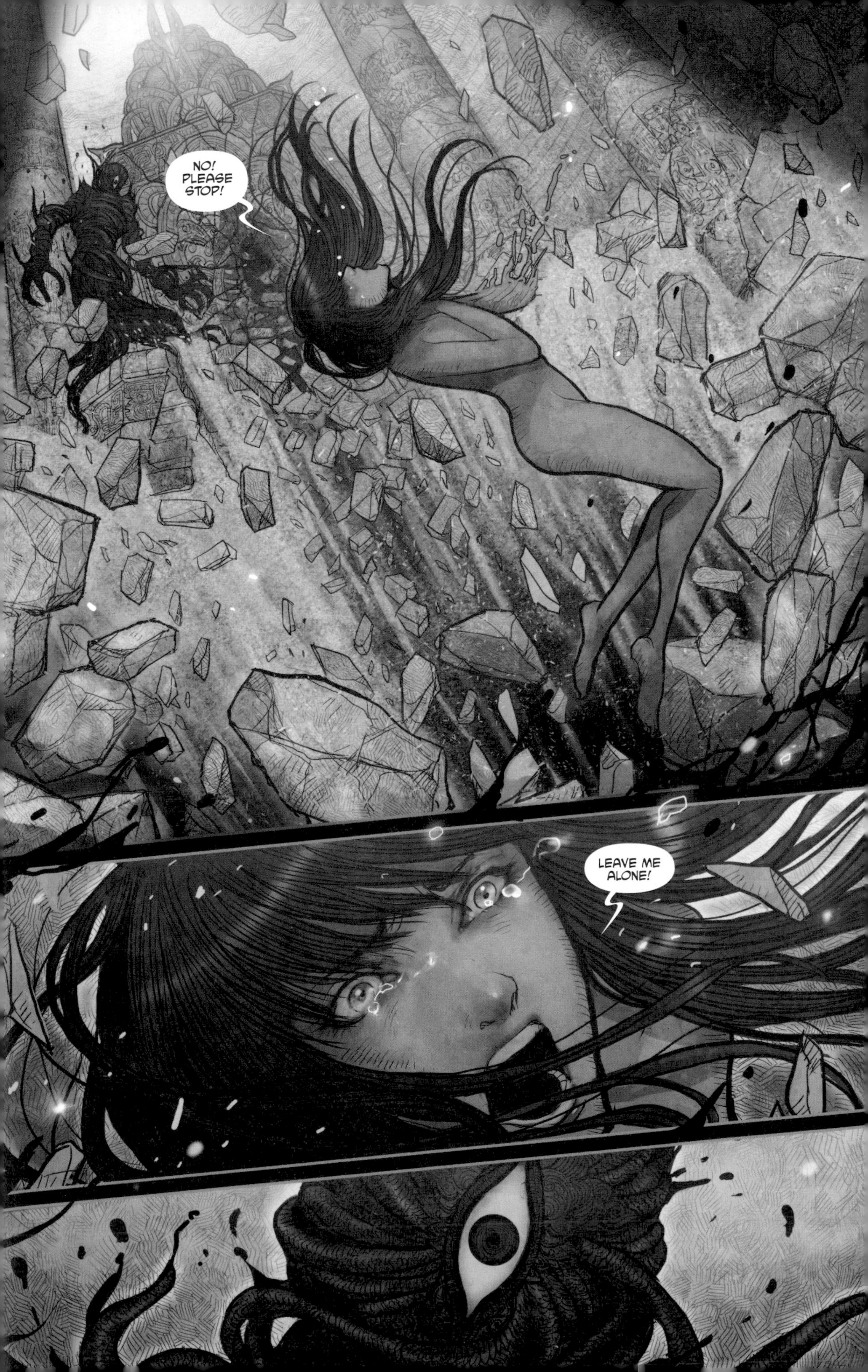
NO! PLEASE STOP!
LEAVE ME ALONE!

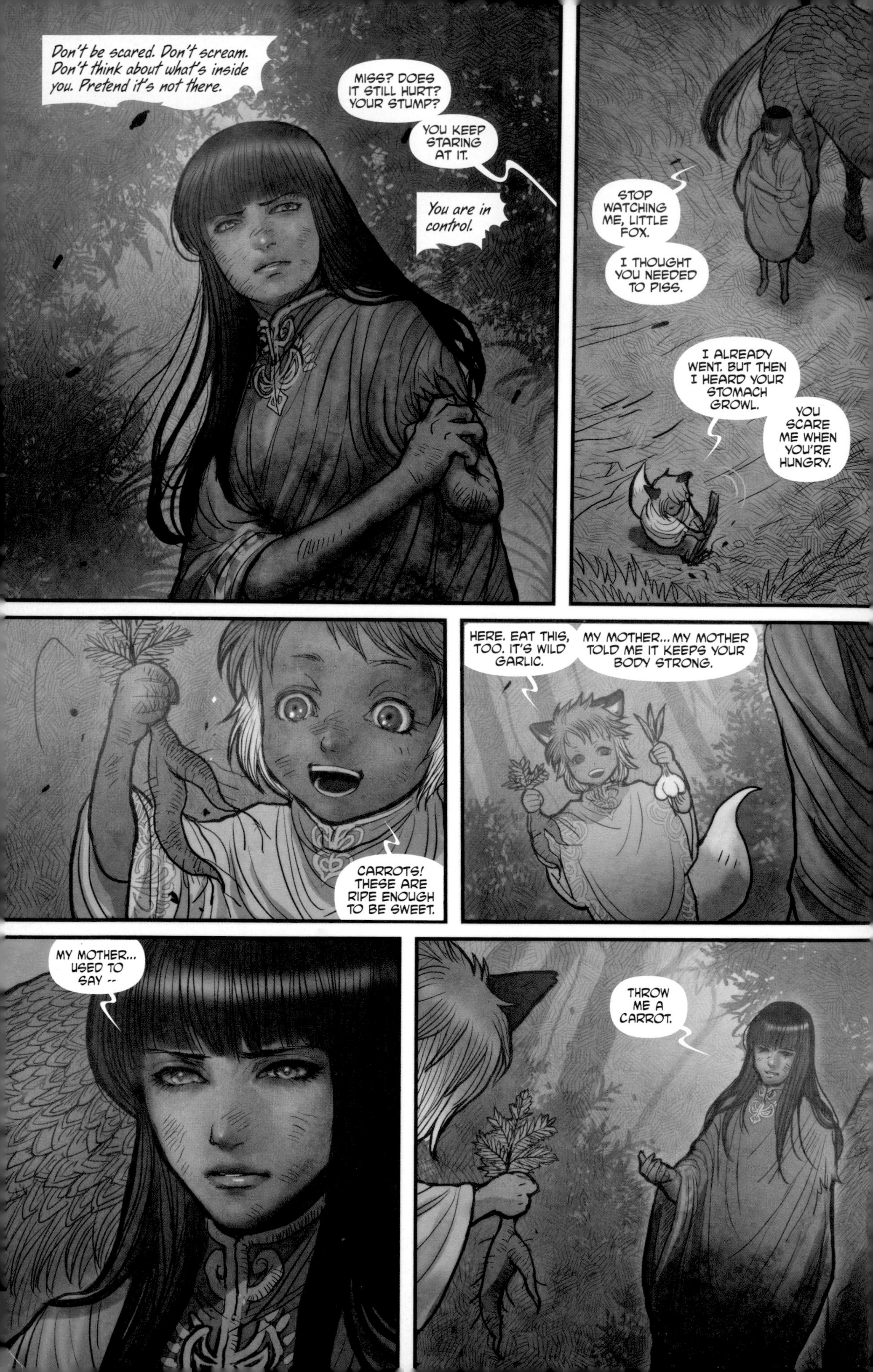
Don't be scared. Don't scream. Don't think about what's inside you. Pretend it's not there.
MISS? DOES IT STILL HURT? YOUR STUMP?
YOU KEEP STARING AT IT.
You are in control.
STOP WATCHING ME, LITTLE FOX.
I THOUGHT YOU NEEDED TO PISS.
I ALREADY WENT. BUT THEN I HEARD YOUR STOMACH GROWL.
YOU SCARE ME WHEN YOU'RE HUNGRY.
CARROTS! THESE ARE RIPE ENOUGH TO BE SWEET.
HERE. EAT THIS, TOO. IT'S WILD GARLIC.
MY MOTHER... MY MOTHER TOLD ME IT KEEPS YOUR BODY STRONG.
MY MOTHER... USED TO SAY --
THROW ME A CARROT.

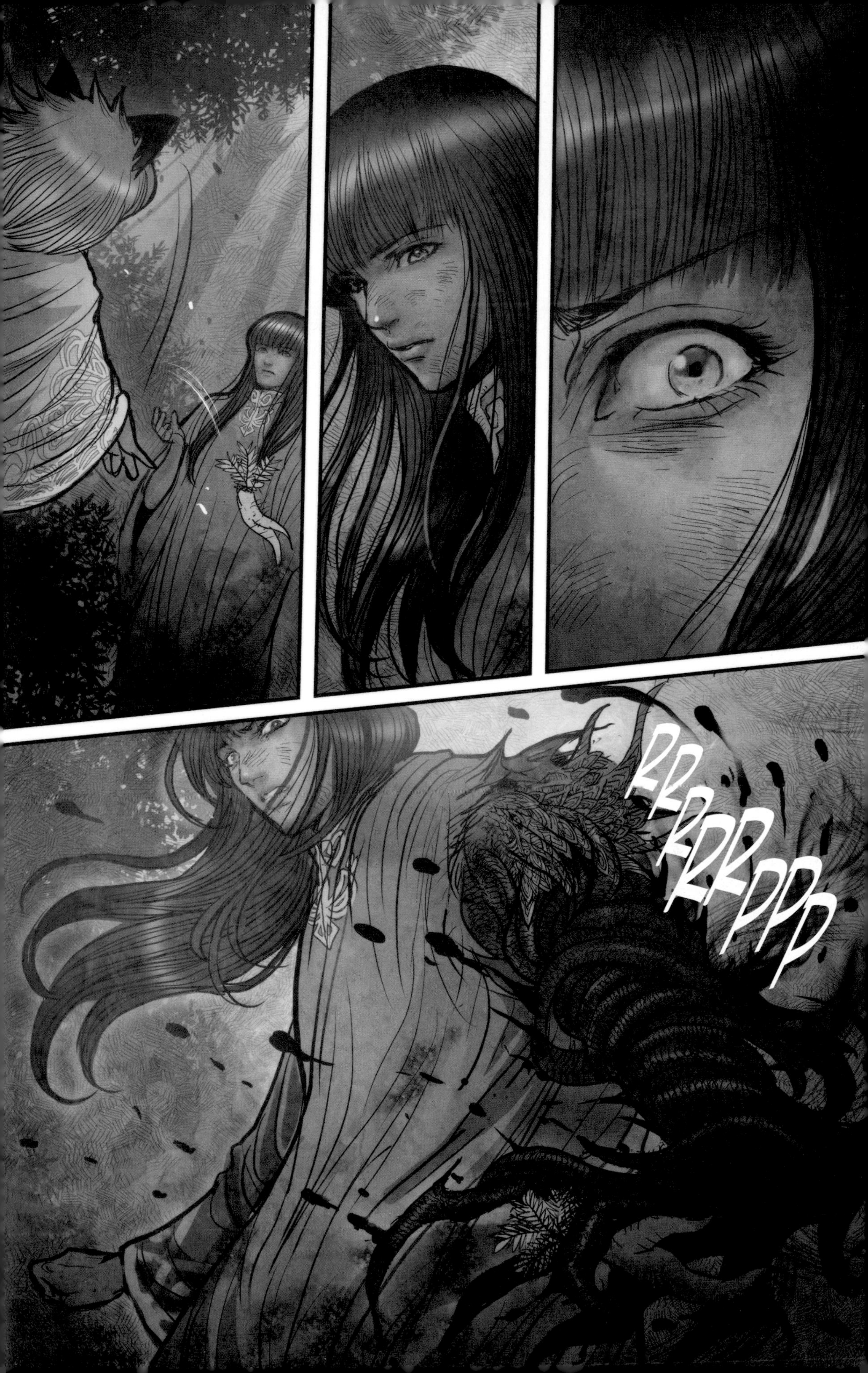
RRRRRRRPPPP

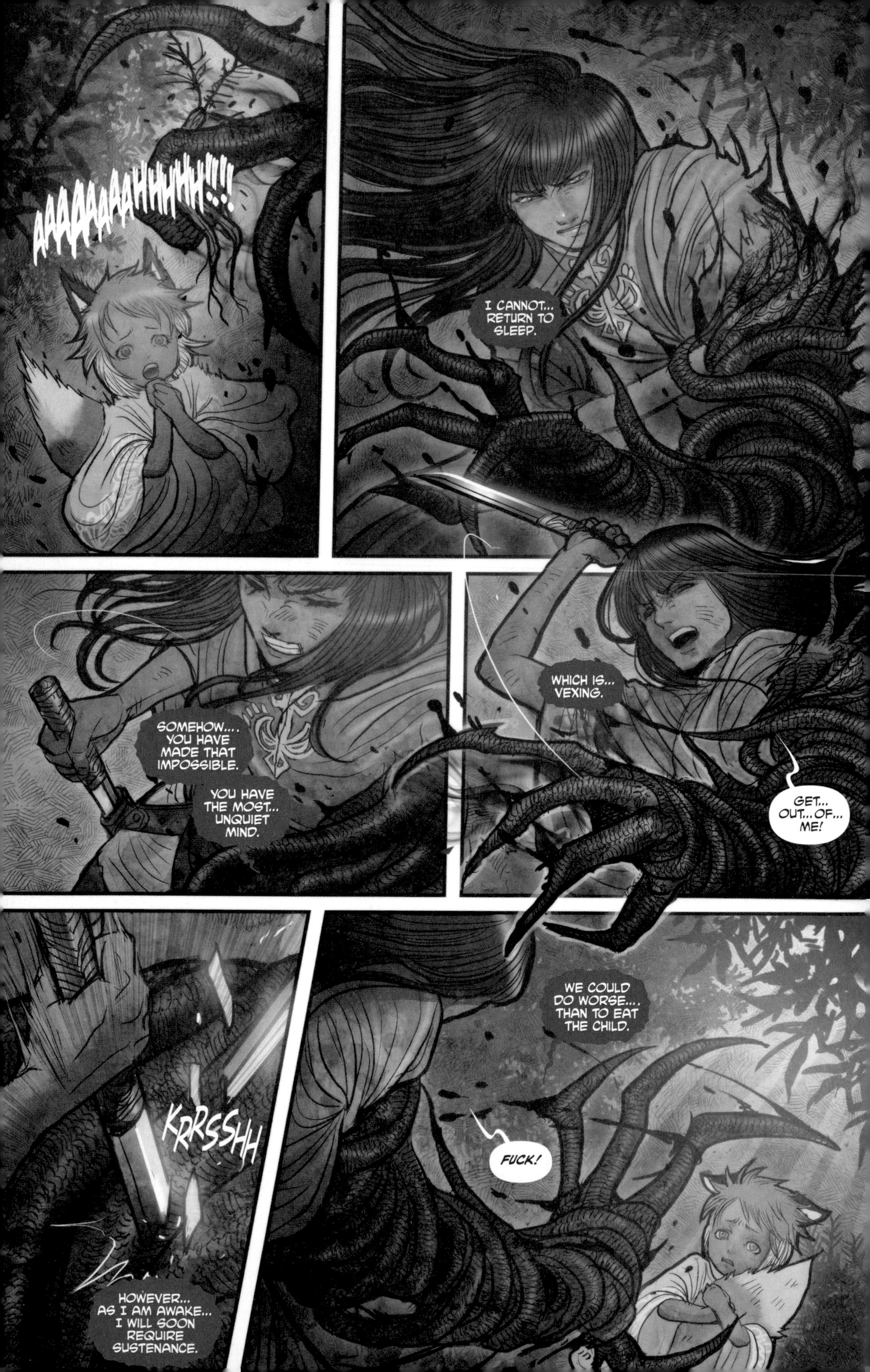
AAAAAAAAHHHHHH!!!!
I CANNOT... RETURN TO SLEEP.
SOMEHOW... YOU HAVE MADE THAT IMPOSSIBLE.
YOU HAVE THE MOST... UNQUIET MIND.
WHICH IS... VEXING.
GET... OUT... OF... ME!
KRRSSHH
HOWEVER... AS I AM AWAKE... I WILL SOON REQUIRE SUSTENANCE.
WE COULD DO WORSE... THAN TO EAT THE CHILD.
FUCK!

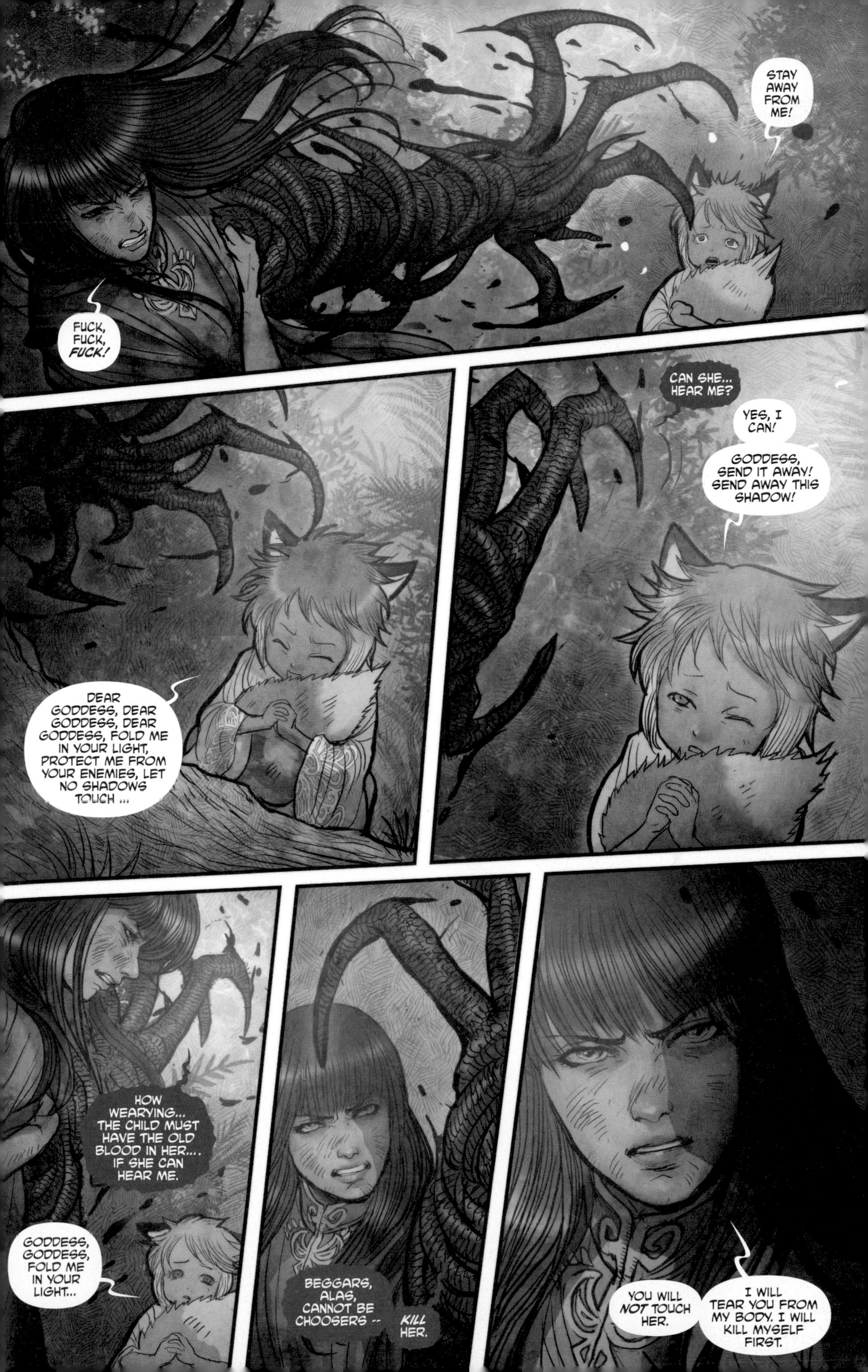

STAY AWAY FROM ME!
FUCK, FUCK, *FUCK!*
DEAR GODDESS, DEAR GODDESS, DEAR GODDESS, FOLD ME IN YOUR LIGHT, PROTECT ME FROM YOUR ENEMIES, LET NO SHADOWS TOUCH ...
CAN SHE... HEAR ME?
YES, I CAN!
GODDESS, SEND IT AWAY! SEND AWAY THIS SHADOW!
HOW WEARYING... THE CHILD MUST HAVE THE OLD BLOOD IN HER... IF SHE CAN HEAR ME.
GODDESS, GODDESS, FOLD ME IN YOUR LIGHT...
BEGGARS, ALAS, CANNOT BE CHOOSERS --
KILL HER.
YOU WILL *NOT* TOUCH HER.
I WILL TEAR YOU FROM MY BODY. I WILL KILL MYSELF FIRST.

YOU... CANNOT STOP ME. YOU... HAVE NO POWER OVER ME.

I AM A GOD.

SPIT ON THAT. IF YOU'RE SO GODLIKE THEN WHY THE *FUCK* ARE YOU LIVING INSIDE *ME?*

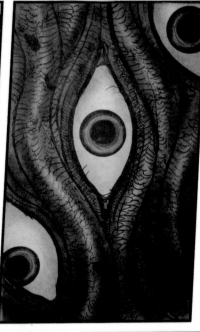

RIGHT.

STAY HERE, KIPPA. AND KEEP PRAYING.

I'M GOING HUNTING.

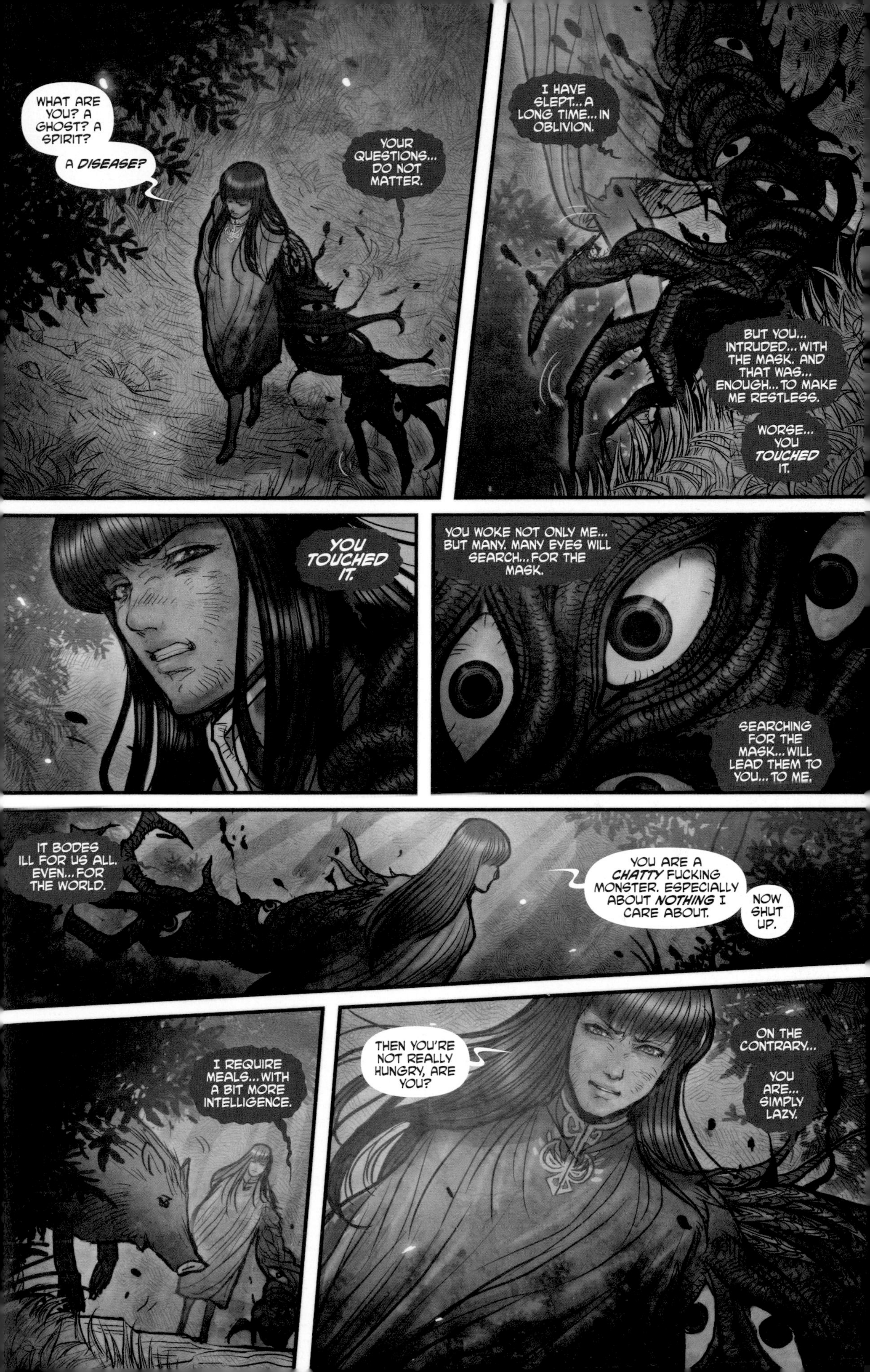
WHAT ARE YOU? A GHOST? A SPIRIT?
A DISEASE?
YOUR QUESTIONS... DO NOT MATTER.
I HAVE SLEPT... A LONG TIME... IN OBLIVION.
BUT YOU... INTRUDED... WITH THE MASK. AND THAT WAS... ENOUGH... TO MAKE ME RESTLESS.
WORSE... YOU TOUCHED IT.
YOU TOUCHED IT.
YOU WOKE NOT ONLY ME... BUT MANY. MANY EYES WILL SEARCH... FOR THE MASK.
SEARCHING FOR THE MASK... WILL LEAD THEM TO YOU... TO ME.
IT BODES ILL FOR US ALL. EVEN... FOR THE WORLD.
YOU ARE A CHATTY FUCKING MONSTER. ESPECIALLY ABOUT NOTHING I CARE ABOUT.
NOW SHUT UP.
I REQUIRE MEALS... WITH A BIT MORE INTELLIGENCE.
THEN YOU'RE NOT REALLY HUNGRY, ARE YOU?
ON THE CONTRARY...
YOU ARE... SIMPLY LAZY.

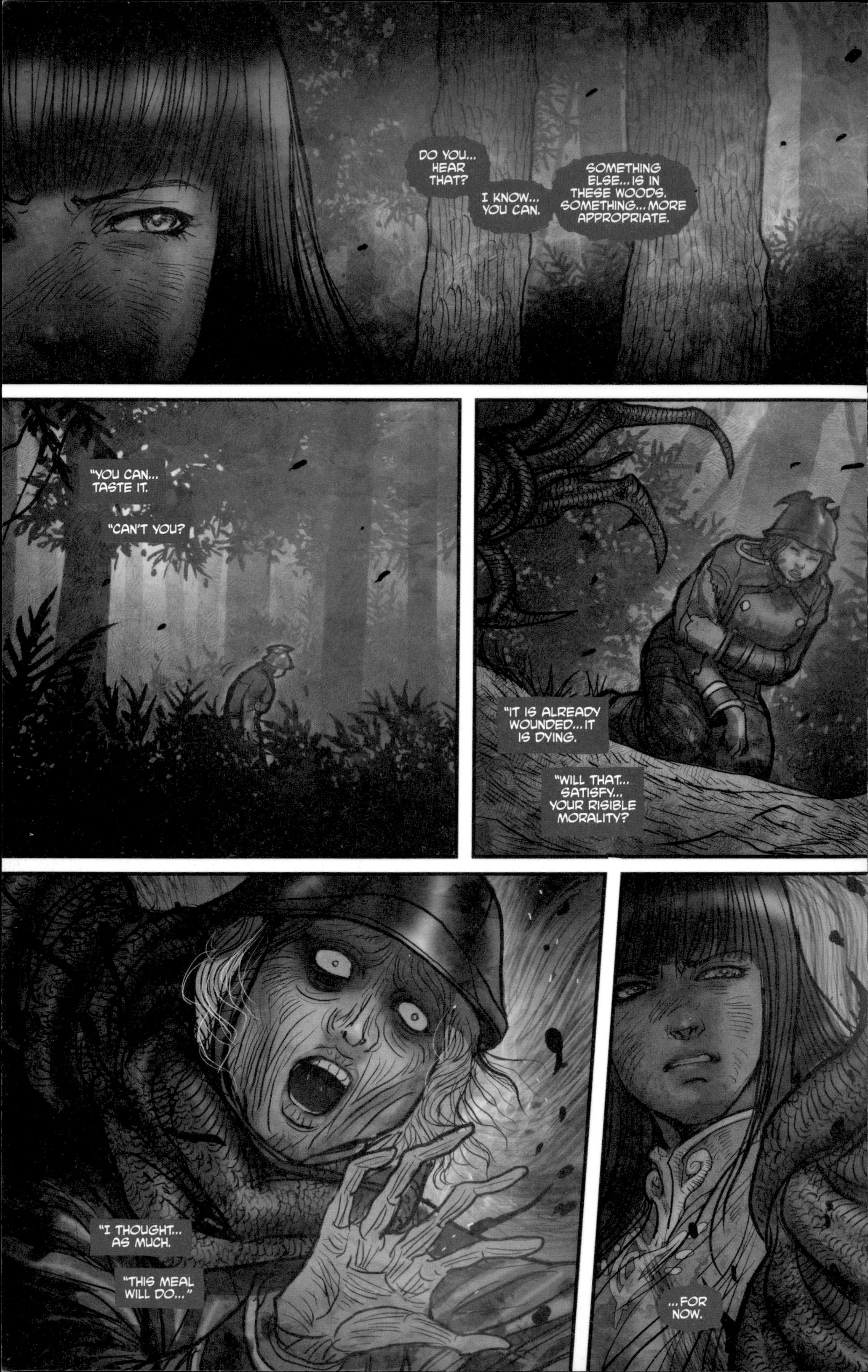
DO YOU... HEAR THAT?
I KNOW... YOU CAN.
SOMETHING ELSE... IS IN THESE WOODS. SOMETHING... MORE APPROPRIATE.
"YOU CAN... TASTE IT.
"CAN'T YOU?
"IT IS ALREADY WOUNDED... IT IS DYING.
"WILL THAT... SATISFY... YOUR RISIBLE MORALITY?
"I THOUGHT... AS MUCH.
"THIS MEAL WILL DO..."
...FOR NOW.

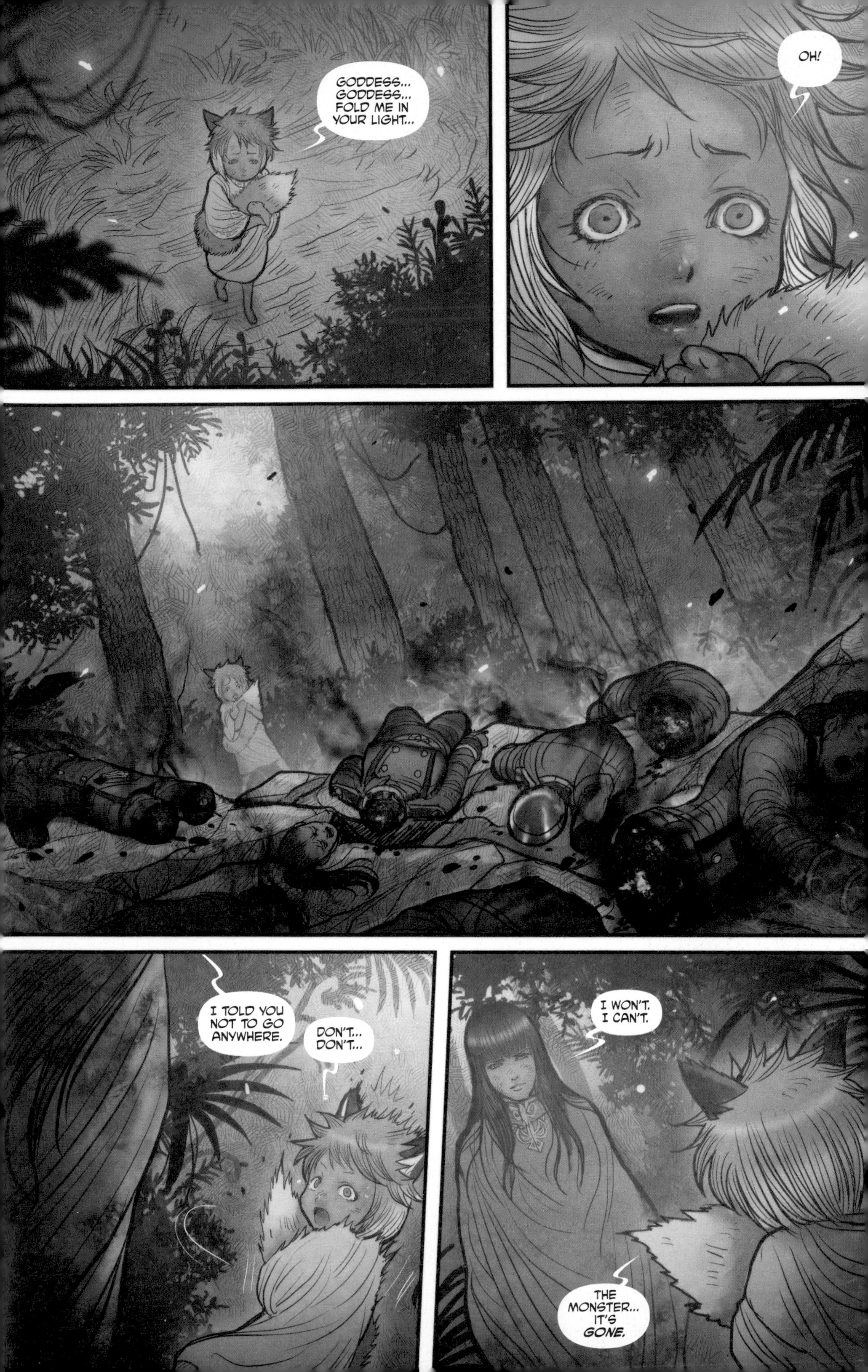
GODDESS... GODDESS... FOLD ME IN YOUR LIGHT...
OH!
I TOLD YOU NOT TO GO ANYWHERE.
DON'T... DON'T...
I WON'T. I CAN'T.
THE MONSTER... IT'S *GONE.*

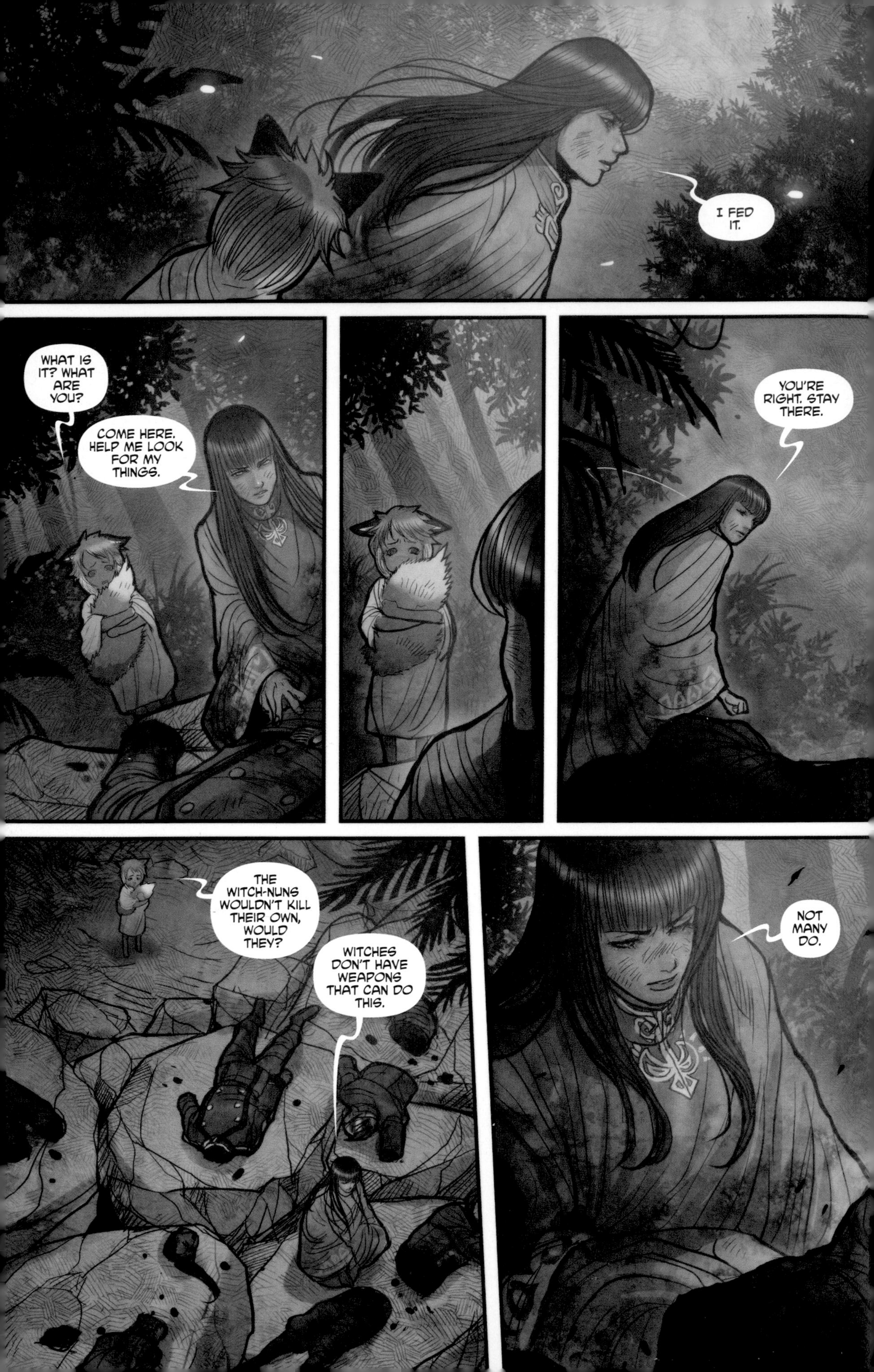
I FED IT.
WHAT IS IT? WHAT ARE YOU?
COME HERE. HELP ME LOOK FOR MY THINGS.
YOU'RE RIGHT. STAY THERE.
THE WITCH-NUNS WOULDN'T KILL THEIR OWN, WOULD THEY?
WITCHES DON'T HAVE WEAPONS THAT CAN DO THIS.
NOT MANY DO.

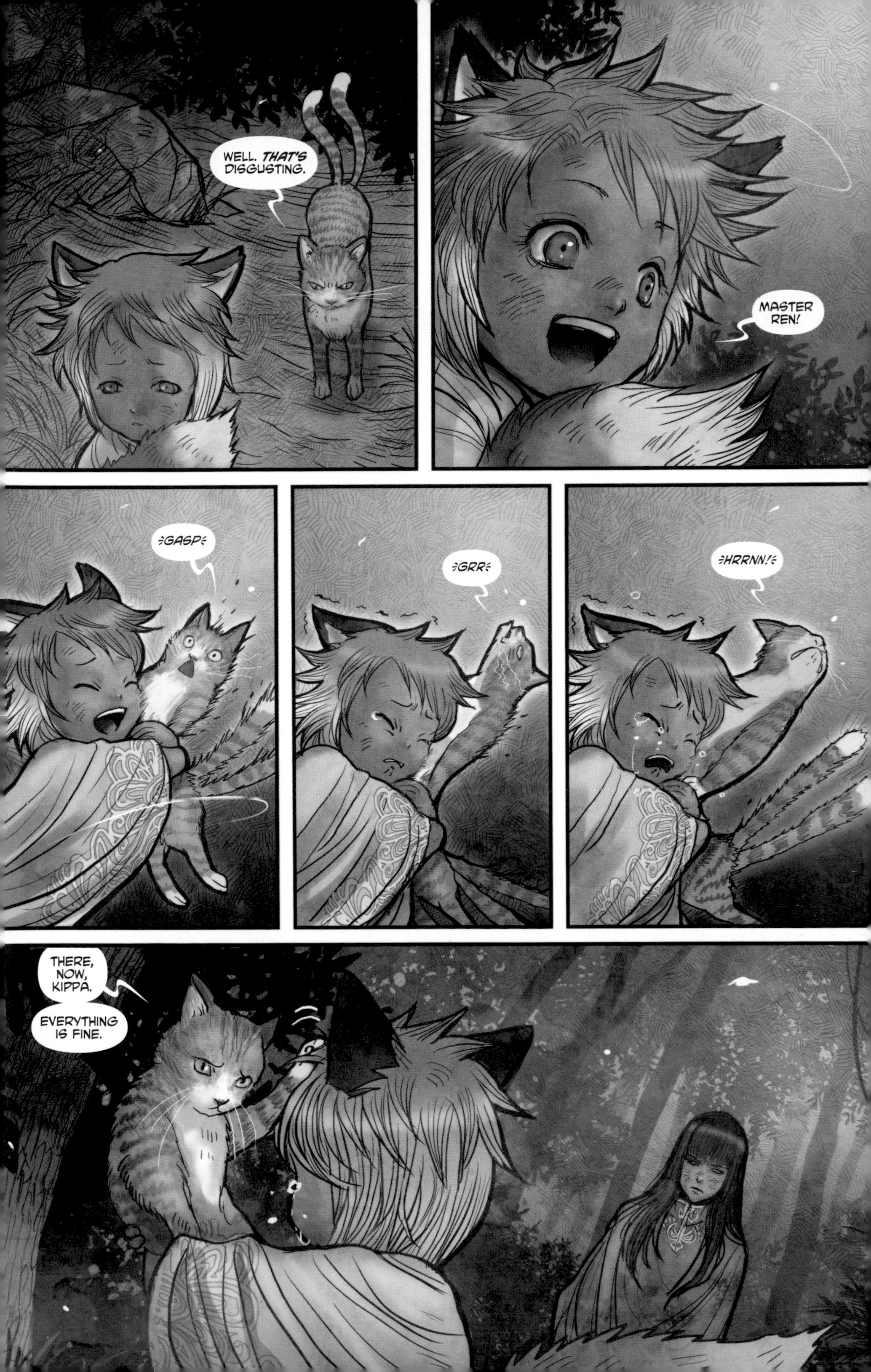
WELL. *THAT'S* DISGUSTING.
MASTER REN!
GASP
GRR
HRRNN!
THERE, NOW, KIPPA.
EVERYTHING IS FINE.

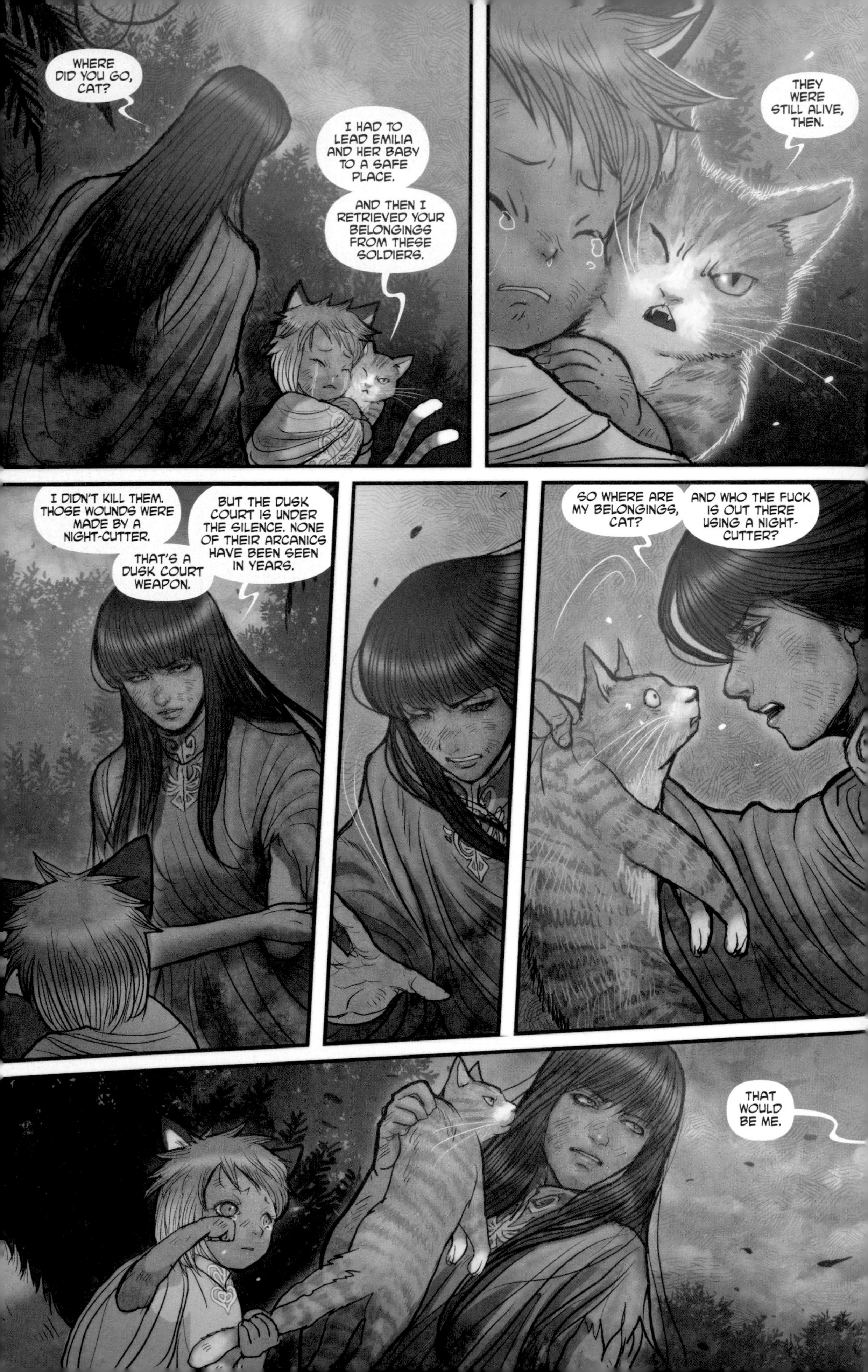
WHERE DID YOU GO, CAT?
I HAD TO LEAD EMILIA AND HER BABY TO A SAFE PLACE.
AND THEN I RETRIEVED YOUR BELONGINGS FROM THESE SOLDIERS.
THEY WERE STILL ALIVE, THEN.
I DIDN'T KILL THEM. THOSE WOUNDS WERE MADE BY A NIGHT-CUTTER.
THAT'S A DUSK COURT WEAPON.
BUT THE DUSK COURT IS UNDER THE SILENCE. NONE OF THEIR ARCANICS HAVE BEEN SEEN IN YEARS.
SO WHERE ARE MY BELONGINGS, CAT?
AND WHO THE FUCK IS OUT THERE USING A NIGHT-CUTTER?
THAT WOULD BE ME.

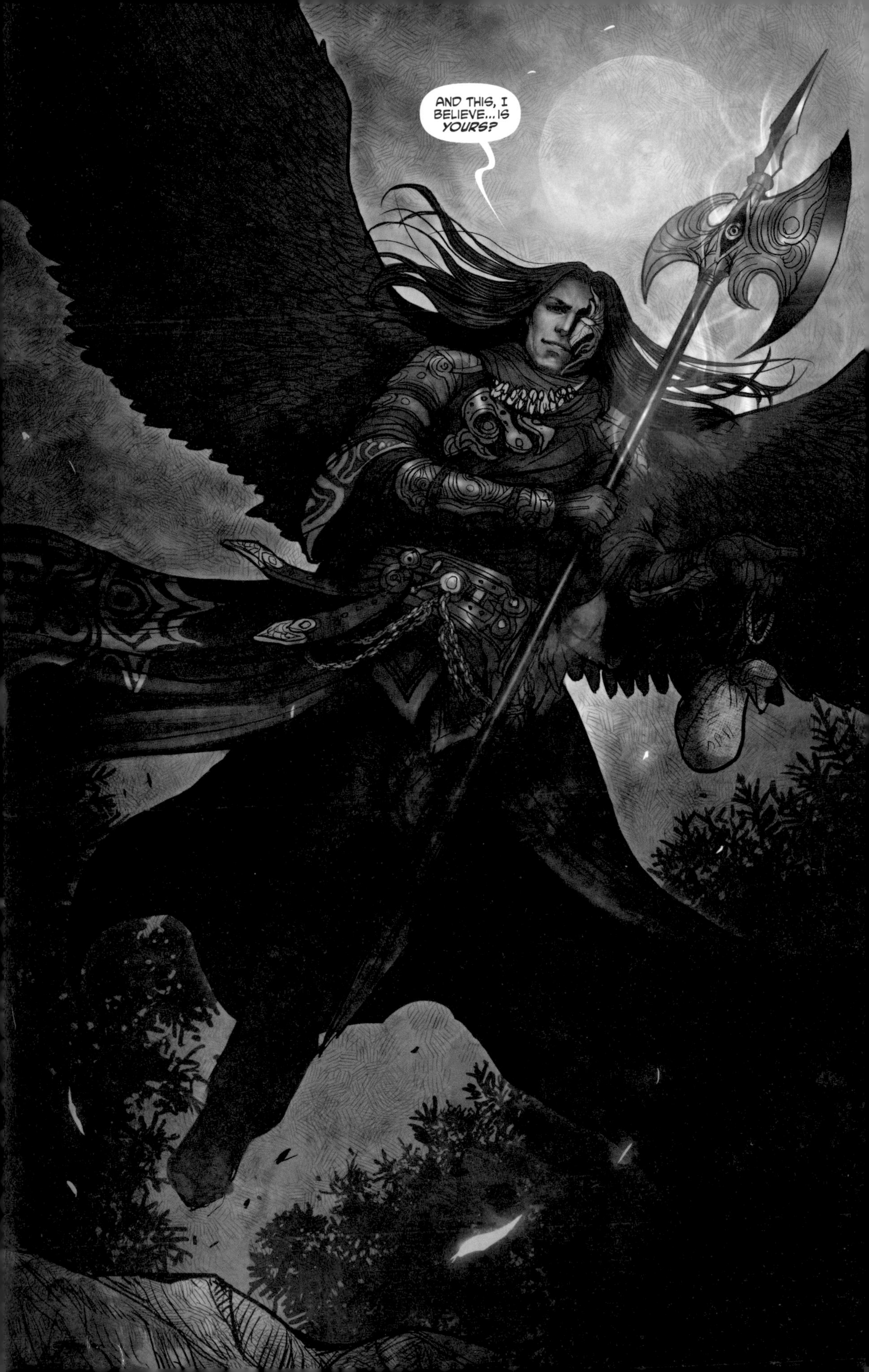
AND THIS, I BELIEVE...IS *YOURS?*

AN EXCERPT OF A LECTURE FROM THE ESTEEMED **PROFESSOR TAM TAM**, FORMER FIRST RECORD-KEEPER OF THE IS'HAMI TEMPLE, AND LEARNED CONTEMPORARY OF NAMRON BLACK CLAW...

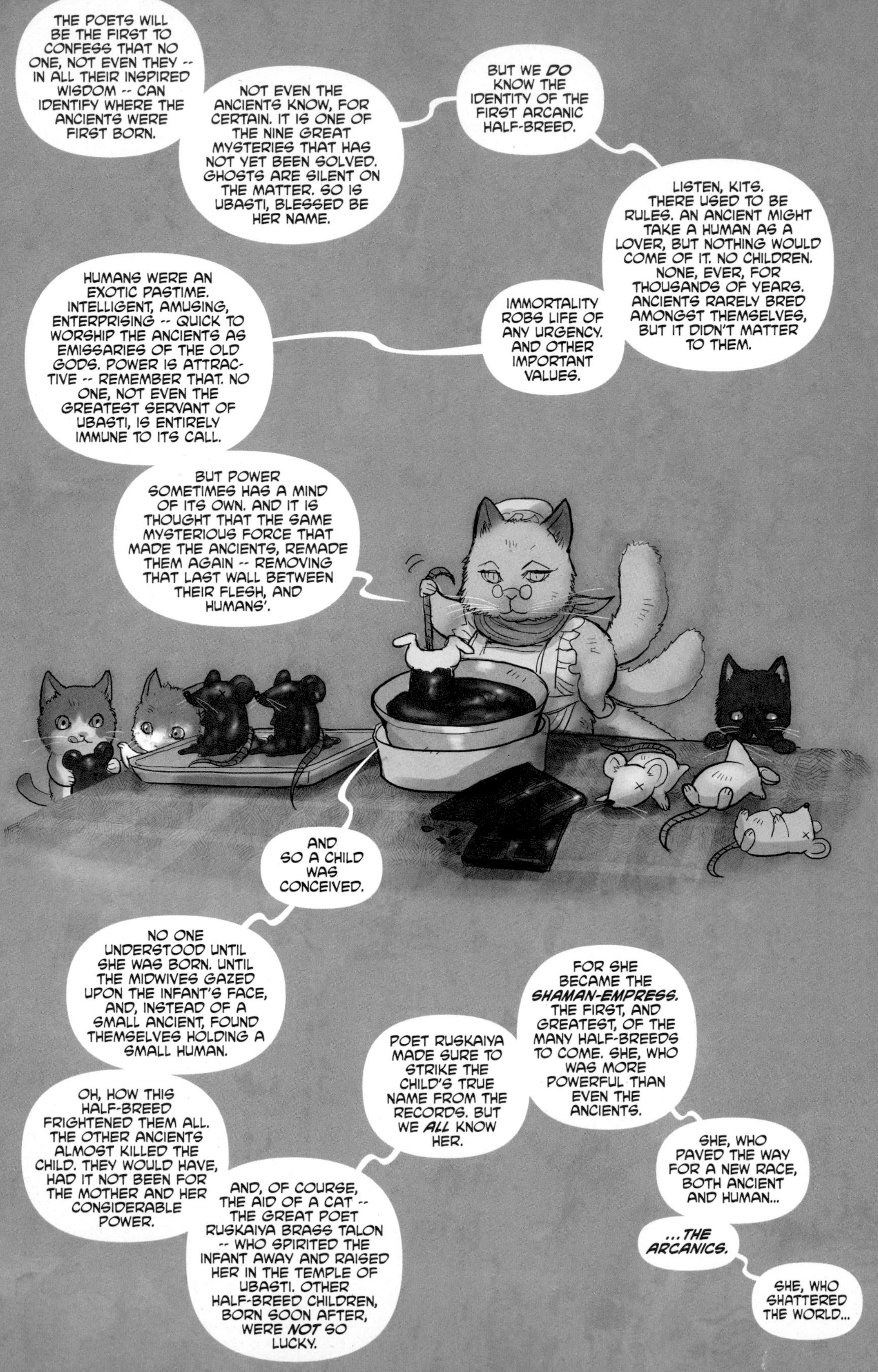
THE POETS WILL BE THE FIRST TO CONFESS THAT NO ONE, NOT EVEN THEY -- IN ALL THEIR INSPIRED WISDOM -- CAN IDENTIFY WHERE THE ANCIENTS WERE FIRST BORN.
NOT EVEN THE ANCIENTS KNOW, FOR CERTAIN. IT IS ONE OF THE NINE GREAT MYSTERIES THAT HAS NOT YET BEEN SOLVED. GHOSTS ARE SILENT ON THE MATTER. SO IS UBASTI, BLESSED BE HER NAME.
BUT WE *DO* KNOW THE IDENTITY OF THE FIRST ARCANIC HALF-BREED.
LISTEN, KITS. THERE USED TO BE RULES. AN ANCIENT MIGHT TAKE A HUMAN AS A LOVER, BUT NOTHING WOULD COME OF IT. NO CHILDREN. NONE, EVER, FOR THOUSANDS OF YEARS. ANCIENTS RARELY BRED AMONGST THEMSELVES, BUT IT DIDN'T MATTER TO THEM.
IMMORTALITY ROBS LIFE OF ANY URGENCY. AND OTHER IMPORTANT VALUES.
HUMANS WERE AN EXOTIC PASTIME. INTELLIGENT, AMUSING, ENTERPRISING -- QUICK TO WORSHIP THE ANCIENTS AS EMISSARIES OF THE OLD GODS. POWER IS ATTRACTIVE -- REMEMBER THAT. NO ONE, NOT EVEN THE GREATEST SERVANT OF UBASTI, IS ENTIRELY IMMUNE TO ITS CALL.
BUT POWER SOMETIMES HAS A MIND OF ITS OWN. AND IT IS THOUGHT THAT THE SAME MYSTERIOUS FORCE THAT MADE THE ANCIENTS, REMADE THEM AGAIN -- REMOVING THAT LAST WALL BETWEEN THEIR FLESH, AND HUMANS'.
AND SO A CHILD WAS CONCEIVED.
NO ONE UNDERSTOOD UNTIL SHE WAS BORN. UNTIL THE MIDWIVES GAZED UPON THE INFANT'S FACE, AND, INSTEAD OF A SMALL ANCIENT, FOUND THEMSELVES HOLDING A SMALL HUMAN.
OH, HOW THIS HALF-BREED FRIGHTENED THEM ALL. THE OTHER ANCIENTS ALMOST KILLED THE CHILD. THEY WOULD HAVE, HAD IT NOT BEEN FOR THE MOTHER AND HER CONSIDERABLE POWER.
AND, OF COURSE, THE AID OF A CAT -- THE GREAT POET RUSKAIYA BRASS TALON -- WHO SPIRITED THE INFANT AWAY AND RAISED HER IN THE TEMPLE OF UBASTI. OTHER HALF-BREED CHILDREN, BORN SOON AFTER, WERE *NOT* SO LUCKY.
POET RUSKAIYA MADE SURE TO STRIKE THE CHILD'S TRUE NAME FROM THE RECORDS. BUT WE *ALL* KNOW HER.
FOR SHE BECAME THE *SHAMAN-EMPRESS.* THE FIRST, AND GREATEST, OF THE MANY HALF-BREEDS TO COME. SHE, WHO WAS MORE POWERFUL THAN EVEN THE ANCIENTS.
SHE, WHO PAVED THE WAY FOR A NEW RACE, BOTH ANCIENT AND HUMAN...
...THE ARCANICS.
SHE, WHO SHATTERED THE WORLD...

CHAPTER FIVE

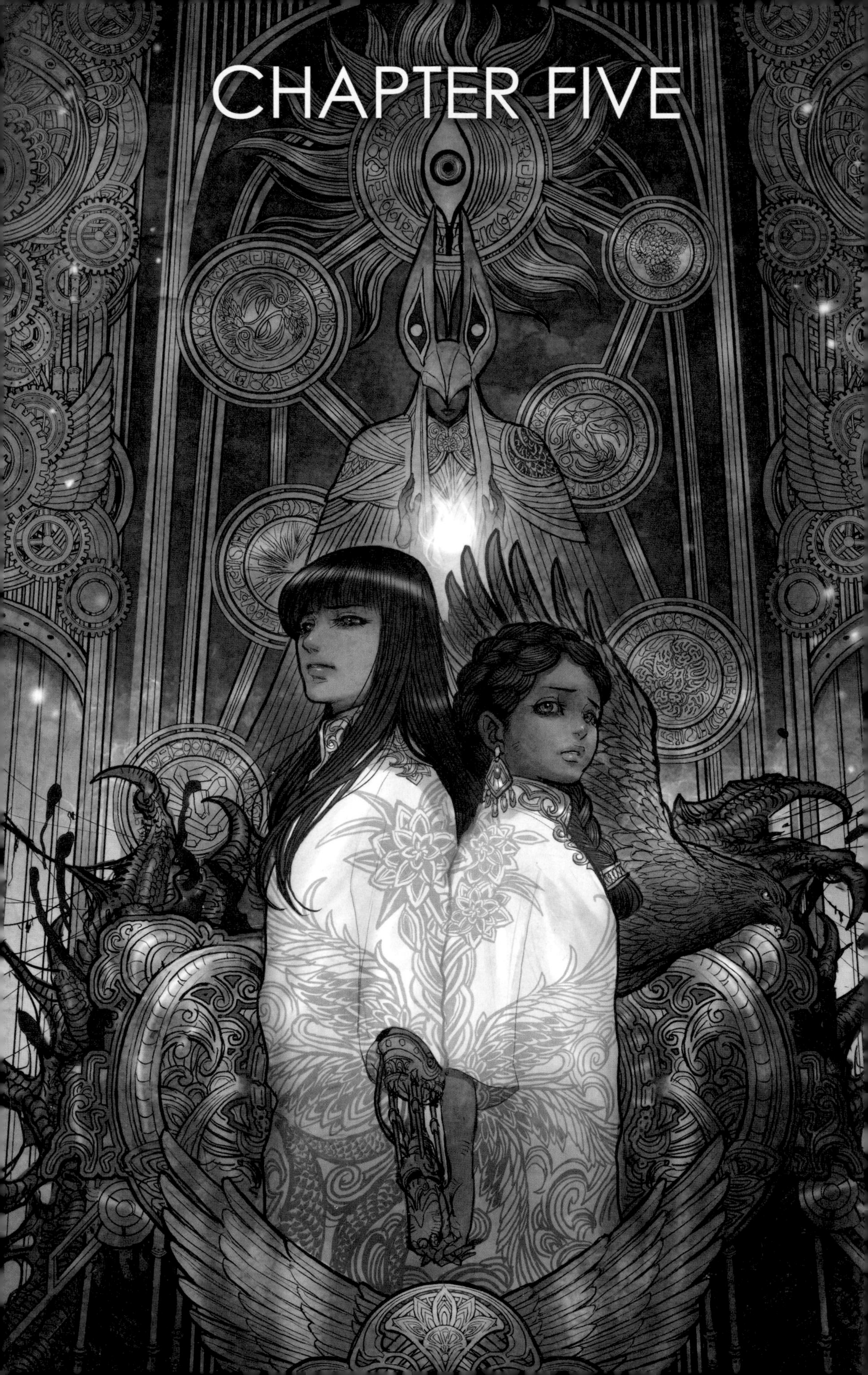

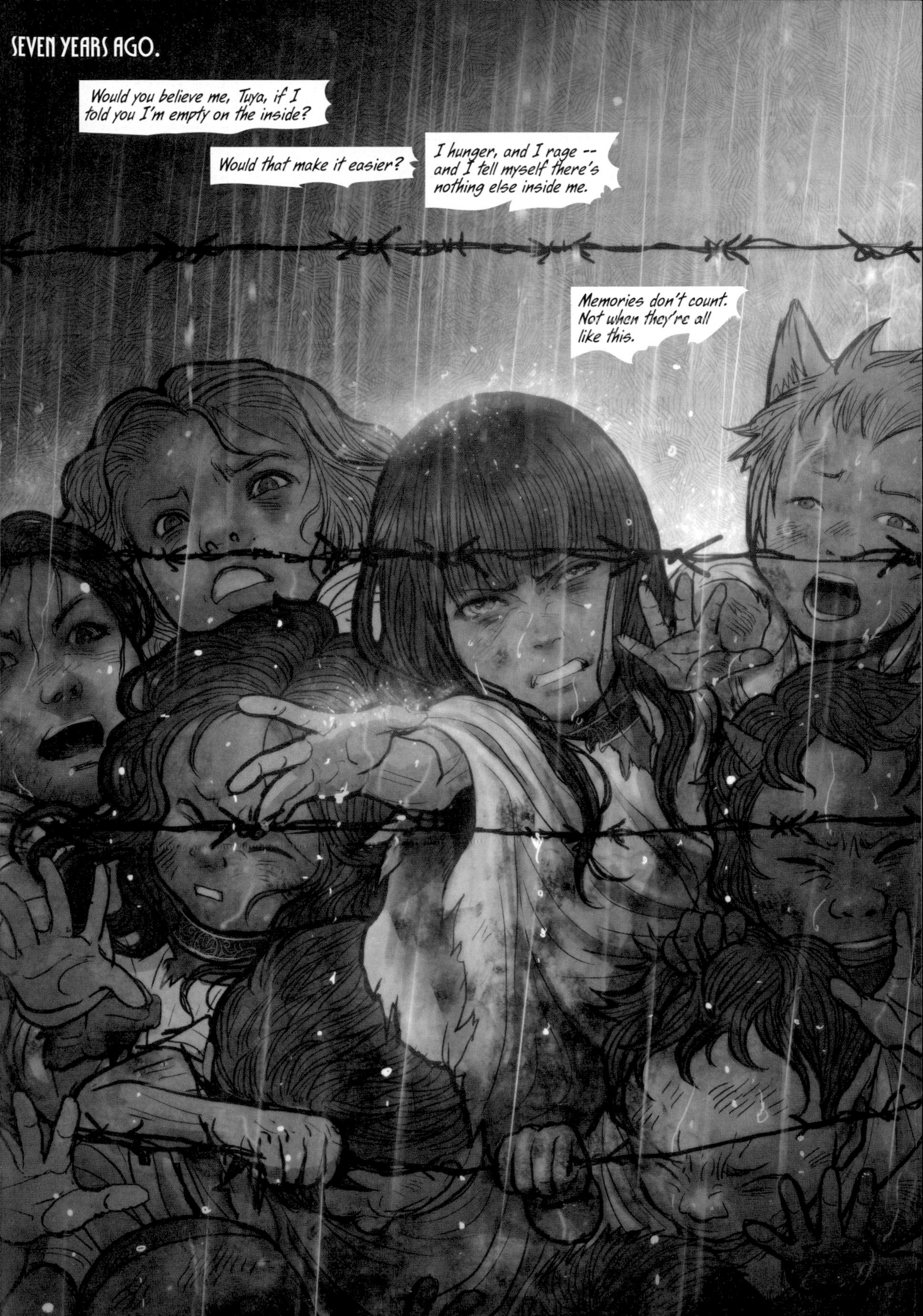
SEVEN YEARS AGO.
Would you believe me, Tuya, if I told you I'm empty on the inside?
Would that make it easier?
I hunger, and I rage -- and I tell myself there's nothing else inside me.
Memories don't count. Not when they're all like this.

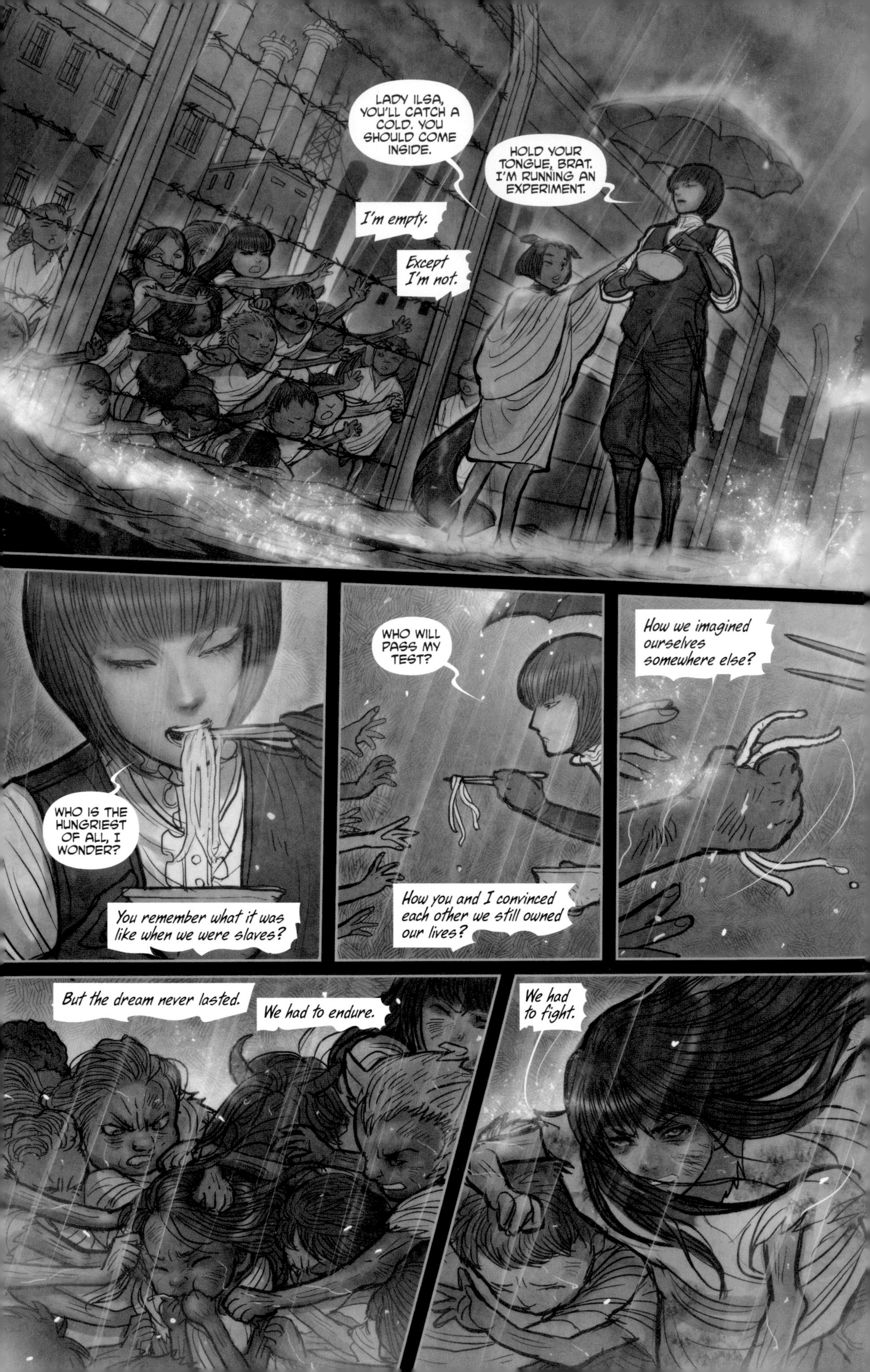
LADY ILSA, YOU'LL CATCH A COLD. YOU SHOULD COME INSIDE.
HOLD YOUR TONGUE, BRAT. I'M RUNNING AN EXPERIMENT.
I'm empty.
Except I'm not.
WHO IS THE HUNGRIEST OF ALL, I WONDER?
You remember what it was like when we were slaves?
WHO WILL PASS MY TEST?
How you and I convinced each other we still owned our lives?
How we imagined ourselves somewhere else?
But the dream never lasted.
We had to endure.
We had to fight.

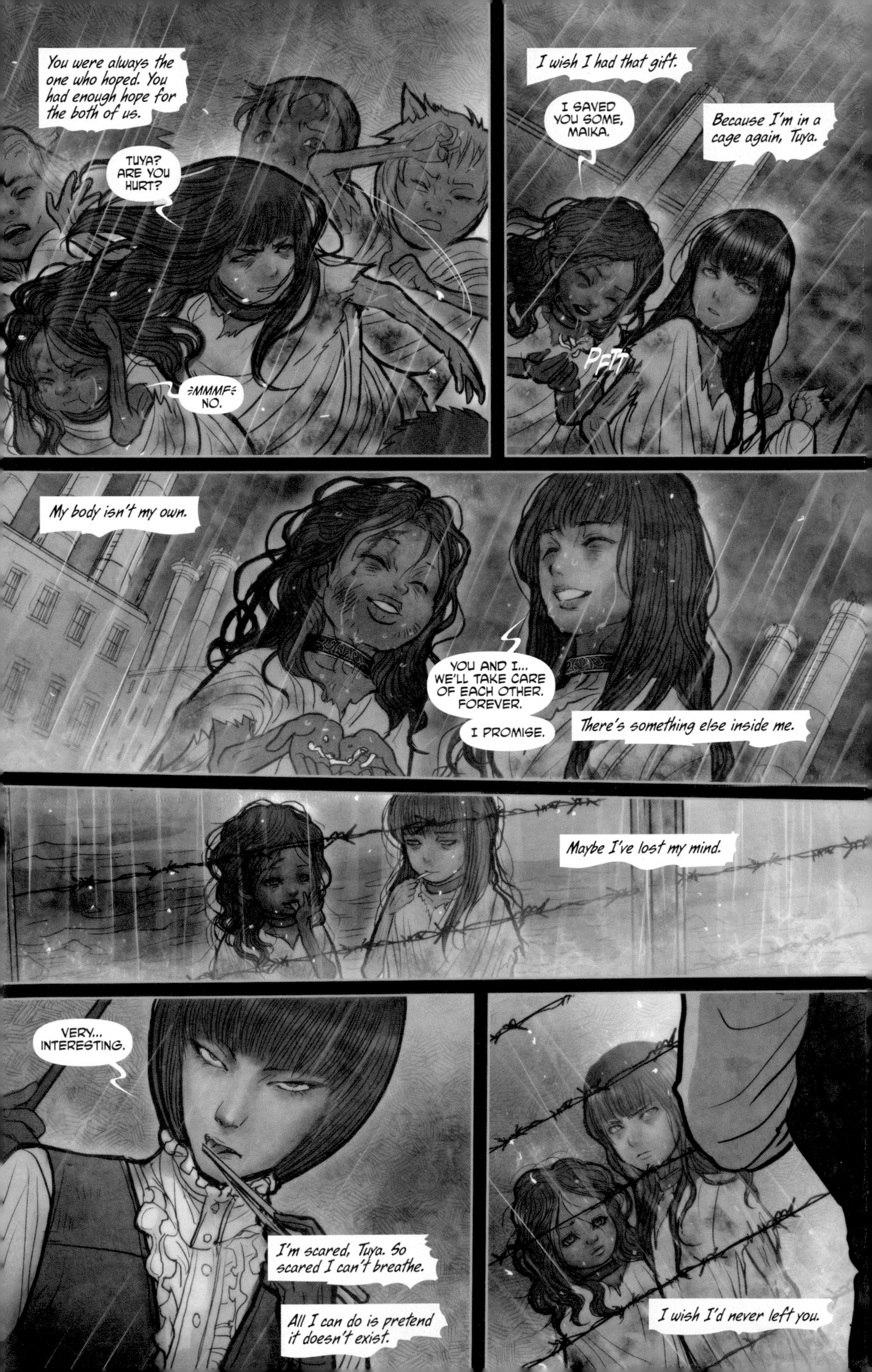

You were always the one who hoped. You had enough hope for the both of us.
TUYA? ARE YOU HURT?
MMMF NO.
I wish I had that gift.
I SAVED YOU SOME, MAIKA.
Because I'm in a cage again, Tuya.
PFFT
My body isn't my own.
YOU AND I... WE'LL TAKE CARE OF EACH OTHER. FOREVER.
I PROMISE.
There's something else inside me.
Maybe I've lost my mind.
VERY... INTERESTING.
I'm scared, Tuya. So scared I can't breathe.
All I can do is pretend it doesn't exist.
I wish I'd never left you.

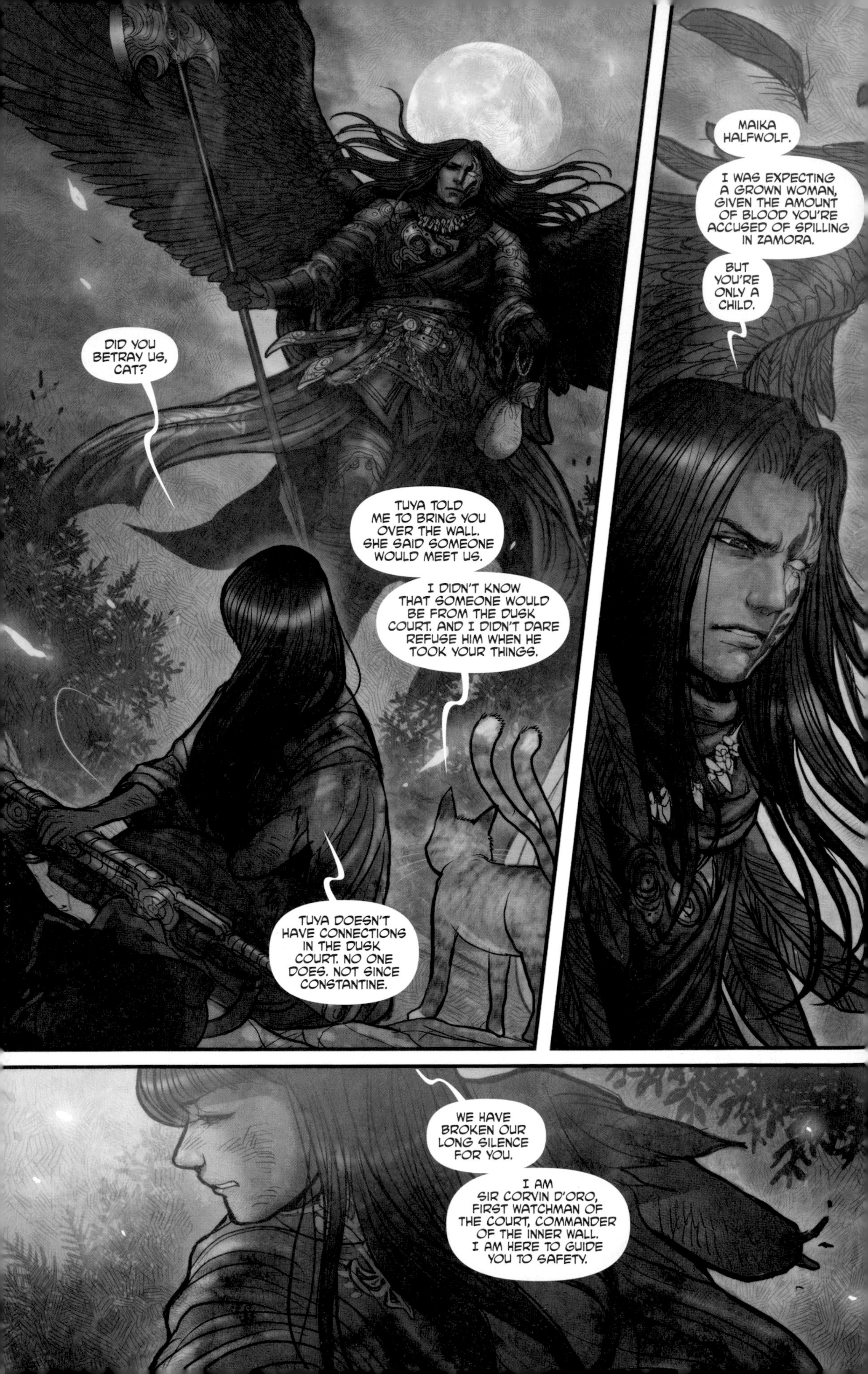
DID YOU BETRAY US, CAT?
TUYA TOLD ME TO BRING YOU OVER THE WALL. SHE SAID SOMEONE WOULD MEET US.
I DIDN'T KNOW THAT SOMEONE WOULD BE FROM THE DUSK COURT. AND I DIDN'T DARE REFUSE HIM WHEN HE TOOK YOUR THINGS.
TUYA DOESN'T HAVE CONNECTIONS IN THE DUSK COURT. NO ONE DOES. NOT SINCE CONSTANTINE.
MAIKA HALFWOLF.
I WAS EXPECTING A GROWN WOMAN, GIVEN THE AMOUNT OF BLOOD YOU'RE ACCUSED OF SPILLING IN ZAMORA.
BUT YOU'RE ONLY A CHILD.
WE HAVE BROKEN OUR LONG SILENCE FOR YOU.
I AM SIR CORVIN D'ORO, FIRST WATCHMAN OF THE COURT, COMMANDER OF THE INNER WALL. I AM HERE TO GUIDE YOU TO SAFETY.

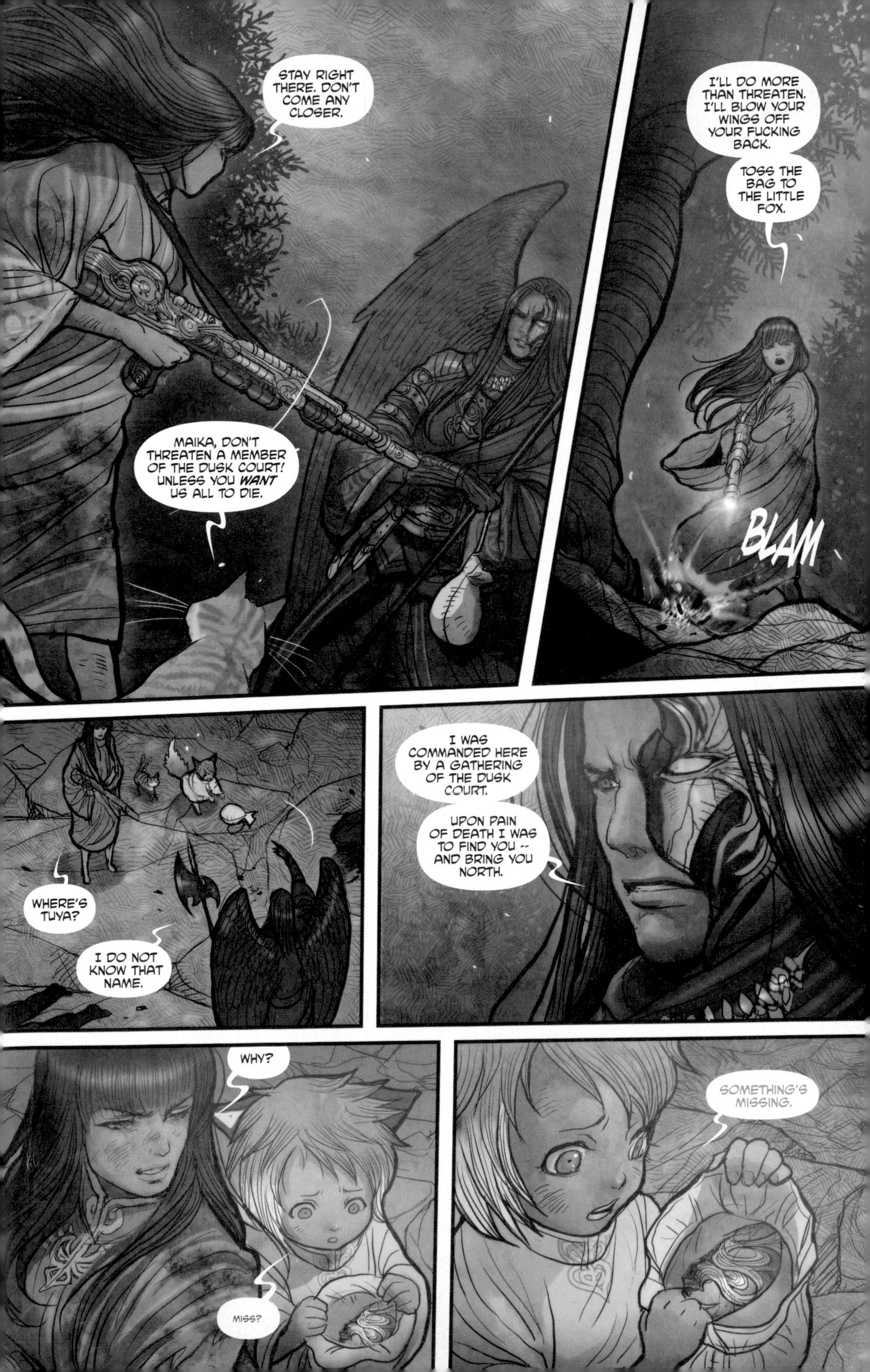
STAY RIGHT THERE. DON'T COME ANY CLOSER.
MAIKA, DON'T THREATEN A MEMBER OF THE DUSK COURT! UNLESS YOU *WANT* US ALL TO DIE.
I'LL DO MORE THAN THREATEN. I'LL BLOW YOUR WINGS OFF YOUR FUCKING BACK.
TOSS THE BAG TO THE LITTLE FOX.
BLAM
WHERE'S TUYA?
I DO NOT KNOW THAT NAME.
I WAS COMMANDED HERE BY A GATHERING OF THE DUSK COURT.
UPON PAIN OF DEATH I WAS TO FIND YOU -- AND BRING YOU NORTH.
WHY?
MISS?
SOMETHING'S MISSING.

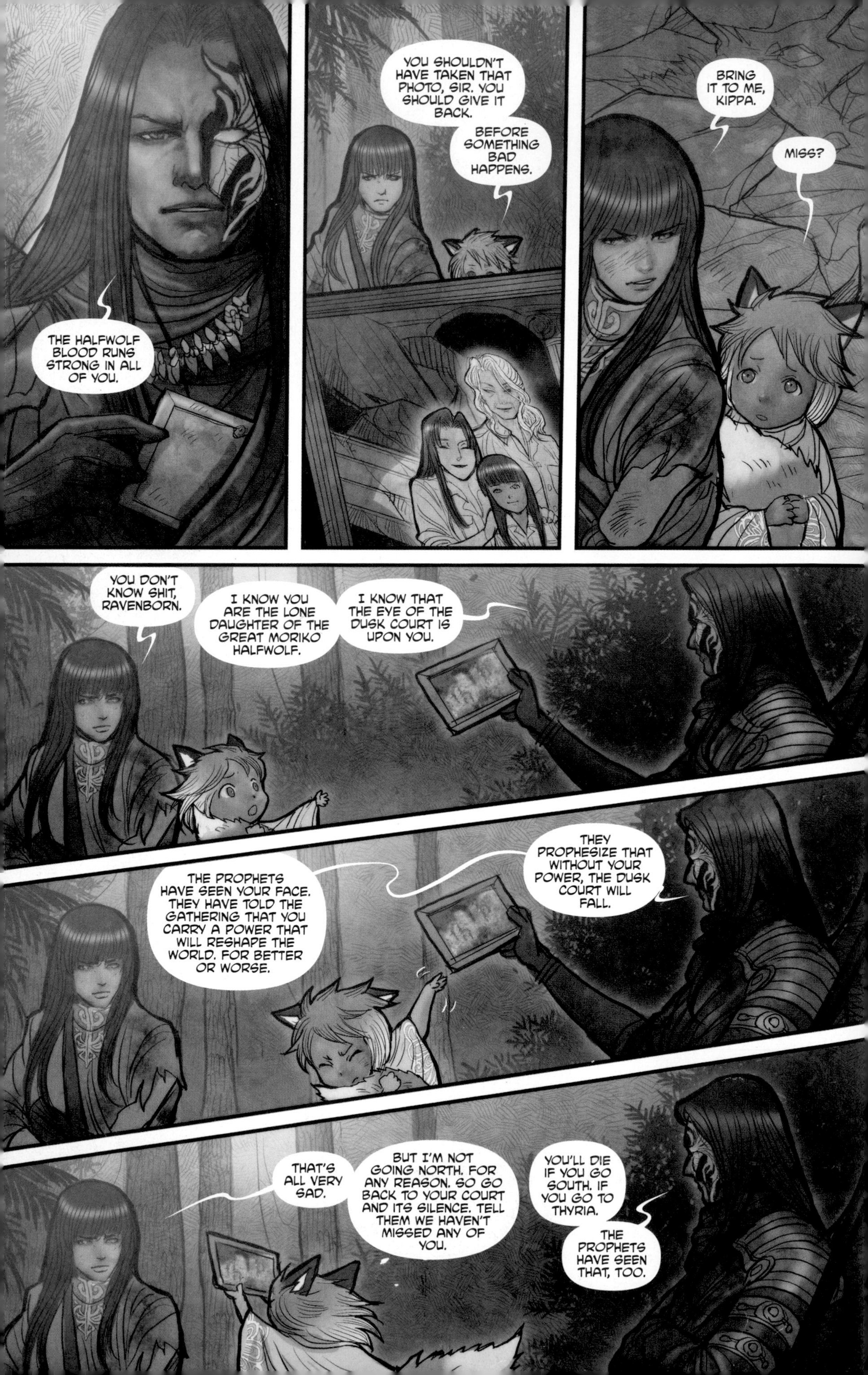
THE HALFWOLF BLOOD RUNS STRONG IN ALL OF YOU.
YOU SHOULDN'T HAVE TAKEN THAT PHOTO, SIR. YOU SHOULD GIVE IT BACK.
BEFORE SOMETHING BAD HAPPENS.
BRING IT TO ME, KIPPA.
MISS?
YOU DON'T KNOW SHIT, RAVENBORN.
I KNOW YOU ARE THE LONE DAUGHTER OF THE GREAT MORIKO HALFWOLF.
I KNOW THAT THE EYE OF THE DUSK COURT IS UPON YOU.
THE PROPHETS HAVE SEEN YOUR FACE. THEY HAVE TOLD THE GATHERING THAT YOU CARRY A POWER THAT WILL RESHAPE THE WORLD. FOR BETTER OR WORSE.
THEY PROPHESIZE THAT WITHOUT YOUR POWER, THE DUSK COURT WILL FALL.
THAT'S ALL VERY SAD.
BUT I'M NOT GOING NORTH. FOR ANY REASON. SO GO BACK TO YOUR COURT AND ITS SILENCE. TELL THEM WE HAVEN'T MISSED ANY OF YOU.
YOU'LL DIE IF YOU GO SOUTH. IF YOU GO TO THYRIA.
THE PROPHETS HAVE SEEN THAT, TOO.

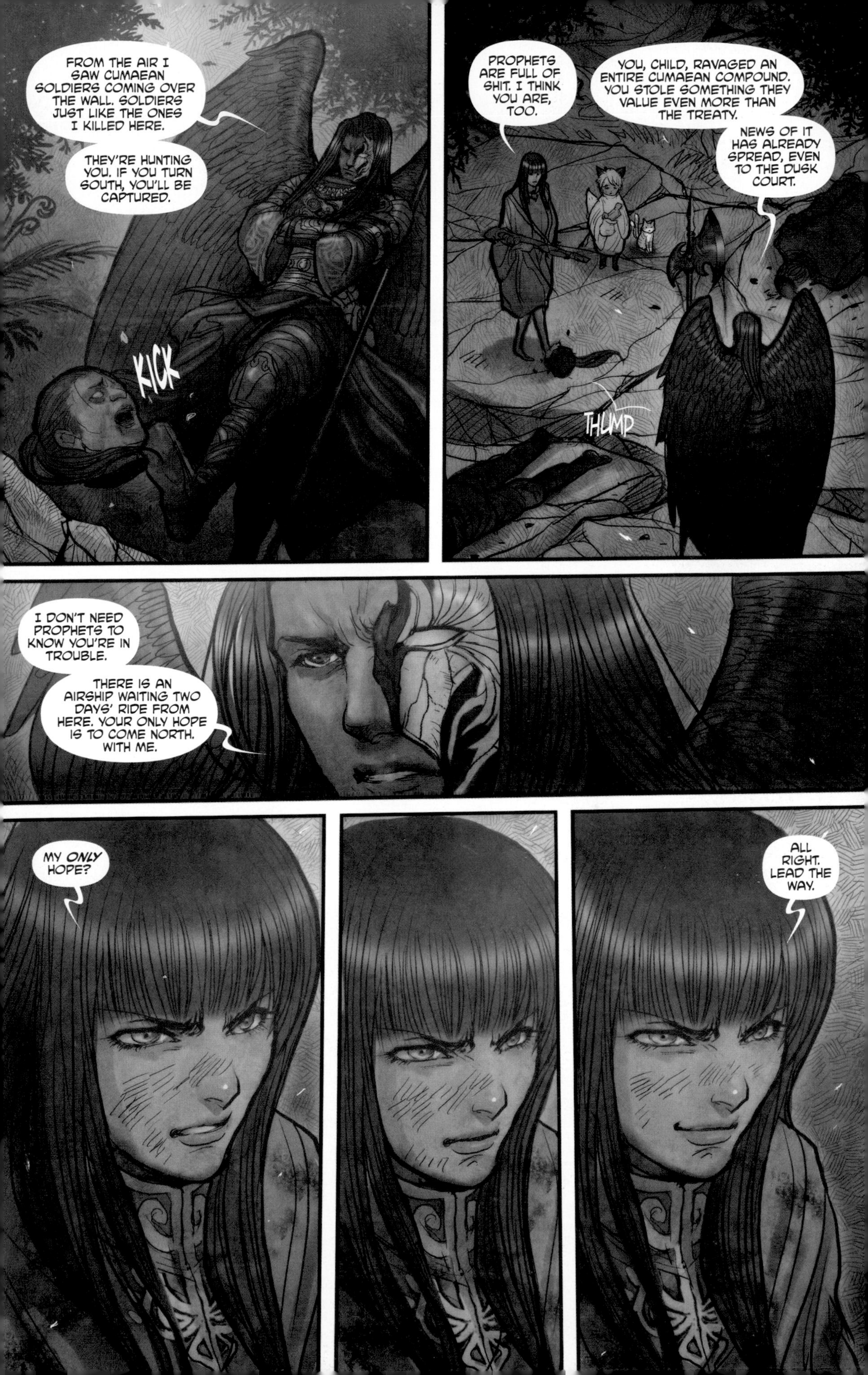
FROM THE AIR I SAW CUMAEAN SOLDIERS COMING OVER THE WALL. SOLDIERS JUST LIKE THE ONES I KILLED HERE.
THEY'RE HUNTING YOU. IF YOU TURN SOUTH, YOU'LL BE CAPTURED.
KICK
PROPHETS ARE FULL OF SHIT. I THINK YOU ARE, TOO.
YOU, CHILD, RAVAGED AN ENTIRE CUMAEAN COMPOUND. YOU STOLE SOMETHING THEY VALUE EVEN MORE THAN THE TREATY.
NEWS OF IT HAS ALREADY SPREAD, EVEN TO THE DUSK COURT.
THUMP
I DON'T NEED PROPHETS TO KNOW YOU'RE IN TROUBLE.
THERE IS AN AIRSHIP WAITING TWO DAYS' RIDE FROM HERE. YOUR ONLY HOPE IS TO COME NORTH. WITH ME.
MY *ONLY* HOPE?
ALL RIGHT. LEAD THE WAY.

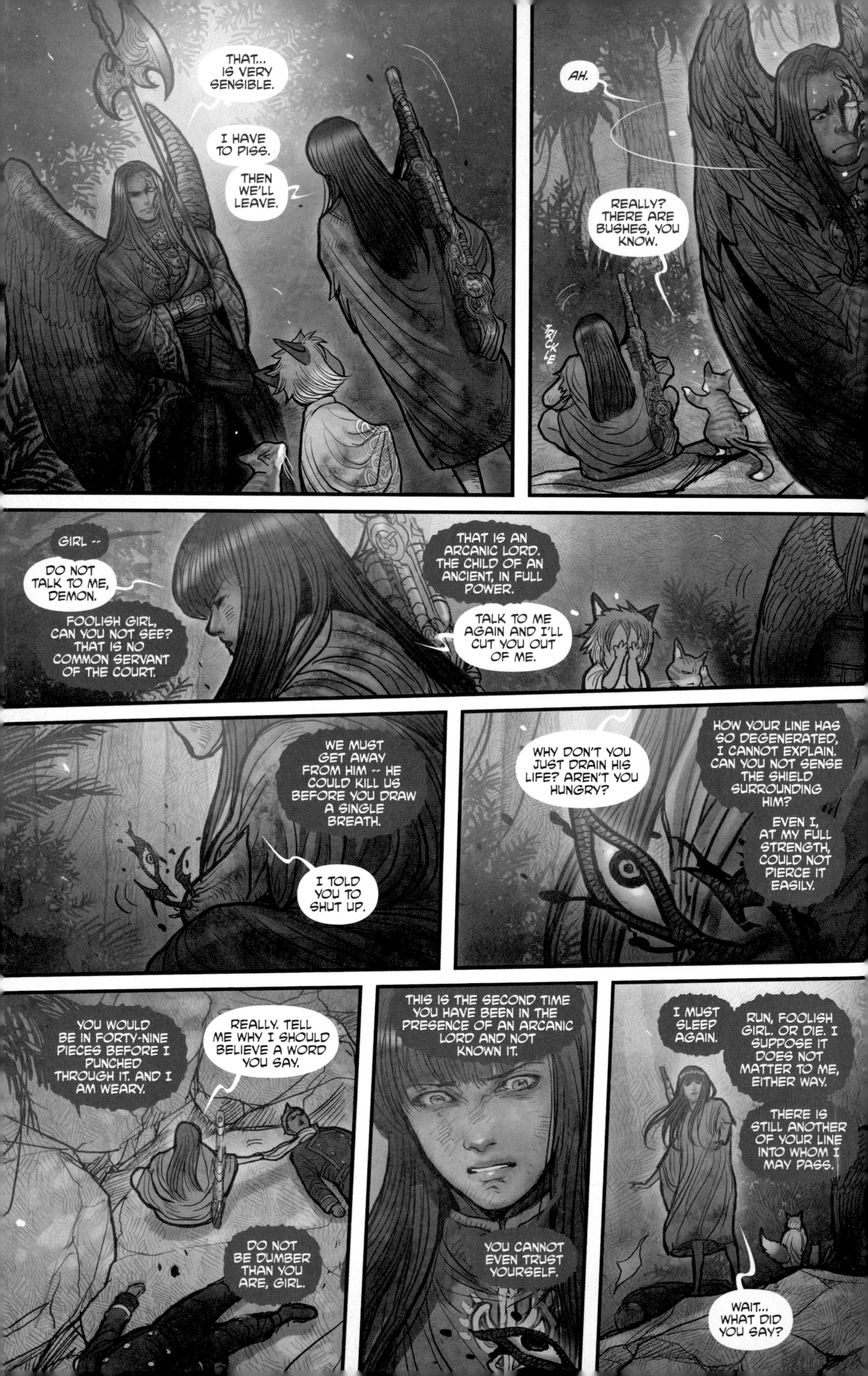
THAT... IS VERY SENSIBLE.
I HAVE TO PISS.
THEN WE'LL LEAVE.
AH.
REALLY? THERE ARE BUSHES, YOU KNOW.
TRICKLE
GIRL --
DO NOT TALK TO ME, DEMON.
FOOLISH GIRL, CAN YOU NOT SEE? THAT IS NO COMMON SERVANT OF THE COURT.
THAT IS AN ARCANIC LORD. THE CHILD OF AN ANCIENT, IN FULL POWER.
TALK TO ME AGAIN AND I'LL CUT YOU OUT OF ME.
WE MUST GET AWAY FROM HIM -- HE COULD KILL US BEFORE YOU DRAW A SINGLE BREATH.
I TOLD YOU TO SHUT UP.
WHY DON'T YOU JUST DRAIN HIS LIFE? AREN'T YOU HUNGRY?
HOW YOUR LINE HAS SO DEGENERATED, I CANNOT EXPLAIN. CAN YOU NOT SENSE THE SHIELD SURROUNDING HIM?
EVEN I, AT MY FULL STRENGTH, COULD NOT PIERCE IT EASILY.
YOU WOULD BE IN FORTY-NINE PIECES BEFORE I PUNCHED THROUGH IT. AND I AM WEARY.
REALLY. TELL ME WHY I SHOULD BELIEVE A WORD YOU SAY.
DO NOT BE DUMBER THAN YOU ARE, GIRL.
THIS IS THE SECOND TIME YOU HAVE BEEN IN THE PRESENCE OF AN ARCANIC LORD AND NOT KNOWN IT.
YOU CANNOT EVEN TRUST YOURSELF.
I MUST SLEEP AGAIN.
RUN, FOOLISH GIRL, OR DIE. I SUPPOSE IT DOES NOT MATTER TO ME, EITHER WAY.
THERE IS STILL ANOTHER OF YOUR LINE INTO WHOM I MAY PASS.
WAIT... WHAT DID YOU SAY?

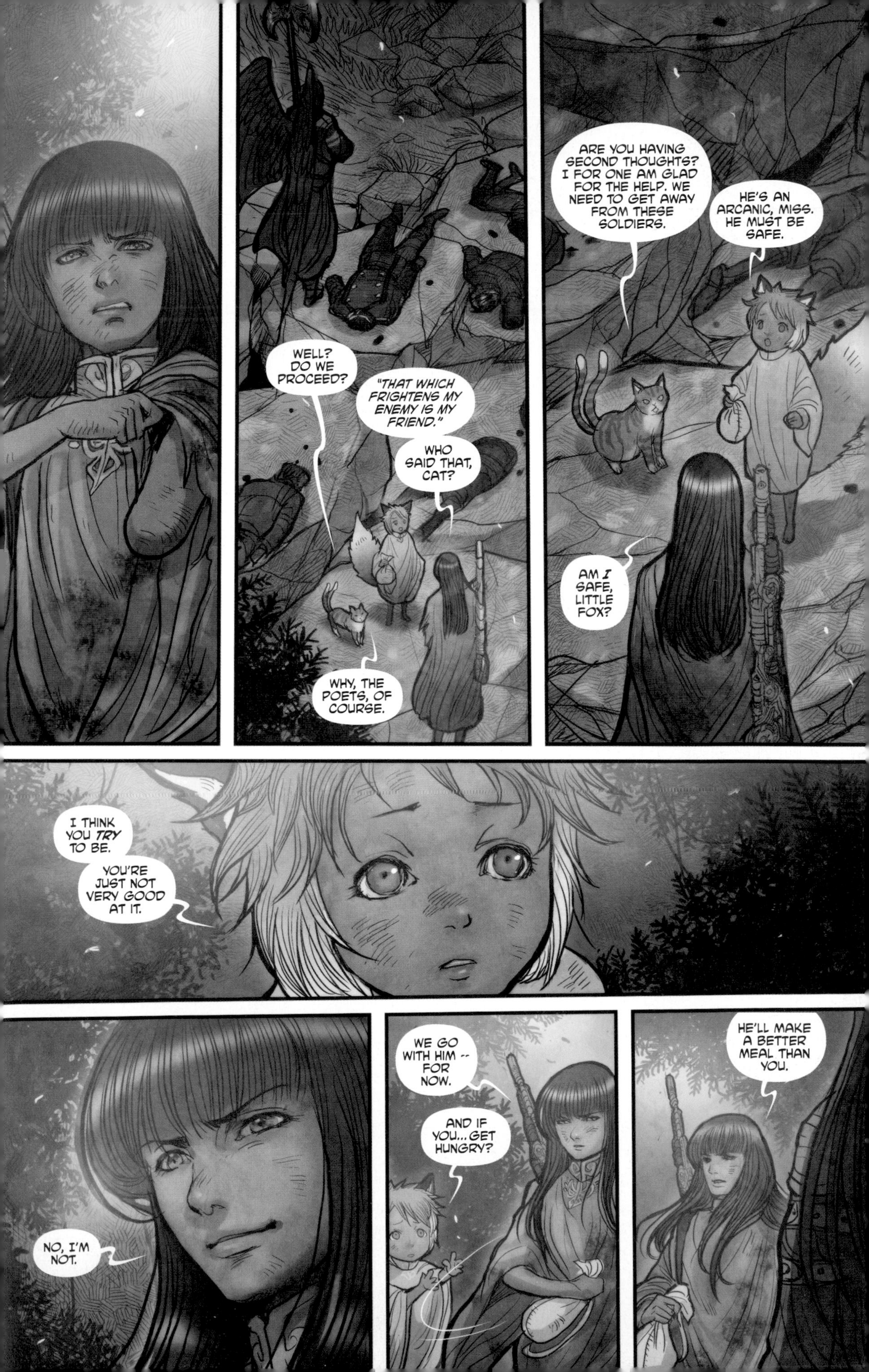
WELL? DO WE PROCEED?
"THAT WHICH FRIGHTENS MY ENEMY IS MY FRIEND."
WHO SAID THAT, CAT?
WHY, THE POETS, OF COURSE.
ARE YOU HAVING SECOND THOUGHTS? I FOR ONE AM GLAD FOR THE HELP. WE NEED TO GET AWAY FROM THESE SOLDIERS.
HE'S AN ARCANIC, MISS. HE MUST BE SAFE.
AM *I* SAFE, LITTLE FOX?
I THINK YOU *TRY* TO BE.
YOU'RE JUST NOT VERY GOOD AT IT.
NO, I'M NOT.
WE GO WITH HIM -- FOR NOW.
AND IF YOU... GET HUNGRY?
HE'LL MAKE A BETTER MEAL THAN YOU.

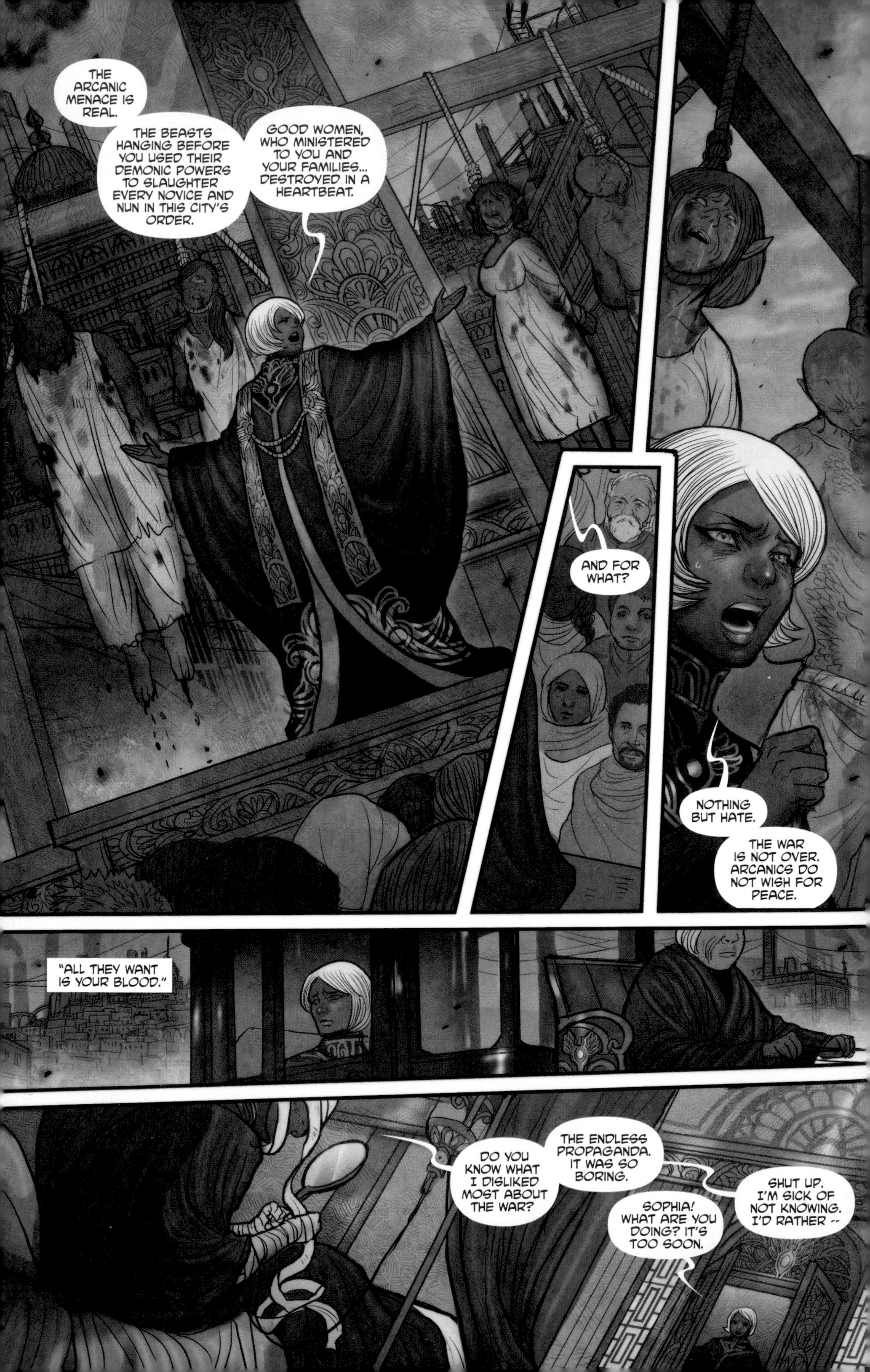
THE ARCANIC MENACE IS REAL.
THE BEASTS HANGING BEFORE YOU USED THEIR DEMONIC POWERS TO SLAUGHTER EVERY NOVICE AND NUN IN THIS CITY'S ORDER.
GOOD WOMEN, WHO MINISTERED TO YOU AND YOUR FAMILIES... DESTROYED IN A HEARTBEAT.
AND FOR WHAT?
NOTHING BUT HATE.
THE WAR IS NOT OVER. ARCANICS DO NOT WISH FOR PEACE.
"ALL THEY WANT IS YOUR BLOOD."
DO YOU KNOW WHAT I DISLIKED MOST ABOUT THE WAR?
THE ENDLESS PROPAGANDA. IT WAS SO BORING.
SOPHIA! WHAT ARE YOU DOING? IT'S TOO SOON.
SHUT UP. I'M SICK OF NOT KNOWING. I'D RATHER --

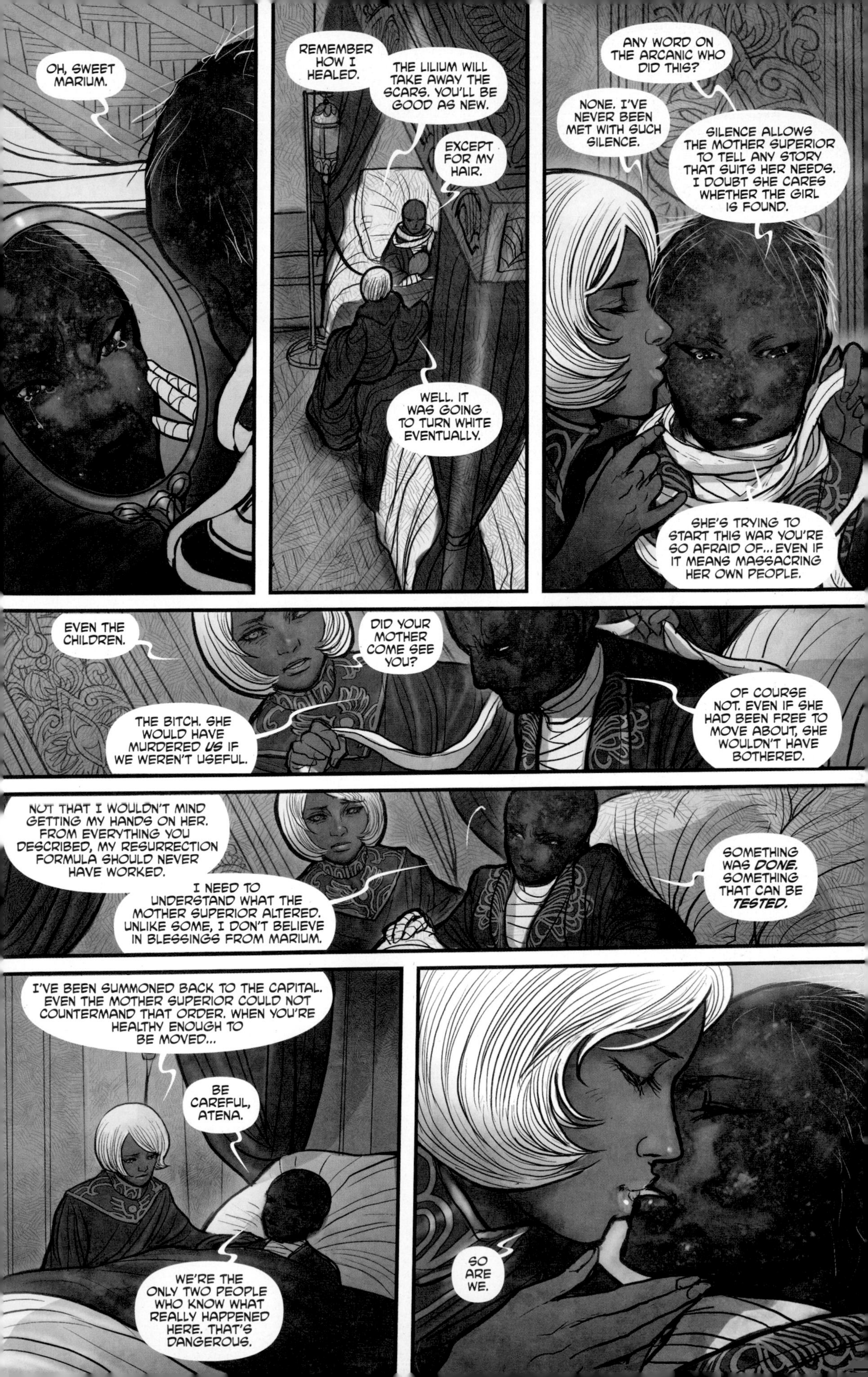
OH, SWEET MARIUM.
REMEMBER HOW I HEALED.
THE LILIUM WILL TAKE AWAY THE SCARS. YOU'LL BE GOOD AS NEW.
EXCEPT FOR MY HAIR.
WELL. IT WAS GOING TO TURN WHITE EVENTUALLY.
ANY WORD ON THE ARCANIC WHO DID THIS?
NONE. I'VE NEVER BEEN MET WITH SUCH SILENCE.
SILENCE ALLOWS THE MOTHER SUPERIOR TO TELL ANY STORY THAT SUITS HER NEEDS. I DOUBT SHE CARES WHETHER THE GIRL IS FOUND.
SHE'S TRYING TO START THIS WAR YOU'RE SO AFRAID OF... EVEN IF IT MEANS MASSACRING HER OWN PEOPLE.
EVEN THE CHILDREN.
DID YOUR MOTHER COME SEE YOU?
THE BITCH. SHE WOULD HAVE MURDERED *US* IF WE WEREN'T USEFUL.
OF COURSE NOT. EVEN IF SHE HAD BEEN FREE TO MOVE ABOUT, SHE WOULDN'T HAVE BOTHERED.
NOT THAT I WOULDN'T MIND GETTING MY HANDS ON HER. FROM EVERYTHING YOU DESCRIBED, MY RESURRECTION FORMULA SHOULD NEVER HAVE WORKED.
I NEED TO UNDERSTAND WHAT THE MOTHER SUPERIOR ALTERED. UNLIKE SOME, I DON'T BELIEVE IN BLESSINGS FROM MARIUM.
SOMETHING WAS ***DONE.*** SOMETHING THAT CAN BE ***TESTED.***
I'VE BEEN SUMMONED BACK TO THE CAPITAL. EVEN THE MOTHER SUPERIOR COULD NOT COUNTERMAND THAT ORDER. WHEN YOU'RE HEALTHY ENOUGH TO BE MOVED...
BE CAREFUL, ATENA.
WE'RE THE ONLY TWO PEOPLE WHO KNOW WHAT REALLY HAPPENED HERE. THAT'S DANGEROUS.
SO ARE WE.

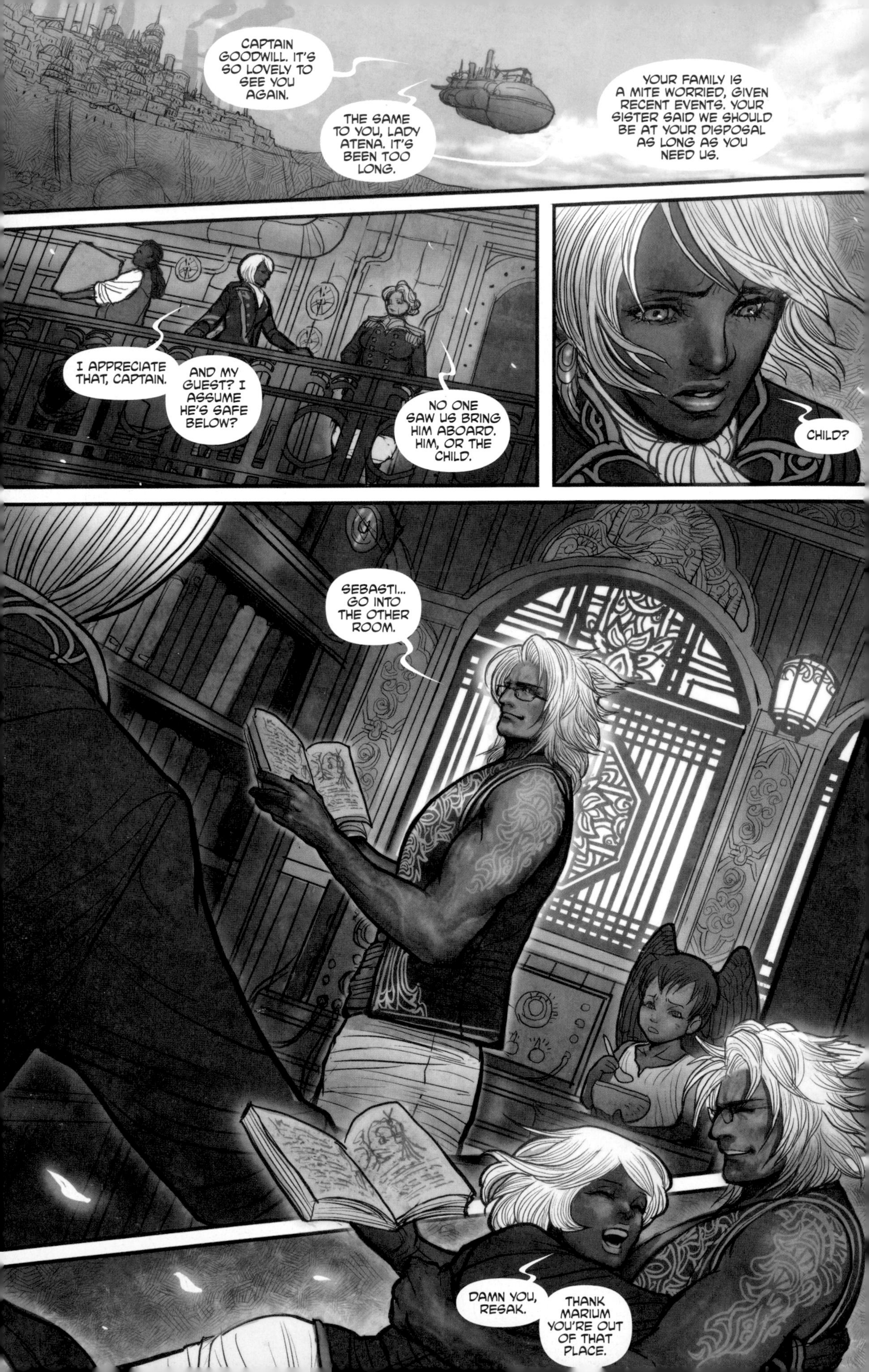
CAPTAIN GOODWILL. IT'S SO LOVELY TO SEE YOU AGAIN.
THE SAME TO YOU, LADY ATENA. IT'S BEEN TOO LONG.
YOUR FAMILY IS A MITE WORRIED, GIVEN RECENT EVENTS. YOUR SISTER SAID WE SHOULD BE AT YOUR DISPOSAL AS LONG AS YOU NEED US.
I APPRECIATE THAT, CAPTAIN.
AND MY GUEST? I ASSUME HE'S SAFE BELOW?
NO ONE SAW US BRING HIM ABOARD. HIM, OR THE CHILD.
CHILD?
SEBASTI... GO INTO THE OTHER ROOM.
DAMN YOU, RESAK.
THANK MARIUM YOU'RE OUT OF THAT PLACE.

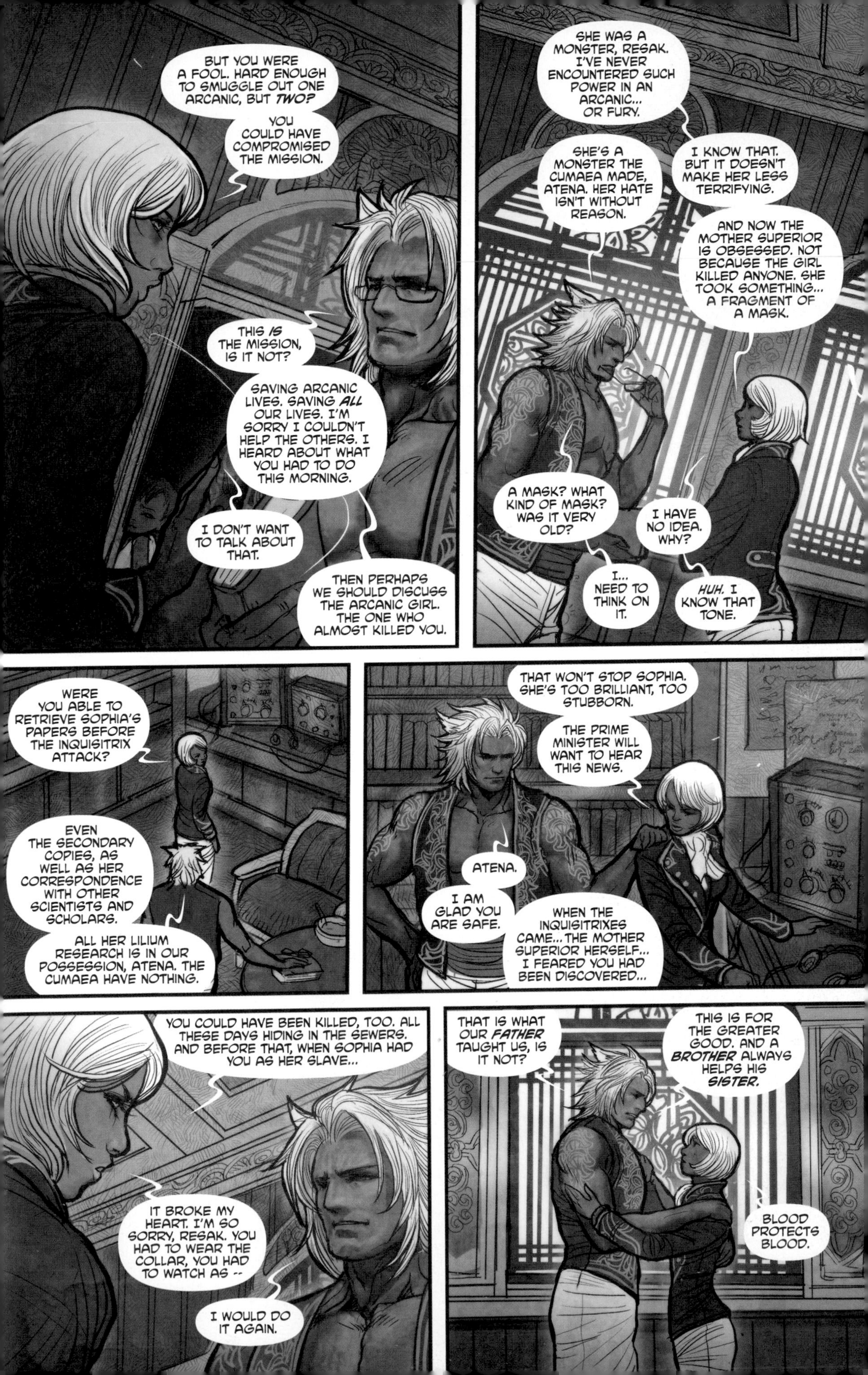

BUT YOU WERE A FOOL. HARD ENOUGH TO SMUGGLE OUT ONE ARCANIC, BUT *TWO?*
YOU COULD HAVE COMPROMISED THE MISSION.
THIS *IS* THE MISSION, IS IT NOT?
SAVING ARCANIC LIVES. SAVING *ALL* OUR LIVES. I'M SORRY I COULDN'T HELP THE OTHERS. I HEARD ABOUT WHAT YOU HAD TO DO THIS MORNING.
I DON'T WANT TO TALK ABOUT THAT.
THEN PERHAPS WE SHOULD DISCUSS THE ARCANIC GIRL. THE ONE WHO ALMOST KILLED YOU.
SHE WAS A MONSTER, RESAK. I'VE NEVER ENCOUNTERED SUCH POWER IN AN ARCANIC... OR FURY.
SHE'S A MONSTER THE CUMAEA MADE, ATENA. HER HATE ISN'T WITHOUT REASON.
I KNOW THAT. BUT IT DOESN'T MAKE HER LESS TERRIFYING.
AND NOW THE MOTHER SUPERIOR IS OBSESSED. NOT BECAUSE THE GIRL KILLED ANYONE. SHE TOOK SOMETHING... A FRAGMENT OF A MASK.
A MASK? WHAT KIND OF MASK? WAS IT VERY OLD?
I HAVE NO IDEA. WHY?
I... NEED TO THINK ON IT.
HUH. I KNOW THAT TONE.
WERE YOU ABLE TO RETRIEVE SOPHIA'S PAPERS BEFORE THE INQUISITRIX ATTACK?
EVEN THE SECONDARY COPIES, AS WELL AS HER CORRESPONDENCE WITH OTHER SCIENTISTS AND SCHOLARS.
ALL HER LILIUM RESEARCH IS IN OUR POSSESSION, ATENA. THE CUMAEA HAVE NOTHING.
THAT WON'T STOP SOPHIA. SHE'S TOO BRILLIANT, TOO STUBBORN.
THE PRIME MINISTER WILL WANT TO HEAR THIS NEWS.
ATENA.
I AM GLAD YOU ARE SAFE.
WHEN THE INQUISITRIXES CAME... THE MOTHER SUPERIOR HERSELF... I FEARED YOU HAD BEEN DISCOVERED...
YOU COULD HAVE BEEN KILLED, TOO. ALL THESE DAYS HIDING IN THE SEWERS. AND BEFORE THAT, WHEN SOPHIA HAD YOU AS HER SLAVE...
IT BROKE MY HEART. I'M SO SORRY, RESAK. YOU HAD TO WEAR THE COLLAR, YOU HAD TO WATCH AS --
I WOULD DO IT AGAIN.
THAT IS WHAT OUR *FATHER* TAUGHT US, IS IT NOT?
THIS IS FOR THE GREATER GOOD. AND A *BROTHER* ALWAYS HELPS HIS *SISTER.*
BLOOD PROTECTS BLOOD.

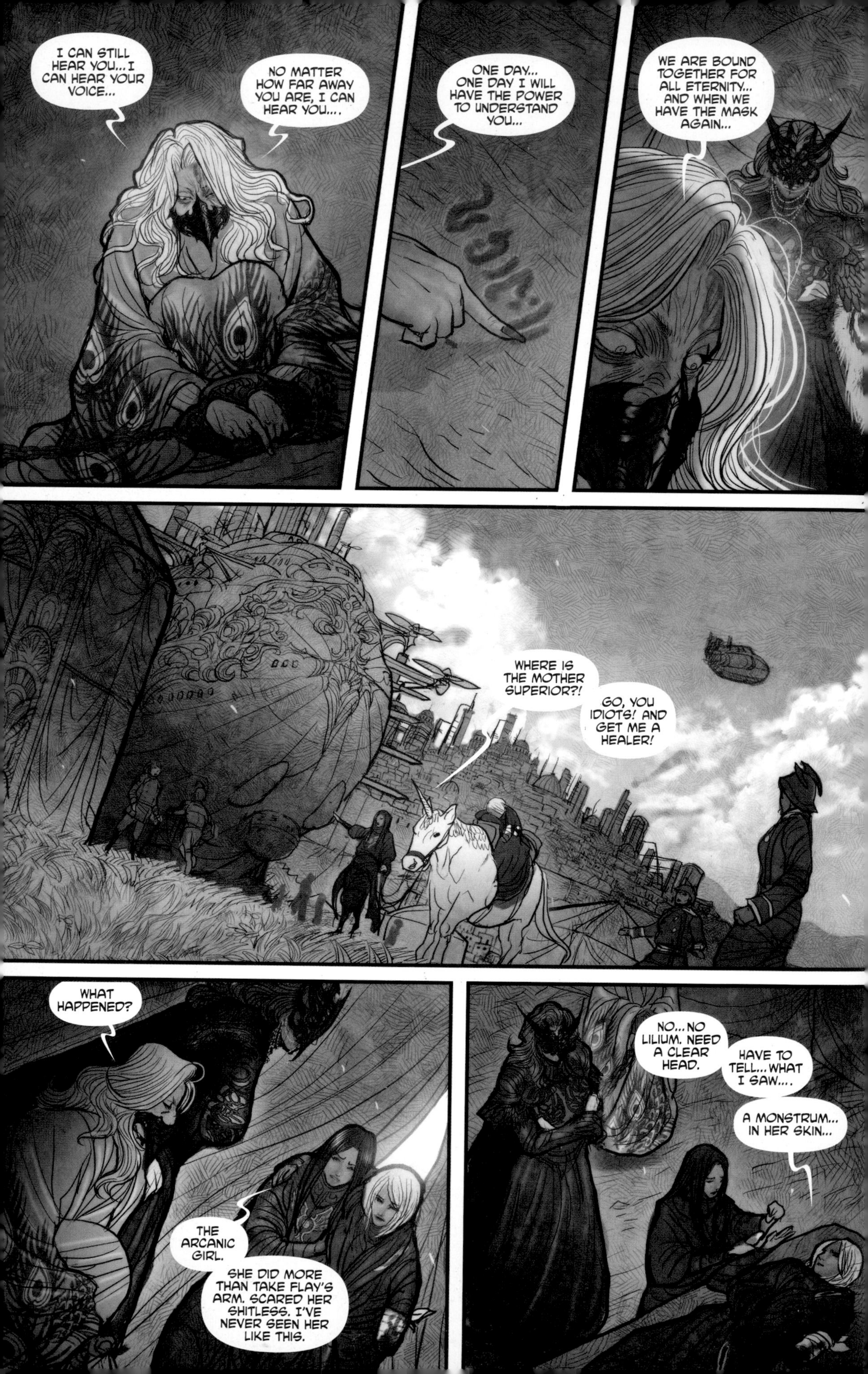
I CAN STILL HEAR YOU... I CAN HEAR YOUR VOICE...
NO MATTER HOW FAR AWAY YOU ARE, I CAN HEAR YOU....
ONE DAY... ONE DAY I WILL HAVE THE POWER TO UNDERSTAND YOU...
WE ARE BOUND TOGETHER FOR ALL ETERNITY... AND WHEN WE HAVE THE MASK AGAIN...
WHERE IS THE MOTHER SUPERIOR?!
GO, YOU IDIOTS! AND GET ME A HEALER!
WHAT HAPPENED?
THE ARCANIC GIRL.
SHE DID MORE THAN TAKE FLAY'S ARM. SCARED HER SHITLESS. I'VE NEVER SEEN HER LIKE THIS.
NO... NO LILIUM. NEED A CLEAR HEAD.
HAVE TO TELL... WHAT I SAW....
A MONSTRUM... IN HER SKIN...

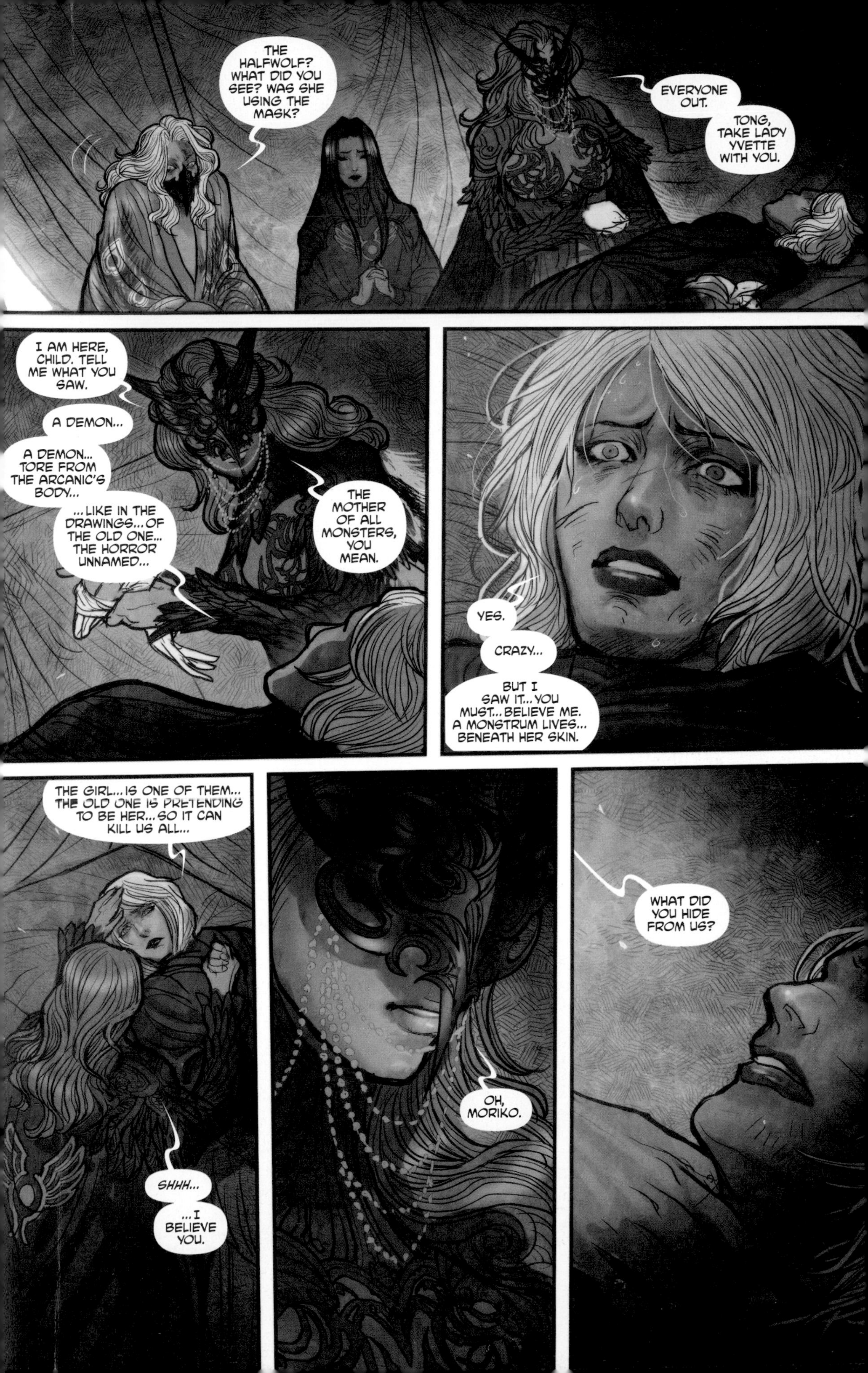
THE HALFWOLF? WHAT DID YOU SEE? WAS SHE USING THE MASK?
EVERYONE OUT.
TONG, TAKE LADY YVETTE WITH YOU.
I AM HERE, CHILD. TELL ME WHAT YOU SAW.
A DEMON...
A DEMON... TORE FROM THE ARCANIC'S BODY...
...LIKE IN THE DRAWINGS... OF THE OLD ONE... THE HORROR UNNAMED...
THE MOTHER OF ALL MONSTERS, YOU MEAN.
YES.
CRAZY...
BUT I SAW IT... YOU MUST... BELIEVE ME. A MONSTRUM LIVES... BENEATH HER SKIN.
THE GIRL... IS ONE OF THEM... THE OLD ONE IS PRETENDING TO BE HER... SO IT CAN KILL US ALL...
SHHH...
...I BELIEVE YOU.
OH, MORIKO.
WHAT DID YOU HIDE FROM US?

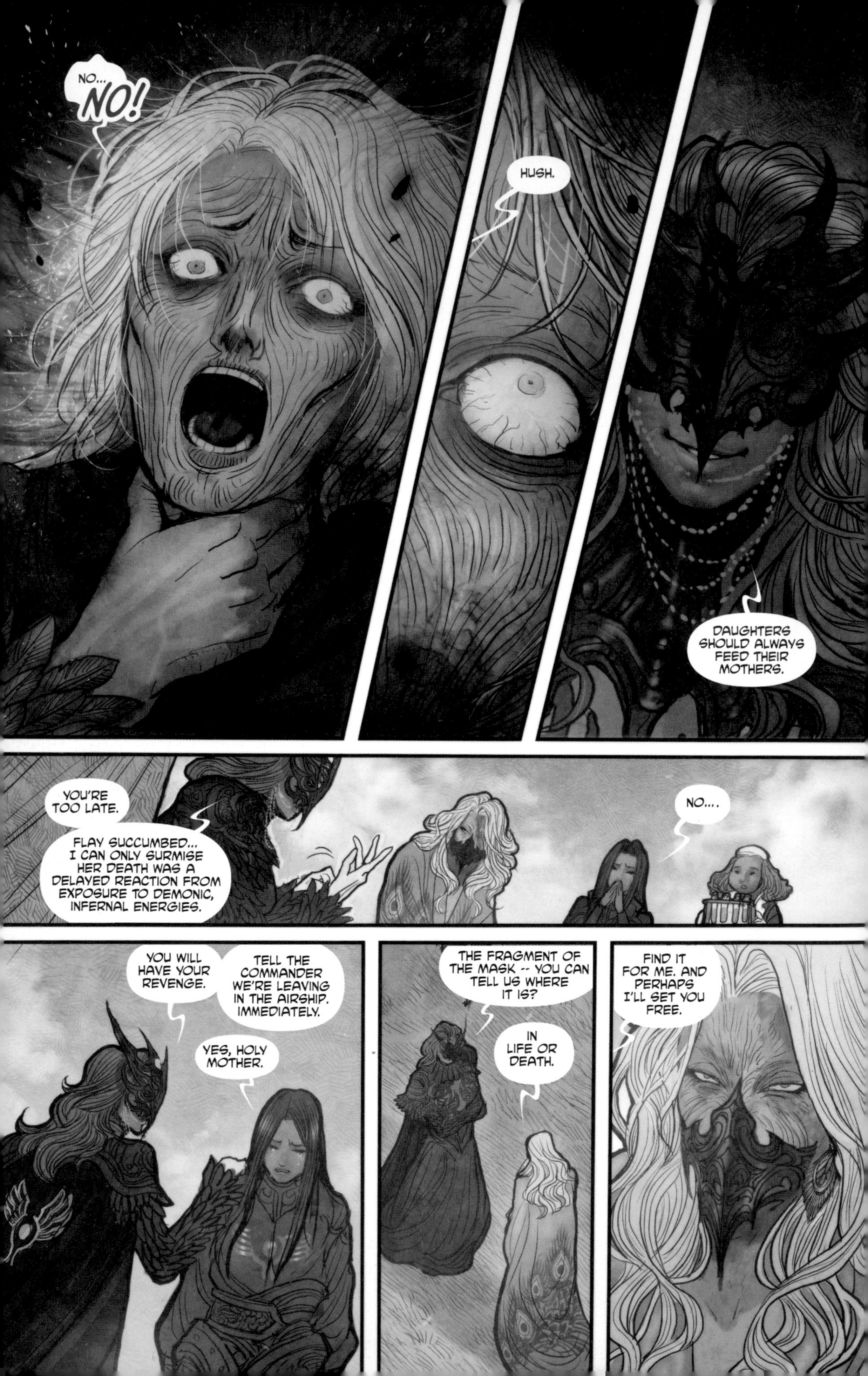
NO... NO!
HUSH.
DAUGHTERS SHOULD ALWAYS FEED THEIR MOTHERS.
YOU'RE TOO LATE.
FLAY SUCCUMBED... I CAN ONLY SURMISE HER DEATH WAS A DELAYED REACTION FROM EXPOSURE TO DEMONIC, INFERNAL ENERGIES.
NO....
YOU WILL HAVE YOUR REVENGE.
TELL THE COMMANDER WE'RE LEAVING IN THE AIRSHIP. IMMEDIATELY.
YES, HOLY MOTHER.
THE FRAGMENT OF THE MASK -- YOU CAN TELL US WHERE IT IS?
IN LIFE OR DEATH.
FIND IT FOR ME. AND PERHAPS I'LL SET YOU FREE.

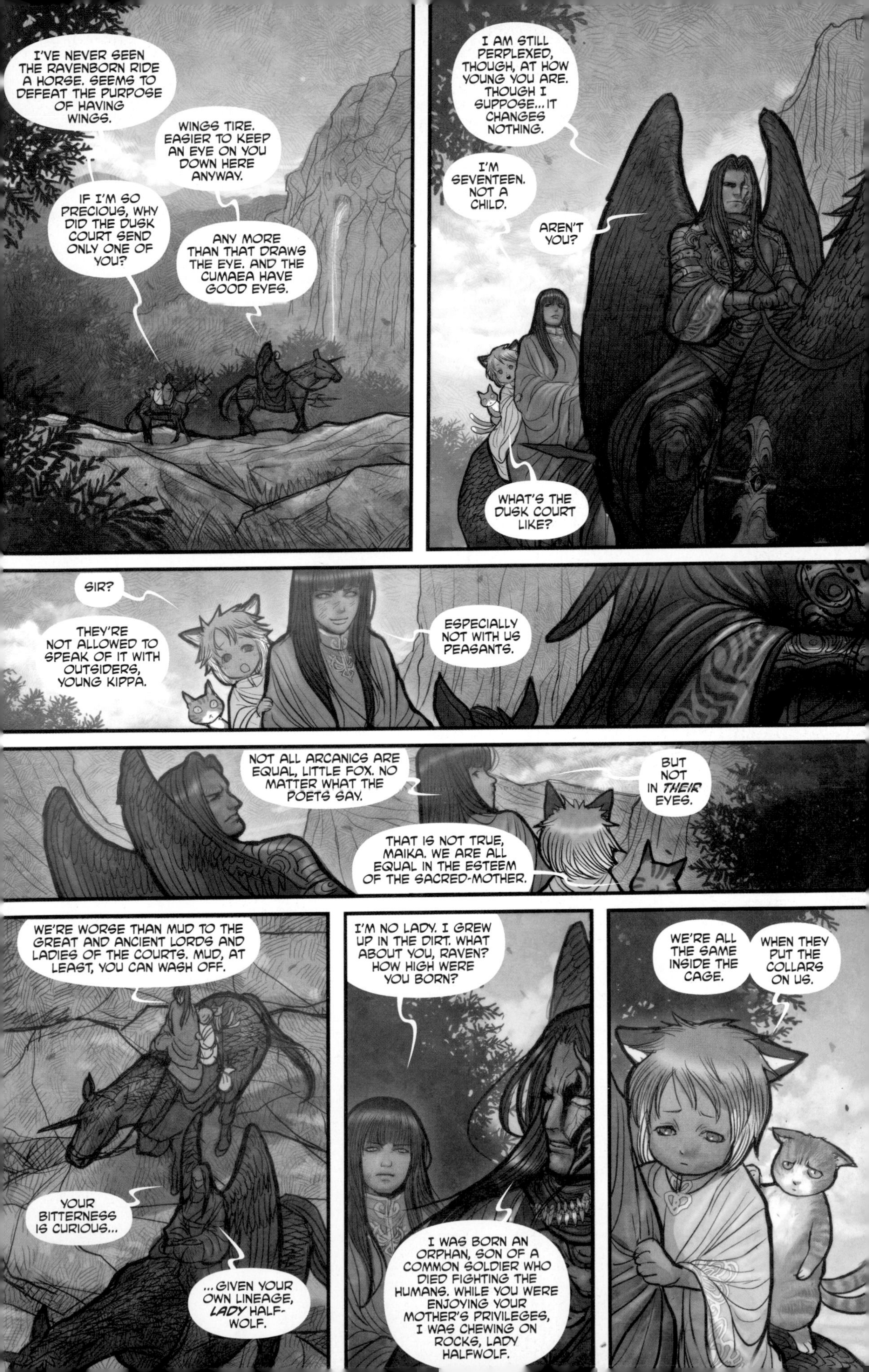
I'VE NEVER SEEN THE RAVENBORN RIDE A HORSE. SEEMS TO DEFEAT THE PURPOSE OF HAVING WINGS.
WINGS TIRE. EASIER TO KEEP AN EYE ON YOU DOWN HERE ANYWAY.
IF I'M SO PRECIOUS, WHY DID THE DUSK COURT SEND ONLY ONE OF YOU?
ANY MORE THAN THAT DRAWS THE EYE. AND THE CUMAEA HAVE GOOD EYES.
I AM STILL PERPLEXED, THOUGH, AT HOW YOUNG YOU ARE. THOUGH I SUPPOSE... IT CHANGES NOTHING.
I'M SEVENTEEN. NOT A CHILD.
AREN'T YOU?
WHAT'S THE DUSK COURT LIKE?
SIR?
THEY'RE NOT ALLOWED TO SPEAK OF IT WITH OUTSIDERS, YOUNG KIPPA.
ESPECIALLY NOT WITH US PEASANTS.
NOT ALL ARCANICS ARE EQUAL, LITTLE FOX. NO MATTER WHAT THE POETS SAY.
BUT NOT IN *THEIR* EYES.
THAT IS NOT TRUE, MAIKA. WE ARE ALL EQUAL IN THE ESTEEM OF THE SACRED-MOTHER.
WE'RE WORSE THAN MUD TO THE GREAT AND ANCIENT LORDS AND LADIES OF THE COURTS. MUD, AT LEAST, YOU CAN WASH OFF.
YOUR BITTERNESS IS CURIOUS...
...GIVEN YOUR OWN LINEAGE, *LADY* HALF-WOLF.
I'M NO LADY. I GREW UP IN THE DIRT. WHAT ABOUT YOU, RAVEN? HOW HIGH WERE YOU BORN?
I WAS BORN AN ORPHAN, SON OF A COMMON SOLDIER WHO DIED FIGHTING THE HUMANS. WHILE YOU WERE ENJOYING YOUR MOTHER'S PRIVILEGES, I WAS CHEWING ON ROCKS, LADY HALFWOLF.
WE'RE ALL THE SAME INSIDE THE CAGE.
WHEN THEY PUT THE COLLARS ON US.

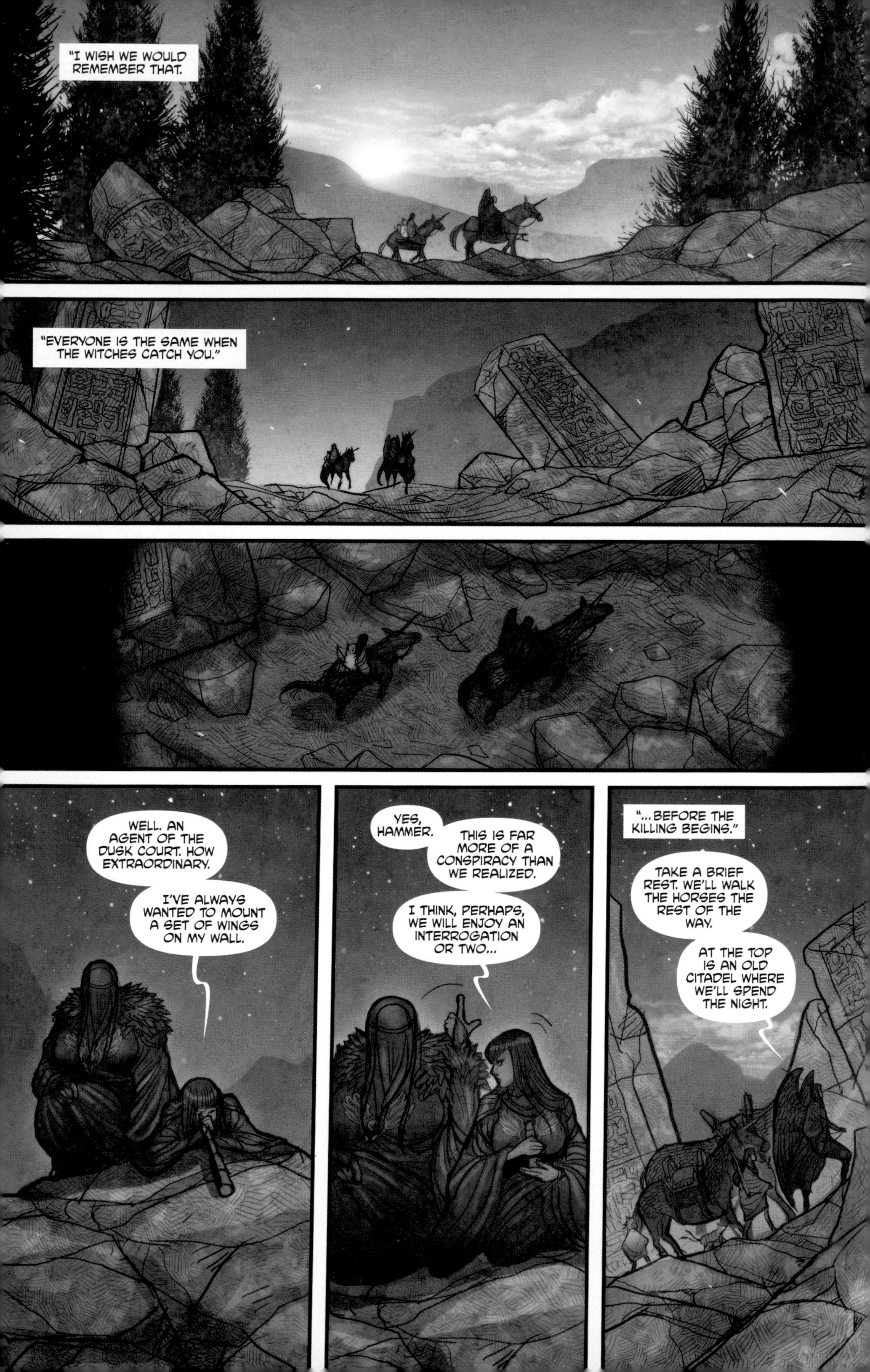
"I WISH WE WOULD REMEMBER THAT.
"EVERYONE IS THE SAME WHEN THE WITCHES CATCH YOU."
WELL. AN AGENT OF THE DUSK COURT. HOW EXTRAORDINARY.
I'VE ALWAYS WANTED TO MOUNT A SET OF WINGS ON MY WALL.
YES, HAMMER.
THIS IS FAR MORE OF A CONSPIRACY THAN WE REALIZED.
I THINK, PERHAPS, WE WILL ENJOY AN INTERROGATION OR TWO...
"...BEFORE THE KILLING BEGINS."
TAKE A BRIEF REST. WE'LL WALK THE HORSES THE REST OF THE WAY.
AT THE TOP IS AN OLD CITADEL WHERE WE'LL SPEND THE NIGHT.

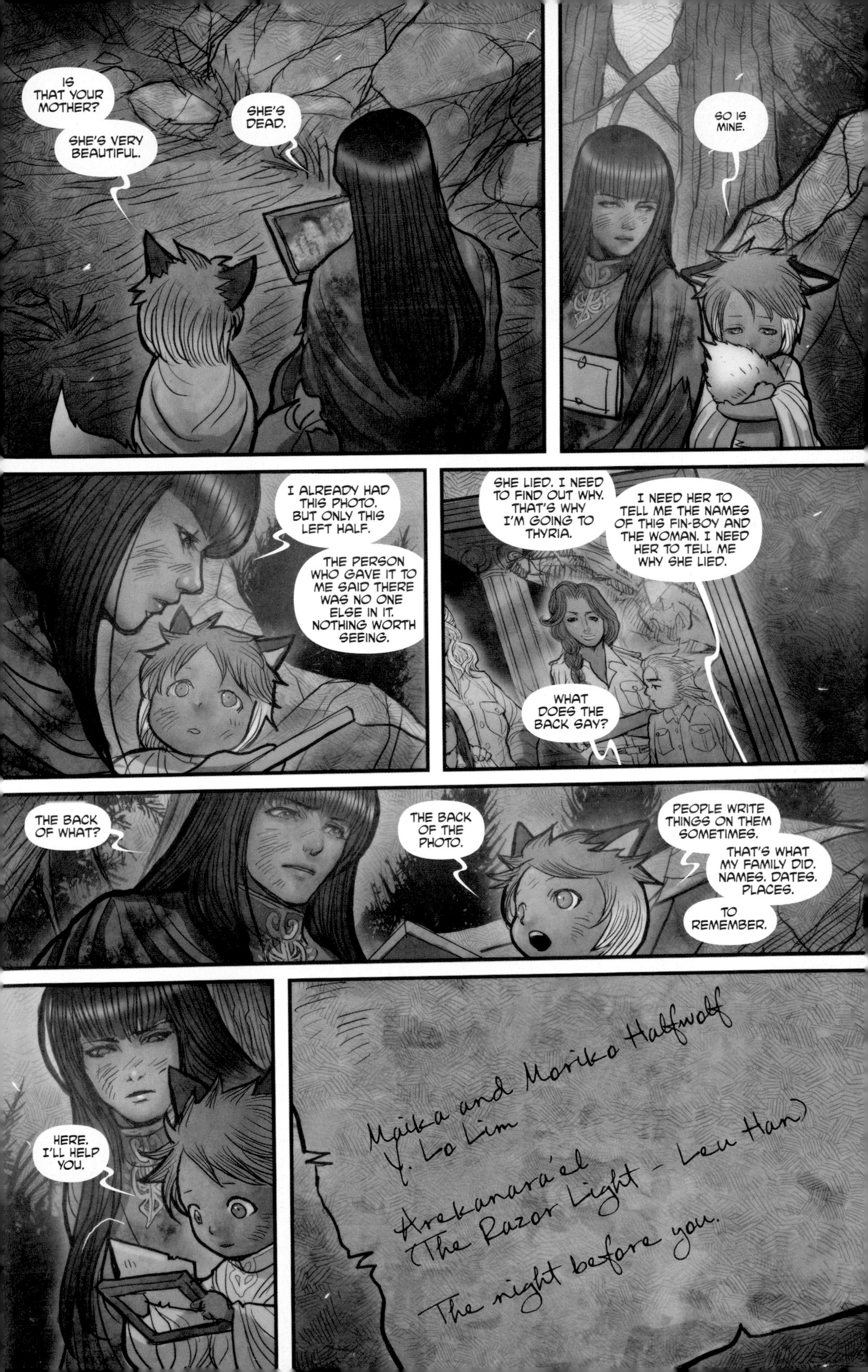
IS THAT YOUR MOTHER?
SHE'S VERY BEAUTIFUL.
SHE'S DEAD.
SO IS MINE.
I ALREADY HAD THIS PHOTO. BUT ONLY THIS LEFT HALF.
THE PERSON WHO GAVE IT TO ME SAID THERE WAS NO ONE ELSE IN IT. NOTHING WORTH SEEING.
SHE LIED. I NEED TO FIND OUT WHY. THAT'S WHY I'M GOING TO THYRIA.
I NEED HER TO TELL ME THE NAMES OF THIS FIN-BOY AND THE WOMAN. I NEED HER TO TELL ME WHY SHE LIED.
WHAT DOES THE BACK SAY?
THE BACK OF WHAT?
THE BACK OF THE PHOTO.
PEOPLE WRITE THINGS ON THEM SOMETIMES.
THAT'S WHAT MY FAMILY DID. NAMES. DATES. PLACES.
TO REMEMBER.
HERE. I'LL HELP YOU.
Maika and Moriko Halfwolf
Y. Lo Lim
Arekanara'el
(The Razor Light - Leu Han)
The night before you.

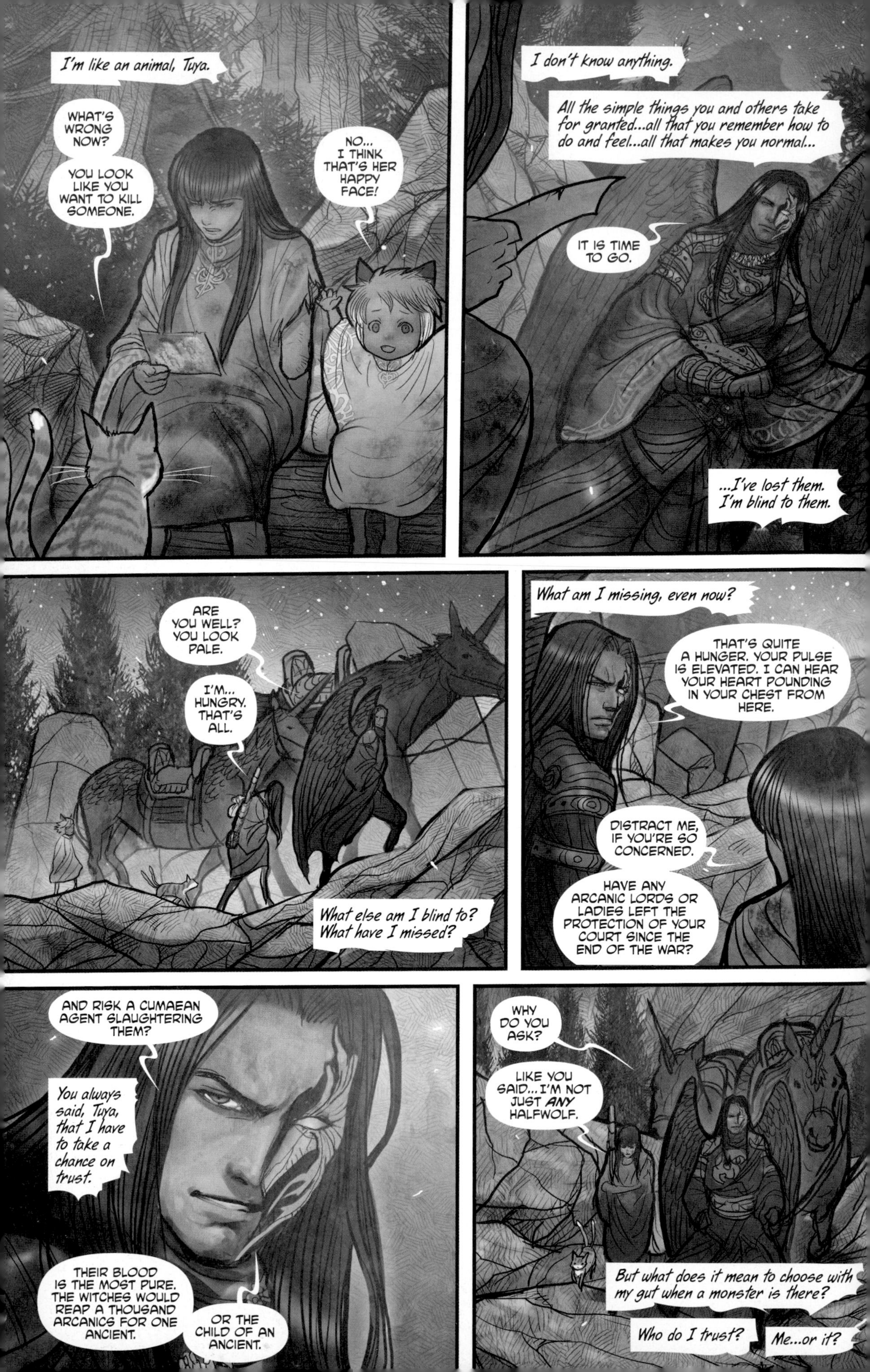
I'm like an animal, Tuya.
WHAT'S WRONG NOW?
YOU LOOK LIKE YOU WANT TO KILL SOMEONE.
NO... I THINK THAT'S HER HAPPY FACE!
I don't know anything.
All the simple things you and others take for granted...all that you remember how to do and feel...all that makes you normal...
IT IS TIME TO GO.
...I've lost them. I'm blind to them.
ARE YOU WELL? YOU LOOK PALE.
I'M... HUNGRY. THAT'S ALL.
What else am I blind to? What have I missed?
What am I missing, even now?
THAT'S QUITE A HUNGER. YOUR PULSE IS ELEVATED. I CAN HEAR YOUR HEART POUNDING IN YOUR CHEST FROM HERE.
DISTRACT ME, IF YOU'RE SO CONCERNED.
HAVE ANY ARCANIC LORDS OR LADIES LEFT THE PROTECTION OF YOUR COURT SINCE THE END OF THE WAR?
AND RISK A CUMAEAN AGENT SLAUGHTERING THEM?
You always said, Tuya, that I have to take a chance on trust.
THEIR BLOOD IS THE MOST PURE. THE WITCHES WOULD REAP A THOUSAND ARCANICS FOR ONE ANCIENT.
OR THE CHILD OF AN ANCIENT.
WHY DO YOU ASK?
LIKE YOU SAID...I'M NOT JUST ANY HALFWOLF.
But what does it mean to choose with my gut when a monster is there?
Who do I trust?
Me...or it?

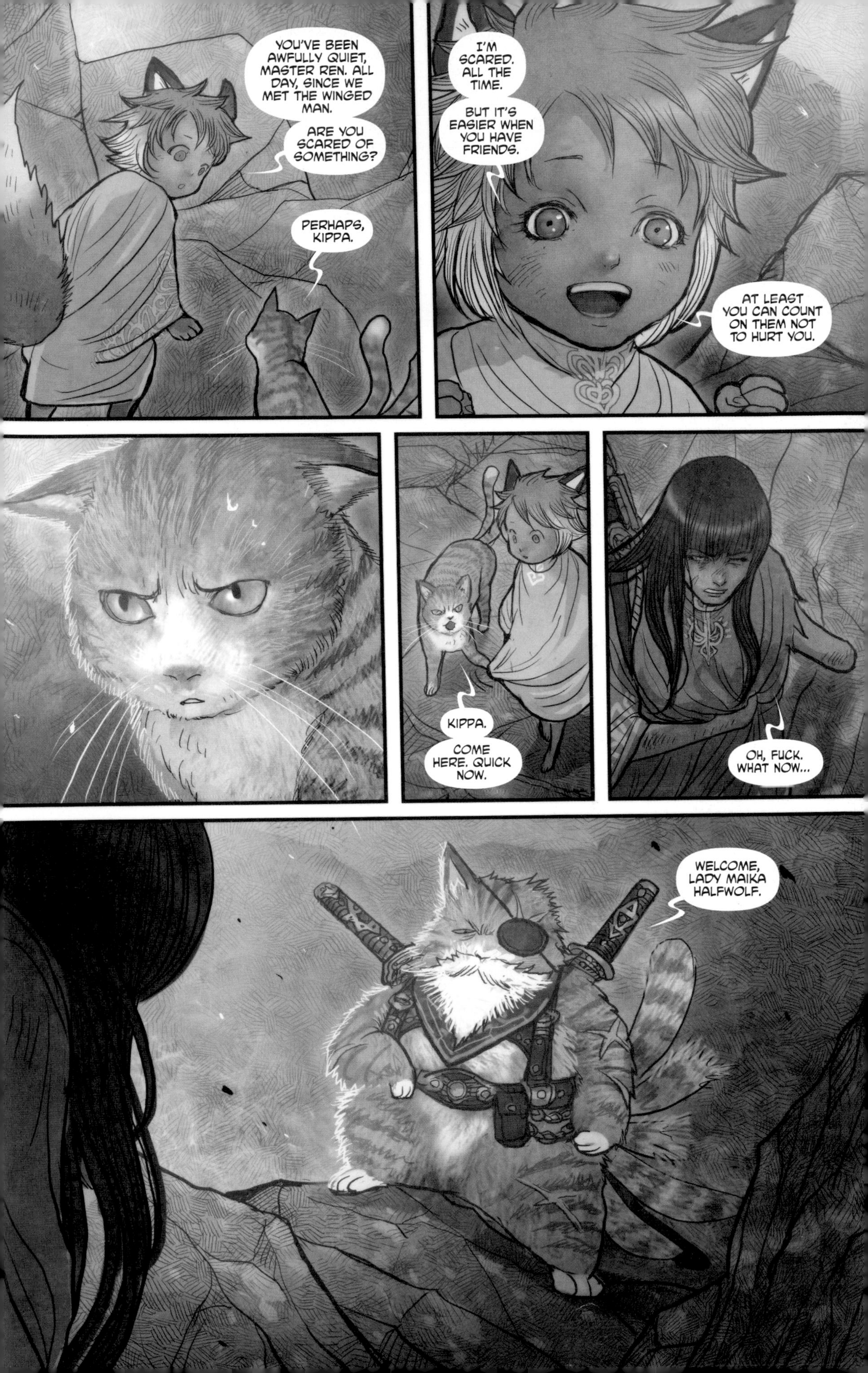
YOU'VE BEEN AWFULLY QUIET, MASTER REN. ALL DAY, SINCE WE MET THE WINGED MAN.
ARE YOU SCARED OF SOMETHING?
PERHAPS, KIPPA.
I'M SCARED. ALL THE TIME.
BUT IT'S EASIER WHEN YOU HAVE FRIENDS.
AT LEAST YOU CAN COUNT ON THEM NOT TO HURT YOU.
KIPPA.
COME HERE. QUICK NOW.
OH, FUCK. WHAT NOW...
WELCOME, LADY MAIKA HALFWOLF.

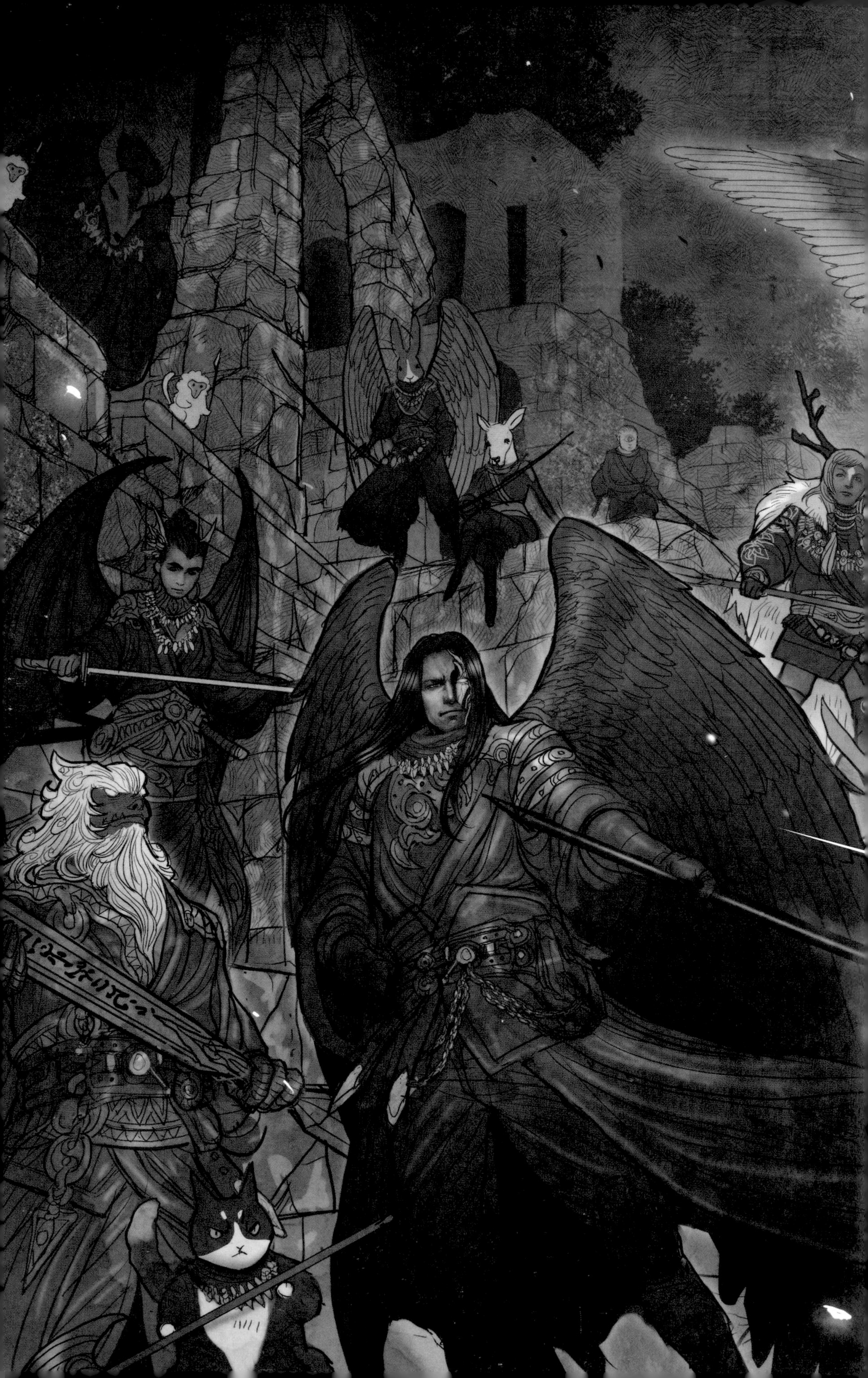

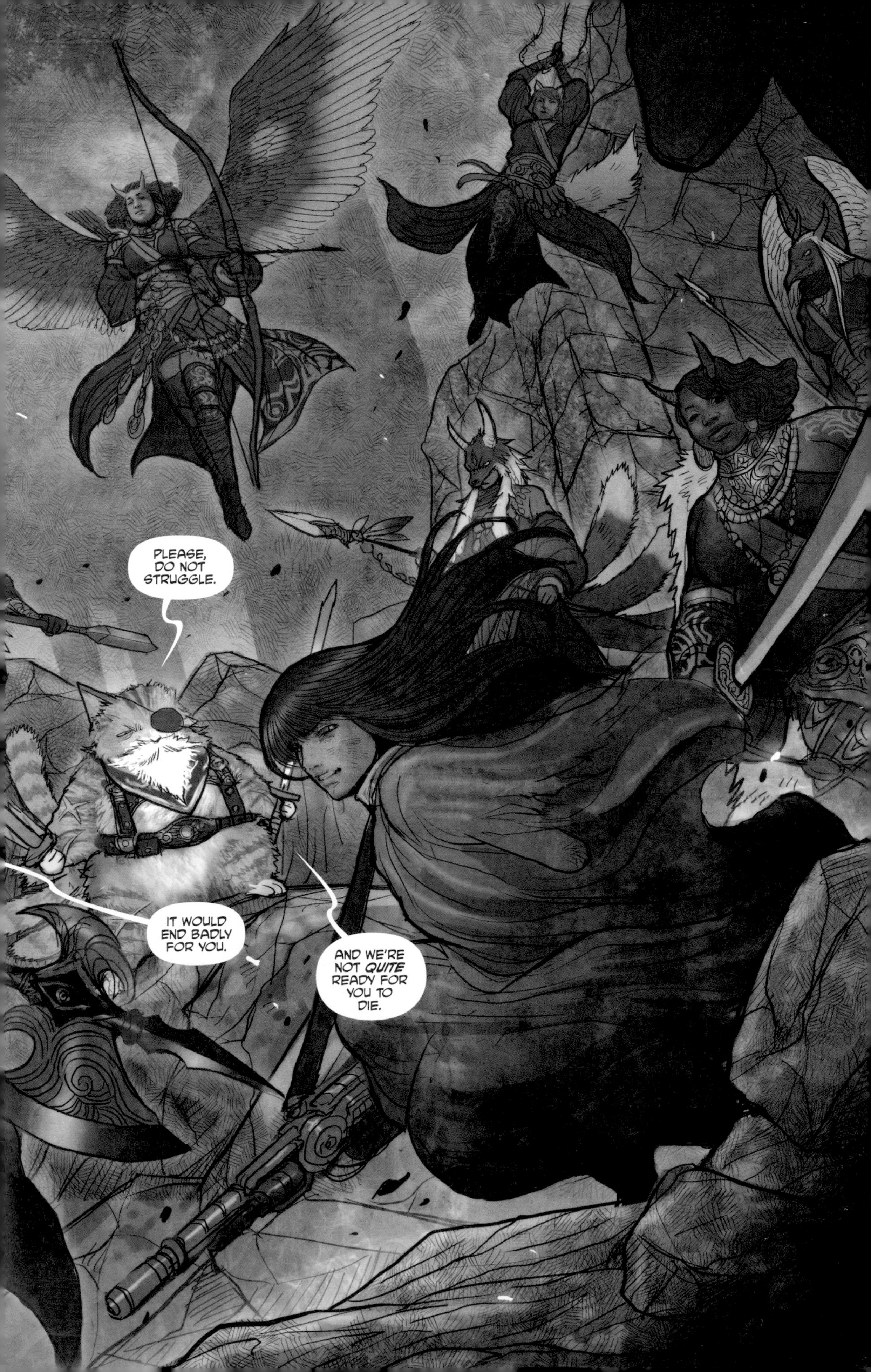
PLEASE, DO NOT STRUGGLE.
IT WOULD END BADLY FOR YOU.
AND WE'RE NOT *QUITE* READY FOR YOU TO DIE.

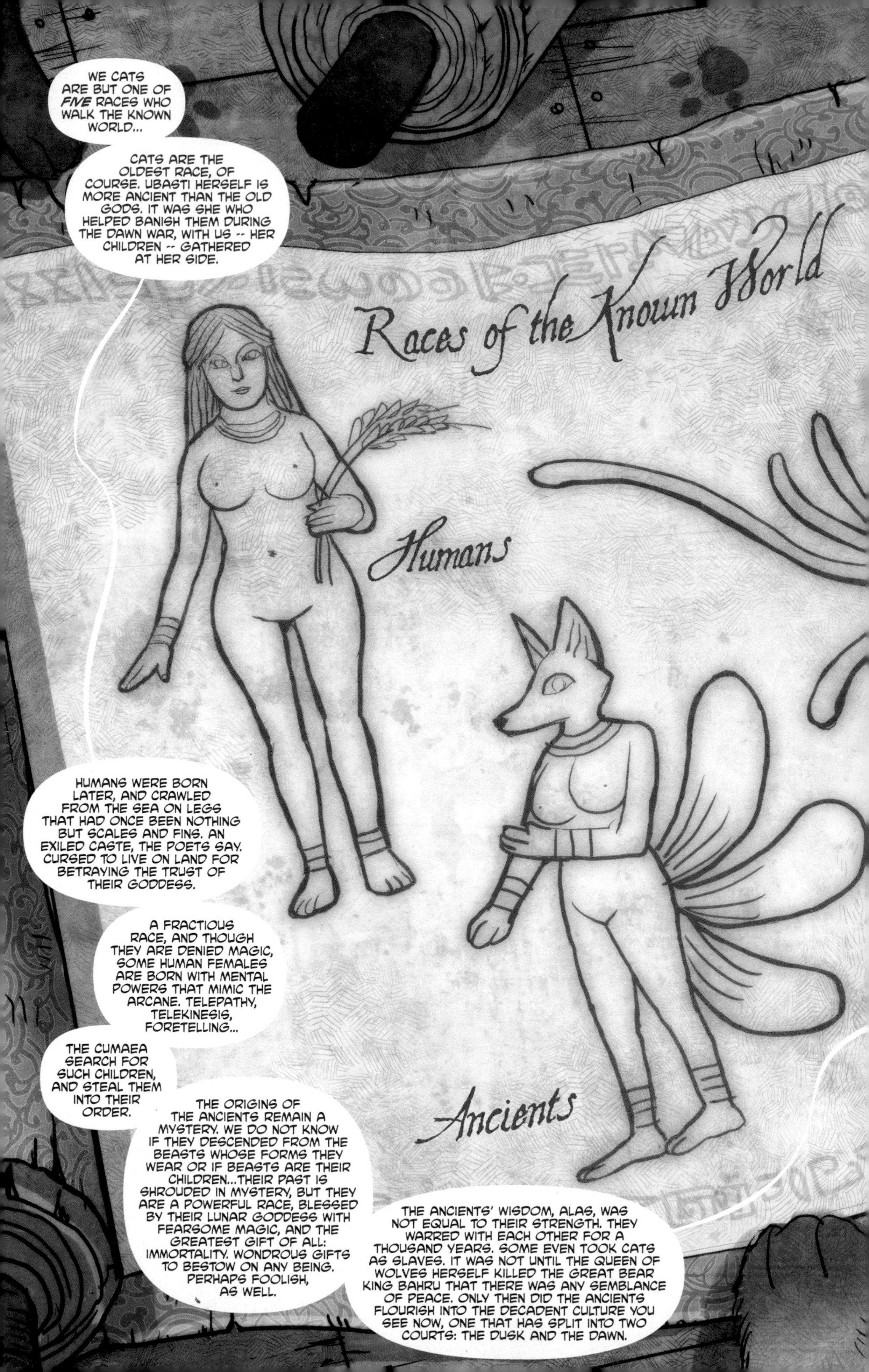
WE CATS ARE BUT ONE OF FIVE RACES WHO WALK THE KNOWN WORLD...
CATS ARE THE OLDEST RACE, OF COURSE. UBASTI HERSELF IS MORE ANCIENT THAN THE OLD GODS. IT WAS SHE WHO HELPED BANISH THEM DURING THE DAWN WAR, WITH US -- HER CHILDREN -- GATHERED AT HER SIDE.
Races of the Known World
Humans
HUMANS WERE BORN LATER, AND CRAWLED FROM THE SEA ON LEGS THAT HAD ONCE BEEN NOTHING BUT SCALES AND FINS. AN EXILED CASTE, THE POETS SAY. CURSED TO LIVE ON LAND FOR BETRAYING THE TRUST OF THEIR GODDESS.
A FRACTIOUS RACE, AND THOUGH THEY ARE DENIED MAGIC, SOME HUMAN FEMALES ARE BORN WITH MENTAL POWERS THAT MIMIC THE ARCANE. TELEPATHY, TELEKINESIS, FORETELLING...
THE CUMAEA SEARCH FOR SUCH CHILDREN, AND STEAL THEM INTO THEIR ORDER.
Ancients
THE ORIGINS OF THE ANCIENTS REMAIN A MYSTERY. WE DO NOT KNOW IF THEY DESCENDED FROM THE BEASTS WHOSE FORMS THEY WEAR OR IF BEASTS ARE THEIR CHILDREN...THEIR PAST IS SHROUDED IN MYSTERY, BUT THEY ARE A POWERFUL RACE, BLESSED BY THEIR LUNAR GODDESS WITH FEARSOME MAGIC, AND THE GREATEST GIFT OF ALL: IMMORTALITY. WONDROUS GIFTS TO BESTOW ON ANY BEING. PERHAPS FOOLISH, AS WELL.
THE ANCIENTS' WISDOM, ALAS, WAS NOT EQUAL TO THEIR STRENGTH. THEY WARRED WITH EACH OTHER FOR A THOUSAND YEARS. SOME EVEN TOOK CATS AS SLAVES. IT WAS NOT UNTIL THE QUEEN OF WOLVES HERSELF KILLED THE GREAT BEAR KING BAHRU THAT THERE WAS ANY SEMBLANCE OF PEACE. ONLY THEN DID THE ANCIENTS FLOURISH INTO THE DECADENT CULTURE YOU SEE NOW, ONE THAT HAS SPLIT INTO TWO COURTS: THE DUSK AND THE DAWN.

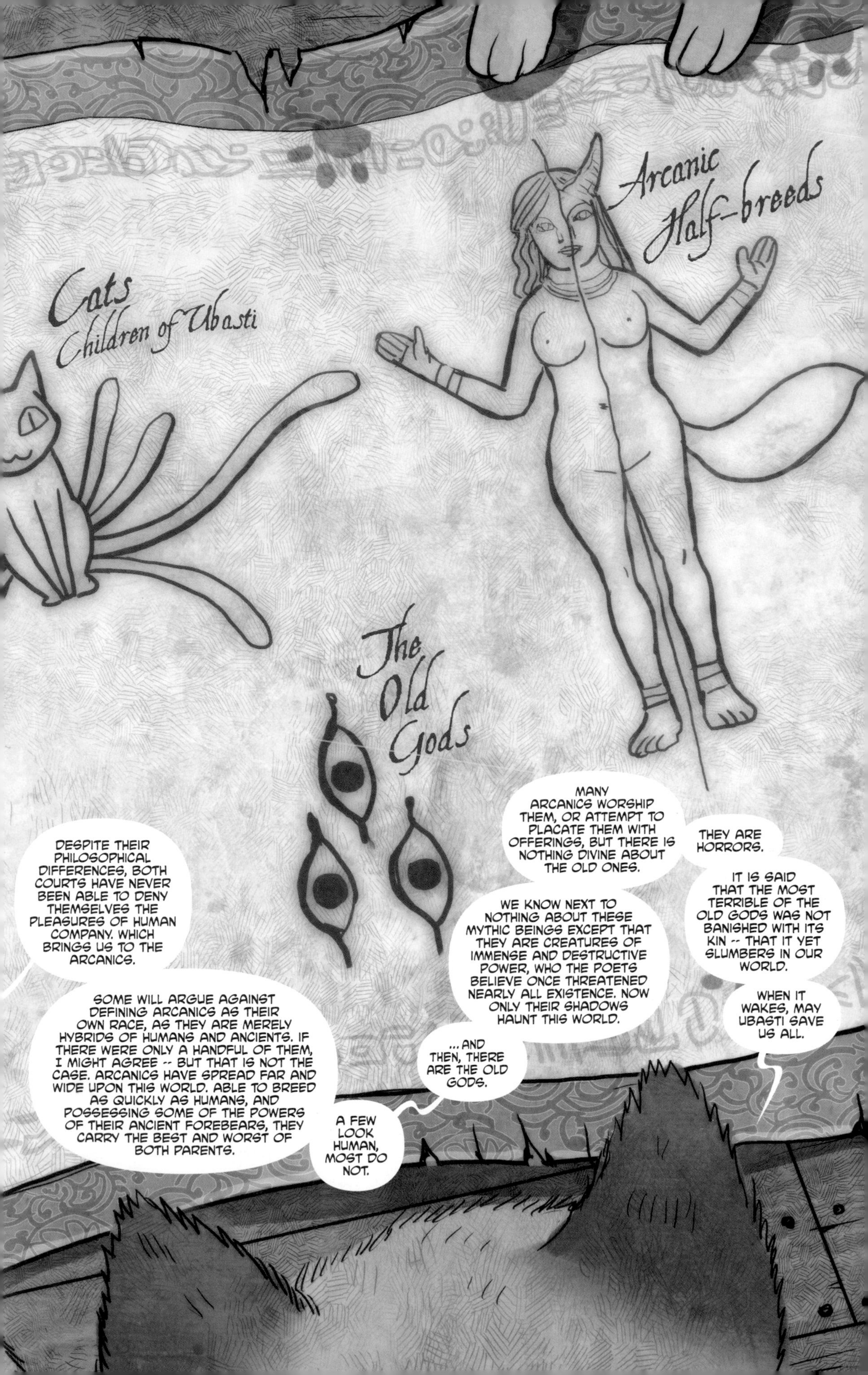
Cats
Children of Ubasti
Arcanic Half-breeds
The Old Gods
DESPITE THEIR PHILOSOPHICAL DIFFERENCES, BOTH COURTS HAVE NEVER BEEN ABLE TO DENY THEMSELVES THE PLEASURES OF HUMAN COMPANY. WHICH BRINGS US TO THE ARCANICS.
SOME WILL ARGUE AGAINST DEFINING ARCANICS AS THEIR OWN RACE, AS THEY ARE MERELY HYBRIDS OF HUMANS AND ANCIENTS. IF THERE WERE ONLY A HANDFUL OF THEM, I MIGHT AGREE -- BUT THAT IS NOT THE CASE. ARCANICS HAVE SPREAD FAR AND WIDE UPON THIS WORLD. ABLE TO BREED AS QUICKLY AS HUMANS, AND POSSESSING SOME OF THE POWERS OF THEIR ANCIENT FOREBEARS, THEY CARRY THE BEST AND WORST OF BOTH PARENTS.
A FEW LOOK HUMAN, MOST DO NOT.
...AND THEN, THERE ARE THE OLD GODS.
WE KNOW NEXT TO NOTHING ABOUT THESE MYTHIC BEINGS EXCEPT THAT THEY ARE CREATURES OF IMMENSE AND DESTRUCTIVE POWER, WHO THE POETS BELIEVE ONCE THREATENED NEARLY ALL EXISTENCE. NOW ONLY THEIR SHADOWS HAUNT THIS WORLD.
MANY ARCANICS WORSHIP THEM, OR ATTEMPT TO PLACATE THEM WITH OFFERINGS, BUT THERE IS NOTHING DIVINE ABOUT THE OLD ONES.
THEY ARE HORRORS.
IT IS SAID THAT THE MOST TERRIBLE OF THE OLD GODS WAS NOT BANISHED WITH ITS KIN -- THAT IT YET SLUMBERS IN OUR WORLD.
WHEN IT WAKES, MAY UBASTI SAVE US ALL.

CHAPTER SIX

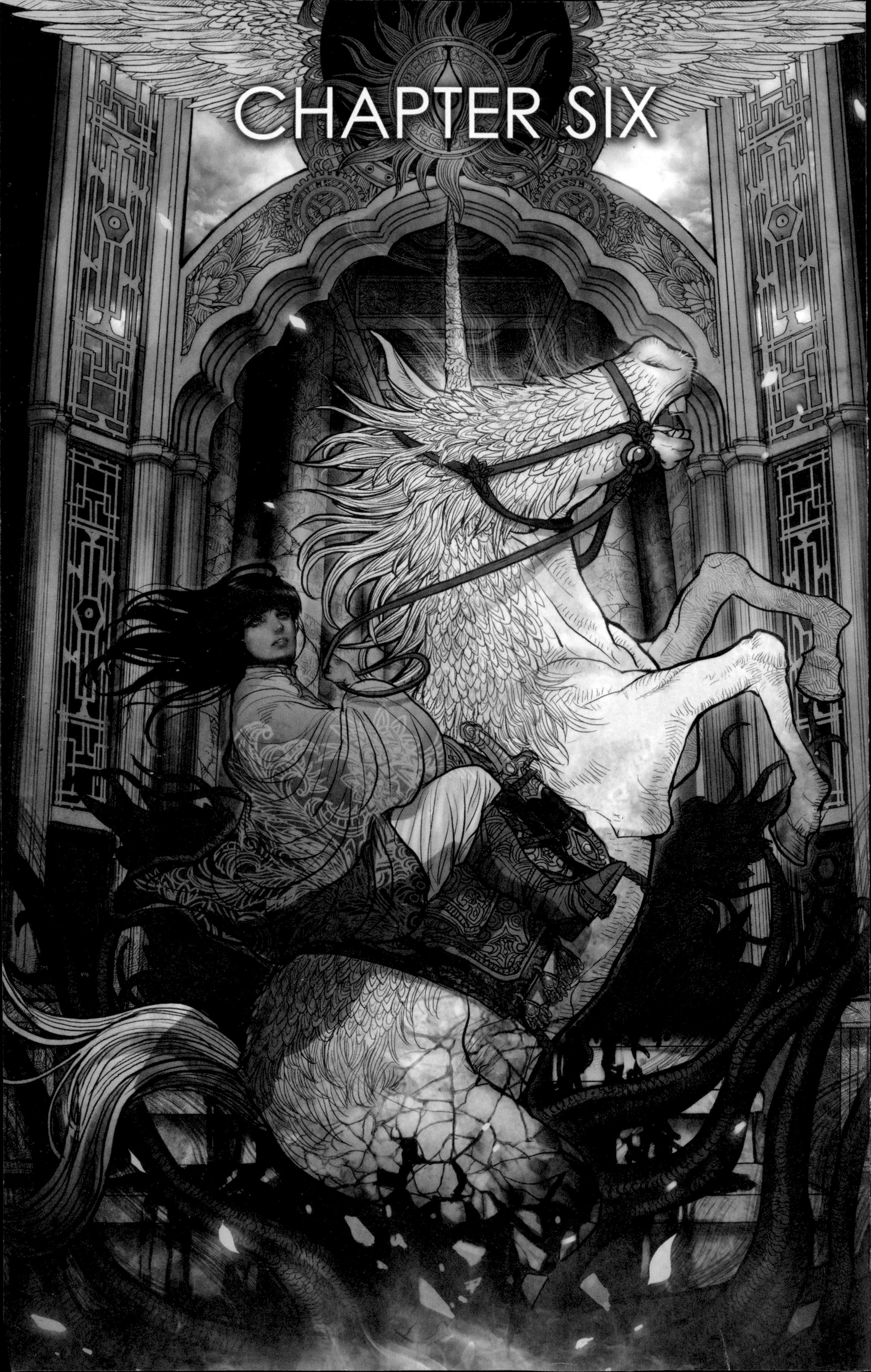

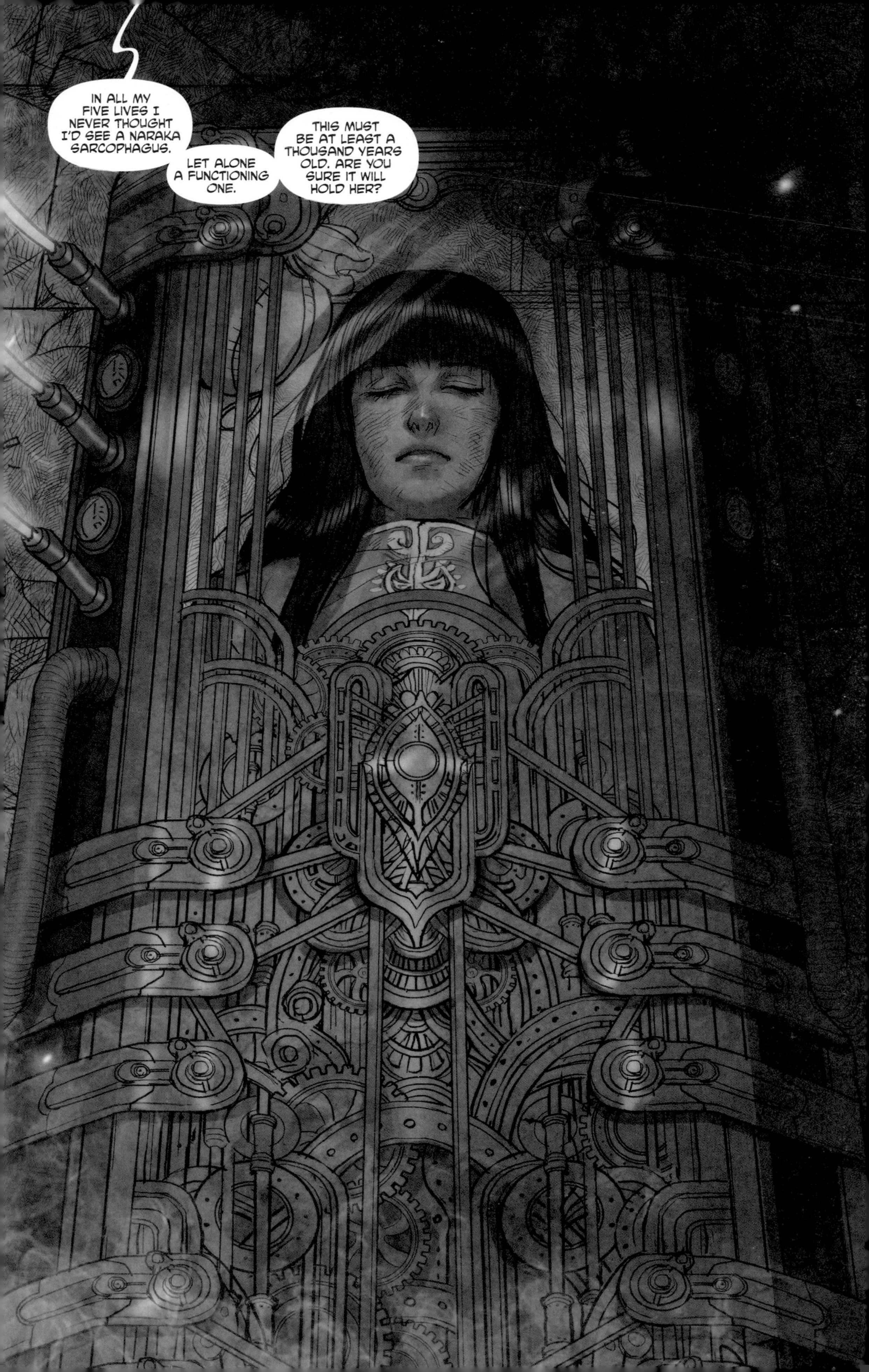
IN ALL MY FIVE LIVES I NEVER THOUGHT I'D SEE A NARAKA SARCOPHAGUS.
LET ALONE A FUNCTIONING ONE.
THIS MUST BE AT LEAST A THOUSAND YEARS OLD. ARE YOU SURE IT WILL HOLD HER?

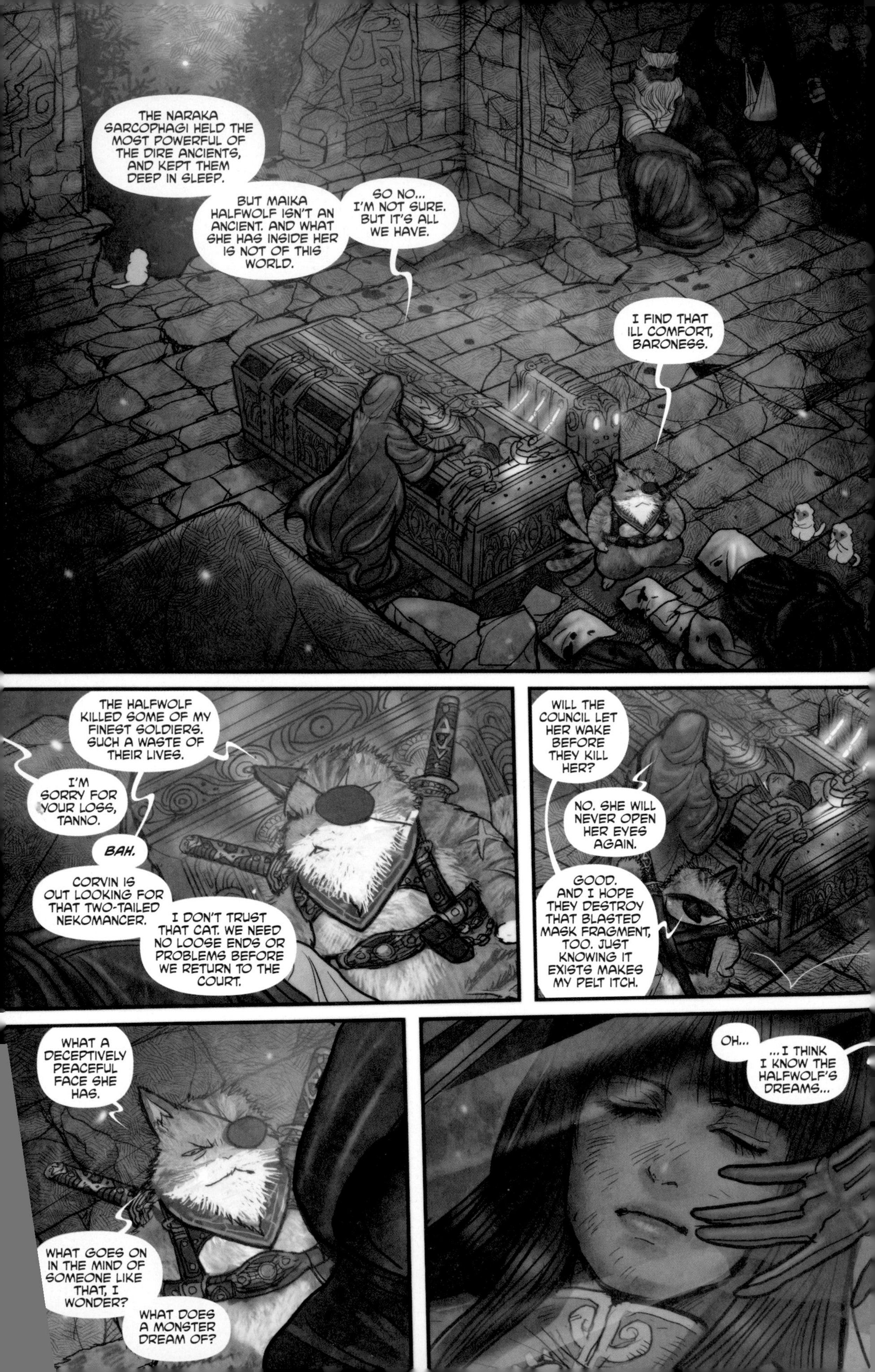
THE NARAKA SARCOPHAGI HELD THE MOST POWERFUL OF THE DIRE ANCIENTS, AND KEPT THEM DEEP IN SLEEP.
BUT MAIKA HALFWOLF ISN'T AN ANCIENT. AND WHAT SHE HAS INSIDE HER IS NOT OF THIS WORLD.
SO NO... I'M NOT SURE. BUT IT'S ALL WE HAVE.
I FIND THAT ILL COMFORT, BARONESS.
THE HALFWOLF KILLED SOME OF MY FINEST SOLDIERS. SUCH A WASTE OF THEIR LIVES.
I'M SORRY FOR YOUR LOSS, TANNO.
BAH.
CORVIN IS OUT LOOKING FOR THAT TWO-TAILED NEKOMANCER.
I DON'T TRUST THAT CAT. WE NEED NO LOOSE ENDS OR PROBLEMS BEFORE WE RETURN TO THE COURT.
WILL THE COUNCIL LET HER WAKE BEFORE THEY KILL HER?
NO. SHE WILL NEVER OPEN HER EYES AGAIN.
GOOD. AND I HOPE THEY DESTROY THAT BLASTED MASK FRAGMENT, TOO. JUST KNOWING IT EXISTS MAKES MY PELT ITCH.
WHAT A DECEPTIVELY PEACEFUL FACE SHE HAS.
WHAT GOES ON IN THE MIND OF SOMEONE LIKE THAT, I WONDER?
WHAT DOES A MONSTER DREAM OF?
OH...
...I THINK I KNOW THE HALFWOLF'S DREAMS...

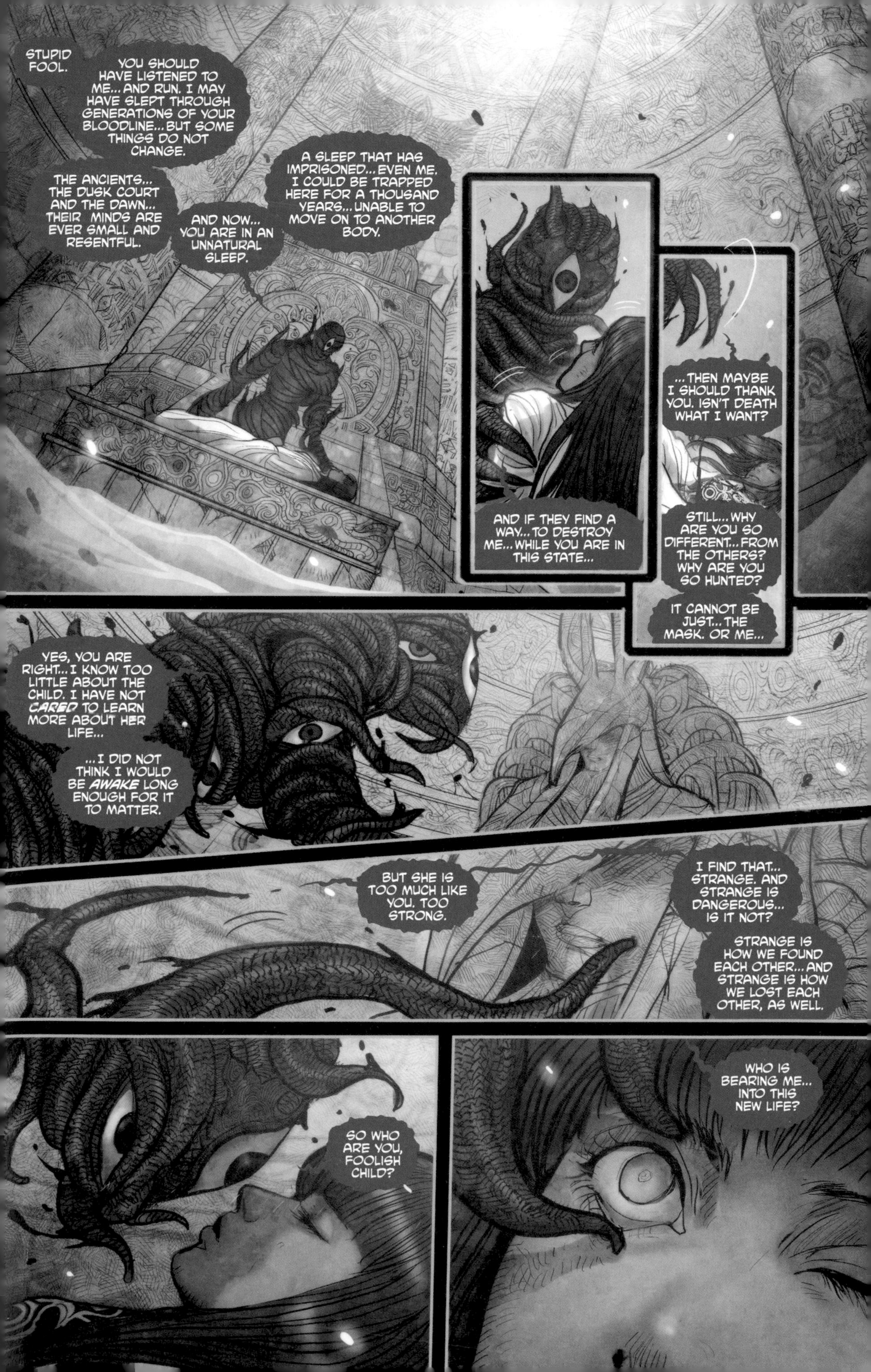
STUPID FOOL.
YOU SHOULD HAVE LISTENED TO ME... AND RUN. I MAY HAVE SLEPT THROUGH GENERATIONS OF YOUR BLOODLINE... BUT SOME THINGS DO NOT CHANGE.
THE ANCIENTS... THE DUSK COURT AND THE DAWN... THEIR MINDS ARE EVER SMALL AND RESENTFUL.
AND NOW... YOU ARE IN AN UNNATURAL SLEEP.
A SLEEP THAT HAS IMPRISONED... EVEN ME. I COULD BE TRAPPED HERE FOR A THOUSAND YEARS... UNABLE TO MOVE ON TO ANOTHER BODY.
AND IF THEY FIND A WAY... TO DESTROY ME... WHILE YOU ARE IN THIS STATE...
...THEN MAYBE I SHOULD THANK YOU. ISN'T DEATH WHAT I WANT?
STILL... WHY ARE YOU SO DIFFERENT... FROM THE OTHERS? WHY ARE YOU SO HUNTED?
IT CANNOT BE JUST... THE MASK. OR ME...
YES, YOU ARE RIGHT... I KNOW TOO LITTLE ABOUT THE CHILD. I HAVE NOT CARED TO LEARN MORE ABOUT HER LIFE...
...I DID NOT THINK I WOULD BE AWAKE LONG ENOUGH FOR IT TO MATTER.
BUT SHE IS TOO MUCH LIKE YOU. TOO STRONG.
I FIND THAT... STRANGE. AND STRANGE IS DANGEROUS... IS IT NOT?
STRANGE IS HOW WE FOUND EACH OTHER... AND STRANGE IS HOW WE LOST EACH OTHER, AS WELL.
SO WHO ARE YOU, FOOLISH CHILD?
WHO IS BEARING ME... INTO THIS NEW LIFE?

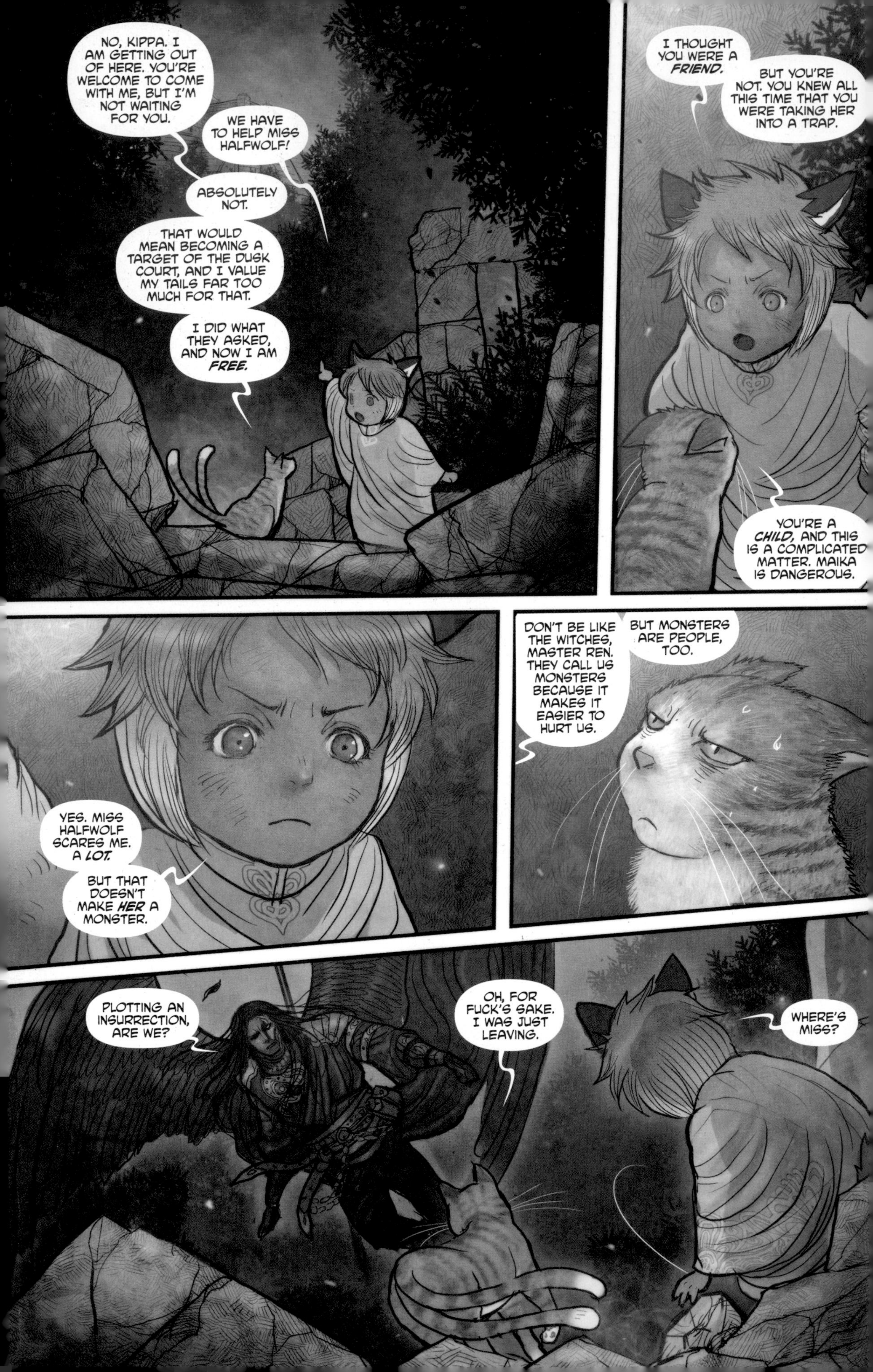
NO, KIPPA. I AM GETTING OUT OF HERE. YOU'RE WELCOME TO COME WITH ME, BUT I'M NOT WAITING FOR YOU.
WE HAVE TO HELP MISS HALFWOLF!
ABSOLUTELY NOT.
THAT WOULD MEAN BECOMING A TARGET OF THE DUSK COURT, AND I VALUE MY TAILS FAR TOO MUCH FOR THAT.
I DID WHAT THEY ASKED, AND NOW I AM *FREE.*
I THOUGHT YOU WERE A *FRIEND.*
BUT YOU'RE NOT. YOU KNEW ALL THIS TIME THAT YOU WERE TAKING HER INTO A TRAP.
YOU'RE A *CHILD,* AND THIS IS A COMPLICATED MATTER. MAIKA IS DANGEROUS.
YES. MISS HALFWOLF SCARES ME. A *LOT.*
BUT THAT DOESN'T MAKE *HER* A MONSTER.
DON'T BE LIKE THE WITCHES, MASTER REN. THEY CALL US MONSTERS BECAUSE IT MAKES IT EASIER TO HURT US.
BUT MONSTERS ARE PEOPLE, TOO.
PLOTTING AN INSURRECTION, ARE WE?
OH, FOR FUCK'S SAKE. I WAS JUST LEAVING.
WHERE'S MISS?

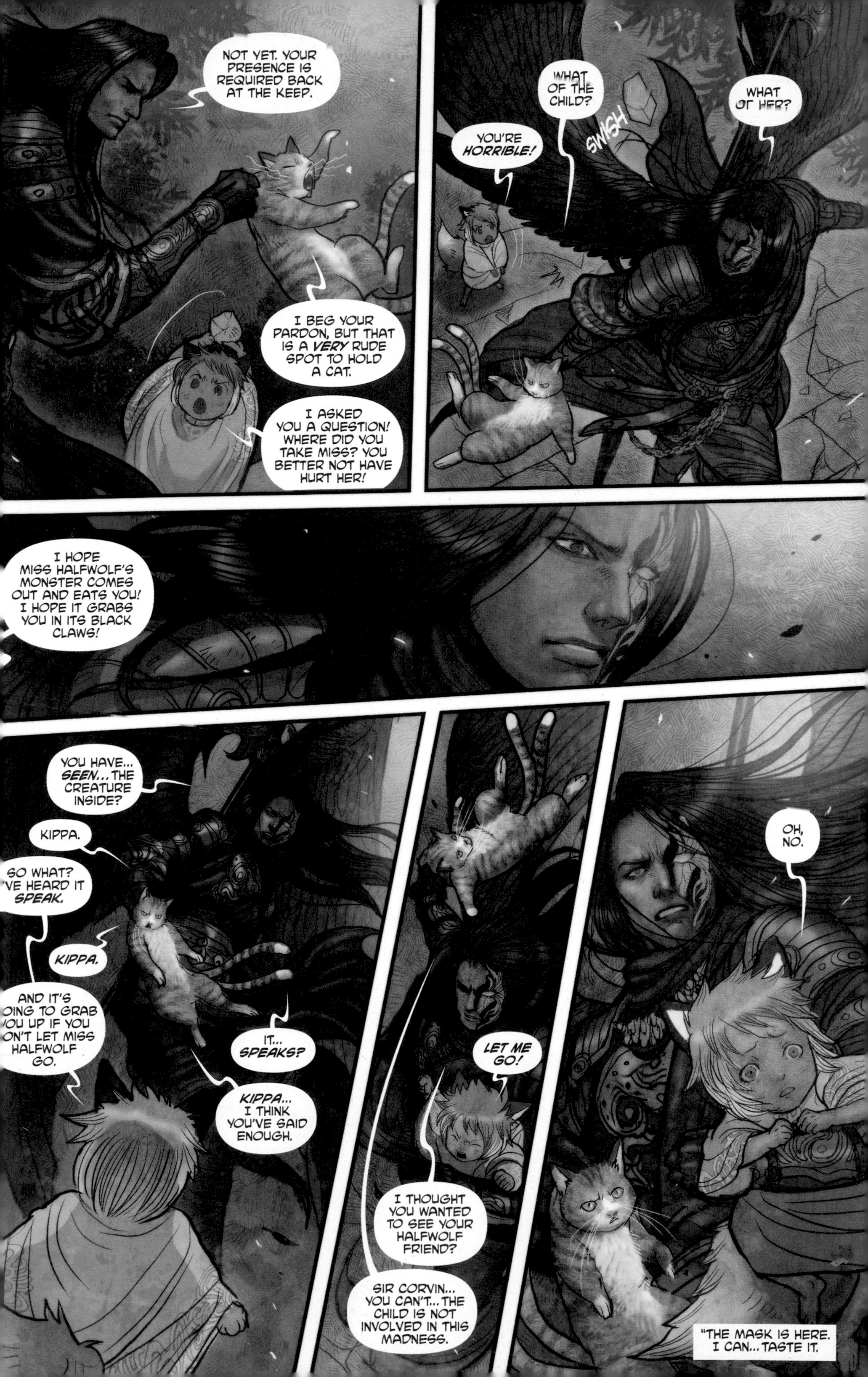
NOT YET. YOUR PRESENCE IS REQUIRED BACK AT THE KEEP.
I BEG YOUR PARDON, BUT THAT IS A *VERY* RUDE SPOT TO HOLD A CAT.
I ASKED YOU A QUESTION! WHERE DID YOU TAKE MISS? YOU BETTER NOT HAVE HURT HER!
WHAT OF THE CHILD?
WHAT OF HER?
SWISH
YOU'RE *HORRIBLE!*
I HOPE MISS HALFWOLF'S MONSTER COMES OUT AND EATS YOU! I HOPE IT GRABS YOU IN ITS BLACK CLAWS!
YOU HAVE... *SEEN*... THE CREATURE INSIDE?
KIPPA.
SO WHAT? 'VE HEARD IT *SPEAK.*
KIPPA.
AND IT'S OING TO GRAB OU UP IF YOU ON'T LET MISS HALFWOLF GO.
IT... *SPEAKS?*
KIPPA... I THINK YOU'VE SAID ENOUGH.
LET ME GO!
I THOUGHT YOU WANTED TO SEE YOUR HALFWOLF FRIEND?
SIR CORVIN... YOU CAN'T... THE CHILD IS NOT INVOLVED IN THIS MADNESS.
OH, NO.
"THE MASK IS HERE. I CAN... TASTE IT.

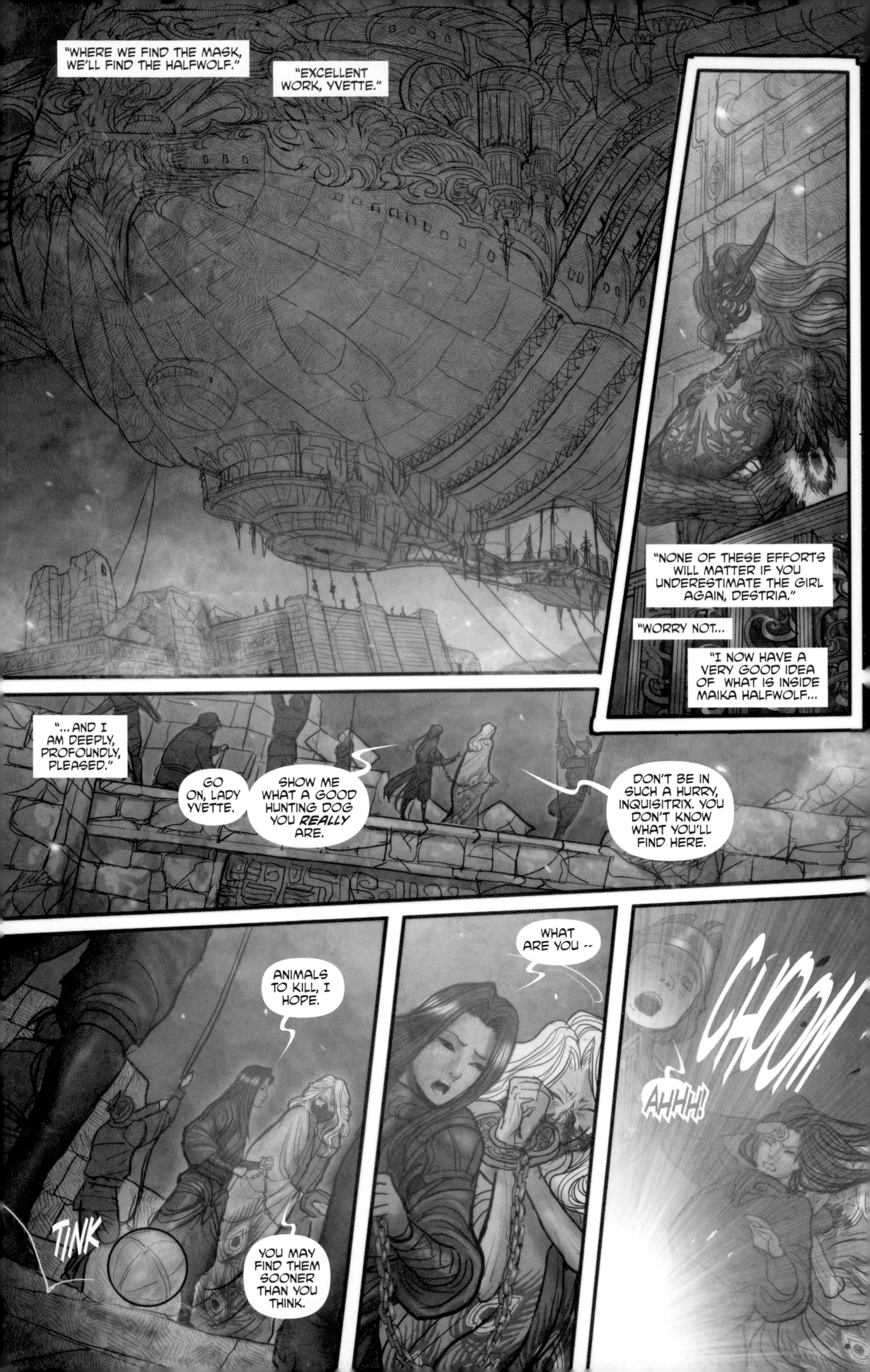
"WHERE WE FIND THE MASK, WE'LL FIND THE HALFWOLF."
"EXCELLENT WORK, YVETTE."
"NONE OF THESE EFFORTS WILL MATTER IF YOU UNDERESTIMATE THE GIRL AGAIN, DESTRIA."
"WORRY NOT...
"I NOW HAVE A VERY GOOD IDEA OF WHAT IS INSIDE MAIKA HALFWOLF...
"...AND I AM DEEPLY, PROFOUNDLY, PLEASED."
GO ON, LADY YVETTE.
SHOW ME WHAT A GOOD HUNTING DOG YOU *REALLY* ARE.
DON'T BE IN SUCH A HURRY, INQUISITRIX. YOU DON'T KNOW WHAT YOU'LL FIND HERE.
ANIMALS TO KILL, I HOPE.
YOU MAY FIND THEM SOONER THAN YOU THINK.
TINK
WHAT ARE YOU --
CHOOM
AHHH!

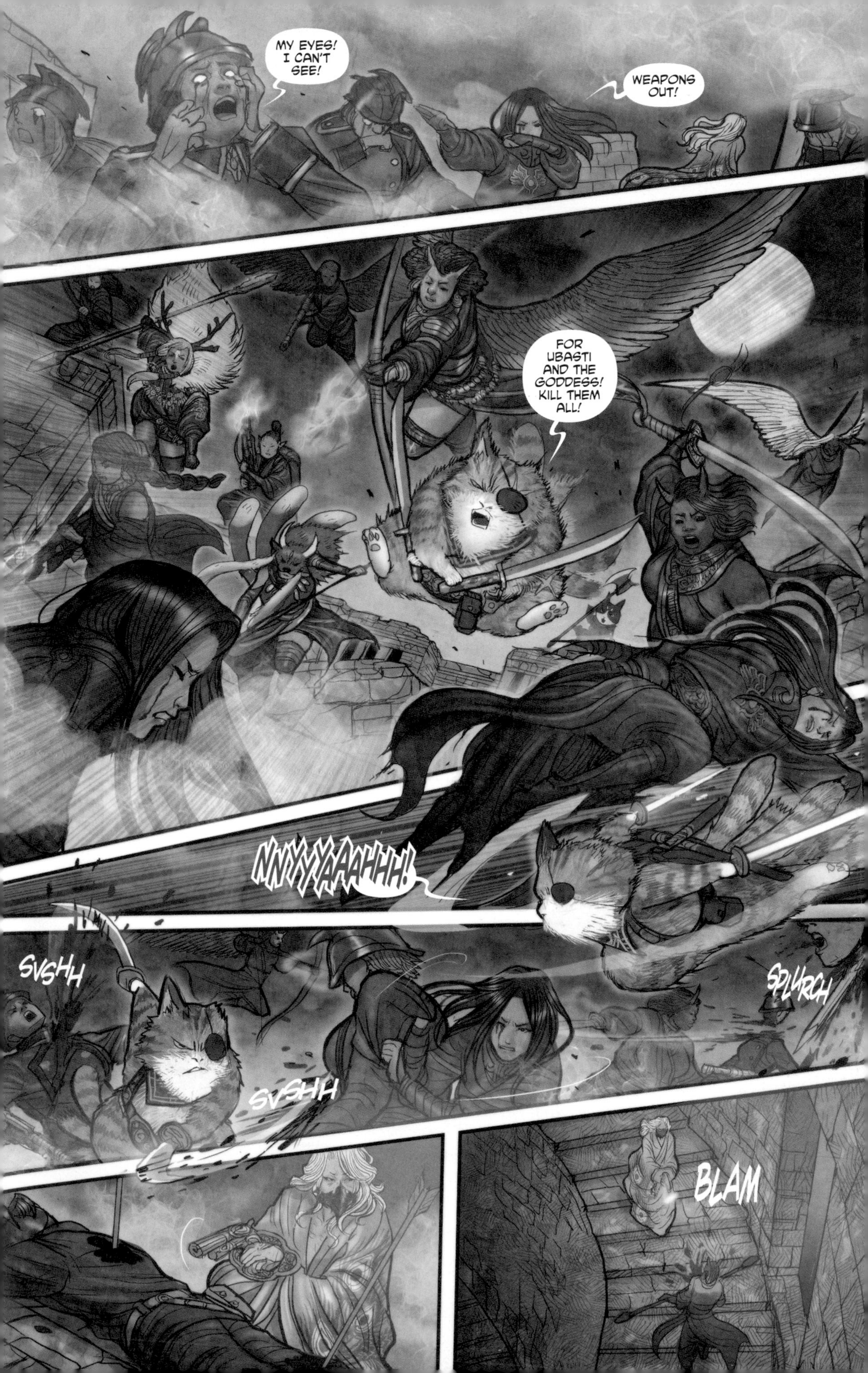
MY EYES! I CAN'T SEE!
WEAPONS OUT!
FOR UBASTI AND THE GODDESS! KILL THEM ALL!
NNYYAAAHHH!
SVSHH
SVSHH
SPLURCH
BLAM

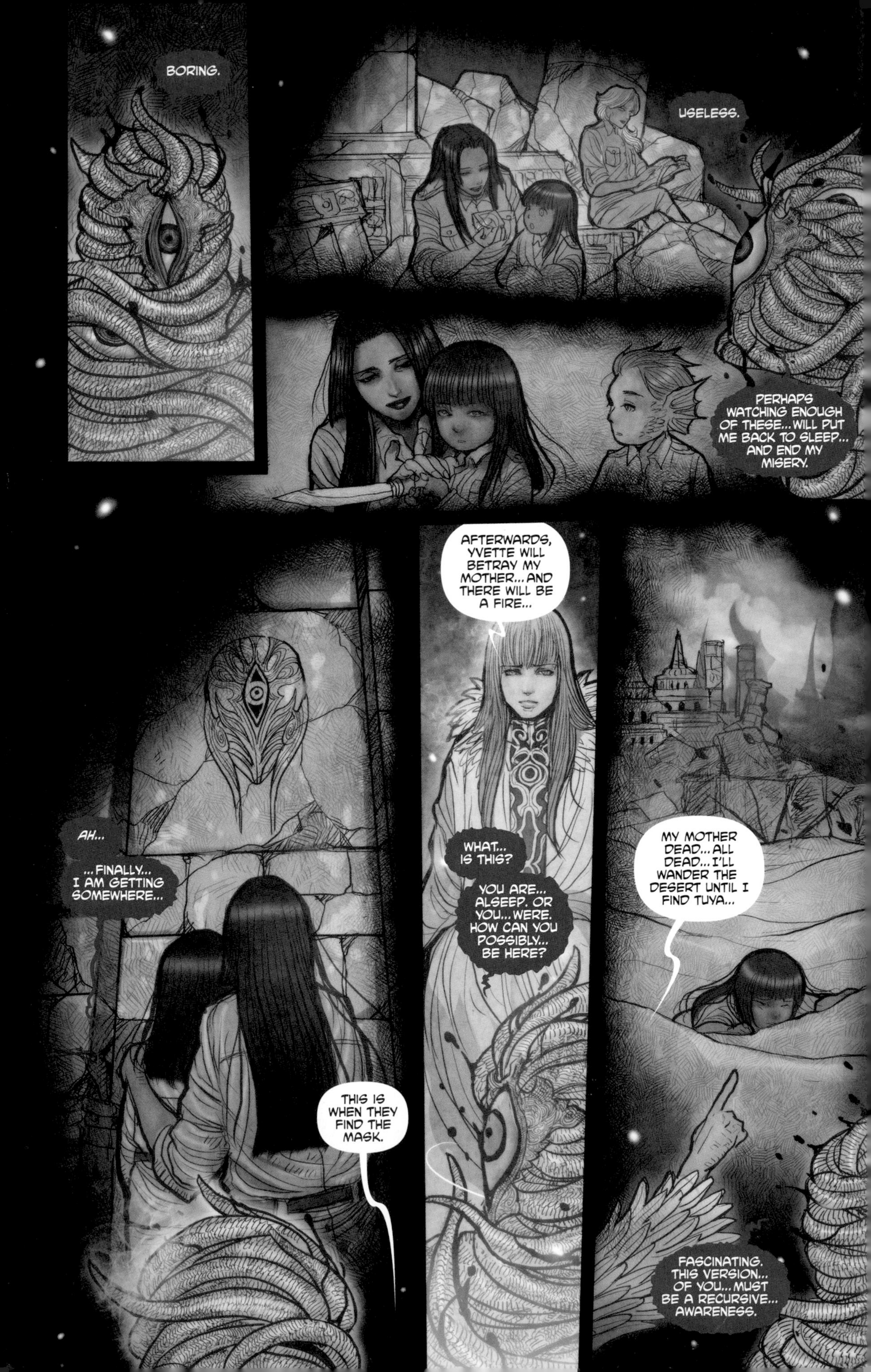
BORING.
USELESS.
PERHAPS WATCHING ENOUGH OF THESE... WILL PUT ME BACK TO SLEEP... AND END MY MISERY.
AH...
...FINALLY... I AM GETTING SOMEWHERE...
THIS IS WHEN THEY FIND THE MASK.
AFTERWARDS, YVETTE WILL BETRAY MY MOTHER... AND THERE WILL BE A FIRE...
WHAT... IS THIS?
YOU ARE... ALSEEP. OR YOU... WERE. HOW CAN YOU POSSIBLY... BE HERE?
MY MOTHER DEAD... ALL DEAD... I'LL WANDER THE DESERT UNTIL I FIND TUYA...
FASCINATING. THIS VERSION... OF YOU... MUST BE A RECURSIVE... AWARENESS.

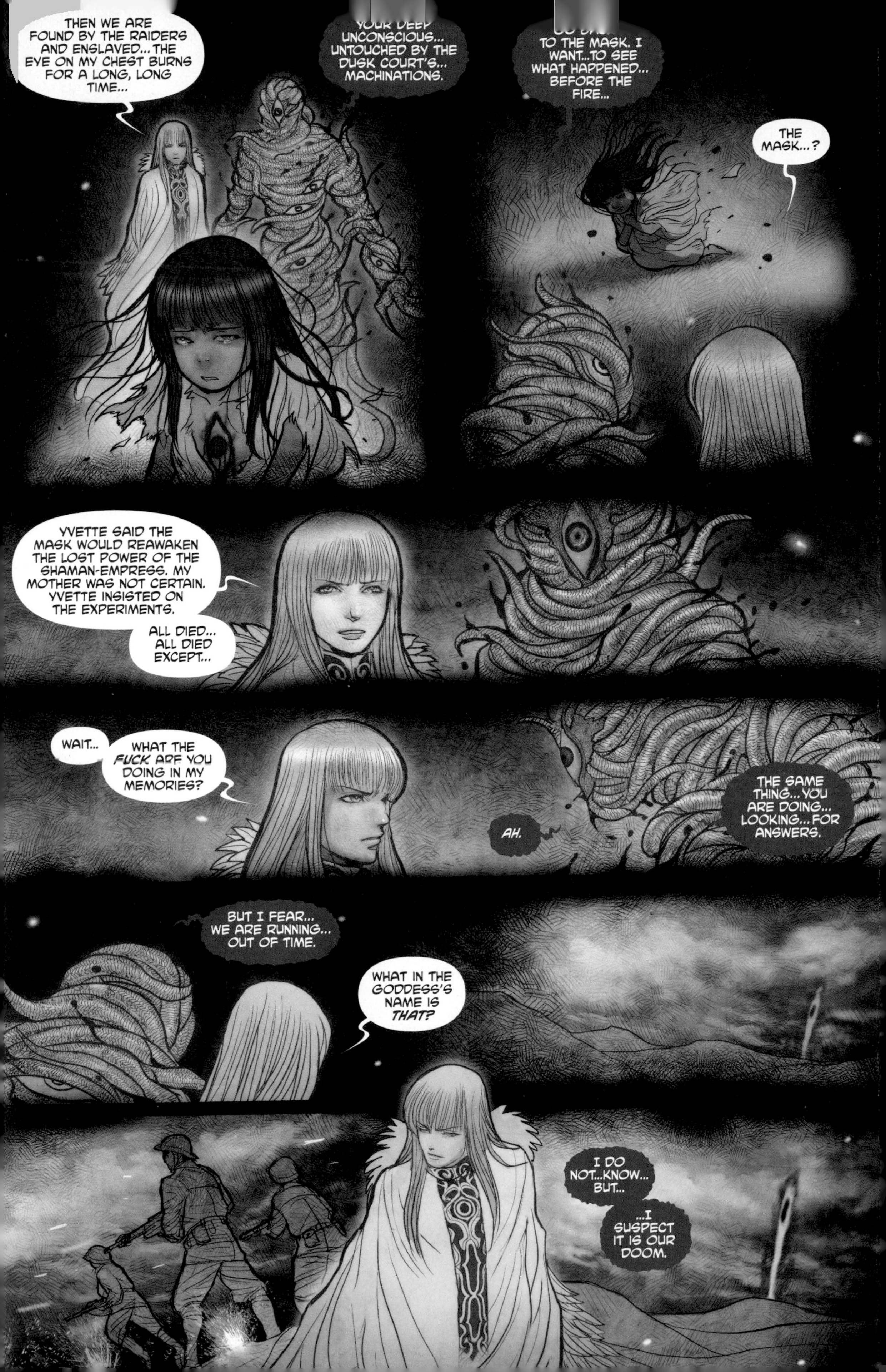
THEN WE ARE FOUND BY THE RAIDERS AND ENSLAVED... THE EYE ON MY CHEST BURNS FOR A LONG, LONG TIME...
YOUR DEEP UNCONSCIOUS... UNTOUCHED BY THE DUSK COURT'S... MACHINATIONS.
TO THE MASK. I WANT...TO SEE WHAT HAPPENED... BEFORE THE FIRE...
THE MASK...?
YVETTE SAID THE MASK WOULD REAWAKEN THE LOST POWER OF THE SHAMAN-EMPRESS. MY MOTHER WAS NOT CERTAIN. YVETTE INSISTED ON THE EXPERIMENTS.
ALL DIED... ALL DIED EXCEPT...
WAIT...
WHAT THE *FUCK* ARE YOU DOING IN MY MEMORIES?
AH.
THE SAME THING... YOU ARE DOING... LOOKING... FOR ANSWERS.
BUT I FEAR... WE ARE RUNNING... OUT OF TIME.
WHAT IN THE GODDESS'S NAME IS *THAT?*
I DO NOT...KNOW... BUT...
...I SUSPECT IT IS OUR DOOM.

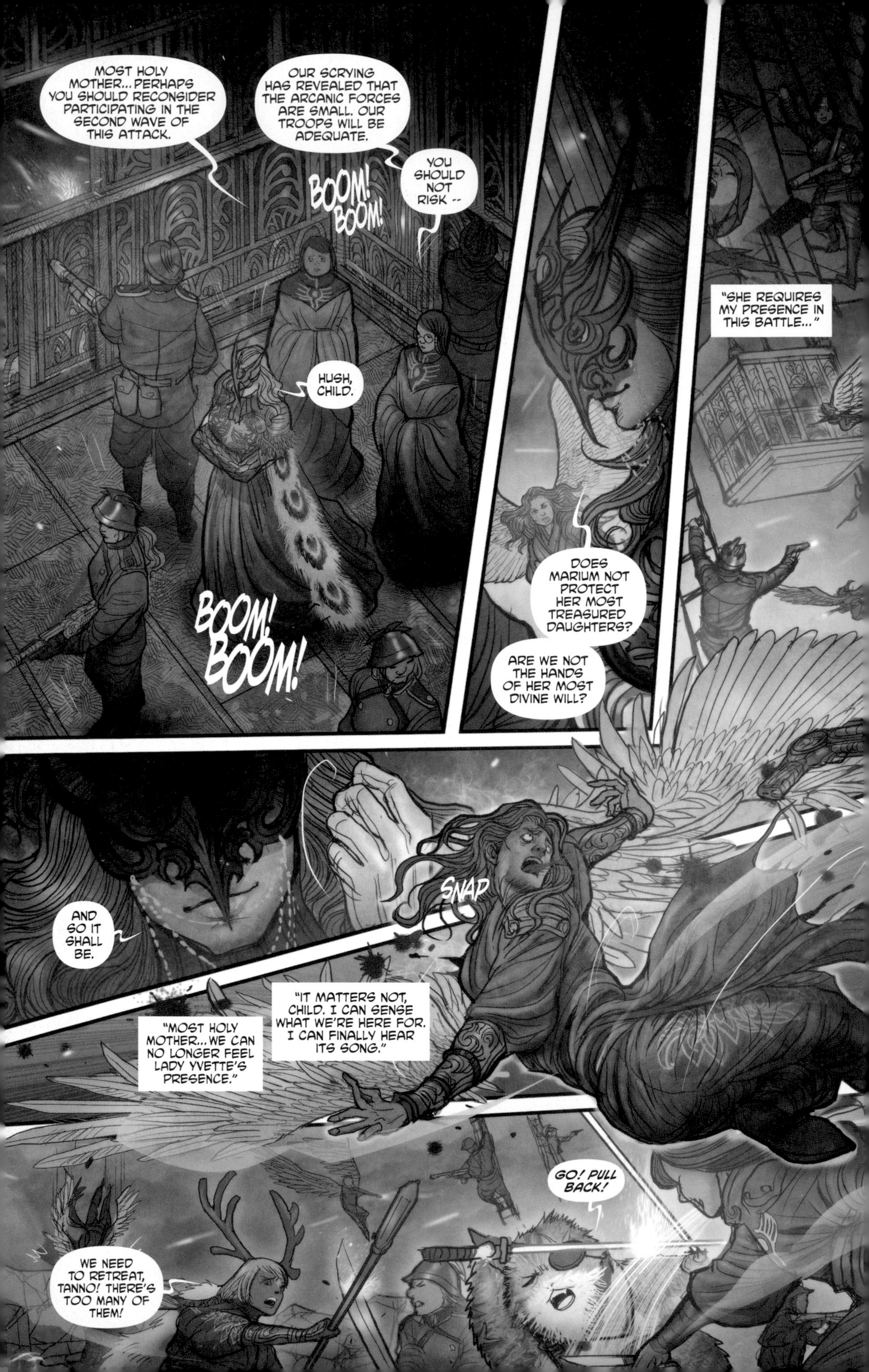
MOST HOLY MOTHER... PERHAPS YOU SHOULD RECONSIDER PARTICIPATING IN THE SECOND WAVE OF THIS ATTACK.
OUR SCRYING HAS REVEALED THAT THE ARCANIC FORCES ARE SMALL. OUR TROOPS WILL BE ADEQUATE.
BOOM! BOOM!
YOU SHOULD NOT RISK --
HUSH, CHILD.
BOOM! BOOM!
"SHE REQUIRES MY PRESENCE IN THIS BATTLE..."
DOES MARIUM NOT PROTECT HER MOST TREASURED DAUGHTERS?
ARE WE NOT THE HANDS OF HER MOST DIVINE WILL?
AND SO IT SHALL BE.
SNAP
"MOST HOLY MOTHER... WE CAN NO LONGER FEEL LADY YVETTE'S PRESENCE."
"IT MATTERS NOT, CHILD. I CAN SENSE WHAT WE'RE HERE FOR. I CAN FINALLY HEAR ITS SONG."
GO! PULL BACK!
WE NEED TO RETREAT, TANNO! THERE'S TOO MANY OF THEM!

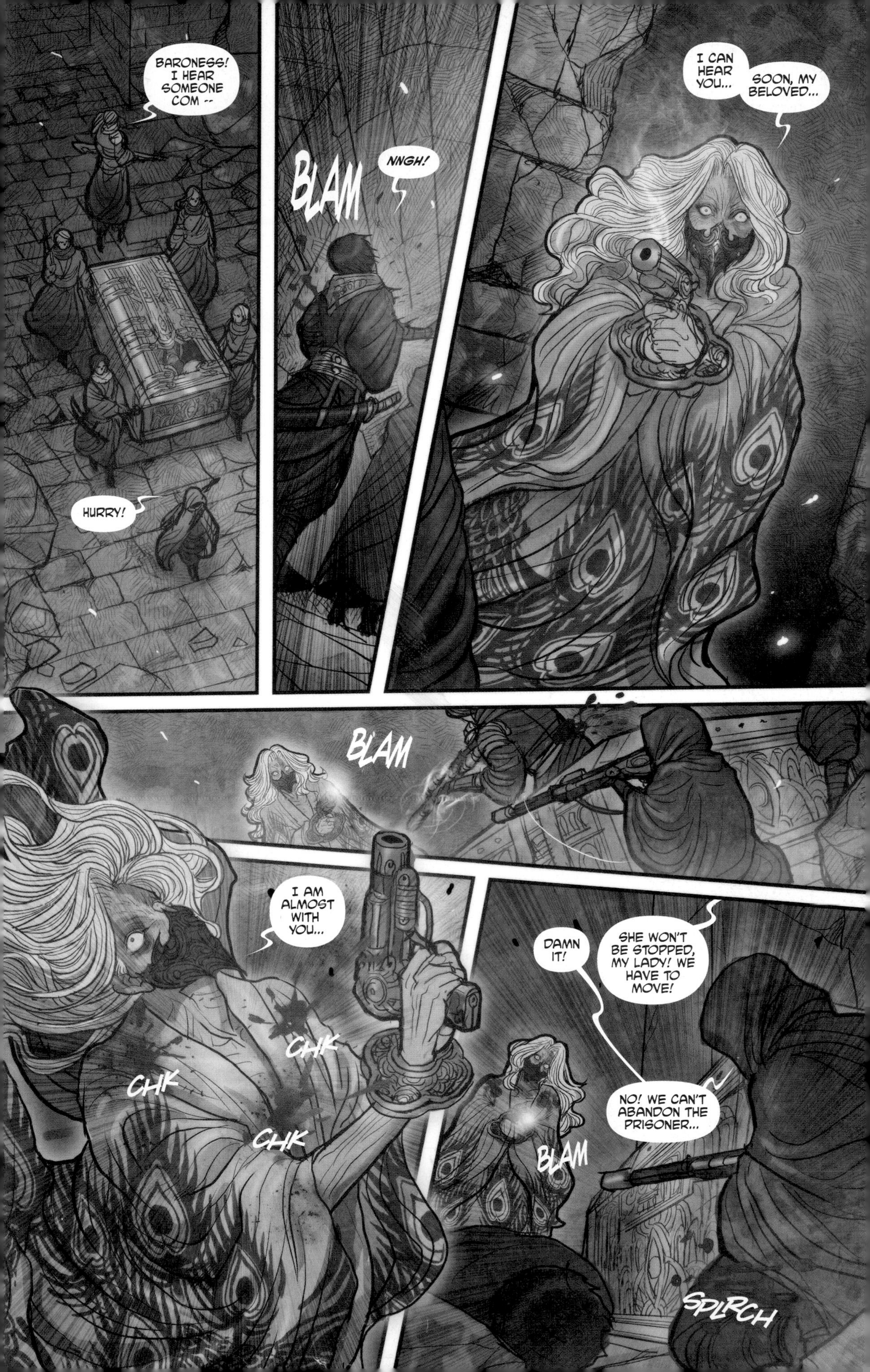
BARONESS! I HEAR SOMEONE COM --
HURRY!
BLAM
NNGH!
I CAN HEAR YOU...
SOON, MY BELOVED...
BLAM
I AM ALMOST WITH YOU...
CHK
CHK
CHK
DAMN IT!
SHE WON'T BE STOPPED, MY LADY! WE HAVE TO MOVE!
NO! WE CAN'T ABANDON THE PRISONER...
BLAM
SPLRCH

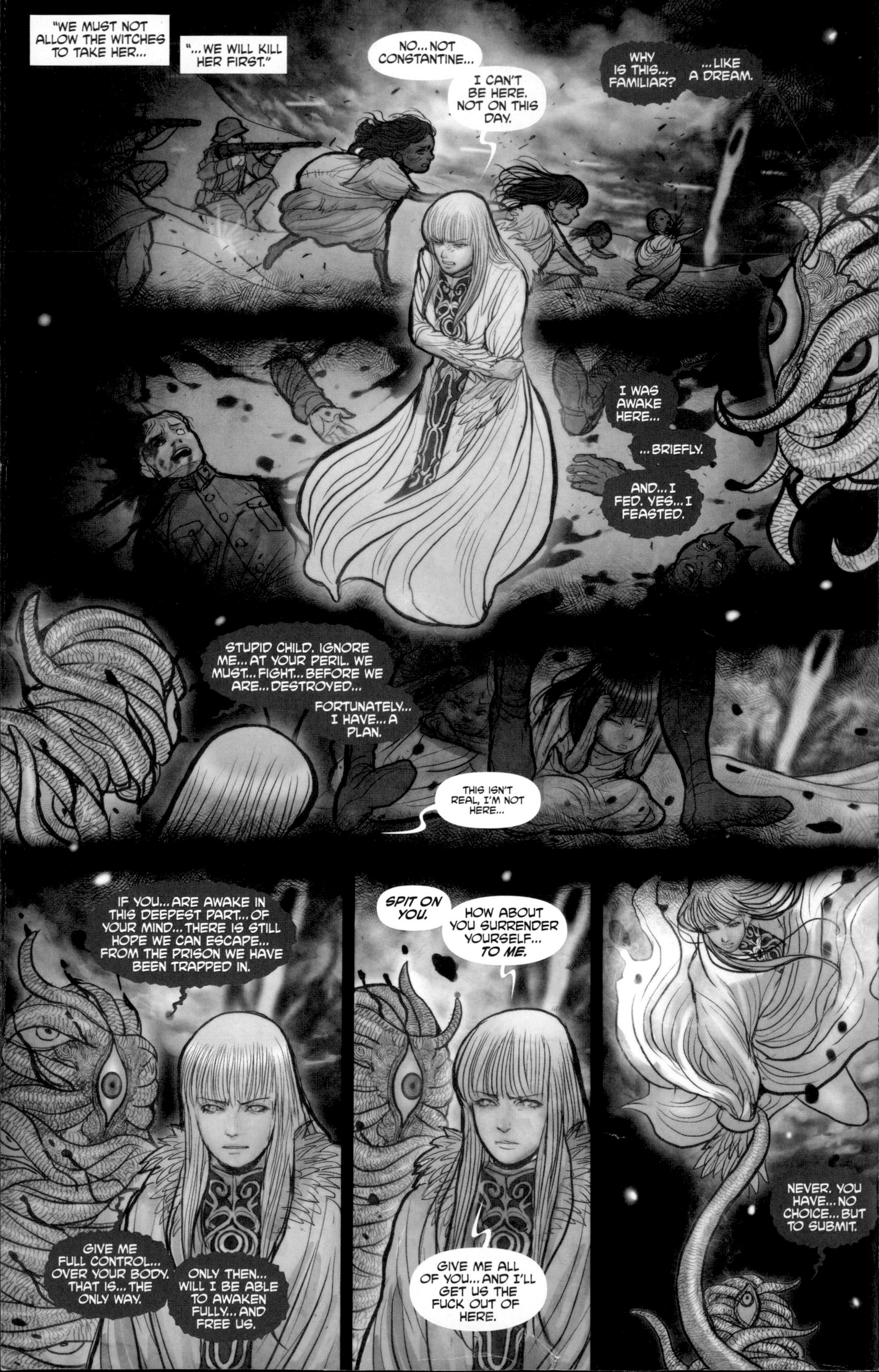
"WE MUST NOT ALLOW THE WITCHES TO TAKE HER...
"...WE WILL KILL HER FIRST."
NO...NOT CONSTANTINE...
I CAN'T BE HERE. NOT ON THIS DAY.
WHY IS THIS... FAMILIAR?
...LIKE A DREAM.
I WAS AWAKE HERE...
...BRIEFLY.
AND...I FED. YES...I FEASTED.
STUPID CHILD. IGNORE ME...AT YOUR PERIL. WE MUST...FIGHT...BEFORE WE ARE...DESTROYED...
FORTUNATELY... I HAVE...A PLAN.
THIS ISN'T REAL, I'M NOT HERE...
IF YOU...ARE AWAKE IN THIS DEEPEST PART...OF YOUR MIND...THERE IS STILL HOPE WE CAN ESCAPE... FROM THE PRISON WE HAVE BEEN TRAPPED IN.
GIVE ME FULL CONTROL... OVER YOUR BODY. THAT IS...THE ONLY WAY.
ONLY THEN... WILL I BE ABLE TO AWAKEN FULLY...AND FREE US.
SPIT ON YOU.
HOW ABOUT YOU SURRENDER YOURSELF... TO ME.
GIVE ME ALL OF YOU...AND I'LL GET US THE FUCK OUT OF HERE.
NEVER. YOU HAVE...NO CHOICE...BUT TO SUBMIT.

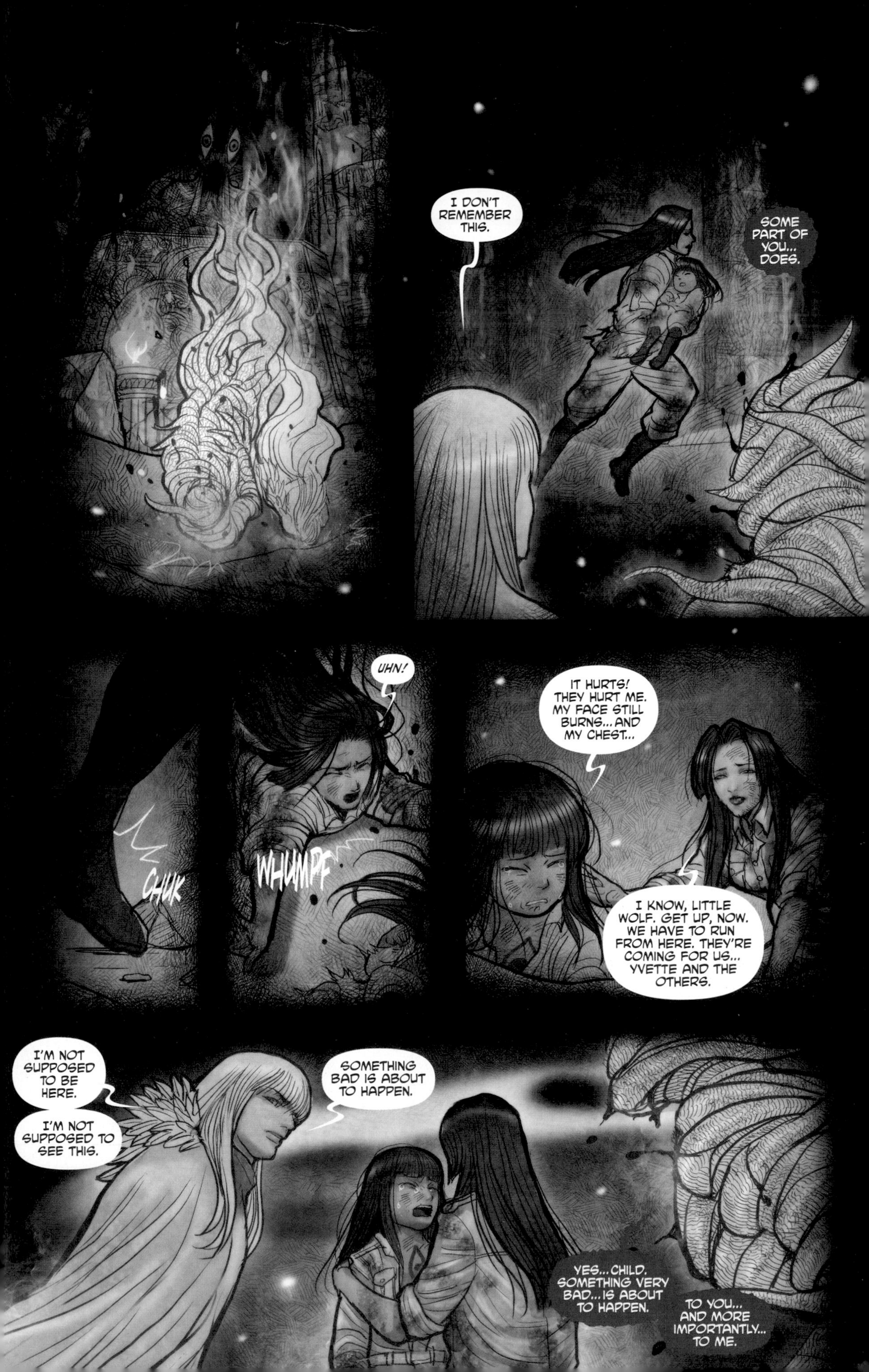
I DON'T REMEMBER THIS.
SOME PART OF YOU... DOES.
UHN!
CHUK
WHUMPF
IT HURTS! THEY HURT ME. MY FACE STILL BURNS... AND MY CHEST...
I KNOW, LITTLE WOLF. GET UP, NOW. WE HAVE TO RUN FROM HERE. THEY'RE COMING FOR US... YVETTE AND THE OTHERS.
I'M NOT SUPPOSED TO BE HERE.
I'M NOT SUPPOSED TO SEE THIS.
SOMETHING BAD IS ABOUT TO HAPPEN.
YES... CHILD. SOMETHING VERY BAD... IS ABOUT TO HAPPEN.
TO YOU... AND MORE IMPORTANTLY... TO ME.

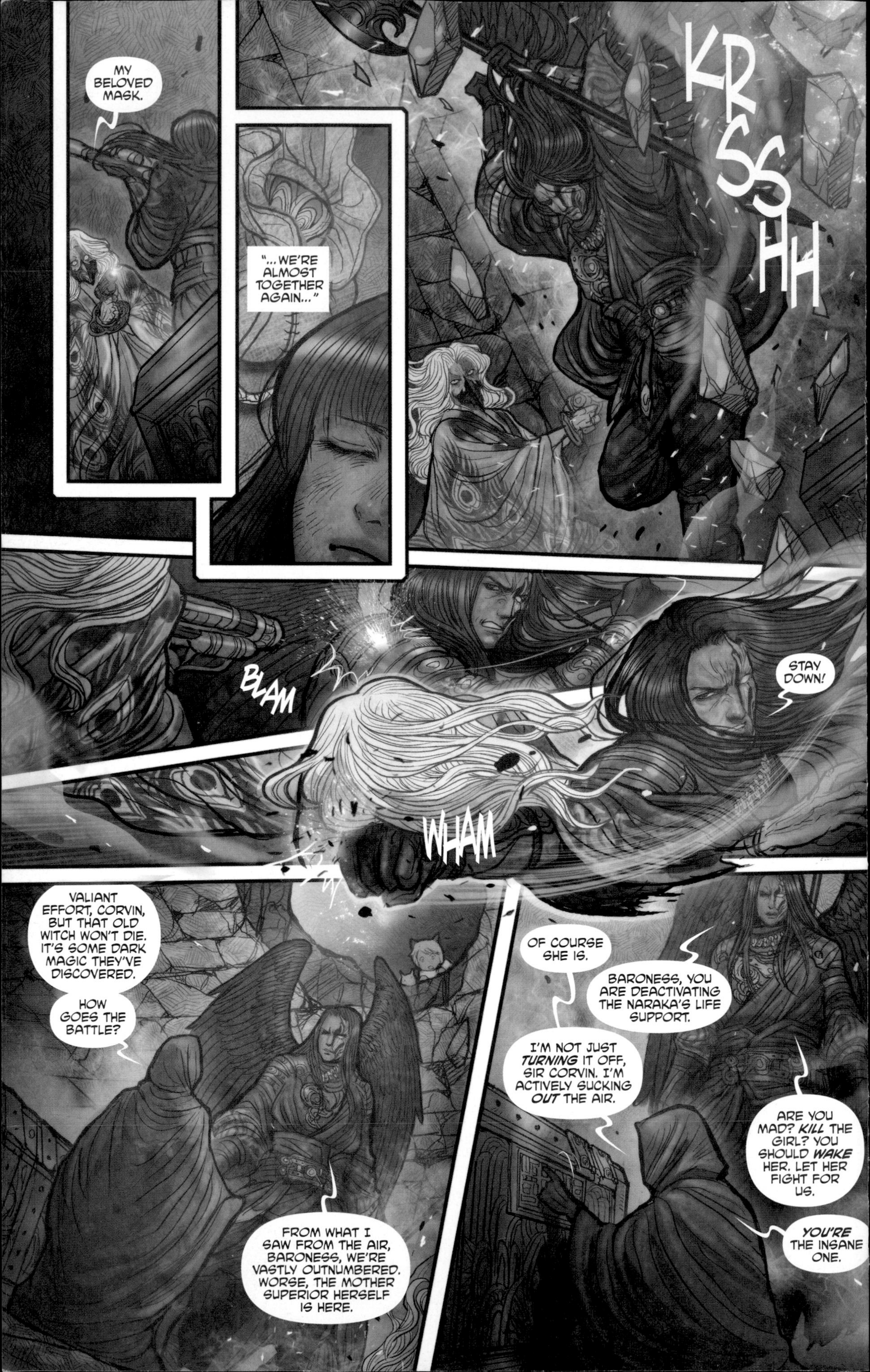
MY BELOVED MASK.
"...WE'RE ALMOST TOGETHER AGAIN..."
KRSSHH
BLAM
STAY DOWN!
WHAM
VALIANT EFFORT, CORVIN, BUT THAT OLD WITCH WON'T DIE. IT'S SOME DARK MAGIC THEY'VE DISCOVERED.
HOW GOES THE BATTLE?
FROM WHAT I SAW FROM THE AIR, BARONESS, WE'RE VASTLY OUTNUMBERED. WORSE, THE MOTHER SUPERIOR HERSELF IS HERE.
OF COURSE SHE IS.
BARONESS, YOU ARE DEACTIVATING THE NARAKA'S LIFE SUPPORT.
I'M NOT JUST *TURNING* IT OFF, SIR CORVIN. I'M ACTIVELY SUCKING *OUT* THE AIR.
ARE YOU MAD? *KILL* THE GIRL? YOU SHOULD *WAKE* HER. LET HER FIGHT FOR US.
YOU'RE THE INSANE ONE.

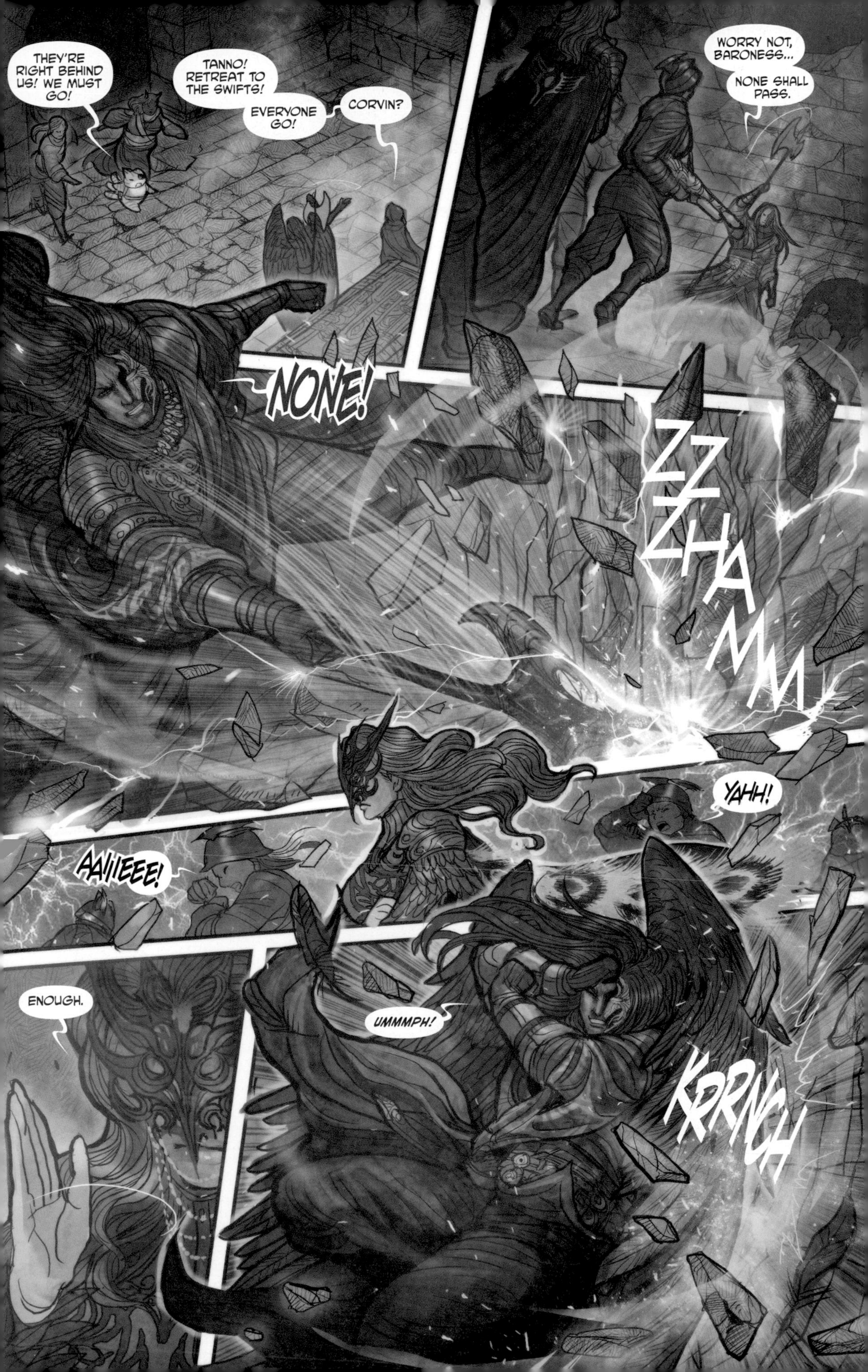
THEY'RE RIGHT BEHIND US! WE MUST GO!
TANNO! RETREAT TO THE SWIFTS!
EVERYONE GO!
CORVIN?
WORRY NOT, BARONESS...
NONE SHALL PASS.
NONE!
ZZHAMMM
YAHH!
AAIIIEEE!
ENOUGH.
UMMMPH!
KRRNCH

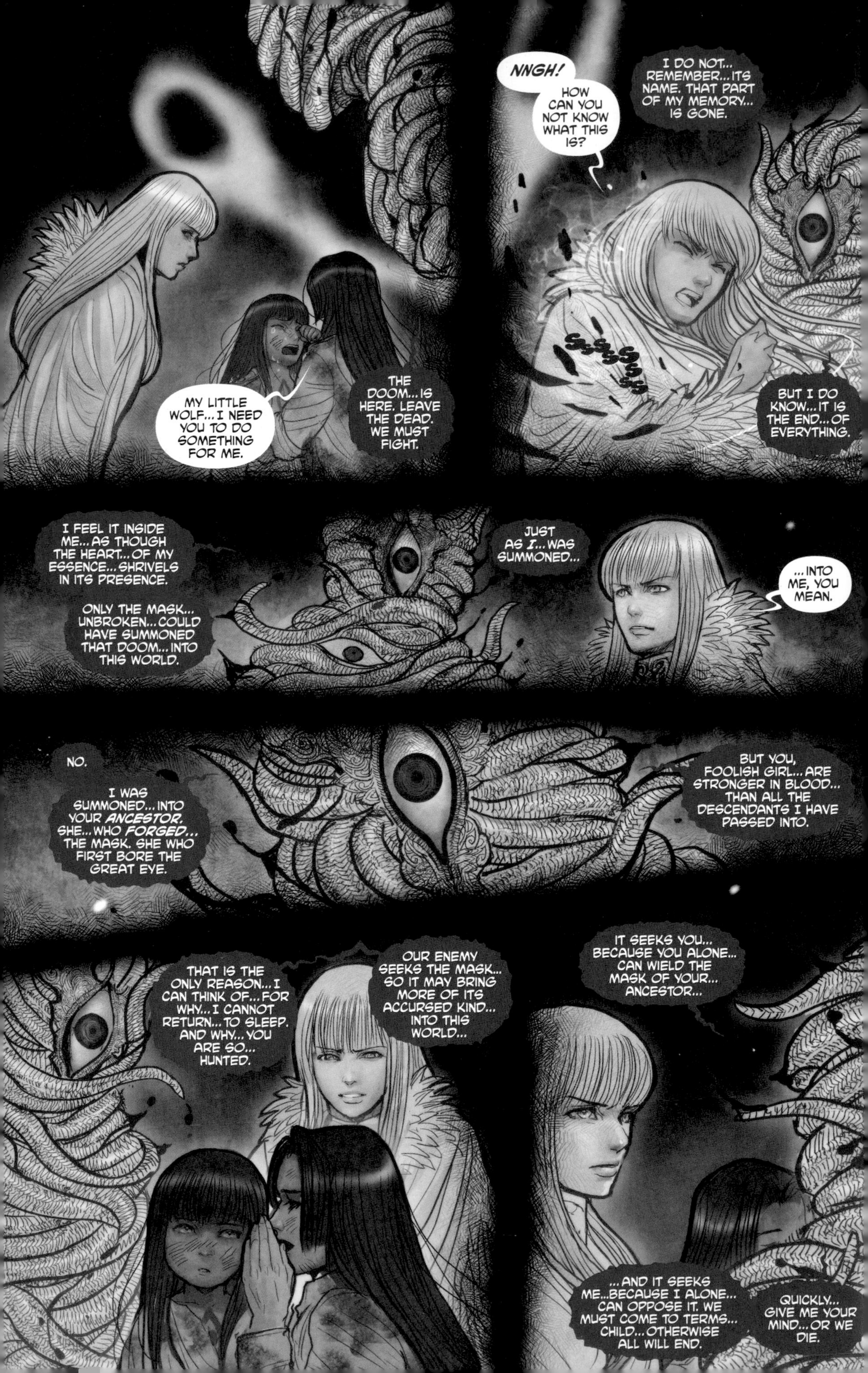
MY LITTLE WOLF... I NEED YOU TO DO SOMETHING FOR ME.
THE DOOM... IS HERE. LEAVE THE DEAD. WE MUST FIGHT.
NNGH!
HOW CAN YOU NOT KNOW WHAT THIS IS?
I DO NOT... REMEMBER... ITS NAME. THAT PART OF MY MEMORY... IS GONE.
BUT I DO KNOW... IT IS THE END... OF EVERYTHING.
I FEEL IT INSIDE ME... AS THOUGH THE HEART... OF MY ESSENCE... SHRIVELS IN ITS PRESENCE.
ONLY THE MASK... UNBROKEN... COULD HAVE SUMMONED THAT DOOM... INTO THIS WORLD.
JUST AS I... WAS SUMMONED...
...INTO ME, YOU MEAN.
NO.
I WAS SUMMONED... INTO YOUR ANCESTOR. SHE... WHO FORGED... THE MASK. SHE WHO FIRST BORE THE GREAT EYE.
BUT YOU, FOOLISH GIRL... ARE STRONGER IN BLOOD... THAN ALL THE DESCENDANTS I HAVE PASSED INTO.
THAT IS THE ONLY REASON... I CAN THINK OF... FOR WHY... I CANNOT RETURN... TO SLEEP. AND WHY... YOU ARE SO... HUNTED.
OUR ENEMY SEEKS THE MASK... SO IT MAY BRING MORE OF ITS ACCURSED KIND... INTO THIS WORLD...
IT SEEKS YOU... BECAUSE YOU ALONE... CAN WIELD THE MASK OF YOUR... ANCESTOR...
...AND IT SEEKS ME...BECAUSE I ALONE... CAN OPPOSE IT. WE MUST COME TO TERMS... CHILD... OTHERWISE ALL WILL END.
QUICKLY... GIVE ME YOUR MIND... OR WE DIE.

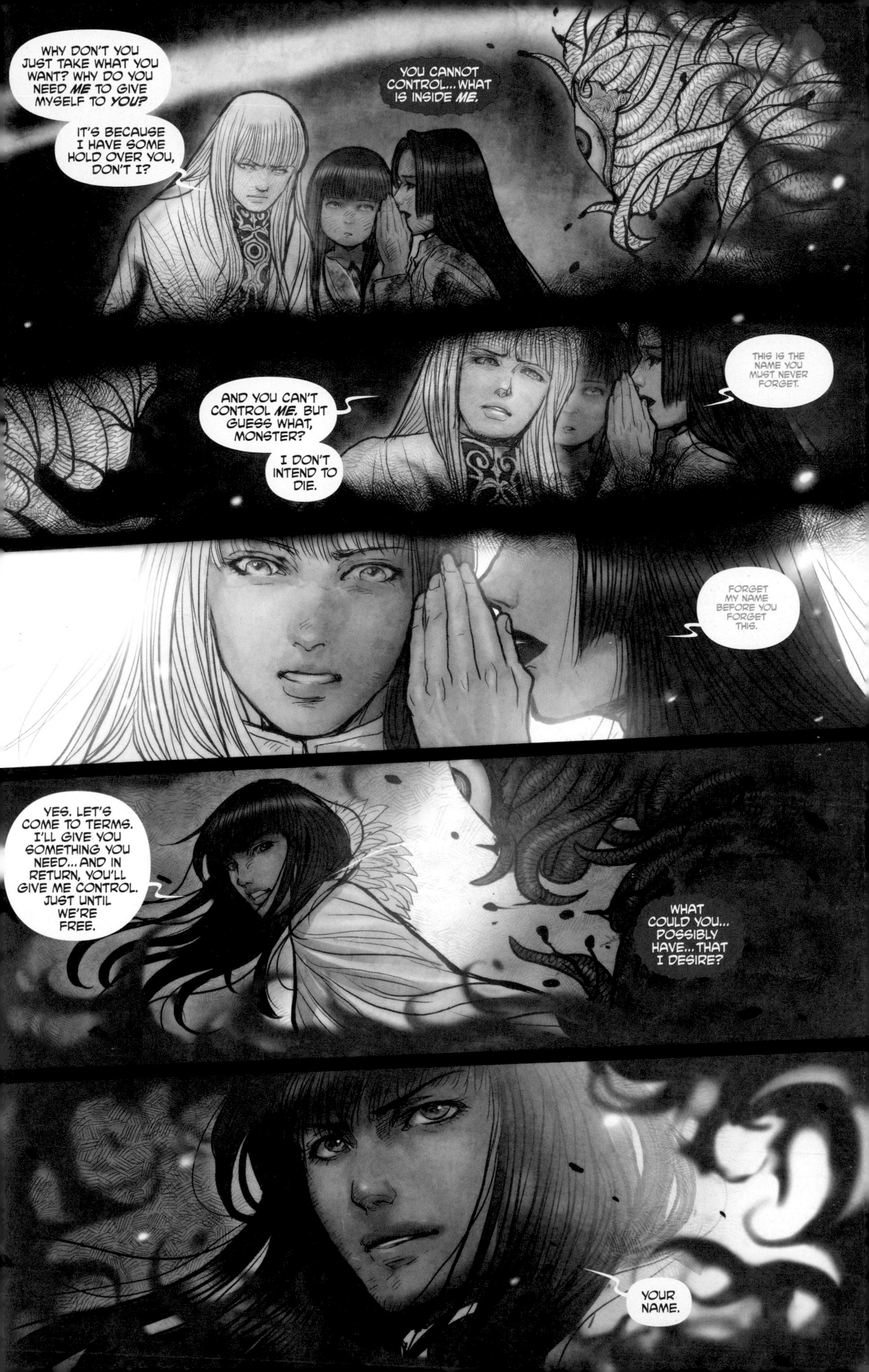
WHY DON'T YOU JUST TAKE WHAT YOU WANT? WHY DO YOU NEED *ME* TO GIVE MYSELF TO *YOU?*
IT'S BECAUSE I HAVE SOME HOLD OVER YOU, DON'T I?
YOU CANNOT CONTROL... WHAT IS INSIDE *ME.*
AND YOU CAN'T CONTROL *ME.* BUT GUESS WHAT, MONSTER?
I DON'T INTEND TO DIE.
THIS IS THE NAME YOU MUST NEVER FORGET.
FORGET MY NAME BEFORE YOU FORGET THIS.
YES. LET'S COME TO TERMS. I'LL GIVE YOU SOMETHING YOU NEED... AND IN RETURN, YOU'LL GIVE ME CONTROL. JUST UNTIL WE'RE FREE.
WHAT COULD YOU... POSSIBLY HAVE... THAT I DESIRE?
YOUR NAME.

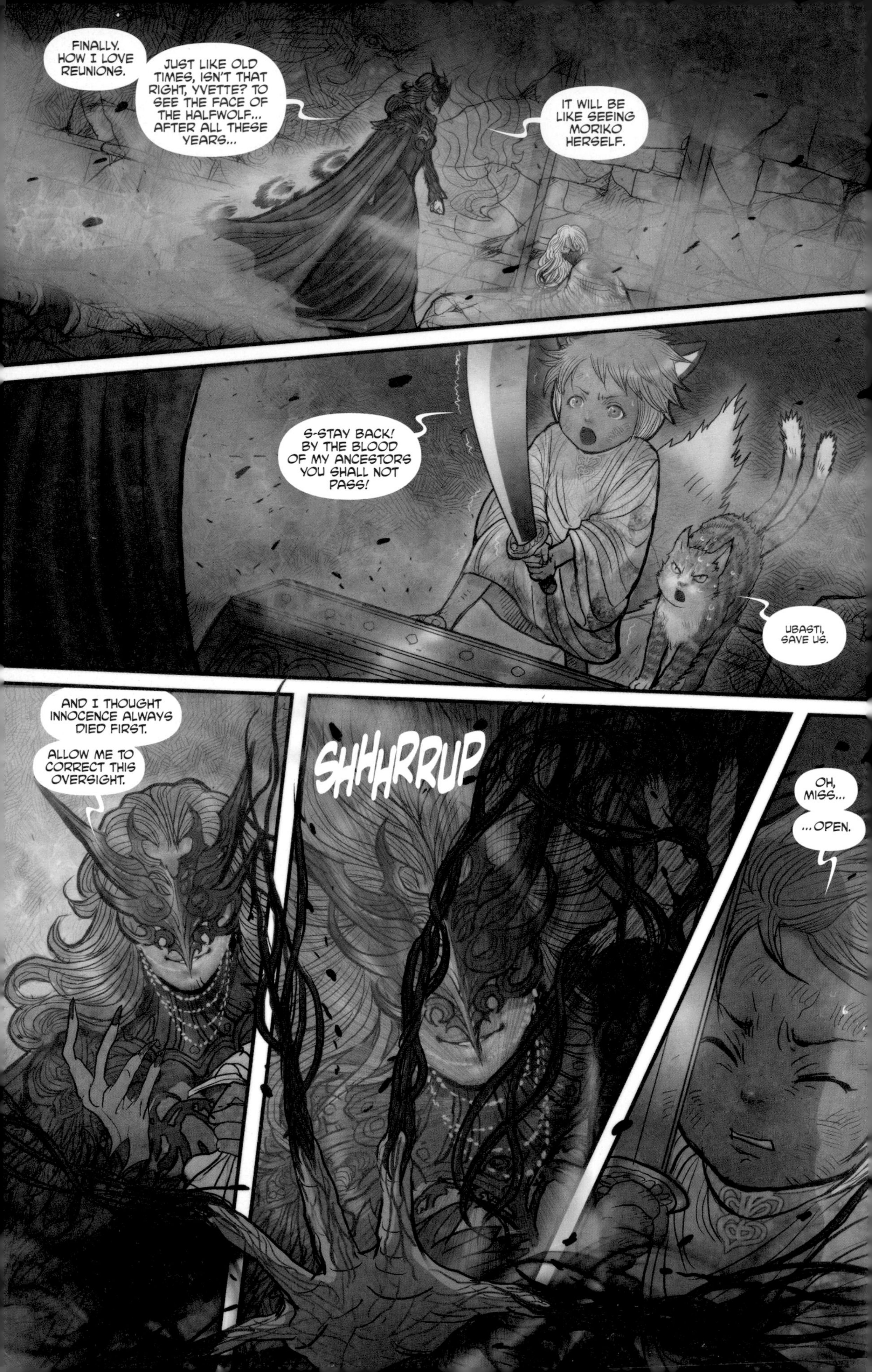
FINALLY. HOW I LOVE REUNIONS.
JUST LIKE OLD TIMES, ISN'T THAT RIGHT, YVETTE? TO SEE THE FACE OF THE HALFWOLF... AFTER ALL THESE YEARS...
IT WILL BE LIKE SEEING MORIKO HERSELF.
S-STAY BACK! BY THE BLOOD OF MY ANCESTORS YOU SHALL NOT PASS!
UBASTI, SAVE US.
AND I THOUGHT INNOCENCE ALWAYS DIED FIRST.
ALLOW ME TO CORRECT THIS OVERSIGHT.
SHHHRRUP
OH, MISS...
...OPEN.

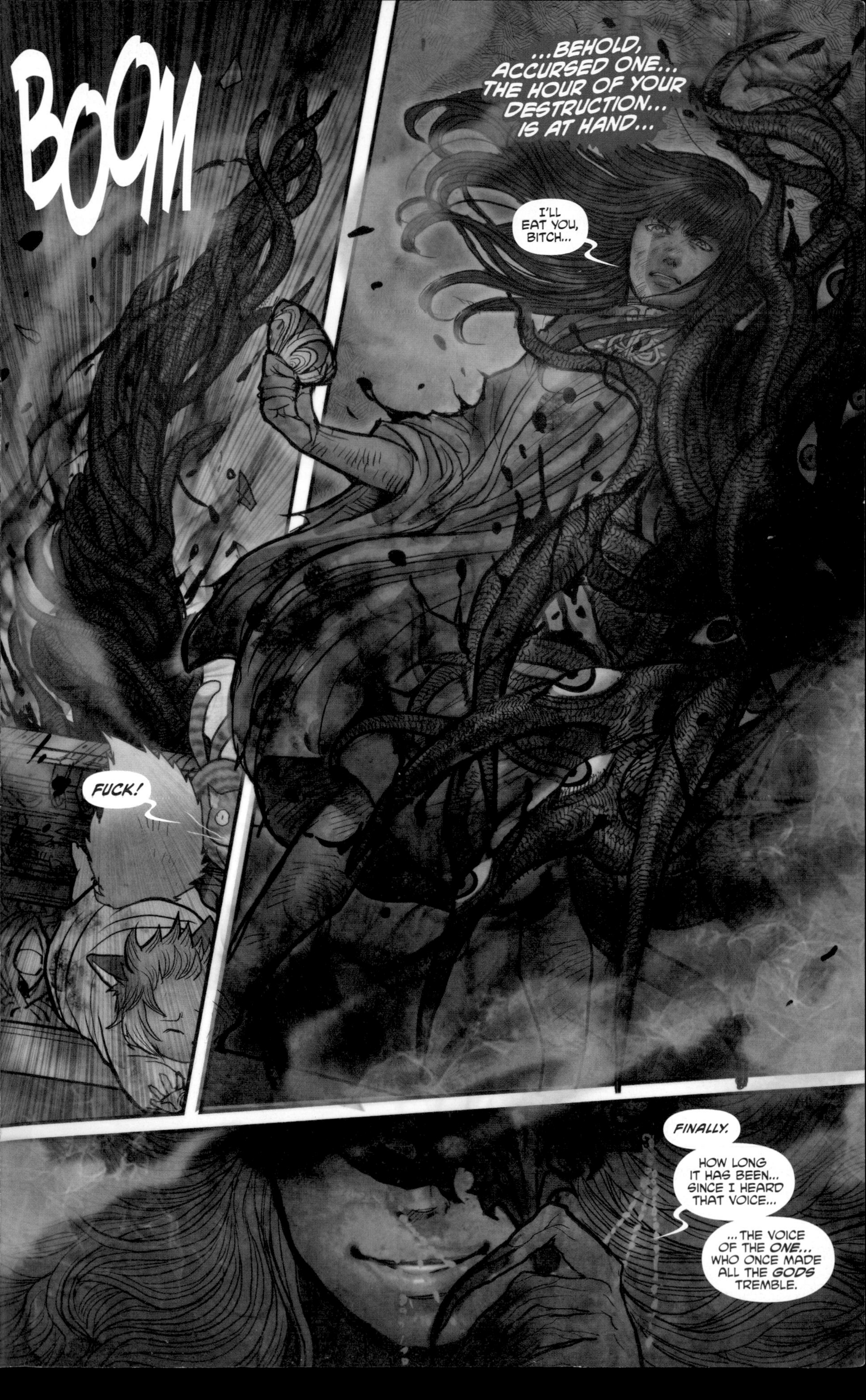
BOOM
...BEHOLD, ACCURSED ONE... THE HOUR OF YOUR DESTRUCTION... IS AT HAND...
I'LL EAT YOU, BITCH...
FUCK!
FINALLY.
HOW LONG IT HAS BEEN... SINCE I HEARD THAT VOICE...
...THE VOICE OF THE ONE... WHO ONCE MADE ALL THE GODS TREMBLE.

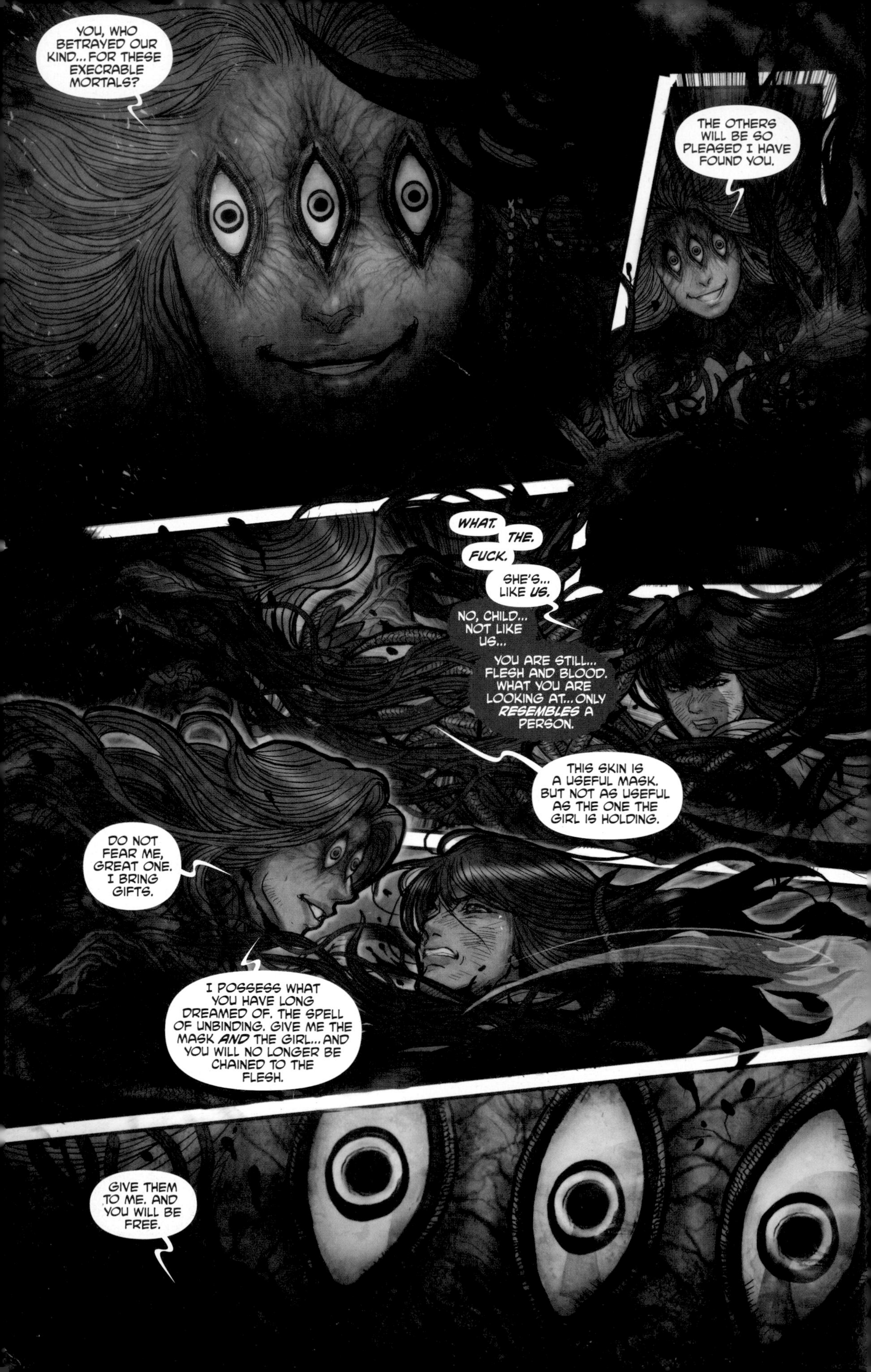
YOU, WHO BETRAYED OUR KIND... FOR THESE EXECRABLE MORTALS?
THE OTHERS WILL BE SO PLEASED I HAVE FOUND YOU.
WHAT.
THE.
FUCK.
SHE'S... LIKE US.
NO, CHILD... NOT LIKE US...
YOU ARE STILL... FLESH AND BLOOD. WHAT YOU ARE LOOKING AT... ONLY RESEMBLES A PERSON.
THIS SKIN IS A USEFUL MASK. BUT NOT AS USEFUL AS THE ONE THE GIRL IS HOLDING.
DO NOT FEAR ME, GREAT ONE. I BRING GIFTS.
I POSSESS WHAT YOU HAVE LONG DREAMED OF. THE SPELL OF UNBINDING. GIVE ME THE MASK AND THE GIRL... AND YOU WILL NO LONGER BE CHAINED TO THE FLESH.
GIVE THEM TO ME. AND YOU WILL BE FREE.

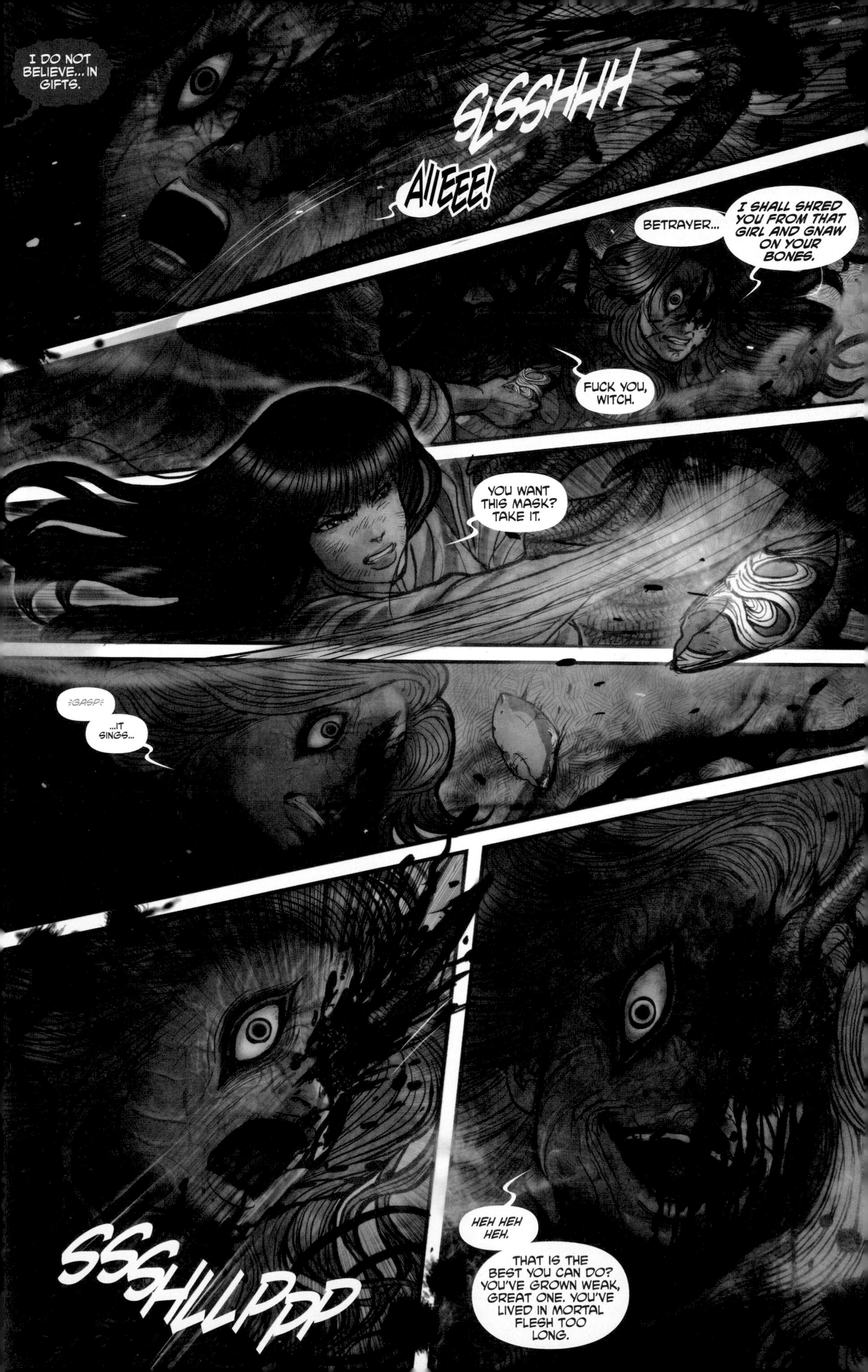
I DO NOT BELIEVE... IN GIFTS.
SLSSHHH
AIIEEE!
BETRAYER...
I SHALL SHRED YOU FROM THAT GIRL AND GNAW ON YOUR BONES.
FUCK YOU, WITCH.
YOU WANT THIS MASK? TAKE IT.
GASP
...IT SINGS...
SSSHLLPPP
HEH HEH HEH.
THAT IS THE BEST YOU CAN DO? YOU'VE GROWN WEAK, GREAT ONE. YOU'VE LIVED IN MORTAL FLESH TOO LONG.

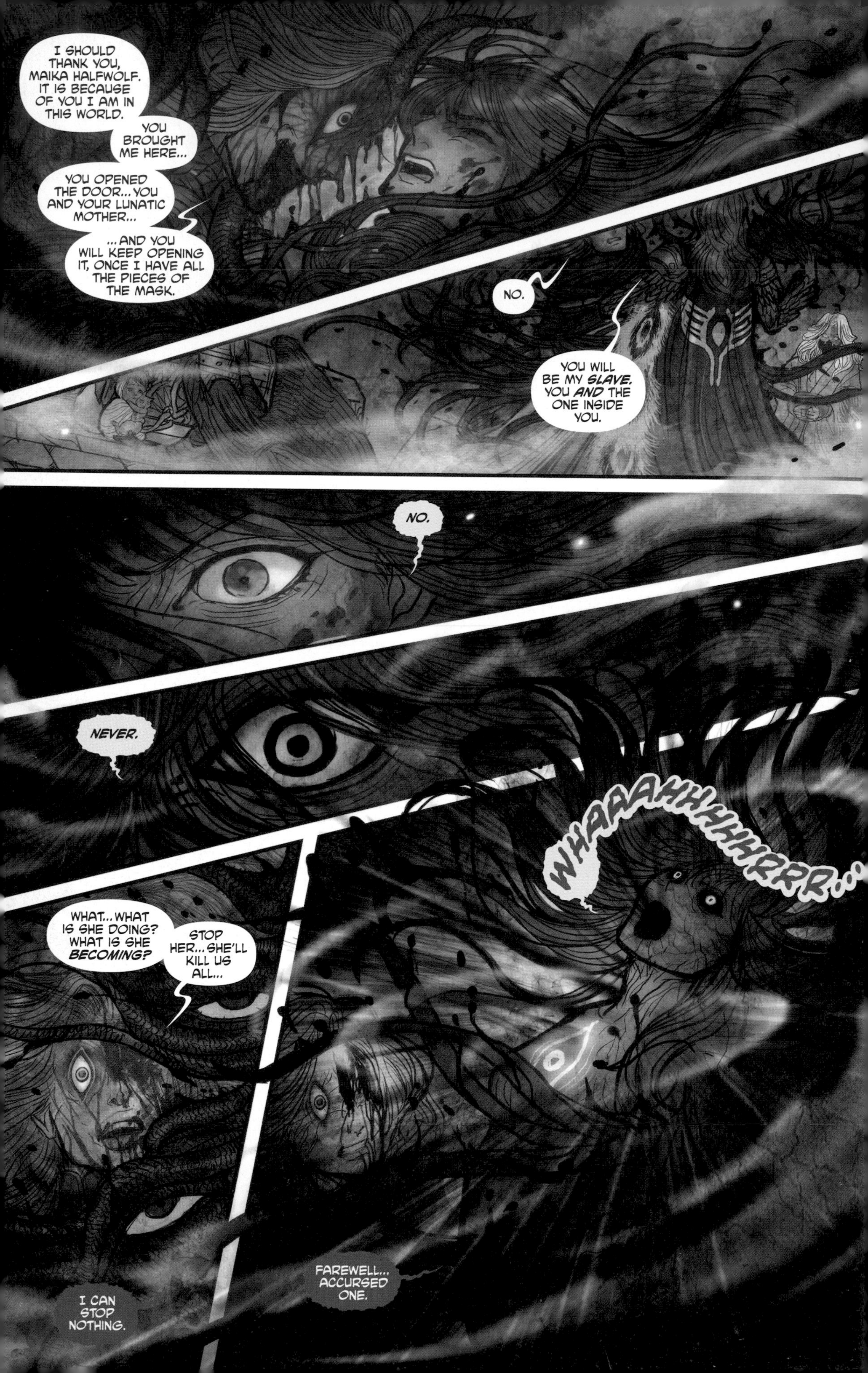
I SHOULD THANK YOU, MAIKA HALFWOLF. IT IS BECAUSE OF YOU I AM IN THIS WORLD.
YOU BROUGHT ME HERE...
YOU OPENED THE DOOR... YOU AND YOUR LUNATIC MOTHER...
...AND YOU WILL KEEP OPENING IT, ONCE I HAVE ALL THE PIECES OF THE MASK.
NO.
YOU WILL BE MY SLAVE. YOU AND THE ONE INSIDE YOU.
NO.
NEVER.
WHAAAAHHHHRRRR...
WHAT... WHAT IS SHE DOING? WHAT IS SHE BECOMING?
STOP HER... SHE'LL KILL US ALL...
I CAN STOP NOTHING.
FAREWELL... ACCURSED ONE.

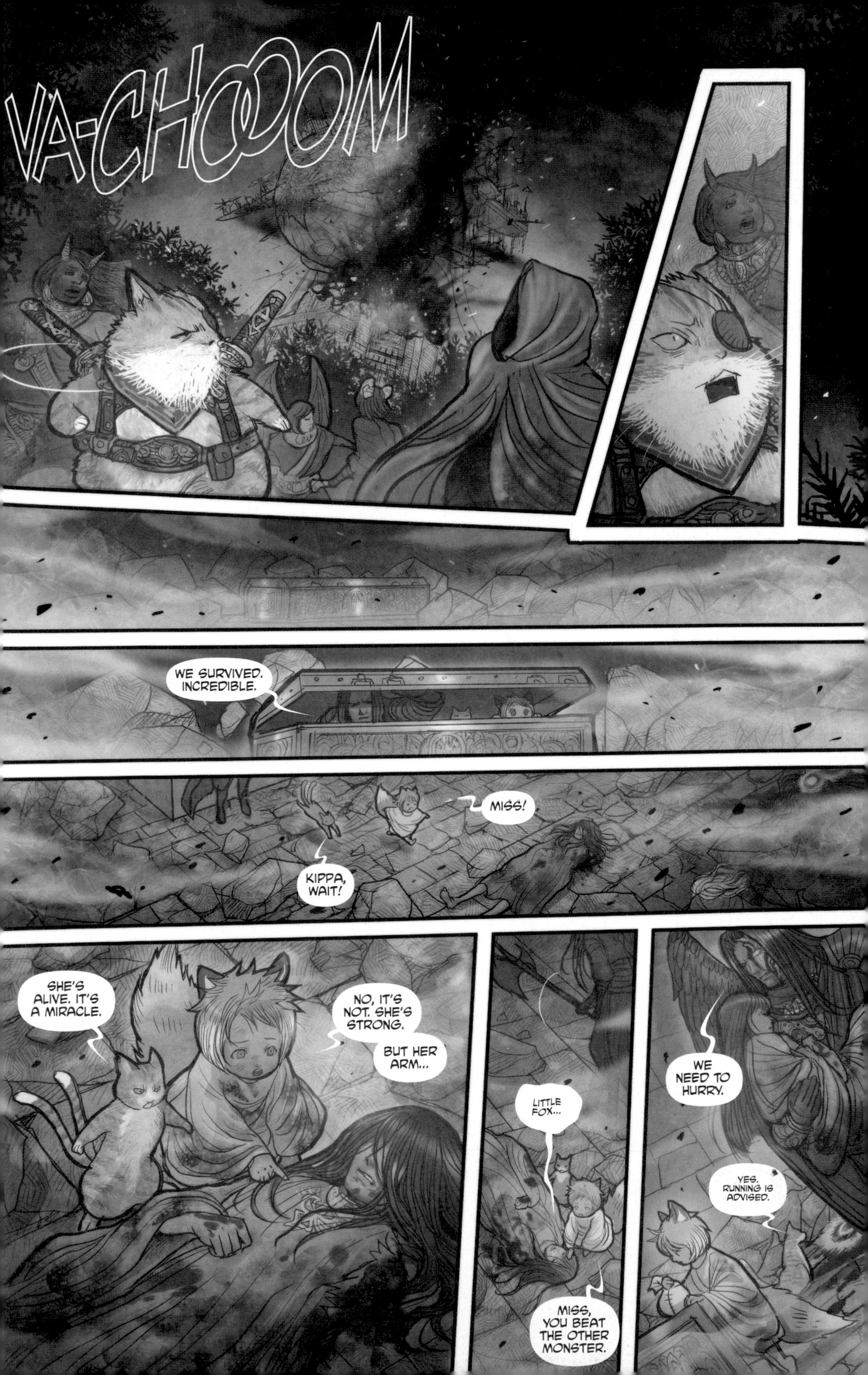
VA-CHOOOM
WE SURVIVED. INCREDIBLE.
MISS!
KIPPA, WAIT!
SHE'S ALIVE. IT'S A MIRACLE.
NO, IT'S NOT. SHE'S STRONG.
BUT HER ARM...
LITTLE FOX...
MISS, YOU BEAT THE OTHER MONSTER.
WE NEED TO HURRY.
YES. RUNNING IS ADVISED.

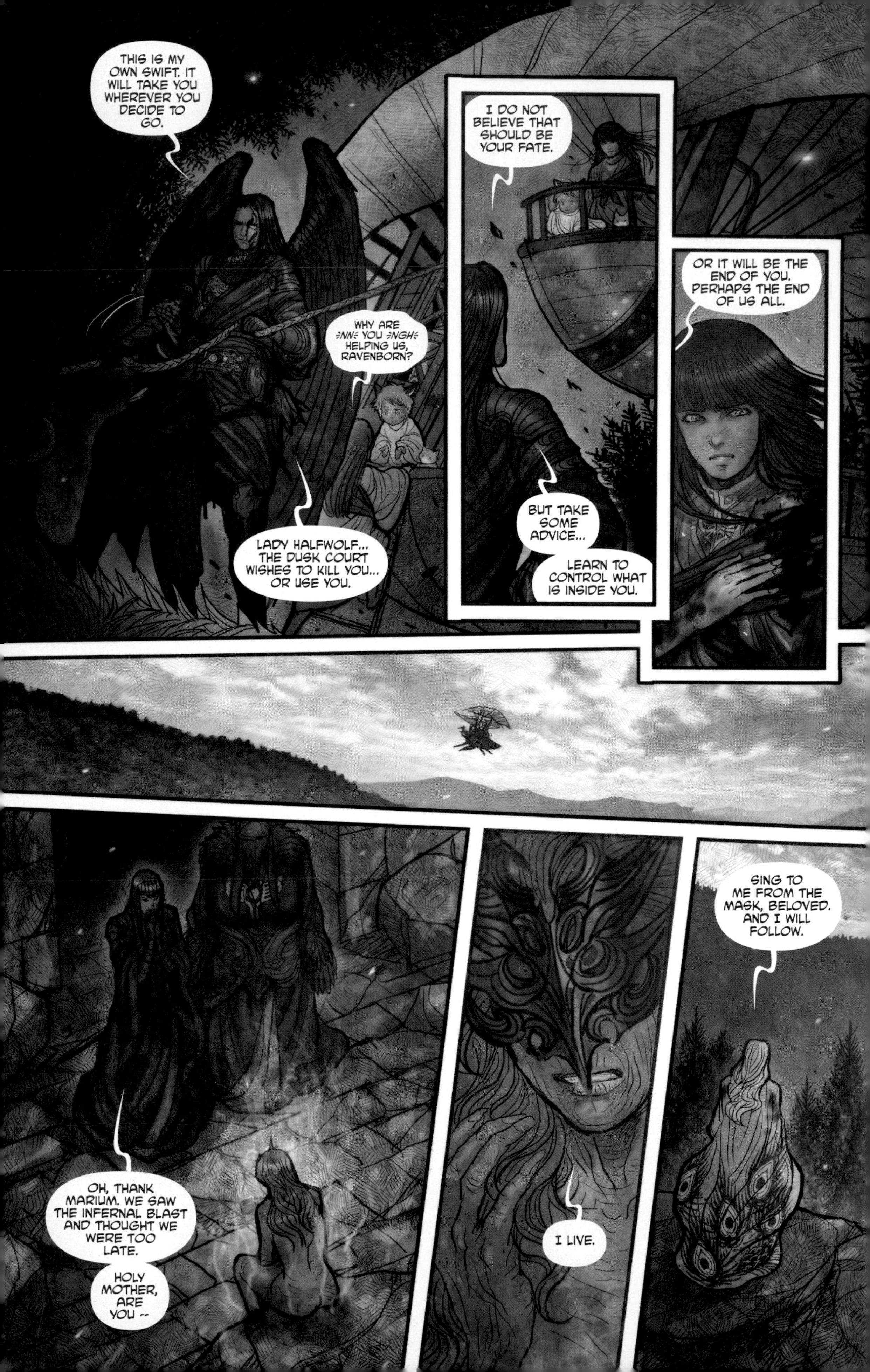
THIS IS MY OWN SWIFT. IT WILL TAKE YOU WHEREVER YOU DECIDE TO GO.
WHY ARE =NN= YOU =NGH= HELPING US, RAVENBORN?
LADY HALFWOLF... THE DUSK COURT WISHES TO KILL YOU... OR USE YOU.
I DO NOT BELIEVE THAT SHOULD BE YOUR FATE.
BUT TAKE SOME ADVICE...
LEARN TO CONTROL WHAT IS INSIDE YOU.
OR IT WILL BE THE END OF YOU. PERHAPS THE END OF US ALL.
OH, THANK MARIUM. WE SAW THE INFERNAL BLAST AND THOUGHT WE WERE TOO LATE.
HOLY MOTHER, ARE YOU --
I LIVE.
SING TO ME FROM THE MASK, BELOVED. AND I WILL FOLLOW.

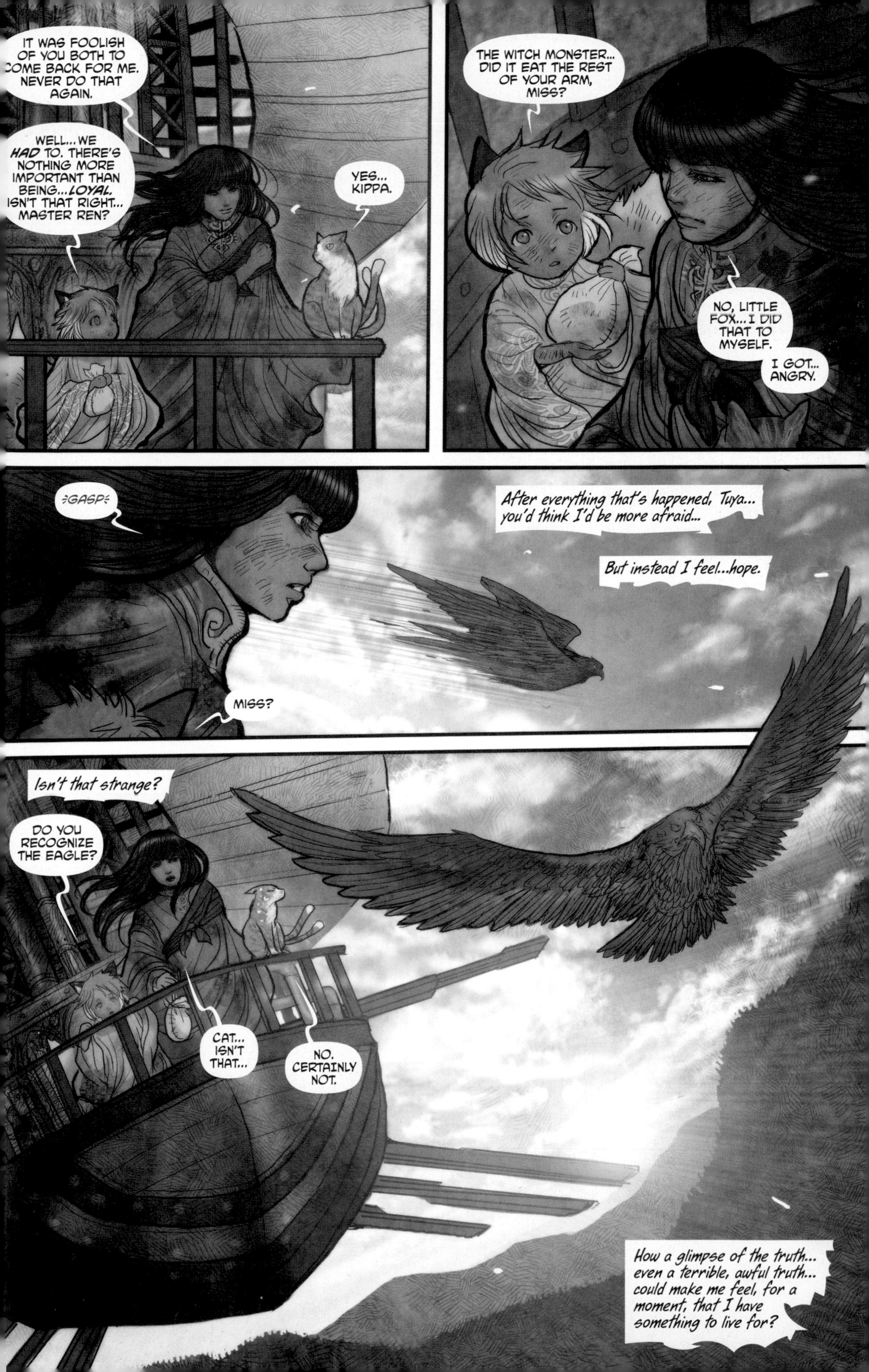
IT WAS FOOLISH OF YOU BOTH TO COME BACK FOR ME. NEVER DO THAT AGAIN.
WELL...WE HAD TO. THERE'S NOTHING MORE IMPORTANT THAN BEING...LOYAL. ISN'T THAT RIGHT... MASTER REN?
YES... KIPPA.
THE WITCH MONSTER... DID IT EAT THE REST OF YOUR ARM, MISS?
NO, LITTLE FOX...I DID THAT TO MYSELF.
I GOT... ANGRY.
GASP
After everything that's happened, Tuya... you'd think I'd be more afraid...
But instead I feel...hope.
MISS?
Isn't that strange?
DO YOU RECOGNIZE THE EAGLE?
CAT... ISN'T THAT...
NO. CERTAINLY NOT.
How a glimpse of the truth... even a terrible, awful truth... could make me feel, for a moment, that I have something to live for?

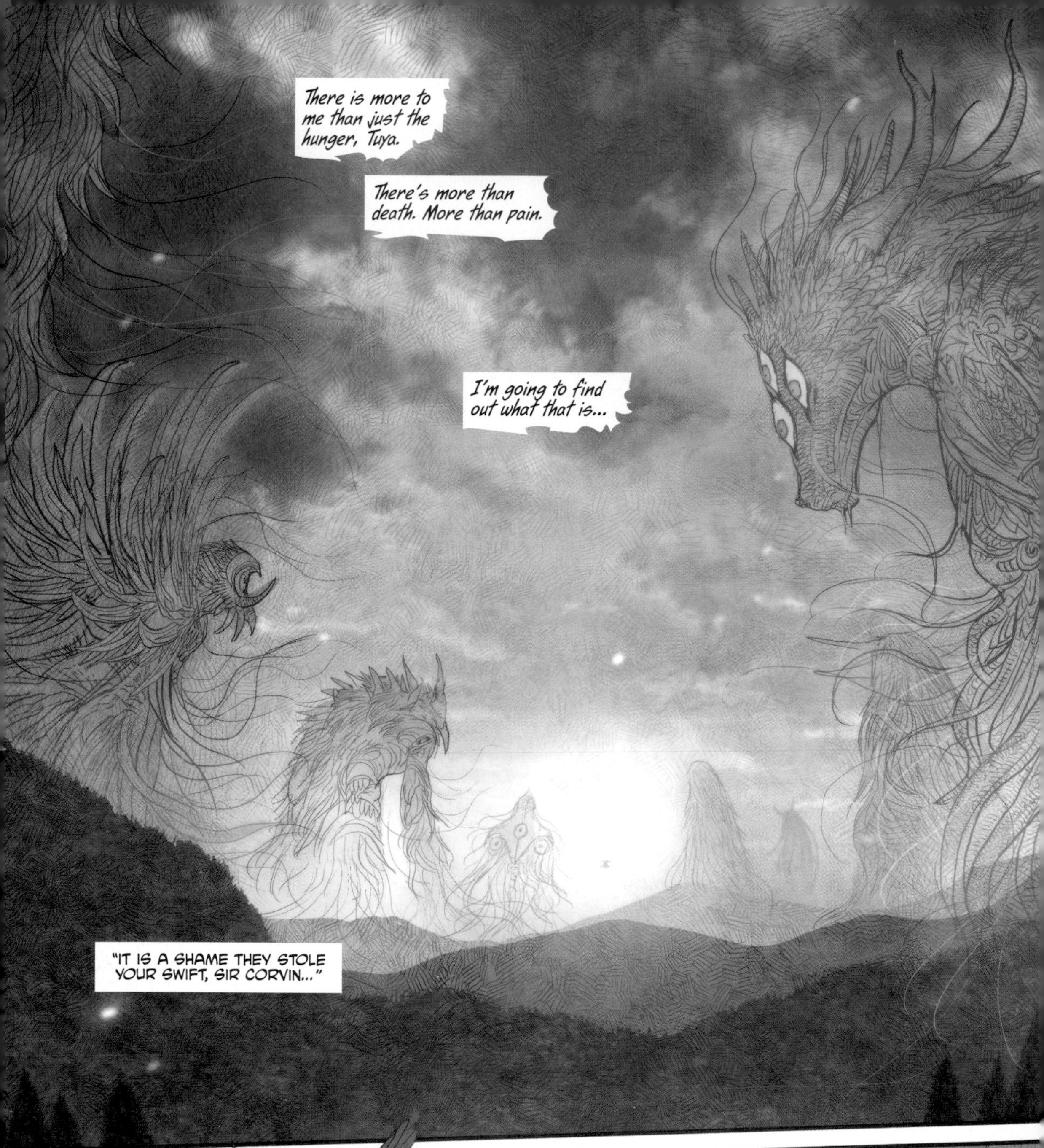
There is more to me than just the hunger, Tuya.
There's more than death. More than pain.
I'm going to find out what that is...
"IT IS A SHAME THEY STOLE YOUR SWIFT, SIR CORVIN..."

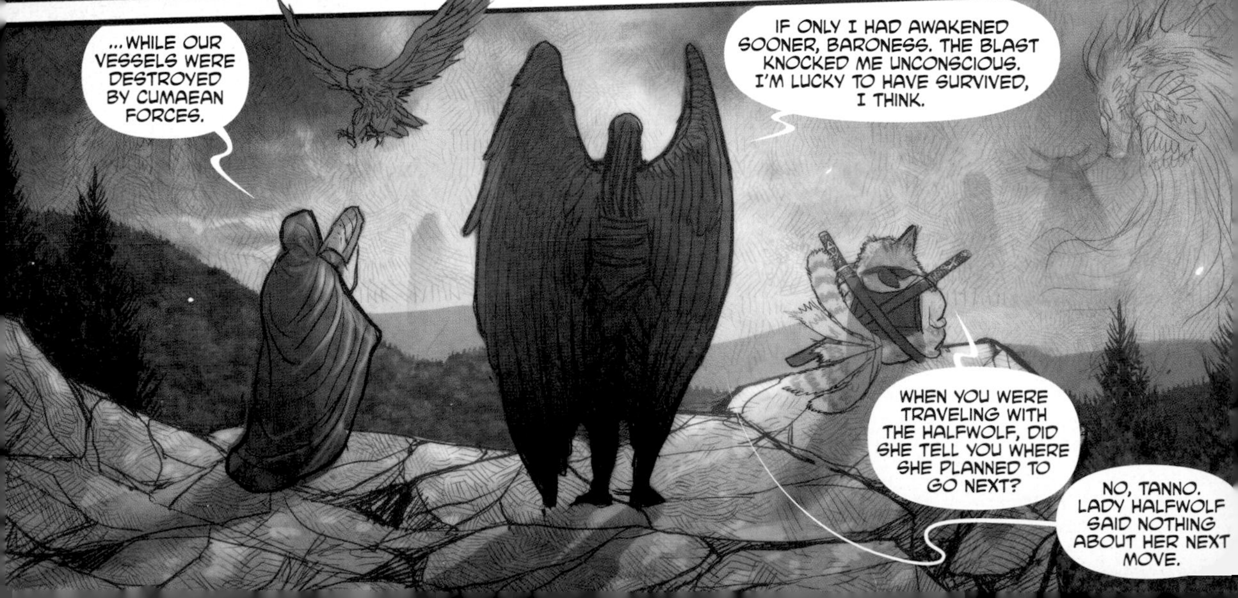
...WHILE OUR VESSELS WERE DESTROYED BY CUMAEAN FORCES.
IF ONLY I HAD AWAKENED SOONER, BARONESS. THE BLAST KNOCKED ME UNCONSCIOUS. I'M LUCKY TO HAVE SURVIVED, I THINK.
WHEN YOU WERE TRAVELING WITH THE HALFWOLF, DID SHE TELL YOU WHERE SHE PLANNED TO GO NEXT?
NO, TANNO. LADY HALFWOLF SAID NOTHING ABOUT HER NEXT MOVE.

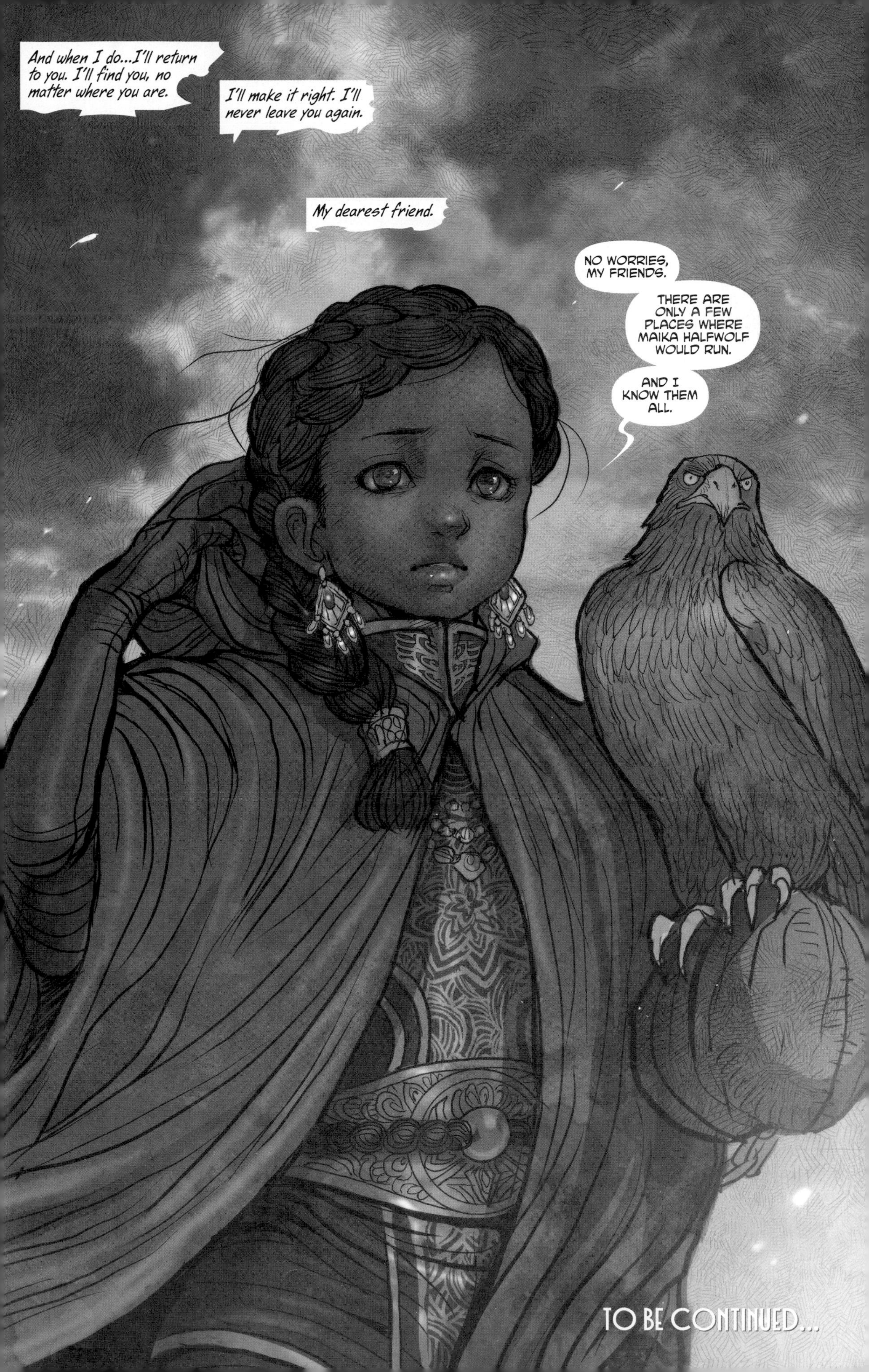
And when I do...I'll return to you. I'll find you, no matter where you are.
I'll make it right. I'll never leave you again.
My dearest friend.
NO WORRIES, MY FRIENDS.
THERE ARE ONLY A FEW PLACES WHERE MAIKA HALFWOLF WOULD RUN.
AND I KNOW THEM ALL.
TO BE CONTINUED...

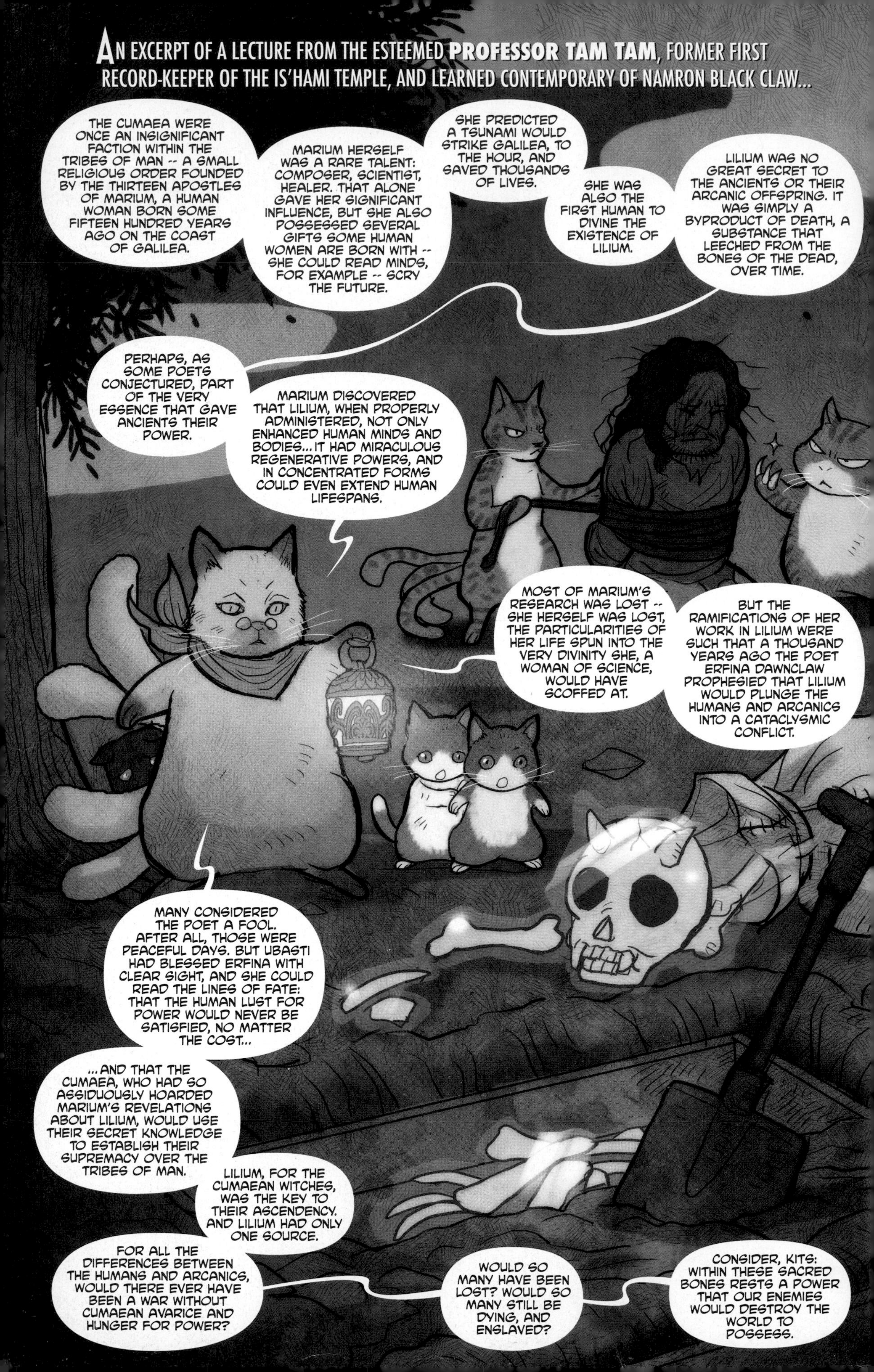

AN EXCERPT OF A LECTURE FROM THE ESTEEMED PROFESSOR TAM TAM, FORMER FIRST RECORD-KEEPER OF THE IS'HAMI TEMPLE, AND LEARNED CONTEMPORARY OF NAMRON BLACK CLAW...
THE CUMAEA WERE ONCE AN INSIGNIFICANT FACTION WITHIN THE TRIBES OF MAN -- A SMALL RELIGIOUS ORDER FOUNDED BY THE THIRTEEN APOSTLES OF MARIUM, A HUMAN WOMAN BORN SOME FIFTEEN HUNDRED YEARS AGO ON THE COAST OF GALILEA.
MARIUM HERSELF WAS A RARE TALENT: COMPOSER, SCIENTIST, HEALER. THAT ALONE GAVE HER SIGNIFICANT INFLUENCE, BUT SHE ALSO POSSESSED SEVERAL GIFTS SOME HUMAN WOMEN ARE BORN WITH -- SHE COULD READ MINDS, FOR EXAMPLE -- SCRY THE FUTURE.
SHE PREDICTED A TSUNAMI WOULD STRIKE GALILEA, TO THE HOUR, AND SAVED THOUSANDS OF LIVES.
SHE WAS ALSO THE FIRST HUMAN TO DIVINE THE EXISTENCE OF LILIUM.
LILIUM WAS NO GREAT SECRET TO THE ANCIENTS OR THEIR ARCANIC OFFSPRING. IT WAS SIMPLY A BYPRODUCT OF DEATH, A SUBSTANCE THAT LEECHED FROM THE BONES OF THE DEAD, OVER TIME.
PERHAPS, AS SOME POETS CONJECTURED, PART OF THE VERY ESSENCE THAT GAVE ANCIENTS THEIR POWER.
MARIUM DISCOVERED THAT LILIUM, WHEN PROPERLY ADMINISTERED, NOT ONLY ENHANCED HUMAN MINDS AND BODIES... IT HAD MIRACULOUS REGENERATIVE POWERS, AND IN CONCENTRATED FORMS COULD EVEN EXTEND HUMAN LIFESPANS.
MOST OF MARIUM'S RESEARCH WAS LOST -- SHE HERSELF WAS LOST, THE PARTICULARITIES OF HER LIFE SPUN INTO THE VERY DIVINITY SHE, A WOMAN OF SCIENCE, WOULD HAVE SCOFFED AT.
BUT THE RAMIFICATIONS OF HER WORK IN LILIUM WERE SUCH THAT A THOUSAND YEARS AGO THE POET ERFINA DAWNCLAW PROPHESIED THAT LILIUM WOULD PLUNGE THE HUMANS AND ARCANICS INTO A CATACLYSMIC CONFLICT.
MANY CONSIDERED THE POET A FOOL. AFTER ALL, THOSE WERE PEACEFUL DAYS. BUT UBASTI HAD BLESSED ERFINA WITH CLEAR SIGHT, AND SHE COULD READ THE LINES OF FATE: THAT THE HUMAN LUST FOR POWER WOULD NEVER BE SATISFIED, NO MATTER THE COST...
...AND THAT THE CUMAEA, WHO HAD SO ASSIDUOUSLY HOARDED MARIUM'S REVELATIONS ABOUT LILIUM, WOULD USE THEIR SECRET KNOWLEDGE TO ESTABLISH THEIR SUPREMACY OVER THE TRIBES OF MAN.
LILIUM, FOR THE CUMAEAN WITCHES, WAS THE KEY TO THEIR ASCENDENCY. AND LILIUM HAD ONLY ONE SOURCE.
FOR ALL THE DIFFERENCES BETWEEN THE HUMANS AND ARCANICS, WOULD THERE EVER HAVE BEEN A WAR WITHOUT CUMAEAN AVARICE AND HUNGER FOR POWER?
WOULD SO MANY HAVE BEEN LOST? WOULD SO MANY STILL BE DYING, AND ENSLAVED?
CONSIDER, KITS: WITHIN THESE SACRED BONES RESTS A POWER THAT OUR ENEMIES WOULD DESTROY THE WORLD TO POSSESS.

CREATORS

MARJORIE LIU is an attorney and *New York Times* bestselling author of over seventeen novels. Her comic book work includes *X-23*, *Black Widow*, *Dark Wolverine*, and *Astonishing X-Men*, for which she was nominated for a GLAAD Media Award for outstanding media images of the lesbian, gay, bisexual and transgender community. She teaches a course on comic book writing at MIT, and lives in Cambridge, MA.

SANA TAKEDA is an illustrator and comic book artist who was born in Niigata, and now resides in Tokyo, Japan. At age 20 she started out as a 3D CGI designer for SEGA, a Japanese video game company, and became a freelance artist when she was 25. She is still an artist, and has worked on titles such as *X-23* and *Ms. Marvel* for Marvel Comics, and is an illustrator for trading card games in Japan.